The Pyromancer's SCROLL

Jeremy P. Madsen

Iron Rock Press

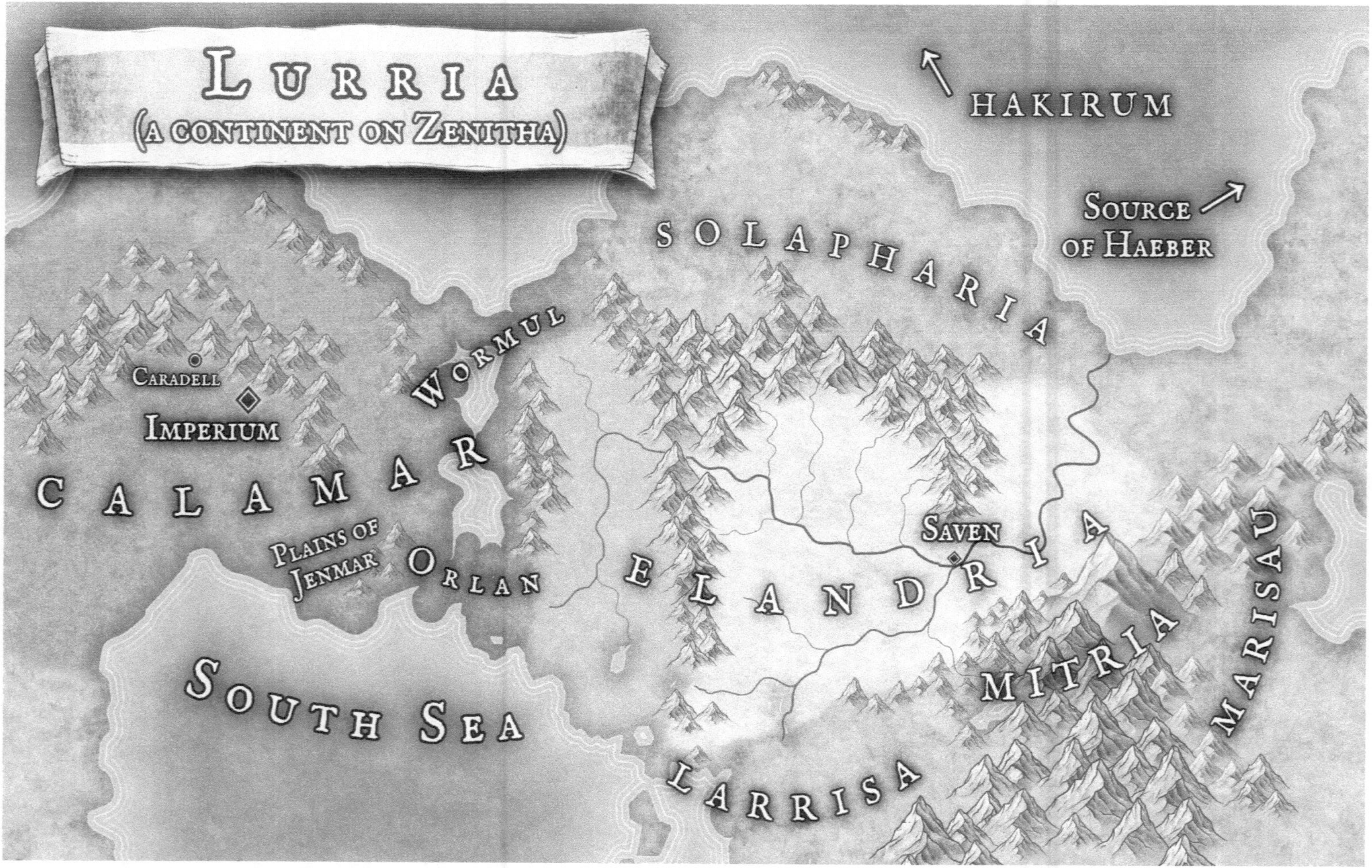

LURRIA
(A CONTINENT ON ZENITHA)
HAKIRUM
SOURCE OF HAEBER
SOLAPHARIA
CARADELL
IMPERIUM
CALAMAR
WORMUL
Plains of JENMAR
ORLAN
SAVEN
BLANDRIA
MITRIA
SOUTH SEA
LARRISA
MARISAU

Close-Up of Elandria
Rugeran Mountains
Mount Terramor
Bastion of Memory
Emerald Lake
Sanctum of Kings
Saven
Irongate Isle
Arnon Plains
Silvermoss
Nidar
Angerflood
Monine
Wivern Way
Meradov
Mera Valley
Penandre Pass
Quimar
Lindor
Elandria
Western Elandria
(Occupied by Calamar)
Larrisa
Mithria
Marisau

Glossary

Avirs A race similar to humans but more petite. Their eyes and skin tone change color depending on their emotions.

Griffins A race with the wings, head, and talons of an eagle and the hind limbs of a lion. Married griffins are fiercely loyal to their spouse ("wingmate").

Humans The hardiest and strongest race in Zenitha.

Korriks A warlike, reptilian race, with clawed hands and thick, scaly hide. Korriks have a short childhood, a long young adult life where they frequently stick close to their siblings (their "broodmates"), then a short adult life. They live to be 60–70.

Merfins An aquatic race with a finned tail instead of legs. They are air-breathers like other mammals, so they build their communities in rivers, lakes, and coastline instead of deep ocean. They can live to be as old as 150.

Snippens A race similar to squirrels but around the size of housecats. They are very dexterous, agile, and creative. Snippens live to be only 30–35. They typically live in large extended-family groups in underground burrows.

Swifters Fast, lithe creatures, a combination of wolves and cheetahs. They can run for long periods of time and have excellent senses of hearing and smell.

Aquamancy The power of water, channeled through potions

Pyromancy The power of fire, channeled through motion

Terramancy The power of earth, channeled through objects

Verbomancy The power of air, channeled through speech

Vivamancy The power of life, channeled through song

*For Tyler, whose epic ideas and inspiring
example made this book possible.*

The Pyromancer

When killing kings and sparking wars, Archivous preferred to wait till nightfall—but late afternoon could work in a pinch. The archdemon stalked down the cobblestone street, invisible to the riffraff around him. Yes—he had caused the death of at least a dozen kings in his long and nefarious career. And the wars? He had stopped counting: they were so pathetically easy to spark. Aggressive leaders, resource scarcity, what have you: it usually didn't take much to bathe swords in blood.

Today's war, however, was proving stubborn.

Archivous prowled around the edge of a crowded marketplace, keeping to the long shadows cast by the setting Sun. He passed straight through carts and wagons in his way. They posed no obstacle—they existed only on the physical plane, while he inhabited the unseen plane.

Emotions swirled around him, flowing to his senses from each mortal he passed. There were the usual ones: stress, desire, hunger, boredom. But today, bubbling under the surface, he felt apprehension. People were lingering in the streets a little longer than usual, despite the setting Sun. Whispers flew that the king was about to issue a fateful decree. He smirked. Today's news would be far more fateful than any of them anticipated.

One strand of emotion stood out from the rest: blazing ambition, focused to a keen point and tipped with fury. It emanated from the figure that Archivous was shadowing, a tall human in a scarlet cloak. The human had nearly reached the end of the market, two dozen yards ahead.

Confound it, that pyromancer was *fast*. Archivous opened his wings and launched into the air, flapping heavily, like an enormous vulture bat with horns. A screech of pain escaped his fangs as his full wingspan was scorched by the sunlight. (The Sun's ray—to Archivous's perpetual annoyance—fully inhabited both the physical *and* the unseen plane.) As soon as Archivous caught up to the human, he snapped his wings closed and retreated to the shadows.

"You'd think I could get a little cloud cover," Archivous grumbled to himself. "It's not like I'm at the climax of a seven-decade masterpiece of geopolitical calamity or anything."

Archivous's protégé left the busy streets behind and began threading his way between large stone manors. Once away from the crowds, the human moved low to the ground at a near run, never pausing as he wound through the maze of narrow streets.

"No need to go so fast," Archivous growled, bending his will upon the human's thoughts. "There's nothing to lose by striking after nightfall."

He knew an echo of his suggestion reached the man's mind. But the human only glanced at the position of the Sun in the sky and redoubled his pace.

Archivous rolled his eyes. Curse these mortals and their inconveniently correct superstitions.

After a few minutes, they passed into the shade of the palace acropolis. At last.

The human accelerated toward the last house in his way. Thrill radiated from the man's heart as he leapt fifteen feet into the air, clearing the wall easily. Traces of fire flashed in his wake.

The manor's roof adjoined the rocky hill that supported the palace. Up this slope the man climbed, moving with speed beyond any normal ability. His scabbard rapped against the rocks as he sprang from ledge to ledge.

Archivous took to the air again, keeping to the hill's shadow. He breathed deeply, drinking in the man's intoxicating emotions.

A clarion voice interrupted his sadistic glee. "You have no place here, demon."

Archivous pivoted in midair, smirk vanishing as he glared at the luminous being hovering a short distance away. An angel. Just his luck.

"Don't you have anything less irritating to do?" Archivous griped.

The angel kept a wary distance, her shimmering wings beating the air rhythmically. She looked young—perhaps only a century or two. Her sash held only a scroll, not a sword. Well, that was fortunate at least. He lacked both the time and patience today for a scuffle.

"The Sun has not yet set," the angel said. "You have no right to claim until then!"

"But I can still tempt," Archivous said. "Can't I?"

The angel, ignoring his question, pointed at the man ascending the cliff. "What mischief is he about?"

"Why don't you tag along and see?" Archivous goaded. As annoying as that would be, it would be much preferable to the angel going to find help. The last thing he needed today was to fight off an angelic patrol in daylight.

The man reached the top of the cliff and placed his back to the thirty-foot walls of the palace. From his belt, he unhooked a grappling spike and began twirling it, his other hand holding coils of rope for quick deployment. With a flick of his wrist, he launched the spike upward. It arced through the air, slipping into a crenelation at the top of the wall and sticking fast.

"Masterful, isn't he?" Archivous said, flying close to the human and sizing him up like a work of art. "I've been grooming him for this mission for years. He's served me well as a spy, thief, saboteur. And now, finally, an assassin."

"Assassin?!" the angel cried. "Who is his target?"

Archivous smirked. "Who do you think, quill brain?"

The angel gazed at the man, likely straining to pick up an echo of his thoughts. Her eyes widened. "No!"

"Quite yes," Archivous said, smirking as he saw the panic in her face.

The angel glanced at the reddening sky. "If the king dies before sunset, his soul is ours to claim!"

"Take him," Archivous spat. "I couldn't care less for that self-righteous sprig of a soul." It was a lie: Archivous would *love* to drag that stubborn monarch to the Void—maybe throw him into a particularly agonizing pit in return for all the trouble the king had caused him the last decade. But the archdemon had an even more savory prize in his sights.

"Besides," Archivous said, gesturing to the man already twenty feet up the rope, "After today, Durrin's soul is mine forever."

For a moment the angel wavered, and Archivous worried she'd bolt to find help. But instead, she flew up to whisper into Durrin's mind.

"Think!" she pleaded. *"Think about what you are doing!"*

Archivous rolled his eyes. "Do you think he can hear you? He has ignored your comrades for years now. He hears only me."

Archivous flew so close his horns would have impaled the human's head, had they not been immaterial. *"The battlement is clear. Now is your chance."*

Durrin vaulted over the crenellated balustrade, landing in a crouch. His eyes roved over the palace complex: a landscape of towers, roofs, and courtyards. Then he ran down the walkway, doubled over. His sword hissed from its sheath. Fire flickered along its edge.

"I could appear, and stop him," the angel warned.

"You would risk that?" Archivous said, holding her gaze to show he wasn't intimidated in the slightest. "You know the ancient law. Step through the curtain of sight, and I won't be far behind."

"The Sun still reigns in the sky," the angel said. "I would wield its power."

"So?" Archivous scoffed. "Even were it high noon, do you think *you* could stop me?" His voice grew. "Are you an archangel? You carry not even a sword. Do you know who *I* am?"

"You are an outcast," the angel said.

Archivous roared, spreading his wings to their full thirty feet of webbed expanse. "I am Archivous! I have crushed armies and conquered kingdoms! I have slaughtered souls and scattered stars! None are mightier than I!"

The angel stood her ground. "There is the Eldest."

Archivous snapped his wings closed. "The Eldest will never come."

"Think what you will," the angel said. "But if I can't stop the pyromancer, at least I can warn the king." She dove through the stones beneath her, disappearing.

Archivous chuckled to himself. "Go ahead. It won't help."

Yavenya—the angel—twisted and turned, darting through the palace as fast as her wings could propel her. Tapestries whizzed by, scarcely more than blurs. No mortal door impeded her; she passed through each with ease.

The assassin. Durrin. She had never seen him in this city before, but just now she had glimpsed his soul: a shard hard as steel, fueled by unremitting ambition, and armed with terrible pyromantic power. His soul terrified her.

She came to a pair of guards. Both were korriks: a short, stocky race, with reptilian features and scaly hide instead of skin. Their clawed hands and martial spirit made them a natural choice for militaries across the world.

"Danger!" Yavenya cried, projecting the idea toward their minds. *"An assassin! The king is in peril!"*

The korriks came alert, turning as if they had heard something, their emotions turning to confused alarm. But that was all. Like most mortals, the guards could only hear the faintest echo of her voice. She flew on.

As she flew, her supernatural hearing picked up a chilling sound, echoing through the stones above her: a shout of alarm, followed by a clash of metal and roar of fire. The assassin was fighting his way across the roof of the palace.

Yavenya burst into the throne room, a vast circular chamber. Massive pillars stretched fifty feet high, supporting a magnificent dome. The light of the setting Sun streamed through clerestory windows at the dome's base.

The king sat on his throne, conversing with officials of various species. He was an avir—an elegant race, more delicately built than humans. His shoulder-length hair framed the crisp, angular features of his face.

At his side was a young avir girl, scarcely ten or eleven. She sat awkwardly in a chair much too big for her, her fingers tracing the embroidery of her dress as she watched the conversation intently.

". . . angry when they hear the decree," one of the king's counselors was saying, as Yavenya flew across the spacious room.

"Most certainly," the king replied, his tone grim. "But I would rather face riots at home than war on our—"

"Your Majesty!" Yavenya cried. *"Beware!"*

The king looked up in alarm, eyes sweeping the room.

"Assassin! Fire! Sword!" she warned, pressing the mental images upon him.

"Your Majesty?" a counselor murmured.

The king held up a hand, bidding silence. Listening. Listening to *her*. Yavenya's heart leapt. Not for decades had she felt a soul so attuned to her voice. *"A pyromancer comes!"* she said. *"He's breached the walls!"*

The king's face drained of color, turning ashen white. It was a trait unique to avirs: the pigment of their skin responded dramatically to their emotions.

"We're in danger," the king said, rising from his throne. He looked at two of his guards. "Escort my daughter and counselors to the front gates."

The guards saluted. "Yes, Your Majesty."

The young avir girl stood. "What's wrong?" she asked, her face also growing pale.

"I'm not sure," said the king. He wrapped her hands in his as he met her frightened gaze. "But remember, Adara: You are stronger than your fears. Now go!"

The king pushed his daughter toward the throne room doors. Adara paused for a moment, looking back one last time. Then the guards ushered her out with the king's counselors.

"Flee!" Yavenya cried.

The king remained with three guards, all of whom were korriks. He signaled for them to follow as he strode toward a small door at the back of the throne room. "To the treasury," he said. "It's more secure than here."

Yavenya's heart surged.

"Too late," a voice snarled.

Yavenya spun to see the archdemon step out of the wall like a fiendish mural come to life. He smirked at her, gesturing upward. "My triumph is at hand."

A window on the roof exploded.

Glass showered down from the ceiling. A fireball came a moment later, engulfing the rear door in flames moments before the king reached it. Last came the pyromancer. Fifty feet he dropped, plummeting from his perch on the broken window sill, scarlet cloak billowing in his wake. Midway through his descent, he twisted in midair, fire erupting from his outstretched hands to slow his fall. He landed in a crouch before the main throne room doors.

Straightening, he drew his sword and pointed it at the king's heart. "Today you taste the sword of Calamar, King Everborn."

For a moment, all was silent, save the crackle of flames.

Then the guards shouted to each other and charged, spearpoints leveled.

The pyromancer showed no sign of alarm as the spears closed in. With a practiced motion, he twisted his sword in an intricate pattern above his head, then leveled it at his opponents. Lightning crackled along the blade's length, popping and jumping before shooting outward. It coursed through all three guards, leaping from point to point on their bronze armor as their bodies convulsed. A thunderous crack split the air.

"No!" Yavenya cried, darting across the room.

Two of the guards dropped to the ground, the clatter of their weapons inaudible amid the echoes of the thunderclap. But the one closest to Yavenya only staggered. She took a measure of his pain into herself—all she could do in her incorporeal form. She screamed as his agony coursed through her. She'd nearly forgotten what it felt like. To be mortal. To face such consuming pain. She collapsed to her knees, gasping.

On the far side of the room, the king fought to open the blazing rear door, crying out in pain as the heat singed his arms.

The guard that Yavenya had helped, a korrik with a decorated crest on his helm, regained his footing. He touched the tip of his spear, causing it to come alight with a hard red glow. Then he charged, a battle cry roaring from his throat. "ELANDRIAAA!"

But the pyromancer was ready for him. Side-stepping the spear thrust, Durrin summoned a blast of fire with his free hand, causing the guard captain to recoil. Durrin darted forward, thrusting with his sword, but the korrik nearly impaled him with his spear. For a moment they danced in counterpointing thrusts of bronze and fire, as Durrin slowly gave ground.

Then Archivous, invisible to the combatants, stepped up behind the pyromancer. Yavenya trembled as she felt the demon pour confidence and fury into his protégé. Durrin snatched the shaft of the captain's spear as it drove toward him, then twisted and unleashed a spinning mid-air kick into the korrik's face.

The korrik captain staggered backward. Durrin wrenched the spear from the captain's grip, then whirled it around and rammed the glowing tip into the captain's breastplate. A flash of blue light shunted the spear aside, leaving the breastplate unharmed. The captain reached for his short sword, but Durrin used the spear to knock the korrik's feet out from under him. Stepping over him, Durrin drove the spear downward. The first blow was again deflected away from the korrik's breastplate. The second blow sliced across the korrik's cheek, shunted aside by a flash of blue light but still leaving a deep gash. The third blow punched through the side of the captain's chainmail hauberk and buried itself a foot into the stone floor, leaving him pinned.

"No," Yavenya whispered, rising to her feet. But there was nothing more she could do now, except be a witness.

The pyromancer strode forward.

The king stood at the back of the room, alone and unarmed. His hands were burned and his robes scorched from his attempts to escape out the burning door, but he stood tall. The fearful pallor of earlier had disappeared. Now his expression showed neither pain nor panic—only the hard bronze hue of resolve.

The assassin approached. "Walls and guards cannot save you from the sword of Calamar, Your Majesty."

The king raised a blistered hand, the palm outward. "In neither walls nor guards do I trust. I trust in the hosts of the Sun."

The assassin closed the final feet between them. With a lightning-fast thrust, he drove the point of his sword into the king's chest.

The king fell to his knees, his eyes growing wide as his breath escaped him.

"Then where are your angels now?" the pyromancer whispered as he pulled the sword free.

On the other side of the curtain of sight, Archivous grinned, triumphant, as he watched the regicide unfolding before him.

Beside him, the angel watched with wide, horrified eyes.

"This will spark war," the angel said.

"Yes," said Archivous, licking his fangs. "This death is but the first of thousands, maybe millions." He gestured at Durrin. "And this man the next in a long line of my victims, stained forever with innocent blood." Archivous laughed. "Try as you might, even with all the wisdom of the Hosts of the Sun, you can never control the choices of mortals!"

The angel pulled a scroll from her robe and rolled it open, pausing to wipe tears from her cheeks.

"We cannot, because we will not," she said. She summoned a glowing quill and set it to the parchment, but paused to look at the demon. Her eyes glinted with determination. "But neither will you."

Tears mingled with blood-red ink on the angel's parchment. "You think you have won this day," she said as she wrote. "You think this is a fateful day. An evil day. A day of fire, blood, and tears. But today is not the end of Durrin's story. I am now the one who keeps his scroll. And his scroll is not yet sealed."

Part One

The Price of Justice

Chapter 1

The Prisoner

Seven years later.

Durrin woke to the sound of rattling keys.

He snapped his eyes open, though in the darkness of his cell, that didn't improve his vision much. He lay still, listening. Information had always been his most valuable commodity. Here, in this dungeon, it was his *only* commodity.

The rattle of keys drew nearer.

Durrin slipped off his cot, planting his feet on the freezing stone pavers. Through the tiny window of his cell door, a faint light was growing brighter. Durrin picked out seven, maybe eight sets of footsteps. Two squads of guards in the middle of the night? Strange.

The footsteps stopped outside his door.

"What do you think the magistrate wants him for?" a low voice muttered.

"Execution, I hope," a gravelly voice responded. "About time."

Durrin flexed his fingers as he recognized the voice of the warden. It didn't surprise him in the slightest that the man wanted him dead. Foiling eleven escape attempts in seven years had that effect.

"Can't be execution," said another guard's voice. "It's the dead of night. The magistrate would never authorize that."

"So?" said the warden. "Demons take that firebrand and be done with him, I say."

So not only would the warden kill him without a second thought—if allowed—but he would gladly doom Durrin to eternal damnation as well. Durrin filed the information away with the hundred or so other reasons he hated the man. He didn't let himself feel angry. The anger was there, of course, but he kept it buried under steely focus. Anger was a knife, best kept sheathed until it could be used.

Durrin crept to the door, careful not to clank the chains binding his wrists. He reached the barred window just as the warden's face appeared in it. Durrin spat at him.

"Shadows!" the warden cursed, wiping his cheek. "I'll have you—"

"That's for three days ago," Durrin said.

His defiant statement cut the warden short. "What?"

"Three days ago, for keeping me in the yard past dinner," Durrin said, giving the warden a self-justified smirk.

The warden scowled. "That was for insubordination. You refused to work."

"And you refused to get me a sharper axe," Durrin responded. "How am I supposed to chop wood with a dull axe?"

The warden held up a finger. "I know you too well, Durrin Rendhart. You wanted the axe for a new escape plan."

The warden was exactly right, but Durrin shook his head. "All I—"

"Shut up and get out here," the warden said, shoving the door open and stepping back. The guards leveled their spears in a perimeter around the doorway. "And no devilry, Rendhart, or you'll sleep with the shadows tonight."

Durrin stepped casually into the circle of spears, eyeing the guards. Four of them, and the warden, were humans like Durrin. The other four were korriks, the stocky creatures each coming up to Durrin's chest. Green, scaly skin glimmered beneath their armor.

Durrin raised an eyebrow at the warden. "*Eight* guards? Really?" Antagonizing the man had been one of his only joys the last seven years. "Seems a bit excessive."

"Get moving," the warden snapped. His air of bravado didn't fool Durrin—not when the warden was deliberately keeping two of the beefiest guards between them.

Durrin fell into step, four guards in front of him and four behind with spears leveled at his back. The warden took up the rear.

As he walked, Durrin took advantage of the lamplight to study the shackles around his wrists. It wasn't the chain that posed the real obstacle—it was the pure black stones set into the metal restraints. No light reflected off the black stones' surfaces: they were as dark as a starless sky.

Voidstones they were called. They sucked relentlessly at Durrin's powers, inhibiting him from wielding fire or any other pyromantic abilities. Their influence was like a cord wrapped around his heart, never squeezing hard enough to stop it, but never letting it beat freely. In a very real sense, those stones were his real prison. The walls around him only locked up his body. The voidstones locked up part of his very being.

For the thousandth time in seven years, he cursed those stones.

Durrin turned his eyes from the voidstone shackles to the guards, gauging their abilities. Though he lacked his powers, the hard labor of prison life had kept his muscles strong. Given the right moment, with the right distraction . . . Durrin mentally reviewed the passages ahead of them, thinking through possibilities. He needed more information.

"So where are we going?" Durrin asked casually.

"Silence!" the warden snapped.

They passed a tiny window set into the prison's thick walls. In the middle of the night, it admitted no light, just a musty breeze and the constant murmur of the river. The Silvermoss. The second of Durrin's obstacles. Two of his escape attempts would have worked if he hadn't been caught swimming the river's wide expanse.

Irongate Isle, this prison was aptly named. Perched on a hunk of rock in the middle of the Silvermoss, the prison had once been a fortress, built to protect Elandria's capital city, Saven, from invasion. Now it protected the capital from the most dangerous dregs of its own populace. As a foreigner, Durrin was somewhat of an anomaly.

They passed through a guarded checkpoint and turned down another row of cells. A handful of grizzled faces peered out behind bars as they passed. Durrin ignored them. Most of these inmates—lowlifes and criminals from the bottom rungs of Elandria's society—had tried to beat him up at one time or another. None had yet to succeed.

They entered a section of the prison Durrin had never seen before. By the looks of things, these were administrative offices. He scanned the area for possible exits. If he could access the outer walls, he could make a jump for the water, then swim to shore under cover of darkness . . .

The warden knocked on a heavy oak door. "We have the prisoner, sir," he barked.

"Good work," said a quiet voice. "Send him in."

The warden hesitated. "Alone, sir?" he said, scowling in Durrin's direction.

"Alone, officer."

The warden's scowl somehow deepened. He jerked his hand, and the guards shoved Durrin forward until the warden could grab Durrin by the tattered collar of his tunic.

"One wrong move in there," the warden growled, "and the Sun will rise on your dead body floating in the river."

"Good morning to you, too," said Durrin cheekily. "*Officer.*"

The warden yanked open the door and shoved Durrin inside, slamming the door behind him. Durrin stumbled for a moment, then stood and instinctively put his back to the door, blinking to adjust his eyes to the sudden light.

"Welcome, Durrin," said the same soft voice as before. "Please. Have a seat."

Durrin scanned his surroundings. Light from a half dozen lamps illuminated shelves packed with tablets and scrolls. This must be the prison's archive room. Two windows were set into the far wall, but their small size ruled them out as potential escape routes.

At a large table sat an elderly figure dressed in long white robes. He was an avir, the same species as King Everborn. The king Durrin had slain seven years before.

The avir gazed at Durrin, neither smiling nor frowning. Durrin studied his face. An avir's eyes and skin tone changed to match their mood, making them pathetically transparent in a conversation. This avir's skin was a neutral olive brown, indicating calmness. His eyes were bright brown with keen focus, indicating neither hostility nor welcome. So this was the "magistrate." He seemed . . . underwhelming.

Durrin ignored the proffered seat: remaining standing gave him far more tactical options. Could he hold this avir hostage? Use him as leverage to get to the outer walls? Worth considering. For now, he may as well see what the magistrate wanted.

A moment passed in silence. The avir kept his eyes locked on Durrin, studying him. For a few seconds Durrin stared back, then he let his eyes roam the room, taking in small details. A modest satchel. A stack of clay ledgers. Quills, styluses, ink bottles. Nothing truly useful.

A full minute passed. The avir continued to study Durrin, his face an unbroken wall of perfect composure.

"If you're here to interrogate me," Durrin said finally, "let's get it over with."

The avir shook his head. "I'm not here to interrogate you," he said softly. He finally broke his gaze, looking down at a parchment as he dipped a quill in ink. "Allow me to introduce myself. I am Cymer." As he spoke, he began writing in flowing cursive script. "I am a mage in the Luminant Order, and by the appointment of the co-regents of Elandria I am the chief magistrate of justice. And you are Durrin Rendhart, of the Empire of Calamar. According to prison records, you have been imprisoned here seven years for the murder of a minor landowner."

According to prison records. It was a deliberate hedge, one that Durrin decided to follow up on. He wasn't in the mood for pretenses.

"I assume you know what I'm *actually* here for," Durrin said.

Cymer paused, looking up. "I do," he said quietly. A hint of color flashed across his face, too fast for Durrin to pinpoint the exact emotion.

Durrin gestured at the closed door behind him. "I take it even the warden doesn't know?"

Cymer shook his head. "Only a handful of people in the kingdom know the truth."

"Why?" Durrin said.

The avir blinked. "Why what?"

Durrin hadn't meant to ask the question. But he had wondered for seven years, and this might be his only chance. "Why cover it up? Everyone I've talked to here, guards and prisoners alike, thinks that King Everborn died in an accident. Why did you hide what really happened that day?"

The avir studied him. "Are you angry about it?"

Was he?

"It probably kept me alive these past seven years," Durrin conceded. If his true crime had been known by the prison guards—or even the other inmates—they would have lynched him in a matter of days.

"I believe it's more than that," Cymer said. The avir's eyes had turned a darker shade of brown. That usually meant displeasure, or perhaps suspicion. "You feel robbed. You wanted the credit. The glory."

"I wanted the results," Durrin snapped. "Everborn's death was supposed to be done publicly, in the name of Calamar. The whole world was supposed to see the consequences of opposing us."

"So you are proud of what you did."

"I—" Durrin paused. How *did* he feel? His past self, seven years earlier, had not exactly relished the assignment. And if he had known he would be captured, he never would have carried it out. But the old avir didn't need to know any of that. Durrin cleared his throat. "I am proud to have been the one skilled enough to do it."

"I see," said Cymer. And Durrin couldn't help but wonder if the magistrate had seen more than Durrin had intended.

Before the avir could pursue the topic further, Durrin turned to another question he had long puzzled over. "If you were intent to keep the assassination a secret—why did you let me live?"

It took the magistrate some time to reply. For almost a minute, he gazed at the wall, lost in thought. Finally, he wet his lips. "What is justice, Durrin?"

Durrin stared at the shackles binding his wrists. "Justice is when a man receives what he deserves."

"What would have been *just* for you to receive, then, for your deed seven years ago?"

Durrin pushed the bracers up his forearms as far as they'd go, to let the raw skin underneath have a chance to dry out. "A life for a life. I slew your king. You had every cause to kill me in return."

Cymer shook his head. "You are not talking about justice. You are talking about retaliation."

"How is that different?"

Instead of answering, the avir asked another question. "You told me what justice would have demanded *here*. How about if you had escaped and returned to Calamar?"

Durrin straightened his shoulders. "I would have been hailed a hero. Richly rewarded."

"Quite the opposite of facing the noose," Cymer said. "But you still aren't talking about justice. What would have been *just* for you to receive?"

Durrin shook his head. "Stop speaking in riddles."

"Very well." Cymer reached into the satchel beside him, pulling out a ceramic oil lamp, beautifully painted with dancing angels. He hefted it. "What is this, Durrin?"

"A lamp."

"Is it important to you?"

"Not unless I could barter it for a warmer cell."

"Well, it means a great deal to me," said Cymer. "I've kept it close for forty-eight years. Does this lamp follow any laws?"

"No."

"Are you sure?"

Durrin shrugged. "What can it do, raid the treasury?"

Cymer dropped the lamp. It smashed into a hundred pieces on the floor.

"What did you do that for!" Durrin cried, involuntarily taking a step forward.

"You said it didn't follow any laws," said Cymer. "So I figured I could let it go without consequences."

"That's ludicrous," said Durrin.

"No," said Cymer. And once again he fixed Durrin with his unsearchable gaze. "*That* is justice."

Durrin looked down at the shards. Half buried in the wreckage, the broken face of an angel stared blankly up at him.

Anger simmered deep in his heart. *Justice?* he thought bitterly, wishing he could shout his thoughts without revealing too much. *Justice?! I was never supposed to be in this dungeon! I was to return to Calamar in triumph. I had a reward waiting, a prize that would make me the greatest pyromancer in Calamar—perhaps the greatest pyromancer of this age!*

"The world is never just," he spat.

"I know," said Cymer. "And that is what gives me hope."

For a long minute, they filled the room with uneasy silence.

"Back to the reason I came," Cymer said. He re-dipped his quill and resumed writing. "By the ancient laws of Elandria, given to us centuries ago by Arnon the Wise, the punishment for murder is fourteen years in prison. As magistrate of justice, I am to review prisoners' conduct. Depending on their behavior, I can reduce or increase their penalty by up to a factor of two."

Durrin dug his nails into the pad of his thumb, staring at the imprint each left. The warden had repeatedly warned him that every escape attempt would lengthen his sentence. Durrin had figured that those who knew his true crime would never let him walk free regardless, so the threat hadn't stopped him in the slightest. This "behavior review," he knew, was only a formality.

Cymer kept writing. "Durrin Rendhart, by the authority vested in me by the co-regents to the queen elect, I reduce your penalty from fourteen years to seven. As today marks the seventh year to the day since your arrest, you have hereby fulfilled the extent of your term."

What?

Cymer blotted the parchment with a wad of cloth, then rolled it up. He rose and walked around the table, holding out the scroll. "This will certify your freedom to any who ask."

Durrin numbly accepted the scroll. His mind reeled in free-fall.

Cymer handed him a small but heavy bag. "You had about a hundred shekels on your person when you were arrested. This bag has that amount restored in full."

Next, Cymer produced a key and fiddled with the bracers around Durrin's arms, working the key past seven years of rust. "A supply boat should be stopping by soon. It will take you to the capital. From there, you are on your own. Without these."

The shackles fell to the floor with a resounding clang.

Durrin stared at his pale and wrinkled wrists. He hefted his arms. Without the bracers, they felt unnaturally light. He rubbed his wrists, wincing in pain.

Then he felt it: a spark, deep inside him, freed from the voidstone's remorseless vice. It started as a tiny flicker, so faint he feared he only imagined it. But as the seconds passed, it grew ever so slowly stronger. Durrin breathed deeply, closing his eyes as he reached inward. He had forgotten how it matched his heartbeat.

I'm free. Durrin barely dared raise the thought, as if thinking it would cause him to wake and find himself back in his cell. He fingered the scroll the avir had given him, then held it close to his chest.

Cymer strode to the door. "I will explain my decision to the warden and have guards escort you to the quay."

"Wait," said Durrin. His mind still reeled with a hundred questions, but one had risen to the fore.

The magistrate turned, meeting his gaze one more time.

"Why?" Durrin whispered.

Cymer's eyes gained their distant look again. Finally, he refocused on Durrin, his face as inscrutable as when Durrin had first entered the room.

"We will see."

Chapter 2

The General

Six days earlier, three hundred miles west of Durrin's rocky prison, a general fought for his kingdom—and his life.

"To me! To me! Elandrians, to me!"

General Volthorn Skarr ducked under a spear thrust, then caught the blow of a mace on his shield. Blades flashed around him.

"To me! Elandriaaa!"

He thrust and hacked with his short sword, its glowing red blade cutting into armor and leather far deeper than any normal weapon. Spears and swords rammed into his armor only to rebound back, repulsed by bursts of blue light.

"To me!"

The hilltop around him was a melee of shouts and weapons. A spear knocked into his collarbone so hard it nearly knocked him over, despite the enchantments on his armor deflecting most of its energy. Volthorn was running out of time—he could feel his armor draining of terracharge with each blow. He dispatched the spearman that had struck him, then glanced about, looking for the green surcoat of an ally. All he saw were the red colors of Calamar.

This was it. If his soldiers could hold this hilltop, their daring charge had a chance to succeed. On this charge hung the fate of his left flank, the whole battle, perhaps the city of Meradov and an entire Elandrian province.

"Volthorn!"

The chaos behind him parted as a pair of korriks pushed up the hill, shields and spearpoints out as they fought back-to-back.

"Kelzern! Trazar!" Volthorn called. As always, his broodmate brothers were never far behind him. "The battle is nearly ours!"

His broodmates stood around him, giving him a moment's reprieve. He spotted a fallen green standard and snatched it from the ground, hoisting it into the air. "To me! Elandrians!"

The hilltop was a roiling mass of soldiers: korriks, avirs, and humans each locked in one-on-one struggles with sword or spear. But as he waved his standard, his soldiers came to him. A trio of men clad in heavy armor charged up to stand by Volthorn's brothers, using their height and long spears to drive the enemy back. Then a band of five korrik broodmates joined them, pushing their way through the intervening opponents with a bloodcurdling war cry.

"Form a shield wall!" Volthorn bellowed. "The hill is ours!"

More soldiers came, fighting their way up the hill to join Volthorn's vanguard. In the charge that he had led a moment ago, he had outstripped his infantry. But now they were catching up to him, sweeping away the Calamarvans on their side of the hill.

"Reinforce the line!" Volthorn yelled, pointing to the growing shield wall in front of him as more and more soldiers arrived. "Don't let—"

Something rammed into Volthorn's helmet, knocking him over. Sky tipped and ground rolled as his vision jerked violently, then filled with a wincing flash of blue light.

"Kraack's beard!" Volthorn cursed.

He rolled over onto his hands and knees, head swimming as he struggled back to his feet.

"Griffins, General!" someone yelled nearby. "Keep down!"

"I know a talon strike when I feel one!" Volthorn snapped. He glanced at the sky. Griffins circled and dove, over a score of them, harassing the soldiers in the shield wall with outstretched claws. Red dye on their plumage identified them as Calamar's forces.

"Sloppy," he muttered, feeling the dent on the back of his helmet. By rights, the blow from the griffin's talon should have snapped his neck— or the boulder that broke his fall should have—had it not been for the enchantments on his armor. He closed his eyes, concentrating. While the rest of his armor still vibrated with an invisible hum, his helmet had been completely depleted.

He touched a sapphire in his belt, drawing power from the jewel into his clawed fingers. *Terracharge* the power was called—the heartbeat of the earth, captured and channeled through metal and stone. As he absorbed the energy, his skin began to tingle and glow with a faint blue light. Then he pressed his fingers to his helmet, letting the metal soak up the energy like a sponge.

The cries of battle snapped Volthorn back to his surroundings. Griffins still wheeled overhead, but a platoon of archers was already jogging up to drive them away. With the efficiency born from three years of war, the archers set up in two lines and began launching volleys into the air. As they reloaded, accompanying spear bearers presented a porcupine of bronze points to any griffin that tried to dive for an attack.

How was the larger battle faring? Volthorn leapt atop the boulder he'd just cracked his head against and surveyed the hill. Despite the griffin assault, the shield wall was still holding and was even beginning to push back the red standards of Calamar. Periodic blasts of fire or flashes of light marked the presence of pyromancers and terramancers in the fray.

Volthorn turned to look downhill. Besides scattered units of soldiers still moving upward, the hillside was strewn with the carnage of the assault he had led minutes earlier. Bodies from both sides lay scattered on the rock and grass. Among them moved several dozen figures clad in blue, working furiously to dress wounds or move the injured onto stretchers.

Through the chaos came a swifter, running up the hillside with no sign that the incline offered any impediment. Part feline, part canine in form, swifters were as lithe as cheetahs and as strong as wolves. Their long legs could propel them at incredible speeds. While little use in pitched battle, swifters made excellent messengers and scouts.

"Lieutenant Silverpaw!" Volthorn bellowed, waving him over. The lieutenant came to a halt with barely a sign of being winded.

"General," Silverpaw said, dropping his tail in the swifter version of a military salute. "The right flank holds. Green Pine Battalion is standing strong, despite heavy casualties."

"And the rest of the line?"

"Iron Thicket Battalion is faring better. Cavalry and swifters have the riverbank secured. As I ran over, the center looked strong as well."

"Thank the stars," Volthorn said, feeling a knot of tension in his chest give way to relief. The rest of the army had held firm during his daring charge on the left flank. His mind went to work, thinking through his strategic options, projecting a half dozen ways the remainder of the battle could play out. He made up his mind. "Have Captain Mern commit all our remaining reserves on the right flank. Order them to press hard. We will save Meradov yet!"

The swifter sprinted away. Other aides and messengers were arriving, finally catching up to their general. Volthorn spent the next several minutes hearing reports and sending orders. Every update confirmed his hopes: the battle was swinging in the Elandrians' favor. The Calamarvans, their flank splintered by Volthorn's unexpected assault, were on the point of collapse. If he could route them here, the road would be clear to relieve the besieged city of Meradov, only seven miles away.

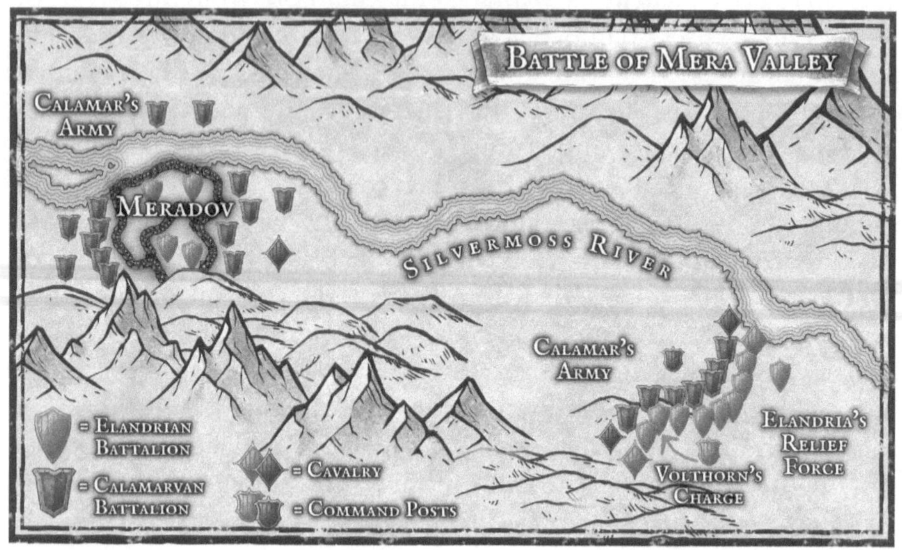

"How is the air battle?" Volthorn asked a griffin captain that landed in front of him.

"Your reckless charge outstripped us for a few minutes there," the griffin said, lifting his wing so an avir could wrap a bandage around his hind leg. "But Calamar has only committed several dozen flights to this battle: the rest of their griffins must be supporting their assault on Meradov. My squadrons will have air mastery soon."

"Once you do, target their standard-bearers on the right flank," Volthorn said. "If we can throw them in confusion, our cavalry can get around to their rear and carry the day."

The griffin glanced at the sky. "May we carry the day while the day is still with us."

Volthorn cursed as he followed the griffin's gaze westward. In the thick of battle he had lost track of time. When had the Sun sunk so low in the sky? If he couldn't score a decisive victory by sunset, the enemy could slip away and regroup during the night.

Volthorn left his aides and strode downhill toward one of the wound-dressers. The young avir lad was kneeling over a half-conscious soldier, tying off a quickly reddening bandage on the soldier's leg. The avir's once-blue tunic was splattered with mud and dirt. Besides a kit of bandages and salves, he carried a ram's horn slung over his shoulder.

"Dawn Warden," Volthorn called, referring to the religious order that the avir belonged to. "How much daylight is left?"

The avir looked up, his face a nearly colorless gray with exhaustion. He glanced at the Sun's position in the sky. "Too little," he said, then turned back to trimming the bandage.

"I need something more exact," Volthorn said. "When will you sound your horns?"

This time the avir—who looked to still be in his teens—pointed to one of the western mountain peaks. "The moment the Sun hits that mountain, we blow. Maybe . . . half an hour."

"That's not enough time," Volthorn said. "The shadow of a mountain shouldn't count as true dusk. We'd have an extra hour if the horizon was flat."

The avir held up his hands. "My apologies, General. But that's the Dawn Warden code. We can't deviate from it."

"We need more time!" Volthorn said. "An extra half hour of fighting, and we could encircle the enemy and force their surrender. Then tomorrow we could lift the siege around Meradov."

"And what is that worth, General?" said a female voice. Another Dawn Warden had joined them, a middle-aged woman who carried herself with grim confidence. She carried a horn identical to the avir's, as well as several waterskins, one of which she handed to her companion.

"Is it worth the souls of our troops?" she continued. "Is a fleeting victory worth the eternal torment of those dragged by demons to the Void?"

"All I'm asking—" Volthorn said.

The Dawn Warden held up her hand. "You know we cannot make exceptions. Neither can the Dawn Wardens behind Calamar's lines. We blow when we blow. Not before, and stars forbid not after. Enough wounded will die during the night as it is, may demons never find them." She turned to the avir. "Come. We need a hand with a stretcher."

They moved down the hill, leaving Volthorn to grind his teeth in frustration. He had no authority over the Dawn Wardens. They moved with the army but were separate from it, with their own leadership and even their own supply chain. Their independence was deliberate—it prevented exactly the kind of exception-making that he had just demanded.

Part of him knew they were right. Each minute a battle dragged on past dusk, the greater the risk that the souls of the fallen would be claimed by the demons that haunted the night.

"Shadows," he cursed, kicking a fallen shield before stomping back up the hill.

Volthorn returned to his cluster of aides and resumed hearing reports. As he had hoped, the reserves were tipping the tide on the right flank.

Coupled with his successful charge on the left flank, the Elandrian army was slowly encircling their opponents.

But time was not on their side.

A long blast of a horn sounded from the far side of the battlefield, where the mountain's long shadow was creeping over the terrain. The call spread into a symphony, as dozens of Dawn Wardens behind both armies' lines lifted their horns. From his vantage on the hill, Volthorn could see the effects ripple across the battlefield. Gaps opened between opposing ranks of soldiers. Arcs of fire and flashes of light faded as mancerers on both sides disengaged. The cries of war fell away, replaced by the monolithic blowing of horns.

"So close," Volthorn said, staring out over the battlefield. He kicked at the ground again. "So close! Seven thousand enemy soldiers, almost within our grasp."

"What are your orders?" asked one of his officers.

Volthorn removed his helmet, feeling the welcome relief of cool air around his head. He took a deep breath, thinking through and prioritizing the many orders he would need to give tonight. "The wounded are our highest priority," he said. "Once each squad sees to its dead and wounded, it can make camp. Have casualty reports sent to my brother Trazar."

"Yes, General Skarr."

The horn blasts were finally fading, their last echoes reverberating off the sides of the valley. In their wake came a new sound: bells. All across the field, Dawn Wardens were standing over the bodies of the fallen, ringing small silver bells in their hands.

A breeze wrapped itself around Volthorn, wicking away the sweat of battle on his scaly head. His eyes followed the breeze as it picked up the fringes of banners farther down the hill. Not for the first time, he willed his vision to see the unseeable. Did the breeze mark the presence of angels as they winged across the battlefield, summoned by the sound of bells to gather the souls of the fallen? Or was the breeze just a breeze?

His exchange with the Dawn Wardens replayed in his mind. It was easy to dismiss the souls at stake in the heat of battle and the light of a full Sun. But in the gathering dusk, as daylight gave way to darkness, he found himself feeling a hint of the frantic urgency the angels must feel, as they worked to gather souls before night fell.

"General," an officer said, breaking into his reflections. "You'll want to hear this."

Volthorn turned. Two griffins had just landed on the hilltop, their chests heaving from their flight.

"Report," Volthorn said.

"Meradov, General," gasped one of the griffins. "The city has fallen."

He stared at the griffins, trying to process what they had just said.

"Calamar breached the west gates earlier this afternoon," the griffin continued. "We tried to drive them back but failed. Within an hour they had taken most of the lower city, cutting off two battalions still manning the outer walls."

"You still had the inner walls," Volthorn said.

"A squad of enemy pyromancers set the inner city afire," the griffin said. "We surrendered just before dusk. It was either that or perish."

"We're scarcely seven miles away!" Volthorn shouted, more to the skies than to the messengers. "Commander Gerren couldn't hold out one more day?"

"Commander Gerren is dead," the other griffin said.

The words hit like punches to the ribs.

"He fell earlier today, trying to retake the west gates," the griffin continued. "We were the first messengers who could get through with the news. I'm sorry, General."

Volthorn sat down on a boulder to process the sobering news. Commander Gerren had been the chief commander over all of Elandria's forces, answering directly to the co-regents. Volthorn had fought under him for the entire length of the war. And now he was gone.

Eventually, Volthorn pulled his mind back to the present moment. "Gerren was a valiant leader," he said for the benefit of his staff, though words felt like a hollow cover for the numb emptiness he felt inside. "Loyal to his kingdom, kind to his troops, honorable to a fault. May angels find him."

"May angels find him," the gathered officers murmured, faces downcast.

It was the ever-pragmatic Trazar that broke the silence. "What now?"

Volthorn put his hand to his temples, kneading his scaly skin with his claws as he put his mind to work. Pieces moved around on his mental map, predicting the ways the next few days could play out. "Meradov has fallen. Our objective is now obsolete. With the siege no longer tying up Calamar's forces, they'll be upon us tomorrow with a force double what we faced today. Tell every company to bed early and prepare to rise two hours before dawn. Our only option now is to retreat back down the Mera Valley."

"I'll send a flight back to the capital, to bear the news," said Kelzern.

"Send a flight," Volthorn said. "But tell the co-regents I'm coming in person."

"What?" Kelzern said. "That's a week's journey. We need you here."

"Now that Meradov has fallen, the course of the war has changed," Volthorn said. "With Commander Gerren dead, I'm next in seniority. The co-regents will want to meet with me to devise a new strategy."

The co-regents. The royal palace. How long had it been since he'd last been there? Not since before the war. He did his utmost to avoid the place.

For a moment, his mind fell back to that cursed day, seven years before. Glass showering from the ceiling. Fire and lightning. A figure in red.

Volthorn absently brushed a scar running along his cheek, the result of a spear thrust that had nearly killed him. He should have acted faster. He should have posted more guards. He should have foreseen—

Stop it, Volthorn barked to himself. *The past has passed.*

"Saddle my horse," Volthorn said. "I'll leave tonight."

Chapter 3

Freed

Six days and six nights later, the bump of a boat against a dock jolted Volthorn awake. Stone walls towered over him, framed by a purple sky.

"We're almost there, General," said a sailor at Volthorn's side, deft hands tying a mooring rope to the gunnel. "Just making a quick stop at Irongate Isle."

Volthorn rolled into a sitting position, groaning as his stiff muscles resisted. It had been a long six days. Two of those he had spent in the saddle, galloping east down the Mera Valley, trading his horse out at army way stations. The last four he'd spent on a barge, sailing day and night down the Silvermoss River.

He stared at the cliffs towering above them. Irongate Isle, a hunk of rock in the middle of the Silvermoss, was where Elandria held its most dangerous prisoners. He had seen the prison many times from a distance, but his military duties had never brought him inside. Irongate Isle was administered by the ministry of justice, not the army.

"Hold steady, lads! That's the way! Hand me some of those boxes!"

The deckhands were unloading a couple crates of fresh provisions for the guards and their prisoners. Volthorn shivered in the early morning chill, wrapping himself deeper into his travel blanket.

The boat rocked as three people stepped aboard from the quay. Two were avirs in guards' uniforms, probably leaving the island to enjoy a couple days off-duty. The third was a tall, thin human wearing a tattered tunic and trousers—most likely a prisoner just released. His features were nearly indistinguishable in the semidarkness.

Volthorn shifted. Something about this man set him ill at ease—a memory, tugging at the edges of his consciousness. He tugged his blanket over his head to cast his face in shadow as he studied the stranger.

The man also appeared to be avoiding attention. He stood alone at the prow, gazing out over the dark river, his face turned away from the eyes of anyone in the boat. Volthorn studied his stance. The man seemed to be a trained warrior, keeping his feet well placed, neither too close together nor too far apart.

The barge cast off from the isle. Soon the sailors were calling to each other, reporting on distances as they guided the barge toward the docks of the city Saven. Even as the barge pitched with the waves, the man stood erect, his legs bending and straightening in rhythm with the boat's rocking.

As they approached the shore, the sailors' calls were answered by dockhands on the bank. For a moment, the light of a lantern on shore caught the stranger's face as he turned, illuminating a sharp nose, chiseled chin, and keen eyes. Fiery eyes.

In a flash, the memory clicked into place. The assassin. The pyromancer that had burst into the palace seven years before and murdered Volthorn's king. The man who should have been killed for his crime—but wasn't.

"Rendhart," Volthorn breathed. Confusion mixed with alarm in his thoughts. What was Rendhart doing here? Why was he walking free?

The man leapt ashore, clearing the four feet still between the dock and the boat.

Volthorn sprang to his feet. "Stop him!"

The man slipped through the gathered dockhands, moving like a wisp of smoke.

Sailors looked about in confusion. Volthorn pushed past them, stumbling over crates and ropes in the semidarkness. "That man!" he said. "Seize him!"

Rendhart reached the edge of the quay and broke into a run.

Volthorn leapt from the boat to the dock. He stumbled, banging his knee into the wood, but straightened and charged through the dockhands. He stopped at the edge of the dock, looking around. Darkness and shadow lay before him—an impenetrable maze of buildings and narrow alleys. He saw no sign of the man.

"Tyrant's horns," Volthorn cursed.

"Sir," said a voice behind him. "Is something amiss?"

Volthorn pivoted, coming face-to-face with one of the prison guards that had been on the barge.

"Why is Rendhart free?" Volthorn demanded.

"That man?" said the guard. "He was released early this morning."

"On whose command?"

"By special order of the chief magistrate."

"Cymer?"

The guard shrugged. "I believe so, sir."

Volthorn clenched his fist. Of course this disaster would be Cymer's doing. What was the chief magistrate thinking?

The barge captain jogged up to join them. "General Skarr," he said, saluting. "Is everything all right?"

Volthorn turned, searching the dark riverfront one more time. His mind began to calculate all the harm Rendhart was capable of inflicting in the coming hours—and what Volthorn would need to do to counter it. "No," he replied finally. "Something is wrong. Something is very wrong indeed."

Durrin kept to the shadows, passing from alley to alley, moving at a brisk walk. He paused at a corner, listening for any sign of pursuit.

Nothing.

He kept walking, choosing his route erratically, but always away from the river. Who was the korrik that had pursued him as he left the boat? Was his sudden freedom too good to be true—had there been a mistake? Any minute, he expected to hear soldiers' cries behind him, an alarm raised, lanterns flashing in the dark. Just like seven years ago. He had run through these same streets then—an assassin, fleeing the scene of his success. Was this the corner where the arrow had scathed his arm? Was that the street where he had torched the wagon to block his pursuers?

Once clear of the river district, Durrin ducked into a corner, clothing himself in darkness. He patted the purse Cymer had given him, tied to his belt. A hundred shekels. Enough to get him all the way back to Calamar, if he used it carefully.

Back to Calamar. Back to the prize that awaited him, seven years overdue. Back to his destiny.

The thought sent thrills down his spine.

Durrin returned to the streets. People were starting to come out in the early morning light: craftsmen, tools in hand as they headed to their shops; children with buckets to fetch water; merchants pushing carts, heading to market squares.

He rounded a corner and came face-to-face with a squad of soldiers. For a moment, he froze, about to turn and flee. But his mind worked quickly. Too little time had passed since his flight from the docks for this to be an organized dragnet for him. These soldiers had to be just a regular street patrol. He regained his composure and walked by, earning barely a glance. His heart started to slow.

As he walked, he planned. He itched to be out of this city as fast as he could, but first he needed three things: a horse, supplies, and information.

His stomach rumbled. And a bite to eat. Four things.

Saven was not the city Durrin remembered. It had once been known for its clean and tidy streets. Now he had to step carefully to avoid piles of refuse and debris. Where in a previous decade he had passed through plazas and city squares, he now wound his way through crowded tenements, each wooden hut more ramshackle than the last. The chatter of children and the cries of infants leaked through the thin walls, betraying the crowded conditions inside. Refugees from the war, most likely. Thousands of them.

He had admired this city once. His assignments had taken him here on occasion, typically to gather intel on Elandria's troop numbers or to deliver a clandestine message to one of Calamar's many field agents. Saven had always struck him as a pleasant, well-run city, despite the musty river smell that often pervaded it. Now, the whole city felt crowded, dirty, and overburdened.

Durrin did not remember seeing so many soldiers seven years ago. They patrolled the streets in squads of four, set apart by their green surcoats and bronze armor. Whenever they came near, Durrin would shrink into the shadows, trudging along with his head down, shoulders bowed. He knew how to avoid attention.

Something was happening today. There was an energy in the air, an excitement he could sense in those he passed. He crossed a wide street and noticed garland and banners strung from house to house. Preparations for a parade? That might explain so many soldiers.

As soon as it grew late enough for shops to open, Durrin stopped at a market, quickly ordering only the essentials he would need for his journey: A travel cloak. A pack. A week's supply of victuals. At a blacksmith, he bought a couple small metal tools—the best substitute for a lock pick set he could manage under the circumstances.

His side itched to have a sword hanging from his belt. But that would cost too much and attract too much attention. The sword would have to wait.

A horse, however, couldn't. Neither could information. And he knew a good place to find both.

Volthorn Skarr strode briskly through the city streets, while a nervous captain tried his best to keep up. "Send messengers to each city gate,"

Volthorn ordered. "Have the watch screen every adult male human who attempts to leave, detaining any who match that man's description. We must not let him escape the city."

"Yes, General," the captain said. "Shall I order a search of the streets?"

Volthorn paused, considering. Then he shook his head. "In a city this big, you would never find him. And we can't afford the soldiers, not today." He lowered his voice. "Besides—I don't want to draw too much attention to our search. The chief magistrate and I may have . . . *differing* opinions about Rendhart's fate."

The captain looked confused, but he didn't ask further questions. He was a good soldier.

"Lastly," Volthorn said, "I want the processional guard for today doubled."

The captain nearly missed a step. "Doubled?" he said. "I already have three entire companies."

"Then make it six," Volthorn said. "I want a wall of soldiers between the princess and the crowd at all times. And have archers stationed on rooftops along the route." He ran a finger across the scar on his cheek. "I will not make the same mistake a second time," he murmured.

Inns. Best places to get information.

Durrin stopped at a large, two-story structure, only a short distance from the west gate of the city. The inn's sign labeled it the Dozing Donkey, complete with a corresponding caricature. He nodded, satisfied. He preferred large inns over smaller ones; he would attract less attention.

Inside, the main tavern room was warm and snug, with a fire already kindled in the hearth. Behind the counter he found a young avir with a mop of red hair spilling from beneath his cap. He was probably the innkeeper's son. Durrin plopped a small piece of silver on the counter. "A bite of breakfast when it's ready," he said, careful to speak with the crisp consonants of an Elandrian accent.

"Anything else?" the assistant said, sweeping the silver into a pocket of his apron.

"I'm looking for a horse," Durrin said. "Any for sale?"

"Only one mare," the avir said. "And she'll cost you eighty shekels."

Durrin bit back a curse. Eighty shekels for a horse? Wartime prices. After his earlier purchases, he barely had eighty shekels left in his bag, and he would need much of that on the road. "She better be worth that much," Durrin said. "Let me see her."

The redhead led Durrin through a couple doors, past a small courtyard, and into a stable. As they entered, two swifters looked up from a bed of hay, their pointed ears pricking up. Swifters had few possessions (being unable to carry anything except in their jaws), so most found lodging in the lofts or barns of other dwellings. These two swifters probably lived in the stable for free, in return for keeping an eye on the animals. Once they saw the avir with Durrin, they settled back down.

True to the inn's name, the stable held several dozing donkeys, as well as a handful of horses. The innkeeper's assistant showed Durrin the one for sale. It was old and small, probably passed up for military use. Still, it looked fit enough to hold Durrin's weight. And he wasn't in a position to pay top shekel.

"For that mangy piece of leather, I'll give you thirty shekels," Durrin said.

"The price is eighty shekels," the boy said. "No use haggling with me—my father doesn't let me. Says I'm too young."

That was obviously a lie, and an expert way to begin the haggle. This boy knew what he was about.

"No deal then," Durrin retorted. "Last night I met a merchant who would sell me a horse half as old as this for thirty-five shekels."

The boy didn't bat an eye. "Then you're a fool not to have taken him up on it. At such a bargain, it's surely sold by now. Eighty shekels."

"Go find your father and tell him I'll pay him forty shekels, no more," said Durrin.

The boy hesitated. Hah! Durrin had called his bluff; the boy was fully authorized to negotiate, and retreating behind his father was a blow to his pride he was unwilling to take. "He's busy attending to travelers," the boy said finally. "But tell you what: Since today is a holiday, I'll take three shekels off the price."

Durrin shook his head. "You really expect someone to buy this mare for seventy-five shekels? Only a fool would pay more than forty-five for her, and a desperate fool at that."

"You must be desperate, then, to be offering forty-five shekels," the boy said.

"I'm offering forty-two," Durrin said. "Or no deal."

The boy held up his hands. "My father would be furious if I sold the mare for less than seventy-five."

Durrin turned to leave. "Very well. I'll look elsewhere."

He exited the stable and was about to reenter the main inn when the boy caught up to him. "Seventy," he said breathlessly. "Take it or leave it."

"Listen," said Durrin, turning in the doorway. "I have to get all the way to Solapharia in the next month, and I have only so much money to get me there. The most I can afford for her is forty-five shekels." All of which was true, except for his destination.

The redhead put his hands on his hips. "And you think we're sitting on piles of money here? We paid good silver for this mare, and we're not going to sell ourselves short just because you're a cheapskate. But seeing you're in a bind, I'll be generous and sell her for sixty-five shekels."

"Fifty," said Durrin.

This time it was the boy who turned to go. "Sixty-five is my best offer," he said over his shoulder. "I have chores to do."

Durrin felt no need to look desperate by giving chase. Before the boy could leave the courtyard, Durrin called, "Fifty-five."

The boy hesitated. "Sixty."

"Deal," Durrin said.

They shook hands, then returned to the inn. "I'll pay for the horse now," Durrin said. "Then I want some food."

The boy put a balance on the counter, then placed a fifty-shekel weight and a ten-shekel weight on one of the balance's two trays.

Durrin opened the purse of money that Cymer had given him. Digging around, he found three chunks of silver that he guessed weighed roughly fifteen shekels each. He drew them out. "Three twenty-shekel pieces," he said.

As Durrin placed the silver on the empty tray, he began subtly twitching the smallest finger of his hand. Deep inside him, the spark of pyromancy, dormant for so many years, flickered with feeble life. Invisible threads of energy began to wrap around his hand.

With the silver counterbalancing the weights, the balance's arm began to straighten, the arrow in the middle swinging closer to the center—but still fifteen shekels short of reaching it.

Before the arm had come to rest, however, Durrin twisted his wrist. Like a doll on invisible strings, the tray was pulled downward, the chords of its momentum entwined with those swirling around Durrin's fingers. Finally, it stabilized at equilibrium for a second. Then two seconds.

"Nice weights," Durrin said, picking up the fifty-shekel weighing stone and examining it. The trays fell out of balance with a loud clang. "Granite?" he guessed.

"Diorite," the boy said, sweeping Durrin's silver off the tray and stowing it beneath the counter. "Shipped from Orlan."

"A good investment," Durrin said, setting the weight back on the counter. "Now about that breakfast."

As the boy disappeared around the corner, Durrin let his muscles sag. Altering the momentum of the balance hadn't required much pyromantic strength—the trick was mainly technique—but in his current state, he didn't have much strength to give. The spark inside him felt drained, like a dying ember in a cold hearth.

As far as Durrin knew, he was the only pyromancer to ever think of using his powers to cheat a set of scales. He had learned the trick back at the Academy, one particular year when he spent the bulk of his savings on scrolls and codices instead of food. Quite a few merchants had found themselves short-changed that year. Since then, he'd grown more cautious with the technique. Using it now, with his spark so weak, had nearly been a mistake. But sixty shekels for a *horse*? Durrin had standards.

He had his gear, he had his horse, and he was about to get his meal. That just left Durrin with his most important need: information. While he waited for his meal, he sunk onto a stool by the counter, letting his eyes rove across the common room. The inn had a sprinkling of the usual menagerie: merchants, soldiers, travelers. What surprised him were the large number of families. He counted at least a dozen children crouched over games or running around chasing each other, while their parents did their best to keep them quiet.

"Baked lentils, with some bread on the side," the innkeeper's assistant said, setting the meal in front of him.

"Many thanks," Durrin said. He nodded toward the common room. "Quite a busy morning you're having."

"Aye," the young avir said, dropping a pile of platters into a bucket of water. "Lots of folk come in from the countryside for the coronation."

So that explained all the soldiers—a wartime coronation. He imagined security would be tight. "When do the ceremonies start?" he said, veiling the fact that he lacked the remotest idea of who was even being crowned.

"An hour or so before noon," said the avir, scrubbing furiously at his dishes. "A procession will lead Princess Adara down from the palace to the Silvermoss. Will you watch?"

"Hmm," Durrin grunted. "Not sure."

As he ate his lentils—which needed more salt—Durrin processed what the avir had told him. Adara, he recalled, was the daughter of the late king. Seven years ago, she'd been only a girl, meaning she would now be in her late teens. Impressive—had the throne really remained vacant for seven years, waiting for the rightful heir to come of age? Kingdoms rarely enjoyed such stability.

He studied the handful of soldiers and officers in the room. Many appeared to be veterans, with well-worn uniforms bleached by the Sun.

They looked much different from the fresh-faced, smartly dressed guards Durrin had encountered seven years ago.

From conversations he'd had with other prisoners at Irongate Isle, Durrin knew that a war had been raging for three years between Elandria and Calamar. He needed to get more intel about the safest routes back to his homeland. But if his questions were too probing, the redhead might report him as a spy or informant. This would require subtly.

"I couldn't believe the news from the front the other day," Durrin said, deliberately being as vague as possible.

The redhead shook his head. "I couldn't believe it either. My dad said that Meradov would never fall. He'd been there once. Said the walls were thicker than a house."

Durrin's countrymen had taken Meradov? The news surprised and impressed him. Meradov was scarcely a two-week's march from Saven, and nowhere near the traditional border between Calamar and Elandria. If Calamar's armies were there, it meant Calamar had taken at least a third of Elandria's territory. Durrin felt a thrill of satisfaction. His country had always excelled at war.

Outwardly, however, Durrin frowned. "Such a blow," he said. "I heard we lost nearly thirty thousand." He invented a specific number in hopes it would garner a specific response. He was right.

The avir waved a hand. "Embellishments. I heard some officers talking just last night. Two or three thousand dead, the rest of the garrison captured. Four thousand or so. Most of our army wasn't in the city when it came under siege. That's why it fell so quickly."

Durrin took another bite of lentils. This news made his journey a little . . . difficult. The city of Meradov controlled the most direct road back to Calamar. But it sounded like that area was a hotbed currently. He would need to find an alternate route.

A teenage girl joined the boy, probably his sister judging by the shared red hair. "Did you hear they're watching the gates?" she said. "They're stopping any human males from going out. I think they're looking for someone."

"As if today wasn't crazy enough," the boy said, rolling his eyes.

Durrin finished his last bite of bread. The gate watch had to be looking for him. Who else? He had suspected escaping this country wouldn't be so easy.

Durrin waited until the boy and girl had their backs turned, then slipped upstairs, fingering the tools in his pack. Seeing the officers in the common area had sparked an idea.

CHAPTER 4

ON GUARD

Volthorn strode through the palace grounds. Around him were exquisite gardens—but instead of appreciating their beauty, he eyed them critically. Should the palace ever be assaulted, they would prove a liability: the trees blocked important lines of fire, and the greenery would go up in flames if struck by incendiary missiles. Volthorn would have to order their removal if Saven ever became threatened.

Eight soldiers greeted Volthorn at the palace doors. He had sent orders ahead to double the guard: he was pleased to see they had already complied. The sergeant on duty snapped a salute. "General Skarr, *sir!*"

Volthorn came to a stop. "Have we met?"

"No, *sir!*"

"Then how did you know I was General Skarr?"

The sergeant paused, then continued. "By the mark on your face, *sir!*"

Volthorn's frown deepened. He had long ago gotten used to the fact that his most salient feature was the dark red line scoring his cheek. It had even given him his nomen of *Skarr*. But sometimes he still had trouble accepting the fact.

"So that's what the army knows me for . . ." Volthorn muttered.

"It's a battle wound, sir," said the sergeant. "A badge of honor."

A badge of honor? Volthorn thought as he strode past them. *More like a sign of failure.*

The palace halls were thronged with chatting aristocrats, bustling servants, and stressed officers. Volthorn corralled a swifter racing past. "Where can I can find Magistrate Cymer?"

"Banquet hall, I believe, sir," the swifter said, then darted away.

Volthorn wound his way to the specified room, a long, many-pillared hall already set with dozens of tables. There he found the old avir conversing with several companions. All were clad in long white robes, each tied with sashes of gold, blue, or silver. As Volthorn approached, Magistrate Cymer turned.

"General!" the old avir said, bowing. His eyes shone bright blue with pleasant delight.

"Your Magistrate," Volthorn said. "A word with you. Please."

"Of course," Cymer said, a frown appearing on his face as his eye color darkened. He bowed to the others and excused himself.

Volthorn stomped into an adjoining hallway, which was empty save for a few passing servants. Cymer followed more slowly, his brow furrowed. "General Skarr, is everything all right?"

"All right?" Volthorn snapped, turning to face him. "*All right?* Our kingdom is at war, if you haven't noticed!"

Cymer's eyes lost the rest of their blue hue, turning dark brown instead. "Trust me, General. I've noticed."

"Then explain to me," Volthorn said, growling each word, "why you released *Durrin Rendhart* from Irongate Isle!" The mere mention of the name caused Volthorn's blood to boil. "In the past, Cymer, the regents and the military have turned a blind eye to your generous pardons. But this? This is the last straw."

Cymer strode over to a window, looking out over the city. "Sometimes the best way to heal old wounds isn't to lock people up, General."

"I'm not trying to heal old wounds," Volthorn said. He gestured to a pair of guards patrolling past. "I'm trying to keep our kingdom safe! Releasing some petty thieves and vagabonds is one thing. But Rendhart? *Rendhart*?! He should have been executed seven years ago!"

"Durrin Rendhart was punished according to our law," Cymer said, turning. "He committed murder, and for that he was sentenced to fourteen years in prison. In my capacity as chief magistrate, I reduced his term by half."

Volthorn could barely believe his ears. Had Cymer forgotten what Rendhart was capable of? The turmoil and chaos that man had brought upon their nation in a single day? Maybe it was easier to forget when you didn't have a scar etched across your face. "Rendhart is a threat to our kingdom's security," he said, breathing deeply as he struggled to stay calm. "The military should have been consulted before you released him—and *especially* before releasing him *the morning of Adara's coronation!*"

Cymer studied him. "Do you expect him to cause a problem?"

"Yes!" Volthorn nearly punctured a tapestry with his claws. "I've ordered six hundred troops to line every inch of the processional route from here to the river!"

Cymer shook his head, his gaze becoming distant. "I can assure you, General. Durrin will not pose a threat to Her Majesty today. His path will take him far from Saven."

"If so," said Volthorn, "Then I bet a thousand shekels he'll head straight back to Calamar, to resume his service to their murderous cause."

"You don't know he will," Cymer said softly.

"And you don't know he won't!" Volthorn growled.

Cymer laid a hand on Volthorn's shoulder. "Peace, Volthorn. Do you think I have forgotten the harm Durrin dealt our kingdom? Releasing him was no light matter. What I did, I did with great cause."

Volthorn searched for any sign of duplicity in the old avir's eyes. He found none. "What was that cause?"

Cymer pursed his lips. "I cannot say. Not yet."

Before Volthorn could protest, a swifter messenger, attired in a pure white vest and golden sash, padded to a halt in front of Cymer. She bowed reverently.

"*Ku aveli do vera ti,*" she said. Volthorn recognized it as a common greeting in an ancient language called the Numinous Tongue. The language was used frequently by members of the Luminant Order, in which he knew Cymer was a prominent leader.

Cymer bowed in reply. "*Ku avara to kima di,*" he said before reverting to Lurrian. "What tidings do you bear?"

"The glade is ready. It's time we gathered."

Cymer turned back to Volthorn. "We'll have to continue our conversation later, General Skarr. I must prepare for the coronation ceremony."

Volthorn scowled. "If you insist, Magistrate." Inwardly, Volthorn's mind was already at work, planning and preparing. Cymer's words had done little to assuage his fears. Rendhart was still a threat, as volatile as fire. And if Cymer felt he had the authority to release that fire, Volthorn felt justified using *his* authority to contain it.

As the avir glided away with the swifter, a soldier marched up to Volthorn and saluted. "General Skarr! The High Chancellor requests your presence in the council room."

"Can it wait?" Volthorn said. He itched to be overseeing the hunt for Rendhart, not wasting time in meetings.

"He is the High Chancellor, sir. One of the co-regents."

And one of the ones I'll be meeting with to decide the direction of the war, Volthorn thought grudgingly. "Very well. Let's hope he doesn't talk my ears off."

"We can always hope, *sir,*" the sergeant said. Volthorn caught the hint of a smile behind his salute.

Volthorn took a moment to get his bearings, then picked what he hoped was the right corridor. It had been two years since he'd been to the palace. He tried to avoid coming here—it brought back too many memories. He passed a section where the wood paneling was noticeably newer and the stones under his foot were stained black with fire.

Nearly a fourth of the palace had burned that fateful day. Volthorn remembered stumbling through these corridors, gasping at servants to fetch buckets to put out the flames, wondering if his stinging eyes were wet from smoke or from tears.

After only one wrong turn, he arrived. Much smaller than either the banquet hall or the majestic throne room, the council room was a cozy, circular chamber, well furnished with chairs and pillows. In the center, a recessed floor held a table spread with a large map of the kingdom, currently littered with a variety of drinks and hors d'oeuvres.

Several bored-looking dignitaries occupied the room, all held captive by the locutions of a gray-haired swifter: Chancellor Skagar, the busiest administrator Volthorn had ever seen. As one of the kingdom's co-regents, Skagar had been the driving force behind the kingdom's management for the last seven years, working from well before dawn to well after dusk each day. Volthorn had seen the aging swifter keep four scribes busy simultaneously, dictating four different letters at the same time. Unfortunately, this practice had carried over into his day-to-day conversations—including the current one.

". . . but regardless, I'm sure today's ceremony will be absolutely stunning. I assume you read the last letter I sent you? The streets will be lined with banners, over a hundred of them. I apologize for the letter's length; I get a little carried away with my instructions sometimes. And the royal barge has stood the tests of time quite well, much better than Lady Luviana feared. In that letter, I failed to commend the eastern provinces for surpassing their recruitment quota. Ah! And here is General Skarr."

"You wanted to speak with me, Chancellor?" Volthorn grunted.

With the pause in the conversation, the aristocrats in the room seized their chance, muttering excuses as they escaped out the door. Good. Volthorn wanted a private conversation, anyway.

"Volthorn Skarr," Skagar said, his tail swishing as he paced. "You must tell me all about your journey."

"It was boring," Volthorn said. "As I hoped." He found himself a glass to pour some wine. "How is the princess?"

"She'll do all right," Skagar said. "Though I shouldn't have left so much of her tutelage to Lady Luviana's care. Adara's etiquette is impeccable and her diplomatic skills extensive, but I fear she falls short in legal knowledge and economic theory."

Well that wasn't exactly a helpful answer.

"No, I meant how *is* she." Volthorn had barely seen the princess over the last seven years. When he thought of her, he still pictured the eager, excited girl that had often walked at her father's side—when she wasn't running ahead, anyway, which would have annoyed the royal bodyguard more if it hadn't been so endearing.

The swifter frowned. "I'm worried about her, Volthorn. I can smell her anxiety whenever she enters the room. Our kingdom at war, armies marching across our lands—a child shouldn't have to deal with such problems."

"A child?" Volthorn said. "She's turning eighteen today. I had fought in three campaigns by the time I was her age."

"She's an avir," Skagar said. "You're a korrik. It's different."

"And you're a swifter," Volthorn said. "You probably had raised a brood by the time you were eighteen."

"Two," Skagar sniffed.

"Which just supports my point," Volthorn said. "She has had seven years to prepare. If she's anything like her father, she'll do just fine." He took a gulp of wine. When he resumed, he dropped his voice to barely more than a whisper. "On that note, Chancellor—has she found out the truth?"

Skagar froze, one paw raised in mid-stride. "About . . . his death?"

Volthorn glanced at the door to make sure it was closed before nodding.

Skagar shook his head. "She doesn't suspect anything, as far as I can tell. The few who know the truth have done an excellent job of keeping to the narrative we all decided upon."

"Good," said Volthorn.

"Why do you bring it up?" the swifter said. "I smell fear about you. Worry."

Rendhart. The name echoed in Volthorn's mind.

He shook his head. "I'm just nervous for today. As a precaution, I've doubled the processional guard."

"Yes, I heard you had taken that liberty." Skagar said. He stopped directly in front of Volthorn. "Last time I checked, I don't believe the city garrison was under your jurisdiction."

"Do you care?" Volthorn said, sinking down into a chair. "Commander Gerren is dead. We both know the only two viable replacements you have are me and General Orrin. And, as I have heard you yourself complain several times about General Orrin's overcautiousness, and seeing you have not bothered to summon him to the capital, I figure that you have already made your choice."

The chancellor scowled. "Well . . . perhaps. But even so, a command is a command, General. Don't overstep your authority."

"With all due respect, Chancellor," Volthorn said, leaning forward, "proper protocol is low on my list of priorities right now."

They met each other's eyes. Technically, Volthorn should have looked away after a second—high nobility outranked military officers—but instead he met the swifter's gaze for a pregnant moment.

"Rendhart is free," Volthorn announced.

The hair rose all along the swifter's neck. "He escaped?"

"No. *Somebody* decided it was a good idea to pardon him. This morning."

Skagar pivoted to resume his pacing, moving quicker this time. "Stars above, Cymer," he muttered. "Why?"

"Cymer wouldn't specify. He said he had good reasons."

"Where is Rendhart now?"

"Somewhere in the city. I have guards watching for him at every gate."

"We must call off the coronation, postpone it until he is found," Skagar said instantly, then shook his head. "No, no, we can't do that. Adara will ask questions. Everyone will. Could we cancel just the procession? Hold the ceremony in the palace? No, Adara would insist on tradition."

"Can someone be her double?" Volthorn suggested. "Just for the procession?"

Skagar shook his head. "We have none prepared. No one who could pass as her, not with hair as dark as hers. No, we have to proceed as planned. You've already doubled the processional guard. We don't even know if Rendhart will try something. It's been seven years. He was released just this morning—his powers will still be at a trickle. And if we take any extreme precaution, Adara will ask too many questions."

"Then we proceed with the ceremony?"

"We proceed."

"Then I will don my gear and personally escort the princess," Volthorn said, standing. *Right beside the monarch. Captain of the guard. The final line of defense.*

Like last time.

He only hoped the outcome would be different this time.

Chapter 5

Silence and Shouts

Princess Adara Everborn, Queen Elect of Elandria, began her coronation with an hour of silence.

She spent the hour alone, sitting cross-legged in a chamber deep within the palace. The room, a perfect circle of stone, held no windows to let in the hubbub from the outside world. The only light came from a flickering candle.

Breathe. She let the thought fill her mind, mirroring the air in her lungs. *Release.*

The hour of silence was an ancient tradition, one that had accompanied the coronation of Elandrian kings and queens for hundreds of years. For a species whose skin showed their every emotion, the ritual was crucial to helping them present a calm, collected countenance to the people they were to rule.

Adara breathed again, slowly, rhythmically, emptying her lungs completely before drawing in a new breath. For the last several months, Adara had practiced weekly for this ordeal, carving out time from her packed schedule to train her body and her mind on how to sit perfectly still.

Waking. She let the concept fill her mind with the next breath, then let its opposite accompany the exhale. Sleeping.

Her legs ached from sitting folded so long. Carefully, quietly, she shifted her posture, extending one leg straight while keeping the other tucked beneath her—the only movement she had allowed herself in the last hour.

The candlelight caught the diamonds of her necklace, filling the room with a flickering mosaic of colors. Her dress, brilliantly white, fell in pleats around her like a cascade. Her only other adornment was a glistening pair of white rings on her right hand. For now, she wore no crown.

Dawn. *Breathe.* Dusk. *Release.*

A torrent of thoughts barraged her mind, in sharp contrast to the quiescence around her. By far, the hardest aspect of this trial was mental, not physical. She had not anticipated that.

Learning. *Breathe.* What was the opposite of learning? Ignorance. *Release.*

How long had it been? Surely an hour had passed already. Had the bell sounded and she had missed it? Could she even hear it so deep in the palace? What if she missed the procession? Surely Skagar would send someone if she failed to be punctual.

Focus!

Patience. *Breathe.* Impatience—no, that antonym seemed like a cop-out. Worry? No, better: Haste. *Release.*

She glanced at her hands, noting with satisfaction the pigment of her skin: a deep, solid, neutral tan. No frightened shade of white, no scattered freckles from stress, no hints of blue from grief or green from nervousness. Just a calm, composed, royal hue of bronze.

Regal. *Breathe.* Childish. *Release.*

The walls of the chamber were lined with stone alcoves: fourteen of them, as she had counted several times in the last hour. Each held a miniature statue of a bygone ruler of Elandria. According to one of her tutors, the real purpose of this ritual, beyond stilling her emotions, was to hear the voices of those who preceded her. What did they have to say?

Remember. *Breathe.* Forget. *Release.*

Her gaze returned, as it had a hundred times in the last hour, to the alcove directly in front of her. Nestled inside was the statue of a tall avir, his features pointed and strong. In one hand he held a scroll; in the other, an olive leaf. His eyes gazed upward, as if he were looking at something distant. Something unattainable.

Love. *Breathe.* Loss. *Release.*

For a minute she stared at the statue. In the shifting light it almost seemed alive, as if the head would turn to smile at her at any moment, the eyes rekindling with a once-familiar glow.

Adara held her breath. In the utter silence, she could almost hear her father's last words to her, echoing from the past:

You are stronger than your fears.

"I will not fail you, Father," she mouthed without breaking the silence. "I promise."

A bell tolled somewhere above her, making her jump. It was muted, but the sudden sound was startling after so long a stretch of stillness.

High noon. It was time.

One last ritual remained, one she knew by heart. She shifted into a kneeling position, gasping slightly from the pain shooting through one leg that had fallen asleep. Adara touched her heart and her forehead with one hand, as from her lips fell a familiar prayer:

> *"Father of Stars, hear me.*
> *Shower thy peace on our land.*
> *Give us the strength of angels.*
> *Guide us. Heal us. Save us."*

Part of her yearned to linger, to say more, to listen. But her people awaited her. Her coronation was at hand.

Adara stood and strode to the door.

The palace courtyard was alive with energy. The whole coronation procession was standing at the ready as Adara stepped out into the midday Sun. At her appearance, the assembly went silent, each person turning to face her and kneeling or bowing their head in respect. She stopped in her steps, caught off guard by the sudden attention.

Encouraged. *Breathe.* Intimidated. *Release.*

Chancellor Skagar padded over to her. "I just consulted the sundial," he said as servants brought up Adara's horse, a beautiful white mare. "We're right on schedule."

"He's nearly paced us all to death," said a gruff voice as a stout korrik joined them, dressed in gleaming bronzium plate and mail.

Adara smiled deeply. Ever since Volthorn had led her father's bodyguard, his sturdy presence had always been reassuring. "General Skarr," she said with a slight curtsy. "I hope you were accompanied by angels on your journey."

"I came with all speed," Volthorn said. "My trip was—" he paused for the briefest of moments. "Uneventful."

"Your colleagues have highly recommended you," said Adara. "As has your track record on the battlefield. It has been decided that you will be promoted to chief commander, to fill the absence left by Commander Gerren, may he rest in the light."

Volthorn bowed. "It is . . . an honor, Your Highness."

Skagar paced beside them, the corners of his mouth turning in a frown. "We planned to tell you this afternoon, General, after the coronation. It was to be Her Highness's first official royal act."

Adara felt her skin start to redden as she blushed with embarrassment. Not now! Confidence. *Breathe.* Embarrassment. *Release.* "The formal decree will still be issued this afternoon, Chancellor," she said, keeping her head erect but her tone conciliatory. "I just thought Commander Skarr would like to know in advance."

"I suppose it's for the best," Skagar sighed. "In any case, General Skarr, we want to hold a war council tomorrow, first thing in the morning. Can you prepare a strategic plan for the rest of the summer?"

Volthorn bowed. "I shall see to it."

Two assistants helped Adara mount. Ahead and behind her, the members of the procession tidied up their lines. A great hush fell on the whole assembly.

Adara looked to where a line of heralds stood on the battlements, eyes trained on her, rams horns in hand. One nod from her, and they would blow.

She held her breath.

"Your Highness," said Skagar. "Are you ready?"

Eagerness mixed with nervousness in her veins. Was she ready? Truly ready? Seven years she had spent preparing for this day. She had mastered lessons by rote, read shelves upon shelves of scrolls, and reviewed diplomatic case studies until she could rehearse them in her sleep. But was that enough? For a kingdom embroiled in war, what could an eighteen-year-old girl bring that two seasoned regents could not?

Fear. *Release.* Faith. *Breathe.*

Adara nodded.

Durrin's ears filled with the blast of a dozen horns, followed by the roar of a thousand voices.

He reined his horse to a halt and looked toward the sound. Buildings impeded his view, but he could still make out a line of green banners issuing from the palace.

More horns. More shouts.

The tattered clothes of his imprisonment were gone. Now he wore the armor and uniform of an Elandrian officer, pilfered a half-hour before from the officer's quarters. And a good thing, too—the streets around Durrin were deserted. Everyone in the city had congregated to the processional route. In his prison tunic, he would have been as conspicuous as a flame in a field of snow.

More shouts. Durrin could make out the words now, roared by the gathered throngs: "Hail, Adara, Crown Elect! Hail, Adara, Crown Elect!"

He hadn't intended to watch the procession—it wasn't on the short list of things he still needed to do before he could escape this city. But observation brought information. And information, used in the right way, could be incredibly potent.

His horse stirred, nervous. Durrin hushed it with a hand on its neck. Then, making up his mind, he nudged it toward the noise.

"Hail, Adara, Crown Elect!"

Adara rode, flanked by knights and nobility, as horns proclaimed their fanfare across the city. In echo, belltowers rang from a dozen directions, filling the air with the clamor of joy.

"Hail, Her Majesty! Hail, Adara, Crown Elect!"

So many people! They filled the streets and packed every window. Parents held children on their shoulders. Griffins and snippens perched on the rooftops. Ten thousand eyes were upon her, every throat roaring her name.

"Hail, Adara, Crown Elect!"

As tradition dictated, Adara waved no greeting to the crowd. Despite the cheers, this ride was not yet a triumphal march. She was not yet crowned, and until she was, ancient rules of ritual demanded that she stay perfectly still, focused on her destination. Still, she couldn't help but let her eyes roam in wonder across the gathered throng.

As the bells and horn blasts finally faded, a mystic song took their place. Before Adara walked a dozen musicians: harpists, trumpeters, and singers. These were not simple performers—they were vivamancers, wielders of the power of life channeled through music. Together they performed a song that soared in its heights and swooped in its depths, filled with an energy that lit a fire in Adara's chest. Her heart sang along with the music, pumping her veins full of equal parts resolve and wonder. As her procession advanced through the streets, she could see the effects of the magical melody rippling through the crowd, lifting shoulders, brightening eyes, and raising the volume of the cheers.

"Hail, Adara, Crown Elect!"

In front of the musicians walked four standard-bearers, their banners snapping in the breeze. Behind Adara rode the rest of her retinue: nobility in glittering robes, officers in full dress uniform, and high-ranking royal officials. Chancellor Skagar paced to her left, General Volthorn to her right.

"Are all the soldiers necessary?" Adara said without turning her head, just loud enough for Volthorn and Skagar to hear. Besides the platoon that marched in front of them, soldiers lined both sides of the street, jostling with the crowd to keep a wide strip open to either side of her procession.

"We are at war, after all," Skagar said, his words barely reaching her ears.

"One can never be too prepared," Volthorn added.

The procession turned from the palace hill, curving in a long arc through the city as it descended toward the river. Every turn revealed another street thronged with cheering crowds.

"There must be forty thousand people here, at least," Adara said, struggling to wrap her mind around the sight.

"The whole city and surrounding countryside turned out to see you," Skagar said. "It's been a long seven years."

Adara had never seen so many people together in one place. At the insistence of her advisors, her public appearances had been rare in the years since her father's death. Most of her time had been spent at a remote sanctuary in the mountains, absorbed by her intense schedule of tutoring. What was the greatest number of people she'd ever addressed? Maybe a hundred?

Faces jumped out at her as she rode. A trio of korrik blacksmiths, banging their tools together in celebration. An old human matron, her wrinkled face almost pleading as she joined in the shouts. A young pair of avir parents, eyes aglow as they raised their children in their arms to catch a glimpse of their passing queen elect.

They believe in me, Adara thought, sitting up straighter as she felt the weight of so much expectation settle on her shoulders. *I am their ruler. I am their hope.*

Like my father.

If only she knew how to live up to her father's legacy.

Durrin watched the procession from afar.

He sat astride his horse, perched on a side street with just enough elevation to allow him to gaze above the crowd. Over the roar of the cheers, the processional music wafted to his ears, enticing him to give in to its euphoric spell.

He pushed back, angrily. Vivamancy had its uses, and he was not one to pass up a relaxing performance in a tavern or theater. But he would not let his emotions be swayed by its power today. Not by his enemies.

First the standard-bearers passed into his view, then the band of vivamancers. Next came a young avir maiden astride a brilliantly white horse, the brightness of its coat exceeded only by the spotless dress of the rider. Durrin took note of the princess's hair color: dark brown, laced with traces of deep blue. For an avir, that meant a lifestyle sparse on laughter but heavy with loss.

"Adara Everborn, daughter of King Arvanon," Durrin murmured, watching her with narrowed eyes. "What kind of ruler will you be? You are embroiled in war with the most powerful empire in all of Zenitha. Will you know what's good for you and back away from a fight you can't win? Or will you choose to be a thorn in Calamar's side, and bear the consequences?"

He turned his horse away. With a snap of his fingers, he summoned a flame in his hand and stared into its depths.

"Like your father."

Chapter 6

Anointing by Fire

Volthorn's eyes were getting tired.

His gaze shifted from face to face in the crowd, zeroing in on every human male. He ruled out one after another. Not him. Not him. Not Rendhart.

Once, he thought he saw something—a distant face, half visible behind the throngs—but in a moment it passed, leaving Volthorn searching in vain. Had it been just an invention of his nerves?

After the longest half hour of Volthorn's life, the procession reached the Silvermoss River. There, moored at a dock, waited a magnificent boat sheathed in gold. The prow was carved into an exquisite angel, her hands holding a sword tucked to her chest. Her wings extended behind her to form the sides of the boat, until they gave way to carvings of fruit-laden trees. On the stern was an emblem of the rising Sun. The boat, named the *Fortune Bringer*, was reserved for only the most exceptional occasions.

As the procession reached the quay, Volthorn stepped aside, joining the perimeter of soldiers keeping the crowds back. Now that Adara was out on the dock, she was well out of range of a sudden attack. Volthorn breathed a little easier.

As the princess boarded the ship, a herald said in a clear, ringing voice, "Farewell, Crown Elect! May angels bring thee safely beyond, and safely back to us again."

The crowd took up the call in a rippling wave. "Farewell, Crown Elect! Farewell, Crown Elect!"

Adara took her place at the prow as the deckhands pushed off from the dock. The roar of the crowd reached its peak, reverberating up and down the Silvermoss, sending great flocks of birds rising to the skies.

"Farewell, Crown Elect!"

Volthorn surveyed the scene: The nobles dressed in their finery. The countless throngs with hope alive in their eyes. Adara, riding in regal splendor on a vessel of gold. For a moment, everything seemed perfect.

Yet everything was wrong.

The soldiers stationed in front of the crowd were not for ceremony or show. They were there to guard their queen in a time of war, a time when any throng could harbor an assassin.

Among the dignitaries, the ranks of foreign ambassadors were conspicuously empty. Embroiled in war with such a powerful enemy, Elandria had become a political pariah, devoid of allies.

Volthorn took a long look at the *Fortune Bringer*. Once its role in today's ceremonies was completed, the boat would be taken downriver to an enclosed dock. There it would be stripped of its ornamental plating, the gold melted down to buttress Elandria's nearly bankrupt coffers.

Volthorn's mind turned to the memory of a cold evening, seven years ago. He had stood on this same dock that day. But then his face had been covered with bandages, his armor broken, his eyes fixed on a shrouded body laid out on the ship's deck. There had been no cheers that day, only the pealing of bells and the haunting cry of a single herald: "Farewell, King Everborn, Crown Departed! May angels bear thee to the Halls of the Sun, never to return again."

Wrapped in the painful memories of the past, Volthorn watched the *Fortune Bringer* approach the far shore. The shouts of the crowd began to ebb as the throng lost its energy.

Then the shouts changed.

"Fire!"

"Smoke!"

People were pointing to the west. Volthorn sprang up a pile of boxes to get a clearer view. A pillar of black smoke was blossoming above the cityscape, maybe five blocks away.

The docks burst into commotion. Volthorn sprang off the pile of boxes and found a squad of soldiers. "Each of you grab an able-bodied civilian and take them to the source of the fire. Put it out."

"Yes, General."

He pushed them on their way, then fought his way through the crowd to another squad. "Patrol the streets around the fire. Detain anyone who you find alone."

"At once, General."

Volthorn spotted a horse tethered to a post outside a storefront. He ran up and untied it.

"I'm requisitioning this horse for military use," he announced to any-one in earshot, not waiting to see if the owner was among them before mounting. Luckily the horse was small enough for korriks to ride—he would have needed a stool to mount anything taller. Digging his heels into the horse's flanks, he galloped toward the pillar of smoke.

Several blocks away, Durrin Rendhart reined his horse to a stop before the city gates. The armor he had stolen clanked unfamiliarly as he pointed behind him. "Fire! Fire in the West Quarter!"

Several soldiers stepped out of the shadow of the gatehouse. "What was that?" said a soldier, identified as a sergeant by the insignia on his surcoat. "A fire?"

Durrin pointed at a plume of smoke just becoming visible two blocks away. "The armory is afire—but we can still save it with a bucket chain!"

"There's a pond just outside the gates," the sergeant ordered. "Korvan, Marv, search the gatehouse for buckets. Move!"

The soldiers sprang into action, two korriks running inside the gate-house while two humans unbarred the heavy gates. Durrin dismounted, grabbed a bucket in one hand, and lead his horse with the other hand as he joined the squad of soldiers streaming through the gates.

The sergeant stopped the last two members of his squad. "Stay here and don't let anyone in or out. If this was an act of arson, we can't let the perpetrator escape."

Durrin dropped his bucket and swung back into the saddle. He edged his horse away from the gate. "I wouldn't worry too much about the per-petrator escaping, sergeant," he said.

The sergeant turned toward him. "Why's that, soldier?"

"Because," said Durrin, giving a two-finger salute as he turned his horse toward the highway and dug his heels into its ribs. "I already did."

Volthorn found a set of buildings smoldering, the fire nearly extin-guished by several bucket brigades already at work. An officer, spotting him, ran through the crowds to meet him.

"What burned?" Volthorn asked.

"An armory, General. Second biggest in the city."

"Who was over the watch today?"

"I was, General. We normally have ten men on guard at all times. But with the procession's need for soldiers, we only had three today. A fire started around the back, behind the smithy. By the time we spotted it, it was out of control."

"Arson?"

"Must have been, General. There was no source of open flame around." The soldier removed his helmet and took a knee. "I should have been more vigilant, General. I hereby resign my commission."

I should have been more vigilant.

Fire. Falling glass. A flash of lightning.

I should have been more vigilant.

"You'll do no such thing," said Volthorn. "You were understaffed and had no warning. Now put that helmet back on and get to work salvaging what weapons and equipment you can."

"Yes, General," the captain said.

Volthorn surveyed the smoking scene. It had rained throughout the last week, so the buildings and their surroundings were not very dry. A regular arson's fire could never have spread so quickly. This had to have been a pyromancer's work. And Volthorn had a prime suspect.

A griffin landed next to him. "General. The co-regents seek your counsel. They want to know whether it is safe to proceed with the coronation ceremony."

"Is everything quiet on the far bank?"

"It was when they sent me."

Volthorn's thoughts turned to the river. The normally well-trafficked waterway was empty of boats due to the day's festivities. If Rendhart had meant for the fire to be a distraction so he could do additional harm today, he'd have difficulty finding a way to cross the river. Or was this a coordinated assault with other operatives? Could Rendhart have gotten in touch with Calamarvan agents so quickly? Volthorn thought for a moment, weighing the contingencies, estimating the odds.

"Tell them I recommend they proceed as planned," Volthorn said. "Whoever instigated this, let's not give them the satisfaction of disrupting today's ceremony."

The griffin bowed, turned, and launched into a running takeoff. Volthorn stepped into the still-smoking ruins, examining the extent of the damage. He had just picked up the charred haft of a spear when a human officer marched up to him. "General Volthorn, *sir*" he said, saluting.

"Report," Volthorn said, turning the spear over in his hands.

The captain swallowed. "The human you sent orders last night to watch for. I was just informed that he slipped out the West Gate a few minutes ago, right after the fire started."

Volthorn snapped the spear in half with a sudden crack. "Was the gate not being watched?" he demanded.

The captain nodded vigorously. "It was, sir. But he was wearing an officer's uniform, most likely stolen. In the confusion when the fire was spotted, he slipped out the gate and galloped off. The sergeant on duty didn't have any mounts or swifters on hand to chase him, and by the time they had a griffin in the air, he had disappeared."

As the news fell, pressure began to build up in Volthorn's chest. He strode to the wall of the building, pressing a hand against the masonry and digging into it with his claws, channeling his anger into the rock.

"We await your orders, General."

Volthorn fought to clear his thoughts. What did this mean? What was Rendhart's intentions? He pieced together a possible narrative for the events of the morning. Rendhart, finding himself suddenly freed, had tried to leave the city, just as Magistrate Cymer had predicted. But finding that Volthorn had set a watch for him, he had started the fire as a distraction, creating an opportunity to slip out the gates.

Volthorn suspected that though escape may have been Rendhart's primary goal, destroying an Elandrian weapon depot and casting a cloud over the coronation had likely been icing on the cake for the man.

Eventually, Volthorn loosened his grip on the wall and turned back to the captain. "If he slipped out the gates, then he won't commit any more mischief in the city today. That's good enough for now."

"And for later?"

Volthorn mentally tallied the forces present in the city. Most would need to leave immediately for the front. He had so few to spare. "My guess is he is returning to Calamar. Dispatch a flight of griffins to scan the roads heading west for the next fifty miles. Later today, I'll have messages sent to all the border patrols to keep an eye out for him."

Volthorn turned, staring to the west. "You will not escape again, Rendhart."

Across the river, Princess Adara stood still, once again ringed by a circle of silence. Unlike the shrine in the palace, this circle was ringed not by stone walls, but by trees. And rather than the silent statues of the dead, this glade held a circle of living beings, of various races, each dressed in white. Sunlight streamed into the glade from directly overhead.

At the far end of the glade waited Cymer. The old avir stood wrapped in a white robe tied with a golden sash.

"Adara Everborn," Cymer said, his voice resounding with a strength that defied his age. "Daughter of His Highness King Arvanon Everborn and Her Highness Queen Illanya Everborn, may they dwell in the Sun."

Adara took a deep breath. "I am ready."

Cymer nodded. "I stand before you now not as Elandria's chief magistrate, but as a mage of the Luminant Order."

Adara nodded.

"When you stepped into this glade, you left Elandria," Cymer continued. "You left time and space itself. For this clearing is a holy circle, a sanctum of the Luminant Order. This Order is more ancient than the Everborn house; more ancient than Elandria. More ancient than the world of Zenitha itself. It is the Luminant Order, and the power of Light that it wields, that your mantle of queenship comes from."

On a small golden table next to Cymer sat a trio of glittering objects: a horn of oil, crafted from silver; a scepter, molten from gold; and an intricate crown, forged from a pure white metal called eternium. Adara knew that crown well. It was the crown her father had worn: the Everborn crown, fashioned eight centuries ago at the very edge of the world.

At a signal from Cymer, the others in the glade began singing a wordless song, its harmonies winding through the stone pillars and the trunks of the towering trees. With the music came Cymer's voice, singing loud and true and free.

> *"Light is my order, and Cymer my name,*
> *Serving the Father who rules in the sky.*
> *He now anoints thee queen of thy people,*
> *To stand in the stead of the ones who did die."*

Adara mouthed along as Cymer spoke, missing not a word. This song she knew by heart. She had read it, pondered it, every night for the past two weeks.

Adara knelt before Cymer. The old mage unstopped the horn of oil, letting its earthy fragrance wash over Adara as he let seven drops fall onto the crown of her head. She felt the cool drops of oil soak into her hair as Cymer continued his song.

"Wisdom I give thee: the prudence of yore,
To govern; to rule; to direct; to decry.
Courage I give thee: the braveness of heart,
To know when to fight, or to speak, or to fly."

Cymer placed the scepter in Adara's right hand. Its golden sheen gleamed in the noonday light.

"Queenship I give thee: the burden of rule
Trust in this mantle to guide and sustain.
Look to the Light! Its precepts obey,
Seek for the Eldest to counsel thy reign."

Cymer raised the crown of eternium, its jewels catching the light and sending sparks of red, blue, and green throughout the glade. Adara bowed her head, feeling the weight of the crown settle upon her.

"Make thy decisions with patience and sight,
Fathom the thoughts, and counsel impart.
Know who to trust with the care of thy life,
Speak with the power to sway deed and heart."

Cymer's voice rose to a crescendo, resounding off the trees. For a moment, it seemed Adara could hear a mighty chorus of voices joining with him, though she knew he sang alone.

"Stand with thy forebears of centuries past,
Anointed with power and wisdom and might,
Rule as you serve the Father of Stars.
Adara thou art, so shine with the Light!"

At the last word, Cymer clapped his hands above his head. Light flooded the glade, seeming to originate from his hands, yet filling the whole glade evenly, leaving no shadow. For the briefest of moments, Adara thought she saw the glade filled with luminous beings, dozens of them, circling her in rank upon rank. Each wore robes of dazzling gold, with glistening wings tucked behind them. Some held staffs, some scrolls, and others gleaming swords. She could almost hear their voices, raised in a mighty joyous shout that exceeded any mortal cry.

Then the light faded, Adara blinked, and the scene was gone.

Cymer let his hands fall to his sides. The chant faded away, returning the glade to silence.

"Rise, Queen Adara," Cymer said.

Adara stood. Her eyes searched the glade, looking for any sign, any echo of the fleeting vision she had glimpsed. Finally her questioning gaze met Cymer's. The old avir smiled, and in that smile, she knew that he knew what she had seen.

"Always remember what you were shown today," the old avir whispered. "Trials are coming. There will be times, not far off, when all seems lost and you are surrounded by only enemies. But remember today. Remember that you are never truly alone."

CHAPTER 7

AWAKENING SPARKS

Alone at last, Durrin thought.

He stood in a glade, surrounded by oaks and maples. The nearest road lay a half mile away, much too far for any sight or sound from this spot to reach there. Even the eyes of griffins would fail to pierce the canopy above him. He let out a deep sigh. He felt truly alone for the first time since before his imprisonment.

His horse roamed at the edge of the glade, looking for grass in range of its tether. The mare, though old, had turned out to be half-decent. It had kept up its strength the last two days, despite Durrin driving it hard. <u>Almost</u> worth the forty-five shekels he'd paid for it. Almost.

After leaving Saven, Durrin had turned north. In the past, he would have gone straight west, heading across Elandria's central provinces to the Mera Valley, the only easy route through a formidable mountain range called the Rugeran Mountains. But with the Mera Valley the site of a recent battle, that whole area was likely crawling with troops. He'd decided that his best bet was to circle around and cut through the Rugeran Mountains well to the north of the Mera Valley. The road would be rocky and treacherous. Durrin didn't particularly care.

The reward awaiting him in Calamar would be worth it.

Durrin shed his cloak and strode to the center of the glade. After seven years wasting away in a dungeon, it was time to begin climbing back to greatness. It was time to re-master the first Kymar routine.

Kymar Roline had been a legendary pyromancer from centuries earlier—perhaps the greatest pyromancer to ever live. He had founded the school where Durrin had studied—the Imperial Pyromantic Academy of Calamar—and made its pyromancy program the finest in the world. The linchpin of Kymar's pedagogy was his series of five acrobatic routines, designed to build up students' speed and prowess as they advanced from beginner to master.

Durrin closed his eyes, breathing in deeply through his nose, then letting it out slowly through his mouth. He stood with feet apart, hands relaxed at his sides, and listened with his mind.

Pyromancy was heat. It was motion. It was passion.

Pyromancy was power.

As he focused, Durrin could sense that power around him. It pulsed in the beats of his heart. It vibrated in the air. It hummed in the ground. Everything in the world had energy: it only needed to be found and controlled. Unleashed.

He began moving the tips of his fingers in infinitesimal circles. After a few seconds, he let the movement spread to larger arcs with his hand, then his whole arm. Each motion followed a subtle pattern, memorized by years upon years of patient practice. As his movements built, he felt the air around him begin to bristle. Chords of invisible energy wrapped around his fingers, coaxed out of their dormant state by every pass of his arm. He could feel the weight of that energy resisting the pull of his hand through the air.

The corners of his mouth turned in a smile as a familiar thrill filled his body.

Deep inside Durrin, his spark pulsed, allowing him to both feel the energy around him and control it. For seven years, that spark had been dormant, smothered by voidstone shackles. Even now, after two days of freedom, it was weak, like a coal smoldering in a burned-out fire. But with each growing motion, he coaxed it back to life.

The energy around him gave an audible crackle. Now. It was time.

He poured passion into his spark. It leapt in response, sending energy coursing through his nerves and up his arm, where it met the chords of energy wrapped around his fingertips and set them alight. A torrent of fire erupted around his hand. He felt no pain; the fire did nothing to his skin. He *was* fire.

For the first time in seven years, he felt truly alive.

He felt unstoppable.

Durrin danced through the steps of the routine, muscle memory from a thousand rehearsals flooding back to his limbs. Spinning and twirling, he passed the ball of fire from hand to hand, slowly gaining speed until the flame became a streak of light spinning around his figure.

Then, only halfway through his routine, the spark inside him flickered.

He stumbled. The fireball slipped from his fingers. It careened through the air and slammed into a nearby bush, sending daggers of flame in every direction.

Durrin doubled over, the breath knocked out of him from losing control of so much energy so abruptly. He gasped for a couple seconds, hands on his knees. Then he staggered over to the bush. It had caught fire, its branches crackling and popping.

If he let the bush burn, the smoke might betray his presence—or, worse, start a forest fire. Durrin held his hand over the bush, concentrating until he could feel the invisible rivulets of power and heat coursing outward. With a curl of his fingers, he drew some of that heat into the palm of his hand. As he did, the flames wavered and diminished. Opening his fingers, he let the power dissipate, causing the air above his hand to shimmer from the column of heat.

He drew power from the bush twice more, until the flames had died and the branches were reduced to smoldering twigs. Each effort left his spark feeling even more drained.

Finally, Durrin stepped away from the bush and stretched, letting out a groan. His horse looked up at him, idly flipping her tail.

"Unimpressed?" Durrin said. "So would be my classmates." He stumbled over to his canteen. "Imagine it: Cadet Rendhart—the Academy's three-time champion for the fifth Kymar routine. And now he can't even execute the first."

The horse snorted and returned to her grass.

Durrin sipped at his canteen, his thoughts turning to what awaited him at his destination. According to legend, Kymar Roline had developed not five, but six pyromancy routines. The Imperial Academy had only taught up to the fifth. The final routine—Kymar's sixth—was written on a secret scroll, kept in a forbidden vault in the heart of Calamar, its potent knowledge restricted to an elite few.

That scroll awaited him. He'd earned it seven years before.

Durrin returned to the middle of the glade, assessing his performance. He had failed to complete the beginner routine, yes—but for his first attempt in seven years, he hadn't done bad. His spark was growing in strength. A lifetime of training was coming back to him—slowly, but not as slowly as he had feared. When he had started at the Academy two decades ago, the first Kymar routine had taken him months of daily practice to master.

And daily practice would be how he'd master it again.

Durrin took a deep breath, resumed his stance, and began the first routine a second time.

※

Volthorn hated beginning a meeting with bad news.

He strode into the royal council room, his helmet under his arm. The other three participants in the war council were already waiting for him. Queen Adara, arrayed in a long silk dress, sat with perfect posture, her eyes bright with attention—but Volthorn couldn't help thinking she looked a size too small for the spacious throne she occupied.

Skagar paced around the edge of the room, blessedly silent for once.

To Adara's left was her other advisor and former co-regent, Lady Luviana. The elderly merfin rested in a pewter basin half filled with water.

Merfins were an aquatic species, humanoid from their torso upward but with dolphin-like tails instead of legs. Most lived in rivers, lakes, or oceans. Merfins such as Luviana, who chose to interact regularly with "land-walkers," were rare. And for good reason—transporting the royal advisor around the palace and maintaining her various reclining pools required an entire team of servants.

In Lady Luviana's case, her contributions far outweighed the labor costs she incurred. She had been a royal advisor for over ninety years, spanning five rulers' reigns—merfins were known for their incredible longevity. She also graced the court with her talent in vivamancy.

Lady Luviana held a small harp in her hands, plucking the conclusion of a wistful refrain as Volthorn entered. He could feel the spell it cast as he walked in. The music tugged on his body, urging his muscles to relax and his emotions to quiet.

Queen Adara rose to her feet. "Commander Skarr," she said, a warm smile on her face. "Welcome."

Volthorn bowed to all three. "Your Highness, Lady, Chancellor." He turned back to Luviana. "An interesting choice of music to precede a council of war. I would expect something more rousing."

"Stirring sagas are for the moment of battle, Commander," Luviana said, her voice almost as musically enchanting as her harp. "When planning what battles to fight, you must be calm as the morning wind."

"Unfortunately, today does not bring calming news," Volthorn said, striding to the middle of the room, where a huge map occupied the central table. He set his helmet down with a clang, dispersing the last vestiges of Luviana's vivamantic spell. "A messenger griffin just flew in. Calamar's hosts have left Meradov and are marching east. I fear Saven is their destination."

The queen's face turned a shade paler.

"So soon?" Skagar asked. "They've occupied the city scarcely a week."

"It's their haste that tells me they intend to capture Saven by mid-autumn," Volthorn said. High summer had just passed, leaving autumn just a few weeks away.

"What are their numbers?" Skagar said.

Luviana coughed, interrupting them. She gestured to the queen. "For the sake of Her Majesty, I think a quick overview of the present situation would be helpful, Commander."

Volthorn looked to Queen Adara for approval. She pursed her lips. "I believe I already have a good grasp, my lady. I do not need a refresher."

An awkward silence filled the council room. Finally, Lady Luviana nodded. "Of course, Your Majesty. It was just a suggestion; I wasn't sure how long it has been since your last briefing."

"Meradov fell six days ago," Queen Adara said, pointing to the city's location on the map. "With it, Calamar now has uncontested control of the Mera Valley, the upper Silvermoss, and its tributaries. This cements their hold over all our western provinces, which has been their main object for the last three years."

"Exactly, Your Majesty," said Volthorn, pleased with how Adara had stood up to Luviana's skepticism. "I expected Calamar to take the next month to shore up their new holdings. Today's news reveals that their plans are much more ambitious. They mean to capture the capital and end the war before the year is up." Volthorn used a long rod to slide troop markers across the map. "Scouts report that the host leaving Meradov numbers around fifty thousand."

"Nights alive, Commander," Skagar exclaimed. "We can't marshal half that number. How will we—"

"We can," Volthorn said, scowling at the interruption. "For the last three years, my predecessor, Commander Garren—may he rest in the light—has adopted a strategy of spreading our forces out, trying to hold various cities, win small victories here and there, and force the enemy to guard their flanks."

Volthorn pounded his fist on the table. "But those are not the results we need. Garren's strategy was a recipe for a long, slow death, as Meradov's fall makes all too clear. If we are to defeat Calamar, we must combine our forces and smash their army in battle."

Skagar opened his mouth, but Volthorn hurried on before he could interrupt again. "With your approval, I plan to gather nearly all our battalions and garrisons to the Arnon Plains—here." Volthorn pointed to the plains at the mouth of the Mera Valley, about a hundred miles west of Saven and fifty miles east of the Calamarvan army at Meradov. "All told, we will number around twenty-eight thousand. Yes, Skagar, our numbers are few. But they will have to suffice."

Volthorn used his rod to push the Calamarvan army down the Mera Valley. "I am fairly certain Calamar will try to cut straight across the Arnon Plains and capture Saven. They have just over a month to do it, before much of their army will have to march home for the fall harvest."

"As will much of ours," Skagar reminded him.

"Yes," Volthorn said. "But Calamar's conscript soldiers have farther to travel, and so must leave earlier. Only their professional soldiers—around ten thousand—will remain for the winter. If they haven't won the war by then, they'll have to hunker down in fortified cities until the spring."

Volthorn indicated the Arnon Plains with his rod. "Over the next month, my army will do all we can to slow them down without engaging in direct battle. We'll harass their flanks, burn bridges, plan ambushes. We know the terrain better, so we'll be able to dance away if they try to pin us down.

"I'm hoping this will lead to one of two possibilities. First, Calamar might split their army for faster travel, allowing us to isolate and defeat each division piecemeal. Second, there might be a brief window where their conscript farmers have departed and their professional army is exposed outside of any fortified city. If that happens, we can cut off their retreat and defeat their professional soldiers in a single battle."

With a flourish, Volthorn swept the Calamarvan armies off the map. "Either possibility could end this war."

He looked up at Queen Adara and her two advisors. Luviana's face was creased with concerned wrinkles. Skagar's tail was twitching in agitation. The queen's eyes were fixed on the map, her hands fidgeting absently with the hem of her long sleeves.

"Your Majesty?" Volthorn ventured.

Adara's eyes flitted from the map to Volthorn, then to her lap, then back to the map. Finally she wet her lips and looked to Skagar. "Chancellor? Any thoughts?"

Skagar spoke up without hesitation. "Your Majesty, I have deep concerns. Commander Skarr's audacity threatens our very existence. He proposes facing down an army twice his size on the open plains, without any walled cities to protect him. One poor maneuver, and our whole army could be wiped out!"

Volthorn felt his blood turning hot. He pushed it down. "My plans are perfectly viable, Chancellor. Calamar's forces will be slow, unfamiliar with the terrain and tied down by their supply lines. My troops will have no problem keeping out of reach until the moment I decide to engage.

"There are far less risky options," Skagar growled. "Pull our forces across the Silvermoss to Monine." He gestured to a city about halfway between Saven and Meradov. "It has strong walls, a defensible position. Calamar can't simply pass you by."

"But they *can* put me under siege with half their army," Volthorn objected, "and march the rest toward Saven. If I try to break out, they'll cut me to pieces battalion by battalion as I march them out the gates. No, Chancellor. If we let them pin us down, we're doomed. We must defeat them in open battle."

Luviana raised a webbed hand, nodding in agreement with Volthorn. "Commander Skarr has a point, Chancellor."

"It's a toss of dice with unfavorable odds," Skagar said, settling down on his haunches as he stared at the map, tail twitching. "I fear you are overly optimistic about our military's ability to pull off impossible victories."

Volthorn opened his mouth, ready to defend his troops, but the queen spoke first.

"What about negotiation?"

The room fell quiet as Skagar, Volthorn, and Luviana turned to look at her.

Queen Adara sat up straighter in the throne. "Battles and troop movements . . . is this our only option? I was thinking last night—*feeling* last night—that perhaps we could contact the emperor. Ask for a truce, or a treaty, or something."

"Arrange for a diplomatic end of the hostilities," Skagar translated.

"Yes," Adara said, her voice growing firmer. "Emperor Stoneclaw and my father were close friends once. We could appeal to that friendship, and—"

"Your Majesty," Skagar interrupted, "may I remind you that it is *Emperor Stoneclaw* who has claimed a third of our territory in the last three years. Any supposed friendship has been long since forgotten."

"Yet in the years before the war," Adara said, "Emperor Stoneclaw was often willing to come to terms when our two nations had disputes."

"*Willing* might be too strong a term, Your Majesty," Lady Luviana said, the water in her basin splashing as she shifted to a new position. "I was the one handling most of those disputes, if you recall. Calamar's disposition was anything but friendly."

"But I recall you yourself maintaining that the driving force behind the hostilities was not the emperor himself, but a faction within his government," Adara objected.

"If the emperor wanted peace, he would have sent us overtures long before now," Skagar said. "He has not. And I don't blame him. If my armies were having a fraction of the success that his have had, I wouldn't dream of stopping."

"And that's why we must proceed with my plan," Volthorn said, tapping the map with his rod. "As long as Calamar's armies march unchecked, they'll turn a deaf ear to any negotiations. Only if we score a decisive victory will they be willing to come to the table."

"Will they?" Adara said. "Or will they dig in their heels? Skagar, you taught me once that war is as much about prestige as territory or treasure. Perhaps Calamar can't afford to lose prestige on the international stage."

"Then we come to my plan regardless," Volthorn said. "If they won't back down when things are going well, nor when things are going wrong, then we must defeat them so decisively they have no *choice* but to sue for peace."

"Assuming you can do so without getting our army ripped to shreds," Skagar muttered.

Before Volthorn could verbalize a retort, Adara spoke again. "When were our last negotiations with Calamar?"

Luviana and Skagar exchanged embarrassed glances. Skagar's tail dipped nervously. "I believe it was right before the war started, Your Highness."

Adara's eyes widened. "We haven't had talks with them in three years?"

"No, Your Highness."

Adara sank back in her throne. "Then we should send Emperor Stoneclaw a letter immediately. It shall be an overture of peace, issued by my royal decree, as one of my first acts as queen."

Skagar scrunched his eyes shut. "Your Highness," he said, sighing. "Wartime negotiations are not to be treated lightly."

"Which is why you will help me draft it," Adara said. "If we send the message with a griffin tomorrow, it can reach Imperium in less than a week."

Volthorn scowled. "And *if* the emperor chooses to reply, it will be another week before we hear of it, or longer. What do you want me to do in the meantime? Let Calamar march toward our capital unchecked? We *need* to *fight*, Your Highness."

"I'm afraid the commander is right," said Luviana. "Don't put all your faith in negotiations, Your Highness. We can try, but prepare to be disappointed."

Adara stared at the map. Then she took a deep breath. "Very well, Commander. While we wait for an answer from Imperium, you may proceed with your plan."

Volthorn gave a deep bow. "Then with all due respect, Your Highness, I must see to my orders." He picked up his helmet and strode toward the door.

"Commander Skarr?"

Volthorn turned impatiently. "Yes, Your Highness?"

Adara's eyes seemed to stare into emptiness for a moment before refocusing on him. "May angels attend you, and may you only fight in the light."

Volthorn bowed and strode from the room.

CHAPTER 8

WYVERN WAY

A shadow fell over Durrin's horse.

Durrin leapt from the saddle, landing in a crouch on the ground, scanning the skies.

Nothing. Just a small cloud, skirting its way across the rising Sun.

His horse looked at him and snorted, then continued plodding up the mountain trail. Durrin scanned the skies again, then caught up to his mount.

"Don't be amused," he said, grabbing the reins. "You won't be laughing when I'm safe on the ground and you're being carried off by an oversized flying lizard."

He'd finally settled on a name for his horse: Raggedy Ruby. *Raggedy* because she wasn't exactly the youngest horse on the block, and *Ruby* for a touch of red hair in her mane.

As Durrin heaved himself back into Raggedy Ruby's saddle, his eyes involuntarily swept the skies again. The map called this route *Wyvern Way*: a weather-beaten trail, barely more than a path, that wound its way through the Rugeran Mountains fifty miles north of the Mera Valley.

When he had chosen this route, back in the security of the plains, he had hoped the pass lived up to its name. Wyverns were massive, two-legged flying reptiles, the apex predators of the skies. If this section of mountains truly held wyverns, their presence would deter griffin flights and small ground patrols, giving Durrin his best chance of slipping into Calamarvan territory unimpeded.

But now, with every movement in his peripheral vision making him jump, he was beginning to regret his choice. Wyverns were known to prey on deer, cows, reptilians, and even moose. A lone horse and rider, on an exposed path, would make a tempting target.

Eight days had passed since Durrin had left Saven. His skin had begun to tan—pyromancers didn't get sunburns, thankfully—and the long hours of riding, coupled with daily attempts at the first Kymar routine, were toning his muscles. He had left his stolen armor and uniform behind, opting instead for less conspicuous traveling clothes.

As he had ridden into higher and higher foothills, settlements had grown sparser, giving way to isolated ranches. Now the mouth of a rocky canyon gaped before him, its depths shrouded in shadow as the Sun hid behind the towering mountains around it. Scraggly pines stuck out of the sides of the canyon like rows of prickly teeth.

Into that mouth he rode, plunging into the twilight.

As his horse trotted along, Durrin reached within himself and found the flame flickering deep inside his chest. Then, taking a deep breath, he reached out with his mind.

Every pyromancer had a sixth sense—called *pyrosense*—that allowed them to detect the energy within living beings around them. Immediately, Durrin felt the powerful thrum of Raggedy Ruby beneath him, pulsing with each beat of her heart. He reached farther. Gradually, his mind became aware of a low, throbbing pulse, the lifeforce of a thousand plants around him, all living, all growing at once. Against that tapestry were faint sparks of animal life: perhaps a squirrel, a bird, or a mouse. His mind sensed them all, dimly, although he could not easily pinpoint in which direction or how far away.

He rode for some time, winding his way up the track, listening to the world around him with his mind. Every locale had a different pattern of sparks. Some places, like plains and fields, were serene as a gentle breeze. But these mountains were wild, young, and unpredictable.

He also watched with his eyes, scouting the path ahead, the woods to either side, and the skies above. Besides the occasional sparrow, nothing flew overhead. No griffins. And no wyverns.

"We may just slip through unnoticed," Durrin said, patting Ruby's neck.

Then he felt it—a new spark out of the myriad. This one was stronger and brighter than the others. It wasn't a wyvern—it was far too small for that, and too intelligent. Perhaps a snippen or a swifter, posted as a sentry to watch the road.

Durrin kept riding, displaying no reaction. In a situation like this, pyromancy was an advantage best kept secret for as long as possible. As he rode, he surreptitiously snapped his fingers, summoning a flame in his palm. He focused his mind on the creature he had detected, willing the flame to flicker in its direction.

The flame flickered to his left. A casual glance revealed a rocky crag jutting out from the canyon wall, its towering crest crowded with bushes.

It was the perfect sentry point. A lookout there could command a view nearly half a mile down the canyon. It was too late to hide: any half-decent sentry would have already spotted him.

His suspicion was confirmed when, a few seconds later, he heard a high-pitched bird call echo off the canyon walls. Five seconds later, another bird call answered it, issuing from somewhere up ahead. Both were well-crafted fakes. He should know—his mimicry teacher at the Academy had drilled him for two weeks on those exact calls.

"Here we go," Durrin murmured, shifting in his saddle. He reached out with his pyrosense, looking for the sparks that would indicate a patrol's presence. There they were, a hundred yards or so farther up the trail. As he rode closer, he could pick out their numbers. Eight. Nine. Ten. Maybe twelve warriors, moving toward him further up the trail.

"Demons' wings," Durrin quietly cursed. In his prime, he could have taken that many, sowing mayhem with fire and sword. But not today. In his current state, he couldn't handle more than three or four.

Durrin briefly considered turning his horse off the path in an attempt to dodge the trap. But the incline on one side of the trail was steep and rocky, while the other side dropped off toward the creek at the bottom of the canyon. Raggedy Ruby wouldn't get ten paces without spraining an ankle or falling. Turning back now would just invite pursuit. Durrin took a deep breath. "No way around but through, I guess."

He turned the next corner. A dozen warriors blocked his path.

"Halt!" the lead soldier cried. "Dismount and identify yourself!"

Durrin complied, his eyes sweeping over the patrol. By the style of their armor, they were Elandrians, not Calamarvans. Five had arrows nocked; the others hefted shields and spears. He'd have to buy some time, wait until they had let down their guard before making a break for it. Time for some acting.

Durrin fumbled to pull back his cloak, showing his empty belt. "I am unarmed," he said, pitching his voice higher and adding a slight warble. "My name is Roland Ridnur, just a merchant passing through." The name had been one of his go-to aliases when doing espionage work before his imprisonment. He wished he could let a bit of a Solapharian accent slip into his speech, but he was out of practice with that particular dialect, so he stuck with an Elandrian inflection.

The squad leader, a tall and lanky avir, stepped forward. His eyes were deep brown with suspicion. "Where are you from?"

"Marlay, a small town in Solapharia," Durrin responded. "I'm traveling there now."

"Solapharia?" the soldier said. "But that's north of here, not west."

Durrin heaved a sigh. "Marlay is on the far western end of Solapharia. This Sun-forsaken track is the fastest route from Modine—or at least it is now, with Meradov up in a flurry." That was hardly true—there were much better routes to the north. He was banking on the lad failing his impromptu geography test.

The avir flunked. "All right. What exactly are you transporting?" The avir looked askance at Durrin's horse. "Rags?"

"Don't be ridiculous," Durrin said. "I come down every spring with mules loaded with tin, sell the whole lot at Modine for hard silver, then head home." He pulled open one of his saddlebags, showing it was nearly empty. "Unfortunately, some thieves snuck into my camp three days ago and stole my whole year's earnings. Don't know how my wife and kids will be getting through the winter."

The squad leader kept frowning at him. Durrin looked down and scratched the back of his neck, doing his best to look like a merchant fallen on tough times.

"Well, Roland, I'm afraid I have bad news for you," the sergeant said. "Due to the war with Calamar, this pass is closed. And we're under orders to arrest anyone who attempts to cross."

The warrior in Durrin urged him to lash out at this helmed beanpole in front of him and make a break for the trees. But he pushed the urge down. It wasn't time yet. "Under arrest?" Durrin said, increasing the tremor in his voice. "For trying to get to my homeland? I wish you'd reconsider." He fumbled for the sack of coins at his belt. "The thieves didn't take all my earnings. Perhaps for a small fee . . ."

The sergeant's eyes flashed red. "Bribery won't work on me, scum pan. I'm here for my kingdom, not for silver. Crenick, Tvert, bind him."

Two korriks stepped forward, grabbed Durrin's arms with sharp claws, and lashed his wrists behind his back. Durrin gave some token resistance, crying out as they landed a couple kicks.

"Take him back to camp," the sergeant said.

Durrin let the squad of soldiers escort him up the path. After a hundred yards or so, they came to the patrol's camp, strategically situated in front of a natural chokepoint. Here, the canyon walls narrowed to within ten feet of each other, creating a ravine barely wide enough for the canyon's burbling creek. It was the perfect location for an outpost. If a Calamarvan force tried to move down the canyon from farther upstream, they could be held off nearly indefinitely by a small band of soldiers at the ravine's mouth.

Plus, the tall cliffs to one side and the pines on three others likely prevented wyvern attacks.

The camp, set up outside the ravine's mouth, consisted of just a few tents around a fire pit. It looked like the patrol had no horses. That would make his escape easier. The only real obstacle would be the single swifter among them.

Most of the soldiers went back to various tasks around the camp, leaving only a few soldiers still guarding him. He could wait longer for an ideal time to escape, but why? He was losing daylight.

Durrin turned so that none of the guards could see his hands tied behind his back. He then began moving the tips of his fingers in subtle circles, gathering invisible cords of momentum. With a sharp flick, he transformed the energy into a burst of searing heat, channeled into his bonds. One of the loops burned completely through, and the tension in the ropes around his wrists vanished. One shake, and they'd drop to the ground. But for the moment, they still resembled proper bonds.

"Search his bags, and confiscate anything suspicious," the sergeant was directing. "We'll send him down the canyon tomorrow morning."

"That really won't be necessary," Durrin said, still adopting his mercantile tremor.

"I'm afraid it will," the sergeant snapped.

Durrin dropped the accent. "I'm afraid you're wrong."

Durrin lashed out with his hands, snapping his bonds and striking both of his korrik escorts at the same time. Then he spun, flames shooting out from his whirling hands and spraying throughout the camp, catching dry leaves and tent fabric on fire. Soldiers ducked or shielded their eyes.

"Stop!"

"He's loose!"

Durrin sprang across the camp to Raggedy Ruby, kicking the soldier guarding her and leaping into the saddle. He dug his heels into Ruby's flanks. The mare must have understood the urgency, because she took off like a shooting star, faster than she'd ever bothered to run for Durrin before.

The soldiers scrambled to block his escape. But most made a major blunder; they ran to block the way back down the canyon. Durrin instead steered his horse straight toward the ravine leading farther up Wyvern Way.

Only the squad leader had the sense—and the long legs—to get in Durrin's way. He dashed to the ravine's mouth, raised a spear, and launched it at Durrin's chest.

But there was a reason Durrin had won the Kymar championship three years running. Even if it was over a decade ago.

Durrin shifted his arm upward, releasing a wave of energy that knocked the spear inches off course. The spear tip grazed his ribcage, ripping through the fabric of his jerkin but missing his skin. As it flashed by, he brought his hand up, closing his fingers around the shaft.

Durrin swept his hand over his head, whipping the spear around in a half circle. The haft clanged into the avir's helmet, knocking him off balance.

Durrin could easily have killed the sergeant. It would only have taken readjusting his grip on the spear and delivering a well-aimed thrust.

But this was just a soldier, doing his job. He didn't need to die today.

Instead, Durrin tucked the spear to his chest and leaned forward, digging his heels into the mare's sides. The wind whistled around him as Raggedy Ruby accelerated into a full gallop up the ravine, her hooves pummeling the creek bed. The shouts behind him grew fainter. Two arrows whizzed past him, clattering off rocks. After a few seconds, he rounded a bend and fell out of range.

"Well, that was easy enough," Durrin said, letting his horse slow a touch.

Then a swifter's howl echoed off the sides of the ravine.

Durrin drove his heels into Raggedy Ruby's flanks again, cursing. He'd forgotten about the swifter. Normally, a horseman wouldn't have much to worry about a pursuing swifter. While swifters could outrun any horse, they weren't big enough to take down a mounted rider, especially while dodging spear thrusts. But he needed to put enough distance between him and the rest of the patrol so that they wouldn't catch up while he dealt with the swifter.

Durrin glanced behind him and saw a streak of brown fur, barely forty yards behind him and gaining quickly. Shadows, but those creatures were *fast*. He snapped the fingers of his left hand, summoning a spike of flame that he winged behind him. The swifter dodged it effortlessly without even breaking stride.

Very well. Durrin spun his spear, summoning a swirling whirlwind of flames. Then he flung the fiery vortex at the swifter behind him.

The swifter drew up short, mouthing something too distant for Durrin to hear. The ball of flames came within three yards of its target, then shattered, fragments of flame fanning out to either side like they had hit an invisible wall.

Confound it. *Verbomancy.*

It was one of the five branches of magic, parallel to pyromancy and terramancy. Verbomancers could manipulate the air itself with their words, causing gusts of wind, influencing the weather, or—in this case—creating a wall of solidified air.

In Durrin's experience, verbomancers always meant trouble.

Only a moment later, Raggedy Ruby stumbled, as if she had galloped into an invisible tripwire—which, thanks to the verbomancer, she probably had. Sky and earth tipped in Durrin's vision as he pitched forward. Then his training kicked in, and he channeled his momentum into a ball of fire that he winged blindly behind him. A yelp told him the flaming projectile had hit its target.

Raggedy Ruby faltered, then got gingerly back to her feet. She got off to an uncertain trot, then, apparently assured that her limbs were still intact, eased back into a true gallop. Durrin glanced behind him. The swifter was only thirty yards away now, some fur singed but otherwise undeterred.

The trail climbed upwards as the ravine widened out into a proper canyon again. Durrin hunched over his horse's neck, slitting his eyes against the wind. His horse would tire soon, long before the swifter would, leaving him at the mercy of an opponent who could surround him with invisible walls if given enough time. *Options. Options . . .*

The tree line broke. He rode out onto a flat stretch of rock, interrupted by only the occasional bush or patch of grass. Mighty flanks of mountains rose to either side, while rows of peaks and valleys cascaded before him: the eastern side of the Rugeran Mountains, with a distant flat line of plains far beyond. He had reached the summit of the pass, higher than even trees grew.

Raggedy Ruby fell into a comfortable rhythm as she streaked across the pass. Tears from the cold air welled in Durrin's eyes, blurring his vision. Every few seconds, he impatiently wiped them away, but they would come back a moment later. Unable to see clearly how far away the swifter was, Durrin hunched over in the saddle and focused instead on his pyrosense.

The world came to life around him. The horse beneath him was a roaring flame of sinew and strength. Behind him, growing steadily closer, he sensed an unflickering fountain of energy indicating his swifter pursuer. These two sparks, the horse and the swifter, were the only animals in the vicinity, two blazing fireballs against a scattered backdrop of grass and shrubs.

Then he felt a third spark. It was faint, meaning it was far away. But it was unlike any spark he'd felt before. Primal. Fierce. *Huge.*

And growing nearer. Rapidly.

Sudden panic coursed through Durrin, freezing his muscles.

Then the image of a scroll in a sealed vault flashed across his mind. No, he wasn't going to let his panic stop him. He hadn't survived seven years in a dungeon and traveled two hundred miles to end up as a reptile's lunch.

Durrin jerked the reins with all his weight, yanking Raggedy Ruby's head up and cutting off her gallop. He swept his spear in a twisting arc that caught the wave of misplaced momentum and channeled it into a blast of fire above him.

A primal scream split the sky. Something dark, winged, and scaly sliced through the air in front of him, talons as long as Durrin's hand raking the air mere feet from his head. The creature plowed through the inferno he had summoned, scattering heat and flames like a battering ram.

Then the danger passed. The creature, its wingspan as long as a cottage, retreated into the sky, screaming as it went. Raggedy Ruby bucked then, and it was all Durrin could do to avoid flying off.

It took Durrin half a minute to calm his steed. Ruby's eyes were rolling, sweat pouring down her glossy neck as she skittered back and forth, neighing loud enough to wake the deaf. In the commotion, Durrin barely noticed the swifter dash back to the tree line and disappear.

"Scared of a wee little wyvern, are we?" he called after it, feeling defiantly emboldened in the wake of the sudden attack and its unexpected outcome. "Be thankful they find swifters too scrawny to bother!"

Finally Raggedy Ruby came to a stop, her muscles spasming every couple seconds as she heaved huge breaths. Durrin breathed heavily too, his heart still hammering in his chest like a woodpecker. He scanned the sky, all senses trained for movement.

Nothing.

"Well, not too bad, not too bad," Durrin said, patting his horse's neck. "We scared off a wyvern and let it scare off our pursuer at the same time. Now as long as our racing hearts don't kill us, we just have a long descent through the mountains, a few checkpoints, and nine hundred miles of roads, then we should arrive at Imperium in just about two weeks."

Raggedy Ruby gave him a look that was decidedly unappreciative.

CHAPTER 9

DESPERATE TIMES, DARING PLANS

Two days later.

Volthorn had lied to Queen Adara.

He hadn't meant to. At the time, sitting inside Saven's mighty walls and riding the euphoria of the coronation, Volthorn had felt aglow with confidence. It was with that confidence that he had assured the queen and her counselors that he and his army could pull off the impossible.

But now, back at the front after a long week of riding, he saw things more realistically.

They were trying to pull off the *impossible*.

"Next," he growled, planting his claws in the dust of the training yard.

His latest opponent advanced cautiously. An avir lad, probably no older than nineteen, his face was white under his helm with nervousness.

"You have the longer reach," Volthorn reminded him. "Use it."

The recent recruit leveled his blunted spear and charged. Volthorn stepped back, dancing to the side as he knocked the thrust away with his shield. Volthorn maneuvered to keep himself on the avir's right side, where it was more difficult for the avir to turn his spear. "Come on," Volthorn coached. "Your spear tip will reach me long before my sword reaches you. Keep thrusting."

The avir stepped forward, spear driving toward Volthorn's face. Volthorn brought his shield up, deflecting the blow. Stepping forward under the cover of his shield, he slammed the blunted tip of his wooden practice sword into the soldier's leg.

"Out!" Volthorn said. "In a real fight, you'd be on the ground with a life-threatening wound."

The avir rubbed his thigh, wincing. "How do I improve, Commander? You said to thrust, but it left me wide open."

"Thrust, then withdraw," said Volthorn, demonstrating with his sword. "Step forward, step back. Be ready to block the moment your attack ends. Understand?"

"Yes, Commander Skarr."

"Good. Keep drilling."

Volthorn turned away, removing his helmet and wiping the sweat from the scales of his face. He stepped to the side of the yard, where the captain over training waited.

The captain saluted. "Your assessment, Commander?"

"You have them on the right track," Volthorn said. "These recruits have good hearts, all of them. A few more weeks of training, and they would become capable soldiers."

The implication hung in the air until the training captain picked it out and voiced it aloud. ". . . But we don't have a few more weeks, do we."

"We have three days, at most, before we're either on the march or in battle," said Volthorn. He handed his training sword to an aide and retrieved his real gear, including his terramancy gems and equipment. "Practice is what they need most. Relieve the new squads of all other camp duties and double their training time. Ten hours per day."

"I'll see to it, Commander," said the captain.

Volthorn left the training grounds and stepped briskly through the war camp, weaving his way through patches of tents and fleets of wagons. The air was alive with the clang of blacksmiths' tools, the smoke of cooking fires, and the wind of griffins' wings.

After a few minutes, his brother Kelzern jogged up to him. "There you are," he said. "I was looking all over for you?"

"I had some time open up and thought I'd review the newest recruits," said Volthorn. "Anything to report?"

"The garrison from Modine just arrived," Kelzern said. "Two thousand strong. They left none behind, just as you ordered."

"Good," Volthorn said. "What else?"

"Afternoon flight reports came in. Calamar's host will have advanced another ten miles down the Mera Valley today."

Volthorn ran the number through his brain and processed the implications. The Calamarvans were just two days' march away now. He had even less time than he had thought.

"Is that all?"

"There's something else," said Kelzern.

Something about Kelzern's tone made Volthorn stop and look at him. "What is it?"

"News from one of our border patrols," said Kelzern, looking unsettled. "They've been guarding an obscure pass called Wyvern Way, about fifty miles north of here. Two days ago, they detained a man trying to cross over to Calamar's side of the pass."

Volthorn tightened his claws around the pommel of his sword. "And?"

"He turned out to be a pyromancer. He broke free and escaped."

Volthorn dug the claws of his foot into the ground underneath him. "Do you think it was Rendhart?" he questioned.

"Based on their description, most likely," Kelzern said.

Volthorn's brother knew the significance as well as Volthorn did. Kelzern had been there that same fateful day, knocked out by the assassin's initial burst of lightning. It had taken him over a week to recover.

"I should never have reduced the border patrols," said Volthorn, resuming his walk. "They were at half strength and in no condition to fight a skilled pyromancer."

"But you need the troops here more," Kelzern said. "Be fair to yourself, Volthorn. You had no idea which route Rendhart was going to take."

Volthorn nodded reluctantly. "You're right." He did his best to let the matter go. For better or for worse, Rendhart was now out of Elandria's reach.

Still, Volthorn couldn't help but feeling like he had made a miscalculation.

By the time Volthorn and Kelzern reached the command tent, their brother Trazar was waiting for them, along with all four of Volthorn's generals: Generals Orrin and Branoc, both humans; General Embertail, a red-tailed griffin; and General Snarltooth, a swifter. Each general would be commanding a different division of the army in the coming campaign.

Volthorn saluted each of his officers, exchanging greetings and pleasantries. Beneath his smile, he studied each of them carefully. Just over a week ago, he'd been their same rank. How did they feel about getting passed over, and now having to take orders from him?

"Let's get started," Volthorn said. He turned to Kelzern. "Run perimeter on the tent. Don't let anyone come within twenty paces, not staff nor messenger nor even a snippen. And *especially* no keen-eared swifters."

Kelzern nodded and slipped back outside.

Volthorn turned to Trazar. "My precautions."

His brother handed him an oddly shaped piece of pink quartzite, with a wide base, a twisted stem, and a knobby top. Volthorn touched his hand to a jewel on his belt, sucking terracharge from the gem into his fingers. Then he brought his fingers into contact with the quartzite, transferring the energy into the rock. He closed his eyes, using his mind to measure the subtle throb of energy now vibrating in the rock. Good—that should last several hours.

Volthorn flexed his muscles and snapped the quartzite at its narrowest point, releasing a loud bang. In its wake, the stone began glowing with a soft pink light.

His generals watched in curiosity. "Commander," the swifter hazarded. "May I ask—"

"Quartzite beacon," Volthorn answered. "It emits a terracharge field that interrupts other terramantic devices. That includes any listening stone that a spy may have placed in here."

Volthorn's brother handed him a vial of green fluid and a piece of leather incised with an intricate pattern. "This is an anti-eavesdropping rune," Volthorn explained. "I had one of our camp aquamancers prepare it this morning. It should stop any verbomancer from using a spell to overhear us."

Volthorn placed the piece of leather on the table, straightening its corners. Then he unstopped the vial and dripped the liquid carefully onto the rune. The droplets filled the etched lines with a slight hiss, sending up a cloud of steam smelling faintly of cloves.

"I hope it works," Volthorn said, eyeing the empty vial. "I have no idea what's in it, but the aquamancer assured me it was all very expensive ingredients."

"They always say that," General Orrin said, snorting. The others laughed.

Volthorn looked over the objects on the table. *I've blocked any attempt to spy using terramancy and verbomancy. Aquamancy and vivamancy have no way to listen long-distance, so they pose no threat. That just leaves pyromancy.* Pyromancers had incredible hearing, a side effect of their sensitivity to the slightest waves of energy. *The camp is full of noise, and Kelzern is making sure no one comes near this tent. That will have to suffice.*

The thought made his worries about Rendhart resurface. The man may not pose a threat for the moment. But once he resumed serving under Calamar's banner, what then? Would he return to Elandria as a spy? Or worse—as an assassin once again?

He'd worry about that later. "Generals," Volthorn said, planting his clawed hands on the war table, where a large map was laid out. "I assume you've each studied the battleplans I sent you?"

The generals each nodded.

"Good," said Volthorn. "Forget all about them." He watched as surprise flashed across their faces. "Those plans were only diversions. For security reasons, I'm acting under the assumption that someone in one of our many staff positions may be a spy for Calamar. Written plans are dangerous—which is why all our key strategy meetings will be strictly in person, under precautions such as I've taken today."

General Branoc, his aging cavalry general, muttered something about a poor memory. Volthorn made a mental note to review everything with him a second time.

Volthorn pointed to the map in front of him. "The latest reports place Calamar's host here, halfway down the Mera Valley. Between their vanguard, their marching columns, and their rearguard, they total fifty-five thousand troops."

"More than we expected," General Orrin said, rubbing his sideburns thoughtfully.

"Yes," Volthorn admitted. "I was anticipating they'd leave more behind to garrison Meradov. Instead, they are committing everything to this campaign."

He tapped the map where their forces were camped, where the Mera Valley emptied out onto the Arnon Plains. "But so are we. With our force from Modine that arrived today, plus two more garrisons that are arriving tomorrow, we will have twenty-five thousand fighting troops, plus about three thousand swifters and griffins."

Volthorn took a deep breath. He knew what he was about to propose would be controversial. "Because of the desperate situation, I plan to order the four battalions holding the Penandre Valley to march north to reinforce us."

The Penandre Valley was on the south-western corner of Elandria's territory. Besides the Mera Valley, it was the only other gap in the Rugeran Mountains, making it the only other easy route from Calamar to Elandria.

General Orrin immediately shook his head. "That valley is critical to our defense," he said. "If we pull out those troops, we'll have a second Calamarvan host marching unopposed right up the Angerflood."

"From all our reports, there's no buildup of Calamarvan troops anywhere near the Penandre," Volthorn said. "They seem to be channeling all their resources up here. Once they get word that our forces have pulled out of the Penandre, it will be too late to mount any offensive down there before winter sets in."

His generals mulled this over. "What about next spring?" the swifter named Snarltooth asked, sitting up on his back paws to get a better view of the map.

"I hope to win the war by then," Volthorn said. "If not, we can reposition our forces over the winter and have the Penandre Valley guarded again by the first thaws."

General Embertail—a sleek, red-tailed griffin—cocked her feathered head, her keen eyes roving over the map. "I don't like it. It's too risky."

"War is risky," Volthorn said. "You win by balancing risks. By increasing the slight risk of invasion on our southwest border, I decrease the *massive* risk that our army here will be wiped out by a force nearly twice its size. Perhaps we will need those troops there. But we *know* we need them here."

He glanced over at the anti-eavesdropping rune. It was still emitting a steady supply of steam, at least for now. The aquamancer had said it should last around two hours. "We need to move on. Any last objections?"

"Have you run this by Her Majesty?" asked General Branoc.

Volthorn paused, frowning. "No," he finally said. "It hadn't occurred to me."

"This is not a minor troop movement," General Branoc said. He shifted in his seat, popping the aging joints of his back. "This needs royal approval."

"Sending a messenger to the palace will add at least a day's delay, if not two," Volthorn said. "And in any case, Queen Adara is too young to understand the strategic situation."

"With all due respect," said General Branoc, "Her Highness is our anointed queen. She must be the one to approve a risk like this."

Volthorn looked around. The other generals each nodded their agreement.

"Very well," Volthorn finally said. "I will run it by Her Majesty. Any *other* objections?"

His generals kept silent.

"Good. Moving on." Volthorn moved his finger across the map, tapping four rivers that cut north to south across the Arnon Plains. "These tributaries are key. They represent four lines of defense between here and Saven. As long as each river can buy us a week of time, we can survive. And I intend to make the best use of them as possible."

For the next hour and a half, Volthorn talked his generals through the details of his strategic plan, including troop deployment, logistics, defensive positions, and battlefield tactics. They discussed supply lines, chains of command, and the best way to deploy the army's hundred or so mancerers in battle.

Volthorn's strategy relied on extensive coordination. The army's infantry, numbering about twenty-four thousand avirs, humans, and korriks on foot, would be split between three divisions, commanded by General Orrin, General Snarltooth, and Volthorn himself. These divisions would be in a near constant state of retreat, keeping just out of reach of Calamar's army as it advanced. As one division withdrew, the second would deploy behind it, ready to beat back any forays by the Calamarvan vanguard. This left the third division free to march either to the right or to the left in a series of feints meant to keep the Calamarvan host constantly vigilant about being outflanked.

As the three infantry divisions performed their dance of precision, General Branoc would lead the cavalry division—three thousand humans and avirs on horseback, with supporting units of swifters—in hit-and-run raids, meant to harass the Calamarvan flanks or interrupt their supply line. The key would be for General Branoc to stay close enough to the main army to rush to their aid in the event of a battle, and to not get himself trapped. Volthorn was not too worried: the grizzled general knew the Arnon Plains like the laces of his boots.

Key to all of this would be the reconnaissance division, commanded by General Embertail. Composed of griffin flights in the sky and swifter packs on the ground, the reconnaissance branch had a two-fold duty: first, keep tabs on the enemy's movements, and second, prevent the enemy from scouting the Elandrians' movement. The battle for superiority in the air and on the ground would be constant, bloody, and relentless, as griffins fought each other beak-to-claw and swifter packs hunted each other across the countryside. But the results could easily spell the triumph or ruin of the entire campaign.

Near the end of the meeting, as his generals hammered out the details of battalion reassignments, Volthorn took a step back and surveyed them all: a cadre of veteran officers, the brightest minds in Elandria's military, discussing how to harass and defeat an army twice their size.

Who knew? They might even have a chance of pulling it off.

CHAPTER 10

LORD SALIDAR

Red banners greeted Durrin on the other side of Wyvern Way.
He had forgotten just how much he missed seeing that color.
Red—the color of strength and courage. The color of Calamar.
The color of home.

At the foothills of the mountain pass, he came to a Calamarvan outpost, its red banners snapping proudly above a wooden stockade. The soldiers were initially suspicious, and rightfully so: Who was this cloaked figure, riding alone out of Elandrian territory? But their hostility had disappeared with the drop of a name.

"I am on the special errand of His Excellency, Lord Salidar Aram," Durrin announced. "He will not be pleased if I am delayed."

The soldiers immediately responded with bows, apologies, and fresh provisions.

Over the next few days, Durrin rode through the plains and highlands of Western Elandria, its war-ravished towns now flying the red banners of Calamar. Then he crossed a low mountain range into a prosperous, bustling province of Calamar called Wormul. Wormul had once been a collection of independent city states, until trade wars devolved into actual wars two decades before. To keep the trade routes flowing, Calamar had been forced to step in and annex the whole region. Durrin still remembered his disappointment as a young lad, when the conflict had ended before he could enlist.

From Wormul, he and Raggedy Ruby took a barge upriver into the heartland of Calamar. After a week of sailing, they reached the capital, Imperium.

No other city in the world rivaled Imperium in size—some said as many as a million people lived within its walls. It had only grown in Durrin's seven-year absence. As his barge approached, he passed hundreds of laborers raising a wall to enclose a new urban sector.

Where the river met the city, a splendid new statue greeted him: a magnificent swifter, carved from one massive slab of red marble thirty feet high, its regal mouth turned in a snarl to ward off Calamar's enemies. An inscription at its base identified it as a depiction of Emperor Stoneclaw's eldest son, Crown Prince Thundertail.

Imperium sprawled across a plain, with the river on the south and a mountain range on the north. Four massive spurs of rock jutted out from that range, extending like fingers into the city. Those spurs defined both the physical and the social hierarchy of the city.

Crowning the easternmost and tallest spur was the Imperial Palace: a soaring complex of columns and arches, brimming with rooftop gardens and hanging ivy.

The second spur, not quite as tall but sticking farther out into the city, was dominated by a palace built in a markedly different style: monolithic walls instead of columned porticos, blocky battlements instead of gardens, with the balustrades decorated with carved reliefs rather than ivy. Though *technically* smaller than the Imperial Palace, its towering profile made it appear bigger to those walking the streets below—no doubt the intent of its architect. This was the palace of Salidar Aram, high vizier to the emperor himself.

Imperium's third spur was adorned by an ascending series of columned structures. These were the archives, sanctuaries, and courts of the Knights Vigilant, Calamar's dominant religious order and the administrator of its laws.

The fourth and final ridge held schools dedicated to each of the five mancery arts. From the docks, Durrin could barely see the spires of his alma mater, the Imperial Pyromantic Academy.

In the shadow of these towering buildings, the sides of each spur held estates and manor houses: the domain of the wealthy. In the valleys between each spur, and in the plain spreading out to the river, lived the city's poorest classes—craftsmen, laborers, and slaves, packed into ramshackle neighborhoods.

Durrin didn't hesitate. Once off the boat, he steered his horse through the crowded streets, charting a course straight toward the palace on the second spur.

It was time to reunite with his old master.

Memories flooded him as the door guards admitted him into the fore-chamber of Salidar's palace. How many times had he come here, hooded and cloaked as he was now, to report on a mission or accept a new assignment? And yet the palace was not without its changes. He strode to the wall to study a new mural. It depicted a battle in ferocious detail, probably one of Calamar's triumphs in the war with Elandria. In the center of the mural, painted larger than any other figure, towered a man in golden armor: Salidar. He held his arm outstretched to order his troops onward, as terrified Elandrians turned and fled before him.

Footsteps sounded on the cold stones. Durrin turned to see a stocky human enter the chamber, a scowl engraved upon his face. He wore an immaculate suit of blue livery with purple highlights.

Durrin leaned back against the mural. "Yorid! What a surprise. I hope you haven't been glowering like that since I last saw you seven years ago."

The steward stopped and scanned Durrin up and down. Finally, he let out a grunt. "I thought I was rid of you."

Durrin shrugged. "No such luck." He gestured at Yorid's elaborate clothes. "I see your uniform has seen an upgrade."

"Your manners haven't."

Societal rules demanded that Durrin keep his head bowed in Yorid's presence. Yorid, as the chief steward of a high nobleman, was several social tiers above Durrin, who was in effect still just a tradesman. Seven years before, when Yorid had been a mid-level servant, they'd been on roughly equal footing.

Durrin made an overly elaborate bow. "My greatest apologies, my liege. Would it please my liege to inform his liege that my liege's humble servant requests an audience with my liege's liege?"

Yorid's frown didn't budge. "I'll tell His Excellency that you're alive—somehow—and you want to talk to him." He turned to leave. "And no snooping around while you're here, Rendhart. I don't want to find you in the treasury again."

"That was eleven years ago," Durrin said. "And besides, I was exploring, not snooping."

"You picked two locks and impersonated a guard," Yorid grunted as he stomped away.

"I could have sworn it was three," Durrin said to himself.

In the steward's absence, Durrin wandered over to a window and looked out over the city. In the last half hour, something had appeared over the city's fourth spur. Ascending straight up from the crown of the ridge was a column of pulsating light, swirling like a multicolored ribbon until it disappeared into the clouds.

The phenomenon was called a leyline beacon: a natural fountain of terramantic energy, one of a hundred or so dotted across the world. Leyline beacons were essential for the operation of terramancy: every terramantic talisman had to derive its charge from a leyline. As a result, nearly every leyline beacon in the world—except for a few in extremely remote locations—was highly coveted, heavily fortified, and rigorously taxed.

Imperium's leyline beacon appeared consistently every late afternoon. It was the strongest and steadiest in the entire empire—and the main reason Imperium had been built here centuries ago.

The long blast of a horn shook Durrin out of his thoughts. The crowded streets below were alive with voices and the clack of wood on stone as storekeepers closed their shops and carts rumbled toward their final destinations for the day. Dusk was approaching. Soon the Knights Vigilant would blow the second evening horn, marking the onset of night.

In Imperium, no one stayed out at night. Night was the domain of cutthroats, thieves, and demons.

Not that that had ever stopped Durrin.

The stomp of surly feet marked Yorid's return. "His Excellency has decided, contrary to my most strident objections, to admit you into his presence. Follow me."

Durrin shadowed Yorid up a staircase, through a dining hall bustling with servants cleaning up a meal, and to an armed checkpoint, where Durrin was searched for weapons.

"Seven years ago, I was exempted from these searches," Durrin grumbled as a guard patted him down.

"So were a lot of people," Yorid grunted. "His Excellency doesn't take chances anymore."

Yorid paused at an ornate set of bronze doors. "Don't take too much of His Excellency's time. He just entertained the emperor for supper and was hoping to enjoy some quiet reflection."

The guards opened the door, and Yorid gestured for Durrin to enter.

Walking into Salidar's office was like stepping into another world. The glow from a chandelier reflected off a hundred gilded treasures and thousands of precious jewels. Each wall boasted an exotic array of weapons, statues, and paintings—the trophies of forty years of military triumphs.

In the center of the glistening room, clothed in velvets so fine that they were worth their weight in gold, stood Lord Salidar Aram, Governor of the Western Provinces, Captain of the Host of Ten Thousand, and High Vizier of the Eternal Empire of Calamar.

Salidar waited for Yorid to exit, then swept toward Durrin with arms outstretched. "Durrin Rendhart," he announced, his voice as magnanimous as seven years ago. "Welcome back, my most talented and loyal friend."

Durrin pulled back his hood and gave a slight bow. "It's been a long time, Your Excellency."

Salidar put an arm around Durrin's shoulders, steering him further into the room. "Who would have believed that the legendary Rendhart has been alive all these years? I thought for sure those treacherous Elandrians had somehow managed to kill you."

"No such luck," Durrin replied wryly. "Imprisonment was the best they could offer."

"But you have escaped at last!" Salidar said.

"And I came straight to my old patron," Durrin said. No sense in correcting the vizier. Durrin himself still could make no sense of his inexplicable release. Salidar would react to that detail only with suspicion.

Salidar noticed Durrin holding his gaze and frowned. "Given your long captivity, Durrin, I will forgive your lack of propriety this once."

Durrin quickly averted his eyes. In Calamar, to look a superior in the eyes was a serious affront, punishable by law. Eyes betrayed motive and emotion, and to see one's eyes was therefore to have power. "Forgive me, Your Excellency. I fear I have forgotten old habits."

Durrin studied the room's furnishings instead, conscious of the vizier looking him up and down. Durrin gestured to a set of throwing darts on a table. "I see you've taken up a new hobby."

"Ah, the darts? Yes." Salidar picked one up, hefting it expertly in his fingers before pivoting and throwing it at a map on the far wall, where it struck, quivering. "A simple game, but a diverting one. But I imagine you did not come here for small talk. What is on your mind?"

Durrin snapped his fingers, summoning a flame that he held in his hand, staring into its depths. "I have come to claim what you promised me."

Salidar threw another dart. "Kymar's scrolls, I recall?"

"Kymar's *scroll*," Durrin said, feeling his heart surge at the mention. "His sixth scroll. The last scroll."

"Ah, yes, the scroll forbidden to all but the masters of the Pyromancers' Guild," said Salidar. "The scroll held in the deepest vaults of the Pyromantic Academy. The scroll that not even I—nor even the emperor himself—has access to." The implication behind Salidar's words was clear. If *he* could not access that scroll, how could he give it to Durrin?

"You made me a promise, Your Excellency," Durrin said, forcing himself to keep his voice even. "If I carried out the emperor's order, you would make sure I became a guild master, with all its privileges—including access to that scroll."

Salidar did not immediately reply. Instead he glided his way to a table set with tea, figs, and tarts. "Guild mastership . . . is not an easy favor to grant at the moment," he said as he poured them each a cup.

Durrin stayed where he was. "A deal is a deal," he said. "I earned it, did I not?"

"Yes, earned it and double, my old friend and ally," Salidar said. "What you pulled off, seven years ago . . ." Salidar shook his head. "No one else possessed the combination of skill, patriotism, and unflinching courage that the task required. You neutralized an enemy of Calamar mere hours before he would have unleashed irrevocable harm on our people."

"And the scroll?"

Salidar sighed, then took a long draught of tea before resuming. "My relationship with the guild masters has not gone unchanged these last seven years. Some have grown slightly . . . discontented with me of late. Persuading them to elevate you to their ranks, whom some do not know, and whom others remember only with jealousy, will be difficult."

Durrin raised his eyebrow. "You're talking as though you were no longer the undisputed master of Calamar."

"Then let me be frank," said Salidar. "I am not. Much has changed in seven years, Durrin. Yes, my power and wealth have grown. For almost two decades now I have been the grand vizier, right-hand man to the emperor himself. Under my care, Calamar has become stronger and wealthier than ever before. The brigands on the South Sea have been quashed. We have expanded west, north, and east, subduing tribes of raiders and civilizing the populations. We have built bridges and roads, cities and harbors. Trade is blossoming, and the markets are busy."

Salidar stepped over to the map. "But Elandria has been a thorn in our side. They fear us, Durrin; they fear our power and prosperity. So they seek to deny us the resource that we most need, hoping to make barren our fields and starve our people."

"Haeber crystals," Durrin said.

He was well-acquainted with haeber, and its strategic importance, from both lectures at the Academy and his subsequent career collecting intel for Salidar. Haeber was a precious commodity, mined at the edge of the world and then shipped thousands of miles over sea and land, at great expense. Haeber came in the form of soft, pale-white crystals, about the size of a fist. Farmers the world over ground the crystals down into a fine powder and sowed the powder in their fields before planting. Every field needed a sprinkling of haeber every couple of years, or the crops would begin to fail. In Calamar, most of the haeber supply came overland through Elandria.

Salidar nodded. "Yes. For over a decade Elandria has created a shortage. In the years before the war, shipments over the border steadily dwindled to almost nothing. For a long time, I advocated taking a harsher line against Elandria. But there are some in the court who harbor sympathies to the Elandrian nobility. When war finally came three years ago, it was much later than it should have."

"What sparked the conflict?" Durrin asked, still piecing together the events of recent history. The other inmates at Irongate Isle hadn't exactly been the best sources of international political analysis.

"Elandria broke the terms of a treaty and halted all haeber shipments to us," said Salidar. "They intended to starve us. We had to fight back. Our armies have already seized haeber crystals sufficient for all our farms in the central provinces, as well as much grain and livestock. Once we conquer their capital and assimilate Elandria as a new territory, we'll be able to secure the trade routes once and for all."

Salidar set down his cup and began to pace, his hands clasped behind his back. "But the war has not gone as well as the emperor and I hoped. Thanks to the incompetence of our generals and the cunning of theirs, it has dragged on for three years now. Some in the court have grown weary. They petition the emperor for us to surrender and retreat. Others have grown envious of me and are attempting to undercut the war, denying my army sufficient supplies or troops.

"And amidst it all, we have received this!" Salidar held up a scroll, sealed with the royal crest of the Everborn family. "It arrived just a few days before you did, carried by an official envoy of Elandria." He dropped it contemptuously. "The young offspring of Everborn has been crowned queen, and now she thinks she can parley with us on equal terms. A ludicrous notion, but if some at court catch wind of it, they may twist it to their advantage."

Durrin didn't ask what Salidar was doing with an official message meant only for the emperor. Some questions were better left unanswered.

Salidar turned back to him. "I hope that helps you understand my position, Durrin. I want nothing more than to help you become the most powerful pyromancer in Calamar—the most powerful pyromancer in the world! But that requires a level of influence with the Pyromancer's Guild that I do not currently possess—not until we win this war."

Durrin stared into his cup. "So how can I help you win it?"

He could hear Salidar smile. "Ah, *that* is the right question, Durrin."

The vizier selected another dart, turning back to his map. "You may have wondered why I throw at a map, not a target. It is a matter of aim. Unlike a target, where the bullseye is painted for you, the trick to war and politics is not just striking accurately, but knowing *where* to strike."

Salidar stepped closer to the map, examining the kingdom of Elandria. "Our armies are already marching on their capital. They have gathered to stop us, but we outnumber them two to one. A crushing victory on the field of battle is imminent."

"That will not be enough," Durrin said. "I have spent many years among the Elandrians. They are not the type to surrender."

"Not while a member of their precious Everborn family sits on the throne," said Salidar. Quick as a snake, he sunk the dart into the capital city of Saven. "So that is where we must strike. The blow will be bitter. To lose their queen, mere weeks after her coronation . . ."

"Your Excellency, she is only eighteen," Durrin said, a pit forming in his stomach. His mind returned to the young figure he had seen through the crowd. "Surely a youth on the throne is an asset to us, not a threat."

"*Any* Everborn, no matter their age, is a threat," Salidar said. "There are old sympathies in the imperial court that her name alone threatens to revive. No. She must be removed. The only question is how. If her death is traced back to Calamar, her people may only become more entrenched in their lost cause."

Salidar began to pace again. "Your timing could not have been better, Durrin. I have ideas of how to solve this problem, but I have needed someone to take the lead, someone with great skill whom I could trust. Someone like you."

"You're too kind," Durrin said, hiding his unease. He didn't like where this conversation was going.

"My options have been severely limited of late," Salidar continued. "My enemies in the court have formidable coffers, and I can no longer trust all my servants. Many of my operatives are being watched. But none of my enemies will know that you have escaped. Few even remember your existence. This opens whole new avenues . . ."

"Any assassination, no matter how subtle, will be pinned on Calamar," Durrin said.

"And if it resembles an accident?"

Durrin shook his head. "The Elandrians will not be so naive a second time."

"Then we must pin the blame on a different group," said Salidar. "You have relations with the Mitrian tribes, do you not? Perhaps we could hire a strike team—"

"The Mitrians would never agree to that," Durrin interrupted. "Their chiefs have made a pact of peace with Elandria. And they are a people of honor."

"Then I will need some time to think and plan," Salidar said. "In the meantime, lie low, and let no one know who you are."

"I have old colleagues I was hoping to connect with," Durrin objected. "Alumni of the Academy. Contacts. Former clients."

"I'm afraid that is not an option," said Salidar. "Not yet, anyway. No one must know you have returned. Can you do that for me, Durrin?"

Disappointment flared within him. No reunion with old friends. No public recognition for the seven years he had suffered in a cell for his country.

No scroll.

"I guess I have no choice," Durrin muttered.

"Then start preparing for a long and dangerous expedition," Salidar said. "Are you short on silver?"

"I just escaped from a dungeon, Your Excellency," Durrin pointed out. It was an exaggeration—he should still have a line of credit with some banking houses in the city, but there was no point in passing up the generosity of the richest man in the world.

"I'll have Yorid give you twenty pounds of silver," Salidar said, scribbling on a scrap of parchment. "Outfit yourself with the best weapons and provisions, then come back in five days' time." He handed the note to Durrin. "Until then."

Durrin took the note. So that was it. He was back in Salidar's service, no more than a hired sword, still no closer to his goal than seven years before.

"Until then."

He bowed stiffly, threw the cowl of his cloak back over his head, and strode angrily from the room.

CHAPTER 11

THE BURDEN OF RULE

Adara had often imagined what ruling a kingdom would be like. Before her father died, she had seen mainly the ceremonial aspects: Parades. Feasts. Cheering crowds.

After his death, Adara had spent most of her time at a royal sanctuary tucked away in the hills, far from the capital. The mountain clime and the idealism of her tutors had given her a somewhat romanticized vision of ruling: Signing decrees with a flowery signature. Negotiating with emissaries from far-off lands. Delivering passionate speeches to vast audiences.

Both views could not be farther removed from the reality of the last week: Hour . . . after hour . . . after hour . . . of meetings.

Adara was, by her best count, currently in the seventeenth meeting of the day. She had already met with her morning intelligence officer, the chancellor of the treasury, the captain of the palace guard, the ministry of agriculture, the vice-chancellor of the treasury, her afternoon intelligence officer, her wardrobe specialists, the Saven city elders, her chief scribe, the assistant-vice-chancellor of the treasury . . .

"Your Majesty. Your Majesty!"

Adara jolted back to the present. She was in the royal suite, which acted as her office whenever an occasion didn't require the throne room or the council room. The walls were hidden behind shelves sagging with a decade of scrolls and clay tablets. Skagar and Luviana had used these chambers for archival space while co-regents, and neither was the most . . . organized. Crammed between the shelves were crates of personal effects that Adara had brought from her mountain sanctuary. She had intended to organize and redecorate, but she hadn't had the time to touch a single box since her coronation.

She sat in a meeting with Skagar—well, *she* sat, while the seemingly tireless swifter paced the breadth and width of the crowded room, his tail threatening to topple piles of parchment with each wag. Two snippen scribes sat in a corner, their noses twitching as they kept their styluses ready to record any needed order or letter.

Skagar shook his head. "Your Majesty, I need you to focus. This is important."

"I'm sorry," Adara said, shifting in her chair, which was almost as oversized as the one in the council room. "What were you saying?"

"The message we received earlier today from the provincial secretary-royale. You'll remember that I told you about her last Tuesday, she's a snippen I hold in the highest esteem, the daughter of a talented accountant, himself the son of a decorated statesman I taught in my days at the Sumian Academy, though he passed before you were born. Anyway, Vallia asked—"

"Wait, who's Vallia?" Adara interrupted.

Skagar sighed. "I just *told* you. She's the secretary-royale to Governor Kodric."

"Governor—of the Arnon Province," Adara clarified.

"Exactly," said Skagar. "Anyway, Vallia is seeking your guidance about the evacuation of items of historical or cultural value from any administrative repositories located inside the borders of the Arnon Province, in light of the ongoing advance of the hosts of Calamar: collections such as literary archives, court records, artwork, and the like. On the one hand, Vallia is concerned about their destruction should they fall into enemy hands. On the other hand, she is keenly aware of the need to conserve resources, the shortage of wagons due to military acquisitions, and the impact on morale it may have on the populace for the government to be seen preparing for the prospect of the enemy acquisition of territory."

Adara closed her eyes tight, her tired brain parsing her counselor's rambling sentences. "The governor of the Arnon Plains wants to know . . . if he should be evacuating records so that Calamar doesn't destroy them."

"Precisely, Your Highness," Skagar said, still pacing. "As I see it, it is a question of how likely we see the possibility of Calamar's armies claiming the Arnon Plains this fall. Should Commander Volthorn prove successful, we may repulse their advances at the second or third tributary. But should he fail, it might—"

"Of course we need to evacuate such items," Adara said. "Naturally, we hope Calamar won't seize the Arnon Plains. But there's a good chance they will. It's far better to move a scroll a hundred miles and then move it back later, than to lose it forever to plunder. I thought we learned that lesson two years ago when the great library at Lindor went up in flames."

"Please remember the shortage of personnel, Your Majesty," Skagar pontificated. "Vallia's staff at the provincial capital is already stretched thin, and military recruitment has caused labor shortages throughout the countryside. Not to mention the expense of hiring wagons and workers, when you know as well as the assistant vice chancellor to the treasury just how thin our finances are."

Adara winced at the mention of the assistant vice chancellor to the treasury. That had *not* been a pleasant meeting.

"Then tell Vallia to save whatever they can," Adara said. "Prioritize what's most important. What's most irreplaceable."

Skagar looked over a clay tablet on a table. "Very well. Vallia provided a list of the various archives and their contents. I'll read them off and you can specify the order of criticality for their relocation. First, indexes of grain prices across provincial sectors for the last eight years. Second . . ."

Adara rubbed her eyes. Was she hearing this right? Was *she* being expected to appraise the value of archival documents? Never in all her tutelage had she been told that ruling a kingdom would involve such minutia.

"Chancellor," Adara said. She gestured at the scribes waiting at the side of the room. "Are these details something you could perhaps work out with Wiflin and Niflin?"

Skagar looked up, looking somewhat startled. "What? Ah. Yes. Of course, Your Majesty. We shall see to it."

As the chancellor talked with the two snippens, Adara stood, straightening her tired legs. Her back felt like someone had jabbed a haeber crystal into it. She reached her arms up in a stretch, caught one of the scribes glancing quizzically in her direction, and quickly resumed a more dignified pose.

Sitting back down, Adara fished around her cluttered desk until she found the draft of a speech she was supposed to give the next morning. Her speechwriter had dropped it off two days prior. Certain sections of the speech were still blank, waiting for Adara to insert her own wording. She'd been trying to finish the speech between meetings all day.

Adara dipped her quill and scanned the parchment, frowning. Were the opening words too stiff? She had asked her speechwriter to make it sound dignified—like her father's speeches. But did it just sound pretentious instead? She scribbled an alternative opening in the margin, then crossed it out and wrote another one.

A piece of the chancellor's conversation drifted her way, and she looked up. "Skagar," she called. "Repeat that again, please."

The swifter turned, his ears pricked in surprise. "I was just directing them, Your Highness, to prioritize census records."

"Yes, but over what?"

"I believe we were just discussing the archives of lore in the Sanctum of Kings."

Adara set her quill down. "You are going to save census records over ancient lore?"

"You asked us to prioritize what's most irreplaceable, Your Highness," said Skagar. "Many of the manuscripts in the Sanctum have copies elsewhere, including in this very palace."

"Many, yes, but some are the only extant copies," said Adara. "Treasures of knowledge from distant millennia. And you find census records more valuable?"

One of the scribes—Wiflin, probably—spoke up. "The census records are essential for administering our taxes, Your Highness. No records, no taxes, no revenue."

"Yes," said Adara. "But if Calamar seizes the province, then we won't be collecting taxes anyway, will we?"

"Your Majesty," Skagar said, sounding slightly annoyed. "I believe you asked Niflin, Wiflin, and I to establish priorities as we see fit, so we could take something off your plate."

Well, I thought I could trust you to make sensible decisions, Adara thought to herself. Out loud, she said, "Prioritize works of art and literature, anything of ancient date, and any ritual texts. *Before* administrative records."

"Yes, Your Majesty," the scribes said, busily smoothing out the clay tablets they had been engraving marks into. Skagar only sighed loudly, his ears flicking in annoyance.

Adara sat back in her chair. A wave of exhaustion suddenly hit her, like someone had pulled a plug in her feet and all her energy was draining out.

One of her maidservants entered, trimming the room's lights. Instead of candles or oil lanterns for light, the palace used lumen—a special type of moss that glowed with a warm, steady light when wet. Lumen was more expensive than its alternatives, but ever since her father's death, the palace avoided open flames whenever possible.

Adara glanced out the window to where the sky was rapidly darkening. So late already? How early had she risen? It had been before dawn.

Adara covered a yawn, picked up her quill, and turned back to her speech. She reread her latest opening line, scribbled it out, and wrote a fourth version. She was running out of margin.

A knock sounded at the door, then an officer poked his head inside. "Your Majesty—pardon the intrusion—but a message just arrived from the front."

Adara glanced at her speech. "Can it wait?"

"I'm afraid not, Your Majesty. Commander Volthorn is seeking authorization for a troop reassignment. The request is urgent."

"Troop reassignment?" Skagar asked, his tail quickening with interest.

The soldier entered the room and saluted. "Commander Volthorn seeks royal permission to transfer the Snow Paw, Thunderbolt, White Hill, and Fire Storm Battalions from the Penandre Pass to the Arnon Plains, to reinforce his army before he faces battle."

Adara kneaded her face with her fingers. She could barely think straight, she was so tired. "Approved," she murmured.

"Your Majesty, one moment," Skagar said. "The Penandre Pass? If we move those battalions, the pass will be left defenseless."

"Commander Volthorn plans to reinforce the pass by the winter," the officer said. "No enemy host is anywhere near the Penandre. The battalions, in their present position, are useless. He needs them up north."

"The Penandre garrison protects all our southern provinces from invasion," Skagar said, shaking his head. "We cannot authorize this."

The officer cleared his throat. "No offense, Chancellor, but that decision is not yours to make. Only Her Majesty has authority over Chief Commander Skarr."

"I am Her Majesty's chancellor and royal advisor," Skagar said, his fur bristling. "I have the right to express myself."

"The Commander said—"

"Show Her Majesty the actual order," Skagar directed.

The officer offered Adara a piece of parchment, still crinkled from being tied to a griffin's leg. She smoothed it out, squinting to make out the tiny scrawl of characters. Midway through the scroll, she paused, realizing she couldn't recall what the previous sentences had said.

I can't do this right now. Her brain felt crowded with numbers, dates, and locations. She'd done so much just today. But her kingdom needed her. She had to do this. Focus!

She read the letter over again. Troop movements. It would leave Elandria's south-west border exposed. But Volthorn needed the troops on the Arnon Plains. Four battalions. Four thousand troops. That could tip the scales of battle. But it carried a risk. How great of a risk? Volthorn said it was minimal. Skagar thought otherwise. It was up to her.

But why was *she* the one to make this decision? Why couldn't someone else make it for her? Adara closed her eyes, trying to quiet her mind.

I need more time.

She looked up, painfully aware of how gray her skin was. "Can I sleep on this, and decide in the morning?"

"You'll notice at the end of the letter that Commander Volthorn needs the request approved immediately," the officer said. "Even a day's delay could determine whether the reinforcements reach him in time or too late."

Skagar was saying something, but Adara couldn't focus on his words. The writing on the parchment swam in her vision. Volthorn knew the risk he was taking. He wouldn't take it lightly. Who was she to delay what he needed so urgently? Who was she to countermand him, when she was the one who had given him authority in the first place?

"Approved, by my royal decree," Adara said, fumbling to detach the top of her scepter. She pressed the scepter's engraved pattern firmly onto the parchment, leaving the indentation of the royal seal.

The officer saluted and retrieved the order. "We'll send this to the Penandre garrison at once. Thank you, Your Majesty."

The door closed behind him, and Adara instantly sank back in her chair.

"Your Highness?" Skagar asked softly, approaching her chair with a light step. "Are you feeling all right?"

"I need to rest," Adara said. "Just a few minutes." Had she eaten dinner? When was the last time she'd had even a drink of water? She could scarcely remember.

She heard the clatter of the scribes gathering up their tablets and styluses. "Certainly, Your Majesty," Skagar said. "We'll finalize this list tonight and send it off to Vallia. I was hoping to run by you the draft of our petition to General Grimbold, but that can wait until the morning. And I'll tell your evening briefing officer . . ."

Adara didn't hear the rest as she sank into a fitful sleep.

"Please, Daddy! I'll sit still. You won't even notice me."

Adara, eleven years old, twirled her dress as she looked up, her eyes pleading.

Her father laughed, running a hand through her hair, his fingers warm even in the dream. "How can I *not* notice you? You are my daughter. My princess."

She walked down a corridor of the palace with him. In the dream, their surroundings seemed to fade away, leaving just the two of them.

"You've let me sit in the throne room before," Adara said.

"Yes," her father replied. His eyes gained a touch of brown. "But today is different. There are decisions I must make today, weighty ones.

Complex ones. I'm uneasy, Adara. It's not that you're too young. It's . . . I don't know."

"I want to watch you," Adara said. "I want to learn."

Her father stopped and closed his eyes. He let out a long breath, stood in silence for three heartbeats, then breathed in deeply.

"Very well," he said, resuming his pace. "It would be good for you to understand the situation. I'll be hearing various groups today. First the haeber merchants."

"There's been a shortage of haeber," Adara said.

Her father nodded. "You are quick to observe. The haeber supply is governed by far-off factors beyond our control: weather, winds, war. It has always waxed and waned from year to year. But lately it has only waned. Calamar is demanding more haeber. They threaten our merchants, accusing them of destroying some of the supply to hike up costs."

"Are the merchants doing that?" Adara asked.

Her father snorted. "Of course not. The root of the shortage is far east of us. By the time the trickle of haeber gets here, our own farmers buy the bulk of it before it can ever reach Calamar. Which brings up the second group I'll be hearing today: representatives from various farming towns."

"What do they want?"

"They want me to pass a decree halting all exports of haeber to Calamar," her father said. They turned a corner and walked down a set of stairs. "They warn that only by keeping all the haeber here will we have enough for our own fields. Otherwise, we face the risk of famine."

Adara tightened her grip on his hand. "I don't want a famine, Father." She remembered a famine. It had been four years earlier, after a devastating late frost. As a member of the royal family, she herself had never gone truly hungry. But she was still haunted at night by the memory of people begging for food in the streets, their cheeks sunken and their limbs as thin as sticks.

"Neither do I," her father said. "But Calamar's farmers need haeber, too. Denying it to them would mean war. You have not experienced war, my princess. It is worse than famine."

"Then we face either war or famine," said Adara. "How can you ever be expected to decide?"

How can you ever be expected to decide?

⁂

Adara drifted awake. The room was nearly dark. The lumen lanterns gave only a faint glow, their moss nearly dried out. Someone, perhaps one of her handmaids, had draped a blanket over her at some point.

What time was it? Adara rose, her limbs feeling covered in molasses, and walked out onto her balcony. Above her, the sky glittered with a myriad of stars. Just above the western horizon, the Near Moon floated in the sky like a lumen globe, casting its yellow light on the cityscape before her. The Far Moon, with its red, pockmarked surface, drifted high overhead. Adara leaned out to catch a glimpse around the corner of the palace wall of the last object in the sky: the Void. It hung in the sky above the eastern horizon, a black circle of perfect darkness, standing in sharp contrast to the glorious tapestry of stars around it.

The Near Moon, the Far Moon, and the Void each followed the same path as the Sun, their orbits each spaced four hours apart. So since the Near Moon was about to set, it meant the Sun had set four hours earlier.

"End of the first watch," Adara mumbled. Only a third of the way through the night. She could still get a good night's sleep if she made it to her bed upstairs.

Then everything from the day crashed into her. The Penandre garrison. Having to micromanage Skagar. Her unfinished speech. Other concerns from her many other meetings—orders to be sent, decisions to be made, reports to process. The full weight of the seemingly infinite responsibilities fell upon her, filling her eyes with tears. She grasped the railing for support as her body shook with sudden, wrenching sobs. She wiped tear after tear from her face, until the sleeve of her dress was soaked.

"Handkerchief, Your Majesty?" came a soft voice behind her.

Adara turned to see her chief magistrate, Cymer, standing in the doorway, proffering her a square of cloth.

"Oh, Cymer—" she said, taking the handkerchief and dabbing at her eyes. There was no mirror handy to check her reflection, but based on the hue of her hands, her whole complexion was probably deep blue. "You shouldn't have to see me like this."

The old avir stepped beside her, looking out over the darkened city. "On the contrary, Your Majesty. I came exactly for that purpose. To see you. Like this."

Adara tucked loose hairs back under her crown. "Chancellor Skagar sent for you?"

Cymer shook his head. "No. I just came."

He continued to gaze out over the city. Adara's eyes finally dried up, and she found herself looking out as well. There was something comforting about having the old avir there beside her. He was a fountain of resolve that she could almost tangibly sense.

The city before them was dark. A few lumen lanterns still shone in the more well-to-do sections of the city, but they were growing fainter as they dried out. Here and there, a tavern or inn still shone with firelight, snippets of songs and laughter brought by the occasional gust of wind.

Then came a new song on the breeze: a haunting siren of pain and grief, rising and falling in great waves as it split the night air. After a few seconds, a second voice joined in, interweaving its melody with the first. A song of loss. A mourning dirge.

Adara's eyes swept the city for the source. There—not far from the palace, a house shone with light, candles and lanterns lining every windowsill. The wailing dirge rose from there. After a minute, the dirge was joined by handbells, perhaps a dozen of them, ringing with wild abandon.

She knew what was happening inside that house: someone had just died. Now, in desperation, the family was lighting every candle, wetting every lumen globe, and splitting the air with ritual sounds—all to keep at bay the demons that walked the night, hunting for disembodied souls to drag to the Void.

Cymer also was watching, his brow furrowed with concern.

"Do the songs and candles work?" Adara asked. It was a question she had wondered many times throughout her childhood, though she had never voiced it out loud until now. "Can they really keep the demons at bay until the dawn comes?"

Cymer took a deep breath. "The different orders disagree. The Dawn Wardens believe strongly in the power of sound. The dirge you hear is a common one in their tradition. I imagine the household called one or two wardens to stand vigil with them tonight. They also believe in the power of bells."

"And what do you think?" Adara asked.

"I have never felt a demon quail at the ringing of a bell," Cymer said. "Nor at the singing of a dirge. Those beliefs come from ancient texts revered as sacred by the Dawn Wardens but not by my order, the Luminant Order. But perhaps I am wrong? I do not pretend to know everything. We know so little of things beyond the veil of sight."

"The lights are a strong tradition of the Luminant Order," Adara observed.

"Yes," Cymer said. "It appears this household is embracing both orders' teachings. That is good. There is power in the light. Great power."

Cymer closed his eyes, whispering a prayer for the deceased. After a minute he opened his eyes. "Will it be enough? The night is long, and the servants of the Void are persistent. But some souls are harder for them to seize than others. Pray that the light will be enough."

They stared out over the city again. Eventually the wind shifted, carrying the dirge and the ringing of bells away.

Finally, Adara was ready to voice the fears weighing on her heart. "I can't do this, Cymer."

He looked at her gently. "Can't do what?"

Adara dabbed at her eyes again with the loaned handkerchief. "*Everything.* The meetings. The reports. The problems I'm supposed to fix. The decisions I'm expected to make." She took a deep breath, trying to push back the panic rising again within her. "What if I'm making the wrong decisions? What if I'm leading this people to ruin?"

Cymer nodded slowly, his face solemn. "Do you remember your coronation?"

A vision of glowing figures danced in her memory. "Yes," she said, straightening.

Cymer tapped the crown of eternium on Adara's brow. "When you were anointed, you were given the gift of wisdom. That is not some fanciful notion, Adara. It is a *real power*, promised by ancient prophecy to the heir of the Everborn House. That is why we waited seven years for you to come of age, instead of giving the throne to another. That is why we look to you for guidance, though you are so young. The gift of wisdom is your right. It is your duty."

"If it is real, then I don't feel it," said Adara. "I don't feel wise, Cymer. I don't feel smart, or even capable. I just feel exhausted, and overwhelmed, *all* the *time.*"

"You will feel it with practice," said Cymer. His eyes brimmed with intensity. "Bring your questions to the Light, Adara. Be still. Listen to the voice that speaks in your heart. If your heart is pure—and I know it is—then the Sky Father will not let you lead your people astray."

"I wish I could believe that," said Adara.

"You can," said Cymer.

CHAPTER 12

NAMES FROM THE PAST

Eleven hundred miles away in Imperium, Durrin couldn't sleep.

It was the day after his meeting with Salidar. He had spent the morning shopping for supplies and gear, before a wave of exhaustion hit him in the afternoon—the cumulative weariness of three weeks of travel. Intent on catching up on much-needed sleep, Durrin bunked down early. But though his whole body felt exhausted, sleep eluded him.

Perhaps there was too much light in his tavern room. He shuttered the windows and jammed a cloth into the cracks.

He still couldn't sleep.

Was it his pillow? It was old and lumpy. He asked a servant for a new one.

Still couldn't sleep.

He mentally counted up to a hundred goats. Nope. Backwards? Nope. In Mitrian? Still nope.

Something troubled him that he could not shake.

He stared up at the beams of the ceiling, the conversation with Salidar replaying in his head. Why had he agreed to another mission? He had done Calamar's dirty work once. He had already earned that scroll.

He turned his mind to the mission before him. Assassination. Again. How would he pull it off? There would be many more guards this time. Could he strike at night? No, too obvious. During an event outside the palace? Perhaps. Maybe while the queen—

Queen—not a king this time. Not a seasoned ruler whose decrees threatened Durrin's country, but a youth, barely eighteen years old, only weeks into her reign.

His memories turned to that fateful day, seven years ago. To the pain and shock in the king's eyes as Durrin's blade had struck. Durrin had gone on many perilous missions, fought in many skirmishes and sorties. But King Everborn's had been the first and only life he had taken in cold blood.

The Pyromancy Guild had a code, one he'd repeated a hundred times at the Academy. *Kill if kill you must,* the last line read, *but never after dusk.*

It wasn't the most scrupulous of codes, but even pyromancers had their standards.

Never after dusk. Durrin had honored that. He had even rushed his attack to make sure he struck in the afternoon, well before twilight—so that the king's soul could be claimed by angels and taken to the Halls of the Sun, not left to be seized by demons.

He had followed the code. So why did the deed still haunt him?

Durrin forced his mind to turn to other thoughts. He relived his years studying at the Academy, recalling faces long past. Tutors. Classmates. Friends. People he hadn't seen in over seven years.

Salidar had ordered him not to let anyone know he had returned. But surely there was *someone* from his past he could see, someone who could keep a secret. Where were they all now? Many were probably fighting in the war. Others would have found jobs in the city or elsewhere in the empire.

Luckily, he knew where to find such intel.

Giving up any last hope of an early bedtime, Durrin gathered up some gear and slipped out into the streets, wrapped in a dark cloak.

Two hours later, under the cover of dusk, Durrin stood on a rooftop, surveying the Imperial Pyromantic Academy of Calamar.

The Academy stood atop the city's fourth spur, in company with buildings dedicated to the other four mancery arts. Each structure's architecture was designed to reflect its subject. The Pyromantic Academy boasted towering spires and steep gables, all constructed from orange tiles and rust-red bricks—the whole complex conjuring the image of a raging fire.

Behind Durrin pulsed the shimmering column of light that marked the city's leyline beacon. At the moment, it glimmered orange and red, lighting up the spires of the Pyromantic Academy as if the building truly was aflame.

Durrin hadn't bothered with the Academy's front gate—that would require revealing his identity, against Salidar's orders. Besides, where was the fun in that?

Instead, he had scaled the northern wing of the College of Terramancy—which was built directly underneath the leyline, adjacent to the Pyromantic Academy. He crept along its rooftop, then broke into a run for the last few yards.

As he picked up speed, Durrin marshalled invisible currents of power around him, a wave of potential energy waiting to be unleashed. As he hurled himself off the edge of the roof, the spark within him surged, transforming that energy into extra momentum that propelled him across the twenty-foot gap. Fire flickered in his wake as whisps of excess energy burnt off.

His feet caught purchase on a small ledge halfway up the wall of the Pyromantic Academy. Before gravity could claim him, he hauled himself upward by grabbing small protrusions in the stonework. After a nerve-racking couple of seconds, he pulled himself up onto the Academy rooftop and lay there, spread flat on the tiles.

He listened, chest heaving, waiting for the call of a nightwatchman to split the darkness. Nothing.

Not bad, he thought. He had discovered this route of entry back as a cadet. It had taken careful study, repeated attempts in daylight, quite a few bruises, and a broken leg before he had mastered the jump to the ledge and the subsequent climb. Muscle memory, it appeared, had not forsaken him during his imprisonment.

Satisfied that he had gone undetected, Durrin crept along the rooftop, weaving his way between garrets and spires, avoiding the ridgeline where his silhouette would be visible against the starry sky. Soon the Academy's courtyard opened out below him. After checking for watchmen one more time, he grabbed the edge of the roof and swung down to a second-story walkway below.

The courtyard stretched below him. At the moment, it was empty, just a uniform expanse of flagstones (no shrubs or flowers—too flammable) and a fountain in the corner (for when cadets caught their clothes on fire).

But to Durrin's eyes, the courtyard was brimming with memories. Here he had launched fire from his hands in endless drills. Here he had competed in the annual Kymar competition, winning first place for the level-one routine, then the level-two routine, working his way upward year by year until he won first place at the fifth and highest level—a title he held three years in a row. Here he had become the greatest of his class, a rising star, a legend in the making.

Here the Council had turned him down, three times, for guild mastership.

Focus.

Durrin turned away, creeping down the balcony. When he reached the door he was looking for, he produced a lockpick set—a purchase he'd made earlier in the day—and opened the door in seconds. The next door, a couple of rooms later, took more work. After several unsuccessful attempts, he grew impatient and melted the lock's interior into slag. It would be noticed, of course, but not before he was long gone.

Beyond that door lay the Academy archive—the mundane one, not the secret vaults buried deep beneath the building. He had worked here in his first years at the Academy—back when filing paperwork wasn't beneath him—so he knew his way around. He used a pitcher of water to wet a lumen globe for light, then ran his finger down a shelf until he found a large, leather-bound tome, which he hauled over to a lectern and opened.

The codex listed all the cadets admitted to the Academy from the prior decade. Each cadet had their own page dedicated to tracking their progress and status. As he thumbed through, some pages were full, crowded with reports of Academy performance and updates on the graduate's subsequent career. Others were largely empty, ending with a terse note about the cadet's dismissal or withdrawal.

Soon he reached the section for his graduating cohort. He eagerly scanned each page, focusing on the name at the top and the most recent entry at the bottom.

Jorman "Firebrand" Tallaway . . . Independent blacksmith in Killia.

That was a surprise. The Firebrand had become a blacksmith? Jorman had sworn he would never settle down and work a "low" pyromancy job. How Durrin would love to see that. But Killia was a two-weeks' journey to the west. Too far for a visit. Durrin turned to the next entry.

Swiftwing, of Greendarrow . . . Lieutenant, South Sea fleet, three decorations of bravery.

Trusty ol' Swiftwing. Good to see she was making a name for herself. Durrin turned the page, smiling as he saw the name of a close friend.

Marvin Junger . . . Killed by Elandrian cavalry in the Battle of Lindor. Cremated with full honors.

His smile vanished. He read the last line again and again. Marvin? Good-natured, prankster Marvin? How could he be dead?

Durrin's pace through the book quickened. Every second or third page he stopped, reading and re-reading a classmate's final entry.

Died of the yellow plague while on campaign in Elandria. Buried in a mass grave.

Killed in the second assault on Erlenmir. Cremated with full honors.

Disappeared while scouting the Penandre Pass. Presumed dead or imprisoned.

Wounded in the Battle of Twisted River. Died eight days later of infection. Cremated.

Caught retreating during the Battle of Seven Heights. Executed. Buried with dishonor.

Each name brought a host of memories. These were men—boys—he had studied beside, competed against, sparred with, pulled pranks on. And now four, five, six of them were dead?

No, not just dead. Killed in the war.

The war *he* had helped to start.

On his journey back to Imperium, he had seen the devastation in Western Elandria firsthand. Salidar had mentioned the war had not gone as smoothly as he had hoped. But until now, Durrin hadn't stopped to consider the full cost of Calamar's "victories." Elandria was far larger than the tribes and minor city-states that Calamar had conquered in previous wars. Both Elandria and Calamar were large enough to field armies in the tens of thousands. How many pitched battles had been fought in the last three years? How many of his countrymen had died?

He stopped at the next page.

Halorn Venarim

"Halorn," Durrin whispered. Halorn, a fellow human, had been one of Durrin's closest friends. They had spent many afternoons together, practicing, studying, or talking—always talking—of ideas and questions and stories.

The first half of the page was full of glowing reports of Halorn's diligence and achievements at the Academy. One year, he had even won the fourth-level Kymar championship.

Then came a few entries of his subsequent career for the Guild. Durrin smiled at one:

Nearly bungled a job for Nachimans the Aquamancer, resulting in a public scandal and a formal complaint from the City Chancellery. Censured.

Halorn had asked for Durrin's help getting through that mess. It had involved a hilarious fight with a punctilious snippen, then a near run-in with an old man and a crossbow. Good times.

The page ended abruptly with three entries. The first was dated to the fourteenth year of Emperor Stoneclaw's reign, the same year Durrin had undertaken his ill-fated mission to Saven.

June 8, Fourteenth Regnal Year — Halorn's whereabouts unknown. Appears to have left Imperium and is purposefully evading detection. Investigation opened.

December 2, Fourteenth Regnal Year — Search for Halorn unfruitful. Investigation suspended.

September 12, Seventeenth Regnal Year — Investigation reopened at the Guild Council's request.

June 17, Eighteenth Regnal Year — Halorn located on a small farm in Caradell. Claims he has renounced pyromancy. Deemed to pose no security threat. Investigation closed.

Durrin stared at the page, relief mixing with confusion in his gut. Halorn, at least, was still alive. But what did these entries mean? "Purposefully evading detection"? "Renounced pyromancy"? Yes, Halorn had been uncomfortable with certain types of work the Guild assigned. But he had absolutely loved the art of pyromancy itself.

Durrin crossed the room to where a large map hung on the wall. Caradell—there it was, little more than a village, about a day and a half's ride from Imperium. He could journey there and back in three days and still make his appointment with Salidar.

Durrin was about to return the volume to the shelf when a thought came to him. Opening the codex again, Durrin thumbed through the pages, glancing only at the names. Reaching the end of his cohort, he frowned and looked through the section again, careful to not skip any pages.

His name wasn't there.

He leafed through the section one more time, slowly. Halfway through, a ragged line of paper marked where a page had been torn out.

His page.

He fingered the stub of paper left, examining the torn edge. It looked like the page had been ripped out a long time ago—several years ago, most likely.

Durrin stared at the torn page for several heartbeats. Then he slammed the book closed, returned it to its shelf, and strode to the door.

It was time to find an old friend. And when he did, he had some questions.

Besides—if he stuck around in Imperium with nothing to do, who knew what trouble he could get himself into? He might do something rash, like break into the Academy archives.

CHAPTER 13

TWIN GIRLS AND A BOY NAMED QUEASLE

Two days later, Durrin rode through the streets of Caradell—or more specifically, the *street* of Caradell. There was a smithy, a mill, a cooper, and a carpentry shop. That was it. There wasn't even a tavern. Everything else in the area was farms.

Durrin made some inquiries for Halorn. At first, the villagers only looked at him, a hooded city-dweller, with suspicion. He had expected as much, but it was still mildly frustrating. Finally, after Durrin flashed a few coins, the blacksmith pointed him in the direction of Halorn's farm.

Durrin followed the man's directions, leaving the village and riding up a narrow trail into the hills. Raggedy Ruby pushed through fields of tall, ripe hay, which coated the edges of Durrin's cloak with seed husks. The late afternoon Sun drifted from cloud to cloud, casting long swaths of alternating light and shadow across the rolling hills.

This is ridiculous, a voice said in his mind. Durrin had spent the last seven years in a dungeon. Would Halorn even recognize him? And if he did, why would Halorn even want to talk to him? For some reason, Halorn had renounced pyromancy and turned to a life of farming. He had chosen a new life—a life where Durrin had no place. It had been foolish to come here.

Durrin reined his horse to a stop, about to turn back.

"Durrin!"

Farther up the path, a figure was bounding toward him, kicking up dust and straw. A figure he knew.

"Halorn!"

His old friend had not changed. He still had that same subtle lope to his step, and as he got closer, Durrin could make out the same twist to his grin.

Durrin dismounted and held out a hand, but Halorn nearly tackled him in an embrace. With that embrace, something within Durrin, something he had held tight for seven long years, broke. And he wept. Tears poured down his face as he shook in his friend's arms.

For a moment, Durrin tried to pull away, ashamed of his tears. But Halorn only hugged him tighter. That was when Durrin realized why he cried. For the first time since his release, someone acted truly relieved to see him. For the first time, someone made him feel like he truly had been freed.

Durrin hugged Halorn back, letting seven years of bottled loneliness pour out of him.

After a long moment, Halorn pulled away and held Durrin's shoulders at arm's length, grinning at him. "Welcome home, Durrin."

Durrin wiped his cheek with the edge of his cloak—an action completely foreign to him. He hadn't wept like this since . . . he had no clue when.

"I hope you're hungry," Halorn said, grabbing the reins of Durrin's horse. "We have supper ready for you."

Durrin followed him, bewildered. "You were expecting me?"

Halorn nodded. "I dreamed last night that you would come."

In the next half-hour, Durrin realized he had been mistaken. Halorn *had* changed.

He no longer wore the sable and scarlet robes of the Academy, but the simple tunic and trousers of a farmer. His arms were sinewy instead of lithe, his hands calloused from years of heavy labor.

As they crested the rise, they came upon a cluster of small stone buildings. Smoke rose from a chimney, and herds of sheep and goats gazed sleepily at them as they approached.

"Well-maintained," Durrin noted.

Halorn nodded, his face beaming. "Well-staffed, too. Beyond the hill lives a pack of swifters; they herd the sheep and goats, almost six hundred head. A family of avirs lives in that one-story cottage, and underneath the barn lives a full burrow of snippens to help with odd jobs. I live in the two-story structure."

"Who owns the land?" Durrin said. "A nobleman from Elain?"

Halorn shook his head. "I do. Outright."

Durrin stopped, pleasantly surprised. "You mean you *own* this whole farm?"

Halorn nodded.

"How much is it worth?"

Halorn looked toward the main house. "Not as much as these darlings."

A door slammed. Two young girls were running toward them, their apron strings flying in the wind. "Papa! Papa!"

Halorn caught them both in his arms, swinging them through the air and laughing. "On the lookout, are we? How's—hey! No tickles!"

He went down in the tall grass, his daughters on top of him, all three laughing hysterically.

Halorn had a *family*? Durrin took a closer look at his friend. On Halorn's left hand glistened a white wedding ring, forged from eternium. How had Durrin not noticed that before?

Something tugged at Durrin's cloak. He spun, ready to disarm the would-be pickpocket. But no, it was only a little boy, no older than three. He stared up at Durrin with big blue eyes. "Why 'ello!" he said, giving Durrin the happiest grin he had ever seen.

"Um, hello," Durrin said, feeling thoroughly out of his wheelhouse. He hadn't been surrounded by small children since . . . well . . . since he was a small child.

"Who you?" the boy chirped.

". . . I'm Durrin."

"You're doing what?"

"No. *Durrin.*"

The boy's smile got even bigger. "Ahhh! . . . You're doing 'dat during what?"

"No. My name is *Durrin.*"

The boy's eyes became as big as saucers. "*Ohh!* . . . My name is Queasle!"

Queasle? What kind of a name was that?

"Sorry," Halorn said, dragging himself over to Durrin, a girl latched onto each leg. "Let me introduce you. Children, this is Durrin. He's an old friend of mine. We knew each other before you were even born!"

"Dad, when was I born?" one of the girls said.

"I was born before you!" the other said.

"No! We were born at the same time!"

"No, I was born first. By *five* minutes. Mama said so!"

Halorn smiled. "These are the twins, Janea and Anjea. They're both four. And the boy's Quin, but his sisters called him Queasle once, and now we can't get the name out of his head. Let's tie up your horse and head inside. Girls, let go of my legs, please."

Inside the main house, a tall woman was taking flatbread out of a small brick kiln. She looked up as they entered and greeted Durrin with a smile and a bow.

"This is my wife, Elianna," Halorn said. "Elianna, this is Durrin Rendhart."

"I've heard a lot about you, Master Durrin," Elianna said, laying the bread out on the table, joining a bowl of figs and a jar of olive oil.

"You have much to tell!" Halorn said as he began to slice a wedge of cheese. "I've thought for seven years that you were dead!"

Someone tugged at Durrin's cloak again. It was Queasle. "Are you the *fire mage?*" he asked, wonder in his face.

"Uh. . ." Durrin blinked. He'd never been called a fire mage before, but that was what pyromancy was. "Yes?"

"You're in Daddy's bedtime stories!" Janea chirped. Or maybe it was Anjea.

Durrin's head was spinning. Too many people were talking at once. He turned back to Elianna. "Don't call me 'master,'" he said. "I never became a guild master."

"But you deserve to be one!" said Halorn. "And that's what matters."

"You're a guild master in Daddy's stories," Anjea said. "You're Master Rendhart, the Hero Who Never Laughs."

Durrin lifted his eyebrows at Halorn. "Never laughs?"

"Well, it's true."

After Halorn got everyone to sit down at the table—a mighty feat in and of itself—he looked at one of his daughters. "Anjea? Could you do the honors?"

The little girl scrunched up her eyes, rapidly touching her heart and then her head before reciting at a breathless pace, "Father of Stars, who gave what is ours, thanks do we give, by thee do we live. Done!"

"You can't say it that fast!" Janea chided.

"Your sister's right," Halorn said. He looked sheepishly at Durrin. "We try."

Durrin awkwardly waited until the others started grabbing food before reaching for the bowl of figs. It had been many, many years since he had heard a prayer of thanksgiving before a meal, and he didn't want to misstep by starting too early.

Durrin had been riding most of the day with only a scant lunch. He dug into the food, devouring half a loaf of bread and a bowl of figs in short order. Food had not tasted so good in a long time. As he ate, Anjea and Janea bombarded him with half a hundred questions.

"Are you really seven feet tall?"

"Well, I—"

"Did you once burn up an entire forest with a single sneeze?"

"That's impossible, for starters, and—"

"I found a grasshopper today in the grass. Do you want to see it?"

"Um—"

"Master Rendhart! Master Rendhart!"

"Yes?"

". . . I forgot. Oh! I remember! Do you like my hair bow?"

"Well, I guess it's quite—"

"Master Rendhart! Is it true that you and Daddy once welded shut the hinges to the schoolmaster's office?"

Durrin shot Halorn a glare. "You *told* them about that? We made a vow of secrecy!"

Halorn shrugged. "I ran out of ideas! *You* try telling a bedtime story on the spot. Every single night."

While Durrin started in on a second helping—he felt like he'd never be full—Halorn rose and began cleaning up while his wife climbed a ladder to care for a newborn who had started wailing upstairs. Then one of the twins asked a question that made Durrin pause.

"Master Rendhart! Can you do some pyrop—pyrum—can you do some fire magic for us?"

The room became expectant. Durrin looked to Halorn, the words from the Academy log fresh in his mind: *renounced pyromancy.* "That depends. What does your father say?"

Anjea, Janea, and Queasle all turned to look at their dad. "Papa! Pleeease?"

Halorn kept his focus on the dishes he was scrubbing. "Master Durrin is a pyromancer. Of course he can do a display for you." His tone was even—he wasn't shutting down the idea, but he didn't seem excited.

Three little heads turned back around. "Do it! Do it!"

Durrin, still watching his old friend out of the corner of his eye, spun his hand in a circle and brought a flame to life in his fingers. He tossed the flame back and forth between his hands, garnering "oohs" and "aahs" from his young audience. Each toss sent the flame higher and higher, until with a final twirl of his fingers, he sent the flame spiraling upward until it winked out near the ceiling.

The children were silent for a moment. Halorn watched the display with an unreadable expression.

Then Anjea and Janea said simultaneously, "That was boring."

"Boring?" Durrin said. That was a third-year trick!

"I thought you would make a tiger out of flame," said Anjea.

"Or set your hair on fire," said Janea.

"Or create a new star in the sky," said Anjea.

"Or turn yourself invisible," said Janea.

"More cheese!" said Queasle, banging his empty plate on the table.

Durrin held up his hands. "Sorry, I can't do much indoors. I might catch something on fire."

To his surprise, Halorn spoke up, a new energy in his voice. Perhaps Durrin's display was reigniting fond memories. "Then we'll go outside! Perhaps Durrin can favor us with a repeat of his Kymer championship performance from eleven years ago."

The girls' eyes got even wider. "Yes! Yes! Yes!"

As Halorn shepherded them all outside into the courtyard between farm buildings, Durrin whispered, "I'm not up to the fifth routine right now. I just barely re-mastered the first and moved on to the second."

Halorn winked at him. "The twins won't know the difference."

After repeated warnings from both Durrin and Halorn to stay well back, the three children got seated on a log about ten yards from Durrin. Taking a deep breath, he launched into the second Kymar routine.

Whereas the first routine built up power and speed gradually, the second started flashy. With a clap of his hands, Durrin summoned twin rivulets of fire. These trailed in the wake of his hands as he spun, weaving the flames like trailing ribbons on a pair of sticks; around his torso and head, between his legs, intwined together. Periodically he would throw both rivulets of fire high into the air, perform a somersault or front-flip, and land in time to catch them in his hands. The routine was flashy, fast, and fiery—exactly what Halorn's children were looking for.

Feeling his strength waning, Durrin cut off the routine early, skipping the last round and snuffing out his flames with an explosion of cascading sparks. As the children burst into squeals and wild applause, Durrin held his final pose, his chest heaving. He'd impressed even himself—he'd started to relearn the second routine only a couple days before, yet his execution just now had been nearly flawless. He smiled. He always performed better with a crowd.

"Again!" the twins squealed. "Again!"

"I think that's enough," Halorn said. "We must let Master Rendhart have a break. Besides, it's time for chores."

"Awww!"

"No awws."

"Please??"

"None of that, either. Hurry on, now!"

After quite a bit more *awws* and *pleases*, the girls finally ran back inside, Queasle toddling behind them.

In their absence, a sudden stillness presided. Halorn turned to Durrin, motioning toward a footpath lit with long shadows by the sinking Sun. "As for you, my old friend, it's time we had a talk."

CHAPTER 14

·OF ANGELS AND DEMONS

Before Durrin and Halorn left the circle of farm buildings, Halorn ducked inside a barn and emerged with two strange-looking implements: wooden poles, about as long as quarterstaffs, with rectangular pieces of metal mounted on one end.

"What are these?" Durrin said, taking one and examining it. "Some sort of weapon?"

Halorn raised an eyebrow. "You mean you've never seen a hoe before?"

"Hoe?"

"It's for weeding."

Now it was Durrin's turn to raise an eyebrow. "Weeding?"

Halorn started down the path, the hoe over his shoulder. "I figure we can walk and talk or we can work and talk. Come on, it's not as hard as city folk make it out to be."

Durrin shrugged and followed. Soon they left the path and plunged into a field of plants. Durrin looked around. "Which ones are weeds?"

Halorn pointed out one of the long green stalks. "Do you see this? Tall, straight, with giant green leaves growing out of it? That's corn." He gestured to a scraggly plant near the stalk's base. "Anything else is a weed, and it goes."

"But why weed now, if the corn is already grown?"

Halorn began scrapping his hoe through the dirt, catching and uprooting two or three weeds with each pass. "Because every weed now turns into ten next spring. Now, are you going to stand there and keep asking questions about horticulture until the four World Anchors crumble and Zenitha cracks like an egg, or . . ." He gestured toward the hoe.

Durrin heaved a sigh, heaved the hoe off his shoulder, and started pushing the end through the dirt. It bumped and jounced along the ground, doing nothing to the weeds in its path. Halorn made it look so easy.

"Don't push," Halorn said after a moment. "Pull. Pull toward you, then take a step forward and pull again."

They worked in silence for a minute as Durrin got the hang of it. A cool breeze blew across the field, rustling the corn all around them.

"So," Halorn said. "You have a story seven years long to tell. Last I knew, you were running missions for High Vizier Salidar, representing his interests in Elandria and Mitria. Then you disappeared."

Representing was a judicious word for it. Durrin had traveled throughout Elandria undercover, gathering intel for Lord Salidar and performing the occasional act of strategic arson. His frequent trips to the Mitrian Mountains were in a more official capacity, building a relationship with tribal leaders that Salidar had hoped could pave the way for future alliances.

Halorn continued. "I also know you had reapplied to the Guild Council for guild mastership, to no avail."

Durrin yanked his hoe through a particularly hard clump of dirt. "Three times, Halorn. I applied *three times*. That was after I had won the Kymar championship, the Sable Hunt, *and* the Mancery Mayhem cup. But they still rejected me."

"They feared you," said Halorn. "They knew you were better than any of them. Guild mastership was the only thing they could keep back from you."

They didn't want me to get my hands on Kymar's sixth scroll, Durrin thought silently. *They knew it would have made me unstoppable.*

Durrin began to get into a rhythm with the hoe. It was easier work than it had first looked. "At the time, Lord Salidar had the clout to help me gain guild mastership. He and I struck an agreement. If I completed a dangerous mission for him, he would make sure I joined the Guild Council." *And gain access to the Council's vaults,* he added silently.

Halorn paused, looking over at him. "What was the mission?"

For a moment, Durrin considered telling Halorn the truth. He needed to share it with someone, needed to unload the growing guilt he felt.

No. The mission for the emperor had been top secret.

Instead, Durrin used a variant of the story that the Elandrian leadership had fabricated. "Salidar sent me on the trail of a spice merchant who had swindled him. After several months, I finally caught up to him in Elandria. But he caught wind that I was on his trail. As I was breaking into his manor to gather evidence, he swarmed me with guards, then turned me over to the Elandrian courts with claims I had come to assassinate him. They locked me up for seven years."

Durrin fell silent, working his hoe rhythmically. Memories of Irongate Isle bubbled up, trying to break out. The freezing winters and the scorching summers. The backbreaking labor chopping logs or making bricks in the courtyard. The suffocating darkness.

"I'm sorry," Halorn whispered.

"I survived," Durrin said. He tried to say more but couldn't without his throat constricting.

Finishing their row, they pivoted and moved on to the next.

Finally, Durrin cleared his throat. "After seven years, they released me." He detailed his adventures getting back to Calamar, including his narrow escape in Wyvern Way, which prompted a laugh from Halorn.

"Always one to dance at death's edge!" Halorn said. "Now I have another story to add to my bedtime arsenal."

He grew more serious, pausing and looking at Durrin intently. "Have you been back to the Academy?"

Durrin shrugged. "*Technically* yes, but I didn't exactly use the front door."

Halorn shook his head. "I'm not surprised. So the Guild doesn't know you're back. Does Lord Salidar know?"

Durrin had already broken Salidar's orders by visiting Halorn. He shouldn't push his luck with his employer further. "You're the only one who knows. And I need you to keep this visit a secret—at least for several months. No one else can know, for now, that I'm still alive."

"So you *have* seen Lord Salidar."

Durrin kept his eyes trained on his hoe. "I didn't say that."

"You may as well have." Halorn's voice became cynical. "How convenient for him to have an agent that no one remembers exists. What mission does he have planned for you next?"

"I haven't seen the vizier," Durrin insisted, looking up and raising his tone slightly as if he were annoyed.

Halorn straightened, looking him in the eyes. "You're a good liar, Durrin. But not that good."

Durrin resisted the urge to smirk. Halorn had no idea how much of Durrin's story had been a lie.

"Fine," Durrin said. "*Perhaps* I'm working for the vizier. Not a word to anyone."

Halorn gestured to the desolate terrain around them. "Careful. These hills are just crawling with spies."

"Which brings up *your* story," Durrin said, seizing the opportunity to change the topic. "How did you go from one of the Guild's rising stars to a farmer in the middle of nowhere?"

Halorn spent a minute hoeing before he answered. When he did, he spoke slowly. "The same summer you disappeared, I began to question my career path. I was becoming disillusioned with pyromancy, and with the

Guild in particular. There's only so many occupations that the Guild prepares you for. Did I really want to become a bodyguard? A spy? A thief?"

"Guild members aren't thieves," Durrin snapped.

"Oh? And that job we did on Renner Street? Breaking into that aquamancer's shop?"

"We were gathering information."

"We *stole* his trade secret," Halorn snapped. "And we almost burned his shop to the ground in the process."

"I wouldn't be too worried about the old man," Durrin said. "I passed his shop two days ago. He looked like he's still doing fine."

"That's not the point," Halorn said. "It was *wrong*. And I hated every minute of that assignment. But you know how the Guild works. If you're assigned a job, you do it. No questions asked."

"That's not true. You can always decline."

"And if you decline too many?" Halorn asked. "You face Guild discipline. I know. I faced it. Twice. I felt trapped, Durrin. Trapped between my conscience and my identity. I was a pyromancer! I was literally *born* a pyromancer! I had given it my life, and I loved it. But it was leading me down a path that I hated more and more with each step."

Halorn began swinging his hoe with greater force. "Finally, I couldn't take it anymore. So I fled. I knew they'd come after me, but my integrity was worth more than my life."

"Where did you go?" Durrin said.

"Everywhere," Halorn said. "I knew all the tricks, and I knew the Guild's investigators knew them better. My only hope was to make the chase more effort than it was worth. I hopped from town to town and city to city, covering my tracks as best I could, even drawing lots to make my path as randomly erratic as possible.

"Eventually, after a year of running, I figured they'd given up. So I settled down with some goat herders, up in the Northern Provinces. There I lived life as I had never lived it before: On the mountainside, day in and day out. Sleeping under the stars, with no more shelter than a cave or a tarp. And living with the most humble people you could ever know."

"Sounds pleasant," Durrin said. Personally, though, he wasn't sure if he'd prefer Irongate Isle to that kind of deprivation.

"I got to know their lore keeper," Halorn continued. "Her mind was a library, Durrin! Hundreds and hundreds of stories, all memorized! I would sit at her feet for hours and just listen."

Halorn leaned on his hoe as he looked out over the sea of corn, turned to gold by the setting Sun. "Her stories opened my understanding of the world. What do you understand about demons and angels, Durrin?"

Durrin paused, rubbing his hands where the hoe was threatening to leave blisters. "What we're all taught, I suppose." He quoted the common nursery rhyme:

"They who die in the day, angels speed on their way.
They who die in the gloom, demons drag to their doom."

"And do you believe it?" Halorn asked.

"Why wouldn't I?" Durrin had known that nursery rhyme since he was a child. Everyone had. His whole life, he had heard the horns of the Knights Vigilant or the Dawn Wardens, warning of the onset of twilight. The daily schedule of their whole civilization revolved around the time-table of demons and angels, dusk and dawn, day and night.

"No," said Halorn, catching Durrin's gaze. There was an intensity in Halorn's eyes that hadn't been there before. "Do you really, *truly* believe that, Durrin Rendhart? That there really are angels, all around us, during the day? And demons at night, stalking us?"

The question gave Durrin pause. He rested on his hoe and looked out toward the east. Past the fields of corn. Past the hills. Past the horizon. To the first glimpse of the Void, rising opposite the setting Sun, its pitch blackness impenetrable by the dying rays of twilight. How many hundreds of times had he seen it haunting the night sky? Yet right now, it was like he was staring into that well of darkness for the first time.

"I've never really thought about it," Durrin admitted.

"Most people don't," Halorn said. "Until death draws near. But do you think that's all that angels and demons can do? Just stand by and wait for us to die?"

"That's what we are taught," Durrin said.

Halorn shook his head. "No. That's what the *Knights Vigilant* teach."

The Knights Vigilant were one of three religious orders common throughout Zenitha, along with the Dawn Wardens and the Luminant Order. In Calamar, only the Knights Vigilant and the Dawn Wardens were active. The third, the Luminant Order, had been expelled, their texts burned, when Durrin had been a young boy.

"Do you disagree with Vigilant doctrine?" Durrin warned. "You know the punishment for heresy."

"I am not disagreeing with it," Halorn said. "I'm only saying that there's more. So much more. Let me start by sharing a longer version of that nursery couplet:

> *"They who die in the day, angels guard from the fray:*
> *They who die in the night, against demons must fight.*
> *Those who've valiantly won see the Halls of the Sun,*
> *With the Eldest to fly to the Father of Sky.*
> *Those with honor or fear go to moons far and near;*
> *Those who live lives of gloom, demons drag to their doom.*
> *Act; do not wait. Seal the scroll of your fate.*
> *Deal rightly with all, or to the Void you will fall."*

"The lore keeper taught me that angels are around us, all the time," Halorn continued. "They watch us unseen, nudging our thoughts, elevating our spirits. And they keep a record. It's an ongoing account of all you have ever done: your successes, your failures, every act, good and bad."

"Like the Academy's codices?" Durrin asked.

Halorn nodded. "Yes, but far more accurate. The Academy can only record what they know about you. But the angels see all. Everything. This is what the poem refers to by 'the scroll of your fate.'"

"The scroll of your fate," Durrin repeated, pondering the phrase. "Your fate . . . when you die?"

"Yes," said Halorn. "Your eternal destination. The halls of the Sun are not for everyone. They are only for the just and good. When you die, the angels will read your scroll. If you lived a decent life but did not prove yourself valiant enough for the halls of the Sun, they will take you to the Near Moon or the Far Moon—places of safety and rest, but far short of endless splendor."

Durrin glanced up at the two moons in the sky. "And for those who have not lived a decent life?"

"Those whose scroll of fate is stained with acts of theft and lies, cruelty and violence, tyranny and murder—such souls the angels cannot and will not claim."

"Even should they die under the Sun?" Durrin said.

Halorn nodded. "Even should they die at noonday."

Durrin turned back to his hoeing, though his mind was fully fixed on the ideas coming from Halorn's mouth. "Then what happens to them?"

"Their disembodied soul is left to wander the earth until sundown," Halorn said. "Then, when night falls and the Void rises, they are hunted down by demons, chained, and dragged to the Void."

Durrin glanced east again. The last rays of the Sun had slipped below the hills, leaving the earth and sky in a dull blue twilight. The Void was now fully visible, looming over the eastern horizon, its darkness as impenetrable as if a gaping hole had been ripped out of the fabric of the sky.

"What about those who die at night?" Durrin asked.

"That part all the orders agree upon," Halorn said. "The servants of the Void will attempt to catch any soul they can find, noble or vile. *Every* soul they snatch is a victory for them. But that is not the extent of their ambition. They haunt the darkness, whispering corrupt thoughts into our minds, stoking our basest inclinations. Because if they can get us to become depraved—"

"Then the angels will not claim us," said Durrin.

"And we are left in the demons' clutches, no matter where the Sun sits in the sky when we die," Halorn said.

Halorn's words echoed in Durrin's mind.

Tyranny and murder.

The angels see all. Everything.

Durrin had never truly contemplated the day he would die. While most people feared the night, he had never been able to afford to: his assignments had too often required nocturnal expeditions. As illogical as he now realized it sounded, he had always counted on dying during the day. But what if that wasn't enough?

His breathing began to quicken. What if, by killing King Everborn, he had crossed a line that could not be un-crossed? According to everything Halorn had said, Durrin was most likely already doomed for the Void.

Unless.

Unless Halorn was wrong.

"How do you know this is all true?" Durrin said. "You heard it all from a goat shepherd in some backwater mountain valley. Not exactly the most reliable source."

"Why not?" said Halorn.

"Truth is found in the consensus, the mainstream—not the lone voice in the fringes," Durrin said. "Truth is verifiable and provable. Truth is found in the academies, the universities, the halls of knowledge."

"That may be so with something you can experiment with, like mancery or farming," said Halorn. "But you can't experiment with death. You get one shot, and it's a one-way trip."

"You're flirting around dangerous dogma," Durrin objected. "The moment you begin to dictate what people must do to escape the Void, you have power over them. You could tell them to do or not do whatever meets your fancy—or fills your pocket. That's why the Luminant Order was forbidden four decades ago. And rightfully so—I've seen firsthand how much political power they wield in nations that still harbor them, like Elandria."

Halorn stopped hoeing and looked at him. "So which is worse, Durrin? A philosophy that says you need to live a good life? Or a philosophy that says it's okay to steal and lie and even kill, as long as you never kill after dark?"

Durrin froze.

The last line of the Pyromantic Code echoed in his memory. *Kill if kill you must—but never after dusk.*

His mind flashed with the image of his sword, wet with a king's blood, reflecting the light of a late afternoon Sun.

Durrin shook his head and retreated to his hoeing. This was all too much for him to think about right now. "We're off topic. Last we left you, you were tending sheep and goats on a mountainside up north."

Halorn didn't immediately respond, and Durrin worried he would drag the conversation back to talk of angels and demons. But eventually, Halorn shrugged. "Right. Sheep. Goats."

Halorn resumed hoeing. "I reflected a lot on that mountainside: about who I really was, and who I really wanted to be. I decided that pyromancy was only a danger to me. I had been trained to use my powers to take advantage of others. And I lived in a society that expected such. The only way I could be free was to start over with a clean slate. So I renounced pyromancy."

"But you haven't truly abandoned the art itself, right? Just the profession?" Durrin reflected on how dull and lifeless he had felt when cut off from his powers in Irongate Isle. He couldn't imagine willingly letting his talent fade.

"I meant what I said," said Halorn.

Halorn had to be bluffing. Durrin snapped his fingers, summoning a flame into existence. He tossed it at Halorn. They had often played this game at the Academy, tossing flames back and forth with carefree abandon.

Instead of catching it, however, Halorn stepped aside. The flame sizzled into the ground, where he stamped it out with his boot. "I renounced it, Durrin. Forever. I am no longer a pyromancer."

"But you were so skilled!"

"And that was why I had to give it up," Halorn said. "No matter what honorable employment I found, people would always be approaching me with requests and 'special assignments.'"

"Then you just say no to anything shady," Durrin said.

"You should know it's not so easy," Halorn said. "Where do you draw the line? What do you do if you're threatened or blackmailed? And then there's the prestige and wealth that's always tantalizingly within reach. No—I decided it was better to get out of the boat entirely than to keep patching leaks.

"I gave the Guild a year to despair of their search. Then I ventured back into central Calamar, where I met my wife and started working at this farm."

Durrin thought back on the Halorn he had known: so skilled, so passionate about new techniques or stories of famous pyromancers of old. Durrin shook his head in disappointment. "I always thought you'd reach great heights. Not a humble farmer."

"I don't mind being humble," Halorn said.

They each hoed in silence for a minute. They were close to the end of a row, and Durrin was redoubling his efforts to finish before it became too dark to see.

"Stay with us," Halorn said suddenly.

"What?"

"Stay here," Halorn repeated. "We could use another hand for the harvest, and we have enough supplies to feed you during the winter. In the spring, if you decide you're not cut out for farming, you could get employment in Caradell. I'm sure the blacksmith would take you on."

Durrin examined the corners of Halorn's mouth to see if he was joking. He wasn't.

"Leave the Guild?" Durrin said. "Abandon everything I've worked for my whole life? For scratching in the dirt for a living?"

Halorn's voice was even, but it simmered with intensity. "And what has the Guild brought you thus far, Durrin? Seven years rotting in a cell?"

Durrin threw down the hoe. Reaching out his hands, he aimed a spike of pure heat at the soil in front of him, shriveling up the remaining weeds in his row in seconds. Then he spun to face Halorn. "I *will* become a guild master. But that's not all. I will become the greatest pyromancer who walks the earth—maybe the greatest that has ever lived. Greater even than Kymar Roline. Because unlike you, I'm not afraid to do what it takes. *Whatever* it takes."

Halorn met his gaze. There was a depth in his friend's eyes that Durrin didn't remember being there seven years ago.

"I cannot control your choices," Halorn said finally. "I can only tell you what I know: if you pursue your goal"—he pointed at the orb of pure darkness hanging in the sky—"*that* is what awaits you."

Durrin turned away. "You can keep your fables to yourself."

He walked a dozen yards before Halorn called out, "Will you at least stay the night? The twins will never forgive me if you don't tell them a bedside story!"

Durrin paused for only a moment. Then he kept walking, channeling his anger, frustration, and confusion into each footstep. "I'm afraid I can't stay. I have an appointment back in Imperium."

Chapter 15

Pirates of the Skies

Pirates!

Cutlass-wielding, swash-buckling, trouble-making terrors, they roamed the trade routes, preying on lone vessels or the stragglers in caravans. Merchants feared them, militaries fought them, and rulers despised them.

Lord Salidar Aram prided himself on belonging firmly in that third category. He had dealt with many pirates in his day. Before his political career, he had served as an admiral in the South Sea, clearing the salt trade of brigands.

But *aerial* pirates? This was new.

Salidar stood on a platform overlooking Imperium's merchant sector. The platform was part of a series of elevated wooden docks, built to service the loading and unloading of one of Zenitha's marvels—cloudships.

A cloudship was a flying craft, consisting of a gondola hanging beneath a large, pill-shaped balloon. Every few weeks, a caravan of cloudships would sail over the mountains from the far north and dock in Imperium. Their crews would unload furs, pearls, and amber in exchange for sugar and crafted goods, then follow the prevailing winds to lands farther east. All cloudships came from a far northern people called the Hakiru, who carefully guarded the secrets of their airships.

But the cloudship now docked in front of Salidar was different than any he had seen before. It was much smaller, and its sleeker shape and host of outlying fins and sails gave it an aura of speed and agility that the giant merchant ships lacked. Its gondola was small, only thirty feet long. Salidar wondered how the crew, twenty or so in number, ever found enough space to sleep comfortably on its deck.

Most striking about the cloudship was its warlike character. Rows of brightly painted shields hung from the rails on starboard and port, like seafaring pirate vessels that Salidar had seen in the South Sea. The bow and stern sported mounted ballista, lurking like vultures in their pivots. The gondola's wood was scored with gouges and burn marks, and its balloon was riddled with patches. A couple arrows stuck out at odd angles from the wood of the gondola, as if left from previous engagements just to add character.

"Most barbaric," Salidar said to no one in particular.

As Salidar and his bodyguards strode down the platform toward the cloudship, a crewman on the dock turned from where he had been sawing a plank. It was the first Hakiru Salidar had seen up close. The man was massive, towering well over six feet. He wore a green tunic that stretched taut across his muscular chest, a fur cloak tied with a brooch around his shoulders, and enough weapons to equip a platoon. One cheek was defaced from an old scar. He folded his arms over his chest, gazing confidently at Salidar's party as they approached.

"I've come to speak to your captain," Salidar announced, unfazed by the man's daunting size. Few things fazed Lord Salidar.

The man shook his head, tapping his ears and uttering something in a strange language.

One of Salidar's aides leaned close to him. "Most of the crew only speak Hakiru, my lord."

The massive man turned toward the ship and clapped twice. A moment later, a snippen vaulted over the edge of the gondola, ran down a mooring rope, and scurried up to Salidar. She sported a garish red scarf, an assortment of knives and tools in her belt, and the air of someone who didn't care what Salidar thought. Well. That would soon change.

"Lord of Calamar," the snippen said, deliberately staring Salidar in the eyes before bowing ridiculously low. "We are honored at your presence. You may call me Ensign Twigly. I'll be serving as your translator." She spoke Lurrian fluently, with a local accent. How had she come to join a Hakiru crew from the far north?

"You hail from Calamar?" Salidar sniffed.

"Imperium itself, to be precise," the snippen said. She added in a low voice, "Think I even had a job in your scullery for a day or two, 'til I broke something."

"I see you have forgotten your native customs of respect," Salidar said.

The snippen didn't get the hint, instead continuing to stare straight into Salidar's face. She smiled, as if enjoying her insolence. "The Hakiru have a saying, my lord. 'All are equal in the sky.'"

"An interesting sentiment," Salidar said, removing his signet ring and rolling it between his fingers as he studied its depths. "I have often thought the same, but of the grave."

The snippen opened her mouth, a retort likely on her lips, but something about Salidar's tone of voice, or maybe the fact that his signet ring identified him as the second most powerful person in the empire, shut her up. Salidar smirked. He loved winning games.

"Bring me your captain," Salidar said. "I wish to speak to him."

The snippen whistled, and a moment later, a griffin swooped down next to them. Salidar had heard somewhere that in the Hakiru culture, every cloudship had to be captained by a griffin. That only made sense, although it rendered the motto "a captain must go down with his ship" rather moot.

"Name?" Salidar said, like he would to a servant. No sense in maintaining a fiction of equality.

The snippen translated, the griffin responded in Hakiru, and the snippen translated back into Lurrian. "Wingcaptain Bladebeak, my lord."

Salidar cut to the point of why he had come. "The city officials told me that they suspect you of practicing piracy. How do you answer?"

More translation, then the snippen's response. "Some might call us pirates, my lord. Others call us outlaws or mercenaries. We call ourselves adventurers. We have no fealty but to ourselves, no homeland but the open sky."

Salidar clicked his tongue. "That doesn't answer my question. Have you ever attacked an unarmed merchant vessel?"

The snippen smiled. "If we said no, my lord, we'd be pulling your tail, except you ain't got one."

Cheeky. Salidar didn't get that behavior around him very often. Normally he'd respond with an execution order, but thankfully for this insolent little rodent and the rest of the crew, he had other plans today.

"Do you work for silver?"

"Aye, we work for silver, gold, potatoes."

"What brings you to Calamar?"

"A storm, my lord. Wicked nor'easter hit us by surprise from the northwest. We came here to trade for supplies and make repairs before following more friendly winds east."

Salidar brought his fingertips to his chin. "You realize that Calamarvan law forbids giving harbor to or making trade with pirates. One word from me, and I could have your ship seized, your crew tried in the courts of the Knights Vigilant, and all of you executed before the week is out."

The snippen translated this to the griffin, followed by an agitated exchange between the two.

"*Or*," said Salidar, emphasizing the word. Both of them looked at him curiously. "I have a business proposition to make. Have you ever performed a kidnapping?"

A thousand miles away, the struggle for the Arnon Plains had commenced.

Volthorn stood at the bank of the first tributary—Elandria's first line of defense—watching his army retreat. Wagons and horses tramped across to his side of the river on a large stone bridge, while humans, avirs, korriks, and swifters crossed on a series of temporary pontoon bridges built just downstream.

His eyes swept over the ranks, noting the many wounded. These were battalions from his Third Division. Earlier that day, they had fought in a short engagement with the vanguard of Calamar's army. The engagement had been indecisive, with Elandria withdrawing before Calamar could bring up reinforcements. Perhaps Volthorn could have scored a tactical victory by pressing to the attack. But with the main bulk of Calamar's army rapidly closing in, it would have been strategic suicide. Volthorn's withdrawal across the river would be dicey enough as it was.

He turned to his command staff. "News from the Second Division?"

"They're in battle array a half-mile west as you ordered, shielding the Third Division's withdrawal," an officer said. "Calamar's vanguard is in sight but not yet engaging."

"Then we may just slip out of their claws." He turned to his brother Kelzern. "How much of the Third Division is across the river?"

"About half. Trazar's doing his best to speed them up."

Volthorn ran calculations in his head, estimating how long it would take for the rest of the Third Division to cross and what needed to happen in the meantime. He turned back to the first officer. "In half an hour, have General Snarltooth pull the Second Division back to the river, prepared to cross as soon as this division is over. Have their heavy infantry hold the rear and be the last across. Captain Walkren?"

Captain Walkren, head of the army's engineers, stepped forward. "I have crews standing by to dismantle the pontoon bridges. Three crews to a bridge."

Volthorn nodded. "Good. And the stone bridge?"

"I took your suggestion, Commander. My terramancers have planted liquidation grenades at the base of each arch." A liquidation grenade was a particularly useful terramancy talisman for demolitions. When activated—which could be done at a distance through a paired talisman—it turned the stone around it to the consistency of sludge for several dozen seconds. The effect on the bridge would be . . . messy.

"Excellent," said Volthorn. "What do you think about waiting to activate them until the first Calamarvan soldiers are halfway across? Give them a little surprise dip in the river?"

Kelzern grinned at the image, but Captain Walkren frowned. "Too risky. They'll be expecting that. What if they bring up a quartzite beacon?"

Now it was Volthorn's turn to frown. A quartzite beacon—the same device he used to ensure privacy in his war councils—would disrupt the signals needed to activate the liquidation grenades. "Good thinking," he said. "Better blow the bridge as soon as our last battalions are across."

Their discussion was cut off by an earsplitting scream from the skies.

"Griffin fight!" someone called. "Archers!"

Volthorn scanned the skies. Three Elandrian griffins, their plumage dyed green, shot out of the clouds overhead, their wings tucked in a full dive. In the next second, eight red-dyed Calamarvan griffins appeared in hot pursuit.

"Clear a landing space!" Volthorn bellowed. But the griffins were diving too fast to land. Instead, they pulled up sharply just before impacting the river, their wings skimming the water's edge as they turned upstream.

A moment later, Calamar's eight griffins dropped from the skies, slamming into Elandria's three griffins from above. The river exploded in spray as the griffins plunged into the water, scratching and biting in a melee of wings and claws.

Soldiers plunged into the water, splashing toward the commotion. Officers shouted orders and archers took aim. But nobody could tell one griffin from another in the mad throes.

The fight lasted only a couple seconds. Then Calamar's griffins disengaged and burst free of the water, scattering droplets in every direction as their wings fought for altitude. Arrows hissed through the air. One enemy griffin screamed and plunged from the sky as an arrow found its mark. But the others wove and turned, evading shots until they escaped out of range.

In the river, several soldiers were helping the Elandrian griffins reach the shore. Volthorn waded into the shallows to assist them. The water ran red with blood.

"Medics!" Volthorn shouted. "We'll need medics and a surgeon!"

"I'm afraid it's too late for this one," a soldier said. The griffin in his arms was limp, the down of his neck stained red with blood from multiple wounds.

"Thunderbeak! No!" cried one of the other griffins. She struggled to her feet in the shallow water, shaking free of the soldiers trying to help her as she pushed her way over. Her desperate eyes landed on the dead griffin in the soldier's arms, searching for any sign of life.

"I'm . . . sorry," Volthorn said, as he failed to find a heartbeat. "He's gone."

The griffin lifted her head and let out a piercing cry. It split the air, echoing off the stone bridge and reverberating through Volthorn's bones. He had heard that cry before with griffins. It was the heartbroken cry of losing their second half.

After the scream had died away, Volthorn asked softly, "He was your mate?"

"Of sixteen years." The griffin nuzzled her dead companion with her beak. "We raised two broods together."

Volthorn bowed his head in respect. His thoughts turned to his brothers, Trazar and Kelzern, and how devastated he would feel to lose one of them. And yet it was said that the bond between griffin mates was even stronger than between korrik brood brothers. Was that what it would feel like one day when he parted with his brothers to find a mate of his own?

Volthorn shook himself out of his thoughts and turned to a pair of soldiers. "Help her move him to shore, then give her some space to mourn."

"Yes, Commander."

Volthorn splashed through the shallows to the riverbank, where the third griffin was getting a gash on his wing dressed and wrapped by a blue-clad medic from the Dawn Wardens. "How do you fare?" Volthorn asked.

The griffin looked up wearily. Volthorn recognized him as a flight captain, one of about thirty in the army. "We can't keep on like this," the griffin said despondently. "They have fresh griffins arriving every day. I was taking a wing pair on a routine patrol downriver—not even directly over their army—when they closed on us from three directions. We couldn't outfly them."

"Why weren't there more patrols nearby to back you up?"

The griffin shook his head. "We're spread too thin. We have to keep tabs on their entire army, alerting you of any breakoff sorties and reporting the movements of each division. And we're doing our best to screen our own army's movements. We're covering a front fifty to a hundred miles wide and twenty miles deep, and we've got fewer than five hundred griffins to do it. And that has to be divided into four shifts." The griffin gestured toward his wing. "And now I'll be grounded for a week. Not that that compares at all to the loss of Thunderbeak."

Volthorn listened. He kept his face stoic, but inside, his spirits were sinking. General Embertail had reported that the air battle was an ongoing struggle, but hearing and seeing the details firsthand made the grim reality all too clear.

"I'll reassess our strategy," Volthorn said. They couldn't afford to lose their griffins one by one to enemy raids. Neither could they afford to leave the skies directly above their own army undefended. He'd have to pull back griffin patrols to a perimeter immediately around their army. And that would significantly curtail their ability to gather intelligence. It would save more griffin lives but would put the whole army in greater danger of being outmaneuvered.

Tradeoffs. War was a series of unpleasant tradeoffs, constantly hoping that whatever decision he made would lead to the fewest precious lives being lost.

"Rest well this week," Volthorn said to the flight captain. "You've earned it."

He looked up at the wound-littered squadrons of soldiers still crossing the river. "We've all earned it," he added to himself. "But this campaign is just beginning."

A series of mental dominoes fell into place in Volthorn's mind. The last couple days had been too relentless. His griffin flights weren't the only units exhausted: his cavalry, his swifters, and his officers were all near the point of collapse from the campaign's relentless maneuvers. They needed to put some distance between them and the enemy so they could have a day or two of reprieve.

He clambered up the riverbank, back to his cadre of officers and aides. "Change of plans," he said, wiping the mud from his boots. "Inform each general that as soon as the Third Division and Second Division are across, we're withdrawing east at a quick march. Calamar has won this river. We're pulling back to the second tributary."

Chapter 16

Details

Saven may have changed. Halorn may have changed. The whole world may have changed in the last seven years. But Durrin, at least, finally felt like his old self again.

Upon returning from Caradell, he spent another day shopping in Imperium's finest markets. After spending a good portion of the silver Lord Salidar had given him, Durrin was as fully equipped as he'd been in his best days in the past. He wore a newly tailored combat outfit: a highly crafted blend of chainmail and padded leather, adorned with red silk highlights. The outfit would afford him a decent degree of protection while not overly restricting his movement.

A new sword hung from his belt. The long saber had an intricate pattern of curves etched along the blade and the hand guard. It was specifically designed to be a pyromancer's weapon, with the curves helping to capture and channel energy. It had taken some hunting to find a capable swordsmith who wouldn't recognize him, but at last he'd found one who had recently moved to the capital.

Durrin had traded his tattered travel cloak for a new one of the traditional pyromantic design: one side scarlet, one side sable black.

He wore the scarlet side out as he strode along an aerial dock built high above the city's streets. An airship was tethered at the end of the dock, its crew busy making repairs to some fins on the port side.

Interesting, Durrin thought as he took in the strange ship. This was the first time he'd seen one up close. How exactly did it defy gravity to stay aloft? Looking more closely, he saw a large fire pan in the middle of the boat, directly underneath a fabric funnel leading to the giant balloon above. Did the fire pan heat the air in the balloon? He knew that hot air rose while cooler air sank. But would hot air really be enough to keep the massive vessel in the sky?

He looked over the crew. While many looked to be Hakiru by their manner of dress, the rest were a motley assortment of different nationalities. But, based on the confident way they held their weapons and moved about the ship, these were all trained warriors who knew what they were about. Salidar had chosen well.

"Hail, pyromancer!" said a small voice. Durrin looked down to see a garishly dressed snippen scurry towards him. "Are you the skilled professional we are expecting?"

He bowed. "You may call me Rendhart."

"Ensign Twigly." The snippen bowed with a flourish. "I'll be serving as your interpreter." She gestured toward a griffin swooping down for a landing on the dock. "This is our leader, Wingcaptain Bladebeak. And here comes our navigator."

A male avir was climbing down the rope ladder, whistling as he came. He was easily the fanciest-dressed member of the whole crew, with a tailored vest and kilt made from a checkerboard green and red cloth. Durrin recognized the fabric as a textile called a *tartan*, from a land far to the east.

The avir gave a jaunty smile and reached out a hand. "Name es Tadgh MacLery," he said, his accent thick. "I be afraid I don't know Lurrian tah well. Still learning Hakiru, as mattah of fact."

Durrin stared at Tadgh's outstretched hand, confused. Did the man want something? Money?

Tadgh rolled his eyes. "Yeh shake it." He grabbed his hand with his other hand and gave it a firm shake. "Lahk this. Ach. Yeh westerners will neveh understand a good handshake."

"Tadgh comes from a Dorinian clan across the First Eastern Sea," Twigly explained. "He had developed a reputation there as one of their finest navigators, until we picked him up a year ago."

Tadgh winked. "They kidnapped me."

The snippen folded her furry arms over her chest. "More like, we gave you an offer you couldn't refuse. With an emphasis on the *couldn't refuse* part. But we're wasting sunbeams. What's the plan, Rendhart?"

Durrin looked around, making sure there was no one else on the dock besides the pirates. "We must talk discretely. This city is full of spies, many of whom are talented mancerers who could eavesdrop from afar. I assume the basics of this job have already been explained to you?"

Twigly turned and exchanged a few words with Bladebeak in Hakiru. Durrin had never studied that language—it sounded like total gibberish to his ears, completely unrelated to Lurrian, Mitrian, or any other language Durrin had studied.

Twigly turned back. "You sail with us to the city of Wherever. We kidnap the Fancy-Schmancy leader of Wherever. Sail back. Turn her over to our employer for two hundred pounds of gold. Straightforward."

Durrin nodded, reaching into his pack and pulling out a couple of maps. "Yes, but let's go over some details."

"Ach," said Tadgh, the Dorinian navigator. "Details. The demons ah always in the details."

Demons. The conversation with Halorn from three days earlier flashed through Durrin's mind. He resisted the urge to look over his shoulder. It was broad daylight. No demons would be out during daylight.

"First, let's talk about our approach to the capital of Wherever," Durrin said, spreading out a detailed map of central Elandria.

Tadgh shook his head. "No good. You're on a cloud frigate nah, not a horse. You need a propah wind chart. Lucky for you, I came prepared." He pulled a map out of his satchel, spreading it out on the boardwalk and laying weights on the corners. While Durrin vaguely recognized the terrain of Elandria from various landmarks, the chart was covered with an unintelligible sprawl of lines, arrows, and annotations.

"These show the wind currents over our target," Tadgh explained, pointing out various markings. "The rest ach notes about storm conditions, weather patterns, updrafts and downdrafts, likely pressure fronts, and useful waystations." He indicated the Rugeran Mountains, which formed the northern and western borders of central Elandria. "This range is a natural barrier. Hard ta get over. We typically stay west o south of it. But there ah some half-treacherous avenues that we can use."

"Half-treacherous," Durrin repeated, glancing at the Dorinian and raising an eyebrow. "Not sure I like the sound of that. I already had one brush with death in those mountains. Would it be safer to go around?"

"Sure as beetles 'twould be," the Dorinian said, shrugging. "But where's the fun in that?"

Durrin stared at Tadgh for a second. Then he smiled. "You lot are my kind of sailors."

Durrin turned back to the map, studying the route Tadgh had indicated. "The trick will be approaching the capital without being seen," he commented. "They can't know we're coming."

"We're not too concerned about being spotted," Twigly interjected. "Cloudships are an uncommon sight in Wherever, true, but common enough that anyone will just think us to be a merchant vessel straying off the normal trade routes. As long as our final approach to the target is kept on the down-low, we'll have a decent shot. That's where your expertise comes in, Rendhart."

Durrin tapped a point on the map. "I recommend approaching the capital from due north. That way we'll avoid the Silvermoss and Angerflood and all the major roads and settlements, and travel over some sparsely populated hill country."

Tadgh examined the map. "The winds ah pathetic for a north approach. But if we tack and churn, we could make it work."

Durrin had no idea what *tack* and *churn* meant, but he continued on as if he knew exactly what the Dorinian navigator was talking about. "Right. We'll want to approach at night, circle round the palace on the east side, then come to the southernmost tower." He pulled out a second map, this one specifically of the palace complex in Saven. "The living quarters for our target are relatively isolated in a free-standing tower on the south side. Most of the garrison is quartered at the north side, by the palace gates. If we strike quickly and silently, we can overwhelm any guards in the south wing, seize our target, and slip away."

Twigly sucked on her paw as she stared at the map. She didn't seem to be doing much translation anymore. "We'll have to work out some more specific tactics, but that can be done on the flight over. What do we do once we have our target?"

"Slip away fast," Durrin said. "Could you escape griffin pursuit at night?"

"We've developed some tricks," the snippen said, waving her paw dismissively. "With cloud cover, it would be a breeze. But we could manage even without."

"Excellent," Durrin said. "We'll leave a ransom note behind, setting up a time and place for one of our griffins to meet with them to discuss terms of payment."

"But I thought we're taking our target back here," Twigly said.

"We are," said Durrin. "But her people mustn't know that. We need to make it seem like you're acting independently, just kidnapping her so you can exchange her for a hefty price. They can't be any the wiser until we've returned here and handed the target over to your employer."

"And once she's brought here, will she ever be returned to her people? Or is she a prisoner for life?"

"That's up to your employer to decide," Durrin said. The real answer sat uncomfortably in his gut. Lord Salidar had given him secret orders to ensure Queen Everborn didn't reach *any* destination alive.

Twigly frowned, then turned to the griffin and exchanged a long back-and-forth with him. Then she turned back. "It seems a little cruel, to rob a kingdom of their queen and a queen of her kingdom."

"You're pirates," said Durrin flatly. "Don't you do cruel things all the time?"

Twigly brushed a speck of dirt from her scarf. "Only when occupationally necessary."

"Well, this is occupationally necessary," said Durrin.

Twigly nodded thoughtfully, studying the maps as she tapped absently on the stones under her paws. "That's a long flight back here, with few favorable air currents," she said. "What's to say we simplify things somewhat, and just ransom her back to her own people? I'm sure they'll pay a similar price as His Excellency, if not higher, and it saves us quite a bit of sailing." She winked at him. "We could give you a hefty cut of the profits."

Durrin opened his mouth, but he didn't have a reply ready. This option had never occurred to him. From the pirates' perspective, Twigly's alternative *was* much more attractive. But not to Durrin. He wasn't doing this for the gold. If he double-crossed Salidar, Kymar's scroll would be forever out of his reach.

Twigly leaned forward and rapped playfully on Durrin's knee. "I'm just kidding with you, Rendhart. We made a deal with His Excellency. And a deal's a deal."

Durrin studied the snippen carefully. He wasn't sure he fully trusted her. The griffin and the navigator, at least, seemed straightforward. But this snippen—she was a little too cavalier for his liking.

Durrin shrugged the thought aside. All *he* needed was for the pirates to help him successfully kidnap Adara. After that, it wouldn't matter what *their* plans were. *His* plans would take precedence.

"That sums things up." Durrin folded up his maps. "We'll discuss more in the air, when we're well away from any listening ears. When will you be ready to depart?"

"This very afternoon," said Twigly. "We'll have the last rigging in tip-top shape within the hour, and we're already victualed and watered."

So they were punctual, too—ready the exact day Salidar had asked them to be. "I'll return shortly," Durrin said. "I just want to check on my horse again, make sure the stable hands are taking good care of her."

"Why leave her here?" Twigly asked. "We can take her on board with us."

Durrin glanced between her and the cloudship's tiny gondola, not sure how to respond to such a ludicrous proposal. "Are you sure? It's a full-grown mare, and we have a long—"

He paused, noticing the smile trying to escape from the snippen's mouth. "Very funny," he finally said.

"I'm just trying to get you to laugh, Rendhart," Twigly smirked, taking out one of her many daggers and twirling it on her paw. "It's good for your health!"

Durrin stood and shouldered his pack. "I'm afraid professional pyromancers don't laugh unless paid double. It's an added service."

Durrin strode back down the dock, descended a set of stairs to an alley that would lead back to the main street—and found himself face-to-face with a familiar but completely unexpected face.

"Halorn!" Durrin said, startled.

"Hello again." Halorn had an old traveling cloak and a travel pack, but otherwise was still dressed in his simple farming garb.

"Why—"

"I didn't tell you everything," Halorn said quickly. "Back at Caradell. There was more I needed to say."

Durrin glanced up at the aerial docks. How had Halorn tracked him here? He'd taken extra precautions to make sure he hadn't been followed through the city. And how would Halorn have even found him in the first place?

"You lied the other day," Durrin concluded. "You must still dabble in pyromancy. You used it to track me here."

Halorn shook his head.

No pyromancer? Well, there were other ways of tracking someone. "Then you hid a tracking gem in my pack when I visited your farm."

Again, Halorn shook his head.

Durrin was at a loss. "Then . . ."

"I used a power higher than mancery," said Halorn. "I used the power of Light."

It took a second for Durrin to process what Halorn was alluding to. When he did, he took a step back in alarm, summoning a crackling flame of fire.

"You've joined the Luminant Order," Durrin said. "That shepherd in the mountains was more than a storyteller; she must have been an adherent of the Order that escaped the Empire's purge. It was through the Order's arcane powers that you tracked me down."

Halorn's face showed no sign of fear. "The Order is not corrupt, Durrin. We have been persecuted out of fear and jealousy, and because our allegiance is to an authority beyond Calamar's throne."

"You know the Luminant Order is forbidden." Durrin increased the flame in his hand until it roared over a foot tall. "Anyone discovered to be an adherent is to be arrested and imprisoned. I could turn you in."

"But you won't," said Halorn.

Durrin stared at his friend for a few seconds, his thoughts jumbled. Then he realized that Halorn was right. He relaxed his stance and let the flame in his hand die. "What do you need to tell me?" he said grudgingly.

"I didn't give the whole truth about why I left the Guild seven years ago," Halorn said. "Yes, I was getting disillusioned. But mainly, I left . . . because I didn't want to become like you."

Something twisted deep within Durrin's heart.

"What do you mean?" Durrin whispered.

"You were my best friend," Halorn explained. "You were my role model, my inspiration. You faced every challenge with nothing but confidence. You made the hardest pyromantic tricks look like child's play. Every day, I thought about how much I wanted to be like you.

Halorn's face gained a look of pain and loss. "But then the Guild changed you, Durrin. You *let* it change you. As you grew in skill, you naturally acquired the hardest jobs—which were inevitably the most scurrilous. I saw how you stooped to anything that would increase your power and further your career. You became a pawn of Lord Salidar, doing his dirty work with scarcely a thought about those you harmed. I saw how those tasks started to make you hard, cold, and ruthless."

Halorn looked down at his feet. "But what scared me most was realizing I was walking that same path. You had once been a man of honor. So had I. But then you began to stoop to tasks far below your honor. So was I."

Halorn took a deep breath. When he resumed, his voice was tight with barely constrained emotion. "I began to wonder just how far you were willing to go. And that was when you killed King Everborn."

Durrin's insides twisted harder.

"How did you know?" The words escaped him before he could stop them.

"First, I guessed," said Halorn. "The timing seemed too coincidental. You disappeared without a trace. One month later, the king of Elandria was dead, supposedly killed by a tragic fire. So first I just put two and two together. But I kept my ears open. And soon I overheard—well, *eavesdropped* on—two guild masters speculating on whether you had been killed by Everborn's guards."

So his best friend knew he was a murderer. Durrin's legs began to shake. He sunk down on a barrel, placed his hands on his knees, and stared at the cobblestones. "You knew," he whispered. "You knew this whole time." He looked up. "Who else knows?"

"I have no idea." Halorn shrugged. "Many I'm sure suspected. But the guild masters were exceedingly careful to keep your mission a secret. They had to be, if they wanted their plan to succeed."

Durrin furrowed his brow in confusion. "But it already had."

Halorn shook his head. "That wasn't their whole plan. Like Salidar, they wanted King Everborn assassinated, yes. But they also wanted to absolve themselves of any involvement. And, perhaps most importantly for them, they wanted you dead."

Durrin grew chill.

Halorn continued. "I assume you haven't heard about what happened here after you left?"

Durrin shook his head.

"Soon after you disappeared, but before King Everborn's death, the Guild Council denounced you."

"Denounced me?"

"They issued a declaration. It was read in the Academy and posted in several city squares. They declared that you had become dangerous and deranged, and so had been evicted from the Guild, barred from any employment, and placed under warrant of arrest. They said you had disappeared, and that they had reason to suspect you were going to attempt something crazy if not found and captured."

Durrin stared into the shadows of the alley, letting the information sink in.

Halorn kept talking. "You were only a tool, Durrin. But you were a dangerous and ambitious tool that they needed to get rid of as soon as it had done its job. They and Lord Salidar wanted King Everborn dead—to spark a war that would further Calamar's interests—but they wanted to obscure any evidence of their involvement."

"So they cut all their ties with me," Durrin realized. "It all makes sense now, Halorn. My instructions were to assassinate King Everborn in a public, showy fashion, declaring that I had been sent by Calamar."

Halorn nodded. "I suspected as much."

Durrin began to pace, thinking out loud. "Whether I succeeded or not, they wanted Elandria to accuse Calamar of being behind the assassination. The emperor, the vizier, and the Guild would all deny it. Denouncing me was a necessity. 'Rendhart?' they would say. 'Ah, yes, look at this edict we issued. We knew he was dangerous, and we tried to capture him. We're so sorry this happened.'"

Halorn nodded again. "Our citizens would believe the lie. Elandria's wouldn't. And so war would ensue, with Elandria perceived as the unjustified aggressor."

"But instead," Durrin said, "King Everborn's advisors decided to hush up the assassination and pretend the king died in an accident."

Halorn nodded. "And they were wise. It bought them four more years of unstable peace, until war finally broke out three years ago."

Puzzle pieces from seven years ago began falling into place in Durrin's head. "I didn't travel to Saven alone. I went with another member of the Guild. The day I raided the palace, he was supposed to be waiting at the river with a boat, to help me slip away. But when I arrived at the docks, with pursuit hot on my tail—he was gone."

"All part of the guild masters' plan, most likely," Halorn said. "They wanted Elandria to capture you and find out who sent you. And then they wanted you dead."

Emotions ripped through Durrin. Betrayal. Anger. Hate. He summoned a flame, a thin column of intense heat that rose three feet above his hand. Then he let his hatred pour into it like oil, stoking it hotter and hotter until the core burned blue.

"They will pay," Durrin spat. "Those cowards will pay."

Halorn approached Durrin—carefully skirting around his incinerating inferno—and put a hand on Durrin's shoulder. "Durrin. I didn't tell you this so that you could get revenge."

"Revenge?" Durrin snarled. "Or justice? They sought my life. Why should I not seek theirs?"

"Because it will destroy you." Halorn passed a hand through Durrin's column of fire. In an instant, the flame died. Durrin had never felt anything like it before. There was no counter spell, no competing pyromantic pull, not even the suck of voidstone. The heat and energy just . . . *vanished*.

Durrin sprang backward, staring in shock at his friend. "How did you do that?"

"By the same power I knew where to find you." Halorn fixed Durrin with his intense gaze. "Now I have one more question, Durrin. What have you thought about what I shared with you? About angels and demons? About the Void? About your eternal soul?

Hatred and anger towards the men who had betrayed him still coursed through his mind. "What does that have to do with anything?" Durrin snapped.

"Everything." Halorn placed a finger on Durrin's chest. "You are no mere mortal, Durrin. None of us are. We are infinite beings. And you need to decide where you want to *spend* infinity." Halorn pointed up at the afternoon sky. "In the Halls of the Sun?" He pointed down. "Or in the pits of the Void?"

Durrin shook his head. "That's not—"

"Don't you see?" Halorn cried. "Don't you understand? You murdered a king in cold blood! You helped spark a war that has claimed tens of thousands of lives! And you think when you die that these abominable acts won't matter?"

"I did not start this war," Durrin said.

"Oh?" said Halorn. "What did you *think* you were doing, seven years ago?"

Durrin had no answer. He had told himself he had killed Everborn to defend Calamar's interests, to give Elandria a warning, to fulfill the Emperor's wishes. But he had never fully thought through what his act would bring upon the world. The truth was, he had done it solely so he could get his hands on Kymar's scroll.

The silence weighed heavily in the air before Halorn continued, his voice barely louder than a whisper. "Then you better think harder this time, Durrin. Before you kill Everborn's daughter."

He can't know. Durrin's mind filled with panic. His meetings with Salidar had been completely private. Salidar always took every precaution. No one, mancerer or otherwise, could have overheard them.

"I know your orders from Salidar," Halorn continued. "Work with the pirates to 'kidnap' Queen Adara. Then set their cloudship on fire and let the queen and the crew burn or fall to their deaths, while you use your pyromantic prowess to leap to safety."

Durrin's mind raced. There was no way Halorn could know. No mechanism by which Halorn could have overheard.

Unless . . .

Unless everything Halorn had said was true. Unless invisible angels really were witnessing Durrin's every act, and they were the source of Halorn's knowledge.

But if *that* part of Halorn's beliefs was true, then everything else was, too.

The angels see all. Everything.

Tyranny and murder.

Act; do not wait. Seal the scroll of your fate. Deal rightly with all, or to the Void you will fall.

In an instant, Durrin's world had tipped upside down. Everything was in pandemonium. He tried in vain to sort through the shambles, grasping at the thousands of questions coursing through him.

Finally, he settled on one. "Why did the guild masters want me dead?"

Halorn reflected for a moment. "I think it was three reasons. First was jealousy—they didn't want you to outshine them. It would have stripped them of their power and influence."

Durrin nodded. He had already gathered as much.

"Second, they knew you wanted something—something they couldn't offer you."

"Kymar's sixth scroll," Durrin said. "They didn't want me to access its secrets."

"Not exactly," said Halorn. "They couldn't offer it to you because they do not have it."

"What?" *What under the million stars was Halorn talking about?*

"Everyone knows that Kymar Roline made only a single copy of his last scroll," Halorn said. "Kymar forbade his acolytes from ever copying it. According to tradition, that scroll was handed down through generations of pyromantic masters, kept in the most secure vaults of the Academy, down to the present."

"Exactly," said Durrin.

"It's a lie," Halorn said. "The lore keeper told me the truth. Kymar didn't entrust the scroll to Calamar. He entrusted it to Elandria."

"Absurdity," Durrin said, shaking his head. "Calamar was Kymar's homeland. Calamar was where he founded his academy."

"Think about it," said Halorn. "In three hundred years, has any master of the Guild displayed the hidden powers that scroll is supposed to unlock?"

"None," said Durrin. "But that's because the powers are too advanced—"

Halorn held up a finger. "Advanced, yes. But not impossible. No. According to tradition, the reason Kymar made a single copy, the reason he ordered it hidden, was because he feared those secrets would make someone too powerful."

"Then why hasn't Elandria used these powers to win the war?"

"Because they understand what Kymar understood," said Halorn. "Power, once placed in the wrong hands, cannot be wrested back. The scroll is kept with utmost secrecy. Only a handful of people know it even exists in their archives."

"And do *you* know where it is?"

"No!" said Halorn. "I didn't tell you this so you could seek it, Durrin. I told you so you would *stop* seeking it. It is out of your grasp. Unattainable."

"Perhaps," Durrin said, the wheels in his head already turning. He knew the layout of the palace at Saven well, including the location of its library. Perhaps, while the pirates kidnapped the queen . . .

"I know what you're thinking," Halorn said. "But the scroll is not in the royal palace. It's not anywhere in Saven. I know that much. Elandria is vast. It could be anywhere within their kingdom. Give up your quest."

Never, Durrin thought. But he did not voice it out loud. "What was the third reason you think the guild masters wanted me dead?"

Halorn looked relieved to be changing the subject. "The third reason was that you were too closely under the thumb of Salidar. While the guild masters share many of His Excellency's foreign policies, they are keen to maintain their independence. Admitting you to their council would have given Salidar too much power over them."

Durrin blew out a breath. "Then His Excellency, at least, is still an ally."

Halorn shook his head. "He is no ally of yours, Durrin. He sees you only as a tool. His favor extends only as far as you are useful to him."

"You do not know His Excellency like I do," said Durrin.

"I know enough," said Halorn. "I know he started a war for no reason than personal power."

"The war is over haeber," Durrin protested.

"There are other ways to fix the haeber shortage than going to war," Halorn said. "Haeber is the excuse. Ambition is the reason. No, Durrin. Salidar has no one's interests in mind except his own. Following him will only lead to pain. And following anything but this—" Halorn tapped Durrin's chest above his heart, "—will only lead to darkness."

Durrin's mind was still drowning in questions. Halorn had answered one but prompted a thousand more. But before he could ask another, Halorn's head jerked up. "Someone is coming," he said. "I must go."

With surprising speed, Halorn slipped farther down the alley, disappearing around a corner. Durrin stood in shock for a moment, still trying to process all that had happened in the last fifteen minutes. Too late, he reached out with his pyrosense to detect what Halorn had. Immediately he felt it—a trio of figures approaching the entrance to the alley, one of whom with a spark that felt very, very familiar.

It was too late to hide as Halorn had. Durrin turned to face the new arrivals as they reached the entrance to the alley. He bowed deeply at their leader. "Greetings, Your Excellency."

"Rendhart," said Lord Salidar, with a hint of surprise. "Impeccable timing. Come. Our plans have changed."

Chapter 17

Unexpected Cargo

Lord Salidar was flanked by two underlings. One was Yorid, his ever-frowning steward, now carrying a recurve bow over his shoulder and a quiver of arrows at his waist. The other, whom Durrin didn't recognize, was a korrik with an impressive array of knives and brass knuckles tucked into his belt and vest. He was probably one of Salidar's bodyguards.

"This is a surprise," Durrin said, his mind still reeling from the conversation he had just had with Halorn.

"Indubitably," said Salidar. "Life is full of surprises." He gestured to the staircase leading up to the aerial docks. "After you."

The docks? Did Salidar want to give some last instructions to the Hakiru pirates before they embarked? But why would he risk associating himself with them right before their mission?

Durrin led the way up the stairs, followed by the korrik, then Yorid, with Salidar taking up the rear.

Durrin could sense the korrik twitching with uneasiness behind him. As they reached a landing, the korrik paused and cleared his throat. "Your Excellency, might I ask—"

"I'm afraid you can't," Lord Salidar said coldly. "Onward."

There was a disdain in Salidar's voice, mixed with a touch of urgency that went beyond his normal brisk demeanor. Something was definitely afoot.

Durrin glanced back to see the korrik eyeing him suspiciously. "And who are you?" the korrik grunted, idly fingering a bludgeon at his belt.

Durrin hesitated, glancing back at Lord Salidar. The nobleman shrugged, as if he didn't particularly care how Durrin responded. Durrin opted for subtle intimidation.

"Just a three-time fifth-level Kymar champion," said Durrin easily. The korrik scowled, leaving Durrin wondering whether he knew what that meant. Pyromantic terminology could be a bit jargony to the uninitiated.

Presently they reached the aerial quay. A strong wind had picked up from the west, and the cloud frigate was groaning like a slumbering giant as it strained against its mooring ropes. As Salidar's retinue approached, the Hakiru pirates spotted them and left off their work on the rigging, climbing down to the gondola's deck or standing at the edges of the quay. Durrin spotted Twigly among the crew, staring at them curiously.

"Your Excellency," the korrik interrupted. "Why are we here? Who are these . . . scallywags?"

"I have always wanted to see Imperium with a griffins-eye view," Salidar said. "These honest Hakiru traders have offered to take me on a short trip."

Durrin glanced at Twigly, who was close enough to overhear the comment. She looked as surprised as he felt. Salidar was coming aboard?

The korrik cursed. "Your Excellency, I must—"

The vizier glared at him. "Can you remind me when I instructed you to make my decisions your concern?"

The korrik shut his mouth.

"Ah," Salidar said. "That's right. I never have." He turned back to Twigly. "Inform your captain that my companions and I will be coming on board for a few minutes."

Twigly turned to the rest of the crew, barking out a few phrases in their strange language. Immediately, a skinny teenage boy among them waved his hands back and forth, his face full of alarm as he jabbered back at Twigly.

Twigly scurried down the ship's ladder, holding up a paw to stop Salidar from starting to climb aboard. "Not so fast, you landlubbing lobber!" she exclaimed, her nose twitching. "You think you can just spring three extra people on us without a moment's notice and expect to waltz on board? You've got to weigh two hundred pounds apiece!"

Salidar stepped back, his eyes widening with afront at the snippen's insolence.

"Our weight-master here says we'll need to jettison some ballast and generate more lift," Twigly said. "Give us ten minutes. Rendhart, could you assist us on board? We could use your pyromancy."

Salidar glowered at her for a moment, then turned away with an angry swish of his cloak. Twigly began babbling to the other pirates again. In moments, the ship was a bustle of activity.

Durrin followed the snippen up the ladder to the gondola. As he did, he examined the cloud frigate more carefully. The balloon was long and sleek with tapered ends, perhaps a hundred and fifty feet long and fifty feet wide and tall. The gondola hanging beneath it had two strange contraptions mounted at the stern. They looked like the blades of a windmill, except thinner and more tapered, and were positioned out away from the hull by long wooden trellises, one on each side.

The deck of the gondola was best described as highly organized chaos. Dozens of lines and ladders stretched upward toward the balloon. Various trapdoors gave access to compartments for storing cargo and supplies. The rest of the deck was crowded with bedding, crates, weapons, and pirates. It was going to be a cramped trip.

Twigly guided Durrin to the middle of the gondola, where a large metal brazier was burning charcoal. Above the brazier was a funnel of cloth leading to the balloon. Durrin nodded in understanding. Fire would heat the air in the balloon, making it expand and rise, providing lift to counteract the weight of the gondola.

"How is the heat enough to keep the balloon afloat?" Durrin asked.

"It's not enough on its own," Twigly said. "Inside the balloon is prime vapor."

"Prime what?"

"Prime vapor. It's a different kind of air. A lighter kind."

"A different . . . kind of air," Durrin repeated. "How do you have a different kind of air?"

Twigly winked. "That's the Hakiru's little secret." She gestured at the brazier. "But we're off topic. Can you make this fire hotter?"

"I can make the air hotter directly, if that's what you're after," said Durrin. He swept his hands in an intricate pattern, then channeled a plume of fire into the funnel. The fabric above them rippled and visibly expanded, and Durrin felt the gondola bob upward in response.

Twigly's eyes were wide. "Stars, but we're going to love having you on board, Rendhart," she said. "Keep it up. We'll be bringing the rest of the crew on board soon, along with our three surprise passengers, so we'll need as much lift as we can."

Durrin continued for the next five minutes. The gondola bobbed up each time he released a plume of fire and bobbed down each time another crew member came on board—particularly the humans, who were the heaviest. The cloud frigate preserved a delicate equilibrium indeed.

Once Salidar, Yorid, and Salidar's bodyguard were on board, Twigly held up a paw. "Hold a moment." The only pirates still on the quay were two other snippens, standing at the ready at the last mooring ropes. "Let her sink a little so we can loosen the lines easier."

Durrin stood at ease, grateful for a break. Gradually, incrementally, the ship began to sink, until the mooring ropes were no longer taut.

For the last ten minutes, Salidar's korrik bodyguard had been scanning the scene with a scowl on his face, muttering curses under his breath and glaring at any pirate who came too close to him. Finally he turned once more to Salidar. "Your Excellency, I stridently object. You cannot entrust your safety to this ramshackle vessel and scurrilous crew. As your chief of security, I—"

Salidar cut him off without even turning to look at him. "Trust me. I know how much you care about my security—or how little."

The korrik looked puzzled.

Durrin, processing the implications of Salidar's words, moved into a battle stance, dropping a hand to his sword hilt.

A moment later, Salidar spun and released a throwing dart he had held unseen in his hand.

The dart hit the korrik in the neck, causing him to recoil. Then anger filled his eyes, and he lunged forward, drawing a knife from his belt. Durrin stepped forward to defend his master, but Yorid was already there, grabbing the korrik's arm and twisting it behind him. After a moment's struggle, the korrik's movements slowed and he collapsed to one knee, clawing at the dart still buried in his neck.

Salidar stood over him. "I would have liked to interrogate you, to find out how long you were in Lord Skyfang's employ. But this will do."

The korrik fell to his hands and knees, wheezing. His eyes, now tinged with red, stared wide-eyed at the nobleman above him. "How . . ." he croaked. Then he crumpled to the floor of the gondola.

The pirates began to shout in angry tones in their indecipherable language. Tadgh, the Dorinian navigator, pushed his way to the scene. "Yeh murdered him!"

"He was planning to murder *me*," Salidar said calmly. He knelt and retrieved his dart from the korrik's neck. "I learned just this morning that he was under the employ of one of my rivals in court, an ambitious politician named Lord Skyfang. Skyfang had ordered him to assassinate me at high noon today. So I struck first."

"But you *killed* him!" Twigly said. She had moved to stand next to Tadgh and was staring at the body with wide eyes.

Salidar carefully tucked the dart into a pouch at his waist, avoiding the tip. "Indeed. Rock viper venom, undiluted, full dose. Works quickly. Highly effective."

"But couldn't you have had him arrested?"

Salidar cocked his head. "Hmm . . . let's see . . . I could arrest him, spend the better part of a month arranging for his trial, and then have him executed. Or I could execute him now."

"But—"

"Enough!" Salidar snapped. "Do not question my actions, scrawny dreg of the aerial seas. Understood?"

Durrin scanned the angry crowd of pirates, his hand still on the hilt of his sword.

For a moment, all was silent except for the thrum of the rigging in the breeze. Twigly glared at Salidar with narrowed eyes, then finally nodded. "We understand."

"Good." Salidar turned away. "Then let's cast off. We leave immediately."

Twigly opened her mouth, a question on her tongue, but stopped herself.

Tadgh asked instead. "How far are yeh coming with us?"

"The whole trip," said Salidar.

Now Twigly couldn't stop herself. "What?!"

Salidar gestured at the floor. "That bodyguard was not the only spy in my household. I recently learned that there are several others, each with orders to assassinate me when the opportunity presents itself."

"Agents of Elandria?" Durrin guessed.

Salidar shook his head. "Agents of Lord Skyfang, or perhaps others like him. I am not without enemies in court. My rivals, too cowardly to confront me openly, are resorting to the basest measures to thwart my glorious vision of Calamar's future."

Salidar strode to the railing, looking out over the city. "It will take several days, if not weeks, for my own agents to root out the assassins and eliminate them. So I needed a way to get out of the city quickly and unexpectedly, without taking a large retinue with me."

"I see," said Durrin.

"You and the pirates will continue exactly as planned, only with me and Yorid on board. You can toss the korrik's body overboard as soon as we're past the city."

Twigly swished her tail angrily. "This is not what we agreed upon."

"I'm afraid the alternative was you returning here with the prize, only to find your employer dead," Salidar said. "Explain to your captain, *ensign*, that every plan requires adaptation."

After glaring at Salidar's back for a second, Twigly turned to the rest of the crew and gibbered to them in Hakiru. This turned into a lengthy and spirited discussion, though Durrin couldn't tell how much the pirates were angry and how much this was the natural animated nature of their language. Finally, with a series of gestures from Wingcaptain Bladebeak, the crew set to work, tightening lines and securing cargo. On the quay below them, snippens scrambled to untie the last mooring ropes keeping the ship anchored to the dock.

Durrin watched the vizier out of the corner of his eye. He was pretty sure he knew an additional, unmentioned motivation behind Salidar's actions: the vizier wanted to personally ensure that Queen Adara's elimination went as planned. Did he not trust Durrin? Or did he not trust the pirates? Either way, his presence would make this mission even more complicated than it already was.

A moment later, Durrin felt the ship jolt. The last mooring rope gave way, and the airship began to drift east, wholly at the mercy of the wind.

"Give her all you got!" Twigly barked to Durrin. "Or we'll crash into some unlucky bloke's palace."

Durrin obliged, channeling massive gusts of heat into the balloon. Slowly at first, then faster and faster, the airship rose. Durrin looked out in amazement as the cityscape of Imperium fell away beneath him. There was the Mancery Mayhem arena, where he had fought in front of crowds of thousands. There was Salidar's castle, brooding over the city. There was the Imperial Palace itself, a majestic mountain of pinnacles and domes, now looking as small as a doll house.

Durrin leaned over the edge of the gondola, studying the streets below them. For a moment, he thought he saw the miniscule figure of a farmer from Caradell, staring up at them from far below. Then the ship caught a gust of wind and turned, causing that particular street to slip from view.

Durrin turned to look east. They were quickly rising above the nearest line of hills. Beyond that was a farther ridge, and then a farther one. And far beyond that, he knew, waited another city. Another palace. Another chance for him to earn the knowledge and power that he sought.

But at what price?

PART TWO

THE FLAME OF TRUTH

CHAPTER 18

TO THINK ON ONE'S FEET

"Let's practice it one more time," Lady Luviana suggested.

"Which part?" said Adara.

"The initial proposition."

The two of them were waiting in the throne room, moments away from a crucial negotiation. Adara's epistles to Emperor Stoneclaw had received no answer, so they had instead written to Calamar's commanding officer at the front. Their letter had been answered, and a griffin emissary had arrived in Saven earlier that morning to commence diplomatic talks.

Adara took a deep breath. To center herself, she took a moment to close her eyes and focus on her other senses: the weight of the Everborn crown on her head. The feel of the scepter in her gloved hand. The rustle of her dress—one of the finest in her wardrobe—as she shifted in her throne.

Adara opened her eyes. "Sir Firewing," she rehearsed, "our royal personage has brought you here to propose a temporary armistice, one that will advance the interest of both our nations. We believe such an armistice—"

"Remember," Lady Luviana interrupted, shifting in her basin of water beside Adara's throne. "Avoid hedging."

"Right." Adara straightened a little. ". . . the interest of both our nations. Such an armistice would—"

"And slow down," Lady Luviana interrupted again, chuckling. "You'll talk his ear off."

Adara took another deep breath, trying to calm her nerves. How could Lady Luviana chuckle at a time like this? The fate of their nation rode on Adara's performance in the next half-hour. She looked around, trying to find a glass to check her appearance. But the throne room, though glistening with crystal and marble, yielded no mirror in the right position for her to see herself. Why had she decided to wear gloves today? Normally she could gauge her appearance by checking the skin tone on her hands.

"You'll do fine," said Lady Luviana, reading Adara's thoughts—or, more likely, her complexion. The merfin leaned out of her basin and patted the queen's arm. "You have your father's blood in you."

A rap came at the door. Adara nodded to her guards, who opened it.

Sir Firewing, the Calamarvan ambassador, pranced into the room with all the grandeur of a prizewinner on race day. The griffin wore a brilliant golden collar, studied with rubies as big as strawberries. His mane and plumage were dyed in vibrant shades of reds, oranges, and yellows, casting the illusion of fire rippling down his neck and shoulders as he walked. He kept his wings slightly open, magnifying his already impressive size.

In Firewing's wake, Chancellor Skagar loped into the room like some naughty kitten in its mother's shadow.

Adara rose from her throne. "Sir Firewing! We extend our royal greeting." She curtsied regally.

To her surprise, the griffin didn't respond with the deep bow that the occasion merited. Instead, he stood straight, holding her gaze for a second as she straightened. Only then did he bow his head—but it was a tiny gesture, the acknowledgement of Adara as an inferior rather than an equal.

"Salutations to Her Majesty, Queen Everborn of Elandria," the griffin announced. His next words boomed around the throne room. ". . . enemy of the Eternal Empire of Calamar."

The phrase, with its implicit antagonism, hung in the air.

Adara fought for words in the wake of the griffin's wholly unexpected greeting. Her insides squirmed. She had not rehearsed any scenario like this. She had to reestablish an equal playing field—somehow. "Sir Firewing! . . . We . . . express our thanks . . . in your willingness to come to this parley."

"Calamar does not parley with thieves and treaty-breakers," Sir Firewing stated.

Adara stole a glance at Luviana, dropping her voice to a whisper. "Thieves?"

"Haeber," Luviana replied out of the corner of her mouth.

Right. Adara remembered that in the years before the war, Calamar had repeatedly claimed that Elandria had been withholding the precious commodity.

Adara cleared her throat. "I—we—have already sworn on past occasions that there was no . . . duplicity in our nation's dealings with your merchants."

Amusement played in Sir Firewing's eyes. "*You* have, Your Majesty?"

Adara was at a loss for a second. Then, realizing her mistake, she backtracked. "Such was sworn by Our Majesty's regents, acting in our name and with our royal authorization."

"Get back on track," Luviana whispered.

"But in any event," Adara continued, trying to ignore the shaking in her legs, "our royal personage has brought you here to suggest—I mean, to propose—a temporary armistice that—"

"No one has brought me here," Sir Firewing interrupted. "I came of my own choice, with one purpose: to issue an ultimatum."

This was not going anywhere near what Adara had planned. She swallowed. "An—ultimatum?"

"Surrender," Sir Firewing declared. "Surrender to the vast military might of the Eternal Empire of Calamar. Surrender to our hosts, numbering in the hundreds of thousands. Surrender to our brilliant strategic masterminds, who have won dozens of victories so far. Surrender to our superiority in technology, mancery, and weaponry. In the face of your most assured defeat, in the face of your capital burning to the ground, in the face of your people enslaved at the point of the sword, surrender!"

A stunned silence filled the throne room. Sir Firewing stood dominant, his wings spread, a fierce light in his eyes. Adara looked to Lady Luviana, then to Skagar. Both displayed a mix of shock and anger on their faces, but neither said anything. All eyes were on Adara. Only she, as Elandria's queen, could answer such a challenge.

Her heart pounded in her chest as she raced through her tutelage. What response did this warrant? If this were a public challenge, meant to dismay her people or her allies, she should rebuff the challenge with a show of strength. But doing that here would only bring the negotiations to a close before they could begin. But *could* they even begin? Sir Firewing showed no intention of discussing the possibility of an armistice. Then why had he come? He must know they would never accept his call to surrender.

Sir Firewing shifted his stance. The movement snapped Adara back to the moment. How long had she been silent? She had to say something—but what?

"I . . ." Adara's mind was still devoid of a response. "We . . ."

Adara closed her eyes and ran her thumb over the head of the Everborn scepter. Her father's scepter. *Her* scepter.

She would make no headway with Firewing until she understood him and saw him as a friend.

But he had shown he was not interested in friendship. He had openly mocked her authority and threatened her people with death and slavery. Volthorn's warning in their last council of war came to mind. *Until we smash them in battle, they will be unwilling to negotiate.*

She opened her eyes. "Sir Firewing, your ultimatum is premature," she said, trying her best to not make it sound like a gasp. She refilled her lungs. "You . . . underestimate our ability to defend our people. The armies of Elandria are strong, brave, and skilled. We will yet meet your hosts in battle, and then we shall see the truth of your words."

Sir Firewing lifted his beak, again holding eye contact with Adara. There was a haughty look in his eye. A knowing look.

"That day may be closer than you think," he said. Then he turned away. "I shall return on the morrow to hear if your answer has changed."

His words carried an implication. Adara's mind raced, thinking through the timing. Calamar's army was encamped a little more than two hundred miles away. For a griffin, traveling that distance would take six to eight hours of flying. Sir Firewing had arrived well before noon, meaning he had left early that morning.

He obviously knew that something was afoot—that a battle between the two armies was imminent. No word of such battle had yet arrived through Elandria's own messengers. Yet Firewing was confident that such news would arrive by tomorrow.

Which meant the Calamarvan army had to have spent the night positioning itself for a battle. A surprise battle. A battle that, by now, was probably well underway.

Earlier that morning.

"Commander! Commander Skarr!"

Volthorn burst out of his tent. He nearly collided with the sentry shouting his name. "What is it?" he barked.

"A scout—" the sentry gasped. "Just returned. Urgent news."

A spike of alarm swept through Volthorn's veins.

"Wake my aides," Volthorn ordered the sentry. "All of them."

The morning was thick with fog, casting everything in a hazy blue light. Volthorn could barely see the other tents in his command circle. The fog, spawned every morning by the river near their camp, seemed even thicker than usual, smothering everything in blind silence.

A couple yards away, a swifter scout was waiting in the clearing between the tents, his sides heaving and his eyes frantic. "Report!" Volthorn said.

"The enemy's crossed the river," the swifter said. "Under cover of darkness. They're on the far side!"

"Slow down," Volthorn said, forcing himself to keep his voice calm, though his muscles screamed at him to act. He wouldn't get anything useful out of this scout unless he could get him to calm down. "Deep breath. Out. In. There we go. Now, let's start again. Where did they cross?"

"Downriver. Nine—maybe ten miles."

"How many?"

"Several battalions of infantry. Perhaps cavalry, too. They built a pontoon bridge during the night."

"Just one bridge?"

The swifter gritted his teeth as he thought. "I'm not sure. I didn't get a good look. My partner and I were patrolling downriver on this bank when we saw them crossing in the fog. We dared not go any further— there were enemy patrols everywhere."

Volthorn cursed. He had run this risk when he had shrunk their perimeter of reconnaissance. Calamar had cast a wide screen of air and ground patrols, then used that cover, combined with the darkness of the night and the fog of the morning, to move part of their army in a deep flank around Volthorn's position. This was bad. This was very, very bad.

"How many troops?"

"We couldn't tell through the mist. But they sounded like a lot. Several thousand."

Volthorn nearly punched a tent. "SPECIFICS! Was it two thousand, or ten thousand?"

"I . . ." The swifter shook his head. "I don't know."

By this time, several of Volthorn's aides were stumbling out of their tents, eyes widening as they caught the tail end of the scout's report. Volthorn turned to one of them, a griffin. "Grab a wingmate, get in the air, and scout out Calamar's main camp. Tell me their position and their movements. What fraction of the army is still there? Are they on the move, and in which direction? Go!"

The griffin opened her wings and launched into a running takeoff, soon disappearing into the fog. Volthorn turned to a cluster of aides. "Rouse the camp—every battalion. You, First division. You, Second. You, Third. Have the whole army ready to march within a half hour. Go!"

The aides ran off. Volthorn forced his muscles to relax. Despite the urgency of their predicament, he had fifteen or twenty minutes now to process and think. There was no point issuing orders before the army was ready to follow them.

While the rest of his staff spilled out of their tents, Volthorn sat down on a stump to think. Panic and alarm swirled within him, but he clamped the emotions down, forcing his mind to think through the situation with pure logic.

Calamar's plan was obvious—and brilliant. They had taken advantage of Volthorn's reduced perimeter to entrap him. Under cover of night, they had marched part of their army around him to the south. Now, with a hastily erected pontoon bridge, they were crossing to the east bank of the river to get behind Volthorn's army, where it was camped on the west bank guarding a major ford.

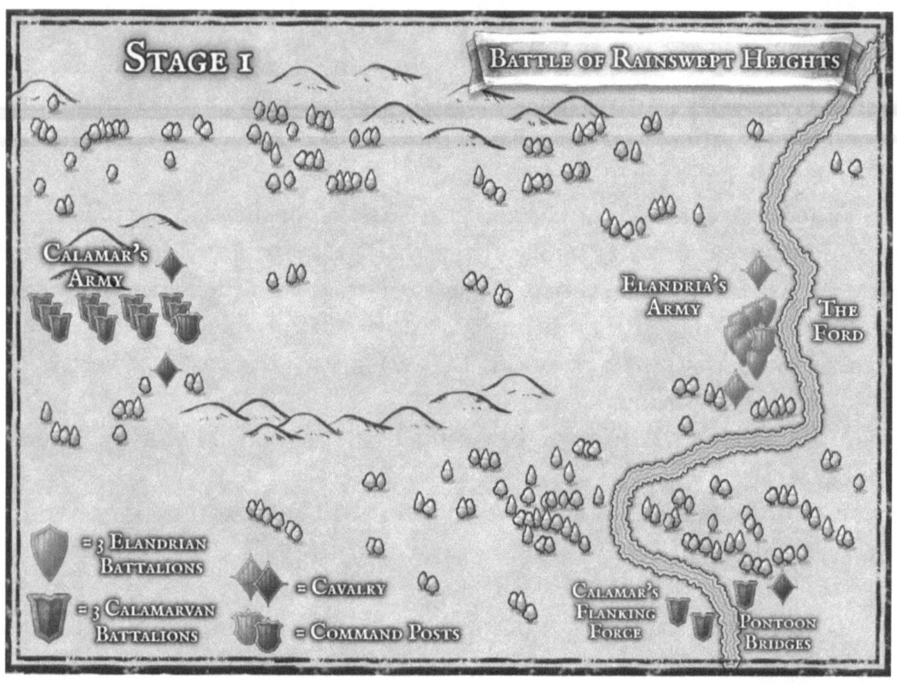

But how many were in the flanking force? That was the million-shekel question.

"We have three options," Volthorn thought out loud, more for his own sake than for his staff's. "Option one: we retreat across the ford to the east bank, to the same side of their flanking force. That force will arrive to block our crossing within two hours or less. We could only get maybe a third of our army, eight thousand troops, across by then. If their flanking force numbers less than that, we could break out quickly and survive. But any more than that, and they'll trap us against the river, while their main force hits the rest of our army from this side."

"Like a hammer and an anvil," his brother Kelzern said.

"A very wet anvil," Volthorn agreed. "Option two: We stay on this side of the river, deploy part of our army to hold the ford at our rear, and prepare the rest of our force to face their main army hitting us from the west. But the outcome is the same—we'd be trapped, with our backs to the river."

"A very wet river," Trazar said.

"Option three," Volthorn said, pointedly ignoring the comment this time. "We march north. This would allow us to dodge the trap entirely—but we would lose the war. They would claim the ford, march across, then make a beeline for Saven and take it before we could catch up to them."

Volthorn's aides and officers looked at him, each face a collage of fear and concentration. Outside their ring of tents, the camp was coming alive with shouts as twenty-six thousand troops readied for battle.

"What do we do?" said Kelzern.

None of the three options would work. Each was exactly what Calamar's generals expected Volthorn to do. Each would lose him the battle or the war.

An alternative popped into his head. He studied it out, thinking through its contours. It would be daring. It would be risky.

But war was all about risk.

"Do you trust me?" Volthorn asked.

Each head in the circle nodded.

A grim smile slowly spread across Volthorn's face. "Then we do option four. We attack."

CHAPTER 19

BATTLE

There was a benefit to the last three weeks of constant maneuvering: it had honed Volthorn's army into a well-oiled machine. Even in the dense blanket of fog, each battalion formed up with near flawless procedure. Soon, under Volthorn's orders, all three divisions were marching west, away from the river. They left their camp behind. Tents and cooking pots could be replaced. Lives could not.

Before leaving camp, Volthorn hastily donned his full combat gear: an enchanted chainmail jerkin for his torso, greaves to cover his shins, spaulders to protect his shoulders, and an open-face helmet with a tall green crest—the mark of Elandria's chief commander. His belt carried a variety of terramantic weapons, as well as jewels and crystals storing large reserves of terracharge.

Trazar gave him a look of disapproval. "You know the military codes prohibit the chief commander from joining in direct combat."

"I know," Volthorn said. The rules were to prevent an army from becoming leaderless in battle. "I don't plan to. But in a battle like today, every soldier will count."

As the army issued from the camp, it spread out into a thin marching column nearly half a mile long. Volthorn, his brothers, and the rest of his command staff rode in the middle of the line, where they could quickly relay orders. The fog was beginning to thin, but the sky overhead was glowering, threatening to drench the land beneath it any second.

"So what's the plan?" Kelzern asked, once the frenzy of getting the army on the march had passed.

Volthorn used his free hand to transfer terracharge from the jewels on his belt to the rings on his hand holding the reins. "Calamar has finally done what I've wanted them to do this entire campaign. Split their army. With around a fourth of their battalions across the river, that leaves their main army significantly smaller, giving us the opportunity to meet them head-on in open battle."

"We'll still be outnumbered," Trazar warned.

"Yes," said Volthorn. "But not *hopelessly* outnumbered."

General Embertail swooped overhead, spreading her wings to catch a headwind that allowed her to glide at Volthorn's pace. "Commander! Scout reports are in. Calamar's main army is marching toward us, perhaps eight miles out."

Volthorn nodded. He had predicted correctly. "Who is winning the fight for air superiority?"

"It's a bit chaotic," said Embertail, flapping her wings to avoid stalling. "It's raining up ahead, and my flights are struggling to tell which griffins are on whose side—if they can even stay aloft in this weather." She swooped away with the next gust of wind.

As if on cue, raindrops began pelting from the sky, causing Volthorn's helmet to ring with tiny impacts. He took it off and tucked it under his shield arm.

An idea sparked in his mind. The rain . . . the fog . . . the visibility . . .

He raced to remember the terrain around them, still fresh in his memory from when they had retreated this way two days before. The land straight ahead was flat, mainly occupied by farms. But just to their left, he remembered there being a low ridgeline . . .

Volthorn turned to a swifter messenger. "Turn the head of the army to the left," he said, the idea still forming in his head even as the orders began coming out of his mouth. "Not a hard turn; just a touch to the south. In a mile or two, we should hit a ridge of low hills. Get the army onto the other side of the ridge, then resume marching due west."

The swifter nodded and darted off toward the front of the marching column.

Volthorn turned to Kelzern. "Send new orders to our griffin and scouting patrols, as well as the Thunder Hooves Cavalry Battalion. Have them attack Calamar's northeast scouting perimeter. We need to draw their attention toward the northeast, and away from our actual position to the southeast. Understood?"

Kelzern nodded and began to ride ahead toward a group of messengers.

The rain began to fall harder, drenching Volthorn from crest to claw. He wiped rain away from his eyes and turned to Trazar. "Calamar picked a fine day for a fight, didn't they?"

The army slogged on. The terrain here was mostly pastureland—now turned to mud—with the occasional grove or thicket. Volthorn could hear the annoyed moos of cows as the lines of marching troops interrupted their grazing.

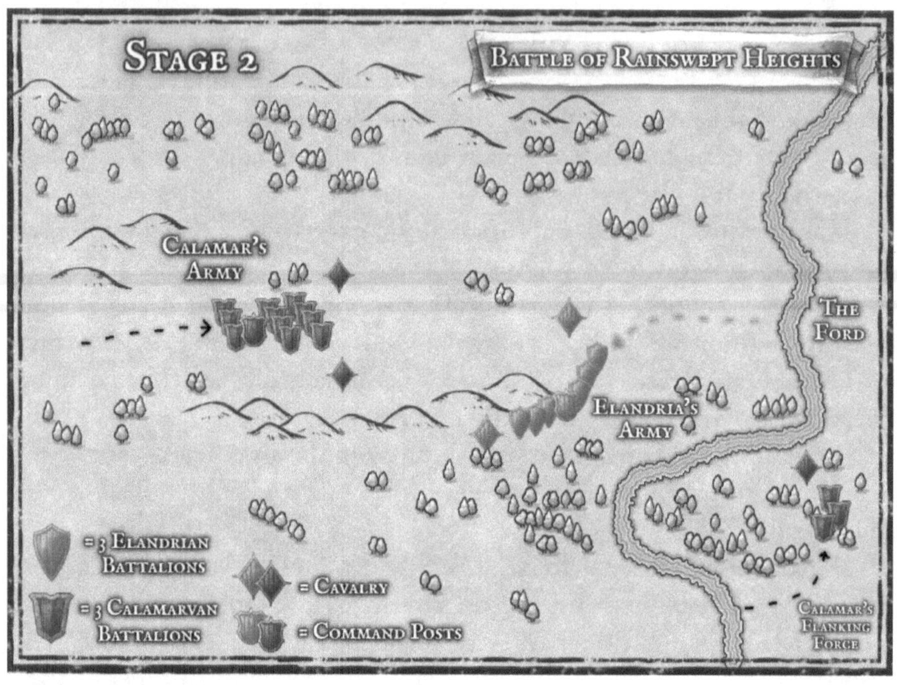

Volthorn looked over to see Trazar studying him quizzically. "Something on your mind?" Volthorn grunted

Trazar nodded. "Yes. I don't understand. You've just thrown away our perimeter guard."

Volthorn shook his head. "No, I'm misdirecting the enemy. The pouring rain will slow down and nearly blind their scouting parties, and every griffin will soon be grounded if this weather keeps up. They'll have to tighten their scouting perimeter closer to their main army. So the way they will know where our army is . . ."

". . . is by finding where our perimeter patrols are," Trazar said, finishing the thought.

"Exactly. When they bump against our patrols on their left, they'll think we're in that direction. And they'll channel all their scouts that way to break through and figure out where exactly we are."

"But they'll never actually find us." Trazar smiled as it dawned on him.

"Right," said Volthorn. "Meanwhile, with the rain and the ridgeline covering us, we should be able to get around their right flank before they realize we're there."

Kelzern returned from dispensing Volthorn's orders, in time to overhear the last part of the conversation. "And what's your plan for dealing with the army behind us, across the river?"

Volthorn frowned. He'd been thinking about that puzzle all morning and still didn't have a good answer. "I'm hoping they'll stay on the far side, to block our retreat across the ford. If they do cross, hopefully they'll get distracted looting our camp and won't chase us—or they won't be able to figure out where we went."

Trazar looked back at the swath of trampled mud in the army's wake. "I wouldn't count on that."

"Then hopefully we can deal with the force in front of us before the force behind us can catch up," said Volthorn.

Kelzern stared at him for a moment, then shook his head. "*That's* your plan?"

"It's my stopgap," Volthorn admitted. "Until I come up with a plan. Do you have any suggestions?"

Kelzern flashed a smile. "Nope. You know me—you get all the fancy ideas; I just order aides around, Trazar handles any math, and together we keep you from getting your head whacked off in battle."

"I *do* appreciate that," Volthorn said with a chuckle.

They fell silent, leaning into the wind as they clutched waterlogged reins.

A half hour later, the ranks ahead of them parted to allow a rider through. He reined up his horse just shy of Volthorn and his brothers, spraying them with mud. "Commander! We just spotted the enemy close at hand—just over the ridge to our right, under half a mile!"

"Do they know we're here?"

A horn sounded in the distance, muffled by the rain. Volthorn recognized the pattern—the Calamarvan signal to form into battle lines.

"I guess they do now," Kelzern said.

Volthorn settled his helmet over his head. "Let them blow. It's too late."

Volthorn realized, as he crested the ridge a few minutes later, that he had achieved what every military commander dreams of: near complete tactical surprise.

The Elandrian army, stretched out in one long marching column, took only a few minutes for each company to turn ninety degrees to their right and march up to the crest of the ridge, until their whole army was in place along the ridgetop, already in battle formation.

In the valley on the far side of the ridge was the Calamarvan army—but facing the wrong way. They had been marching east in a wide formation, expecting to encounter the Elandrian army somewhere between them and the river. But instead the Elandrians had appeared, suddenly, due south of them. And very, very close.

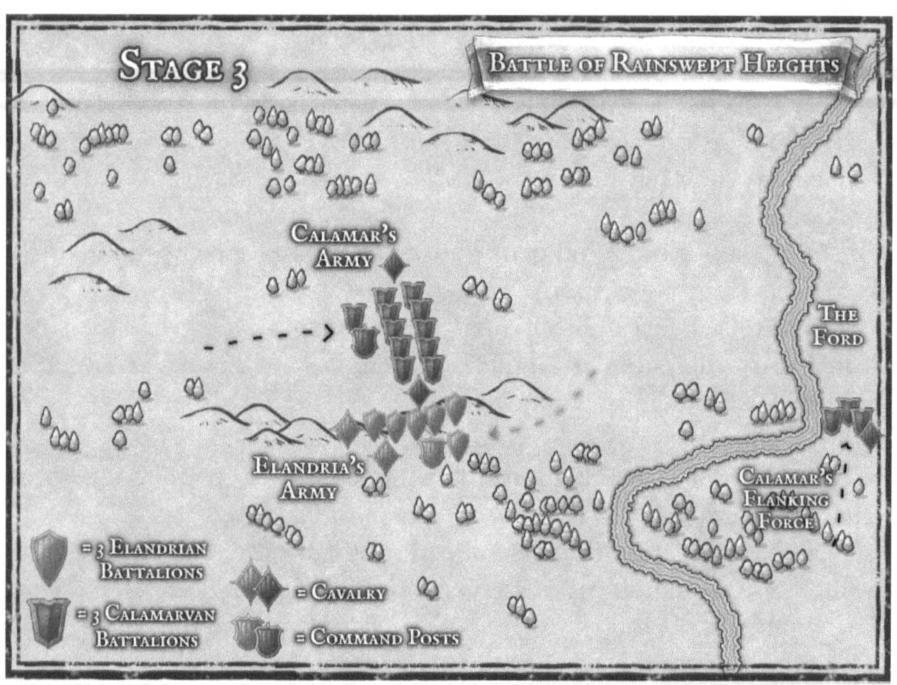

Up and down the ridgeline, Volthorn's officers were at work, smoothing out bulges of men and filling in gaps as they ordered the sodden ranks of soldiers into one long battle line. Their formation stretched nearly a mile long. The infantry formed a dense phalanx of shields and spears, ten to fifteen soldiers deep. Archers occupied the rear, hurriedly stringing their bows. Drums began to pound, up and down the line, making the air throb as their beat melded the army into a single pulsing organism.

In contrast, the Calamarvan army in front of them was in the throes of confusion. Officers were riding back and forth, trying to pivot their battle line, but the tightly-packed formations of soldiers kept getting in each other's way.

The drums, the horns, the day's unexpected reversals—it all filled Volthorn with an energy he could scarcely restrain. He turned to his lead horn-blower. "Sound the charge."

The horn-blower winded his horn in one long blast. More horns up and down the line took up the call. In answer, a roar arose from the throats of humans, korriks, and avirs, over twenty thousand voices raising the same battle cry.

"ELANDRIAAA!!!"

The ranks began to move down the ridge, slowly at first, then faster and faster as the soldiers broke into a light jog. Here and there, a patch of spear points glowed red: the handiwork of terramancers spaced throughout the army, enhancing the weapons of their comrades before going into battle. In the rear of the marching troops, vivamancers played on pipes and drums, filling the air with a battle melody to inspire bravery and quicken reflexes.

Volthorn stayed back on the ridge with his command staff, watching from the vantage point of his horse as his battalions accelerated. The rain was letting up, and a cold wind was at their backs, pushing them onward.

"Commander, *sir!*" said an officer behind him. "Cavalry wants to know their orders."

Volthorn answered without hesitation. "Mass our cavalry on our left flank. Get around the enemy into their rear and wreak havoc."

"Yes, sir!"

Volthorn turned to General Embertail. "And as soon as this rain dies, get your flights airborne again!"

Elandria's ranks were rapidly closing on the enemy. In front of them, the closest Calamarvan battalions had managed to rearrange their ranks to face the unexpected threat. But their hastily erected battle line was thin, and poorly organized. And the rest of Calamar's army was stretched out behind them, their path to the battle blocked by their own soldiers.

Volthorn couldn't have conceived of a better situation if he'd tried.

Archers on both sides began firing volleys. Some hit their mark. Others clanged off the rows of overlapping shields.

Volthorn flinched as a blast of light and noise emanated from one section of the line: some sort of exploding terramantic projectile. It knocked a long furrow in one of Elandria's battalions, killing perhaps half a dozen men and injuring many more, but the gap was quickly filled in as soldiers on either side adjusted their position.

Fifty yards now. More flashes sounded down the line as soldiers on both sides hurled additional terramantic missiles, though none were as powerful as the first. Balls of flame arced through the air, launched by pyromancers in both armies.

Then the ranks collided. The air reverberated with the clash of metal on metal as thousands of spearpoints impacted thousands of shields up and down the mile-long front. The battle cries abruptly died as soldiers turned their attention to thrusting and hacking and blocking and slashing—and all too quickly, the air began to fill with screams of pain.

Volthorn clenched his jaw, trying not to think about how many of his men had died in the last twenty seconds alone.

How quickly the thrill of battle turned to the gruesome reality.

He felt a rush of air as a formation of griffins swooped overhead, climbing in altitude as they screamed their challenge to the wind. The rain had let up, and now griffins were taking to the air all across the battlefield, swooping and diving, scratching and clawing at each other in one-on-one aerial catfights.

Volthorn turned to his aides. "We'll make this hillock our command post. Raise the commander's banner. I want the Iron Thicket Battalion in reserve behind our center, and the Green Pine Battalion ready to reinforce our right flank."

"Yes, Commander."

A platoon of cavalry thundered by. Volthorn watched them ride past. Was he making the best decision, massing his cavalry on his left flank? Was he leaving his right flank too vulnerable?

He shelved the worry. Battles were about balancing risks, not avoiding them.

The morning marched by. Volthorn entertained a constant stream of updates brought by swifters and griffins from each section of the battlefield.

The left flank brought the best news. There Elandria's battle line extended far past Calamar's, allowing them to advance unopposed and inflict chaos on Calamar's flank. Soon enemy battalions began to arrive, crossing from the far end of the battlefield to check the Elandrian assault. But the enemy units were scattered and unorganized, and the Elandrians had momentum. Plus, Elandrian cavalry was harassing the rear of Calamar's army with a series of hammering flanking assaults.

The center quickly turned into a stalemate. After initially losing ground, the Calamarvan army stiffened its resistance, piling more and more soldiers onto the back of the battle line until the mass of men made retreat impossible. The battle here was devolving into a pushing match of shield on shield, as both sides strove to outlast the other.

The biggest problem was on Volthorn's right flank. Most of Calamar's cavalry was on that side of the battlefield, and Volthorn had little cavalry to spare after dispatching most of it to his left flank. Soon rounds of enemy cavalry were smashing into the infantry on Volthorn's right flank. His soldiers were holding firm—for now. But his general on that flank, General Orrin, kept having to thin and lengthen his line, curving it back up toward the top of the ridgeline to avoid getting outflanked.

An hour into the battle, Volthorn ordered the Green Pine Battalion to reinforce the right flank.

"They know we're weakening on our right," Kelzern observed two hours into the battle, after returning from an errand. He joined Volthorn watching the desperate fighting taking place a third of a mile to their right. "They keep sending more units to hammer us there."

"We need to hold a little longer," Volthorn said. "We're routing them on the left. A report just came that their troops are scattering in disorder. A few more minutes, and their center will begin to crumble as well."

"Then it's a race against time," said Kelzern. "Will we hold together longer than they will?"

"We have to," Volthorn said. "Or the war ends here." If his army suffered a route on the field today, there would be nothing standing in between Calamar's armies and the capital.

The rain began to pour down once more. "Krack's crest," Kelzern muttered. "I was just starting to dry off."

Griffins soon began cutting through the mist as they swooped in for landings, pulling back behind the lines before their wings got too sodden to fly.

Volthorn studied the battlefield, both the one in front of him and the one in his mind's eye. "Find a fresh and dry pair of griffin scouts," Volthorn said to his brother. "Send them east and have them find where those other ten thousand soldiers have gotten to."

"Not sure I can guarantee they'll be fresh *or* dry, but I'll do my best," Kelzern called as he trudged away.

An officer galloped up to the command post. "Commander! General Orrin requests more reinforcements on our right flank!"

"Shadows," Volthorn muttered. He only had one reserve battalion left. It was one of his best, the Iron Thicket Battalion. But he was hoping to keep that backing his center.

"Is it desperate?" Volthorn asked.

"We're losing troops left and right. Our men are exhausted and losing morale."

They were interrupted by a griffin, landing beside them with a splash of mud. "Just came in over our right flank, Commander. I saw a fresh enemy battalion moving up the ridge to flank us there."

"Then that does it." Volthorn turned to Trazar. "Dispatch the Iron Thicket Battalion to our right. Send half the troops to reinforce the line, the other half to extend the line further up the ridge, ready to block a fresh assault. Go!"

Soon columns of troops from the Iron Thicket Battalion were marching past his post at a light run. Volthorn waved them on, shouting a war cry.

Scarcely had they passed when a swifter arrived from the left flank. "Six enemy battalions are now in a complete rout, Commander! They're scattering like scared rabbits on hunting day! Our cavalry is now circling around to strike at their center from behind, while our infantry continues scattering their left flank."

"Then we just might make it," Volthorn said with relief. "If our right flank holds another half hour, and if that second army doesn't make it here on time, then maybe, just maybe—"

The ridgeline lit up with a sudden flash of light, blinding his retinas. Seconds afterwards, an explosion shook the ground as a mighty shockwave roared in his ears. A flash of terramantic power rippled through him, released from whatever had caused the explosion.

"The center!" someone cried. "The center!"

Volthorn blinked his eyes, waiting for his vision to recover—and saw a gaping hole in his army's shield wall.

CHAPTER 20

TERRAMANCY DUEL

The gap in the shield wall was about thirty feet wide. Several ranks of soldiers had been killed, knocked down, or thrown clear. Jagged spars of stone protruded from the ground, radiating out from the blast's origin. And in the epicenter, wreathed in residual smoke, towered a warrior in full bronzium plate armor: a master terramancer.

And behind him, a fresh company of heavy infantry, ready to charge.

For a precious second, fear and panic mixed in Volthorn's veins, turning him still as stone as he foresaw his battle line crumbling, his troops pressed from all sides as the gap turned into a torrent and then a flood.

But it was only a second. And then he replaced the emotions with action.

"Follow me!" he roared, snatching his shield from where it lay close at hand. He grabbed the standard marking his command post, yanking it out of the ground and tossing it to an aide. "Follow me! Every last soul!"

He charged forward. The aide took up the call, close on his heels. Then the dozen staff and officers at the command post followed suite, grabbing whatever weapons were near at hand and yelling to the menagerie of messengers, scouts, engineers, and camp assistants that circulated behind the front lines.

"Elandriaaa!" Volthorn bellowed. "Elandriaaaaa!"

He was still a hundred yards out. The enemy terramancer was striding through the gap, dispatching the handful of stunned warriors who tried to get to their feet to oppose him. The enemy infantry followed, forming a tight formation as they charged over the broken ground and began hammering the exposed sides of Elandria's battle line on either side of the gap.

Volthorn needed to buy time for more of his men to arrive! As he ran, he passed his right hand over the talismans at his belt. Rock-shard grenade? No, it required too much precision at this distance. Acrid dust? Only good for close quarters. Double-down stone? *Perfect.*

Volthorn yanked on the slipknot holding the double-down stone to his belt. The stone, a unique strain of pegmatite about the size of an apple, had a hole bored through it for a thong of leather—for both attaching it to his belt and for throwing it. Volthorn pressed a finger to an amethyst on his belt, sucking purple terracharge into his hand, then poured the energy into the stone. His terramantic sixth sense felt the stone come alive with power, just waiting for a rupture to be released. With the leather thong, he swung the stone like a sling, accelerating it with three quick rotations before launching it high into the air.

He was eighty yards out now and closing. Activating and launching the talisman had slowed him down, and his men were catching up to him, taking up his earlier battle cry.

The talisman impacted the ground just ten yards in front of the enemy terramancer. A ring of purple light issued from the impact, sweeping outward until dissipating after about twenty yards. The effect on all those caught in the impact area was immediate. They staggered, their movements suddenly sluggish and labored. Shields and sword tips clanged to the ground, their bearers struggling to lift them back up.

A double-down stone released a force field that temporarily increased gravity. Based on how much terracharge he had poured into this one, it was probably magnified gravity by about fifty percent. Volthorn knew from experimentation the shock the effect had on the body: the sudden increase in weight, the resistance of every limb becoming one and a half times as heavy as normal, the incredible extra attraction that any armor or weapon had for the ground.

All action at the gap ceased almost instantly. The Calamarvan soldiers struggled to take short, halting steps forward. The double-down stone affected friend and foe alike, meaning as Elandrian soldiers on either side of the gap pressed forward into the affected area, they too fell prey to the increase in gravity.

"Ten seconds!" Volthorn shouted to the scattered soldiers behind him. That was about as long as they had before the double-down stone's effect fully wore off—theoretically, anyway. With how many terramantic devices were being thrown around the battlefield, creating hot spots of residual terracharge and disrupting the ground's natural energy field, certainty quickly began to break down.

Ahead of him, soldiers began to move more naturally again, as both the gravity surge decreased and they adapted to the extra strain. The figure in bronzium plate armor cast his spear at a soldier in his way. With a flash of red light, the spear punched through the Elandrian's breastplate like it was a piece of leather.

Volthorn ran straight toward the man in the bronzium armor. "I'll handle the terramancer!" he warned the soldiers behind him. "You keep that infantry busy!"

Thirty yards out now. Volthorn's opponent towered well over six feet, augmented even more by the red plume on his helm. At his belt hung a variety of terramantic tools and weapons. His armor glowed with a green aura.

Volthorn held back a grin. A duel between two terramancers. These could get fun.

With his free hand, Volthorn transferred energy from an emerald and a sapphire to his shield and armor, until the metal hummed around him. Like his opponent, Volthorn wore armor made principally of bronzium. The special alloy was weaker than both iron and normal bronze, but it manifested incredibly useful properties when enchanted with different types of terracharge. Each color of terracharge bestowed a different property. The green terracharge stored in the emerald gave the armor extra hardness, while the blue terracharge from the sapphire created an energy field around the metal that would slow or deflect high-velocity objects.

Turning to face Volthorn, the enemy terramancer touched an orange gem on his right arm. The infusion of orange terracharge—which typically displayed some sort of binding or attractive force—caused the spear he had thrown earlier to pull free of its victim, sailing back into the terramancer's waiting grip. Volthorn drew his short sword in return, running his thumb over a ruby in the hilt to transfer red terracharge into the blade, turning the edge extra sharp.

As Volthorn and the man in bronzium faced off, soldiers on both sides gave Volthorn and the other terramancer a wide berth. Although mancery was employed frequently on the battlefield, duels between two masters were rare spectacles—spectacles easily fatal to those caught in the crossfire.

Volthorn stepped into a crouch, ignoring the rainwater pouring down his face. He kept his eyes trained on the man's spear tip, which was glowing red like Volthorn's sword. How sharp was the enchanted tip? It had sheared through a bronze breastplate as if it were leather—that wasn't promising.

The man feinted toward Volthorn, his spear held low. Volthorn danced backward. *Yes.* Let him make the first move. This was one of Volthorn's favorite strategies; let his opponent take the initiative and attack first, then strike back with concentrated power as soon as a weakness presented itself. He had already applied the tactic on the battlefield today, striking the Calamarvans as soon as they split their army. Time to apply it again.

Volthorn let himself slip on a bit of muddy ground, lowering his shield and exposing his torso. The terramancer took the bait and flung his spear with startling speed. For a moment, Volthorn's life flashed before his eyes; then he raised his shield in time. As the red enchanted spear met the blue enchanted shield, terracharge radiated outward in two thunderous blasts of red and blue light.

The spear fell into the mud in front of Volthorn. Before his opponent had a chance to summon it back, Volthorn used the glowing edge of his sword to cleave the spearhead from the haft.

One weapon down.

Then Volthorn charged, closing the handful of yards between them. The human drew his own sword, but Volthorn rammed him with his shield, attempting to knock him off balance.

His opponent was the much heavier of the two, however, and dug his feet into the broken ground to avoid being knocked over. Then his sword came dancing around the edge of Volthorn's shield, glancing off Volthorn's helmet. Volthorn backed off, trying to fend away the blows with his shield. He could feel the charge in his helmet shredding away with each strike that landed. How much terracharge did that sword *have*?

Volthorn needed to end this. Soon. He darted forward, holding his shield up to cover his head as he slashed his short sword back and forth. It clanged off the metal strips on the Calamarvan's armored skirt, sending sparks of light cascading into the air. Once! Twice! A section of the skirt sheared off, exposing his opponent's abdomen. One more strike would—

A rock smashed into Volthorn from the side.

Volthorn backed away, eyes nearly blinded by the flash of light from his armor as it deflected most of the blow.

He peeked over his shield. The other terramancer held a metal rod in his left hand. Dragging on the ground beside him, as if attached to the rod by an invisible chain, was a rock as big as Volthorn's head. Shadows! His opponent had a boulder mace.

The terramancer swung his rod overhead. In response, the rock lifted off the ground, whistling through the air in an arc headed straight toward Volthorn. He sidestepped to the left, letting the rock smash into the mud with a resounding splat. Then Volthorn's sword swiped, the enchanted blade shaving a chunk off the rock. The chunk fell to the ground, no longer enchanted. Only a single point on the boulder was paired with the guiding rod, so every piece Volthorn could isolate was less mass that could hurt him.

The terramancer jerked his rod, yanking the rock back into the air and whistling it around to come at Volthorn from the side. Volthorn stepped back, letting the rock barely miss him. The terramancer reversed the direction of his rod, but again, Volthorn stepped back, this time raising his sword and cleaving the rock nearly in half. One piece fell to the ground while the other arced to the right, still invisibly tethered to the handle.

Volthorn smirked. Boulder maces! In certain situations, they could be brutal, knocking formations apart in a handful of swings. But in one-on-one duels, especially against other terramancers, they had too many exploitable flaws. He studied his opponent. Any second now and he'd either abandon the mace or sheath his sword to wield it two-handed.

The soldier in bronzium let the rod fall, bringing his other hand toward a gem on the handle to deactivate the terramancy.

Volthorn darted forward, taking advantage of the momentary distraction. He planned his attack in his mind's eye: knock the sword aside with his shield, jab with his own sword, pierce the weak point left by the broken skirt—

The other terramancer stepped back, swinging his mace up. He had only pretended to disarm it! The boulder came swinging at Volthorn's right side, the side not covered by his shield. It was too late to duck, unless he wanted the boulder to smash his head. Instead, Volthorn let the blow take him squarely in the shoulder.

He felt the shockwaves of terramancy sweep around him as the energy field around his armor took some of the blow and then burst, depleted, in a flash of blue light. The blow from the boulder knocked Volthorn to the mud, his sword dropping from his stunned right arm.

Instinctively, he rolled and brought his shield up.

Wham! His opponent's sword smashed down, the red tip biting into the rim of his shield, inches from his head. The sword rose and fell again, completely shaving a corner off Volthorn's shield. Volthorn kicked with his legs, striking against the Calamarvan's boots but failing to knock his opponent over. His eyes were nearly blinded by rain.

Shock filled Volthorn's mind. This was it. He'd been bested. Flat on his back, his enchantments drained, his sword gone, he wouldn't last another two seconds. With him dead, what would happen to the battle? To his army? To his country?

"*Rackatahaaan!*"

The korrik war cry split the air as Kelzern appeared in Volthorn's vision, driving a spear at the enemy terramancer. The Calamarvan stepped back, swinging his sword and clipping the spear in two. In his left hand he smashed his boulder mace into Kelzern's ribs. As Kelzern stumbled from the blow, the Calamarvan stepped forward to finish him off with his sword.

But before he could, Trazar rushed from the opposite side, sweeping past Volthorn and snatching Volthorn's dropped sword from the ground. Knocking away the terramancer's attempted perry, Trazar drove the sword through the gap Volthorn had made in the terramancer's skirt. Light flashed as the sword's enchanted tip pierced the terramancer's last defenses. Then the warrior in bronzium toppled.

Silence fell in that pocket of the battlefield as Volthorn, his brothers, and the surrounding soldiers processed the unexpected reversal.

Then chaos erupted as soldiers from both sides swept into the space occupied by the duelists. Two of Volthorn's officers leapt in front of him, buying him time to get back to his feet as the lines crashed together around them. His mind still recovering from shock, he pushed his way over to where Trazar stood protecting a kneeling Kelzern. "Are you all right?!" Volthorn shouted.

"No—I'm all left!" Kelzern said through clenched teeth, clutching his rib cage. "As in, all that's *left* of me is my *left* side, because my right side just died and went to the Halls of the Sun."

"He's telling jokes," Trazar said as he fended off a probing spear tip. "He'll live."

"That was brave, charging a master terramancer!" Volthorn said. "As foolish as the Far Moon, but brave!"

"You're one to talk!" Kelzern retorted, pushing himself to his feet with the stub that remained of his spear. "Good thing I meant what I said this morning—you do all the thinking, we keep your head from getting whacked!"

"Focus!" Trazar shouted, as a new clump of enemy soldiers rushed them. For a couple minutes, all was a thrashing melee of shields, spear tips, and helmets. A spear pierced the mail on Volthorn's right arm, breaking a couple links as it stabbed his triceps. He'd nearly forgotten what a battle was like without enchanted armor.

After what seemed like forever, a fresh squad of Elandrian infantry arrived behind Volthorn and his brothers. "Commander Skarr!" an officer called. "Get back! We'll handle this!"

Volthorn let a pair of soldiers take his place in the battle line. "I was just starting to enjoy myself!" he called to the officer.

"With that arm, I'm sure!"

Volthorn looked down to see the mail on his right arm stained with blood. "Hardly noticed," he quipped. "I could keep going all day."

But the break reminded him that he had duties far more important than helping one section of the line. He stepped away from the fray and surveyed the battlefield.

The center still held! His duel with the enemy terramancer, and the bravery of his staff, had plugged the gap just long enough to allow soldiers further down the line to rush to their aid. The fighting was still desperate and the battle line thin, but Calamar's momentum had been checked.

Two messengers waited for Volthorn on the sodden hillside. He stomped up to them, wincing as the pain began to set in as his adrenaline ebbed. "Report!" he said.

The first was a swifter with drenched fur. "I just came from the left flank. Calamar's entire flank has collapsed. Battalions in the center are fleeing as well."

"Then the day is won!" Kelzern said.

"Not quite," Volthorn said. "One piece is still in play—the ten thousand enemy soldiers somewhere between us and the river." He turned to the third officer, General Embertail. "Any word?"

"It just came in," Embertail said. She shook water from her wings. "With all this rain, the river's a surging flood, twenty or thirty feet deep. They're trapped on the far side, unable to cross."

Volthorn wrapped the surprised griffin in a hug as he jumped up and down. "Then we've won! We've won! We've won!!"

Chapter 21

Reversals

Sir Firewing disagreed.

"You have not, quote, 'won,' Your Majesty," he quipped.

The Calamarvan ambassador was back in Adara's throne room the next afternoon. News of Volthorn's momentous victory had arrived by griffin messenger that morning, sweeping like wildfire through the streets of Saven. Spontaneous celebrations had erupted across the city.

But in the throne room, the air was as tense as a taut bowstring. While Sir Firewing lacked the calculated bravado—and the flashy ribbons—of the previous day, and while he hadn't yet called Adara a treaty-breaker or thief again, his demeanor was still as icy as a glacier as he stood before her throne.

"You just heard the reports yourself," Adara protested. She glanced at Skagar, who nodded encouragement. "Calamar's army is in full retreat. Several thousand lie dead. Thousands more have been taken prisoners. And that was just where things stood last evening—Volthorn will continue to press his assault on the scattered units that remain, perhaps harassing their retreat all the way back to Meradov."

Sir Firewing shook his head. "I heard *your* reports. How do I know they aren't exaggerated?"

Adara opened her mouth, ready to defend the reliability of her intelligence officers. But Lady Luviana reached up and touched Adara's arm, a pre-arranged signal to let the venerable merfin talk first.

"So, Sir Firewing," Luviana said casually, "have you received any messengers of your own, bringing a differing account of the battle?"

Sir Firewing hesitated, studying the merfin carefully. "Not yet, no."

"Ah? But I believe I heard that a griffin courier arrived for you scarcely half an hour ago."

Of course! Adara remembered that now—it had been one tiny drop of information delivered with a torrent of other reports that morning.

How did Lady Luviana remember all those details—or know what details to pay attention to?"

"So if you really have heard your nation's tally of the battle," continued Luviana, "but you would feign otherwise, then things truly must be as dire as we say—or even more so."

Sir Firewing stood speechless for a moment, his head cocked back and his feathers ruffled. Then his eyes regained their resolve, and he turned to who he probably considered the least skilled opponent in front of him—Adara.

"Perhaps the winds of fortune blew your way yesterday, Your Majesty," said Sir Firewing. "But war is full of reversals. You have won today's battle, yes. You have driven back one army, yes. But you are still weak. Your kingdom is still at the breaking point, as brittle as a dead branch on a hot day. You really think this is the end of the war?"

Adara knew the question was meant to be rhetorical, but she answered it anyway. "It can be."

Sir Firewing's eyes turned quizzical.

Adara searched for the right words. "War doesn't have to be decided with the sword, Sir Firewing. It can be decided with words. *We* can decide it with words. How long must our two nations go on destroying each other? How many souls on either side must perish? How many battlefields must be stained with blood?"

Adara changed the pitch of her voice to a plea. "A brief armistice. That is all I am asking for, Sir Firewing. An armistice until I can speak with your emperor to discuss a more lasting solution."

Sir Firewing weighed her words, his gaze unreadable. Then he cocked his head. "And what advantage, tell me, would Calamar gain from an armistice, Your Majesty?"

"Your armies are being scattered and driven as we speak! Why would you not want to end the death of your own soldiers?"

"Because perhaps they're dying for a cause," Sir Firewing snapped. "Perhaps our soldiers died yesterday fighting for the safety and welfare of Calamar—and for us to slink like cowards to the table of truce would be to spurn their sacrifice."

"Their sacrifice?" Adara said, feeling suddenly angry. She rose to her feet. "Did they die for the safety and welfare of Calamar? Or did they die because they were conscripted to fight a war they never wanted to fight, a war of conquest and plunder?"

Sir Firewing screamed, rearing back on his hind legs, beating his wings, and slicing the air with his talons. Adara stumbled back into her throne, her skin flashing white. Guards sprang forward, weapons ready to defend her.

But the griffin immediately sank back onto all fours, his wings snapping shut. His gaze locked with Adara's, and his words came low and weighed by emotion. "My nest mate died yesterday. I think I should know her motives for fighting better than you."

In the moment of stunned silence that followed, Adara finally saw Sir Firewing for who he was. Yes, he was a staunch believer in his country, his people, and his way of life. Yes, he was a diplomat proud of his powers of persuasion and the service he rendered his emperor. But, above all, he was a person. A person who had just suffered the ultimate loss, at the hands of Adara's own people.

Adara finally understood Sir Firewing. But it was too late.

The griffin ambassador turned and strode toward the doors, the only sound in the room that of his claws clinking on the stone floor. "Farewell, Your Majesty. I'm afraid these negotiations are over. From now on, all you will see from Calamar will be the sword."

Two days later.

Lord Salidar did not take the news of Volthorn's victory well.

"Incompetent fools!" the vizier hissed. "I want General Grimbold sacked for this gaffe, along with his whole command staff!"

The Hakiru cloudship had anchored for a day in a remote valley between Elandria and Wormul, about halfway through their journey. Besides escaping the cramped confines of the gondola for a few hours, the crew needed to restock on fresh water and buy more supplies from a nearby town. (At least, Durrin *assumed* they planned to pay, but with Twigly in charge of that expedition, it was anyone's guess.)

While half the crew got supplies, the rest of the crew and their three Calamarvan passengers were enjoying the luxury of a campfire and a freshly roasted deer—all except Salidar, who was pacing back and forth at the edge of their camp, a stone held near his mouth and another stone pressed to his ear.

No, Salidar had not gone insane. The stones he held were called spy stones. A spy stone was a gemstone terramantically synced with a receiving gemstone. Any sound made in the vicinity of the spy stone would be duplicated by its receiver, even if the two stones were hundreds of miles away.

Spy stones required painstaking calibration and could only be made from a very rare kind of gem. They were among the most expensive terramantic talismans on the market, costing as much as entire castles.

So leave it to Salidar to have not just one, but two sets.

He had brought with him the receiver for one set and the transmitter for the other set, leaving the paired stones with his servants back in Imperium. The setup allowed him to continue leading his vast political machinery even from the middle of nowhere.

"Yes, I know they were outflanked by surprise!" Salidar's angry tones easily reached Durrin's keen ears. "That's exactly why I want Grimbold removed. Who lets an entire army get around your flank? . . . I don't care about the weather—they outnumbered the Elandrians two to one! *Two to one!* I could have won that battle in my sleep."

Salidar was silent for a moment, listening to the reply coming from several hundred miles away. Then he shook his head. "No, no. General Newfang won't do. He's talented, yes, but he's not loyal enough. . . . not to Calamar, to me . . . Lord Skyfang is who. You should already know that. General Newfang fought under Skyfang in the Wormul wars. They're still on close terms."

The pirates were talking and jesting with each other in their strange Hakiru tongue, in good spirits as they dug into their venison. Durrin sat slightly apart from them, staring into the flickering flames. He was concentrating on using his pyromantic powers to magnify the sound waves of Lord Salidar's conversation reaching his ears. His training had taught him to never pass up an opportunity to eavesdrop on something important.

"What about Captain Jarmen?" Salidar was saying. "He's bright and capable, and his terramancy is a bonus . . . Oh. Pity."

The crunch of Salidar's footsteps in the underbrush quickened as his pace accelerated. ". . . No, none of them have enough experience. This is what we'll have to do. Leave General Grimbold in command for now. Tell him to pull back to Meradov with all speed, and to not risk any more engagements, even if they seem advantageous. It's too late in the year for us to take their capital now, even if we did score a victory. Once Grimbold's back at Meradov, he can release the conscript soldiers and keep the professionals garrisoned there for the winter. Next year, I will lead the army myself."

Salidar paused, listening to the reply. ". . . Of course I'll be back by next year! How is the Imperial Council taking my absence? . . . Ah . . . I see . . ." Durrin glanced over to see Salidar's face betraying a smile before he continued. "So Prince Fireclaw is now backing Lord Skyfang? Interesting . . . who else? . . . Oh, he's a surprise. I didn't see that coming. . . . Good,

good. I'm glad the rest are still loyal. Keep telling them the story we agreed upon and note how they respond."

Salidar changed the direction he was pacing. "Now listen. I want conscription orders sent out for another forty thousand troops to be marshalled and trained by next summer . . . I don't care. War involves sacrifice. . . . Ram it through anyway! Declare it a military necessity and bypass the council with a military order. . . . Yes, I'm sure. Forty thousand. And arrange to have the garrisons pulled from the northern border and sent to the front. . . . Honestly, I don't care if there's a few raids up there. Once we have annexed Elandria, we can deal with the raiders. . . . No, not to Meradov. I want them marched to the Penandre."

Durrin's attention was pulled away by one of the Hakiru calling his name. It was a large human named Bjorn, with an old scar defacing his left eye and cheek.

"Rendhart," Bjorn called, his Lurrian broken and awkward. "I and the others wonder. Just how good fighter you are?"

"Good enough," Durrin replied coolly, hoping the vague answer would discourage them from pushing further. But, as usual when this question was raised, he was wrong.

"Let us see," Bjorn called, rising to his feet. "None of us here be mancerers—"

"Hey!" a snippen named Grimbo piped up from the side of the camp, where he was tinkering with a pile of metal, leather, and terramancy gems. He had spent half the flight so far with his hobby, but Durrin had yet to see any successful demonstration of whatever the device was supposed to be.

"None of us be *good* mancerers," Bjorn amended, ignoring the snippen's resulting protests. "How many from us do you think you can battle?"

Durrin thought for a moment. "That depends. In a real-life fight, where I could hit you from twenty feet away with flame hot enough to melt iron, I would say six. But since I'll need to stick to less . . ." he made a show of searching for the right word, ". . . *lethal* tactics, I'll say four."

Bjorn nodded respectfully, looking around at the others and saying something in Hakiru. A quick exchange between several of them followed.

Bjorn turned back to Durrin. "Very well. Let us see if breath of Ky'kiaymon be with you truly. I, Tadgh, Krizmon, and Azura will challenge you."

"Of course you will," Durrin muttered under his breath. "And right after dinner, too." That wouldn't really matter to them—*they* weren't the ones who would be performing flips and somersaults at high speed.

Durrin shed his cloak and his sword, following Bjorn and the other three combatants to a nearby patch of clear ground. The rest of the pirate crew ringed the perimeter, gabbing in their language—probably making bets.

Grimbo scurried over to the cloudship and fetched a set of practice swords—long, wooden rods covered in leather padding. Durrin selected the longest one and tested it. Its design and material made it poorly weighted, with the center of mass in the blade instead of the hilt. He gave it a few practice swings, slicing it back and forth through the air, getting a feel for how it performed both one-handed and two-handed. Dissatisfied, he replaced it and selected a shorter blade with better balance.

Bjorn grabbed the sword Durrin had just rejected, where it looked much more at home in his huge hands. Tadgh, the Dorinian avir, selected a light one-handed sword and swished it elegantly, his face golden and his eyes shining bright blue with excitement.

Both Tadgh and Bjorn carried the distinctive Hakiru-style shield: a long, narrow oval, about three feet tall and a foot and a half wide. The shields were strapped to their left arm, with a handle they could grab with their left hand for extra stability. The design allowed them to keep their left hand free to grab rigging or climb ladders.

Durrin's final opponents, a pair of korrik sisters named Krizmon and Azura, started bickering over the remaining shields.

As their Hakiru jabber grew more and more inflamed, Durrin edged over to stand by Tadgh. "What are they arguing over?" he whispered.

"Color," Tadgh said, rolling his eyes. "Lahk always."

Bjorn pointed to the shields in front of the korrik sisters. "Krizmon say they need red and purple shields, strike fear in enemy chest. Azura say green and blue, to counter to your fire."

"I see," said Durrin. "Does this have anything to do with the fact that Krizmon has a red tattoo on her face, while Azura has a blue tattoo on her face?"

"Purely coincadentahl," Tadgh deadpanned.

Eventually, Krizmon grabbed the red shield and a practice spear. Azura slung the green shield over her back and grabbed a bow and a set of blunted arrows.

Bjorn shook his head. "No arrow. Shoot eye out."

"I'm not worried," Durrin said. "It'll make things interesting."

"Fine," Bjorn grunted. He gestured to Durrin's empty left hand. "You desire shield?"

"I don't need one." In Durrin's style of fighting, shields tended to only get in the way.

Bjorn hefted his practice sword. "Rules be simple. One good hit to torso, or two good hits to arms or legs, and warrior out." He shot a glare at Krizmon. "No hits to head."

Durrin spun his sword artfully with one hand, his earlier reluctance replaced with the thrill of adrenaline. Not counting his escapade at Wyvern Way, this was his first real fight since his days at Irongate Isle. "What is the signal to begin?"

Bjorn looked at his companions, who each nodded. He turned back to Durrin. "Now."

Durrin launched himself across the clearing, gathering a storm of momentum around him as he ran. His four opponents reacted quickly, shouting to each other as they spread out in a half ring, Bjorn to Durrin's left and Tadgh to Durrin's right. In the center, Krizmon covered Azura with her shield as Azura nocked an arrow.

Durrin ran right into the middle of their arc—then launched himself high into the air in a spinning somersault meant to carry him behind the twin korrik sisters.

Krizmon and Azura pivoted in a surprising display of unity, Krizmon holding up her shield to deflect Durrin's coming assault from above and behind. But it never came. While in midair, Durrin twisted, releasing heat and energy to his left to propel him to the right. It was a difficult move, one he could only perform since relearning the third Kymar routine in the last week. He flipped over Tadgh's head, his sword glancing off Tadgh's upraised blade as he almost scored a hit on the surprised avir.

"No head!" Bjorn reminded him, even as he ran forward to help his comrade.

Durrin landed on his feet and instantly pressed to the attack. But Tadgh was a skilled fencer and parried his thrusts with fluid, easy movements.

"You've had some training," Durrin observed as Tadgh pushed him back with a series of attacks. Durrin danced left to keep Tadgh between him and Bjorn.

"I'm the second-son prince of Clan Cleney," Tadgh boasted, one of his thrusts barely missing Durrin's shoulder. "Fencing be in my very blood."

Durrin's pyrosense, running in the background of his mind, picked up a spike of approaching energy to his left. He leapt backward. Azura's arrow whizzed past his chest and disappeared into the trees. The pirates at the edge of the clearing shouted in surprise.

Ah, yes.

The roaring crowds.

The skilled opponents.

Durrin smiled. It was like the Mancery Mayhem arena all over again.

Durrin snapped his left hand, summoning a ribbon of fire—not hot enough to really hurt anybody, but good for intimidation. He spun it in small circles with his left hand, flicking it out toward Tadgh and Bjorn like a whip if they got too close. The two pirates darted forward and back, shying away from the flame but getting a little closer each time.

Azura loosed another arrow. Durrin knocked it out of the air with his sword.

Bjorn and Tadgh finally trapped Durrin between them and moved in. Durrin feinted at Bjorn, then sprang toward Tadgh. The clan-prince-turned-navigator parried Durrin's attack, then stepped forward in a counterattack, swinging his practice sword at an angle that would give him substantially greater leverage than Durrin's parry would have.

But as Durrin swung, he let the flame within him surge, channeling an extra burst of momentum into his sword to knock Tadgh's sword barely off course. Durrin followed up with a lightning-fast thrust, jabbing the avir below the ribs.

"One!" Durrin called, spinning away before Bjorn could strike him from behind. Durrin sprinted across the field, buying some distance between him and his heavyset pursuer.

An arrow barely missed his head.

This was getting annoying.

Durrin turned and charged the korrik sisters. Seeing him coming, Azura dropped her bow and grabbed a practice spear that her sister handed her.

Durrin pulled up short, using his momentum to unleash a ball of fire at the pair of korriks. Krizmon blocked the fireball with her shield. Then she and Azura charged.

Durrin had guessed, from their bickering over shield color, that Krizmon and Azura would have trouble coordinating with each other in a fight.

His assumption nearly cost him a spearpoint in the gut.

The two sisters fought with a synchrony he had never seen before. They seemed to move with one mind as they stuck together, advancing as one, retreating as one, Krizmon covering both of them with her shield as they thrust their spears with flawless coordination.

Durrin found himself on the retreat, fending off the barrage of spear thrusts, unable to land an attack due to the korriks' longer reach. As Bjorn circled behind him, Durrin was forced to use his free hand to create a vortex of flames to keep the large human at bay.

The roar of the onlookers grew in pitch as it looked like Durrin was trapped.

Then he knocked Krizmon's next attack to the side with his sword, using the opening to dart inside the range of their spears. Krizmon raised her shield, expecting an attack from above, but Durrin dropped into a crouch and swung his sword under her shield, smashing into her hip. Scarcely had the blow landed when he pivoted and stabbed Azura in the stomach.

"Three!" Durrin cried.

Krizmon and Azura each began to spout a flurry of angry words, but Durrin was already turning to defend against Bjorn's assault. The constant movement to avoid getting trapped was beginning to wear Durrin down. He parried a series of attacks, but then Bjorn slipped past his guard and slammed his sword into Durrin's left arm. Durrin barely blocked a follow-up to his right, then retreated backward.

"Out?" Bjorn called.

Durrin patted his arm, which was stinging from the blow. "Arm, not torso."

The Hakiru cheered their comrade on.

That's it. Durrin thought, his pride stinging worse than his arm. *Time to show them why you don't fight a pyromancer in real life.* Durrin leapt into the air, blasting a plume of fire toward his opponent with a flying kick. As Bjorn recoiled, ducking behind his shield, Durrin sprang forward. Bjorn attacked, his sword flashing, but Durrin caught his opponent's sword on his own sword's hilt.

As their swords clashed, Durrin stepped forward, closing the gap between them and pushing their locked swords upward. Releasing his sword, he grabbed Bjorn around the waist in a grappling move, lifted the massive warrior bodily into the air, and slammed him down onto his back. A moment later, Durrin held his sword to his opponent's chest.

"Four," Durrin said, his breath coming heavy. "Told you."

Bjorn wheezed, struggling to regain his breath, then took Durrin's proffered hand and rose to his feet. He shook his head and smiled grimly. "By Ky'kiaymon's breath, Rendhart! I be glad you be on our side." Bjorn turned to his comrades and lifted Durrin's hand into the air. "Ai b'kev-etky! To the victor!"

The rest of the crew cheered, then immediately began swapping coins.

Durrin rubbed his arm, which still smarted from Bjorn's blow. He had deliberately gone easy on the pirates during the fight. He could have used pyromancy to make his blows fall far harder and faster. But it wasn't in his interests to let them know *exactly* how good he was.

Azura walked up to him, dragging her sister by the hand. She jabbered something that sounded like a compliment, then nodded her head in a gesture of respect. Krizmon sulked behind her, even when Azura elbowed her pointedly. A moment later, the two were arguing again.

Tadgh strolled up to Durrin, extending his hand. This time, Durrin knew what he wanted and gave his hand a vigorous shake.

"Yah did well," the avir said. "I went easy on yeh, of course, but yeh did well."

"Sure you did," Durrin said dryly. He nodded at Krizmon and Azura. "Those two caught me by surprise back there."

"Ach." Tadgh nodded. "They were joined at birth." He tapped the side of his head. "Stuck together, I mean. What's the word?"

"Conjoined twins?" Durrin supplied.

"Ach, that's right. Stayed that way through their childhood, until a surgeon got them apart somehow. Yeh'd never know it half the time, by the way they quarrel. But they still fight as if they share the same mind."

Durrin studied the two korriks again. They had stopped arguing and were gathering up the practice weapons with movements oddly in sync with each other. The right side of Krizmon's head and the left side of Azura's were deformed where they had once been conjoined.

Durrin looked past them to where Salidar stood near the fire. The vizier had finished his long-distance conversation and now stood alone, coolly watching from a distance.

What was Salidar's plan? With him and Yorid now accompanying the Hakiru on their mission, how had Durrin's role changed? He hadn't had a chance yet to talk to Salidar alone. Was he still supposed to kill the Hakiru along with the princess?

Could he?

He looked around at the laughing, jostling band of warriors around him. They were turning out to be much different than he had expected. Less cruel. More light-hearted. More . . . real.

CHAPTER 22

QUESTIONS EN ROUTE

Summer was surrendering to autumn. Trees were turning to fire. Wheat and corn lay heavy on the stalk. Flocks of birds passed daily over Volthorn's army as they flew southwest, fleeing colder climes to the north and east.

Although Queen Adara had failed to negotiate an official armistice, Volthorn had secured a temporary settlement with Calamar's front-line commander, General Grimbold. Volthorn allowed the ten thousand soldiers in Calamar's flanking division to recross the river and join the remnants of their main army. In exchange, Grimbold agreed to retreat to Meradov immediately, without attempting any more battles or raids that season.

In making the arrangement, Volthorn gave up the possibility of hammering the remnants of Calamar's retreating army. But he also avoided the risk of facing a defeat of his own. Despite his victory, Calamar could still field almost as many battle-ready troops as he could. Many of his battalions had suffered heavy losses, plus he had several thousand prisoners to guard. It was a good thing the Penandre garrison would be arriving in another day or so to reinforce his position.

Another reason was that harvest was near. Between the ongoing haeber shortage and the demands of war, many Elandrian provinces were on the brink of famine. Keeping his conscript farmers another month to score another victory would only mean they'd starve the next spring.

So it was that five days after his victory—which his troops were beginning to call "the Battle of Rainswept Heights"—Volthorn stood watching his last units of seasonal troops march away, disbanded until the next spring. Around six thousand professional full-time soldiers would remain at arms during the winter, encamped in the Arnon Plains.

"Commander Skarr," an aide said, interrupting Volthorn's thoughts. "Intelligence report. We've received an unusual message from a contact in Calamar."

"Unusual?" Volthorn said.

"Peculiar," the aide clarified. "The contact received an anonymous message, written on a note left outside his residence in Imperium. We are puzzled as to its meaning. Here's a transcription."

The aide handed Volthorn a piece of parchment, covered in tidy lines of text:

> *Report to your comrades in yonder land:*
> *Evil stirs in the shadows of the night.*
> *News I bear that you must heed.*
> *Danger from the past returns.*
> *History threatens to repeat.*
> *An avir's life is in peril:*
> *Ruin, fire, and flames.*
> *To the skies, beware.*

Volthorn read the poem several times. "Most obscure," he said. "What do you make of it?"

"We have no idea," the aide said. "The author's identity is unknown, although they are probably associated with Elandrian sympathizers in Imperium. Presumably they wrote in cryptic language so that if the note was discovered, it wouldn't incriminate the recipient or the sender. But we're worried it's some kind of hoax or red herring: counterintelligence meant to lead us onto a false trail."

"If so, it could do a better job of explaining what that trail is," Volthorn quipped. "Let me read it again."

He explored each line carefully. The first: *Report to your comrades in yonder land.* Straightforward. *Evil stirs in the shadows of the night.* Demons? But they always stalked the night. What else could it be referencing? Some sort of enemy operation?

Danger from the past returns. History threatens to repeat. An avir's life is in peril. Those lines seemed to refer to King Everborn's assassination, warning that Adara was in similar danger. But who would know enough to write that? Scarcely two dozen souls in Elandria knew the truth about how King Everborn had died. Who in Calamar would know? Those who had ordered the assassination, of course. But why would they send a message like this, or how would they know who to send it through?

Danger from the past returns. There was only one obvious candidate for what that danger was: Rendhart. And the penultimate line seemed to confirm it: *Ruin, fire, and flames.*

But what did the final line mean? *To the skies, beware.* Was this referring to a griffin attack? To some omen in the skies, like a red sunrise?

"Any idea what it means?" the officer asked.

"I believe it's a warning that Queen Adara is in danger," Volthorn said. "But the exact danger, or what we must do to prevent it, still eludes me." He frowned, thinking. "Inform my staff that my brothers and I will be leaving within the hour. With the campaign season over, and now with this strange portent of danger, I think it's time I returned to the capital."

Once again, Durrin couldn't sleep.

This time, he had plenty of things to blame it on: the cramped deck of the cloud frigate, the snoring of Bjorn next to him, the knowledge that they were several thousand feet above the ground, held aloft by some stunt of aeronautical engineering that he still didn't fully understand.

But he knew the real reason he couldn't sleep. Questions. A hundred thousand questions.

Questions . . . and the shadows of the night.

Durrin rose quietly to his feet, careful not to disturb the sleeping figures around him. He stepped gingerly across the deck, his way barely lit by the faint red light of the Far Moon. As always when the cloud frigate was free floating, he could feel no wind. The cloud frigate flowed at the same pace as the air around it, like a piece of driftwood in a river's current.

Durrin made his way to the prow. There he found Twigly on watch, perched atop the ship's massive ballista. Her long, bushy tail waved in the air behind her, making tiny corrections to keep her perfectly balanced.

Durrin still wasn't sure what to make of Twigly. The snippen was the only member of the crew who spoke fluent Lurrian. Every time he, Salidar, and Yorid conversed among themselves, he got the feeling she was listening in with her large ears. And he could never tell when she was joking and when she was being impudent.

"Couldn't catch any dreams, Rendhart?" the snippen asked as he approached. "Or got caught by nightmares?"

Durrin stood at the prow, grabbing a rigging line for support. He *had* been having nightmares recently: terrible nightmares, of fangs and horns and unending darkness.

But Twigly didn't need to know that. Durrin shrugged. "Questions, mostly."

"Ah." Twigly nodded sagely. "Terrible things, questions. They ruin your appetite, especially when the questions relate to the origin of your supper."

Casting about for small talk to get his mind off his nightmares, Durrin gestured to the darkness in front of them. "What are you watching for?"

"Mountains, mainly," Twigly said. "Terrible things, mountains. Come up on you unawares in the darkness, like a lynx in a field of daisies. We also watch our altimeter."

Twigly pointed to a device stowed under the ballista. Durrin could faintly see a glass tube, illuminated by a small ball of lumen moss. "It shows us our altitude," Twigly explained.

"And it's accurate?"

"Mostly," said Twigly. "Though pressure front fluctuations mean you have to account for the weather patterns, else you can have a high margin of error. Good grief, I sound like my cousin." She shook her head as if to clear herself of the thought. "Where was I? Lynxes. No. Mountains. Right. And we watch for other cloudships. Griffins. Wyverns."

"Do wyverns pose a danger?"

"Not if you're not unlucky. Typically, they're intimidated by our size. Though if you get too close to their nest, they could get defensive and puncture a hole in your balloon."

Twigly patted the ballista beneath her. "Which is one of the reasons we carry these. Wyverns—and dragons."

Durrin snorted. "Dragons are a myth."

"Ah, so you say." Twigly smiled that cocky smile of hers again. "But on the day you're proven wrong, would you rather be caught *with* a giant ballista, or *without* one?"

Durrin stared at her, trying to figure out how serious she was. He shook his head and gave up. "Okay. Next question. You're not really an ensign, are you. You're the captain."

Twigly winked at him. "Whatever gave you that idea?"

"I may not understand Hakiru," Durrin said. "But I can tell who's giving orders and who's receiving them."

"Astute." Twigly twirled, bowing with a flourish. "Indeed, I am! Captain Twigly the Barbaric, at your doorstep."

Durrin raised his eyebrow. "The . . . Barbaric?"

"But of course!" Twigly drew a knife from her belt and spun it in her paw. She stuck the knife between her teeth and talked through it. "Awen't I da most barbaric snippen you've ewer seen?"

Durrin thought about it. "Well . . . you're not wrong," he said. "Why did you pretend otherwise?"

Twigly waved a paw. "I just wanted to pull His Excellency's leg."

"But don't Hakiru cloudships always have to be captained by a griffin?"

Twigly balanced the dagger on one paw. "Traditionally, yes." The dagger slipped, almost plummeting into the darkness before Twigly snatched it at the last moment. "But I have ways of being . . . persuasive."

"You bribed someone, didn't you."

"Nonsense." Twigly tucked the dagger into her vest. "I just made myself so annoying that no one was willing to take on the task of ordering me around. I became captain by default."

Durrin raised his eyebrow. Twigly raised hers in return.

Durrin gave up and changed the subject again. "Twigly—"

"That's *Captain* Twigly, to you," the snippen said. "The Barbaric."

Durrin paused for a moment, then continued with his original wording. "Twigly, you're not even Hakiru. How did you come to join this crew in the first place?"

"The full tale would take half a fortnight," said Twigly. "It involves a lost treasure, seventeen buckets of lard, my great-great-granduncle's belt buckle, and a giant talking penguin. The short version is that I grew up in a rather crowded burrow in Imperium, then after a short and glorious career failing ninety-three different apprenticeships, found myself a member of this crew."

Durrin debated taking the bait and asking about the belt buckle and the giant talking . . . whatever Twigly had said. But his mind was still working through deeper questions, and he didn't feel like listening to a long anecdote.

They fell silent for a minute, each staring out into the night. The ropes around them creaked and groaned in a low, constant chorus.

What was he going to do once they captured Queen Everborn? Could he bring himself to carry out Salidar's orders?

What would Salidar do if he refused?

In the distance, a faint, shimmering light slowly drew nearer. It was like a river of effervescence in the sky, wavering back and forth, its intensity waxing and waning from minute to minute. The phenomenon was called a leyline current—one of many that cut across the sky, linking Zenitha's various leyline beacons into one worldwide network of terramantic energy. Durrin stared at it in awe. It was still high above the ship, but closer than he had ever seen one before.

A young lad climbed down the rigging and hopped down next to Twigly. Durrin knew the lad was named Line, but the language barrier had gotten in the way of knowing any more. So he was caught off guard when Twigly and Line exchanged greetings not in Hakiru, but in a language called Mitrian.

"Wait," Durrin said, switching to the language as well. "You both know Mitrian?"

Line looked at him in surprise.

Twigly nodded. "Aye. We had a Mitrian cook join the crew last year. Terrible chef. His shepherd's pie tasted more like roasted applesauce. But he liked to teach his language to anyone willing to learn—which turned out to be only Line and me. We speak it between us to keep up on it."

"What happened to the Mitrian?"

Twigly scowled darkly. "He burned one too many breakfasts. We made him walk the plank."

Horrified, Durrin glanced over the side of the rail at the ground thousands of feet below them.

"Don't worry!" Line hastily added. "We were grounded at the time. He only fell maybe eight feet. Sprained an ankle but was otherwise fine."

Twigly eyed Durrin curiously. "And how do *you* know Mitrian?"

"I traveled to Mitria often on missions for Lord Salidar," Durrin said. *I was quite fond of their shepherd's pie, actually.* He turned back to Line. "I couldn't help but notice on this voyage how fearless you are with heights."

Line looked away. "It comes with the occupation," he said modestly.

"Everyone else wears a safety rope when they climb up to check the balloon," Durrin said. "But you don't."

Twigly nudged the lad. "Tell'm, Line! He won't bite. Probably."

Line kept his eyes down. "I was raised by griffins," he said just above a whisper.

Twigly elbowed him again. "You gotta tell him more than that."

"It was at the edge of the world," Line added, starting to warm up to the topic. "Go north, to the Hakiru lands beyond the northern seas, and you eventually reach the great sinkholes. Keep going, and the sinkholes give way to massive canyons. Eventually the terrain becomes a broken mess, an endless series of bottomless gorges."

Line grew more animated, his eyes shining. "Even farther north, and land and air invert, until the only solid ground are the skystacks: tall pillars piercing the boundless sky. I was raised there by a tribe of griffins, in a landscape where an endless fall was never more than a few feet away."

Durrin stared at the lad in wonder. He'd heard tall tales of the edge of the world, but had never met an eyewitness. "And your parents?"

Line shrugged. "I never knew them. They disappeared when I was an infant. The griffins raised me until I was twelve or so, then a ship found me and took me farther south. I've been hopping between various Hakiru vessels ever since."

Durrin leaned forward. This was his first chance to talk to a native-born Hakiru—besides Bjorn, whose Lurrian was spotty on a good day. "Line, what are things like up north? In Hakirum?"

Line looked out at the sea of clouds, as if his eye could pierce the thousands of intervening miles. "You would consider it marvelous. We live in balloons much like this one, but bigger, with dozens linked together to form villages and towns, all floating in the air. Most Hakiru sail east and west with the seasons, following great herds of elk and bison that turn the ground dark with their numbers. Some travel south across the sea to the Lurrian continent to trade. Others—" he glanced at Twigly. "—get creative."

Durrin wet his lips, then asked the question most weighing on his mind. "What do the Hakiru believe in? Do you believe in demons and angels, like we do here?"

Line lifted his eyes higher. "We worship the star gods." He pointed to a bright red star near the horizon. "See that? That is Ky'kiaymon, god of pyromancy. And just to the left of the Far Moon, you see that bright blue one? That's Ullyna've, goddess of aquamancy. The others are out of sight behind the balloon, but there's five in all—one for each branch of mancery."

More than one god? Durrin shook his head. "How do you worship them?"

"There are shrines throughout the north—floating shrines, though they are anchored in place—for each of the gods. There, priests burn incense and perform rites to keep us connected to each god, and to maintain the delicate balance of the world."

"And what of angels and demons? And the fate of our souls?"

An arc of light flashed across the sky. Line pointed at it. "You see that shooting star? We believe that a star falls to Zenitha whenever a person is born. That star dwells within us, giving us life and strength. When we die and pass away, the star within us lingers on, dormant and unseen. If its light is truly spent, then a nightwalker—"

"What you and I would call a 'demon,'" Twigly interposed, "though the Hakiru see it as a neutral spirit, not an evil one."

Line nodded. "Then a nightwalker takes it to its final end in the Void. But if a spark of life remains, then a daywalker—"

"An 'angel,' to us," added Twigly.

"—takes it up into the sky, reignites it with the fires of the Sun, and restores it to its place in the night sky. There the star remains until one day it will fall to Zenitha again, to enliven another soul."

Durrin looked out at the sea of stars above them. "So for the Hakiru, the soul doesn't exist past death?"

"No, not in the way you think about it in Calamar," said Line. "To us, the star is just the energy that fuels our existence—like the candle in a lantern—but not our existence in and of itself. We pass away forever when we die."

Durrin pondered the young man's words, comparing them to the different beliefs he was already familiar with. The Knights Vigilant and the Dawn Wardens said your fate was determined solely by whether you died in the daytime or nighttime. The Luminant Order taught that though the time of your death had an impact, more important was the life you lived previously, affecting whether or not the angels would be willing to claim you. The Hakiru said that death was the end of consciousness.

"If we cease to exist when we die," Durrin asked, "Then do our choices in this life matter?"

"Of course they still matter," said Line. "Because the star gods are constantly watching. We must obey their laws or risk throwing the world out of balance."

"What kinds of laws?"

Line shrugged again. "The usual, I guess. No murder. No turning your back on those in need. No cutting a cloudship's anchor lines. No wanton waste of prime vapor. No stealing."

"No stealing?" Durrin glanced at Twigly. "But aren't you guys thieves?"

"We're pirates," Twigly corrected proudly. "What we take, we take by fighting. It's war, not thievery."

Durrin raised his eyebrow skeptically. "And . . . that makes a difference?"

"All the difference in the world," Twigly said. "When you have five gods, it's natural to have a little warfare now and then—as long as you consecrate some of your loot to the god whose banner you won it under."

Line gestured to a long strip of fabric hanging from the spar of the prow. "Right now, we sail a red banner, the banner of the pyromantic god," he explained. "That's because you're on board. If this mission turns a profit, we'll lay aside a tithe to give to the priests of Ky'kiaymon the next time we visit his shrine." He shot a glare at Twigly. "*When* we eventually get there."

Twigly held up her hands unapologetically. "Don't blame me for taking advantage of a zero interest rate. Any star deity worth his salt would have closed that loophole eons ago."

Durrin turned to the flamboyantly dressed snippen. "I take it you've held to your Lurrian beliefs?"

The snippen sighed, turning more serious than he'd ever seen her before. "I don't know, Rendhart. I don't know. In all respects, the Hakiru are my people now. But how can I abandon my belief in the Sky Father? These sky gods—how can I know they are real? Yet, if I can't believe in *them*, why can I believe in the Sky Father? And so I sit on the mooring line, undecided."

Durrin realized he faced the same dilemma. All his life, he had believed the teachings of the Knights Vigilant, without ever giving them much thought. But ever since his conversations with Halorn, he had been confronted with a new reality, one warning him that his crimes had doomed his soul. He couldn't decide which one was true—or how to even tell.

Durrin stared out into the night, pondering everything Twigly and Line had told him. Truth—who could know it? The idea of five star gods instead of one Sky Father seemed ludicrous, but was it just his upbringing that made him feel that way? What did the Hakiru think of people who believed in the Sky Father, or in angels and demons that could carry away your soul after death? What evidence was there one way or the other? How could you know the truth about things that went unseen?

And Halorn—how did he know so much, especially things that he should not know?

Twigly hopped down and wet a lumen globe, casting light over a chart laid out at the foot of the ballista. She studied its features, then hopped back up to the ballista and peered out over the dark landscape. The sky was beginning to brighten in the far east, heralding the dawn.

"We're getting close," Twigly said. "If I'm not mistaken, we just passed Lake Silverhorn to our right. That puts us about a hundred miles out from Saven."

"We can cover that in a day, can't we?" Durrin asked.

Twigly shook her head. "Not with the current winds. We'll have to turn south soon, which will require churning." They had had to "churn" a few times already on their voyage: two swifters on the crew would turn a set of pedals, powering the two propellers mounted off the starboard and port sides. It allowed them to make progress against the wind, or when the wind died.

"So what's our timetable?"

Twigly studied the chart. "If we churn all day today, that will bring us about two-thirds of the way. I think we'll need to stop and rest and re-outfit the vessel tonight, then attack tomorrow night."

"So we'll need a conspicuous place to camp." Durrin knelt to examine the pirates' map. It was a truly high-quality specimen of cartography, showing individual valleys in the hills between them and Saven. He studied it, noting the locations of roads and towns.

"What's this?" Durrin asked, pointing to an unusual icon in an isolated stretch of hills.

Twigly squinted at the writing. "The Hakiru word means a shrine or sanctuary. Probably belongs to the Luminant Order or the Dawn Wardens, I would guess."

Interesting. When serving as Salidar's agent in Elandria, Durrin had studied its geography extensively, becoming familiar with many of its strongholds and cities. But he had never seen this shrine on any map.

Halorn's words from the alleyway played in his mind. *The scroll is kept by the Luminant Order with utmost secrecy. It is not in the palace at Saven. Only a handful of people know where it is.*

Could it . . .?

Durrin pointed to a valley just one ridge over from the mysterious shrine. "Let's camp here."

"Why there?"

"This shrine is a secret sanctuary," Durrin said, "which means not many people come and go. The whole area around it is uninhabited. It's the best place for us to camp without word getting to Saven of our presence."

Twigly shrugged. "Sounds good to me."

Durrin stared out into the slowly brightening pre-dawn sky. The discovery of this secret sanctuary had reignited his passion for Kymar's scroll, which had been somewhat chilled ever since Halorn's news.

But now he found that passion struggling for space amid the torrent of thoughts from his conversation with Line.

What was the state of his soul? What would happen to him when he died?

And if he truly was doomed—was there anything he could do to change that?

Twigly chuckled. "You are indeed haunted by questions, Rendhart. Even in the dark, I can see them scurrying over your thoughts, like a swarm of ants over a dropped piece of lemon cheesecake."

"Lemon . . . cheesecake?"

Twigly winked in the darkness. "It's a delicacy in Solapharia. You should try it sometime. Maybe after you sample laughter."

CHAPTER 23

PERCOLATING FLAMES

Flames. Flames in the palace.

They haunted the hearth of Adara's bedchamber, crackling, spitting, hissing, a mosaic of reds and golds. She contemplated them. They were angry but subdued.

Adara ascended a stairwell. Daylight flooded her. She stood at the pinnacle of the palace, as if at the top of the world. She turned in a circle, taking in the city she had grown to love. The shops. The houses. The people. The many, many, many people. Happy. Prosperous. Peaceful.

Then a wind arose and blew the diorama from her eyes. In its place came a new scene—a terrible one.

Smoke. Destruction. Screams. People running through the streets, scrambling to carry their children. And soldiers. Soldiers everywhere, clad in Calamar's burning scarlet, cutting down all in their path.

And piercing through the terrible scene, a calm but penetrating voice, echoing through her mind:

Report to your comrades in yonder land.

She cast her gaze beyond the walls. There, on the plains normally so beautiful and lush, were trenches and bulwarks of war.

The voice sounded again:

Evil stirs in the shadows of the night.

Beyond the trenches, mighty war engines loomed, towers and trebuchets and battering rams, surrounded by forests of spears, all encircling the city in a ring of terror.

Danger from the past returns.

She fled the horrible scene, casting herself down the stairwell. Her quarters now were ransacked, the furniture broken and splintered, the floor covered with the shattered shards of what had once been a statue of her father.

History threatens to repeat.

She ran now, down another flight of stairs to her fore chambers, then out into a hallway. The flames from the hearth had spread, filling every corner of the stone passage. She ran between those greedy lines of flames, pausing only to stamp out the corners of her dress as they caught fire from stray embers.

An avir's life is in peril.

She reached the throne room. Flames blocked every exit, but that was not all—enemies ringed her on all sides, their blades catching the light of the flames. They wore strange garb and shouted in a language unknown to her. Only the throne was unblocked. She ran to it.

Ruin, fire, and flames.

She stood upon her throne, screaming, but no sound came out of her mouth. The flames were coming closer now, and with them the points of a thousand swords. Scorching heat licked at the palms of her outstretched hands. She closed her eyes.

To the skies—

"Princess! Princess!"

Adara awoke, jerking upright and throwing the covers off her shaking body. Two of her handmaids stood over her, their faces ashen white with concern.

"Fire!" Adara screamed. "Flames!"

"Hush," one of her handmaids murmured. "It was just a nightmare. The palace is safe."

"No, it's not." Adara swung her legs out of bed. "Danger from the past returns!"

A third voice spoke up. "Your Majesty, please, calm yourself."

Adara looked over to see Lady Luviana. The merfin was draped out on a couch in Adara's quarters, her miniature harp in her hands. She must have been brought in hastily, carried by someone instead of transported in her normal traveling basin. A trail of small puddles led from the door to the couch.

"Luviana?" Adara frowned. "What . . . Why . . . are you . . .?"

"You weren't waking up," the merfin explained. "You were crying out and thrashing for a quarter of an hour. Emma and Charlotte tried shaking you, calling to you, even splashing water on you. Eventually, they sent for me to play a vivamantic song to pull you out of sleep."

Adara set her feet on the floor. The cold stone against her bare feet felt remarkably soothing. "A quarter of an hour? But the dream—it lasted barely a couple minutes."

"It seemed to be repeating," one of her handmaids said. "You would start out calm, then slowly grow more agitated until you were kicking and screaming. Then you would calm down again. That happened three or four times. You had us so worried!"

Adara kneaded her forehead, temples, and cheekbones with her fingers. "I don't understand. Why wouldn't I wake up?"

"You were trapped inside the dream," Luviana said. She began idly strumming her harp, plucking a soft but calming melody, like a mountain breeze rippling across a field of wildflowers. "I have heard of such cases, where a dream does not want to end. Often it carries a portent. May I ask what you saw?"

The dream was still remarkably vivid in Adara's mind. She described it as best she could, though as always when retelling dreams, it seemed impossible to transcribe the images in her head into phrases that made any sense. Part of her still felt a terrible sense of urgency, a looming threat that called for her immediate action. But the coolness of the stones beneath her and the melodic strains of the harp were, in conjunction, incredibly soothing.

"There was a voice," Adara finished. "It warned of danger and evil. It said that my life is in peril. *Ruin, fire, and flames*—that was one of the lines." She paused, trying to recall the exact wording of the other lines. "There was more though . . ."

She turned to her two handmaids. "Emma, Charlotte, could you step outside for a moment?"

"Certainly," they said, curtsying and withdrawing. As they opened the door, Adara noticed several worried-looking guards in the stairwell, peeking inside. Her thrashing and cries must have created quite a stir. She felt her face flush with embarrassment.

"What is it, Your Majesty?" Luviana asked once the door had shut and they were alone.

Adara took a deep breath, trying to sort the swirling vortex of thoughts within her. "Tell me again how my father died."

The merfin's fingers paused, skipping a beat of her song. Then the melody resumed. "You were there," Luviana said. "The fire—"

"What caused the fire?" Adara asked.

"We think a vessel of oil got tipped over," Luviana said, talking slowly. She stopped playing. "The tapestries in a hallway caught ablaze, then quickly spread to the paneling in the throne room. Your father worked to make sure everyone got out, but before he could leave himself, the smoke . . ." Luviana broke off in mid-sentence, taking a deep breath. "Pardon me, Your Majesty, but that day brings back many painful memories. I'd rather not talk about it."

"The voice spoke of danger returning from the past, and history repeating itself," said Adara. "Since the end of the dream was me standing on my throne, surrounded by flames, I can't help but wonder . . ."

"I wouldn't worry about a fire," Luviana reassured her. "We have been much more careful about open flames. Mostly we use lumen globes, though they are more expensive."

"There were swords in my dream, too," said Adara. "And the city was under siege. It's not an accident I fear. It's an attack."

Luviana didn't respond immediately. She stared at nothing, a distant look of worry on her face. Finally, she shook her head. "You have had many cares on your mind, Your Majesty. Likely this nightmare was just a reflection of them. I wouldn't worry too much about it."

"Could it have been demons, influencing my dreams?" Adara asked. Some people believed demons were the source of all nightmares.

"Perhaps, Your Majesty. Who knows?"

Adara sat thinking for a minute. She still had so many questions, coupled with a lingering sense of apprehension. Luviana was an excellent source of advice for anything political or social. But in this instance, Adara found the merfin's answers sorely lacking.

"Is Magistrate Cymer near?" Adara asked.

"Alas, he is away on business," Luviana said. "He left the day before yesterday. I believe he is overseeing the evacuation of records from the Sanctum of Kings."

"I see," Adara said, disappointed. She stood and crossed the room to a basin of water, splashing it on her face. There had been one more line to the dream, right before she had awakened. What was it? It had been important . . . something about the skies . . .

"What would you think if I moved my sleeping quarters?" Adara asked. "Perhaps to one of the lower palace rooms? I think I would feel safer there."

"I don't see why not," Luviana said. "But Commander Volthorn might want a say in the matter. He's supposed to arrive late in the afternoon tomorrow—well, I guess today now. We can consult him then. As for now, Your Majesty, you should probably get some more sleep. I can stay here if you wish. This couch is surprisingly comfortable, as far as land-walkers' furniture goes."

"I would like that," Adara said. She strode to the door to thank and dismiss her handmaids, then lay back down. Luviana began strumming a low, quiet tune, supplementing it with a wordless song. Though thoughts and fears still clamored for Adara's attention, the lullaby quickly did its work, and Adara slipped into a deep slumber, devoid of dreams.

The Hakiru pirates were only one day out now.

As Twigly had predicted, they had had to churn their propellors most of the day, fighting to head south against winds blowing west. They were spending their last night anchored in the valley Durrin had found on the map. The plan was to spend the rest of the next day at their camp, then leave in the afternoon, travel the last forty miles to Saven, and attack the palace a couple hours before dawn.

Durrin ate his dinner alone, brooding in the shadows of the trees, watching the pirates banter. He itched to climb the ridge to scout out the shrine on the far side. But not yet. Night had not fully fallen. And besides, he needed to get some answers from a certain nobleman first.

As dinner wrapped up, During stood and strode over to Salidar. "Your Excellency," Durrin murmured. "A word with you, please."

The vizier studied him for a few heartbeats. "If you insist," Salidar said finally, rising and accompanying Durrin into the brush. The under-growth was not very thick, and soon Durrin found a deer trail that wound its way toward the top of the nearby ridge.

As soon as they were out of earshot from the pirates, the vizier sighed. "This isn't about the guild masters denouncing you, is it?"

Durrin held his tongue, but the surprise in his glance must have given him away.

"I should have known someone as talented as you would find out so quickly," Salidar continued. "I assure you that I had absolutely nothing to do with that cowardly betrayal. They acted outside my knowledge and without my permission, and I froze a significant portion of their assets as punishment."

"Why didn't you have the denunciation reversed?" Durrin challenged.

"You know it's not that simple. Recalling a denunciation for no clear reason, immediately after its issuance? That would have severely discredited the Guild."

"And what about discrediting *me*?" Durrin snapped. "How am I supposed to become a guild master now, with an active denunciation hanging over me?"

Of course, if Halorn was right about Kymar's scroll—and Durrin was becoming more and more convinced he was—then guild mastership had nothing to offer Durrin more than a title and a slip of parchment. Still, every time he thought about the Guild's betrayal, it felt like a knife was being twisted in his gut.

Salidar waved a hand dismissively. "It will happen, Rendhart, it will happen. Few people will remember that detail from seven years ago. After this mission is concluded and the war is over, I'll arrange to have you reinstated to the Guild privately. Then we'll give you some high-profile positions, let you ace a couple Kymar competitions, win the Mancery Mayhem cup again, etcetera. With my endorsement, and with your unmatched skills, promoting you to guild master will be quite doable. After all—you are the greatest pyromancer in Imperium, perhaps in the whole empire!"

Durrin ducked under a branch, keeping his eyes ahead of him. Salidar had often given such glowing praise prior to Durrin's fateful mission seven years ago. Back then, it had sounded sincere. Now he saw it for what it was—calculating flattery. Had Salidar always been so manipulative, and Durrin had just gotten wiser? Or had Salidar himself changed?

Either way, it was time to see just where Salidar's priorities lay.

"I learned something else," Durrin said, pausing and looking back at the vizier.

Salidar stopped as well, gazing out at the dark woods around them. "Oh?"

"I heard that the Guild doesn't actually possess Kymar's sixth scroll."

Salidar looked at him sharply. "Who told you that?"

"I have my sources," Durrin said.

"Poppywash," Salidar said. "A baseless rumor meant to discredit the Guild. Or even, perhaps, Elandrian propaganda. If you inform me of the rumor's source, I can ensure its harm doesn't spread."

"My sources will remain anonymous," Durrin said.

Salidar studied him for several seconds. "You've changed, Rendhart," the vizier said eventually. "Ever since the day we set sail, there's been a cloud over you. Tell me. This same source that sought to discredit the Guild: what lies did they have to say about *me*?"

Halorn's words echoed in Durrin's mind. *Salidar is no friend of yours. He has no one's interests in mind except his own. Following him will only lead to pain.*

"Why did you support going to war against Elandria?" Durrin said. "You knew it would be costly."

Salidar resumed walking. The evening was getting darker, so Durrin increased the size of the flame in his hand.

"I saw the writing on the wall a long time ago," Salidar said. "Elandria and Calamar were on a collision course, fighting over resources and influence. Haeber was the biggest flash point. Elandria started reducing haeber shipments about a decade ago, and the shortage in Calamar was beginning to become acute. The Emperor was worried King Everborn would sign an order forbidding *all* haeber exports."

Durrin nodded. The day he had arrived in Saven to make his assault, rumors were spreading in the streets that Everborn would pass such a decree by nightfall. It had been one reason he had struck so hastily.

"Your act of valor thankfully prevented that disastrous decree," Salidar continued. "Everborn's regents, feeling Calamar's sword hanging over them, hastily passed the Guarantee of Trade, making sure haeber still reached our borders. But still, the shipments declined year after year. Tensions frequently flared between our merchants and theirs, and disputes often turned bloody.

"Things finally came to a head three years ago, when their regents ordered that all shipments be cut off entirely. They left us no choice but to invade."

"No choice?" Durrin challenged. "No option other than a long, costly, all-out invasion of their kingdom?"

Salidar stepped over a fallen log. "We had tried negotiations for years. Emperor Stoneclaw was quite resistant to the idea of war. It took a coalition of generals, governors, and members of his own household to convince him that Elandria was no longer a friend. As long as they controlled the trade routes, we would be at their mercy."

"There are other trade routes," Durrin objected. "There's coastal trade through the northern seas, and caravans farther south through Larrisa. Did no haeber arrive through those routes?"

"Not enough," said Salidar. "Nearly thirty million people live in Calamar, Rendhart."

Durrin mulled this over. He had been in Elandria often before his imprisonment. He had seen signs that they themselves were struggling with a haeber shortage. Salidar made it sound like Elandria had acted in malice. But had they? Or was it self-preservation?

Pursuing that line of thought with the Vizier would likely go nowhere, so he shifted topics. "This mission to eliminate Queen Everborn. Is it the emperor's command? Or yours?"

"As high vizier, I represent the emperor's interests," Salidar said.

"That didn't answer my question," Durrin said, turning and facing him. "Did he, or did he not, order you to arrange Queen Everborn's death?"

Salidar stared him in the eyes. "My conversations with His Lordship are sworn to privacy. You should know that."

Durrin folded his arms.

Salidar sighed. "Suffice it to say that I am acting with the same authorization from the emperor that I did seven years ago. Happy?"

So the emperor *was* behind this plot. Durrin switched to the next topic that had been harassing his sleep.

"Now that you and Yorid are on the ship, what is our plan with the Hakiru?"

Salidar paused momentarily and looked back, making sure they were well away from the Hakiru camp. "Are there any sentries close by, Rendhart?"

Durrin swept the area with his pyrosense. "They only have one sentry posted, and he's well out of earshot right now."

Salidar nodded and resumed walking. "Our plans with the pirates remain unchanged. I had briefly thought they could be useful beyond this mission, but Captain Twigly is proving too feisty, and the crew too independent, for them to be trusted long-term. Once Queen Everborn is neutralized and the pirates return us to Calamar, you must eliminate them."

Images flashed through Durrin's mind. Tadgh's friendly handshake. Krizmon and Azura arguing over colors. Twigly's cheeky grin. Line's innocent shrug.

But he knew voicing his qualms to the vizier would accomplish nothing.

"If you insist," Durrin finally said.

They reached the top of the ridgeline. A stiff breeze was blowing, tugging at Durrin's cloak. Through the trees, he could barely make out the silhouette of the next ridge over, a darker black against the star-studded navy blue of the sky. In the valley between the two ridges, Durrin thought he caught a glimpse of a faint light.

Durrin pulled his hood up over his head. "I'm going to patrol our perimeter. Make sure no one is in the area."

"And leave me to bumble back to our camp alone?" Salidar sniffed. "In the dark?"

Durrin found a dead branch in the underbrush and lit its end, offering it to the vizier. "There. Happy?"

Salidar reluctantly took the improvised torch. "If I twist my ankle, it's coming out of your pay."

"Noted."

Durrin started down the far side of the ridge, charting a course toward the distant light. After a few paces, he paused and turned. "Wait . . . you said *Captain* Twigly a minute ago. When did you figure it out?"

"*Please*," said Salidar. "Remember who you're dealing with, Durrin. I knew all along."

CHAPTER 24

FACING THE DARKNESS

Durrin was partway down the ridgeline when he felt the shadow. He sensed it, rather than saw it—a menace behind him, making the hair of his neck stand on end.

He turned with a start, raking his vision across the foliage behind him, flaring the flame in his hand to dispel the shadows of the night.

Nothing.

Nothing he could see, anyway.

He hesitantly turned forward and kept picking his way down the ridge.

He bent his thoughts to Kymar's sixth scroll. This had to be the shrine where it was held. If it was like the first five, the scroll would contain diagrams and figures for a new routine. Notes in the margins would explain how the movements unlocked a new power or energy. What would it be? He had heard tales of Kymar using the routine to generate massive explosive energy. But how—

He whirled around again, certain this time that he had seen something move in the corner of his vision. But again, nothing.

Descending the ridge took forever. The night was nearly completely dark now, with the Near Moon and Far Moon veiled behind clouds. A chill autumn wind blew from the northeast, likely bringing rain in a couple hours. As Durrin drew closer to the shrine, he dared not risk a light, lest it betray his approach. So he pushed cautiously through the dark underbrush, wincing at every rustle he made. The night was chilly, but he found himself sweating, as an irrational sense of haste ate at his gut.

At last he came to the complex. An outer wall, twenty feet high, surrounded a series of buildings inside. He saw no guards. Without bothering to look for a gate, he broke into a run, accelerating over the open ground between the forest and the shrine, then propelled himself up the wall in a surge of pyromancy.

He perched at the top, scanning the complex for guards or sentries. Nothing. Lights shone in several windows, but nobody seemed to be about in the gardens and courtyards. He studied the layout, guessing the purpose of each building. There were the stables, there a kitchen and dining hall, there a set of dorms. One large structure, perfectly circular with a dome for a room, dominated the exact center of the compound. The archives?

Only one way to find out. Durrin leapt off the wall, channeling a blast of heat beneath him to slow his fall, until he landed in an expertly executed tumble. He then stole through the gardens and patios, alert for any sound.

Something dark moved in a portico to his right.

Durrin froze, his hand on the handle of his sword, eyes combing the portico for more movement. After an eternity, he edged forward, then darted into the portico to catch anyone hiding in its shadows.

Nothing.

He shook his head. *Keep moving.*

If he found the scroll, what then? He could return to Salidar, complete the mission, win guild mastership. He would have a secret that no other guild master would have. He would be unstoppable. He could have his revenge.

Was that what he wanted?

Durrin reached a door to the large central structure. Picking the lock in pitch darkness proved nearly impossible, especially since it required two hands so he couldn't summon a flame to light what he was doing. Finally, recalling an old trick, he generated a flame with his breath, crouching so that his fiery exhale illuminated the lock. He had almost run out of patience—and lung support—when the stubborn lock clicked open.

Durrin crept inside, summoning a flame in his hand. Soon he reached a large, circular chamber. The walls were lined with shelves and alcoves, the perfect sizes for scrolls and codices. He stoked the flame in his hand, scattering firelight from his fingers, illuminating . . . nothing.

Every alcove and shelf lay empty.

"No, no, no!" Durrin strode around the room, almost breaking into a run. He shined his light into each nook. Nothing. Just a few discarded scraps of parchment, clay shards from the occasional broken tablet, or empty ink bottles left on scribal tables.

It looked like the archives had been moved—and moved in a hurry. But moved where? And how long ago?

Durrin did another fruitless pass around the room, ending at an ornately carved door. It was set halfway into the floor, accessed by a handful of descending steps. Something drew Durrin to it—some sense of mystery or anticipation.

This door, too, was locked, but it succumbed almost immediately to Durrin's lockpick. It swung open, revealing a curving set of steps, descending downward. Cool, dank air blew past him as it escaped its subterranean confines.

This was ridiculous. The archives had obviously been moved. What did he expect to find? He should slip out before he was discovered, return to Salidar, and focus on completing the upcoming mission.

He flared his light and descended.

The stairs made a half-circle turn, then opened to a large but low-ceilinged chamber built directly underneath the archival room. The ceiling was supported by a forest of vaulted arches, sprouting like branches from rows of columns. The sides of the arches formed a series of nooks around the edge of the room. Each nook contained a large stone box. A sarcophagus.

The entryway bore an inscription:

> *Here lie the fallen of the Everborn House.*
> *May their souls find the light.*

A shiver ran down his spine.

He stood in Elandria's royal crypt.

That same sense of anxious anticipation drove him forward. He crept around the chamber, reading the inscriptions on each tomb. Many names he remembered from his history lessons: Queen Verita, who had expanded Elandria into its western provinces. King Jorman, the longest-reigning king in Elandria's history, dying at a hundred and seven years old. Other names he didn't recognize; princes and princesses who had died before their time, many laid to rest in sarcophagi sized for children.

Finally, he came to the last occupied nook. The inscription here was unsullied by time:

> *King Arvanon Everborn*
> *In peace he reigned.*
> *In flames he perished.*

King Arvanon. The king whose blood had stained Durrin's sword. The king whose piercing blue eyes, devoid of fear, had met Durrin's gaze before his stroke fell.

The king whose daughter was mere days from joining him in this crypt.

Beneath the epigraph was a longer description. Durrin stooped to read it.

Here lies Arvanon, son of Menan and Tiana. Married Queen Mayia of Lindor in his twenty-fifth year. Sired Adara in his twenty-eighth year. Crowned in his twenty-ninth year.

A bringer of peace. Ended the seasonal wars with the Mitrians. Settled a dispute between Larrisa and Marisau. Forged a personal friendship with Emperor Stoneclaw of Calamar. Negotiated with Calamar the Treaty of Everlasting Alliance, signed by Emperor Stoneclaw but never ratified by the Imperial Council.

A peaceful reign, yet a short life filled with grief. Lost a newborn son in his thirty-first year. Lost Queen Mayia to yellow plague in his thirty-sixth year.

In his days arose the great haeber dearth. Implemented rationing during the Long Famine. Negotiated new trade routes through Mitria to raise the dwindling haeber supply. His final royal act, minutes before his death, was to enact the Guarantee of Trade, ensuring continued peace with Calamar.

Fell to sudden flames in his fortieth year.

May angels guard his soul.

"What have I done?" Durrin whispered.

If this inscription was true, then Arvanon was no enemy of Calamar, intent on denying Durrin's homeland of needed resources. This was a leader striking the delicate balance between the demands of his neighbors and the needs of his own people—a man who had devoted his whole life to peace.

And the Guarantee of Trade—it hadn't been signed by co-regents struck with the fear of Calamar in the wake of Durrin's attack. It had been a gesture of peace by Arvanon himself, signed mere moments before Durrin's attack.

What had he done? He had spilled innocent blood. He had allowed himself to become a pawn in Salidar's hand, thrusting their nations closer to devastating war. And he had done it—why? For a seat on the Guild Council? For a mythical scroll?

His thoughts turned to the present. How could he plan to murder a teenager? How could he follow a man who lived a life of intrigue and deception, a man intent on victory in an unjust war? How could Durrin himself have become so cruel, so calloused, so blind?

The shadow—the darkness that had haunted him since sunset—arrived.

It slammed into him, driving him to his knees before King Arvanon's tomb. Overwhelming despair flooded over him, followed by terror and dread and terrible darkness.

What have I done? What have I become?

Memories flashed before his eyes. Meetings, seven years past, with Lord Salidar: missions of an ever more dubious nature, taking him into dark alleyways and secret chambers in far-off lands.

Durrin tried to stand. The world around him tipped. He caught hold of the edge of the sarcophagus to steady himself. Then his arms gave out and he fell flat, prostrate on its cold surface.

How could I have been so blind? He had known. A part of him—the rational, thoughtful part—knew all along that what he was doing was wrong. But another part of him—the part that thought only of himself, that loved to see just how much he could do—saw only the action, the fame, the power.

For years he had waged an unacknowledged war inside himself, until the victory was won, the defeat complete, and the wisest part of his being locked into the deepest recesses of his heart.

But the recent weeks of seeking had given it strength, and now it struggled for dominion.

"I struck before dusk!" he breathed, grasping for something to justify his act. The words were empty. Dusk, dawn, day, night—what did those mean in the face of eternal finalities like good and evil, life and death, justice and fate?

He shivered uncontrollably. Cold? Why did he feel cold? He had not felt this cold since Irongate Isle. He reached inside himself, but where his flame normally burned bright, he found only fear and darkness.

What awaits me?

Strange visions came and went, each lasting only a moment yet seeming to span an eternity. He saw Lord Salidar mocking him in a darkened forest. He saw an avir maiden curled into a ball in a swirling snowstorm, her hair the deep black of utter sadness. He saw a korrik warrior, his face contorted in wrath, his blade raised high.

Durrin gasped and pushed himself upright. He had to get moving— he had to do *something!* He stepped away from the tomb, stumbling in the pitch darkness. He collapsed, shielding his head with his arms.

You are doomed . . .

"I wish I could die," he whispered.

Death . . . In an instant he saw what death would mean. He saw his soul stepping into another dimension, the shell of his body left behind. The Sun shone high; angels filled the sky. One stopped before him. It asked his name. He gave it. The angel unrolled a scroll.

But Durrin already knew what it contained. Dark letters scrawled before his vision, recounting every foul deed, every injustice, every crime. And standing out above them all, the crimson stain of innocent blood.

Doomed.

He saw the angel shudder in horror and fly away. The Sun sank into the undying flames. Night fell. Then he heard the laugh, mocking in triumph; he saw the horns, dipped in blood; the eyes, black as the Void; the claws, stretched out to claim him . . .

You are mine.

"No!" Durrin yelled. He staggered to his feet, but his legs locked up and he fell. A wicked laugh rang in his ears, echoing off the cold walls of the crypt. A shadow seemed to grow before him, stretching from wall to wall, cutting out all light.

He could not move. His tongue was bound. His fingers became talons of stone, rigidly stretched out in unnatural directions. His mind filled with terror and utter despair.

All that remained was a corner of his heart, the portion that he had locked away for most of his life.

Please, he cried, clinging to the brink of utter annihilation. *O Sky Father! Have mercy!*

Darkness closed round him.

A voice pierced the darkness. *"Et ene avara!"*

Light flooded the room. For a moment, Durrin thought he saw a dark shape before him, its foul wings and twisted horns caught in the sudden light. Then it was gone.

"Et ene avara, al Abeam!" The command in the Numinous Tongue came from behind him, from the source of the light. Durrin rolled over, shielding his eyes from the glare.

In the entrance to the vault stood a figure, bathed in light, hands stretched high. The figure's robes shone as if on fire, and power radiated from his being.

Then the figure dropped his hands, and the light faded until Durrin could clearly see his face.

It was Cymer.

CHAPTER 25

FACING THE LIGHT

The old avir stepped quietly forward. No surprise or anger was evident on his face—only the same piercing look from the records room in Irongate Isle.

"Durrin," Cymer said at last. "Arise. Have a seat."

A couple of the stone columns had ledges acting as benches. Durrin numbly rose from the floor and sank down onto one. His head still swam in a sea of emotions, and his muscles felt weak and sore, but the disabling terror and despair had vanished.

Cymer sat on a nearby ledge, facing him. Durrin looked around, puzzled. Cymer hadn't brought any light source with him, but the chamber was lit with a soft glow.

"So," Cymer said. "Do you want to talk?"

A thousand thoughts swirled in Durrin's brain. The truth about Arvanon's reign and the Guarantee of Trade. Halorn's words about the scroll of Durrin's fate. The dark force that had almost destroyed him a moment ago. "I don't know where to begin."

"You broke into a Luminant Order shrine known as the Sanctum of Kings," said Cymer. "You descended into the burial crypt of the royal house of Everborn, came to grips with your conscience, and was emotionally and mentally assaulted by a demon of nearly unspeakable power, bent on your eternal destruction." He smiled slightly. "There. I began for you."

"So the shadow was real?" Durrin asked. "I didn't imagine it?"

"The demon was real," Cymer said. "But not corporal. It did not step through the curtain of sight to inhabit the physical realm. If it had, you and I would likely be dead right now. No, it stayed in the unseen realm. But the depth of your terror allowed you to glimpse its form for a moment."

Durrin stared at the spot where he had seen the shadow. "So everything Halorn said . . . is real," he murmured.

He looked to King Everborn's sarcophagus, then back to Cymer. "The Guarantee of Trade. Why was it revoked three years ago?"

Cymer stood and strode over to the king's burial place. "Each year, the haeber shortage became more severe. We barely had enough for ourselves, much less enough to meet Calamar's needs. But King Arvanon had left a legacy of peace, and our regents did all they could to follow in his footsteps."

"The war hawks in Calamar, however, were relentless. Clashes between merchants became ever more frequent, and Calamar moved more and more battalions to the border. At last, our regents concluded that war was inevitable—and it no longer made sense to sell to our enemies what we needed so badly at home."

Cymer ran a hand over the lid of the sarcophagus. "Our regents were never able to build a relationship with Emperor Stoneclaw. If King Arvanon had still been alive . . . who knows. History is full of what-ifs."

Durrin stared at his hands. Salidar had lied to him and used him. But Durrin held a fair share of the blame. He had lived in Elandria for many months. He had heard of Arvanon's character and knew his reputation among his people for being a peacemaker. But Durrin's insatiable quest for power had muted both his conscience and his reason.

"Cymer—am I doomed?"

"Doomed how?"

"The stain of blood on the scroll of my fate—can that ever be erased? Or is my soul inescapably condemned to the Void?"

He looked up and met the avir's gaze. Cymer stared at him for a long moment, his eyes seeming to pierce to the center of Durrin's being.

"You are not doomed," the avir said at last. "Not yet."

Something kindled in Durrin's chest. It was a fire unlike any he had felt before. *Hope.*

"What must I do?"

"You must change," Cymer said. "You must fix what you have broken. You must replace darkness with light, conflict with peace, hatred with friendship. It will not be easy."

Durrin cast his thoughts to the war gripping both Calamar and Elandria, the thousands in danger of their lives, the millions suffering from famine and deprivation—and the queen in mortal peril.

"Where do I begin?"

"Your heart knows already," said Cymer. "Listen to it."

Chapter 26

You're Welcome

"A pox upon this rain," Twigly muttered. She struck her flint and steel together again, but the sparks failed to ignite the wet grass she was using for kindling. In the last twenty minutes, each member of the crew and tried and failed to start a fire amid the morning's intermittent rain. Breakfast needed cooked, and everyone was getting hungry.

From the edge of the camp, a certain stuck-up Calamarvan nobleman sniffed. "I hope your crew is more competent at kidnapping than at lighting a fire," he said.

"You're welcome to take a turn trying," Twigly said, deliberately catching his gaze. Oh, how she *loved* seeing him bristle when she did that. "If you succeed, maybe we'll make you the ship's cook."

The sound of rustling caused Salidar, Twigly, and the other pirates to look up. The bushes parted as Augerclaw, a swifter that Twigly had posted as sentry, padded into view, his fur glistening with the rain.

"Rendhart is finally returning," Augerclaw reported in Hakiru, as Twigly translated for the vizier. "But he's changed."

"What do you mean, *changed?*" the Calamarvan said, a hint of alarm in his voice.

"He smells . . . different. Yesterday, he reeked of confusion. Now he smells of resolve."

It took Twigly a moment to get a good translation across to the nobleman. Changing Hakiru into Lurrian felt somewhat akin to forcing a cat to take a bath. Once she did, though, Salidar's gaze darkened. "I feared this might happen," he said.

"What?" Twigly asked.

"Durrin has turned against us. He's been acting strangely ever since this voyage started. It's likely one of my opponents found him back in

Imperium and offered a substantial price on my head, and he's finally decided to make good on it."

"Are you sure?" Twigly asked. "That's quite a lot of assumptions you're jumping to."

Salidar nodded. "Nearly. I'll confront him in a moment and find out for sure."

Prancing pumpernickel. Losing Durrin would be a shame. He had become a handy crew member to have around, despite his implacably grim demeanor.

Twigly put a hand to her dirk. "Should I ready the crew for an ambush, then?"

"That won't be necessary," Salidar said. "He'd only see it coming. We only need one." He gestured to his constantly grumpy steward. "Yorid, get in those bushes with your arrows. Keep your scope on Rendhart and fire on my command."

Yorid's scowl deepened. "Are you sure I'm enough, Your Excellency? This is *Rendhart*."

"Then use a voidstone arrow," Salidar said. *Ah, clever.* Weapons tipped with voidstone would rip through any mancery used to deflect or block them.

Salidar's answer didn't seem to fully satisfy Yorid, but he stomped off to do as he'd been told.

Twigly watched the steward retrieve his bow and quiver. "What is the command?" she asked.

"There are three," Salidar said. "If I say, 'I'd be careful if I were you,' Yorid will fire a warning shot. If I say, 'Let me teach you a lesson,' he'll aim to injure. And if I say, 'You have been warned,' he'll aim to kill."

Twigly turned the phrases over in her head. "Useful. Nefarious. I'm borrowing them."

At that moment, Augerclaw sat up on his hind legs and growled an alarm. Twigly turned to see a red cape slashing through the mist.

"Here he comes," Twigly said.

After leaving Cymer, Durrin had found a sheltered grotto and caught a couple hours of sleep. The ground had been hard and cold, but for the first time in days, he had slept without nightmares. The rain had awoken him.

Throughout the hike back over the ridge to the Hakiru camp, Durrin had sorted through the rush of emotions still lingering from the night before. The guilt. The despair. The creeping horror. The shock. The regret. The glimmer of hope.

And he had settled on a plan.

As Durrin strode into the pirates' campsite, he felt a tension that had not been there the night before. No laughter or raucous talk filled the air. The pirates sat around, all absorbed in various tasks. Too absorbed—he'd never seen them so disciplined. His eyes slid over the campsite, counting bodies. He came up short by one.

Between him and the unlit campfire stood Salidar. The nobleman seemed absorbed in throwing darts into a nearby tree trunk. Three darts embedded in the same knothole attested to his impressive accuracy.

Salidar spoke, not bothering to turn from his game. "I was a little concerned that you'd been captured or killed, Durrin," he said. "You were gone the whole night."

Durrin drove straight to the point. "I've decided that I cannot continue as part of your expedition, Your Excellency."

Lord Salidar slowly pivoted. "A most curious turn of events," he said, running a finger along the shaft of the dart in his hand. "I was never informed that anyone back in Imperium had given you a counteroffer. How much are they paying you?"

Did this man think only of money and politics? "It isn't about the rewards, Your Excellency," Durrin said. He retrieved his pack from a pile of gear, conscious of the rest of the pirates watching their conversation closely. "I took a leader from Elandria once. I will not do it again."

Salidar turned back to his game of darts. "Ah, I see now. Don't worry—I'm sure you'll get over your cold feet by nightfall."

Durrin took a step closer, until he had Salidar's attention. "Did you know this whole time who *really* signed the Guarantee of Trade?" he growled.

The shock instead of confusion in Salidar's eyes told him the truth.

"I caused a needless war!" Durrin yelled in the vizier's face. "If King Everborn were still alive, he and Emperor Stoneclaw would be at peace. Haeber would still be flowing over our borders. My classmates would still be alive!"

Salidar stepped backward, drawing himself up to his full height. "Elandria and Calamar were destined to collide. If we had not pursued war on our terms, it would have come on theirs."

Durrin shook his head. "Don't pretend you're impartial in all this. How many thousands of shekels have flowed from Elandrian treasuries into Aram Family coffers? How many of your minions have you rewarded with a cushy post as an occupying governor? How many triumphal parades have you thrown in your own honor with the spoils of a conquered people?"

Salidar parted his lips to show teeth clenched with fury. "You accuse *me* of using violence to further my own interests? Perhaps it's time to look in the mirror."

"I did," Durrin said.

Salidar studied him for a few seconds. "So you refuse to finish your role in this expedition. What will you do instead?"

Durrin checked his bag to make sure his gear and rations were still inside. "I'm leaving. I'm never returning to Calamar—or Elandria for that matter."

Mitria. That was the destination he had settled on that morning. He knew the culture, the language. They would accept him. He could leave behind the corruption of the Guild, renounce the crimes of his past, cut all his ties with Salidar and the war. He could start over. He could build a new life—just as Halorn had.

The vizier tutted, turning back to his game of darts. "Really? You know, it's a shame to think of Kymar's scroll sitting in the Guild's vault, lying unread all these years. So much knowledge never gained. Power never unleashed."

"You and I both know that their vault never held such a scroll," Durrin snapped. "And even if it did, I will not sell my integrity again."

The nobleman turned, his eyes suddenly alight. He stabbed a dart into a stump beside him. "Your integrity? You are one to talk about *integrity* on the day you abandon a critical mission for your people. Have seven years of confinement stripped you of your sense of honor? Remember that Calamar is your country. Every year this war drags on is another year our countrymen die on the battlefield."

Durrin shouldered his pack. "Then tell your diplomats to *end this war!* Have we not conquered enough? Have we not enacted revenge tenfold for any offense Elandria has committed?"

"Elandria is a threat," Salidar said. "Until we control the haeber routes directly, we will always be at their mercy. This war can only end with their annexation."

"You know that's not true," Durrin countered. "You began this war because you wanted power and glory. Well, now you have it—at the blood price of thousands upon thousands of *my* countrymen!"

Salidar drew back. "You know not of what you speak, Rendhart," he hissed. "You did not visit the Northern Provinces five years ago when the famine there grew fierce. You did not see your people cry for food as they perished with hunger. You did not see their children lie starving in the streets!"

"And war is the answer?" Durrin said. "Exchange the misery of our people with the death and bondage of another?"

"If that is what it takes, then yes."

Durrin stepped back, surprised at how openly Salidar had answered.

The vizier's voice softened. "Regardless of its cause, Durrin, the war has come. Nothing can change that now. Whatever your feelings toward it, it will run to its foregone conclusion. What you must decide is whether you will prove a hero to your country, or a traitor."

Once again, the memory of a sword red with a king's blood flashed through Durrin's mind.

"By promoting an unjust war, I betray my country enough," Durrin said.

Salidar's eyes shifted to shrewd calculation. "If you want this war to end so badly, Rendhart, then see this mission through. A leaderless Elandria would surrender quickly, and then the bloodshed you seem to hate so much would be over."

"As I said, I cannot continue with your expedition," Durrin said. "I will not. It is wrong."

"So instead you will run?" Salidar's voice turned to a sneer. "As if you could hide from your crimes in a new land? Oh, no, Durrin." A cold laugh escaped from Salidar's lips. "You cannot escape your past so easily. You must finish the job you started. You must face, not flee, your fears."

Durrin listened to that laugh echo inside him. And he realized Salidar was right. The shadow that pursued him could not be escaped in Mitria. It could not be escaped at the very edge of the world. The demons would always be there, waiting for his death. Flight was futile—which left him two choices.

He could carry through with Salidar's mission, bring about the young queen's demise, and return to Calamar. He could join the guild masters and continue honing his skills. He could achieve greatness, power, fame, and wealth—everything he had ever wanted, short of Kymar's scroll . . . all the while ignoring the shadow lurking in the night, ready to claim his soul the moment he crossed death's door.

Or he could betray his country, find a horse, ride to Saven that very day, and raise the alarm before Salidar could strike.

Durrin wavered on the brink of choice.

Then the memory of the horror in the vault came vividly to his mind, and with perfect clarity he saw that all the fame of the world was but nothing compared to the glory or misery of the hereafter.

He turned his back on Salidar. "I'm leaving."

"Do you think you can just walk away?" Salidar's voice came behind him. "You know too much of our plans. If you were captured and interrogated, our cover would be blown."

Durrin stopped. Those words were not a protest. Out of Salidar's mouth, they constituted a threat. Something played in the back of his mind . . .

The missing member of the camp! Yorid. Durrin reached out with his pyrosense, searching for the man's spark. There it was. Yorid was hidden twenty yards to Durrin's left, where the early morning shadows grew thick under the trees. Durrin could feel the energy building as a yew bow was pulled back. But why hadn't he noticed the archer before? The spark was subdued, as if . . .

Of course. Voidstone. He'd seen some of Yorid's arrows tipped with it. The voidstone was disrupting his pyrosense, muting the vibrations from that direction. Stars, that would make this trickier.

"I am a free man," Durrin called over his shoulder. He began twirling his fingers. "Who is going to stop me?"

"You have been warned," Lord Salidar said.

Durrin twisted to the side, dropped into a crouch, and launched a bolt of fire to his left. An arrow whizzed by his ear, the same spot where his heart had been a moment before. For an instant, his firebolt illuminated Yorid, hidden in the underbrush. Then it connected with the top of Yorid's bow in a blast of heat and sparks, singeing the wood and snapping the rawhide bowstring.

Spinning back to face the camp, Durrin lifted a hand, anticipating the next attack. His fingers snapped closed, snatching a dart out of midair moments before it buried its tip into his neck. Salidar, arm still outstretched from his throw, widened his eyes in surprise and anger.

Durrin examined the pure black point, daubed with a green paste. "Voidstone *and* poison? You have high-end darts."

"Get him!" Salidar hissed. Twigly barked an order in Hakiru, and the camp exploded as the pirates leapt to their feet, reaching for weapons.

Dropping the dart, Durrin swept his hands in a wide arc, summoning a crackling orb of fire and holding it above his head. "No one move another inch!" he bellowed. "Or His Excellency dies here and now!"

The camp froze. Some things didn't need to be translated.

Salidar glanced between the pirates and the fireball in Durrin's hands. "Drop your weapons," he ordered, eyes brimming with anger as he stared at Durrin. "Rendhart has bested me this time."

Twigly translated, and the Hakiru reluctantly set down their weapons and took several steps back. Durrin barked an order and Yorid joined them.

Satisfied, Durrin let the fireball in his hands fade, the heat escaping into the sky with a shimmer. He shot Salidar one last look. "I'm leaving. Forever. Don't try to stop me this time."

Durrin turned away. As he stepped into the trees, Lord Salidar muttered something behind him. Durrin turned. "What was that?"

Lord Salidar had his arm outstretched. ". . . *ai'n enima akura-enojim*," he said, finishing the phrase in the Numinous Tongue. What was he doing? Lord Salidar was no verbomancer. But why else would he be—

Too late, Durrin felt the air around him shimmering with power. Before he could react, the air froze around him, holding him in an invisible casing. He couldn't move his arms to summon fire. He couldn't move his head. He couldn't even wiggle a finger.

Hmm. This was new.

Striding forward, Lord Salidar laughed and spat in Durrin's face. The spittle impacted the invisible shell around him and dripped onto the ground. "Arrogant pyromancer!" Salidar snarled. His voice came muffled through the solidified air. "Where's the power in channeling motion when you can't move?"

Durrin tried to take a breath, but his ribcage only expanded a few fractions of a hair, just enough to deliver a smidgeon of fresh air to his lungs. He tried to speak, but his open mouth wouldn't move.

"You now know one of my closest secrets: my verbomantic abilities," Lord Salidar continued. "I've secretly been developing my skills for decades—for just an occasion such as this."

Durrin stopped listening. Instead, he reached out with his mind, testing the chords of energy binding the air around him. Verbomancy was a tricky kind of magic. It took its power from the words of the Numinous Tongue, operating more as an idea than a force. The vibrations from Salidar's incantation still reverberated in the air, their waves contouring around Durrin's body, holding the air around him perfectly still, hard as iron.

Durrin would have smirked if he could move his mouth. Iron could be broken.

He reached inside himself to his inner fire. It was already raging, spurred by the condescension in Lord Salidar's voice. He stoked it, feeling himself grow hot, vibrating with energy.

Now he needed momentum. His arms and legs couldn't move, but they weren't his only muscles. He focused on his heart, willing it into a faster rhythm until it pounded inside his chest. The internal energy began to build, momentum and heat together, like a tea kettle under pressure. Finally, he let the energy escape, silently puncturing holes in the verbomantic shell around him. He eagerly let his ribcage expand, taking a much-needed breath,

". . . which means you have two options," Lord Salidar was saying. "You can tell me who you're really serving, or Twigly here will have to choose which crew member will kill you."

"A tough choice," Durrin said.

"Indeed," Lord Salidar agreed. Then his eyes widened as he realized Durrin had moved his mouth.

Durrin let the energy explode outward, cracking the air around him into a million shards and scattering the last vestiges of Salidar's verbomancy. Lord Salidar stumbled backward, shouting as the hems of his robe caught fire from the residual heat.

The pirates, who had been watching the exchange with wide eyes, rushed forward to retrieve their weapons and come to the vizier's aid. Before they drew near, however, Durrin swept his hands in a circle and summoned another fireball.

Shouting warnings, the pirates hit the dirt. Salidar cowered on the ground, finishing his incantation—from the feel of things, it was a spell to solidify a shield of air in front of him.

Durrin surveyed his options, then launched the ball of flame high into the air. It arced across the clearing, spinning off tiny licks of flames in all directions, before slamming into the wet tent of firewood in the middle of the campsite, instantly turning it into a raging campfire.

Durrin strode away into the mist. "You're welcome."

Chapter 27

Warnings and Reactions

Later that day.

A bell tinkled as the door to the Dozy Donkey swung open. The red-headed avir at the counter looked up disinterestedly. Then his eyes widened. "You!"

"Me," said Durrin. He dropped a chunk of silver on the counter. "Twenty shekels—what I owe you for the horse, plus interest."

Before the avir could form a response, Durrin turned and strode back out the door.

Adara tapped her foot in the antechamber outside Volthorn's office, looking around. *So this is what it's like to be kept waiting,* she thought. As the only child of royalty, she had normally commanded the instant attention of anyone she needed to talk to.

Sighing, Adara surveyed the smattering of military personnel in the room. They sat nervously at various tables around her, scribbling their way through paperwork. As in many bookkeeping jobs—where size or strength didn't matter—most of them were snippens. They seemed to be doing their very best to look busy and professional with their monarch in the room.

A soldier exited Volthorn's office and bowed low. "The commander is ready now, Your Majesty."

"Thank you, Captain," Adara said, giving a slight nod as she walked past him. It occurred to her that she actually wasn't certain of his exact rank. Interpreting military insignia had never been her strong suit.

Volthorn greeted her inside, showing her the best chair in the room. "Your Majesty," he said, sounding flustered. "I must apologize. As you know, I just arrived after a long ride, and I needed a few minutes to clean up and change my uniform—"

Adara held up a hand. "Please, Commander. It's all right. Waiting won't kill me."

It was a funny thing to say. The sense of urgency and danger from the night before had stayed with her since she'd woken up. All day, as she had waited for Volthorn to arrive at the capital, she had failed to shake the feeling that yes, too much waiting *could* put her very life at risk.

Volthorn sat down behind a large desk, clearing away a smattering of parchments. "What do you need, Your Majesty?"

"I'm concerned about my quarters in the royal wing," Adara said. "I would like to be moved to another part of the palace."

Volthorn frowned, leaning forward. "What, exactly, is your concern?"

"I feel too exposed," Adara said. "I'm in an isolated tower, surrounded by open sky. It just feels . . ." She paused, wondering if she should tell Volthorn about her nightmare. Would he think she was acting out of paranoia? ". . . It just feels wrong," she finished. "Unsafe."

Volthorn nodded slowly, drumming his claws on the table. "I see. But I must reassure you, Your Highness. You're in the royal wing for a reason— not just because of the four-poster feather bed. It's by far the most secure part of the palace. The wing is built at the tallest edge of the acropolis, meaning besides the forty-foot walls of your tower, there's another forty to fifty feet of nearly sheer cliffs beneath that. There's only two entrances to the entire wing, and three guarded checkpoints to get to your quarters. The windows in your room are tempered glass reinforced with iron bars, with voidstone inlays to protect them from magical assault."

Volthorn shifted in his chair. "Now let's compare that to the rest of the palace. Passages and staircases are everywhere. Security is loose at night and nearly unmanageable during the day. Servants and visitors are constantly coming in and out. None of the windows are enforced with voidstone. Only the treasury is heavily secured, and that's hardly a place for a queen to sleep, Your Highness."

Adara frowned. Volthorn's points made sense—but they failed to quench the gnawing worry inside her. "It still doesn't feel right, Commander. It's hard to put into words, but I would feel far more comfortable spending a couple nights away from my usual quarters."

Volthorn leaned back, absently scratching his scalp as he thought. Finally, he straightened. "Your Highness. You know how much your safety means to me. Perhaps *you* would feel more at ease somewhere else—but *I* would not. And neither would my officers. We have had many discussions about ensuring your safety. So please trust me on this one."

Adara studied the sincerity and concern on Volthorn's face. Perhaps he was right. Perhaps she was letting her nightmare, and the emotions from it, cloud her judgment.

"Very well," Adara said. She cracked a smile. "Besides—I do like that feather bed."

"It's better than the hard ground, believe me." Volthorn rose to his feet. "Is that all, Your Highness?"

Your Majesty, Adara silently corrected. "Your Highness" had been her title while she was a princess. Some of her advisors and officers still used it occasionally out of habit.

"That's all for today," Adara said, rising as well. "We'll have many meetings later, I'm sure."

Volthorn opened the door for her, and she stepped out. The room beyond was even more crowded than before, as a griffin messenger had arrived, escorted by an intelligence officer. They both bowed deeply to Adara before entering Volthorn's office.

Poor Commander Skarr, Adara thought, watching as Volthorn admitted the new arrivals and closed the door. *He's probably even busier than I am.*

"Ready, Your Majesty?" one of her two bodyguards asked.

Adara nodded, and the guards escorted her from the room, one in front of her and the other behind. Since her coronation, she had grown used to having a constant bodyguard.

In the corridor outside, Adara and her escorts bumped into a band of six soldiers coming the opposite direction. Amid the soldiers strode a tall man clad in chainmail armor and a long sable cloak.

Adara paused, studying him. His face was unfamiliar—this was no guard or servant from the palace. His boots and the hem of his cloak were caked in mud. But it was his bearing that most caught her eye: the way he carried himself, with confidence and vigor, and with purpose in his grim face. He seemed a battle-worn hero come to life from an ancient epic.

The other party stopped well short of them. The soldier in the lead bowed low, voiding a greeting, but the others only briefly nodded, their attention flicking between Adara and the man they were escorting.

Adara caught the gaze of the tall man. As he noticed her crown and robes, a look of surprise flashed across his face, and he dropped to one knee, bowing his head low.

"What do we have here, Captain?" Adara asked, genuinely curious.

"Just a man with a message for Commander Skarr, Your Majesty," the lead soldier said. "I apologize for delaying you."

"It's all right," said Adara. She couldn't put her finger on exactly why, but something about this man had piqued her curiosity. The guards around him looked uneasy and on edge. But although he looked like a capable warrior, she didn't feel like he posed a threat.

"Who are you?" Adara asked, directing her voice at the kneeling man.

The man hesitated. "Durrin," he finally said.

"You look like you've done a lot of traveling today, Durrin."

He nodded. "The rain has been incessant."

"You traveled far?"

"Around forty-five miles, Your Majesty."

Forty-five miles? In the pouring rain? He must have been driving his horse hard the whole day. "What brought you?" Adara asked.

The man glanced to either side at the soldiers around him. He hesitated for a moment, his mouth open but no words coming out. Before he found a reply, the officer answered for him.

"He has an urgent message for our commander, Your Majesty. Now with your excusal, we won't take up any more of your time."

The officer moved to pass them, but the tall man stayed where he was, still on one knee. "With your permission, Lieutenant," Durrin said, "I'd like to say something to Her Majesty."

The soldier paused, obviously uncomfortable with the request but unsure how to handle it. He looked in Adara's direction, and she held up a hand reassuringly. "Let him talk."

"Your Majesty . . ." The man paused again for several seconds, then continued. ". . . You look very much like your father."

Adara smiled in surprise. "You knew my father?"

The man shook his head quickly. "I did not know him. I only met him. Once. Right before he died. Your Majesty." He paused for a very long time, then continued more slowly, "I'm sorry about your father. Deeply, truly sorry."

Adara had been hearing condoling remarks about her father's death for seven years. Some were sincere, some were not. Some, from close advisors in the days after the accident, had been as charged with emotion as her own poignant feelings. Others, especially from those outside the royal court, were nothing more than meaningless social gestures upon meeting her. That last type had become more and more common over the years. She had come to hate them.

Yet this comment was different from all the others. Yes, it was sincere, but it was something more: this man had an intensity of feeling behind the words, packing each syllable with emotional weight. His voice trembled, as if burdened by the message he was at long last delivering. It was more than a mere condolence. It almost seemed an apology.

"Thank you," Adara said with a tiny voice. She wasn't sure what else to say.

The lieutenant broke the spell with an impressively loud *harrumph*.

The man bowed until his head nearly reached the floor. "Farewell, Your Majesty," he said, before rising to his feet and letting the soldiers sweep him away.

Adara watched them disappear into Volthorn's antechamber. The exchange had stirred within her a strange collection of curiosity, nervousness, and loss. Her heart prodded her to turn back and hear what "urgent message" this hero out of legend bore. But she had business to attend to, tasks to complete, and a kingdom to run. Surely Volthorn could handle it.

Durrin mentally kicked himself in the shins. *Coward!*

He had blown his chance. The queen had been right in front of him. He could have exposed Salidar's plot to her directly.

But he had barely been able to speak. To be confronted by the daughter of the man he had murdered—the girl that he had, less than a day before, been planning to assassinate as well—had left him entirely undone. It had been all he could do to stumble out a half-collected apology.

Pull yourself together. He was about to tell Elandria's chief commander about the plot. Surely that would suffice.

The soldiers around him obviously distrusted him. With his keen hearing, he had overheard every whispered conversation about him since he had arrived at Saven. First the officers at the gate, then the officers at a city command post, then the officers at the palace entrance had all agreed with each other—presumably out of earshot—that this was the "fugitive pyromancer" who had "escaped" from Irongate Isle. It hadn't occurred to anyone yet that Durrin, by giving his actual name, was clearly making no attempt to conceal his identity. Soldiers.

Word had apparently preceded him. The antechamber was a bundle of nerves, with every soldier, officer, and scribe in the room maintaining an uneasy, ever-vigilant silence. What did they think he would do? Take on a dozen opponents in a confined space?

Come to think of it, that did sound like him.

The lieutenant emerged from the commander's office. "You will be seen now," he grunted. He turned to the other soldiers. "Alone."

Durrin felt the many pairs of eyes boring into his back as he strode into the commander's room.

"Sit down, Rendhart," said a cold voice.

Durrin sized up the korrik sitting at the desk. He was short—of course—but stocky, as solid as the earth. Every inch of him, from his scuffed boots to the deep scar on his face, conveyed a battle-hardened veteran. The jeweled rings on his fingers identified him as a terramancer.

Once the door had shut, Durrin cleared his throat. "I am told you are Chief Commander Volthorn Skarr."

"Do you need to be told?" The korrik leaned forward over his desk, his eyes like daggers. "Do you not remember me, Rendhart?"

Durrin studied him, confused. Had this korrik worked at Irongate Isle?

The commander gestured to his face. "You left me this scar as a permanent token of my failure."

The memory clicked. The captain at the palace. The head of the royal guard, whom Durrin had almost killed seven years before with a spear to the face. Durrin's heart sank.

Commander Skarr leaned back in his chair. "I'm curious to hear why you've returned."

"I've come to warn you," Durrin said. "Her Majesty's life is in danger."

"Oh?" said the korrik, raising a scaly eyebrow.

"Listen to me," Durrin pleaded.

Swiftly, Durrin described Lord Salidar's plot, the voyage of the Hakiru pirates, his defection, and the planned assault on the palace. As Durrin spoke, Commander Skarr leaned forward, listening to every word, his eyes never leaving Durrin's face.

"I don't think they know I got here already," Durrin concluded. "If you move the queen to another part of the city, then fill the royal wing with soldiers and griffins, you can catch them by surprise and overwhelm them."

The korrik nodded his head slowly, thoughtfully. "And why exactly, Rendhart, did you decide to warn me?"

Durrin met the korrik's gaze without flinching. "Because I realize now that Calamar's war is unjust. I now understand that what I did seven years ago was deeply, horribly wrong. And I want to set things right."

The korrik studied Durrin for a long time. Finally, after what seemed like an age, Volthorn stirred and learned back in his chair. He cracked his knuckles loudly, then began to clap his hands together. "Nice story, Rendhart."

Durrin's heart sunk. "You don't believe me."

"How can I? The logical flaws are glaring. That Lord Salidar may plot such an escapade, I can believe. But to lead the expedition himself? Entrust his life in the hands of a band of lawless Hakiru, much less run the risk of discovery and failure? Not to mention the foolishness of leaving Imperium and risking the unraveling of the elaborate political web he's built for three decades? Highly unlikely."

"I swear by my life I speak the truth."

Volthorn waved away the oath. "There's more. You expect me to believe that a cloudship has deviated from the normal trade routes and flown to within forty miles of here, without a single griffin patrol seeing it?"

"Who would think to report it? The Hakiru have never posed a threat before."

The korrik chuckled softly, shaking his head. "This is really too much, Rendhart. You can stop trying."

"Trying what?"

"Trying to hoodwink me with this fabrication. It's not working. I must admit, your audacity was ambitious—to come yourself, to lay your biggest card on the table, to tell a story so ludicrous I would be forced to consider it true. But I am no simpleton. You mean to divert me, to tie up precious resources in a vain pursuit."

"A vain pursuit?" Durrin hit the table with his fist, creating a brief flash of fire. "Protecting the queen is a vain pursuit?"

"Massing our whole garrison in the royal wing would be," Volthorn said, his eyes shining. "I see through your plan, Rendhart, thought it was well-crafted. You knew my history. You knew my desire to protect the queen. So with a cryptic, planted message, and now by coming in person, you seek to manipulate me into a foolhardy misallocation of resources. Tell me where your team is actually planning to strike. One of the city gates? The treasury? General acts of arson in the streets?"

"A cryptic, planted message?" Durrin said, confused. "Commander, I swear—"

"Why should I believe a single word you say?" Volthorn nearly spat. "You are a spy and a murderer!"

The words cut to Durrin's core—because he knew they were true.

"Please. Believe me."

The unspoken answer was written plain as day in the korrik's frigid gaze. *Never.*

After several seconds, Volthorn leaned back. "On another note, Rendhart, it's convenient that you turned yourself in."

Fire began to rise in Durrin's chest. "So you'll arrest me? For trying to warn you?"

"No," Volthorn said. "I will arrest you for escaping imprisonment."

"I was set free! By your own chief magistrate!"

Volthorn waved a hand. "He acted without authorization. It's time you finished paying for your crimes."

The fire was raging now. Durrin rose to his feet, sending his chair clattering. "I am a free man. I will defend my right to remain so."

Volthorn stood as well, rising like a surging pile of rock. His armor began to glow as he filled it with terracharge from the gems on his belt. "Perfect. Resist arrest, then. Give me an excuse to kill you."

Durrin let a single lick of fire escape his mouth. Inside, he shook, a volcano about to erupt. He leaned into the korrik's face. "Think very, very carefully about what you're about to do." With a snap of his fingers, he summoned a white-hot flame in his hand. "If I wanted to, I could burn this palace to the ground."

Volthorn didn't blink. "Nudisa semir colem tol," he replied, using a common saying in the Numinous Tongue. *Justice always claims its own.*

For a moment they stood there: the korrik, terramancer of Elandria, stoic and defiant, his armor glowing with power; Durrin, pyromancer of Calamar, tense and quivering, his eyes flaming pits of fire.

They balanced on the scales of choice.

Five seconds passed. Ten.

Then slowly, slowly, Volthorn stepped away. "I will have you escorted out of the province and released. It's more than you deserve."

Durrin let the flame in his hand die, but he still trembled with anger. "You're making a mistake. Salidar will attack tonight. Listen to me!"

"No!" Volthorn snapped. "Do not test my patience again, murderer. Or my mercy."

Durrin stared at him, fire still coursing through his veins. "Very well," he whispered. "Then the blame for tonight will fall entirely upon your head."

CHAPTER 28

ATTACK

Twigly and her crew struck halfway through the second watch.

Their cloudship dropped through the night sky, their fire pan covered to let the air in their balloon cool and shrink. Twigly leaned over the side, gauging the distance between them and the palace lights below. Two hundred yards. One hundred and seventy. One hundred and fifty.

"Steady!" she barked.

Line uncovered the fire pan, letting heat rise back into the balloon. Its downward acceleration slowed, but it was still descending. Rapidly.

Twigly studied the pattern of lights and shadows beneath her. Jutting out from the main palace complex was a large, round tower, connected by a long walkway: the royal wing. That was their target, a tower barely fifty feet wide. If they missed that, it was a long way down to the base of the acropolis.

"Tracking line, deploy!"

Azura and Krizmon unlocked a winch, letting a rope rapidly uncoil from its spool. The end already hung off the side, tied to a wickedly large grappling hook. Grimbo perched on top, ready to hook it fast upon contact. He carried a handful of terramantic contraptions that he had assured her would work this time. They had better. She didn't want another woodpecker fiasco.

One hundred yards. Their fall was slowing as they descended into thicker air. But the timing would still be as finicky as petting a hedgehog.

The rope, hook, and gadget-obsessed snippen had all become lost in the darkness. Briefly, Twigly saw a shadow block out some of the lights below her. That would be Bladebeak, grabbing the rope in his beak to guide it toward its target.

"A hair to the left!" Twigly barked. Tadgh turned the tiller, which rotated a large fin extending behind the ship. She felt the gondola slip slightly to the left in response.

"Seventy yards," she called.

The korriks at the winch applied a brake, slowing the rope's release. "Mark fifty," Azura shouted as a black band on the rope flashed past. "Fifty-five."

A *clack* sounded far below—the sound of metal colliding with roof tile. Twigly leaned over the edge, holding her breath. She'd misjudged the distance by a dozen yards.

A shout in Lurrian broke the night air. "What was that? Who's there?"

Forty yards.

"Reel it in," Twigly said, softer this time. "Keep it taut." She noted the angle of the rope extending from the rail. "A pinch to the right."

Thirty yards.

No more sounds came from below. In the night, the rope would be nearly invisible. And no one ever thought to look up.

Twenty-five. She could see their target clearly now, illuminated by the light of the Far Moon as it flitted between clouds. The royal wing was built like a three-layer cake, three concentric towers stacked on top of each other. The topmost tower, little more than a turret, was just a watch post. She knew from Durrin's schematics that the middle tower had two floors, with the queen's bedchambers on the upper floor and her offices on the lower. The third tower, forming the base of the cake, held peripheral offices and storage. The lower two towers had flat tops, patios with crenelated parapets.

Twigly could see two guards, one on the lower patio and one on the upper. *Only two*—that was a relief. There were more inside, undoubtedly, but two for starters wasn't bad. Maybe her crew could even pull this off without killing anyone. She knew the Hakiru lacked her religious qualms about killing at night. But that didn't make her qualms any less persistent. And no one on her crew wanted unnecessary bloodshed.

Twenty yards.

Twigly raised her paw to her mouth and sounded a shrill whistle. The two guards on the tower both looked up, their alarmed expressions flashing in the light of the lumen lanterns they carried. Then Bladebeak slammed into one, slicing through the darkness without warning. Grimbo jumped onto the other from above, pouring orange terracharge from his fingers into the guard's armor. The guard's movements seized up as his armor locked around him, and he toppled to the ground.

Would you look at that? Grimbo's idea actually worked.

Fifteen yards.

"Anchors away!" Twigly cried.

Krizmon and Azura knocked two more winches loose, and the ship shuddered upward as it was relieved of two iron anchors, each weighing a hundred pounds. They crashed into the stonework below in a chorus of thunderous clangs. If the assault so far had gone unnoticed, that advantage had now ended.

"Over the side!" Twigly shouted, leading the way. Adrenaline spiked in her veins as she wrapped her limbs and tail around one of the anchor ropes, sliding down at a furious but controlled pace. As she approached the top of the lower tower, she drew a long dirk from her belt and stuck it between her teeth.

Pyromancer or no pyromancer on their side, it was time to capture royalty.

A resounding smash shattered Adara's dreams.

She bolted upright in bed, heart pounding. Another smash sounded. The whole room shook from the impact.

What was going on?

Adara slipped out of bed and ran to one of her bedroom windows. Shouts came from outside. A shape flashed past her window, making her start in surprise. A second shape followed a moment later—it looked like a humanoid figure, sliding downward on a rope. The shouts outside multiplied, joined by the clash of metal on metal.

An attack!

The words of her nightmare resounded in her memory: "*An avir's life is in peril. To the skies, beware!*"

Someone pounded on the door to her chamber. "Your Majesty!"

She recognized the voice of one of her guards. "I'm here," she called, running to the door. "What's going on?"

"I don't know. Warriors—invaders—out of nowhere!"

She fumbled for the heavy crossbeam barring the door. "Should we retreat to the lower levels?"

A second guard answered. "No! Stay where you are. The door is strong. We'll hold them off until reinforcements arrive."

It hit Adara then. They were coming for *her*. Whoever they were—Calamarvans, bandits, assassins—they weren't attacking the entire castle, just the royal wing.

Adara looked about the room, unsure what to do. She snatched an overcoat and slippers, putting them on over her nightgown. Somewhere in the distance, a bell clanged in alarm.

Then, in the middle of the shouts and cries and clanging, she heard a most unusual sound: a drip.

Adara turned, sweeping her circular chamber for the source. Close to the wall, opposite the door, the ceiling was bulging downward. As she watched, another fat drop of liquid stone fell. It solidified before it hit the ground, shattering on impact.

She ran back to the door. "They're melting the ceiling!"

There was a pause before the guards responded. "Excuse us, Your Majesty?"

She rephrased. "Terramancy! They're using it to liquify the stone!"

"Then we need to get you out of there!" one of the guards said. "Hurry!"

In the semi-darkness, Adara fumbled at the crossbeam and the two locks on her door. Opening them now seemed to take twice as long as normal. Finally, she flung open the door.

Two korriks were there: Rimrock and Shaq, if she remembered their names correctly. They both had their swords drawn, their faces tight with focus. "Quickly!" Rimrock cried before hurrying down the stairs. Adara followed, clutching the hem of her skirt to avoid falling on the steep steps.

They came to a landing, where two other korriks were waiting. "Someone's coming up!" one warned. Rimrock and Shaq skidded to a halt, and the four korriks filled the stairwell with their short swords and bucklers.

Another guard, an avir, staggered up the stairs, panting. "They're breaking through the door down below!"

"Get behind me!" Rimrock shouted. "Your Majesty, get down!"

Adara found herself boxed into the corner of the landing, the avir covering her with his shield, the korriks in front, their swords out. Her heart pounded in her chest, cold sweat beading on her forehead.

"How many are there?" Shaq asked.

"At least a half dozen," the avir said. "Hakiru bandits, I think."

Hakiru . . . the air traders? Adara had seen their cloudships in the sky on occasion. But she had never met one face-to-face. Why were they after her? Had they made an alliance with Calamar?

Rimrock drew a vial from his pocket, popping the cork out and taking a swig. "Extract of initiative," he said, passing around the aquamantic potion. "Shortens your reaction time."

Adara took a sip. The liquid was sharp and bitter, with a hint of garlic. It sent a shock through her nerves as she swallowed. She blinked. Everything around her seemed to become crisper.

A crash came from above them, reverberating through the stones.

"That would be my bedroom ceiling," Adara warned.

Shaq handed her a dagger. "You may need this."

She gripped the weapon awkwardly in her hand, unsure whether to hold it like a paring knife or a scepter.

Shouts and cries echoed up the stairwell from the chamber below. The pirates must have smashed through the door.

This was it. They were trapped.

Adara looked around her. The potion in her veins seemed to extend each second, allowing her to process tiny details. The avir's chest was heaving, his shield shaking in his hand. His face was white with fear. He was probably a recent recruit, with this his first battle.

The korriks surrounding her held their weapons at the ready, bodies braced to defend. They exchanged glances, smiling. Rimrock even winked at his brother. They seemed eager to fight, even excited, poised like a band of boys ready to begin a footrace.

Adara had never been around korriks before a fight. She'd been told that korriks had a natural affinity for war that other species lacked. She had seen an echo of that zeal many times as the korriks in her retinue sparred with each other or boasted of the battles they had been in. But to see it firsthand unsettled her. She was glad she had been born an avir.

They would die for me, she realized with a mix of gratitude and guilt. All five soldiers were ready to die tonight, without a second thought. This was what they had trained for, this was why they had signed up for the army: to defend their kingdom and their queen. Even if it meant sacrificing their very souls.

"Swords up," Rimrock barked.

The Hakiru came up the stairs silently, sporting heavy fur coats, their cutlasses and oval shields filling the confines of the stairway. She couldn't tell how many there were. They stopped just out of reach of Adara's bodyguard, illuminated by the cold green light of the landing's lumen globes.

"Mikarash sha-ba!" Rimrock shouted, the traditional Korrik war cry reverberating off the stones. His brothers joined in. "Shi-ki-ra maRash!"

"Stand down!" one of the Hakiru shouted. He spoke Lurrian with a thick accent. "No one has to die tonight. It is queen we want. She be safe, though you pay much silver to get her back!"

So that was what they were after—kidnapping and ransom. Were they telling the truth that they wouldn't kill her?

"We'll pay now—with our lives!" Rimrock roared.

The foremost Hakiru parted. Behind them stood a tall human, cloaked in black. He reached out a hand, speaking a torrent of words that could only be the Numinous Tongue. Verbomancy!

Wind filled the corridor. A jet of air, impossibly strong, blasted into Adara's bodyguards. Rimrock caught the blast square on his shield and slid backward from the impact. Adara covered her face with her arm as the stream of air blasted her into the wall behind her.

"Steady!" Shaq shouted.

A bow twanged. Rimrock cried out and fell. Another twang sounded and the avir beside her shuddered. She turned to see an arrow buried in his shoulder. His teeth were clenched. Adara's heart ached to see him in pain. Had he not been covering Adara with his shield, his shoulder would have been protected.

The jet of air swiveled, blasting into Shaq. His sword clanged as he dropped it to grab his shield with both hands.

Things were happening so fast! Three of her guards were already wounded or immobilized, and they had not even swung at the Hakiru. Yet they would keep protecting her until she watched them die in front of her. Die at night—to be claimed by demons.

She made up her mind. She could not demand that ultimate sacrifice.

"Enough!" Adara yelled, stepping out from behind the avir's shield. "I'll go with you!"

One of her korriks grabbed her arm. "Your Majesty!"

"Stand down." Adara shook free and stepped forward. "Take me, but spare my soldiers."

The spray of air stopped. The Hakiru stared at her, their eyes wide. She held her hand forward and dropped her dagger to the floor. Her other hand she raised behind her, forbidding her soldiers from advancing. They obeyed.

"Midsha-la!" one of the Hakiru grunted. They advanced, keeping their swords pointed toward Adara's guards while they grabbed her and pushed her roughly down the stairs. "Move!"

Adara glanced behind her, assuring herself that each of her soldiers still lived.

"Move!"

Volthorn woke to lantern light flooding his chamber.

"Commander Skarr! We're under assault!"

He leapt out of bed, claws reaching instinctively for the sword on his table. The avir carrying the lantern was already turning to run back into the hall.

"Invaders from the skies, sir! They're in the royal wing!" Even as the soldier spoke, a bell tolled somewhere above them: the general alarm.

Fear grabbed hold of Volthorn's heart, squeezing it until it pumped like a racing horse. *The queen!*

He charged out of his room, down the passageway, up a twisting staircase, through a flung-open door, and out onto a balustrade. Other soldiers were stumbling out of various doors, strapping on weapons and wiping sleep from confused eyes.

"Follow me!" Volthorn bellowed, drawing his sword. "To the royal wing! They're after the queen!"

Through the darkness, he could see torchlight on the walkways of the royal wing. Shadows were moving there. Too many shadows. Weapons clashed. The turret at the top of the tower was ablaze. In the dark sky, wreathed in smoke, a darker shape drifted. A cloudship.

"KaRAk rakah!" he cursed.

So Rendhart *had* told the truth. A band of Hakiru attackers had infiltrated the kingdom, the capital, and now the palace itself. Volthorn cursed himself. He'd been a fool. And now the whole kingdom would pay the price.

He charged along the balustrade and down a set of steps, his mind racing through the tactical situation. The royal wing's isolation—normally its greatest strength—was now its fatal weakness. Most of the palace guard was stationed by the front gates, at the far opposite end of the complex. And the single stone causeway connecting the royal wing to the rest of the palace provided a perfect chokepoint.

A swifter running in the opposite direction almost collided with him in the dark. She skidded, regained her footing, and started running alongside him. "They have archers covering the causeway!"

"I fear no archers," Volthorn grunted. He descended the last staircase two at a time, leaping the final six steps and hitting the stones running. As he ran, he touched the gems at his belt, drawing blue terracharge into his fingers and pouring it into his armor.

He reached the causeway. Several soldiers were already there, advancing slowly as they covered themselves with their shields. One lay crumpled on the stones, gasping in pain, an arrow in his side.

"Charge!" Volthorn bellowed, plunging past the other soldiers. "No time for a slow advance. Rush them quickly and we'll overrun them!"

An arrow hissed out of the darkness, glancing away from Volthorn's armor with a flash of blue light. The royal wing was crawling with shadows. Two archers stood on the upper patio, with a clear vantage over the entire causeway. And there were likely more archers on the cloudship hanging above the topmost turret.

"Watch out!" one of Volthorn's soldiers shouted. "They've set an air—"

Volthorn smaked into an invisible barrier at full speed.

"—wall," the soldier finished.

Volthorn slumped to the ground, stars spinning in his vision. *Confounded verbomancy!* One of the attackers must have solidified the air at the end of the causeway into an impassable barrier.

Volthorn stumbled to his feet. He transferred terracharge from a ruby into his sword until the whole blade glowed red. Then he started raining blows into the invisible wall in front of him. His arm shook and stung from each impact, but he kept at it. His goal was not to slice up the wall—verbomancy did not so much bind the air particles into a solid as it did freeze each particle in place. Rather, he hoped the terracharge in his sword would overwhelm the strength of the spell.

With each hit, a hemisphere of red light rippled out from his sword across the solidified air, like a bowl of geletin wobbling when smacked with a spoon. He wondered how effective his blows were: the rules governing interactions between each type of mancery were still largely unknown. With his terrasense, he could feel the power in his sword decreasing with each hit, but the wall in front of him was as invisible to his sixth sense as to his eyes.

A soldier ran up beside him and jumped, trying to scale the invisible wall. His arms and head must have cleared the top, because for a moment he hung in the air, hands thrust forward, scrambling for purchase. But the air, even when solid, yielded no friction or purchase, and a moment later the soldier thumped back onto the stones beside Volthorn.

Desperation added strength to Volthorn's swings. "Your Majesty!" he bellowed. "Adara! Adara!!"

Adara and her kidnappers emerged onto the same balcony where she had talked with Cymer weeks before. Something massive loomed above them in the dark. Dangling from it was a forest of ropes and ladders.

"Get in basket," the pirate behind her barked.

Adara looked around. "Basket?"

"The basket!" The pirate dragged her over to one of the ropes, which was tied to a large wicker basket resting on the stone pavers. The moment Adara had climbed inside, the pirate looked up and shouted something.

After a second, the rope went taut, and the basket lurched upward. As the tower receded below her, Adara could make out the cloudship above her, its gondola sleek and bristling with weaponry. She rolled over and looked over the side of the basket.

The castle below her resembled an ant nest, with scores of figures emerging from doorways and stairwells to converge on the royal wing. But it was too late. Already the rest of the Hakiru were scrambling up the ladders after Adara. Somewhere in the melee, a brazen voice kept shouting her name.

The basket stopped with a jerk. Strong hands grabbed Adara and hauled her onboard the gondola. All was chaos around her: pirates were clambering over the side, cutting lines, loading arrows, and barking orders in their strange tongue. The whole ship jerked, and Adara felt her stomach press into her abdomen. They were rising.

"Adara!" a distant voice cried out. "Your Majesty!" It was Commander Volthorn. She could hear his pain and desperation.

Adara found her feet under her, grabbed the gunwale of the ship, and peered over the edge. The castle lights were sinking into darkness below her.

"I'm all right!" she shouted back, not knowing how far her voice would carry.

A hand pulled her away from the edge.

"Ach. What do we do with the wee gal?" someone said with a strange accent.

"Put her under," a cold voice replied. "We can't risk her screaming."

Someone uncapped a vial and held it under Adara's nose. She struggled, holding her breath as long as she could, but eventually her lungs gave out. As she inhaled, her mind filled with a strange scent. It smelled like sunflowers, and wet grass, and long afternoons. It wasn't that unpleasant, actually. Just . . . a little . . . soporific . . .

CHAPTER 29

MERCY

Durrin woke with a start. He jerked upright on his cot. Where was he? Why was everything dark?

Memories flooded back. After his disastrous meeting with Volthorn, soldiers had escorted him to a military barrack to remain under guard until he could be escorted from the province.

He hadn't intended to comply, of course. His "cell" was only a room with a wooden ceiling. He had planned to burn his way out as soon as night fell, then backtrack to the castle to interrupt Salidar's assault.

What had happened? He remembered lying down exhausted on his cot in the mid-afternoon, intending to take a short nap. Why hadn't he awoken?

Durrin rolled off the cot. Igniting a flame in his hand for light, he peered under the bed. There it was: a small basin of liquid, hidden out of sight in the far corner—an aquamancy sleep aroma, most likely. Its fumes had subtly filled the room that afternoon, luring him into a deep sleep.

"Curse you, Volthorn," Durrin muttered. He rose and went to the tiny window, listening. In the darkness, far away, he heard the panicked clanging of a bell.

"Captain!" he cried, rushing to the door and pounding on it. "Captain! You need to let me out!"

After a moment, an annoyed voice answered. "Captain's asleep. This is Sergeant Barnum."

"Sergeant, you must let me go! Someone's attacking the palace!"

"What in Terramor's tempests are you talking about?"

He didn't have time for this. Talking his way out would take forever. Durrin stepped back into a one-legged crouch and spun, the other leg and his two arms kept straight out horizontally. Heat and energy sucked toward him from each corner of the room. Then he corkscrewed upright, channeling the vortex into the ceiling. Fire erupted from his outstretched hands, blasting into the dry wood.

"What's going on in there?!" the sergeant shouted.

Durrin pulled back his hands. There was now a sizeable hole in the ceiling, the beams around it charred and smoking.

"Should have woken the captain," Durrin said, then gathered energy into his legs and sprung up into the gap.

The night was dark, with a chill wind. Most of the streetlamps had long dried out. He ran across the rooftops, leaping over ten-foot gaps without a second thought. The palace lights twinkled ahead of him, half a mile away. Half a mile! Why did that rock-headed korrik put him so far away? He increased his speed.

The clanging of the bell grew louder. Something was afire on the right side of the palace—the side with the royal wing.

His lungs were burning. How long ago had the attack begun? Three minutes? Five? The raid would be startlingly quick if executed properly, especially if Grimbo's liquidation grenade worked like he said it would.

He redoubled his pace, energy surging around him as the flame in his heart soared. He came to a wide street but cleared it easily, landing with a tumble on the rooftop beyond and rolling back into a run.

Shouting and the clash of weapons sounded up ahead as the palace acropolis rose in front of him. He powered into the ascent, springing from rock to rock, flaring the flames in his hands to better see footholds. The slope increased until it became a cliff, and Durrin scrambled up the face, carried by the wave of momentum.

He reached the top of the cliff and clung to the stonework of the palace wall, his lungs heaving for breath. His hands and arms stung from half a dozen scrapes and lacerations.

As he craned his head upward to find a route of ascent, movement caught his eye. A vast shadow floated in the skies above him, drifting away from the palace as it climbed in altitude. Somewhere above him, a voice bellowed the queen's name.

Durrin collapsed, sinking down with his back to the wall, his legs dangling over the drop. He hung his head between his arms, gasping for air with every ragged breath.

He was too late.

Adara woke slowly from one nightmare into another.

First she became aware of her mouth. It was gagged, with a taut, nasty-tasting cloth digging into the sides of her cheeks. Then she registered the thongs digging into her wrists and ankles.

The cold hit her next. She was shivering uncontrollably, with goose bumps all over her arms and legs. Chill autumn air swept over her, stripping away any shreds of warmth. It was the cold that convinced her she was no longer dreaming.

Adara finally cracked open her eyes, but she saw nothing but darkness. Had she gone blind? Slowly, the darkness gave way to vague shapes. Before her stretched the gondola. Dark figures crouched huddled along its deck.

A thick silence hung everywhere. Adara could almost feel it weighing on her. As hard as she strained her ears, she couldn't hear anything: no wind, no creak of air against canvas, no breathing—only the dull thud of her own heart.

Coldness. Darkness. Silence. A tingle started at the hairs of her neck, rippling up her spine and down her limbs. Coldness. Darkness. Silence. Was this what it was like in the Void?

As panic threatened to take hold, engrained habits kicked in.

Breathe. Release.

Adara focused on her breaths, though they came stifled through her nose.

Light. *Breathe.* Darkness. *Release.*

Memories from the attack ripped through her. She saw, again, the avir falling with an arrow in his shoulder, the Hakiru shoving her toward a basket.

Hope. *Breathe.* Fear. *Release.*

Awful reality sunk upon her. She'd been kidnapped, spirited out of her own castle. Now she lay at the mercy of a barbarous race from the far north, a people that gave no thought to taking lives at night. Would they torture her? Kill her?

Death at night. . . . The fear of it threatened to consume her, crowding out her attempts to calm herself. Visions of demons and endless agony coursed through her.

Breathe. Breathe again. What was the opposite of death?

She shivered in the dark, gripped by terror.

"Well, well," a voice murmured, the sound muffled and sluggish. "Look who's awake."

She struggled to turn her head. In the darkness, she could make out no more than the outline of a tall human standing above her. Unlike the rest of the pirates she had heard, he spoke Lurrian fluently, with the accent of a high-bred aristocrat from Calamar.

"I hope your night has been pleasant." Condescension dripped from his voice. "And I hope your finances are in order. Your kingdom will have to pay a pretty sum to get you back." He stooped at Adara's level, his voice falling to little more than a hiss. "That is, assuming no accident befalls you in the meantime."

The hairs tingled on the back of Adara's neck again. What did he mean by *accident?*

The shadow of a snippen approached. The Calamarvan straightened and turned. "Yes?"

"Keep silence, Your Excellency," the snippen said. Her voice also seemed to come slowly through the air. "Griffins may be near."

The Calamarvan waved his hand. "You doubt the efficacy of my verbomancy needlessly. No one can hear this ship."

"We fear the wind," the snippen said. "It carries sound far, even when muffled by magic." As she spoke, a gust rocked the cloudship. Adara toppled onto her side, unable to catch herself with her hands tied. Something cold hit her cheek. A snowflake?

The buckling deck had no effect on the snippen, but the Calamarvan stumbled, his hand searching for a handhold.

Another human walked up. "This be a wintah gale coming in," he warned. "If we don't land in the next hour, be'en discovered will be the least of our worries."

"Is this a ship on the open sea instead of the sky?" the Calamarvan demanded. "Are we threatened by waves or rocks? What prevents us from simply flying with the wind?"

Another gust rocked the gondola. Adara's stomach lurched as the ship got sucked into a sudden updraft.

"Yeh don't brave a winter gale in a cloudship," the other human said. Adara struggled to place his accent. Dorinian? "It's madness! The slightest change in air could send us rocket'n up or down. We could be driven miles off course, sent crashing into the Mitrian Mountains, or ripped t' pieces by hail."

"I say we're landing," the snippen declared.

The Calamarvan folded his arms. "Landing with a queen that the whole kingdom is looking for?"

"Aye. We're over hill country. There are plenty of places to stow ourselves unseen until the storm blows over."

The Calamarvan turned his back. "I see you are determined. Carry on."

The snippen began barking orders to the crew in a foreign tongue. Soon the ship was alive with activity.

Amid all the commotion, the Calamarvan stood like a monolith, silent and brooding, barely visible in the dark. Then he turned to Adara. "If you think this is your chance for rescue, Your Majesty, you are sadly mistaken. No one beyond this ship has the faintest idea where you are."

Adara could scarcely focus on his words as a new gust of air rocked the ship. She shivered from the cold and the terror. Every inhale brought freezing air into her lungs. She grasped at the pain, letting it guide her thoughts.

Despair. *Release.* Hope. *Breathe.*

Though her mouth was gagged, her mind filled with an unspoken, desperate prayer:

> *Father of Stars, hear me!*
> *Shower thy peace on my heart.*
> *Give me the aid of angels!*
> *Guide me. Help me. Save me!*

In response, her heart filled with a single, quiet phrase. It was a phrase she knew well. Her father had spoken it, long ago.

You are stronger than your fears.

Was she?

Durrin's heart bubbled with wrath. He hated everything. He hated Elandria for getting caught up in this war. He hated Salidar for lying to him. He hated Halorn for telling him the truth. He hated Commander Volthorn—oh, how he hated Volthorn! Prideful, stubborn, stiff-necked reptile!

But most of all, Durrin hated himself.

He stood at the edge of the Silvermoss, staring into the gloom of the night. The cloud frigate had disappeared an hour before, but a new flight of griffins still left in pursuit every few minutes. The light from a city too worried to sleep illuminated the golden undersides of their wings as they sped into the gathering storm. The wind wiped at Durrin's cloak, bringing the first whisps of snow.

Why had he even come to this city? What did he really think he could accomplish?

The trot of a horse heralded someone's approach.

"Ah—Durrin!" said a voice he wished he had never heard. "I thought I might find you around here."

"Go away, Cymer," Durrin snapped.

The avir didn't leave. He dismounted and stepped up beside Durrin, looking across the river as well. "I just arrived at the city," he said, his voice somber. "The night watch filled me in."

Durrin didn't respond.

"What do you think?" Cymer asked after a long silence. "Will they find her?"

Durrin shook his head. "The night is too dark, and with a verbomancer onboard, the Hakiru can travel unheard. And even if they are found, Salidar will not let Queen Everborn escape alive."

A gust of freezing wind wrapped Durrin's cloak around his legs. He felt no cold. The smoldering anger inside him made sure of that.

"You knew their plans?" Cymer asked.

Durrin nodded miserably. "I helped make them. But I tried to stop it. I tried, Cymer! I risked my life facing Salidar. I rode forty miles in half a day. I met with dozens of guards and talked my way into the very palace—for what? To be insulted, ignored, and incarcerated by your own chief commander! I tried, Cymer. I tried and I failed."

A minute passed in silence, the only sound that of the river, ceaselessly flowing down its destined course. Eventually, Cymer walked back to his horse, rummaging for something in his pack.

Durrin hung his head. He had failed. He had botched his chance to rewrite the scroll of his life. He was exactly what Volthorn said he was—a spy and a murderer, doomed for the pits of the Void.

"Ah, here we are," Cymer said.

Durrin turned. The old avir had laid a cloth bundle on the ground and was unwrapping it. There, in a broken heap, lay the shards of Cymer's porcelain oil lamp. The half face of a shattered angel stared up from the pile.

"Tell me, Durrin," Cymer said, spreading out the pieces. "What is justice?"

Durrin's eyes roved across the fragments. In the wreckage of the lamp, he saw his own life—broken, jagged, and shattered into more pieces than he could ever hope to fix. He saw seven years of imprisonment. He saw a career cut short. He saw the Void lurking in every shadow of his future. And finally, he understood.

"I once thought I didn't follow any laws. I thought I could do what I pleased, take what I wanted. But like the lamp, I *do* follow laws—unchangeable laws. If the lamp is dropped, it will fall and break. That is justice. Justice is facing the consequences of the law."

"You are right," said Cymer. "So what was *just* that you receive for what you did seven years ago?"

Tears began to well up in Durrin's eyes as he stared at the broken lamp. "The laws of the Sun are irrevocable. Murderers, thieves, assassins—these cannot enter there. It matters not if we understand the law or not. That is the law. That is justice."

Cymer nodded.

Durrin snapped his head up. "But then you lied last night! You said I could change the scroll of my fate!"

Cymer nodded again. "I did."

"Then how?"

Cymer picked up the largest shard of the lamp. He turned it over in his hands, handling it gingerly to avoid slicing his fingers on the jagged edges. "Do you remember what you said about justice, right after I broke this lamp?"

The memory from Irongate Isle flashed across Durrin's mind. "I said that the world is never just."

"Do you still believe that?"

Durrin thought over his life. He had murdered a king in innocent blood—a horrible act, an act that deserved the most severe consequences. And they had come. Imprisonment for seven years. War upon his nation, claiming the lives of his friends. Losing everything he had aspired to become. And he completely deserved it all.

Once, he had seen the world as vindictive and cruel, dealing out success and failure arbitrarily unless you were strong enough to bend life to your will. But now he saw that all the misery of the last seven years was but the effect of pure, unyielding justice. And that was a prospect far more terrifying.

"Not anymore," Durrin whispered. "I see now that the world is always just."

"Ah," said Cymer, sounding almost eager. "Is it?"

Once again, a memory came to Durrin. "In the prison. After I said things are never just, you agreed with me. Then you said, 'and that is what gives me hope.' What did you mean?"

Cymer's eyes sparkled. "Ah. That is the great secret. Tell me: what is mercy?"

"Mercy is—" Durrin paused, then shook his head. "I guess I don't truly know."

Cymer looked down at the shards of his lamp, then spoke a command in the Numinous Tongue. "Et evinal, al Abeam!"

Light streamed from Cymer's hands, weaving around the pile of broken fragments. The shards began to reform, stacking on top of each other in a perfect reversal of their smash, until they coalesced into a perfect whole in Cymer's hand.

"That," Cymer said, proffering the lamp to Durrin, "is mercy."

Stunned, Durrin took the lamp, turning it over in his hands as he stared at it in unbelief. Not a single crack was evident, not a single chunk missing. "How—where—" he stammered. "No magic in the world can do such a feat!"

"That is because all your life, you have studied only the arcane manceries," said Cymer. "But there is a deeper force. It goes by many names. In the Luminant Order, we simply call it the Light."

"The Light," Durrin repeated, still studying the lamp in wonder.

"It is the source of all creation, the wellspring of all life. By it, the Seven Noble Stars shaped the world at the dawn of time. From it, the arcane manceries draw their power. Through it, all laws are enforced."

Durrin struggled to wrap his mind around Cymer's words. "If what you say is true, then one who wields the Light can control anything!"

"Yes," said Cymer. "But there is only One who controls the Light. I command it not, neither does any other mortal. It is controlled only by the King of the Sun, the one we call the Eldest." His eyes turned bright blue with joy. "It is by the Light that all laws are enforced. That is justice. But by the same power, laws can be reversed. What is broken can be mended. What is wrong can be set right. What is condemned . . ." He looked at Durrin meaningfully, ". . . can be redeemed."

Something bright flickered within Durrin. "Then I can be forgiven?"

Cymer nodded. "You can."

Durrin's heart leapt within him, the flicker growing to fill him with a new resolve. It was an emotion he had never fully experienced before: hope.

"What must I do?"

"You have asked this question before," Cymer said. "The answer is the same."

"I must do what I know I must?"

Cymer nodded.

Durrin set down the lamp. "Then I go to rescue a queen."

Chapter 30

Lost

The first tendrils of winter had arrived.

Volthorn leaned into the howling snow, hugging the neck of his mare. The wind ripped at his hood, seeking the exposed scales of his face. Flurries of snow, picked up by the wind, danced in strange patterns over the path ahead.

He led a band of about forty soldiers—humans, avirs, and korriks—on horseback, with half a dozen swifters following close behind. They were one of more than a dozen parties scouring the countryside for the Hakiru sky pirates. After crossing the Silvermoss shortly after midnight, they had ridden southeast, lighting their way with lumen lanterns hanging from their saddles. Now, as morning turned the dark storm around them to a pale gray, they ascended a winding path into a series of hills.

"Volthorn!" called his brother Kelzern, prodding his horse forward to ride next to Volthorn. "What's our reading?"

Volthorn straightened, shivering as the wind found its way past his cloak. He drew from his pocket a small glass-topped metal disc, with an arrow balanced on a needle inside. After signaling the column of troops to halt, he infused the compass with a small amount of terracharge and held it as steady as he could, studying the needle's direction until it stabilized. He pointed in front of them, slightly to the left. "There."

His brother carried a similar device, still glowing faintly from its last infusion of terracharge. Kelzern pointed to their right. "And that's south."

Volthorn studied the angle made by the two vectors. His brother's compass was a traditional talisman, pointing to the Cosmic Mountain to the south. Volthorn's device was configured to point toward the gem on Queen Adara's signet ring. He had synced the compass with the ring several months before as a safeguard for a situation like this. He had hoped to never have to use it.

"I'd put it at sixty degrees," Volthorn said. "Last measurement was around forty-five degrees."

"Then we're catching up," said Kelzern.

Volthorn shut his eyes, recalling the maps of the area that he had studied, overlaying lines and angles from the various readings they had made. "That depends on how close the pirates are. If they're close, then we're catching up. If they're farther away, they may be stationary, and we'll miss them by several miles. Or they may be even farther away and doubling back up north, getting farther away from us."

One of the other soldiers shook his head. "I don't know how you keep track of all that in your head, Commander," he said respectfully.

"It's easy." Volthorn pocketed the compass. "Didn't you take trigonometry in military school?"

"Trig-a-what?" The soldier looked confused.

"Exactly." Volthorn nodded. "Onward!"

They pressed forward, the wind battering them from different directions. The snow was beginning to pile up as the storm progressed and they gained altitude.

One of the horses slipped, stumbling off the path and down the steep hillside to their right. Two other horses spooked, and all was confusion for a few seconds as their riders fought to calm their mounts without plunging off the track themselves. Finally, the first horse found its footing several dozen yards below, and its rider—who had only sustained minor cuts and bruises—carefully navigated it back up to the safety of the path.

"We can't keep going like this!" Trazar called from the middle of the column. "The storm is picking up, temperatures are plummeting, and the snow is getting deeper. We need to find shelter!"

Volthorn's chattering teeth agreed. But he shook his head. "If we stop now, we might never find the queen!"

"If we keep going, we might all die!" Trazar replied. "Then for sure we'll never find the queen!"

Volthorn looked around at his troops. He saw a group of cold, exhausted, frightened soldiers. He clenched his fist in frustration. "Fine. We'll stop at the next shelter we find."

It was another quarter of an hour before they reached a logging camp, used during the summer months but now vacant. It had a bunkhouse that, with all of them inside, was cramped but snug, with an attached stable for their horses. They had to break the lock on the door, so Volthorn dropped a couple coins on the mantle in payment. Two soldiers got a fire going in the hearth while the others shook the snow from their boots and cloaks.

Volthorn sat down at a small table, spreading a map over the knotted wood and setting his and Kelzern's compasses on the corners to hold them down.

Kelzern sat down opposite him. "Where do you reckon we are?"

Volthorn pointed to a thin line winding its way through the hills southeast of Saven. "We're on this road, I'm fairly sure—somewhere along this stretch after the last village we passed." He studied the compass synced with Adara's ring. "This is showing that Her Majesty is now northeast of us."

Kelzern tapped the tabletop with his fingers. "Northeast? Our last reading was a touch south of east."

"Which, I believe, means they're close," Volthorn said. "Very close. My hunch is that they've had to drop anchor somewhere in the hills nearby to wait out the storm."

Volthorn looked down at the compass again and frowned. It was slowly drifting clockwise. After a few seconds, it stopped, then drifted back to its original position.

"Krack's crest," Volthorn muttered. He stood and examined the chinking in the log walls. "Something's throwing off the calibration."

"Quartzite?"

"Possibly." Volthorn stood and grabbed the compass. "I'll take a step outside, see if the problem clears up away from the lodge."

Kelzern rose as well. "I'll come with you."

"Stay here and stay warm," Volthorn said. "I'm only going a couple yards."

Kelzern shrugged. "Suit yourself."

Volthorn unlatched the door. It swung wide open, letting a blast of freezing air into the lodge. He stepped outside and slammed it shut behind him. The storm instantly claimed him, snow searching for his eyes and face as the wind pierced his cloak.

Volthorn put his back to the lodge and trudged down the path. He went ten yards, then pulled the compass out and studied it. After a minute, once again it wandered a few degrees clockwise, stayed there a few seconds, then wandered back.

Volthorn peered through the snow. Random objects could have an interfering effect on terramantic talismans, especially one so delicately calibrated as this one. Something as innocuous as a nearby boulder with crystal deposits could be throwing it off.

Leaving the path, Volthorn plunged into the trees, ducking under branches and using his sword to hack aside bushes. After a few minutes, he paused and studied the compass again. Finally, it showed a consistent bearing.

Volthorn squinted through the brush back the direction he had come. Where was the lodge? Its windows were shuttered, so he had no light to go by. But it had to be only twenty or thirty yards away. Volthorn spotted a deer trail a few paces away that led in his desired direction, so he pushed through the intervening bushes and followed it back through the trees.

The snow was piling up now—three or four inches in most places, with drifts up to two feet deep. Volthorn paused and looked around. Where was the lodge? Had he passed it already? He glanced at his compass to reorient himself, then closed his eyes and mentally mapped out his route. A dozen yards up the path. Turning and pushing a few dozen yards into the brush. Turning back and following a deer trail for several dozen yards.

The deer trail must have veered off course somewhere and overshot the lodge. Volthorn turned off the trail and plunged back into the underbrush, holding his hands in front of his face as he bulldozed through branches and twigs. His core was overheating, but his extremities were tingling with the cold.

A knot of worry began to tie itself in his gut. Something was wrong. The terrain didn't seem familiar. Why was it sloping downhill? It should be sloping up. He paused and fished out his compass again, then peered through the trees, looking for an opening.

He took a step back and his foot slipped out from under him. He scrambled for traction on the hillside, but his flailing arms only found more snow. Then he was tumbling, the snow sliding down around him. He grabbed at a passing tree trunk but nearly lost his glove. Suddenly, the ground disappeared beneath him, and he dropped into a small ravine, landing with a grunt in the snow.

Volthorn stumbled to his feet, brushing off the snow that had piled on top of him. None of this looked familiar. He tried to climb up the side of the ravine but only slid back down, bringing more snow down on top of him. His stomach filled with a chilling admission.

He was lost.

Chapter 31

A Reluctant Partnership

The cold ate away at Volthorn. It bit at his claws, his nose, his chin. It gnawed at his cheeks and his legs. It caught his lungs in a suffocating grip and slowly squeezed, ever tighter and ever colder.

For what seemed like an eternity, he had struggled through the blizzard, searching desperately for the lodge or any other familiar landmark. But the swirling storm was hopelessly bewildering.

He stumbled in the snow, claws flailing to break his fall. Pain shot through his arms as he landed on a thornbush.

He got back up. Which way was north? Shards of snow stung his eyes. He didn't know.

Shelter. I must find shelter!

He fell again. Shadows! What was wrong with his legs? He hadn't even tripped that time; he'd just tried to take a step.

Something rang in his ears, something other than wind and crackling trees. He pushed himself onto one forearm, squinting into the blinding whiteness. A gust of wind parted the howling snow, and he thought he saw a darker shadow against the trees. Was something moving toward him? In a moment, it was gone. His eyes had to be malfunctioning, like his legs.

Volthorn's arm gave out and he fell back into the snow. But this time it didn't even feel cold. It felt like a warm bed, offering rest from all his cares. He was so tired . . .

Something sounded again at the edge of his consciousness. He didn't care. He was going to sleep . . .

Then a rough hand grabbed the back of his jerkin and hauled him bodily out of the snow. His eyes blinked, then came into focus on an all-too-familiar face.

"My least favorite pyromancer . . ." he groaned deliriously.

"Oh—it's you," Rendhart said, and dropped him unceremoniously back into the snow.

"Never thought I'd see *you* here," Volthorn said once he regained consciousness.

Rendhart snorted. "Neither did I."

Volthorn sat shivering beside a roaring fire, wrapped in the pyromancer's cloak. His own cloak lay suspended from a tree, dripping as the ice melted in the fire's heat. He listened to the chattering of his teeth, trying to distract himself from the pain. His fingers and toes felt like someone was stabbing them with a thousand needles, but at least that meant they hadn't froze. He hoped.

What was Rendhart doing here? He must have followed their patrol from the capital, but why?

"Don't bother thanking me," Rendhart said, as if reading Volthorn's thoughts. He threw some more sticks into the fire. "If your soldiers had mentioned it was *you* out here, I would have stayed warm and dry in the logging camp and left them to continue their fruitless search."

"How did you find us?" Volthorn asked.

Rendhart snorted. "Tracking forty men and horses on a snowy trail? Wasn't that hard."

Volthorn addended his question. "*Why* did you find us?"

Rendhart waved his hand over the struggling fire, causing it to flare up. "Hard as it may be for you to believe, I'm here for the same reason you are—to rescue Her Majesty."

"But you were under guard. How did you—?"

Rendhart shrugged. "You put a pyromancer in a room with a wooden ceiling."

Volthorn snorted. "Not my only mistake in the last twenty-four hours."

"To put it mildly." Rendhart tossed more wood onto the fire.

They each stared at the flames for an awkward minute.

Volthorn shifted, pulling Rendhart's cloak tighter around himself. He hated to admit it, but the pyromancer's cloak was one of the highest quality fabrics he'd ever worn. "I guess we're on the same side now," he said.

"Reluctantly." Rendhart looked up, gauging the wind. "The storm's beginning to pass. We'll wait five more minutes, then head back to the lodge. I should remember the way."

"Ten," Volthorn said. "I'm half frozen."

"Five. The sooner you get moving, the better."

"Fine."

They sat in mutual silence for a couple minutes, watching the fire burn.

"One thing more," Volthorn said, feeling a twinge of embarrassment.

"What?"

"If anyone asks—" Volthorn looked pointedly in the other direction. "We stumbled across each other in the blizzard, but I was never on the point of death."

Rendhart shrugged. "Fine by me."

Salidar was near.

Durrin could feel the energy radiating from the vizier's spark. It was a spark unlike any other—bold, confident, and calculating. A spark Durrin would recognize anywhere. What he felt now was scarcely stronger than an echo. But it was there.

He stopped in his tracks, closing his eyes to focus on the spark.

Commander Skarr nearly walked into him from behind. "Kekogg's crackers, what are you—"

"Shh." Durrin held out his hand and summoned a flame with a snap of his fingers. He breathed energy into the flame, willing it to match the tone of the spark he sought.

"What's going on?" the korrik behind him demanded.

Durrin opened his eyes. The flame in his hand bent slightly to the right. He pointed in that direction. "Salidar and the pirates are close. I think just over that ridge."

"You have to be joking," said Commander Skarr. "How do you know?"

"Trade secret." Durrin turned and strode up the hillside, pushing past branches and underbrush.

The korrik waited for a few seconds, then started after him. "If Salidar's really so close, then we should go get my patrol!"

Durrin shook his head. "Going there and back would take three quarters of an hour or more. I want to see what the pirates are about first."

They struggled up the ridge. Durrin could hear Volthorn blundering behind him, slashing through branches with that magically razor-sharp sword of his. Durrin simply ducked and wove his way through the brush.

He could feel Salidar's spark growing stronger as they approached. Around it, he could sense the sparks of the pirate crew, fluttering around like a flurry of bees. And there was another spark too: a younger, more vulnerable spark.

"Thank the angels," Durrin muttered. The queen was still alive.

As they neared the top of the ridge, Durrin held up a hand. "Wait here."

Volthorn trudged past him. "I'm quite capable of looking over a ridgeline, thank you very much."

Together they crept forward, dropping to their hands and knees as they reached the top of the ridge. The trees gave way to brush, giving them a clear vantage of the ravine beyond.

There they were. The cloud frigate, bucking at its anchors. The pirates, scurrying to break camp. Salidar, brooding. And somewhere down there, Queen Adara.

They had found them.

Volthorn's mind began to churn with the tactical possibilities.

He studied every detail of the scene below him. The pirates' dirigible took up a large portion of the ravine, its mighty balloon shaking in the wind. An array of ropes, strained taut, kept the airship moored to surrounding trees and boulders.

A tall human, clad in black robes, paced back and forth near the airship's gondola. Around him, the crew of aerial pirates were busy at work, collapsing tents, putting out fires, and loading the ship. Volthorn searched their ranks. *Where was Adara?*

There! Although a tent partially blocked his view, Volthorn could see the princess's bright green overcoat. Her hands were tied behind her back, with a rope tethering her wrists to a nearby tree, close to the man in the black robes.

Rendhart leaned close to him. Volthorn wrinkled his nose at the slight hint of sulfur and ash in the pyromancer's breath. "The one in black is Lord Salidar," Rendhart whispered. "The vizier of Calamar."

So Salidar *had* come in person. Another thing Rendhart hadn't lied about. The thought irked Volthorn. "How many pirates are in the crew?"

"Eighteen, plus Salidar and his servant. Most are trained warriors. Many are expert archers."

"How many could you take in a fight?" Volthorn asked.

Rendhart frowned as he surveyed the camp. "Ten. Maybe twelve. It would get dicey. But I'd prefer doing this without killing anyone."

That made things a bit trickier. If they were going to pull this off without bloodshed, they needed a good plan. Volthorn studied the terrain between them and the bottom of the ravine, searching for patterns and gaps in the shrubbery and snow. "I think there's a way down about twenty feet to our left. Do you think you can find it?"

"Sure," said Rendhart.

"It looks like it will let you out onto the ravine's floor just below their camp."

"Okay."

"I need you to create a distraction."

"Can do."

"I'll work my way up above their camp and come at them from the head of the ravine. I need your distraction to be big enough to draw most of them away from the ship. I will then sneak in from the other direction and free the queen."

Rendhart's face was inscrutable. "Simple. Half decent. How do we escape?"

Volthorn pointed to the airship. "With that. If we cut the lines, the ship will jump free in seconds. In this storm, they'll never be able to keep up on foot."

"And you know how to fly that thing? I was on board over a week, and *I* don't know."

Volthorn paused. The pyromancer brought up a good point. But they didn't have any better option. "I can figure out anything," he said, waving his hand vaguely. "It can't be much harder than a boat."

Rendhart's raised eyebrow didn't escape Volthorn's notice.

As the two crawled their way back from the edge, the wind struck up again, harder. Volthorn shivered, wrapping his cloak around him. The claws on his feet still felt frozen. As he fought his way uphill, he glanced behind him to see Rendhart literally leap off the edge of the ridge.

Daredevil. The pyromancer had better play his part well. Or neither of them might ever see Adara again.

Then Volthorn thought of another day, seven years before. Rendhart had played his part well *that* day. Too well.

CHAPTER 32

FIRE IN THE SNOW

Adara could feel the unrelenting gaze of the man named Lord Salidar as he paced in front of her. She had given up making eye contact long ago. Instead, she focused on his boots, watching each one crunch into the snow. Her arms ached from being tied behind her back, and her feet, separated from the snow only by her slippers, felt frozen solid. As much as she dreaded whatever awaited her, she found herself wishing the pirates would hurry up so they could get back aboard the comparatively warm ship.

"Adara," the nobleman said, stopping in front of her. His voice dripped with fake sympathy. "You're shivering. Are you cold?"

She was *freezing* cold. But she would not give him the satisfaction of hearing her say it.

"I spent much of my childhood in the mountains," she whispered. "I'm used to the cold."

Lord Salidar resumed his pacing. "You are so very much like your father, Adara. He refused to acknowledge reality. Stubborn. Prideful. Blind to his own vulnerability."

Adara straightened, defiantly meeting Salidar's gaze. "My father was a great king. He loved his people, and his people loved him. He went to any length to preserve peace and promote prosperity!"

"Doubtless!" Lord Salidar scoffed. "That was why he had to be killed."

Killed?

Adara blinked, stunned.

"My father wasn't killed," she said. "He died in an accident."

Salidar looked at her in surprise. "Died in an accident? You mean your regents hid the truth even from *you?*"

She shivered, but this time not from the cold. "What do you mean?"

Salidar laughed—a cold, chilling laugh. "Your father was murdered. I personally hired the assassin."

The ground seemed to spin out from under Adara. *Killed? Murdered?* Her mind groped for something to grab ahold of in the darkness. It couldn't be true. If it was true, why had no one told her before? Why would Volthorn, Skagar, or Luviana withhold the truth from her?

Memories surfaced. She recalled Skagar's look of devastation when he had brought her the news. He hadn't just looked sad—he'd looked scared. She remembered the anger that glossed over Volthorn's eyes whenever her father's death was mentioned.

Her mind landed in a reality both strange and horribly familiar. No wonder they'd kept her in the mountains in the years after her father's death. No wonder Volthorn placed a heavy emphasis on guards. No wonder the extreme security at her coronation. The shattered image of her past settled into a new picture, leaving her mind to grapple with the implications.

And then she was back in the storm, shivering in the snow, captive to the orchestrator of her father's death. She opened her eyes to see her tears fall, burning holes in the snow. Agony.

"I'm so sorry." Salidar's voice dripped with sarcasm. "It seems my words have had a bit of a shock on you."

Adara looked up into Lord Salidar's smirking face. "You enjoy my pain, don't you?" she whispered. "All you do is torment and afflict. You are no better than a demon."

Lord Salidar flinched. His smile vanished. "I am no demon."

"Then prove it. Let me go."

Lord Salidar let out a sigh and looked away. He resumed pacing. "Adara, Adara. We are both nobility. You care for your kingdom, I care for mine. Calamar must grow; its interests are my chief concern. All who oppose Calamar's welfare must be eliminated. You would do the same in my stead."

"I would never kidnap someone from their home," Adara said. "And in any case, you are wrong. I do not oppose Calamar's welfare. I merely seek to defend my kingdom."

"Your 'kingdom' is a backwater principality infested with radical theology," Lord Salidar sneered. "Calamar is the greatest empire between the four anchors of the world! Its gardens and palaces are the wonders of Zenitha. And by divine fate, I have the privilege to grow its holdings, wealth, and power."

"Through conquest and murder?" Adara asked softly.

Lord Salidar scowled. "You are innocent and naive. This conversation is over."

He turned away, but Adara still had questions. "Why did the emperor order my father's death?"

Lord Salidar stopped and turned. "The emperor? He had no idea. For some reason I still can't fathom, he considered your father a dear friend. I had to go behind his back for the good of the empire. He still believes—"

Salidar's eyes grew wide. Adara heard a crackling roar behind her. Orange light illuminated the snow as a wave of heat washed over her.

Lord Salidar held up his arms, shouting unintelligible words; then a spike of fire roared over Adara's head, impacting a hurriedly summoned shield of air in front of Lord Salidar. Drops of fire rained down around Adara, sizzling as they hit the snowy ground.

Adara twisted around. Halfway up the side of the ravine stood a flashing red figure, wreathed in fire. Even from this distance, she recognized him: the hero from the palace.

Durrin swung his sword in a perfect arc, melting a long stretch of snow into steam and water. Flames licked hungrily at the bushes and trees around him, lighting the whole side of the ravine in a fiery orange hue.

Below him, the camp sprang into turmoil. Pirates scrambled for cover and weapons, shouting to each other in Hakiru.

He had heard everything. The cold wind had brought Adara and Salidar's whole conversation to his mancery-enhanced ears. Salidar had lied to him! Durrin had never been on the emperor's errand. The opposite, in fact—he had murdered the emperor's friend and ally.

In Durrin's shock and rage, he had unleashed his attack early, aiming a blast of fire directly at the vizier.

Let it go! he thought furiously, even as he poured more fire onto the rocky slope. *Focus! Get the queen. Get out.* That's all they had to do.

An arrow whizzed by Durrin's head, missing him by inches. He pivoted behind a tree, moments before two more arrows filled the air with deathly hisses.

Oh. And don't get killed.

He leapt from behind the tree, his sword flashing. The camp below him was in shambles, archers reloading as others grabbed weapons, their yells filling the air. His attack at Salidar had left at least two tents on fire.

Another arrow sped at him, which he deflected with his sword. Impressive. He was fifty yards away still, uphill, and with unpredictable winds. These pirates were good.

Durrin snapped his wrist, shooting bolts of fire down the hillside. They blazed in the cold air as they spiraled down into the camp, exploding on contact. Though none of the firebolts were large enough to be fatal, they could certainly cause burns or catch gear or canvas on fire. He aimed for where the archers crouched, keeping his shots away from Adara and the cloudship.

Something flashed in Durrin's peripheral vision. He spun to see Bladebeak diving at him, the griffin's wings skimming the tops of trees as he swept down the side of the ravine, claws outstretched. Durrin rolled for cover, using the movement to summon a wave of fire above him. Bladebeak careened to avoid it.

"Volthorn, you better carry through," he muttered. This fight was already more dicey than he had anticipated.

Shouts mingled with the hiss of arrows and the roar of flame. Pirates ran in all directions.

Adara looked around. Salidar had disappeared. No one seemed to be paying attention to her in the chaos. Wincing as pain lanced through her numb feet, she scrambled to a nearby outcropping of stone, brushing the snow away with her feet. There—a jagged rock gleamed in the firelight, just as she had noticed earlier when they had tied her to the trees. She knelt with her back to the rock, feeling with her bound hands until she had positioned the knot on top of the most jagged edge. Then she rubbed her hands up and down, sawing away at the knot.

A yelp caused her to glance up. A swifter was dancing around the camp, the tip of her long tail aflame. One of the other pirates grabbed her tail and plunged it into the snow. The flame sputtered out.

Streaks of fire were arcing through the storm, hissing as they buried themselves in the snow. The archers in the crew were crouching behind trees and rocks, while the others were disappearing into the brush surrounding the camp, weapons in hand.

Adara looked up the side of the ravine, toward the source of the firebolts. She could barely make out the pyromancer through the trees, running downhill toward them. A griffin wheeled and circled above him, rending the air with his cries. Each time he dived too close, a flash of fire or a slash of sword warded him off.

Adara's hand slipped, and she bit back a cry of pain as the edge of the rock scraped the skin of her wrist. She resumed the sawing motion, looking around again. No one had noticed her yet. She shifted her angle, her heart thumping as the fibers of the rope slowly gave way.

The knot shifted. She tugged, and her left hand jerked free. Ignoring the bloody scratches on her palm, she twisted around and yanked at the cords still binding her right hand to a nearby tree.

At last, the knot came free. Adara felt around in the snow for a rock—any weapon was better than nothing. Then she gathered up the hem of her nightgown and ran doubled over through the camp. The bulk of the cloudship loomed before her, tossing and straining in the wind. She ducked her head and ran underneath it, her heart pounding, knowing that a downdraft at the wrong second would crush her between the ground and the hull of the gondola. But three heartbeats later, she emerged on the other side, opposite the rest of the camp.

"Going somewhere, Your Majesty?"

Adara spun to see Salidar emerge from the trees, still wrapped in his cloak. A smug smile flitted across his face.

Adara straightened to face the vizier. "They've come to rescue me."

"Who?" Salidar raised an eyebrow. "A pyromaniac with a sword? He faces a score of experienced warriors and will soon be overwhelmed."

"Then why are you cowering over here?" Adara retorted.

"To catch run-away princesses who are too smart for themselves," Salidar taunted, moving closer.

"Catch this, then!" Adara flung the rock she had hidden in the sleeve of her robe. She didn't wait to see if it hit him before darting away toward the trees.

Two seconds later, Salidar barked something in the Numinous Tongue. Adara fell, tripping over the air itself as she ran into an invisible obstacle. She landed in the snow and rolled over, wincing in pain.

Salidar took a step closer, opening his mouth for another spell.

"Mikarash sha-ka!" a voice bellowed.

Salidar spun as a figure crashed from the woods.

"Volthorn!" Adara cried. "Careful! He's a verbomancer!"

The korrik commander didn't hear her as he charged forward, his sword glowing red. "You will curse the day you touched an Everborn!"

A wind picked up around Salidar, stirring the snow and plants around him. It slammed into Volthorn, halting his charge and forcing him to raise a hand in front of his eyes. He took another staggering step forward, then sunk down to his knees to avoid being knocked over.

Salidar changed the tone of his incantation, and the wind began to twist around Volthorn, kicking up snow and leaves in a swirling vortex.

Small rocks and branches pummeled him from all directions, eliciting flashes of light as they impacted his enchanted armor.

Salidar paused his chanting, but the vortex continued. He laughed in triumph. "Now is the day and age of verbomancy. Never before have words wielded such power!"

Volthorn struggled to rise, but a dead tree branch slammed into him, knocking him over. "Adara!" he bellowed. "Run!"

Run? And just abandon him? Adara looked around for a weapon. Verbomancy, though summoned by words, was sustained by thought. If she could break Salidar's concentration—

"Hey!" Adara yelled, facing the side of the ravine and waving her hands. "We're over here! Help!"

Salidar's head whipped around to look at her, then followed the direction of her wave, searching the trees for whoever she was calling to. He searched in vain, for there was no one.

The windstorm around Volthorn ebbed, and he surged forward, thundering a war cry. The vizier backed away, holding his hands in front of him and shouting a hasty command.

Volthorn's sword glanced off an invisible barrier in front of the vizier, releasing a flash of red light. He moved to the right and slashed again, but Salidar pivoted and maintained the shield. Volthorn struck low, sweeping his sword under the invisible barrier and slashing through the hem of Salidar's robe, narrowly missing his legs. Salidar retreated, his chanting growing more desperate as Volthorn continued to rain blows upon his defense. Finally, the vizier turned and darted around the gondola, back toward the camp.

Volthorn turned and beckoned to Adara. "Hurry!"

"How are we getting away?" Had Volthorn brought horses? On foot, they would never outpace the swifters among the Hakiru.

Volthorn grabbed the rungs of a ladder hanging from the cloudship. "On this contraption."

Adara balked. "We're *flying?*"

"Yes!" Volthorn peered under the gondola at the melee still raging in the rest of the camp. "Hurry!"

Salidar's voice bellowed from the far side of the cloudship. "The queen is escaping up the canyon! After her!"

Volthorn sheathed his sword and hauled himself up the ladder. Adara followed, though her arms, still sore from her bonds, screamed in protest.

The ladder bounced as Volthorn sprang over the rail. Adara followed a moment later and joined Volthorn lying flat against the deck. Three seconds later, she heard the patter of footsteps as several pirates ran around the cloudship and disappeared into the trees farther up the ravine. Salidar was still barking instructions in the camp.

Something cold touched her arm. She rolled to see Volthorn handing her a sheathed knife. "Start cutting the mooring lines," he whispered. "They'll be onto us in a minute when the swifters can't find your scent."

Adara nodded and grabbed the knife. She glanced up and down the length of the gondola. Pairs of mooring lines were fastened to both the prow and the stern, and each side held two more, making a total of eight. She ran to the left side—was it starboard or port?—and began slashing at the rope.

The wood beneath her jerked. She turned to see Volthorn move on to the second rope on the right side, having already cut the first. How had he cut his rope so fast? Hers hadn't parted by a single strand.

Adara glanced down at her knife and blushed. She removed the leather sheath. It was in tatters. *Oops.*

An angry cry sounded below them. She glanced over the rail to see the pirates running back through the woods, outrage written on their faces.

The ship rocked again as Volthorn slashed the other rope on the right side. "Your Majesty! Hurry!"

Adara slashed at the rope. This time the knife cut easily through a couple strands. After two more slashes, the rest of the rope snapped from the tension. She raced to the second rope on her side, pausing to grab the ladder and heave it on board.

"The ballast!" she yelled over her shoulder, pointing to large bags of rocks sitting on the deck.

"You get them!" Volthorn hacked at the last rope holding the stern. "Hang on!"

The rope snapped, its split ends whipping the air. The cloudship, now tethered only by the two ropes at the prow, lurched and rocked until its deck tilted sharply forward. Adara lost her footing and landed heavily on the deck, scrambling to grab onto something before she started rolling toward the prow. Branches snapped as the front of the balloon scraped against nearby trees. She hoped the canvas held.

More cries from the pirates turned her eyes back to the camp. They were *all* running toward the cloudship now. Luckily they weren't firing arrows—probably to avoid puncturing the balloon.

Volthorn slid past her, grabbed the railing, and started to haul up the second ladder. "I'll get the last ropes!" he said. "Drop the ballast!"

A garishly dressed snippen appeared on the railing, brandishing a rapier. Volthorn knocked her off the ship with a backhand, sending her spinning into a pile of snow.

Adara scrambled up the deck to where a pile of ballast bags sat in a compartment. She grabbed a bag in both hands and heaved it over the side, aiming at the pirates below her.

Where was the fire-wielding hero?

Scarcely had the thought occurred to her than a flash lit up the scene. The figure in the red cape burst from the woods, his sword gleaming in the light of the flame in his left hand as he dodged past opponents.

The pirates ran to stop him. He blocked a cutlass from a human, landed a kick under his opponent's guard, then swiveled to block a mace swung by a korrik running up behind him. He somersaulted over his opponent, blocked a follow-up swing, and knocked the korrik's feet out from under him.

The ship jolted again. She turned to see Volthorn slash through a rope at the prow. Only one remained now, and it strained like it might break at any moment. Volthorn crossed to it.

"Volthorn!" Adara yelled. The korrik turned, and she pointed at the figure in red below. "Aren't we waiting for him?"

Volthorn scowled. He looked at the melee unfolding in the camp. Then at the rope in his claws. Then back at the melee.

"He's with us, isn't he?" Adara yelled over the hubbub, grabbing another bag of ballast and tossing it overboard. Volthorn nodded, but scowled and looked back at the rope.

Adara frowned. Surely he didn't mean to abandon an ally—did he?

"Your safety is most important!" Volthorn yelled back.

"If we leave him, he'll be killed!" Adara shouted.

A look of indecision passed over Volthorn's face, conflicting emotions wrestling for dominance. After an endless moment, the conflict gave way to resignation.

"Fine," Volthorn grunted. He released the rope, grabbed a bag of ballast, and chucked it overboard at the pirates below, yelling a way cry.

The figure in red ducked and wove through his opponents. An avir ran at him, and without even breaking stride, he grabbed the avir's spear and drove the blunt end into his stomach. Wrenching the spear free, he grabbed it in both hands to block a huge man's attack, then knocked the man over the head with the haft.

Why doesn't he strike at them? Adara wondered. He was certainly deft with weapons, yet she hadn't seen him even draw blood.

Half a dozen pirates remained between the ship and the figure in red. With great sweeps of his captured spear, he summoned two furrows of fire in front of him, creating an avenue between him and the ship. The pirates stumbled to a halt to avoid the flames.

"Cut the rope!" the man yelled, now only a handful of yards from the ship.

Volthorn slashed through the last rope, and the ship lurched free. The man sprang off a boulder and vaulted into the air, pyromancy enhancing his jump to impossible proportions. Twenty feet into the air he leapt, grabbing hold of the ship's railing a moment before it rose out of reach.

Adara ran across the pitching deck, reaching for the man's arms to pull him over the railing and onto the deck. He sat there a few moments, his chest heaving.

Then he looked up, the hint of a smile on his grim face. "Welcome aboard, Your Majesty."

CHAPTER 33

ADRIFT

The next few minutes flashed by. First they had to deal with the griffin in the marooned crew, who screeched with fury as he dove at the ship. The pyromancer—Durrin, as Adara finally remembered from their encounter in the palace—drove the griffin back again and again with sword thrusts and plumes of fire. But only when Volthorn figured out how to fire the ballista at the prow did the griffin finally veer away and disappear into the storm.

Then a mountainside loomed through the clouds, and Volthorn and Adara scrambled to toss additional ballast overboard as Durrin poured heat into the balloon. A horrible crunching sound rent the air as the gondola skimmed the tops of several trees, but then they were rising again, climbing into the sky.

Volthorn slumped against the side of the gondola, his chest rising and falling. "We . . . made it," he said, flashing Adara a grin. "We made it!"

Adara collapsed as well, a laugh escaping her as the tension in her body gave way to relief.

"Don't laugh too soon." Durrin strode to the opposite side of the gondola and started inspecting the rigging.

"But we did it!" Volthorn said. "Against all odds we found the pirates, faced them down, and slipped out from right under their noses!"

"*I* faced them down," Durrin said, still continuing his inspection.

"For which I am extremely grateful," Adara cut in before the exchange escalated. She stood and gave the pyromancer a lot curtsy. She imagined she must be quite a sight, in her tattered coat and thin nightgown. She had lost one of her slippers in the scramble up the ladder. "My life is indebted to both of you."

"Even more than you know." Durrin crossed back to the middle of the gondola and pumped more fire into the balloon. "The pirates kidnapped you to exchange you for ransom, either to Elandria or Calamar. But Lord Salidar—he was planning to kill you at the first opportunity."

Adara recalled Salidar's calculating gaze, and she shivered despite herself. *He killed my father. He tried to kill me, too.*

"But why?" Volthorn said. "Why would he go to all this risk to eliminate Adara? Her Majesty's death would devastate our people, surely, but it wouldn't make us surrender. Salidar must realize that."

Adara's thoughts turned to what Salidar had said about her father. "I think he's afraid of me," she said.

"Afraid?" Durrin frowned. "That doesn't sound like the vizier."

"He's worried I'll contact Emperor Stoneclaw," Adara said. "Stoneclaw and my father were friends. I think he's worried I'll leverage that to negotiate an early end to the war."

Volthorn scoffed. "The emperor doesn't want peace."

"I'm not so sure," said Durrin, wincing as he sat on a bench across from them. "The politics in Calamar are complicated. Salidar himself told me that he had to assemble a pro-war coalition to persuade the emperor to attack Elandria."

"So my hunch earlier this summer was true!" Adara turned to Volthorn. "We might really end this war with negotiations!"

Volthorn didn't respond. His gaze was trained on Durrin. "Rendhart. You're wounded."

"Nothing I can't handle." Durrin undid the clasp of his cloak, letting it fall around him. The whole left side of his combat suit was stained dark red. Adara gasped involuntarily.

"Spear thrust, I think." Durrin gritted his teeth as he pressed a hand to his side. "Pierced the chainmail here, right under my ribcage. I don't think it went too deep."

Volthorn stood. "We should clean and bandage it. Your Majesty, could you find us some water?"

Adara nodded, glad to avert her eyes from the blood. It took some rummaging, but she found a metal mug in a chest of supplies and filled it from one of the water casks onboard.

When she turned back, Volthorn had found a strip of fabric while Durrin had removed his chainmail jerkin and had cut a long strip in his shirt to expose the wound.

"Let me see that water, Your Majesty," Durrin said. She gave him the mug. Holding it in one hand, he passed his other hand around it. After a few seconds, the water began boiling and steaming. Durrin changed the motion of his hand, and the steam from the water diminished.

"What was that for?" Volthorn said.

"Trade secret." Durrin wetted a wad of cloth in the mug and dabbed at his side, wincing with each touch. "Decreases the chance of infection and fever."

Volthorn snorted. "Old bards' tales. Next you'll be asking for leeches to drain your 'blue blood' to compensate for your lost 'red blood.'"

"Can we please stop talking about blood?" Adara said. She felt like she was about to either throw up or faint, despite deliberately not looking at Durrin's wound. There were certain areas where her royal tutelage had left her entirely unprepared. To distract herself, she turned her attention to finding a blanket and some better footwear. Her legs and feet were freezing.

"You lucked out, Durrin," she heard Volthorn comment. "Looks like it just pierced muscle. No organs."

By the time Adara returned with warmer gear, Durrin's bandage was tied neatly in place—though it was already turning red—and he was replacing his chainmail.

Adara sat across from him, wrapping her blanket around her. She studied him. "Who are you exactly, Durrin?"

Durrin's eyes flickered over to Volthorn, then back to Adara. "I am a pyromancer, raised and trained in Calamar," he said. "I used to work for various clients in Calamar, especially Lord Salidar." His face filled with regret. "I committed many horrible deeds. But I have sworn to abandon that path and repair the damage I have caused—as best I can."

"Humph," grunted Volthorn. He got to his feet and stomped off.

"I learned of Salidar's plot," continued Durrin. "And I came here to try to warn you. I came too late."

"But you didn't," Adara said. "I saw you in the palace before the attack." She looked over at where Volthorn stood at the prow. "You were going to see Commander Skarr."

The implication in her words hung in the air, the silence as frosty as the fading storm.

Durrin cleared his throat. "Volthorn did not consider my warning . . . credible enough to warrant action."

Adara turned to Volthorn, feeling her skin flush red with anger. "So you knew! You knew this attack was coming, and you did nothing! Even after I asked to be moved from the royal wing!"

Volthorn kept his back to them. When he replied, it was in an even voice. "In hindsight, my actions were mistaken, yes. But hindsight is not foresight. At the time, I made what I thought was the best decision with the knowledge I had. Durrin was not exactly a trustworthy source of information."

Adara glanced back at Durrin. The pyromancer's eyes bored into Volthorn's back for a few seconds, his mouth turned in a scowl. Then he shook his head slightly. "What is past is past. Arguing will get us nowhere—and especially not back toward civilization."

His words brought Adara to her feet. "That's right. How do we steer this thing?"

Durrin nodded at Volthorn. "Ask Commander Skarr. He assured me he could figure it out."

Adara stared expectantly at Volthorn. He frowned as his eyes scanned the ship and its unfamiliar contraptions and rigging. "Right! Let's see . . . this can't be too hard."

He crossed to the stern and lay a hand on the tiller—a thick wooden beam connected to a fin of fabric protruding behind the stern. He pushed at the tiller, then leaned more weight into it. "This . . . ought too . . ."

"It's locked," Durrin said. "Pin. Underneath."

Volthorn studied the tiller, then found and removed a wooden dowel holding it in place. This time the tiller shifted under his weight, swinging the fin to the left. "There we go," he said. "Just like sailing a boat."

Durrin raised an eyebrow.

Adara glanced around. "I don't think we're turning."

"Of course we're turning," Volthorn said. "You just can't tell because we're surrounded by clouds."

Durrin pointed through the white haze at a slightly whiter circle of luminosity. "The Sun's there. We're probably two hours past noon. Now, Commander, turn the other direction and we'll see what happens."

Volthorn pulled the tiller back toward him. Adara kept her eyes on the Sun, noting its position in reference to the cloudship's rigging. After several seconds, its position remained unchanged.

"I don't understand." Volthorn shook his head. "There has to be a way to steer!"

"Not when free-floating," Durrin said. "Their navigator explained it to me. On a boat, you have two forces acting on your craft: the wind and the water. If the wind is acting on you with a different vector than the water—"

"Vector?" Adara asked.

"A unilateral force with a direction and a magnitude," Durrin said.

Adara shook her head. "You lost me at unilateral."

Durrin took a breath. "If the wind is pushing your boat with a stronger or weaker force than the water, or in a different direction, you can use a rudder to steer. But in an airship, there is no water. We simply float wherever the wind takes us. There's nothing the tiller can find purchase against—it's like trying to steer a boat on a still lake with no wind and no oars."

"Then how do the pirates steer?" Volthorn asked.

"Those propellers." Durrin motioned toward two sets of blades on outriggers. "They give the ship forward momentum through the air, like rowing a ship."

"Well." Volthorn nodded. "Let's give them a try. Your Majesty—I know pedaling is beneath your rank, but Rendhart is wounded . . ."

"I can pedal," Adara said, smiling.

It took them a few minutes to get the hang of the ship's two pedaling contraptions. The pedals were designed for swifters' hind legs, and while they accommodated upright bipeds, it took some experimenting with different handholds before Adara and Volthorn got into a consistent rhythm. The two blades at the stern spun faster and faster until they became blurs, and Adara could feel the air against her face as the ship picked up speed.

"This is what the pirates called 'churning,'" Durrin said from the tiller. "Like churning a butter tub, I guess."

"I've never churned butter," Adara grunted, straining to keep her feet moving quickly. "But if it's anywhere near as hard as this, I'm giving all the milkmaids in the palace a raise."

Volthorn glanced at the Sun's position through the clouds. "We're still heading southeast. Can you turn us around?"

Durrin swung on the tiller and the ship shifted in response, slowly arcing toward the northwest. Clouds still hung all about them, making it so Adara could barely see the front spar of the gondola before it was swallowed by mist. As they turned into the wind, the air battered harder against her face, wicking away the sweat pooling on her brow.

They struggled at the pedals for what felt like forever, but was probably just a quarter of an hour. Adara's legs tired quickly, but it was her lungs that gave out first, aching from inhaling the cold air.

Eventually Durrin insisted that he take a turn despite his wound. Adara took the tiller, blushing with embarrassment. This adventure seemed bent on exposing all her weak points.

After another quarter of an hour, Durrin and Volthorn both began to tire. Sweat dripped from their brows as their legs moved slower and slower, but both seemed intent on outlasting the other.

Finally, Adara spoke up. "This is futile. We're just going to tire ourselves out."

Volthorn and Durrin both staggered off the pedals and collapsed, gratefully accepting mugs of water that Adara proffered them.

"I don't . . . get it," Durrin said. "The swifters . . . made it look . . . so easy."

"They're swifters," Volthorn said. "They're built to run. I've known swifters to sprint five miles without so much as a pause."

"It's the wind," Adara said. "We're heading straight into it. It's like rowing upstream—twice the work for half the gain."

"If we're even gaining at all." Durrin looked out over the vista. "I have the feeling we've still been moving southeast, just at a slower pace. It's hard to tell with these clouds."

Volthorn fished a piece of jerky from a pouch he carried, then passed the pouch around. "We certainly can't 'churn' all the way back to Saven— we'd die from exhaustion first. Stars, but how do these pirates do it?"

"We could land," Durrin said. "Find a village, get some horses, and trek back on foot."

Volthorn shook his head. "We're over the Mitrian Mountains now. Villages are scarce here, and those that do exist are inhabited by the Mitrian tribes."

"I've been among the Mitrians," Durrin said. "They have good relationships with Elandria. I speak their language well and have connections with various chieftains that I could leverage."

"They are a cruel, barbarous, and unpredictable people," Volthorn objected. "I don't trust them. Not with the queen's life, at any rate. Besides, even ignoring the Mitrians, there are bears and reptilians and wyverns."

"And dragons, even," Adara added.

"Dragons are a myth," Durrin said.

Adara folded her arms. "No, they aren't."

"Yes, they are. They're born from people's imaginations, the fanciful combination of a wyvern's wings with a tyrannosaur's size."

"My great-great-grandfather slew a dragon," Adara said. "There's a tapestry in the palace depicting it. And a stained-glass window. And a ballad."

"Show me the beast's skeleton, and I'll believe you," Durrin said.

Adara turned to Volthorn. "Commander, back me up."

Volthorn rolled his eyes. "You're both getting off track," he said. "Dragons or no dragons, I don't want to risk landing."

"Then what else do we do?" Durrin asked. "We can't pedal back northwest, and we can't land. Do we overshoot and land in Marisau? It could take weeks to get back to Elandria from there."

"Well, if we could steer, we wouldn't be in this mess," Volthorn snapped.

"And that's *my* fault?" Durrin glowered at him. "Stealing the airship was *your* idea."

Adara stood up and walked to the prow, away from their bickering. Something was whispering to her from the recesses of her mind: the memory of an idea . . .

She turned. "We need to climb higher."

Durrin and Volthorn stopped mid-sentence and turned to look at her.

"We need to gain altitude," she repeated. "Air currents run in different directions at different heights. If we climb above the storm clouds, we might hit some prevailing winds running north or west."

Volthorn cocked his head. "Are you sure, Your Majesty?"

"Of course," Adara said. The memory was coming back to her. "It was in a lesson one of my tutors gave me."

Volthorn shrugged. "Well, we don't have anything else to try."

Durrin poured more heat into the balloon, and soon they were rising again, slipping between layers of clouds. The temperature dropped the higher they climbed, and soon Adara was wrapped in three blankets, fighting to keep her teeth from chattering.

After a few minutes, they broke out of the last bank of clouds into the glorious light of the Sun. Adara gasped. Around them stretched an infinite expanse of clouds, with towering pillars of gold, deep valleys of shadowy blue, and rolling hills of magnificent white.

"It's so beautiful." She sighed, standing at the railing in raptured awe. "Imagine what it must be like to be a griffin—to soar above the clouds, dipping and gliding through such a wonderland."

"I don't think even griffins can fly this high," Durrin said, joining her at the railing. "The air is thin—can you tell?"

He was right—her breath was coming short and labored, and not just from the breathless vistas before her.

"More importantly," said Volthorn, "Her Majesty was exactly right. Look at the clouds—they're moving away from us. I think we've hit a current running north."

"North's good enough for me," Durrin said. "We can head west later. I don't know about you, but I am about thirty hours overdue for a nap."

Late that afternoon, Volthorn shook Adara awake. "Your Majesty. Wake up."

Adara shifted, unwilling to surrender her warm cocoon of blankets to the chill air around her. How long had she slept? An hour? However long, it hadn't been long enough.

"It's urgent, Your Majesty. We're sinking."

Adara sat bolt upright. "Sinking?" She stood and looked out over the railing. The clouds had largely departed, revealing a mazelike terrain of mountain ridges and deep valleys below them.

"We've been keeping the balloon hot, but the mountaintops are getting nearer," Volthorn said.

Durrin appeared at that moment, climbing down a rope ladder from the balloon above them. If he noticed the drop of thousands and thousands of feet beneath him, he didn't show it.

"There's two small rips in the front of the balloon," he said as he stepped down into the gondola. "Probably from the trees back in the ravine."

"So we're losing air," Volthorn said.

"Prime vapor," Durrin said. "It's a gas that's lighter than air."

Volthorn scrunched up his scaly nose. "Lighter than . . . air?"

Durrin shrugged. "Don't ask me. It's what the pirates called it."

"So we're losing this prime air vapor," Adara said. "Can we patch the holes?"

Durrin shook his head. "Even if I knew how, there's no way to reach them unless we land."

"Then we heat the balloon even hotter to compensate?" Adara suggested.

Durrin looked upward. "Only to a point, or the heat might rip the seams or even set the canvas on fire. I'd rather land now while we can still control our descent."

"I still don't like the idea of landing in this terrain," Volthorn said. "We might be able to make it past the mountains if we keep going."

"The Sun will set in about an hour," Adara said. "I'd rather not crash into a mountain in the dark."

"Aye," Durrin said. "Terrible things, mountains. Creep up on you unawares, like a lynx in a field of daisies."

It was such an uncharacteristic thing for the tall warrior to say that Adara and Volthorn both turned and stared at him.

"Sorry." Durrin shrugged. "Just repeating something I heard once. Never mind."

Adara pointed toward the northern horizon at a larger mass poking above the forest of mountain tops. "What's that?"

Volthorn squinted. "Mount Terramor, most likely. It's the largest mountain in the Mitrian chain. On a clear day, you can see its top from the palace at Saven."

Adara felt a strange earnestness swell within her. "Let's see if, with the propellers and the wind, we can make it there and land before dark. Then we'll at least know where we are."

As Durrin focused on heating the balloon, Adara stared at the mountain in front of them. She had seen its distant peak many times before. But now, for some reason, it was calling to her.

CHAPTER 34

THE BASTION OF MEMORY

Igh Mage Sablewing, guardian of the Bastion of Memory, awoke early.

The griffin rose from her nest, gazing out the windows of her aerie. The library beneath her tower was quiet and dark—still slumbering. The faintest tinges of light were marshalling on the eastern sky, where the library's canyon opened out. In the other three directions, the mighty spurs of Mount Terramor still loomed dark and cold above the library's towers. Soon the rising Sun would bedazzle those rocky flanks as it sparkled on yesterday's snow.

Flinching at the chill air outside her windows, Sablewing decided to forego her usual morning flight and descend the stairs instead. She soon came to the Hall of History, where an early-rising scribe had already lit a series of lumen globes. Lining the southern wall was a row of carved reliefs, preserving in stony memory the history of the world. Each panel was carved in a different style by a different hand. A third of the panels still sat empty.

Sablewing passed through a series of rooms—kitchens, storage rooms, offices—then began another descent. Though she saw no one, she knew she was not alone.

"Thank you for your presence," she murmured, bowing her feathery head as she walked.

It is thy service at this library I must thank. The voice came to her mind rather than to her ears. With it came a feeling of peace that washed over Sablewing, wiping away the last vestiges of sleep.

"What would you say to me?" the griffin asked. Angels never communed with her without a purpose.

A party approaches the gates.

Sablewing nodded, changing her course. "Then I shall meet them."

There is one among them who has committed grievous sins in his past. But he seeks to change. You must let him enter.

"I shall." Sablewing exited the library's main building and took to the air, feeling the cold autumn breeze beneath her wings. Winter was coming early. After a moment, she landed at the main gate of the outer wall. She felt the angelic presence flicker, and she knew her unseen visitor was about to leave.

"Whom have I had the honor of communing with?" Sablewing asked, stopping and bowing again.

Yavenya is my name. I am a keeper of scrolls.

Sablewing looked at the library behind her. "As am I."

My scrolls are of a different nature.

Sablewing opened her beak, wishing to ask a thousand questions she had long wondered about the realms beyond death. But as with previous communions across the veil of sight, she let the question stay on her tongue. The angel had come not to satisfy her curiosity, but to deliver a message.

Instead, Sablewing advanced to the gates, arriving at the precise moment that someone knocked.

The party on the other side of the gate was unlike any Sablewing had ever seen.

There was an avir girl—Elandrian by the shape of her chin—barely past her youth, clad in boots much too big for her, a heavy coat much too coarse, and beneath it the half-shredded hem of a silk nightgown.

Then there was a korrik warrior, perhaps in his thirties, with a deep scar running down his cheek, rough-hewn rings cluttering his fingers with gems, and his clawed hand resting confidently on the pommel of a short sword.

And lastly there was a human, tall and lithe, clad in chainmail and leather, and draped in a fiery red cloak. Though he favored one side, his stance betrayed a deep familiarity with combat.

Behind the trio, the edge of the Sun peeked through the canyon's opening, turning the skies into an inferno of red and gold.

"Welcome," Sablewing said, inclining her head. "What brings you here on this early wintry day?"

No one responded at first. They each looked at each other, as if waiting for someone else to begin. At the insisting nods of the korrik, the avir maiden stepped forward. "You'll find our story quite unbelievable."

"Try me," Sablewing said. "Someone with an incredible story knocks on these doors every week or so, it seems."

The avir took a breath. "I am Queen Adara Everborn, sovereign of Elandria. Two nights ago, I was kidnapped by Hakiru pirates." She motioned to the man and korrik flanking her. "My companions, Volthorn and Durrin, rescued me and we escaped in the pirates' cloudship. Late last evening we crashed about three miles—"

"Crash-landed" interjected the human.

"Crash-landed about three miles down the canyon. We saw the towers of this building from the air last night, and we have come to ask for food, shelter, and aid."

Sablewing blinked. "That *is* quite a story."

"We can prove it," the girl said.

"You already have," Sablewing said. "I can see your signet ring with the Everborn crest quite clearly. And the cloak you wear is obviously of Hakiru make—that twill weave is quite distinctive. Your companion—Volthorn, was it?—bears high-ranking Elandrian insignia on his shoulder. And Durrin." She eyed him critically. "You must have been injured in the fight. I see signs of blood loss in your face."

The three asylum seekers stared at her, looking slightly stunned by the display of information. Sablewing sighed. She tended to have that effect on people.

"You had best enter," she said, stepping back and swinging the gate open with her claws. "There's a gate room to the left that should have food, drink, and chairs. Feel free to light a fire; you should have no difficulty with that, seeing that Durrin's a pyromancer."

The travelers exchanged surprised looks with each other. Sablewing sighed again. "His sword is clearly designed for a pyromancer. Please—rest and replenish. I will fetch someone who can care for your injuries."

"And we need a griffin messenger," grunted the korrik, "to send word to Elandria that Her Majesty is safe."

Sablewing paused and cocked her head. "Hmm . . . I'm sorry. What was that?"

The korrik exchanged a baffled glance with the human.

The avir girl spoke up. "We would be greatly obliged if you could spare a griffin messenger." She curtsied. "Please."

Sablewing smiled. She always liked a display of good manners, especially from royalty. "I will see if someone is willing to make the journey. I'll be back shortly."

※

Sablewing returned to the gate room within a half hour, this time with several others. Sure enough, a hardy fire was roaring in the hearth, and the korrik was busy whipping up some tea to supplement the bread and cheese the hungry trio had already half devoured.

"Your arrival has created quite the stir," Sablewing said. "We don't often get visitors in the late autumn—much less royalty." She introduced the veritable crowd of people behind her. All of them were dressed in simple white robes, the only color that of the blue, red, or green sashes at their waists. "Mariam and her assistant are expert healers; they will look at Durrin's wound, as well as the scrapes and cuts on Her Majesty's hands."

"And my feet," Volthorn said. "I fear some of my claws might be frostbitten."

Sablewing looked at him expectantly.

"If you please, of course," he muttered. "Please."

"After Mariam attends to you, she will show you your rooms," Sablewing said. "We have a number of chambers built into these outer walls where you can stay for as long as you remain here."

"Thank you." Adara curtsied for a second time. "We are indeed grateful to you, and forever in your debt."

Sablewing indicated a pair of young griffins. "Razorclaw and Thunderclaw are willing to take a message to the closest Elandrian outpost this afternoon. We brought parchment and ink so you can write a report."

"Excellent," Volthorn said. "I'll get on that immediately."

Sablewing brought forward a round, pudgy man in his middling years. "Lyman here—"

"I'm a cloudship fanatic," Lyman interrupted, rubbing his hands together furiously. "I've read everything about 'em. Tried to build 'em, but it's devilishly hard."

"Lyman," Sablewing clucked.

"Right, Your Mageship. Sorry. Slip of the tongue. Won't happen again. Anyways, I'm just itching to see the one you came in. Like to get 'er up flying, if'n I can, though I suppose it's in devilishly rough—"

"Lyman."

"Terribly rough shape, I mean. Terribly rough shape. Anyway, I'll take my volunteers down the canyon and have a look, if'n you please." He turned and nodded to a trio of youths, who followed him out the front gate and into the snowy wilderness with postures indicating they'd much rather stay in the warm gatehouse.

"Sablewing," said Adara as she sipped at her tea. "May I ask—what *is* the Bastion of Memory?"

"Surely you've heard of us," Sablewing said. "We sit just beyond your borders."

"I have," Adara said. "But I only know that it's a library for the Luminant Order."

"That it is." Sablewing nodded. "But it is so much more." She beckoned Adara to the gate room's window, which offered a view of the grounds and the Bastion's main structure farther up the canyon. "What do you see?"

"It's a magnificent building," Adara said. "The spires and windows give it the semblance of a palace. The towers resemble those of a fortress. And the overall shape—it reminds me of a mountain."

"You are right in all those things," Sablewing said. "The Bastion is a palace—a residence for any who choose to come here. It is a fortress—a place where truth and knowledge are defended. And it is a mountain—a shadow of the mighty Mount Terramor above it, which itself is only an echo of the Cosmic Mountain, the eternal abode of the Sky Father."

"It is beautiful." Adara gazed at the gleaming marble spires.

"It is a monument to the Light and to the Eldest," Sablewing said. "It has to be beautiful."

"Are we allowed to enter?" Adara asked.

"Only those who are worthy, and who are willing to obey the terms, can enter," Sablewing said.

To Sablewing's surprise, Durrin spoke up from the corner of the room. "What are the terms?"

"The heart must be open to understand," Sablewing said. "The mind must be willing to discard past ideas. The eyes must be ready to see the world anew. And the tongue must know its place and speak only peace. No anger, hate, or malice can enter."

"I would like to enter, and am willing to obey the terms," Adara said eagerly. "I imagine there is much within your walls that I should learn."

"Me too," Volthorn grunted. "If we'll be here a few days while the cloudship is repaired, I may as well make the most of it."

"Your requests are granted," Sablewing said. She looked to the pyromancer, but he sat still in the corner, brow furrowed, mouth turned in a frown. Was he the one the angel had referenced? His gear suggested a Calamarvan origin. What had brought him into the service of Elandria's queen?

She turned back to the others. "After you get some rest this morning, I would be happy to show you around."

Sablewing bowed and left the gatehouse, heading back to the library to commence her day. She hadn't gotten far before she heard the crunch of heavy footsteps in the snow behind her.

Turning, she saw Durrin catching up to her, his face flashing with pain as each step jostled his bandaged side.

"Your Mageship," Durrin said, nearly gasping the words. "I seek admittance as well. I pledge to abide by the terms."

Sablewing looked the man over again. His armor and sword both suggested an affinity for violence. But it was his eyes that grabbed her attention. In their depths, she could see horrible scars.

"From where do you hail, Durrin?"

The man bowed his head. "I am from Calamar. I was trained in the Imperial Pyromantic Academy. But I no longer owe them allegiance."

"Calamar has declared itself an enemy to our order," Sablewing said, frowning. "When they purged us from their borders thirty years ago, many of our shrines were burned by your comrades."

It was then that Durrin did something entirely unexpected. He dropped to his knees.

"Please," he said. "I know I am not worthy to enter. I am a stranger to your ways. I have not won your trust. I have a dark and violent past. Yet I seek answers worth more to me than silver or gold."

Sablewing marveled. In her years as guardian of the Bastion, many proud souls had stood before her. They had demanded entrance, proclaiming their qualifications, offering hefty sums of money, or threatening retaliation if they were excluded. None of those had entered.

Durrin had all the markings of someone like them—his violent past, his advanced training, his expensive gear. But never before had someone asked to enter with such humility.

"You are fortunate, Durrin no longer of Calamar," Sablewing said. "Your arrival was heralded by angels. May your stay at the Bastion bring you the answers you seek."

Chapter 35

Tales of Creation

"I still don't quite understand the difference between the three orders," Durrin said.

He, Adara, and Volthorn walked with Sablewing down a hall of the Bastion. The griffin led them at a slow pace, so that Adara and Volthorn could admire the tapestries and artwork on the walls. Even still, Durrin could barely keep up. He had lost a great deal of blood that morning as the healers had cleaned and dressed his wound, and several hours of rest had failed to revitalize him. Mariam had wanted him to keep resting, but an unquenchable yearning for answers had compelled him to accompany the others.

"There were four orders once," Sablewing explained. "Each was founded at the dawn of time, at the birth of Zenitha itself, before even the Rending. In the beginning, they worked together: four parts of one whole, even as this library has four halls."

"What happened?" Adara asked. She now wore a long blue dress and a fur coat, loaned to her from the Bastion's wardrobes.

"The others lost their way," Sablewing said. "They forgot their true purpose, or they were blinded to it. They set their sights on other ends. Pride followed, and all that it brings: division, envy, contention. The orders gradually drifted apart over the millennia. Rifts emerged as scholars debated how to interpret the ancient texts, or even which texts to consider ancient."

Sablewing gestured to a tapestry showing figures clad in red robes. "The Knights Vigilant went astray first. They used to be the champions of peace. Now they are the enforcers of order. They are obsessed with laws, rank, and protocol. They believe that the more regimented a society, the more safeguards followed, then the fewer souls will die at night and be claimed by the demons."

Durrin nodded. That fit in with what he knew of the Knights Valiant. "They value order above all else."

"That is why the rulers of Calamar support them," Sablewing said. "The Knights Vigilant teach strict obedience to the ruling powers and the established social hierarchy. Their priorities go hand in glove with those of Calamar's nobility."

"And the Dawn Wardens?" Adara asked.

"They are not corrupt like the Knights Vigilant," Sablewing said. "But they have lost their vision. They used to be healers of both body and soul. But they forgot the soul, and now only focus on the body. They do many wonderful works throughout Zenitha: running hospitals and orphanages, feeding the hungry, blowing trumpets to warn of the advent of night. But they lost the healing power that the Sky Father gave them, and now they have only good will."

Sablewing sighed. "Now we, the Luminant Order, are left to carry the burdens of both the Dawn Wardens and the Knights Vigilant. We used to be only the keepers of truth. Now we must spread healing and preserve peace as well. It is an impossible burden."

"You said there was a fourth order," Adara said.

"The Children of the Sky." Sablewing nodded. "Hardly anything is known of them. They disappeared many eons ago, hunted and destroyed by servants of the Void. Of all the orders, the Tyrant King feared them the most."

"What *do* we know about them?" Adara asked.

"Only what they left us here," Sablewing said, leading them into another hall.

Durrin heard Adara gasp as they entered a hall more magnificent than any of the others they had seen. Windows in the ceiling high above them sent light filtering through rows of ornate columns, illuminating shelf upon shelf of scrolls, clay tablets, metal plates, and stone engravings.

"This is the Hall of Lore," Sablewing said reverently. She led them down its length. "Here you will find our most precious records, the ones that tell of our beliefs, of ancient prophecies, and of the very creation of Zenitha."

A magnificent mural occupied the end of the hall. It depicted seven beings swirling above a half-formed disc of rock, elements pouring from their outstretched hands to mix in the vortex of creation. Around them shone a multitude of stars. The stars were inlaid with gems so that they caught and reflected the light, filling the room with points of color.

"This is a depiction of creation," Sablewing said. "Are you familiar with the story, Your Majesty?"

"My father often recited it to me," Adara said breathlessly. "These are the Seven Noble Stars."

"Then you know what they created?"

"They each founded a branch of mancery, and the element that it controls," said Adara. "The first, earth. The second, fire. The third water, the fourth air, and the fifth life."

"That is only five," Durrin said, staring at the mural in awe. "What of the last two?"

"The sixth star created death," Sablewing said.

"Death?" Volthorn objected. "Why—"

"Because death is necessary," Sablewing said. "Each of the elements has its opposite to check it. Earth is checked by air. Water is checked by fire. Life needs a check, too—or else Zenitha would be overrun by plants and trees and insects. And so the sixth created death."

"And the Seventh?" Durrin asked.

"The Seventh Noble Star was more ambitious than them all," Sablewing said. "He approached the Sky Father and asked to create the eternal soul—the spark of eternity that dwells in every intelligent creature. But that was not his to create; only the Sky Father could fashion the eternal soul. And so, at his request, the Sky Father filled the skies with a hundred thousand stars. And every time one falls, it becomes the spark within one of us. Our soul."

Durrin pointed to a spot on the mural, where one of the beings, removed from the others, was at the center of a swirling vortex of blue and black. "The seventh star in this painting," she said. "What is he doing?"

"He is creating darkness," Sablewing said. "Over time, the seventh grew bitter and jealous. He had not the power to create the eternal soul. Nor, he found, could he govern that soul. So he created what *would* give him power: darkness, pain, and despair. And with that power, he swore he would bind and dominate this world."

"But instead he was banished," Adara whispered.

Sablewing nodded. "The Sky Father rebuked him and cast him out. It was then that he became the Tyrant King, fashioning the Void to be his throne and his prison, summoning fallen souls to be his demons to wage war upon the world."

Her tone turned reverent. "But the Sky Father sent his champion: the Eldest, the First of all the stars, the King of Light. The Eldest fashioned the Sun and set it as a check to the Void. He gave wings to those loyal to the Sky Father and appointed them as angels, to battle the demons. So has it been ever since: the Sun and the Void, Darkness and Light, angels and demons, in an endless struggle for the fate of every eternal soul."

Durrin stared at the mural, thinking about his own struggle against the powers of darkness just three nights before.

"The Eldest is not pictured here," Volthorn noted.

"We dare not represent him," Sablewing said. "Nor do we paint the Sky Father. We know not their form. Are they human? Avir? Griffin? Something else entirely? To guess would be sacrilege. For the Seven Noble Stars, there are traditions that ascribe a species to each one. Not all the traditions agree, but they are at least a starting point. But for the Sky Father and the Eldest, we know nothing, other than that they are real."

The hall was quiet as Durrin continued to stare in awe at the painting.

Volthorn cleared his throat. "I appreciate the lesson on your founding myth. But I'm wondering if you have materials on topics I am desperately in need of—tactics and military strategy, perhaps."

"Those would be in our Hall of Learning," Sablewing said. "We passed through it earlier. Go back out this hall and to the left."

"I would appreciate it if you could show me the specific section," Volthorn said, his politeness sounding a bit superficial.

"Of course," said Sablewing. "And Your Majesty—what do you seek?"

"I think I will return to the Hall of Wisdom," said Adara. "It is wisdom I seek most now."

"Ah," Sablewing said somberly. "A wise choice." She turned to face Durrin. "And you?"

"I wish to spend some time here, in the Hall of Lore."

Durrin turned back to the mural as Sablewing led Adara and Volthorn away. Their footsteps faded as he took in every detail, pondering the griffin's words. He had just turned to start perusing the shelves when he paused, as his preternatural hearing overheard an angry whisper from Volthorn.

"You should not have let that man in here," the korrik was saying. He and Sablewing had exited the hall and turned a corner, but sound carried far in this quiet space. Durrin stood perfectly still, listening.

"That was my decision to make," the griffin responded.

"If you knew his past," Volthorn hissed, "the crimes he has committed, the deaths—"

"His past does not concern me," Sablewing said. "Neither does yours, Commander Skarr. What governs entrance to the Bastion is not what people leave behind, but what they bring. Durrin will do no harm while he is here."

"But he is a pyromancer. He is capable of sabotage, arson, theft. Or what if he tells—"

"Volthorn." The griffin's tone had turned stern. "Do you remember the terms? Are you willing to speak only peace, not anger, hate, or malice?"

"Me?" Volthorn asked, sounding confused. "Why turn this on me when he has—"

"Do not concern yourself needlessly over others, Commander Skarr," Sablewing said. "Concern yourself only over yourself."

A few seconds passed where all Durrin could hear was the korrik's labored breathing.

"Come," Sablewing said. "I will show you our treatises on war."

Late the next afternoon, the griffin pair Razorclaw and Thunderclaw returned, bringing tidings from military officials in Elandria. The Hakiru pirates had been discovered, surrounded, and captured. But Lord Salidar had not been among them.

Chapter 36

Darkness and Fears

The last week had not been one of Salidar's favorites.

Never mind that the Elandrian queen had been snatched from his hands on the eve of his triumph. Never mind that his skill in verbomancy, two decades in development under the utmost secrecy, was now common knowledge among his enemies. Never mind that Durrin, one of the world's most talented pyromancers, was now firmly on Elandria's side of the war. Salidar had been *marooned*—and that was unbearable.

As soon as it had become apparent that the pirates would not be retrieving their cloudship, Salidar had found Yorid and slipped away unannounced. A group of twenty stood no chance of escaping Elandria undetected on foot. But two? It could be done.

He and Yorid had charted a course south, staying in the foothills of the Mitrian Mountains, hiding by day and traveling by night to avoid griffin eyes. Temperatures rose slightly after the storm, but the biting cold had nonetheless been their constant companion the last several nights.

The whole debacle was about as nasty of a situation as Salidar could have contrived. Little money. Even less food. Only a sword, two daggers, a bow, and half a quiver of arrows between them. They dared not steal horses, lest the incident be reported and reveal their route.

At least Salidar's verbomancy had come in handy. He used it to shield them from the wind, to keep a pocket of warmer air around them at night, and—one terrifying morning—to stop a trio of reptilian raptors in their tracks. The raptors, each fifteen feet long from snout to tail and coming as high as Salidar's shoulder, had sprung without warning from the brush, claws outstretched and serrated teeth gleaming as they ran across a small glade toward Salidar and Yorid. Salidar had summoned an invisible wall in the nick of time. The raptors had smacked against it and scurried off in fright. Verbomancy certainly had its uses.

Now he sat in a cave—not much more than a rocky alcove—reflecting on the miserable hand fate had dealt him. Yorid was off buying supplies at a nearby village. Hopefully he wouldn't run into another reptilian.

"Capricious fate," Salidar soliloquized, staring out at the wintry weather. "The storm rains on both the wealthy and the worthless. Or snows."

He gauged the position of the Sun behind the clouds. Just past high noon. Time for the daily transmission. Opening his pack, he withdrew a wad of leather, unwrapping it to reveal a gem couched in a metal disc—the receiver for the spy stone held by his underlings in Imperium. He unwrapped another gem in a separate piece of leather, then held it briefly against the first. A soft yellow glow appeared as terracharge transferred between the two upon contact. The glow had been getting fainter each day.

After a minute of silence, the gem in the metal disc hummed with a weak voice. "Your Excellency, are you there?" A pause, then again: "Your Excellency, are you there?"

He could give no response. His own spy stone required a unique gem to charge it— different from the one for the receiver—and his had been left onboard the cloud frigate. Even if he found a terramancer to recharge it, it would need to be recalibrated with its receiver. And *that* could only be done by two highly specialized terramancers who also happened to be twins.

There was a reason spy stones were worth more than entire towns.

After several seconds of silence, the disembodied voice continued. "We hope Your Excellency is still alive and well. We will continue our noon updates, in the hopes that you are listening and will soon be able to respond."

Salidar frowned. It had yet to occur to his underlings that his receiver could have fallen into the wrong hands. Some training would be in order upon his return—maybe even some demotions.

"The situation here has grown dire," the voice continued. "Your extended absence has generated quite a stir, despite our best efforts to the contrary. Many in your extended family believe you are dead. The Aram estate is in shambles. Your nephew Kelvinar vies for the family title, as does his cousin Alivar."

"Fools, both of them," Salidar muttered. "Never even seen a battle."

"We have proposed that any succession be delayed two months," the voice continued. "But we are not optimistic that they will listen. It will take about a week for enough of the family to assemble to form a quorum."

A week. A week before his relatives could vote on if he was dead or not. Well, let them give the reins to Kelvinar. They'd regret their choice a dozen times by the time Salidar returned to restore order.

"The situation in the imperial court is even more delicate," the voice went on. "Some have begun calling for the outright dismantling of the Aram estate and its holdings, claiming they should belong under direct imperial control. This same faction has redoubled their campaign for a premature settlement to the war. They are led, principally, by Chancellor Skyfang, Prince Fireclaw, and High Lord Vandil."

Yes, demotions were *definitely* in order. In Elandrian hands, this information could, if played right, spell the end of the war. Salidar processed the names. Chancellor Skyfang was no surprise—the griffin had been an outspoken rival of Salidar since the beginning. He only opposed the war because *he* was not in charge of it. High Lord Vandil, steward to the emperor himself, had been a consistent voice for peace before the war. Salidar's absence must be making him bold. But Prince Fireclaw, the emperor's second-oldest son—that was news. What were his motives? Jealousy? Ambition?

"The pro-war coalition is still strong, despite your disappearance," the voice resumed. "Your officers present a united front, and we still hold the allegiance of Lord Riesman, Lord Denmir, and most importantly, Crown Prince Thundertail. The emperor shows little sign of changing his mind. But we urge you to return as swiftly as you can. Uncertainty is not on our side. Until next high noon, Your Excellency."

The long interval of silence marked the message's end.

Salidar carefully rewrapped the disc and tucked it back into his pack. Three! Three powerful voices in court, clamoring for an end to everything he had given his life to. And more were likely to follow.

Would his allies stay loyal to him if his enemies bribed them with a share of the Aram family's land holdings? Salidar doubted it. Salidar's officers, though stout supporters of the war, held allegiance to him personally, not to his house. And should Crown Prince Thundertail see the winds shifting, he would switch sides in a heartbeat to secure his future throne against his younger brother.

Politics! The power he had built so carefully for almost three decades, the wealth his forebearers had amassed for five times that length, everything was crumbling before Salidar's eyes. And he was fifteen hundred miles away and could do nothing.

Not nothing.

The thought cut through the turmoil. He paused, trying to figure out why he had thought that. What could he do? Any attempt to either hasten his travel or resume communication would risk his capture or death.

I can help you.

Again, the thought was distinctive, unwarranted, unheralded. And with a chill, Salidar realized it was not his own.

He spun, a defensive spell tumbling out of his lips as he scanned the cave. Nothing. Just shadows.

You can't see me.

It was almost a voice—a low rumble, like far-away thunder echoing across a landscape. But it came to his mind directly, skipping his ears.

"Who are you?" Salidar cried, not sure where to look to direct this unseen being.

I am Archivous. I am shadow incarnate. I wield power unlimited.

Salidar reached out to the wall of the cave to steady himself. "Why should I listen to you?"

Because you need my help.

"And how can a voice inside my head help me?"

The telepathic roar almost brought Salidar to his knees. *I am Archivous, archdemon of the Void! I have crushed armies and conquered kingdoms! I have slaughtered souls and scattered stars! None are mightier than I!*

Salidar took a deep breath. "What do you want?" he whispered.

I would like to make a deal. A solution to your problems—in exchange for a solution to mine.

Salidar stood motionless for several seconds. "I'm listening," he said finally.

I knew you would. You've heard me quite well so far, despite my whisperings being somewhat more . . . subtle.

Salidar frowned. "I don't know what you're talking about."

The many victories you have secured against Calamar's enemies. The brilliant orchestration of King Everborn's death. Your unrivaled success at politics—do you really think you can attribute all this to your own unaided intuition?

Salidar began pacing. "So I have you to thank?"

But of course.

"I see. So I have you to blame for this week's fiasco?"

It was the wrong thing to say to an archdemon. A stab of pain lanced through Salidar's gut, doubling him over in agony. He gasped for breath but found his throat constricting.

You see I have the power to destroy you, the voice thundered in his head. *Do not be impudent with me. Understood?*

"Yes," Salidar croaked.

The unseen power released him.

You have been an excellent servant, Salidar, despite your occasional stubbornness. I have deemed you worthy of more overt instructions—in return for greater power. First, I will restore your political dominance. Who are Fireclaw, Vandil, and Skyfang to me? I shall eliminate them before you even set foot in Imperium.

Second, it's time to finish this pathetic little war. Follow my instructions, and the banner of Calamar shall wave from Saven's towers by next summer's solstice.

Salidar bowed his head, listening to the offer. It was everything he could hope for, and more. "And what is your price?"

It is a minor thing. You know of the Bastion of Memory?

"I do."

Destroy it. Burn it to the ground. Let not one stone remain upon another.

"The Bastion is within the territory of the Mitrian Tribes," Salidar said. "They will not permit an army to invade their lands."

Once Elandria is subdued, the Mitrians will have many reasons to resent and fear you. Opportunity for war will soon present itself. When it does, the Bastion must be your priority.

Everything he needed—in exchange for doing something he likely would have done anyway? "Consider it done," Salidar said.

So you accept the terms of this deal?

"I accept."

In a cackle of demonic laughter, the shadow upon his thoughts vanished.

Salidar stared into space for a few seconds. Beneath the ruffles of his vest, his chest heaved.

Slowly, beginning at his knees, then spreading up his whole body, he began to shake and tremble. He sat down, shivering. One of their travel packs lay close at hand; he opened it and found a nearly empty jug of wine, purchased from the last village. He downed the last of it, barely registering its contents.

For another minute he sat, his eyes staring into space, the shock of what had just transpired finally hitting his brain. He lifted a hand to his face, touching his cheeks, his forehead, his brow.

"What am I doing?" he whispered into the dark.

Durrin woke with a start, reaching instinctively for the sword under his pillow. It wasn't there—and neither was his pillow. He had fallen asleep in an alcove of the library, too exhausted to return to his quarters in the outer wall.

Lantern light and quiet footsteps—what had startled him awake—grew closer, until a small figure appeared, walking alone down the hall.

"Your Majesty," Durrin said. "Couldn't sleep?"

Queen Adara stopped, surprised but not startled. "Apparently neither could you."

"*I* was asleep." Durrin cracked his joints. "Just in the wrong spot." He tried to stand but immediately sat back down, a wave of nausea washing through him. His face felt hot.

"Are you alright?" Adara stepped closer. "How is your wound?"

"It's fine," Durrin lied. Despite the best efforts of the healers, the skin around his wound was bright red with infection, and he had alternated between a fever and chills all day. But he buried the thoughts. "And you? What is driving away your dreams?"

Adara looked torn for a moment, then sat down just outside the alcove, folding her skirts beneath her. "Can I trust you with a secret?"

Trust. So few people had offered that to Durrin in his lifetime. Yes, his clients had trusted he would complete his missions. But that had been trust on a professional, transactional level. Except for Halorn, no one had trusted him with the intimate details of their lives since his youth.

"You have my word," Durrin vowed.

Adara opened her mouth, but before she could begin to speak, she let out a heavy breath and began to shake. Tears seeped from her eyes, glistening in the lantern light before dripping down her cheeks, which were quickly turning blue.

"My father," Adara gasped. "His death—it was no accident. He was murdered. They *killed* him!"

Durrin forced himself to listen. Every part of his being wanted to run, to escape this most painful reminder of his crimes. But for Adara's sake, he could not. He'd given his word.

"Who told you this?"

"Lord Salidar." Adara wiped her cheek. "Right before you rescued me. He said my father was an obstacle that needed to be removed, so he ordered his death. He went behind the back of his own emperor."

She squeezed her eyes shut and shook her head. "But my advisors—that means they lied to me! For seven long years they lied to my face about the death of my own father!"

Durrin cast about for something comforting to say. "I imagine they did it to protect you."

"Protect me from the truth?" Adara replied. "From knowing how my own father died?"

"If Salidar had your father murdered, it was with the intent of sparking a war," Durrin said. "Perhaps your advisors covered it up to prevent one."

Adara bunched up the hem of her dress in her hands, running her thumbs along the embroidered edges. "But why keep it from *me*? Did they not think I was strong enough to handle the truth?"

Durrin stared at the stones in front of him. "The truth is hard to face. Sometimes it can be even harder to share."

Adara took several deep breaths, each one punctuated by half-suppressed sobs. Durrin let her cry. He didn't know what to say or do. What comfort could he offer when he was the reason for her agony? How could he extend solace when each sob that escaped Adara's throat felt like a dagger twisting its way deeper and deeper into his own condemned soul?

Eventually, Adara's sobs subsided into whimpers, and her skin began to return to its neutral bronze hue. She dug a tissue from a pocket of her dress and dabbed at her face.

"Did you know?" she whispered.

"Know what?"

"That Arvanon was murdered. You did not act surprised when I told you."

Durrin shifted, wincing as his bandages moved. He could tell her. He could unload the burden of guilt that every day grew heavier in his heart. How would she react? Cower in fear at finding herself face-to-face with her father's killer? Flee to Volthorn and demand Durrin's death?

No. Even if he knew she could bear the shock, he doubted he had the strength to voice the words.

He let out a deep breath, stalling as he scrambled for a half-truth. "I overheard Salidar's conversation before we rescued you," he said, shrugging. "I've had some time to process it since then."

They sat in silence another minute.

"Who are you, Durrin?" Adara asked. "Who are you, really? You have spent the last two days studying the ancient tomes from dawn to dusk. What are you looking for?"

Durrin summoned a flame in his hand, staring into its flickering depths.

"I am a man who has made mistakes, Your Majesty," he said. "Grave mistakes. I fear I have forfeited my soul. And so I search the tomes for what I must do to pay the redemptive price." He let the flame die. "I will not rest—I cannot rest—until I pay it."

Chapter 37

The Pain of Knowledge

Three days later.

"Something weighs on you, Your Majesty."

Adara looked up from her scroll. "High Mage Sablewing," she said, standing and bowing.

"Please, just Sablewing will do, Your Majesty," Sablewing said.

Adara smiled. "Yet you still call me 'Your Majesty,' despite being no subject of mine."

"Fair enough," said the griffin. "Let me try again. Something weighs on you, Adara."

Adara rolled up the scroll she had been reading. "I guess I'm anxious to return to my people. I've been away too long."

Sablewing nodded. "I was just talking to Lyman this morning. He has finished patching the holes in the balloon, but he'll need more time to reinflate it and repair some damage to the gondola. Perhaps three or four more days. But that's not what's weighing on you."

"My people are at war," Adara said. "I have much to be weighed down by."

Sablewing cocked her head, studying Adara. It felt like the griffin was staring into her very soul.

"You blame yourself," Sablewing said. "For your father's death."

Adara ran her fingers down the edge of the scroll, feeling every mar and blemish in the parchment. It was a welcome distraction from the mars and blemishes inside.

"Before you ask," Sablewing said, "I know the truth about how he died. Cymar confided in me seven years ago. He felt I should know, given my station." She lifted a wing and placed its tip on Adara's shoulder. "I mourn your loss," Sablewing said. "It is a heavy burden."

"I keep reliving that day," Adara said, breathing hard to keep her throat from tightening. "My father was going to hear petitions in the throne room alone. I begged him to let me be present. He didn't want to. He felt uneasy. But he relented."

Her tongue picked up its pace. "Minutes before he died, my father had a premonition that something was wrong—that danger was near. He had time to escape. But instead, his first concern was for me." The words tumbled out now. "He sent me out first while he lingered. If I had not insisted on being there—"

"Adara," Sablewing said gently. "We don't know what would or wouldn't have happened."

"If I hadn't been there, he'd have left the throne room sooner," Adara continued regardless, holding her head in her hands as tears began to flow. "He would have had his full retinue of guards to defend him. That's why I am to blame!"

"Adara," Sablewing rebuked. She stepped forward until her beak hovered a foot from Adara's eyes. "Enough of this nonsense. Were you the one who ordered your father's death?"

"I ignored his wishes," Adara said.

"Answer the question. Did you order your father's death?"

Adara bit her lip. "No."

"Were you the one who carried it out?"

"No."

"Then you are not to blame. And when you insist otherwise, you insist upon a lie."

Adara hung her head, staring at the floor. Her mind replayed again and again that fateful day.

"Perhaps my advisors were right not to tell me," she said softly. "It's consuming me, Sablewing. I've thought of nothing else the last two days."

"That was one of the reasons Cymer confided in me," Sablewing said. "He sought my advice. Your co-regents, Luviana and Skagar, were determined to withhold the truth from you, despite his strong objections. I agreed with his concerns. There is power in knowing the truth. Any time we seek to obfuscate truth, we become weaker and more vulnerable."

Sablewing shook her head. "In the end, Cymer and I decided it was not his place to tell you against the wishes of your regents. And so here you are. Weaker. More vulnerable. Exactly as Cymer had warned."

Adara took a deep breath, running her hands down the length of her dress to smooth it out. Her skin had turned bluish gray with guilt and regret.

"I've been reading many scrolls and tablets," Adara said. "One this morning talked about truth—what you said about it bringing power."

"Ah, yes." Sablewing nodded. "The Accolades. They are attributed to Arnon the Scholar, a tradition I agree with despite the presence of some third-millennium anachronisms in the text . . . but I digress. Yes, Arnon had much to say about truth. What did you learn?"

"One of his poems talked about alignment," said Adara. "He said that to live in truth is to align everything in your life with everything else. That your actions line up with your words. That your words reflect your inner thoughts. That your thoughts match your vision—of yourself, of others, and of the whole world. And that your vision is governed by the truth. Once each part of you is aligned with the truth, you will have power to shape the world."

"And what is the truth about yourself?" Sablewing asked.

Adara looked down at her hands again. The bluish-gray had faded, letting some healthy bronze coloring return. On her left hand, her signet ring sparkled in the light, a constant reminder of her duties. On her right hand, two eternium rings caught her reflection: the filial rings of her father and mother, a constant reminder of their deaths.

"I don't know," Adara whispered.

"Two different identities wage war within you," Sablewing said. "On the one hand, I see a courageous young woman, one who loves her people and will do anything for them. On the other hand, I see a girl consumed by fears and doubts, unsure if she can be trusted with responsibilities of such magnitude."

Adara listened, nodding. "So how do I choose the courageous version and leave the fearful version behind?"

Sablewing looked at her long and hard, her keen yellow eyes unblinking. "Do you truly want to know?"

Adara swallowed. "Yes."

"Then come with me." Sablewing turned and gestured with an outstretched wing.

Adara followed. The griffin led her out of the Hall of Wisdom and into the library's central rotunda, a majestic space crowned by a massive dome. From there, they ascended a set of short, wide stairs to the Hall of Lore. Light filtered in from windows high above, once again illuminating the painting of creation on the far wall.

At the end of the hall, directly underneath the painting, stood a pair of small but ornately decorated doors. Sablewing pressed one paw against the doors. She whispered something too quiet for Adara to hear, and the doors swung inward.

Beyond was a small, straight passageway, sloped slightly upward. Sablewing entered and Adara followed.

"Shut the door," the griffin said.

"We brought no light," Adara said. The passageway lacked any windows. They'd be in complete darkness.

"Shut the door."

Adara obeyed, swinging the heavy panels closed. She saw no lock, nor heard any mechanism engage, but once the doors were shut, they didn't budge. Nor could she see any light around their edges. For a moment she panicked. Would they be able to get out? How would they see?

The alarm lasted only a moment. There was still a faint light in the passage. Carved into the sides of the corridor, about waist-height, were two deep channels lined with faintly glowing lumen moss.

Sablewing was already far down the corridor, and Adara hastened to catch up. As they gradually ascended, the moss grew thicker and cast more light. Up ahead, she could hear the rushing of water.

She ran a hand over the wall as she walked. The stone was cold and smooth to the touch, without any seam or crack. They must be in the bowels of the mountain now, deep inside the mighty cliffs that the library was built against. How many thousands of tons of rock were above them? She tried not to think about it.

Instead, she focused instead on the glowing moss. The channels must be fed by a spring up ahead. The slight incline of the passageway would allow water to slowly seep down each channel, keeping the luminescent moss forever moist.

They came to a pair of thin curtains, the last barrier between them and the rushing sound. The curtains were alight with a strong glow beyond, backlighting the intricate patterns embroidered into them. Sablewing pulled one aside with her paw and ushered Adara through.

She walked into what seemed a dream. A massive chamber spread before her, easily a hundred feet wide and long. Its gleaming walls showed no sign of tool or chisel. Water ran down the sides of the cavern, collecting in pools and nooks before dripping down to a shallow pool at the base.

Everywhere the water touched, lumen moss bloomed—but such moss! It was all colors, blues and greens, reds and golds. Never had Adara seen so many varieties in such abundance. The glow from the moss sparkled off the cascading water and the glistening stone, making the cave dance with light.

At the far end of the chamber, water spilled from an overhang of rock into the pool below, creating a perfectly smooth curtain of water. Behind it danced a flickering source of brilliant, fiery light.

Adara stood for an endless moment, wrapped in the beauty around her.

"It's glorious," she whispered. She found her eyes pulled again and again to the pillar of fire behind the waterfall. "What is that?"

"This is the Curtain of Knowledge." Sablewing's quiet voice barely carried over the thousand ripples of water. "You may step through it, should you wish."

"Step through it? But it's fire!"

"You will not be bodily harmed."

"Is it painful?"

"Knowledge is always painful," Sablewing said. "You must decide whether you prefer its pain to the shackles of ignorance."

Adara stood for a long moment. Did she trust this griffin, whom she had only met a week before? She wanted to. The fire leapt and danced, sending rays of light shooting through every momentary gap that appeared in the rippling water. It was surely no normal fire—a mundane flame would be smothered by so much moisture, and she saw no fuel for it to consume.

She picked her way across the rocky floor as she descended toward the pool. Knowledge—knowledge of what? Of the future? Of the past? Of herself?

She removed her slippers and stepped into the pool. It was shallow and warm, soothing against her bare feet. She strode forward, watching the ripples of each step collide with the ripples expanding from the cascade in front of her.

She stepped up to the curtain of water. The light was almost blinding this close to the flames. She could hear their crackle now, throbbing behind the rushing roar of water.

She extended her hand.

The water parted around it, leaving a gap of air beneath her outstretched arm, through which the leaping flames were fully visible. They were all colors, from brightest blue to deepest red.

She touched the flames.

Raw power ripped through her fingertips, shooting tendrils of shock up her hand and arm, like every particle in her fingers was disintegrating. She cried out and yanked her arm back.

Her fingers were whole, completely unharmed.

Swallowing her fear, Adara plunged forward.

For a moment the water washed over her, pouring down the contours of her face and dousing her shoulders. Then she pressed into the fire. The same burning power as before washed over her, igniting every nerve in a paroxysm of consciousness. For a moment, her mind seemed to move at incredible speed, processing far faster than it should.

Then the sensation faded, and she opened her eyes to find herself . . . in emptiness. All around her was nothing but whiteness, the purest whiteness she could ever imagine.

"Adara," said a voice behind her. A familiar voice. A voice she had not heard for seven years. She turned.

"Father!"

It was him—all of him—alive and whole and *real*. There were his eyes, deep with understanding; his stature, tall with confidence; his smile, tempered by experience. He was clothed in a long, flowing white robe that seemed to meld into the emptiness around her.

She rushed forward, but he held out a hand, stopping her before she could touch him.

"My princess," he said.

"You're alive!" Adara exclaimed, wiping away tears.

"Did you think I ceased to exist when I died?" her father asked, his smile growing by a fraction.

"So you're dead," Adara said, a heaviness returning to her heart.

"Do I look it?" her father replied. She frowned in confusion and he burst out laughing. "Oh, Adara! I died, but I live on, in another form, on a plane where you see me not. You knew this."

She did. She had known it all her life. But *seeing* it—it brought the idea into reality.

"Father—were you really killed, murdered by agents of Calamar?"

King Everborn nodded, with the solemn gravity she remembered from her childhood. "Lord Salidar spoke the truth. I was slain by an assassin under his employ."

Memories of that day rushed back to her, with all the accompanying guilt. "Father—if I hadn't insisted on being there that day . . ."

"Then I would still have perished," he said. "Do not blame yourself. The assassin they sent was deeply skilled. If I had fled the throne room, he would have pursued and killed me, no matter how many guards I had with me—and likely others would have perished as well."

At the mention of the murderer, Adara felt her skin grow hot. So far, her feelings of anger had been directed at Salidar. She had forgotten there was another equally to blame. "Who was the assassin, Father? Where is he now? How can I make sure you are avenged?"

"Adara." Her father's eyes were filled with pain. But she realized, with a start, that the pain was directed not at the one who had killed him, but at her. "Vengeance is the Sky Father's to enact as He sees fit. It is not ours to pursue. If you are not carful, this news will rancor in your soul, breeding hate, fear, and distrust—cutting you off from the light and wisdom you so desperately need. One day, you will know who my murderer is. Before that day comes, you must learn to give your feelings to the Sky Father, or all will be lost. I bear no animosity toward my slayer. Neither must you."

Adara listened to the words, committing them to memory. She swallowed, letting her fists relax, forcing herself to let the anger go. In its place, familiar fears bubbled to the surface, bringing tears to her eyes. She wiped them away, desperate to keep her eyes on her father as long as she could.

"I don't know if I can do this, Father. Our nation is on the brink of destruction. I feel so lost, so often. Every day I fear I'm making irreparable mistakes."

He studied her, his eyes deep wells of love and concern. "Can I share something with you, my princess?"

Adara nodded.

Her father looked out into the whiteness. "If you were to read only the inscriptions and memorials of my reign, you would think I was the perfect ruler, a paragon of peace." He blinked. "But I, too, made mistakes. I could have fortified our northern border more against the Drilandi raiders, rather than neglecting the problem. I could have done more to strengthen our bonds with Calamar."

He took a deep breath. "I should have acted sooner when I saw the warning signs of a haeber shortage. If I had, I could have stockpiled grain in our years of plenty before the Great Famine hit. But I feared the populace, and how they would react. Perhaps, if I had been stronger than my fears, we could have staved off the plague that took your mother's life."

He turned back to Adara, crouching to be at eye level with her. "Do you remember the last words I said to you?"

How could she ever forget? "You said I was stronger than my fears," she said.

He somberly shook his head. "I was wrong."

She had barely registered his shocking declaration before he continued. "Fear gets the better of all of us sometimes. It is the greatest weapon of the Tyrant King, and it is strong. Terribly strong. None of us, *on our own*, can stand against it."

He looked down, as if reliving painful memories. "I stumbled through my reign by clinging to the belief that I was strong enough to overcome my fears and my weaknesses. Since then, I have learned a better way." He straightened. "*We* are not strong enough to overcome our fears. But the Sky Father is."

He gestured to the infinite whiteness around them. "Turn to him, Adara. Turn to the Eldest and his angels. The Light is stronger than your fears."

He turned to go. For the first time, Adara noticed the pair of great wings, with plumage of the purest white, extending from his back. He snapped them open and lifted away, and Adara felt the wind of his flight. On an impulse she rushed forward, her hand outstretched, hoping to grab one feather as a physical reminder of what she had seen—

—and she was stumbling through the Curtain of Knowledge, back into the glistening cavern, filling the pool with the ripples of her splashing feet. She paused, blinking in the sudden dimness of reality. She touched her arms and her dress, marveling. She was neither burned nor wet.

CHAPTER 38

THE PRICE OF IGNORANCE

Two days later.

"I've done all I can," Mariam said to Sablewing, wringing her hands. "Changed the dressing. Washed the wound with vinegar twice a day. Applied honey and cedar bark powder. But the infection is still spreading."

Durrin barely heard them. He was burning up, consumed with fever. Never had he felt so hot, so flushed. His parched lips yearned for water. His limbs lay weak from want of food, but his stomach refused to hold anything down.

"Have you tried vivamancy?" the griffin murmured.

"My assistant has been singing a cooling and strengthening song several times an hour," Mariam said. "At most, it's delayed the onset."

"Aquamantic potions?"

"We've applied aquaheal each morning and evening, but it doesn't do much for wounds once infection has set in. I wish I had some windsbane root to bring down the fever, but we won't get more of that until next spring."

"Hmm," Sablewing looked thoughtful. "And you . . . ?"

Mariam shook her head. "I have asked. I cannot. I was hoping you would . . ."

A pause. "No. Nor I. But I will see about someone else. I'll be back."

Durrin closed his eyes. He barely registered the sound of the infirmary door opening and closing. Then he felt Mariam place a cool, damp cloth over his forehead.

"Appropriate," he mumbled.

"What?" the healer asked, leaning closer.

"Fever," Durrin murmured. "Heat. Appropriate—that I should die—from heat."

"You will not die," Mariam said firmly. "Not under my watch!"

He attempted to shake his head but failed. "I've seen . . . infection . . . in others. I've seen . . . them die." He had caught a glimpse of his wound the last time the dressing had been changed. It had not been pretty.

The prospect of death terrified him. In the half delirium that came with the fever, the shadows of demons and the image of scrolls stained with innocent blood lay constantly at the corners of his vision. What temperature was the Void? Eternal cold or eternal heat? His time at Irongate Isle had instilled in him a terror of the cold. But now he faced the unquenchable heat—burning, all-consuming, overwhelming.

The door opened.

"Aye," said a pudgy voice. "Look at 'im, the poor lad, all laid low like a tumbled tree in an avalanche—"

"Shh," Mariam hissed. "He's not asleep, Lyman."

"Oy! My mistake. Sorry miss, sorry. Still my tongue, I will."

"Lyman,"—Sablewing's voice—"Can you do it?"

"Oh, Your Mageship, I don't know about that. I'm good with fixin' things, right, but that be mechanical stuff, gears and carts and the like. Never been too familiar with the healing arts."

"I didn't ask if you knew what you'd be doing. I asked if you *can*. Are you *allowed* to?"

A long silence.

"Yes, I reckon. Yes." Lyman's voice was soft now, hardly more than a whisper.

"Well, then. Carry on."

The damp cloth on Durrin's forehead was removed, and a pair of calloused hands took their place, covering Durrin's forehead and eyes. Then Lyman's voice uttered an unknown phrase. "*Et evinal, et yidivar, et claminor, al Abeam!*"

In the throes of the fever, Durrin barely registered the touch. But as soon as the words were complete, a current of energy swept through him. It felt like a wave of light, flowing into his head and down his spine, washing before it the pain, the heat, the agony. The light continued to spread until his whole body seemed aglow. Then the hands lifted, and the light faded.

Durrin opened his eyes. The room was bright. His limbs felt new strength. And his wound—

—was gone! Durrin shot upright, grabbing at his waist. There was his bandage, still bloody and soaked, but, tearing it away, he saw the skin on his abdomen was whole, with not even a scar.

He looked up, overwhelmed with shock and amazement. Mariam beamed at him, still clasping her hands, while Sablewing looked on with a smaller but no less joyous smile. Lyman had retreated to the edge of the room and glanced down self-consciously when Durrin looked in his direction.

"I'll, ah, I'll just get back to my work," Lyman stuttered, shuffling his feet. "Almost got the cloud frigate sailing now—maybe fit to sail by tomorrow morning. She's a beauty, she is. Absolute beauty."

Sablewing inclined her head. "Thank you, Lyman."

Lyman bowed awkwardly in return, almost falling over, then retreated from the room. But Durrin caught a smile and a couple of tears on the man's face before he slipped from view.

Later that afternoon, Volthorn found Sablewing in the Hall of Learning. "Your Mageship," he said. "My pardon if now is not a good time . . ."

The griffin cocked her head. "So if it *is* a good time, you wish not to be pardoned?"

Volthorn frowned. Did the griffin always have to be this pedantic? "No . . . I mean, there would be nothing to . . ." He shook his head. "I have come to ask a favor."

Sablewing began pacing down the hall, letting Volthorn follow. "What may I do for you?"

"Queen Adara told me of the chamber you showed her . . . the Curtain of Knowing, I believe she called it."

"The Curtain of Knowledge, yes."

"I was wondering . . . could I perhaps have the privilege of seeing it?"

Sablewing stopped walking and turned to look at him with her piercing yellow eyes. "Why do you seek the Curtain of Knowledge?"

"I . . ." Why *did* he want to see it? "Adara's description roused my curiosity, I guess. I would like to see it for myself."

Sablewing studied him a moment more, then continued walking. "Very well. Though I must give you a warning. The Curtain is not secret—but it *is* sacrosanct. It is not to be treated lightly, or as a mere point of curiosity."

"Forgive my wording, then, Your Mageship. I deeply desire to see the Curtain for myself." Indeed, since Adara had recounted her experience to him, his thoughts had kept returning to that subject. "By the way," he added as an afterthought, "I asked Her Majesty not to tell Rendhart about the Curtain."

Sablewing's tail flicked. "Why is that, Commander Skarr?"

Because he murdered my king, Volthorn thought. But he could not say the words aloud, neither to this griffin nor to Her Majesty. He, Skagar, and Luviana had to maintain the cover story for Arvanon's death. If the truth leaked out now, people would see it only as a retroactive, baseless accusation against Calamar. Not to mention the havoc it might wreak on Adara's psyche.

"Because we still don't know Durrin's intentions, or his allegiance," he said instead. "I've scarcely seen him the last two days—he could be snooping about, gathering intel for—"

Sablewing turned, fixing him with a stern glare. Volthorn stopped in mid-step, recalling the conditions he'd agreed to a week earlier.

They finished their walk in silence.

Sablewing led him to the doors at the end of the Hall of Lore, opening them with a whispered command and leading him through. From there, they traveled up a long stone passageway, through a thin curtain, and into a massive cavern beyond.

Volthorn stood at the brink of the chamber, awestruck by the myriad of lumen lights around him.

"Remarkable," he breathed. He studied the scene for an endless moment. The energy in this space was amazing! His terrasense throbbed, but the power here was different than what he felt when he visited a ley-line beacon. It was deeper, stronger, but at the same, quieter and not as accessible—like a mighty underground river instead of a surface stream.

His gaze settled on the waterfall before him, and the leaping flames behind it.

"Did Adara really touch it?" he said, amazed.

Sablewing nodded. "She passed through it."

"Can I?"

"You may—if you are able. But know that knowledge often comes with pain."

Volthorn touched the scar on his cheek. "I'm not afraid of pain."

He picked his way down the slope, then splashed across the pool until he stood before the veil of water. He reached out a hand, turning it in a circle under the flow of water, watching droplets splay off his claws at every angle. Then he pushed forward.

He instantly snapped his hand back, plunging it into the water at his feet. "This is pure fire!" he screamed. "It's white hot!" He massaged the scaly skin of his hand. "I could have lost my fingers!"

Sablewing watched him calmly. "Was Adara consumed?"

The question gave Volthorn pause. He held up his hand, studying it. The skin still tingled, but he couldn't see any evidence of a burn. Swallowing, he stood and extended his hand again.

Again he snatched it back, screaming in pain. "This is madness! You expect me to plunge my arm into leaping flames?"

"I did not ask you to," Sablewing said solemnly. "Nor do I expect it of you. The choice is yours."

Volthorn studied the water and flames for a long moment, battling between his caution and his curiosity. Again he drew near, steeling himself to plunge through. But after a moment, he turned and retreated to the water's edge at a near run.

"I cannot," he gasped. Tears seeped out of the corners of his eyes. "I cannot."

He was sure he knew why. It must be that only the pure and honorable could pass through the fire safely. But he had a duty to fulfil—a duty he'd been neglecting. By letting a murderer and an assassin walk these halls, he was jeopardizing the safety of the whole library. Well, that ended today.

"Your Mageship, if you would follow me. There is something urgent I must deal with."

Volthorn found Rendhart in the grounds between the main library and the outer wall. An inch of snow still encrusted the ground, but Durrin seemed heedless of the cold as he stood in front of a small audience of library staff, performing some pyromantic tricks. Adara was thankfully not among them. Rendhart paused as he saw them approaching.

Volthorn began talking while still several dozen yards away. "The truth needs to be said," he announced, loud enough for all to hear. "I accept all blame for not saying it earlier. This man is not who you think he is."

"Volthorn," Sablewing said softly from behind him.

He ignored her. "Durrin Rendhart is guilty of political assassination and murder, among other crimes including arson and espionage. He is a long-time agent of Calamar, and though he claims to have abandoned their cause, I suspect his loyalty is still either to them, or to himself. He should never have been allowed to enter the Bastion."

Volthorn stopped three paces from Durrin, eyeing him carefully, expecting the taller warrior to attack. But Durrin stayed perfectly still, his arms at his sides, eyeing Volthorn with an inscrutable glower. No one else said anything.

"Durrin," Sablewing's voice came from behind Volthorn, calm but firm. "How do you answer to this accusation?"

Durrin stared at Volthorn for several seconds, maintaining eye contact even when he opened his mouth to reply. "Commander Skarr is right about who I was," he said solemnly. "I have committed murder and assassination of the darkest kind. I have also committed theft, sabotage, arson, espionage, interrogation, and more. But he is wrong about who I *am*. I have utterly rejected my past. Never again will I serve a cause that leads to war, violence, or injustice."

"And what is your word worth?" Volthorn spat. "How can we trust you not to sell information about the Bastion to its enemies? Or steal some priceless item?"

"I risked my life to save yours," Durrin said, his eyes gleaming with a hint of fire. "I risked it again to save Her Majesty's. Does that mean nothing to you?"

Volthorn shook with wrath. "If you hadn't killed—if you hadn't . . ." He couldn't say anything more past the lump lodged in his throat. He blinked back tears. He had lost so much—*Elandria* had lost so much—because of the man standing in front of him.

"Volthorn," Sablewing said quietly. "Is there another at the Bastion who can vouch for your distrust of Durrin?"

Not Adara. Volthorn shook his head. "No."

"Then until we have another witness, we must allow Durrin to stay. He has committed no infraction of our rules."

A look of smug self-satisfaction passed over Durrin's face. And that was it. For far too long, this criminal had evaded justice. He should have been executed the very day he was first captured seven years ago—but he had not. He should have been kept confined to Irongate Isle—but he had not. He should have been recaptured in the city or on the road—but he had not. And now here he was again, enjoying asylum he had not earned, untouched by the hand of justice.

"Fine," Volthorn snapped. "If you won't act, then I will." He closed the remaining feet between them and landed a resounding slap on the pyromancer's cheek. "Rendhart, I challenge you to a duel!"

Durrin's eyes flashed with fire. He stepped back into a crouch, flames flickering around his hands as he twirled them. Volthorn mirrored him, drawing a long dagger from his jerkin, while his other hand gathered terracharge from a ruby at his waist.

Then Sablewing was between them, filling the space with her black wingspan, clawing the empty air with her front claws as she let out a roar. A wave of light exploded outward from her. Volthorn's muscles grew suddenly numb, the dagger dropping from his grasp as he staggered backward.

Sablewing rounded to face him, somehow seeming to grow in proportions and tower over him. "Volthorn Skarr," she pronounced. "You have brought enmity and strife to the Bastion and have drawn a weapon in threat of open violence. You are hereby confined to the grounds and the rooms of the outer wall for the remainder of your stay."

His fierce intentions from a moment before had vanished. Volthorn found himself powerless—not held immobile, nor stripped of his will—just . . . powerless. Like a naughty kitten rebuked by its mother. He slumped to the ground, eyes wide, mind reeling with what had just happened.

As the others slipped back indoors, the griffin eyed him with a look of sadness. "You are harboring intense anger in your heart, Volthorn. Anger attracts all kinds of darkness: wrath, malice, fear. The more you walk in darkness, the less clearly you will see."

"Am I the blind one?" Volthorn cried. "You'll be sorry when Rendhart betrays you."

Sablewing paused at the entrance to the Bastion. "We shall see."

The doors closed fast, leaving Volthorn alone.

CHAPTER 39

CHOICE

Late that night, Durrin danced to the rhythm of the third Kymar routine.

Danced was the right word, for this one was far more graceful than its two predecessors. It was all about finesse: in movement, in rhythm, and in timing.

He practiced on a patio in the Bastion's grounds. Banks of snow lay all around, made blue by night's darkness, but the patio itself was clear and dry—a common side effect of a pyromantic practice session.

In the middle of the patio, three columns of flame blossomed into the sky. Durrin danced around and between them. Every move of his head, every lift or drop of his hands, every step with his toes or heels tugged the energy onward, feeding its rhythm and tenor, coaxing it to twist its way out of the frigid surroundings and funnel into the columns of flame. Back and forth. In and out. Up and down.

His pyrosense alerted him that someone was approaching. He slowed the rhythm of his dance, letting the energy dissipate back into the surroundings. Unlike the other routines, he felt self-conscious performing the third routine around others. It felt too . . . beautiful. Especially for someone like him to be able to create.

Durrin recognized the approaching spark as Sablewing's. The high mage's spark carried the distinctive energy pattern common to all griffins, but it held something more: some deep, hidden power that Durrin had felt only once before, in Cymer.

Durrin turned and bowed as the griffin landed on the patio. "Your Mageship. You shouldn't be out on a frigid night like this."

"I couldn't agree more," Sablewing said. "Lyman's thermoscope says it's negative six Arnon—but accounting for wind factor, it feels more like negative fourteen. Anyway, let's get inside."

"I'm content to keep practicing," Durrin said. "The cold doesn't trouble me."

"Ah, but I have something to show you." Sablewing turned to walk back toward the library. "Two things, actually."

His curiosity piqued, Durrin jogged to catch up, his boots crunching through the crusty top layer of snow to the soft powder underneath with each step. "This couldn't wait until morning? We aren't supposed to leave until midday."

"I must leave tomorrow myself," said the griffin. "At first light."

"To where?"

"To the far northeast, almost to the edge of the world. I've received tidings about the situation there with the haeber trade—the *source* of the haeber trade, mind you, for the entire world. It appears that our global supply chain crisis has been precipitated by an extremely effective cabal of corsairs."

"Corsairs? That's all that's behind this catastrophe?"

Sablewing held up a paw. "These are not just common pirates. They have become alarmingly organized and powerful in the span of a few short years. They're on the verge of cutting the trade off completely."

That was a piece of alarming news. "Has anyone done anything about it?"

Sablewing nodded. "They've tried. There's been several sea battles already. But the corsairs still grow stronger. They've already overthrown two kingdoms that have tried to stop them. Which is why I must leave tomorrow: to find a way to end the crisis once and for all."

Durrin frowned. "How can you succeed where entire kingdoms have failed?"

"I don't know," Sablewing admitted. "But when you walk in the Light, there will always be a way."

They arrived at the Bastion, shaking the snow from their limbs as they stepped into the welcome warmth. Durrin may not have been bothered by the cold, but that didn't mean he preferred it.

The library was dark and still. They strolled through, leaving a diminishing trail of water behind them as the snow still on their feet and legs melted. Sablewing led him to the Hall of Lore.

"You're taking me to those doors, aren't you," said Durrin. "The ones without any keyhole."

"The doors you have tried to open three times now?"

Durrin thought back on the past week. "Pretty sure it was more than three."

"You could have just asked me, Durrin. I would have shown them to you."

They reached the set of ornate doors. Sablewing opened them and stepped up into the corridor beyond. Durrin stopped at the threshold, listening with both his ears and his mind. He felt something beyond—something more than the rush of falling water. Some source of energy he had never felt before.

He pressed on after the griffin.

They ascended the passageway, the lumen on the walls gradually growing brighter. Sablewing lifted the curtain at the end and ushered Durrin into the cavern beyond. He stopped, overwhelmed with wonder as his eyes took in the glistening array of moss and the cascading patterns of water on the cavern walls.

Gradually, his eyes settled on the wall of water at the end of the chamber, and the iridescent flames behind it. He descended, taking his eyes off the waterfall only for brief moments to pick out his trail on the uneven cavern floor. This was it. The source of the energy. As he came closer, it was almost overwhelming.

Durrin waded into the pool, pausing just a few feet away from the shimmering curtain of water. "What is this place called?" he asked reverently.

Sablewing took to the air, soaring across the chamber and landing gracefully at the pool's edge. "This is the Curtain of Knowledge."

"It is not normal flame," Durrin observed. He knew fire, in all its varieties. This was something higher than fire. The energy radiating through the curtain of water felt more refined, more constant, than anything he had felt before. "What is it?"

"It's light, Durrin. Pure, cleansing, purifying, burning light."

"May I touch it?" Durrin asked.

Sablewing nodded. "You may."

"What will happen?"

"You will gain knowledge."

Durrin took a step closer, his eyes transfixed. "Knowledge about what?"

"Whatever you most need."

Knowledge. Durrin stared into the depths of the glowing waterfall before him. What knowledge did he most need? For the last week, he had spent most of his waking hours in the Hall of Lore, consuming the legends and prophecies of the Luminant Order. But knowledge alone was not enough. Knowledge could not expunge the stain of innocent blood on the scroll of his fate. Only action could do that.

Durrin studied the flames for a moment longer. Then he turned away. "Not yet," he whispered. "Maybe one day. But I am not ready."

Sablewing nodded her head slowly. "When you feel like you are, the Curtain will be waiting."

In silence, they ascended back to the entrance of the chamber and down the long corridor. After the doors had closed behind them, Sablewing cleared her throat. "I have something else to show you. Follow me."

Durrin followed her to the Hall of Learning. At the end of that hall was another set of doors, but these had a conventional keyhole. Sablewing reached her beak into the pocket of a wide belt she wore around her shoulder, retrieving a key and passing it to Durrin. He opened the doors.

Beyond was a small room lined with chests. Sablewing strode inside. "Most of our collection is accessible to any worthy to enter the Bastion. But there are certain records that we keep more restricted. Knowledge is powerful, and not all knowledge is fit to be shared with anyone."

She stopped at the far wall, where a small iron door held an intricately designed pattern lock. She pushed carefully at various parts of the pattern with her beak. "You may have noticed that a group of wagons arrived yesterday. They carried a shipment of tablets, scrolls, and artwork from one of our sister shrines in Elandria. The collection is be kept in safekeeping here until the war with Calamar concludes."

An old but familiar thrill gripped at Durrin's heart. "This shrine—is it the Sanctum of Kings?"

"Yes," Sablewing said, a note of surprise in her eyes. "Light some lumen globes for me, if you please. This lock is tricky in the dark."

Durrin obliged, finding a vessel of water in a nook in the wall and using it to dampen several lumen lanterns in the room. Sablewing studied the lock in the soft glow of the lanterns, then prodded a series of rods until the lock clicked and the heavy door swung open.

"Among the collection was a particular item of great value," Sablewing said, reaching inside the vault. "It is the only one of its kind—and is to remain so, until the Sky Father dictates otherwise." She emerged with a long, narrow box and passed it to Durrin.

Durrin took the box and carefully laid it on a table. His fingers trembled as he undid the clasp and opened the lid. Inside rested a pristine scroll of purest red vellum, sealed with a glob of wax stamped with a fiery symbol. A symbol Durrin knew well.

Kymar's sixth scroll.

He slowly reached inside the box, running his fingers along the smooth vellum. His pulse roared in his ears as the rest of the room seemed to fade away. After all this time. After the studies, the sacrifices, the tournaments, the triumphs. After seven years spent in chains. After all this, the scroll he had spent twenty years trying to obtain had been placed in his hands the week he had ceased looking for it.

"Why are you showing me this?" he whispered.

"When Kymar Roline sealed up this scroll, he made his followers swear to keep it from any who would abuse its power," Sablewing said. "We have followed that strictly, showing the scroll to no one for over three hundred years. But there must come a time when all secrets are shared. I consider you worthy."

Durrin reached inside the box, slipping his fingers underneath the scroll and lifting it out, examining it in the light of the lumen globes. It was breath-taking.

"The scroll must be kept secure," Sablewing said. "I will instruct my assistants that whenever you desire to study it, they will open the vault for you. Then you must remain in this room, the door closed and locked, until you have returned the scroll to its place."

"Mastering a Kymar scroll can take days," Durrin murmured, his eyes still glued to the scroll. "Weeks."

"I would expect no less."

Durrin traced his thumb over the emblem embossed onto the wax seal. He closed his eyes, letting out a long breath.

Then he returned the scroll to its case, closing the lid and snapping the clasp closed.

"I cannot accept this," he whispered. "Her Majesty wishes to leave tomorrow. She requires a pyromancer to operate the cloud frigate."

"You are welcome to return as soon as you see her to safety," Sablewing said.

Durrin shook his head. His mind was clearer now than it had been since his release from Irongate Isle. "Mastering pyromancy is not my path anymore. I have a new quest. Once I return to Elandria, I will be joining their cause."

Durrin placed the box back inside its vault. "If I truly wish to find redemption, then I must do all I can to right my wrongs. I must end the war I helped to start."

Sablewing bowed her head in respect and wordlessly shut the vault door.

Not giving himself a chance to change his mind, Durrin turned and strode from the room, leaving behind the scroll he had once given everything to find.

As he did, he smiled.

Part Three

The Path of Redemption

CHAPTER 40

COUNTERATTACK

Four months later.

Civilization at last!

Lord Salidar had never been so happy to see the red and gold standard of Calamar. Granted, the fortified town it flew above was hardly impressive—a wooden stockade, a poor excuse for a trench, perhaps a couple hundred inhabitants—but it was the first sign of home he'd seen in over four months.

A month before, after a grueling winter trek, he and Yorid had finally slipped across the southern border of Elandria into Larrisa. There, they had located Calamar's embassy and called for a mounted escort to retrieve them.

All things considered, his venture had met with mixed results. Most unfortunately, he had completely failed to eliminate Queen Adara: news had spread of her dramatic return to Saven several weeks before, aboard the very airship that had whisked her away. He had failed to eliminate the pirates, who were in Elandrian custody and liable to spill all sorts of information about him. Durrin Rendhart, one of his most skilled agents, had defected—an incalculable loss. And he had been kept away from Imperium nearly four times longer than he had planned.

But those hadn't been his only objectives.

In his absence, his enemies in court had gotten sloppy, allowing his servants to root out and eliminate several double agents among his staff. And, most importantly, he had created an opportunity for anyone secretly disloyal to tip their hand.

Today, he would harvest the fruit of his victory.

Salidar reined his horse to a stop on a slight rise overlooking the town, the retinue of soldiers in his wake pulling their mounts short.

"So this is Quimar," Salidar said, studying the vista.

"Yes," the lieutenant beside him said proudly. "We took it from Elandria two years ago."

"I know," Salidar said.

He closed his eyes, listening for the now-familiar whisper.

Lord Skyfang has arrived on schedule. All is proceeding as planned. Without fail, the archdemon's voice sent a shiver down his spine. He shook it off and spurred his horse forward.

A full platoon of soldiers waited at the town gate. "Hail, Your Excellency!" the captain shouted, raising his sword in a military salute. "How was your journey?"

"Like a stroll in the park," Salidar replied airily. "I won't deign to mention the near starvation and constant threat of capture, nor the fact that the toes on my left foot have yet to regain any feeling after we swam a half-frozen river."

"Stream," Yorid mumbled behind him, inaudible to all but Salidar.

"Our deepest sympathies." The captain bowed. "You'll be pleased to know that the honorable Lord Skyfang has just arrived to personally greet you. He is awaiting you in the town hall."

Salidar rode up close to the captain. "You received my message, Captain Turlin?" he said in a lower voice, scrutinizing the captain for any sign of treachery.

"Of course, Your Excellency," the captain said. "I've already seen to most of your instructions."

Salidar nodded and rode through the gates. Behind him, he heard Captain Turlin address the commander of the cavalry that had escorted Salidar. "We'll take it from here, Lieutenant. Your squadron can relax and resupply in the barracks. You're off duty for the day."

Presently, Salidar reached the town hall, a building as puny as the rest of the town. Leaving Yorid to see to their horses, he strode to the doors, eyeing the pair of soldiers standing guard on either side.

They are loyal, came the harsh echo in his head. *You doubt me?*

"No," Salidar mouthed. He knew he didn't need to speak out loud for the archdemon to hear.

A thunderous chuckle grated through his mind. *You truly are a good liar.*

Salidar did his best to ignore the icy chill that settled in his gut. Archivous could read his mind more deeply than he had realized.

Lord Skyfang waited for him inside. The griffin aristocrat wore a long, multilayered headdress of purple silk that cascaded down his neck like a mane. His stance suggested confidence, but his head shook every few seconds with a nervous twitch.

"Ah, Lord Salidar," Skyfang said, his rich voice booming in the somewhat underwhelming space. "Welcome back to Calamar." He smiled in a somewhat sardonic way. "Too bad it is not the same Calamar that you left."

"I'm sure it isn't, with imbeciles like you left in charge," Salidar quipped.

Skyfang blinked, pulling his head back slightly at Salidar's unexpected coolness under fire. After a twitch, he resumed. "I'm afraid your political career is over, Your Excellency—if I should still even be using that title. Times have changed. The fortunes have turned. The rabbits have scattered."

"Oh?" Salidar spied some wine set out on a nearby table and poured himself a glass. On second thought, he fiddled with the goblet without drinking anything. "Is there a new vizier?"

"Soon, yes," Skyfang boasted. "I already have the emperor's assurances. Within the month, *you* will be calling *me* Your Excellency."

"Only if the Imperial Council approves," Salidar said. He held up a bowl. "Wine?"

"Yes, thank you," Skyfang said. Salidar filled the bowl and placed it on a pedestal where the griffin could easily lap from it.

"You underestimate your support on the Council," Skyfang said. "High Lord Vandil, Crown Prince Thundertail, and Prince Fireclaw have all forsaken you. They are all fed up with this pet war of yours." The griffin went to sip from the bowl of wine, but froze before he did, his eyes flicking between the bowl and the bottle of wine by Salidar. His head twitched with uncertainty.

Salidar smiled and downed his cup, satisfied the drink hadn't been poisoned. "Even should the Imperial Council back you, the military council can still block it with a two-thirds vote."

"Even there your support has crumbled," Skyfang countered, regaining some of his bravado. "General Grimbold has pledged me his support. He's worried you'll dismiss him for his defeat last fall."

"Astute man," Salidar said.

"General Newfang and General Kryll are willing to desert you as well," Skyfang said.

"Are they now?" Salidar turned to pour another cup of wine to hide his smile.

"It's all over, Salidar," Skyfang said. "Don't you see? Your power is gone. Your failed war is over. Your family's wealth is just one decree away from seizure."

Salidar paced around the side of the room. "Ah. But it appears you have not heard the latest news."

Skyfang took a step back. "What news?"

"I heard it via spy stone just this morning," Salidar said. "Prince Fireclaw was tragically killed yesterday. It appears he was attacked by a wyvern while on a hunting excursion. And just two days before that—it must have been right after you left Imperium to come here—High Lord Vandil fell terribly ill. He's bedridden now, and probably won't last the month."

Salidar's words landed like thunderbolts, exactly like he intended. The griffin staggered back onto his haunches, wings dropping to the ground. Then he shook his head vigorously. "No. You lie. You're trying to trick me."

"Oh, you'll soon hear the truth yourself." Salidar reached the front door and slid it open. "When you return to Imperium to stand trial."

"Stand trial?!"

"Lord Skyfang, you're under arrest for threatening the vizier, impeding the war effort, and sympathizing with Calamar's enemies," Salidar said. "Such a litany of offenses amounts to treason."

Skyfang spread his wings. "You can't arrest me, Salidar. Don't you know why I chose to meet you here? Quimar is garrisoned by elements of the Victory Battalion, troops I've led in over a half dozen campaigns. They'll never agree to arrest me."

Salidar stepped aside as soldiers began filing in through the door. "Is that so? Then why do these soldiers bear the insignia of the Intrepid Battalion?"

A look of pure panic flashed across Skyfang's features. The soldiers surrounded him, leveling their spears.

"Under my orders, two companies from Intrepid arrived just this morning to relieve your precious Victory troops from duty," Salidar said. He turned his back. "I must offer you my thanks. This news about Generals Newfang and Kryll will be quite . . . actionable."

Skyfang let out a scream. "The emperor won't let you get away with this, Salidar!"

"I am sure the emperor can be persuaded to see affairs my way again," Salidar said. He paused in the doorway, turning to look back at Skyfang. He raised an eyebrow.

"Oh—and I believe that's *Your Excellency* to you."

"Fall back!" Volthorn bellowed. "Retreat to the bridge!"

A blow caught him in the ribs, and he stumbled, his vision filling with a flash of light as his terramantic wards deflected the blow. He looked up to see a human in Calamarvan armor gallop past on horseback, heading for another Elandrian soldier.

Oh, no you don't, Volthorn thought. He raised his sword and flung it. It spun end over end before glancing off the mounted soldier's arm, knocking him off-balance a moment before he struck.

Volthorn ran forward, retrieving his sword as the cavalryman circled around for another pass. Volthorn poured terracharge from a ruby into his sword, then sliced the glowing red blade through the cavalryman's saddle straps as he charged past. The soldier toppled off the horse and fell heavily to the ground. Volthorn dispatched him with a quick stab.

He glanced around. His order to fall back had spread up and down the Elandrian line, and soldiers were withdrawing in various stages of chaos.

This was his first visit to the front after Adara's harrowing rescue and safe return. He had come merely to inspect the battalion guarding this bridge. But out of the blue, two companies of enemy cavalry had ridden out of the Mera Valley, slamming into their camp without warning. Amid the chaos, Volthorn and his officers had scrambled to organize a defense, until they had formed a shield line to cover the battalion's retreat across the river.

"Don't turn your backs!" Volthorn yelled. "Keep your eyes on the enemy!"

The Calamarvan cavalry was regrouping, coming in for another assault. Volthorn ran down the length of the line, bellowing at his soldiers to keep up their formation as they withdrew. He ducked into the line a moment before the cavalry was upon them again.

Spears and horse hooves flashed. The human to Volthorn's left cried out and fell. Volthorn's sword was ineffectual in the tight formation, so he sheathed it and grabbed a spear, thrusting forward blindly as he covered his head with his shield.

A moment later, the cavalry was galloping away again, rounding for another assault.

"Keep pulling back!" Volthorn roared. "But stay in your lines! Stay in your lines!" He dropped the spear and turned to the man beside him, who was now doubled up on the ground.

"Get up!" Volthorn barked. The man didn't respond, so Volthorn grabbed him and heaved him to his feet. He wrapped the man's arm around his shoulder and tried to drag him, but the weight of the fully armored man left him exhausted after half a dozen steps.

The man coughed wetly. "Leave me," he croaked.

"Not today." Volthorn flipped open a pouch on his belt, fishing out a rare amethyst. He drew purple terracharge from the gem, then poured it into the man's scale mail until it glowed brightly. His burden instantly decreased as gravity started pushing the breastplate *up* instead of pulling it down. Pocketing the gem, Volthorn pushed onward, half-supporting, half-dragging the man back toward their own lines.

"We're almost there!" Volthorn shouted to his soldiers as they parted to let him through. "Just twenty more yards to the bridge!"

Another round of clashes burst behind him as the cavalry charged again. More screams. He staggered onward, too tired to keep shouting orders.

The bridge was clogged with soldiers and wagons. He waited a moment for the jam to clear, scanning the action behind him. About two hundred Elandrian soldiers remained in the shield line, forming a shrinking perimeter around the bridge. Beyond them, two companies of Calamarvan cavalry harassed them, with a third company riding over a distant hill to reinforce them. Griffins screeched and wheeled overhead.

"Almost there!" Volthorn yelled to his troops. Then he stumbled across the bridge, the soldier he supported getting heavier with each step as the breastplate leaked terracharge. Finally he reached the far side and handed the wounded soldier to a pair of field medics.

Soldiers flowed past him. He waded back in, shoving his way back to the middle of the bridge. "Form up around me!" he yelled. "Spears and pikes forward! Four ranks deep!"

The last soldiers to retreat to the bridge formed up at his orders, presenting a porcupine of spear tips at the enemy cavalry. The riders pulled their horses to a stop at the far side of the bridge, prancing uneasily in place.

"What now, Commander?" a lieutenant called. "Do we charge?"

"No," Volthorn said. "There's too many of them, and too few of us. Stay put and hold the line."

The lieutenant saluted. "With our lives, Commander."

Volthorn slipped through the ranks until he reached the far side of the bridge. Triage and turmoil met his eyes. Medical staff and members of the Dawn Wardens scrambled to dress the dozens of wounded. Officers shouted orders. Soldiers ran every which way. He strode over to a griffin whose plumage markings identified her as a lieutenant.

"Where is Captain Mern?" Volthorn barked.

"Dead, Commander," the griffin answered grimly. "He fell in the first attack on the camp."

Volthorn stood in silence for a moment, shock sweeping through his nerves like cracks across a frozen lake. Mern was dead?

"Commander?"

Volthorn shook his head. "I'm all right. Just . . . I've worked with Captain Mern a long time." How long had it been since they'd trained together as new recruits—over fifteen years? He wouldn't even get to pay his last respects. How many campaigns would it take to numb him of the shock of death's proximity?

He tucked the emotions away for a future moment. "Who's next in command?"

"I believe that's me, Commander," the griffin replied.

"What's our status?"

"Best as I can judge, we're at about half strength. Two or three hundred got cut off and surrendered when the camp was attacked. Another one or two hundred were killed or wounded in our retreat."

Volthorn shook his head. An entire battalion, cut by fifty percent in an hour. And today's losses were full-time troops with years of experience, which he valued at almost double Elandria's less experienced conscript farmers.

"What's our next move, Commander?" the griffin asked.

"The closest reinforcements are a day away," Volthorn said. "And we won't be able to marshal enough force for a counter offensive." Spring planting was still underway—his seasonal troops wouldn't start arriving for another two weeks.

"Do we retreat?"

Volthorn shook his head. "This position is as defensible as any. If we hold the bridge and keep plenty of men at arms on this bank, the cavalry shouldn't attempt another assault today. Set up camp here. I'll dispatch a message for aid. Do you have any pyromancers in your battalion?"

"Two, I believe, if they survived."

"Burn the bridge this evening. Hopefully with that strategic objective removed, their cavalry will withdraw to the safety of the Mera Valley."

"Yes, Commander."

Throughout the afternoon, Volthorn saw to various orders and dispatched several messages. The cavalry on the far bank moved just out of bowshot and stayed there, prancing their horses back and forth in a show of force, taunting him.

That evening, Volthorn dismissed his staff and walked to the riverbank, surveying the scene as he thought about the day's events. The skirmish had been a small but heart-chilling disaster. He'd lost half a battalion of crack troops. Calamar had driven them back across the first tributary that cut across the Arnon Plains, the first step in a repeat of last summer's thrust toward Saven. He had lost Captain Mern, one of his best battalion leaders, along with other irreplaceable officers.

But what most concerned him was that he hadn't even seen the attack coming. He had assumed Calamar would wait to launch any offensive for at least another month, to give time for the weather to warm up, the ground to dry out, and their conscript farmers to begin arriving for the summer season. He had been dead wrong.

What else was he not preparing for?

He found out two days later. Word came speeding through the air on griffins' wings. Three hundred miles to the south, four enemy battalions had marched through the Penandre Pass, cutting down the paltry garrison Volthorn had left there the previous fall. Behind them came wagon after wagon of supplies and equipment, in preparation for a major offensive. Lord Salidar's intentions were all too clear: the attack this summer would come from two sides at once.

CHAPTER **41**

REVERSAL OF FORTUNES

Halorn heaved on the plow, straining. After a moment, it broke through the clod of clay in its path, surging forward before falling back into a steady, bumpy rhythm.

"Good job, Dossie," Halorn called to his horse. "One more row, then I'll give you a rest."

He settled back into stride behind the plow, holding its handles to keep it carving a straight and deep furrow. The cold morning air stung his hands, but the Sun felt warm upon his shoulders, and the air tingled with the fresh smell of spring. He started singing as he walked, a jolly little ditty about seeds sprouting and growing to reach the stars. It was a classic vivamantic tune, sung at planting time to encourage the crops to flourish. He was no vivamancer, so his song would have no magical effect, but he sung the song anyway.

He kept his promise to Dossie, pausing at the end of the next row. He fished a carrot from the bag at his side, breaking off the tip for himself and giving the rest to the horse. He surveyed the half-plowed field. He had felt a strange urgency this whole month to get his seeds in the ground early.

"Halorn!"

He turned, smiling as his wife Elianna approached. Their youngest, Hope, sat in her arms, looking around at the rich brown field with the wide-eyed, half-startled fascination that only six-month-olds can master.

"Honey-roses," Halorn exclaimed, coming to meet her. "How did it go with . . ."

He trailed off as he saw the tears in her eyes.

"A message came from town," Elianna said. She handed Hope to him and wiped her eyes with the hem of her apron. "The quota's been raised this year. You've been—you've been conscripted."

Halorn's throat felt suddenly dry. "When do I report?"

"Next Tuesday."

"Next Tuesday? Most of the conscripts won't be half done with planting!"

Elianna glanced at the half-plowed field. "What about us?"

Halorn closed his eyes, thinking through the fields he had already completed—thank the stars for that sense of urgency!—and what areas still had to be done. "We're ahead of schedule. If we work nonstop, we could finish by then."

Elianna gripped his arm, her face tense. "And if you never return?"

Halorn stared into the distance, trying to empty his heart of the fears that had arisen to choke it. He closed his eyes, seeking to reconnect with the light he had learned to make paramount in his life.

The seed of an idea came to him. He pursued it, raising it to maturity in his mind, exploring its intricacies and ramifications.

He opened his eyes. He stared into his infant daughter's face for a moment; she smiled and cooed, unaware of the life-changing decisions unfolding around her. Then he turned back to his wife.

"Plan on me leaving next Monday. I know what I must do."

"You wanted to meet with us, Your Majesty?" Skagar asked.

"Yes," Adara said. She sat in the council room with Lady Luviana, Chancellor Skagar, and Magistrate Cymer.

Adara swallowed, fingering the head of her scepter to help calm her nerves. "I have been meaning to have this conversation for a while, but I needed to wait until Cymer returned from his winter circuit. There are four things we must discuss."

"Please proceed," Luviana said, shifting positions in her basin of water.

"First," said Adara, "I must ask you to begin trusting me."

Luviana and Skagar each blinked for a few seconds, surprised. Then they started talking over each other in their objections.

"Of course we trust you, Your Majesty."

"What made you think we do not?"

"If I have done anything that—"

Adara raised a hand, stemming their words. "I do not blame you for not trusting me," she said. "How could I expect *you* to trust me when I didn't even trust myself?"

"But Your Majesty," Skagar said. "What gave you the impression we do not trust you?"

"You explain things I already know," Adara said. "You question my decisions. You act annoyed when my conclusions differ from yours. You trust me enough to involve me. But you do not trust me enough to let me truly lead."

Skagar's tail swished with agitation. "If we have acted—"

Adara held up her hand again. "As I said, I do not blame you. You each have years of experience leading this kingdom, and I am only eighteen, after all. I am not rejecting the incredible value of your counsel. What I *am* asking is that you believe in my ability to lead our kingdom. And I will strive to do the same. In the past, I have been the most grievous offender in this regard."

"Your Highness," Lady Luviana said reassuringly. "Do not be too harsh on yourself. I would say that you—"

"And that brings me to my second request," Adara said. "Trusting me means trusting me with the truth. The full and complete truth."

Skagar and Luviana exchanged glances.

"And we have not done so, Your Majesty?" Skagar asked.

"Luviana, take your comment a moment ago," Adara said. "It is true that I have doubted myself in the past. You know it as well as I. But when I stated it just now, you immediately attempted to dismiss or downplay it. How am I to improve if I do not acknowledge the truth about myself? How am I to lead our kingdom if I cannot trust my own advisors to give me the complete picture?"

Adara glanced at Cymer. The old avir's eyes were bright blue as he gave Adara an encouraging smile. She took a deep breath. This was the moment she'd gathered them here today.

"How am I to follow in my father's legacy when I am never told the truth about his death?"

Silence prevailed in the council room. Skagar and Luviana looked at each other in alarm. Then they turned reluctantly back to Adara, guilt written over their features.

"I learned the truth when I was kidnapped," Adara explained. She had had four months now to process the news, but the words still threatened to choke in her throat. "Lord Salidar himself revealed that he ordered my father's assassination. The high mage at the Bastion of Memory confirmed it."

"Your Highness," Skagar said, his tail between his legs. "We had our reasons—"

"I know you hid the truth to prevent war with Calamar," said Adara. "A perfectly understandable motive. I am not here to argue about the past. I am here asking to know the truth *now*. Tell me how my father died. The full story."

After a long pause, Skagar spoke, his voice slow and laden, devoid of all his usual energy. "You remember the guards escorted me and you to safety, with the other counselors," Skagar said.

"Yes."

"After we left, King Everborn headed for the rear door, to try to get to the treasury," Skagar continued. "It was at that moment that an assassin burst through the ceiling—an extremely powerful pyromancer. He blocked the exits and declared that he was sent by Calamar to kill King Everborn. Volthorn and his brothers attacked, but he bested them with fire and lightning."

"The scar on Volthorn's face," Adara recalled. How had she not made that connection? "And I remember hearing a sound like thunder as we reached the courtyard."

Skagar nodded. "The pyromancer pinned Volthorn to the floor with his own spear and knocked out his brothers with lightning. When Volthorn freed himself a few moments later, King Arvanon was lying in his throne, stabbed in the chest, about to breathe his last. The assassin fled, with a fresh contingent of guards in hot pursuit."

Adara straightened in her chair, specific details from Skagar's story catching her attention. The murderer had been a pyromancer. From Calamar. With incredible skills. He would have ties with Salidar, and a deep-seated vendetta with Volthorn.

A flame of wrath kindled in her heart. Could it be . . . ?

Like lightning, her father's words from the Curtain of Knowledge flashed through her mind. *One day, you will know who my murderer is. Before that day comes, you must learn to give your feelings to the Sky Father, or all will be lost.*

Adara forced herself to take a deep breath, burying her feelings. *Breathe.* Hatred. *Release.* Acceptance. She would deal with her anger and suspicions later. For now, she had to see this conversation through.

"What happened then?" Adara forced herself to stutter.

"I arrived a moment later," Skagar continued. "The entrance to the throne room was ablaze, and I almost couldn't get in. I heard your father's last words before he died."

Adara riveted her gaze on her advisor. "What did he say?"

Skagar's eyes had gained a haunted look as he recalled that terrible day. "Your father said, 'Do not lay this to their charge. Do not let this lead to war. Keep my princess safe.' Then he breathed his last."

Adara hung her head. For seven years, she had never known the last words of her father. Now she did. In death, as in life, her father had done all he could to preserve peace. "No wonder you hushed up the assassination," she realized. "My father himself instructed you."

"If our people had known the true cause of his death, they would have insisted on war," Luviana said. "But we were not ready. Our army was poorly trained and poorly equipped. Skagar and I both knew that war would come sooner or later. We tried our hardest to delay it as long as we could while our nation prepared."

Tears pricked at Adara's eyes. She took a deep breath, aware of the blue pigment creeping into her skin as her mind replayed her counselors' story.

Cymer approached with a handkerchief "Take your time to process, Your Majesty. It is not an easy burden to bear."

Her advisors sat in silence while Adara wept. She wept for her father, slain before his time. She wept for herself, deprived of her parents before the age of twelve. She wept for Skagar and Luviana, and all the cares and worries they had carried for so many years. She wept for her people. And in the depths of her weeping, she found resolve.

"Third," she said, wiping the tears from her face and turning to face her advisors again. "It is time to end this war. I learned something else from Salidar, something he will surely regret telling me. It was not the emperor who ordered my father's death. It was Salidar, working behind his back. Nor was the emperor eager for war when it came."

"Your Majesty, we've been through this," Skagar said, twitching his ears in exasperation. "The emperor has not responded to our—"

"Chancellor," Cymer interrupted quietly. "Her Majesty has asked you to trust her."

Adara waited until Skagar had bowed respectfully before she continued. "We sent one epistle last year, at the start of my reign. Yes, it went unanswered. But what if it never arrived? What if Salidar intercepted the message before it reached Emperor Stoneclaw?

"Salidar is away from Imperium now, commanding the assault in the Penandre. Now is the time to recommence our messages. Remind the emperor of his old friendship with my father. Bring up the unratified Treaty of Everlasting Alliance. Call for an armistice and a settlement. Yes, we don't know if he will listen or if we will even get a response. But I will not watch our people be conquered without doing everything in my power to prevent it."

"I will help you pen an epistle this very day," pledged Luviana.

Adara nodded, pleased. "Finally, I want to entreat our neighbors for help. Solapharia, Larrisa, the Mitrian tribes—they each could give aid that could tip the tide of the war."

"We have reached out to them before, with no response beyond excuses," Skagar said.

"Then we shall repeat our appeals, until they grow weary of our messages," Adara said. "This war affects them, too. They will be the next ones in danger should we succumb to Calamar's ambition. We must make them realize that."

They talked for several minutes more of the messages to be sent and the appeals to be made. Eventually, Skagar excused himself to get to work. Luviana clapped her hands, and a trio of servants entered to wheel her basin to another chamber so she could begin dictating letters. Adara remained in the council room, alone with her chief magistrate.

"You did well," Cymer said, his eyes twinkling with pride.

"I feel exhausted," Adara said, allowing herself to slump in her throne.

"The truth is not easy to face." Cymer said, nodding. "But it is far easier than the alternative. What else do you feel?"

Adara studied the skin of her hand, pleased to see it was more bronze and less gray than she expected. "I know what I *don't* feel," she reflected. "I don't feel confused anymore. I don't feel guilty of not doing enough. I don't feel alone."

"You are finally walking the path of truth," Cymer said. "Which means you are ready for something that I have wanted to offer you for quite some time. Are you familiar with the ranks in the Luminant Order?"

Adara had been taught the ranks as part of her tutelage and had come across them again in her readings at the Bastion. "Yes. There are four ranks: Light, Healer, Knight, and Mage."

"Correct. Each rank used to belong to a different order. But when the Dawn Wardens and the Knights Vigilant went astray, and when the Children of the Sky disappeared, we of the Luminant Order adopted the ranks into our own structure. The rank of Light is the first. It is an introductory and preparatory rank, and the one original to the Luminant Order since its founding. Those who accept its mantle vow to be a light to those around them, an example of goodness, and a seeker of truth in all they do. In return, they are promised a portion of the Power of Light, to aid and strengthen them. Do you understand?"

"I believe I do."

"Then, do you seek it?"

"You mean, join the Order?" Adara exclaimed, caught off guard by the idea. "But—I mean, I have my royal duties—"

Cymer smiled. "You will not have to dress in robes and live in a library, if that is what you're wondering. There are many Lights who lead normal lives, save for the touch of illumination they bring to those around them."

Adara thought about it, then nodded. At Cymer's indication, she knelt, and he touched his hand to her forehead, pronouncing words in the Numinous Tongue.

"Rise, Light of the Order," he finished.

Adara stood, searching within herself. She felt unchanged. But for a moment she felt something—some new whisp of light within her, like the faintest echo of the energy she'd experienced passing through the Curtain of Knowledge.

"What can I do with this power?" Adara asked.

"It mainly works unseen," Cymer said. "In a way, it is much like the voice of wisdom you were promised when you were anointed queen. There will be moments where you feel an extra portion of strength, a gift of enlightenment. But there *is* a very direct power you can use on occasion. Do you know the word for 'light' in the Numinous Tongue?"

"It is similar to my name, I believe," Adara said.

Cymer nodded. "Your name, *adara*, means 'life' in the ancient language—a fitting choice on the part of your parents, for you are full of life. The word for 'light' is different by a single letter: *avara*. Say it."

"Avara."

"To turn it into a command, say, 'Et ene avara!' Meaning, *be there light!*"

"Et ene avara."

He fixed her with his intense gaze. "Command it!"

Adara took a deep breath. Was there something she was supposed to harness within herself, like mancerers did when using their powers? She didn't feel any magic stirring deep inside her, so instead she focused her whole will on the words coming out of her mouth. "*Et ene avara!*"

Light sprang into being around her, illuminating every nook and seam in the walls of the council room. Adara looked around, searching for its source. Then she realized *she* was the source. The whisp of energy deep within her was now a roaring current, surging directly through *her*.

The light only lasted a few seconds. Then it faded, and the energy with it. Cymer nodded in approval.

Adara trembled with the shock of what she had just summoned. "Et ene avara," she said again. Nothing happened.

"You will find that the Power of Light is unlike any other force," Cymer said. "It cannot be commanded or controlled, only invited."

"I am only the vessel," Adara realized, staring at her hands.

"Exactly. You do not wield it. It wields you."

✳

It seemed that every decision Volthorn had made in the last month had been wrong.

After receiving word of the attack in the Penandre, Volthorn had initially stayed at the Arnon Plains, assigning a general already in the south to lead the defense. But soon letters began to arrive from other officers, complaining about the man's overbearing leadership style and lack of combat experience. So Volthorn decided to leave the Arnon Plains and take command of the southern front himself.

Then he had bungled the deployment of troops. He assumed that Calamar, by opening a second front, would only be able to keep around fifteen or twenty thousand troops in the Mera Valley. So he ordered half his battalions stationed on the Arnon Plains to march south to handle the second threat. Scarcely had he done so, however, then reports arrived from the Mera Valley, placing the strength of the enemy there at forty thousand. He had grudgingly sent most of the battalions back.

Forty thousand on the northern front! And another thirty-five thousand on the southern front. How could Salidar field such numbers? The Calamarvan war machine must be stretched to the breaking point.

But the Elandrian war machine was already starting to break. Volthorn arrived on the southern front to find a slapped-together army of barely trained farmers, held together by a core of professional soldiers promoted to officer en masse. They faced constant shortages of supplies, clothing, and weapons, and as morale sunk, desertion began to rise.

His attempts to straighten out the camp had only met with more snags. Training staff had chaffed at the demanding regimen he insisted for new recruits. Two different logistics officers had resigned their posts after failing to meet his expectations. He found himself longing for the familiar team of officers he had left behind in the Arnon. At least his brothers were still with him, dependable as always.

Then the campaigning had begun. Calamar's host, led by Lord Salidar himself, had marched confidently toward Volthorn's position. He was not too badly outnumbered: their thirty-five thousand to his twenty-five thousand. But he knew his army was not ready to fight. For two weeks he maneuvered, seeking to find a favorable battleground or to outflank his opponent. But Salidar seemed to anticipate each move, dancing out of Volthorn's traps and marching his army from strong position to strong position.

After an exhausting day of marching over thirty miles, Volthorn slumped into a chair in his command tent. He stared at the stack of reports Kelzern dropped in front of him. "Where do I begin?" he grumbled.

Kelzern indicated a scroll stamped with the royal seal. "I suggest the epistle from the capital."

Volthorn opened it. Two-thirds was taken up by a long and drawling report dictated by Skagar on recruitment and treasury figures; he skimmed it in ten seconds and moved on to the neat rows written in Queen Adara's hand at the bottom.

Commander Skarr,

Our most earnest thoughts accompany you and your army. We trust in your ability to pull off another miracle and save our kingdom once again.

Yesterday we received a visitor: the pyromancer Durrin Rendhart. He has spent the last three months coordinating aid to refugees in the Arnon. Now he wishes to help with the war effort as best he can, short of fighting on the front lines. We thought it best to assign him a post in the training camp at Nidar. There he will oversee the training of newly recruited pyromancers, where we are confident he will excel. Hopefully this is not the sole piece of good news you receive today.

May angels march with you,

Queen Everborn

Volthorn stared at the letter. "Good news," he huffed.

"What's the matter?" Kelzern asked.

"Rendhart. *Again,*" Volthorn said. His two brothers were among the few who knew all the details of how King Everborn had died. "He's manipulated Adara into giving him a command post at Nidar."

Kelzern started running a file down the blade of his knife. "That's . . . odd."

"It's more than odd," Volthorn said. "It's suspicious."

"Maybe he truly has switched sides," Kelzern said. "From what I've heard, he seems sincere."

"He *seems,*" Volthorn said. "But what if this is a charade?"

"He saved the queen's life. What's not sincere about that?"

Volthorn scowled at the letter, as if staring at it hard enough would reveal Rendhart's true intentions. "The politics in Imperium are as complex as the tunnels in a snippen burrow. Who knows? Perhaps he's serving a faction opposed to Salidar. Perhaps he's trying to sabotage Salidar's efforts to win the war but help achieve victory for a rival instead. Or perhaps this was all an extremely complex ruse to plant a double agent in our midst."

"But why would he want a job training our new recruits?"

"Because Nidar is one of our intelligence hubs," Volthorn said. "With his talents, he could spy on any number of confidential meetings. In fact, besides the front lines and the capital itself, I couldn't think of a better place to plant a spy. And it's ideal for someone who wants to keep a low profile." He searched around for quill and ink. "I will write to Her Majesty at once and insist upon his dismissal."

"Under what grounds?" Kelzern asked. "She still doesn't know what he did."

Volthorn paused, the quill suspended above a blank sheet of parchment. "Perhaps it's time to tell her." He shook his head. "No. She has enough on her mind. If she doesn't follow my recommendation, I'll write to the commander at Nidar and tell him to keep close tabs on Rendhart's actions."

He thought for a moment, biting the feathery tip of the quill, then began writing.

To Her Majesty,

My thanks for your expression of confidence. I hope to live up to it.

I urge you to dismiss Rendhart from his post. I am partial to information about his past—information too sensitive to write here. Suffice it to say that he has demonstrated radical loyalty to Calamar and a willingness to deceive and even kill our subjects to further its interests. Despite his seeming sincerity, he cannot be trusted. His position at Nidar jeopardizes our military integrity. Dismiss him with all speed.

The campaign here progresses. This morning, our cavalry saw a light engagement, but it ended quickly and inconclusively. Our infantry's performance in training maneuvers improves each week, but they are still untested in battle, and I worry about their resolve.

To buy us time for further training, I have begun issuing challenges for single combat: Calamar's best champion versus ours. I have now issued four such challenges, invoking the traditional wording established centuries ago. Salidar has ignored all of them like the coward he is.

May you see naught but peace in your corner of our beleaguered nation,

Commander Skarr

Volthorn used a cloth to soak up excess ink, then blew on the parchment to dry it out. He handed the letter to Kelzern to process and deploy to a messenger griffin, then turned to the rest of the reports on his desk.

A sudden wave of weariness washed over him. He let his head sink down to rest on the cold desk. Everything seemed to be turning against him. Where was the confidence and clarity he had felt the previous year? Where was the strategist who had scored the greatest victory of Elandrian military history?

For the rest of the night, through two hours of reports and meetings and then another hour lying awake on his sleeping mat, Volthorn found his thoughts running again and again to Rendhart. What was the man up to? And could he have anything to do with Volthorn's seemingly inexplicable turn of fortunes?

Just before his bone-weary body finally forced his mind into a restless sleep, he remembered the significance of the day's date. It was the fourteenth day of the fifth month. Exactly eight years since Everborn's death.

Chapter 42

Haunting Dreams

Two souls slept fitfully that night. Memory plagued them both.

✳

"You will pay for killing our king," Volthorn spat.

He was a low-ranking captain again. He had been entrusted with the king's guard. And he had failed.

But he would see justice enacted.

They had the murderer cornered. The pyromancer stood with the Silvermoss to his back, tall buildings to either side. Volthorn and a score of soldiers blocked his escape.

An archer in Volthorn's squad raised his bow, sighted, and loosed. The pyromancer knocked the arrow aside with his sword, not even flinching.

"Get up on the rooftop," Volthorn whispered. "Use a voidstone arrow. I'll buy you time."

Volthorn stepped forward, past the line of soldiers blocking the alley. "You've trapped yourself," he called. "Did you expect a boat?" He began envisioning all the man's possible options, mentally countering each one.

"No, I expected to fly out of this cursed city," the man said sarcastically. He gestured to the deep, bloody gash on Volthorn's cheek. "Seems like you have a souvenir."

Volthorn took a step forward, transferring the last of his terracharge into his sword and armor. He should have been prepared with a larger supply. "Who are you?!" he demanded.

The pyromancer only gave an elaborate bow. "Durrin Rendhart, wielder of the sword of Calamar. But after this day, I shall be known as Everborn's Bane."

Volthorn screamed and launched to the attack.

They exchanged blows with both weapons and mancery. Fire and steel flashed and sung in deadly harmony. Again and again Volthorn thrust and slashed, but again and again the pyromancer parried or twisted away. Several times the man scored hits that only glanced off Volthorn's wards.

The assassin used every conventional attack, but Volthorn foresaw them all. He dodged fire, blocked trusts, and avoided feints. Above all, he waited. The pyromancer was tired. He had run through the city for the last half hour, while Volthorn had arrived at the riverside fresh, on horseback. Time was on his side.

After a minute, they disengaged. The pyromancer was panting, and sweat bathed his jerkin.

"We will kill you for what you did," Volthorn growled.

The assassin launched himself at Volthorn again. For a moment Volthorn staggered back, overwhelmed by the sheer force of the attack, the terracharge in his armor running dry as it repelled a series of blows. Then he switched from a defensive posture to a withering series of attacks. The pyromancer fell back, blocking Volthorn's blows with slower and slower movements, until he was backed up to the river.

Volthorn caught movement on the roof in the corner of his eye. He stepped back. The man stood ready with his sword raised, fire licking his fingers, exhaustion written on his face.

A bow twanged. The man twisted too late. A voidstone arrow buried itself in his side, and he fell with a grunt of pain, his sword dropping into the water.

Volthorn stepped forward and planted a clawed foot on the man's neck. He raised his sword high. "For our king!" he cried.

"Captain Volthorn. Desist."

His soldiers parted to reveal the old avir named Cymer, his cloak bearing the insignia of high magisterial office.

Volthorn wiped the sweat from his eyes. "This man murdered our king!"

"I know," Cymer said. He reached Volthorn and laid a hand on the handle of the sword. "But has not enough blood been shed today?"

"He deserves to die!" Volthorn cried in fury.

"Perhaps," Cymer said. "But even if he did, would you kill him at night, Volthorn? Would you condemn him to be claimed by demons?"

Volthorn looked at the darkening sky. The Sun had set a few minutes before. But he didn't care. "This man deserves the deepest pit in the Void!"

"No one deserves the Void," Cymer whispered. He took the sword from Volthorn's claws. "Do not do this, Captain. Do not succumb to hate."

Volthorn awoke, sweat beading on his brow.

He sat upright, putting a hand to his mutilated cheek. The last words of the nightmare echoed through his thoughts. "Hate?" he murmured. "Or justice?"

"Piece of cake," Durrin muttered.

He was thirty-one again, at the height of his career. He was on the verge of earning unmatched power. And he would not fail.

He stood with his back to Saven's palace wall, his toes dangling over an impressive drop to the rooftops thirty feet below. Scaling the rocky sides of the royal acropolis had proven child's play. The walls would be trickier.

He closed his eyes, reaching out with his pyrosense. Several sparks moved about in the rooms on the other side of the wall. But he sensed no one on the battlement above. Perfect.

Durrin unhooked a coil of rope and a grappling hook from his belt. Spinning it expertly, he launched it up toward the battlement. It was a tricky throw: because of the angle, the grappling hook needed to curve away from the wall, then swing back inward toward the battlements, pulled by the tension in the rope. So even he was surprised when, on the first throw, he heard the satisfying clang of metal on stone and the rope held fast.

He froze, listening to hear if anyone reacted to the sound. Nothing.

Durrin sprang up the rope, climbing at lightning speed.

His thoughts raced even faster.

What was he doing? He was rushing into this with scarcely even a plan. He and his wingman had arrived in Saven just a half hour before. Their intent had been to stake out the palace that night, then strike the next morning. But the rumor on the docks was that the king was about to sign, that very afternoon, a decree to block the export of haeber to Calamar. He had to be stopped today. Even now it might already be too late.

Durrin paused near the top of the wall, listening once again. The battlement was clear. Now was his chance.

He flipped over the edge of the battlement and dropped to the stone-work on the other side, keeping his profile low. Before him stretched the rooftops and towers of the palace complex. He drew his sword and hurried down the parapet, glancing around to get his bearings. He'd poured over schematics of the palace in preparation for this mission, but the real thing always tended to look different.

"Hoy there! What was that?"

The voice of a single guard, to Durrin's left. The guard was approaching his battlement from another that met at a right angle. He ran doubled over in that direction, staying out of the guard's line of sight beneath the edge of the parapet. As he ran, he scanned the area with his pyrosense. Good. No other guards.

The guard turned the corner and started with surprise. Durrin straightened and charged, knocking the guard's spear aside with his sword and landing a pyromancy-reinforced upper cut on the guard's jaw with his free hand. The guard stood for a moment, stunned by the blow. Then his eyes rolled back, and his legs crumpled. Durrin caught both the spear and the guard, lowering both to the stonework without a clatter.

He should kill the guard, lest he awake in a minute and sound the alarm.

No. The guard was out cold. By the time he awoke—or was discovered—it would be too late. There was no need to shed more blood today.

Durrin sprang to a rooftop and scaled it, his fiery red cape trailing in the air behind him. He slid down the other side, gathering momentum about him as he fell, then sprang out across a gap to a walkway on the far side. In front of him rose the dome marking the throne room. Almost there.

A guard rushed onto the walkway from a stairwell, spear lowered. "Halt! Stop right there!"

Durrin snapped his hand, releasing a ball of fire. The soldier recoiled, covering his face, and Durrin swept forward, grabbing the spear and twisting. The soldier resisted, leaning his weight into the spear to keep control of it, but Durrin reversed the direction of his pull without warning, spinning the guard past him and launching him off the walkway to a patio ten feet below, where he landed with a clatter of armor.

Durrin sprang forward, spinning his arms to gather a whirlwind of energy around him. He leapt up to the sill of one of the windows set into the base of the dome. He smashed the glass with the pommel of his sword, then released his inferno down into the throne room below, where it exploded against one of the exits. Then he jumped.

Fifty feet he dropped, scarlet cloak billowing in his wake. Halfway through his plummet, he twisted in midair, fire erupting from his outstretched hands to slow his fall. He landed in a crouch blocking the throne room doors.

He always preferred flashy entrances.

Straightening, he drew his sword and pointed it at the king's heart. "Today you taste the sword of Calamar, King Everborn."

Three guards, all korriks, screamed and ran to stop him. Drawing upon an advanced Kymar form, he twisted his sword in an intricate pattern. Energy popped and cackled around him until he channeled it at the approaching guards, his spark leaping within him. Lighting crackled into existence along the blade's length, shooting out at the guards. Two dropped immediately.

The third staggered, then regained his footing and charged, his spear time glowing red with terramantic charge. Durrin dodged, then pressed to the attack. But this korrik was a skilled warrior, and his spear gave him a longer reach—not to mention it could slice through Durrin's armor like butter if it made impact. Durrin was forced on the defensive as the korrik drove him back.

No. He was better than this. He hadn't come two thousand miles to be bested by a mere bodyguard. Durrin anticipated the korrik's next thrust and grabbed the shaft of the spear. With that threat neutralized, he landing a flying kick, then wrenched the spear from the korrik's grasp and used it to swipe the korrik's legs out from under him.

Durrin landed a series of blows with the captured weapon, draining the terracharge in the korrik's armor. Then he rammed the spear tip through the guard's chainmail and into the stone below, pinning him. Durrin wanted a witness.

Durrin strode forward. "Walls and guards cannot save you from the sword of Calamar, Your Majesty."

The king raised a hand, the palm blistered from where he had tried to open the burning rear exit. "In neither walls nor guards do I trust," he said. "I trust in the hosts of the Sun."

For the first time, Durrin looked into the king's face. He saw no fright there, no panic, no fear. Just sorrow. And—calmness. It was a beautiful face, a noble face. The face of a father, a statesman, and a king.

What was he doing? How could he slay another soul in cold blood?

But guild mastership, secret knowledge, unrivaled power—it only awaited his sword to fall.

Don't do it! Durrin's mind screamed, echoing through his dream as if it could go back in time and undo the past.

But the past was done. The sword plunged into the king's chest.

"Then where are your angels now?" Durrin heard himself whisper.

In that instant, the vantage point of the dream changed. Durrin now observed the scene from the side of the throne room, in his present-day body. He watched in muted horror as his past self withdrew the sword. King Everborn fell, slumping back into his chair and gasping in pain.

"Nooo!" roared the captain, still pinned to the floor.

Then the throne room doors burst open and a squad of guards poured into the room. Durrin fled, running to the back entrance and smashing through the half-burned remains of the door. The guards raced after him.

For a moment they shied back, intimidated by the flames engulfing the doorway. Then they pressed forward with a yell.

In the sudden quiet, the guard captain—Volthorn—finally freed himself from the spear and stumbled to the throne. "No, no, no," he cried, reaching out to try and quench the flow of blood. "Everborn. Your Majesty! EVERBORN!"

Durrin watched it all, standing unseen in the corner. Only then did he notice a figure to his left. He turned. A being stood next to him, clothed in shining white robes. From her back extended a pair of long, feathery wings of purest white, like those of a swan. Her features looked vaguely human-like, but were sharper and more distinct.

In her hands she held a scroll and quill. Tears rolled down her cheeks as she wrote on the scroll with ink red as blood.

Durrin didn't need to ask to know whose scroll she bore.

"Why?" he asked the angel—though he wondered if she could hear him, or if she was part of the past. "Why must I relive this?"

The image of the angel shimmered, then split. One version stayed where she was, weeping as she continued to watch the scene in the throne room. The other version turned to answer Durrin.

"Because you have not yet fully addressed what you did that day," the angel answered.

Durrin fell to his knees. "What more must I do? I forsook my career and my ambitions. I saved Everborn's daughter from the brink of death. Now I spend each day training warriors to defend the nation I once attacked. What more?"

"You must confess," the angel declared. "Confess your sin to the one who must hear the truth the most. And seek her forgiveness."

"And the war? How can I help it end?"

The angel gestured to a section of the scroll in her hands—not the fresh line written in red, but the many lines of writing before it. "Your life has prepared you, Durrin. You are in a unique position to bring Elandria aid. But first, confess. Only then will you be shown what to do."

Durrin awoke with the angel's last words ringing in his head: "Do not delay. Time runs short."

CHAPTER 43

TWO UNEXPECTED VISITS

High Lord Vandil, steward to the emperor of Calamar, was dying. The doctors disagreed about how to diagnose the illness that had seized him scarcely a month before. One was convinced it was the yellow plague, based on the boils on his legs and arms. Another insisted it was swamp fever, due to the chills and spells of delirium. Others didn't even try to diagnose it. Every treatment failed, anyhow.

Once it became apparent that Lord Vandil was not contagious, the quarantine was lifted from his household so that nobility could come wish the imperial steward a final goodbye. But few came. Salidar's unexpected return, Prince Fireclaw's death, and Skyfang's arrest had created chaos in imperial politics, like an anthill kicked open. The only visitor of high rank who came to see the dying avir regularly was the emperor himself, to whom Lord Vandil had been a long and loyal friend.

But late one evening, a wholly unexpected visitor arrived.

Lord Vandil's butler emerged from the room and bowed to Halorn. "My lady said you can enter. Please keep your visit short—it is quite late."

Halorn stepped inside. He had traded his normal work attire in favor of the best dress shirt, trousers, and cap he still owned. Still, his humble trappings felt terribly out of place in the ornately decorated room.

Lady Vandil looked up from where she sat by her husband's bedside. A month of long days and longer nights had taken a beating on her nerves, as her pale skin and graying hair made all too clear.

"Halorn," Lady Vandil said, reaching out a hand. "You once worked on my husband's staff, yes?"

"Almost a decade ago," Halorn said, taking the hand and making to kiss it, though his lips never came closer than a few inches away, as the social circumstances dictated. "Your husband is the best master I ever worked for."

"He was," Lady Vandil agreed. She stood and worked her way around the room, trimming the lamps and re-moistening the lumen globes. The chamber held over a dozen of each, clustered around the door and windows but also hanging in each corner and from each bedpost. More lanterns burned in the hallway and at each entrance to the manor. With Lord Vandil so close to death, every precaution had to be taken during those terrible hours between dusk and dawn.

Halorn looked at the middle-aged avir in the bed. His face was deathly pale, and his chest was barely moving with each breath. "How long since he was awake?" Halorn asked in a soft voice.

"Over three days ago." The noble lady resumed her vigil by the bedside, blinking back a fresh round of tears. "You are kind to come and pay your respects."

Halorn knelt at the bedside and looked earnestly into her face. "I did not come to pay my respects, Your Ladyship. With your leave, I have come to heal your husband."

She looked up at him, her eyes flashing light gray in confusion. "Are you a doctor?"

"Not exactly."

"Vivamancer? We have already hired the best in the capital."

Halorn shook his head.

"Then . . . ?"

Halorn's next words came just louder than a whisper. "I know that in years past, you and your husband were amicable toward the Luminant Order. Has that disposition remained unchanged?"

The avir woman glanced at the door, making sure it was firmly shut. When she looked back, her eyes had gained the faintest glow of hope. "Yes. Yes, it has."

"Then do you believe in the coming of the Eldest?"

She looked down. "I used to believe in the Order's teachings . . . my husband and I both. But we buried those feelings when the second purge started."

"I didn't ask if you have believed in the past. I asked if you choose to believe *now*. Right at this moment."

She dabbed at the corner of her eyes, her shoulders shaking with stifled sobs. "Yes. Yes!"

"Then I will see what I can do."

Halorn stood and gathered the sick steward's clammy hands into his own. He closed his eyes, feeling a familiar power surge into him, coursing through his nerves, building up at the tips of his fingers. Then he spoke.

"Et evinal, et yidivar, et claminor, al Abeam!"

It was a command in the Numinous Tongue. *Be whole, be healed, be clean, by the Eldest!*

The power surged from his hands into the dying man. And it was like his mind went with it, his consciousness becoming aware of each organ in Lord Vandil's body. What he encountered nearly shocked him into drawing back.

Blight. Blight like he had never felt before. This was no common fever or plague—this was an illness caused directly by the malignant power of the Void.

Halorn pushed against that darkness with the power of the Light. For a moment it gave way before him, retreating down the length of Lord Vandil's atrophied arms. Halorn pursued it, commanding muscles, skin, and nerves to be healed.

But as his awareness came to Lord Vandil's chest, he felt something change. A malevolent consciousness began to push back, as if it had just arrived on the scene to take active control of the blight in Lord Vandil's body. Halorn bent his will upon it, urging the Light to vanquish it. But the being he battled was strong. Horribly strong.

"Light," Halorn gasped, sweat beginning to bead on his forehead. "Bring more light!"

Lady Vandil stood and dashed into the hallway. Halorn closed his eyes again, pouring his whole consciousness into the invisible battle before him. Inch by inch he gave up ground as the darkness reclaimed its lost territory. His arms trembled, his whole body shaking with the strain.

With the voice of the clanking of a thousand chains, the force he battled spoke to his mind.

What? You think to rob me of my prize so easily? Me? I am Archivous! I have vanquished angels and trampled nations! I have scattered plague and unleashed war!

The darkness had almost regained Lord Vandil's hands. Halorn almost drew away, disengaging before the darkness could spread to him. But then Lady Vandil rushed back into the room, a shining candelabra in each hand, and with the burst of renewed light, Halorn gained strength. Again he spoke.

"Al avara, al niava, al Abeam, et yidivar!"

The darkness faltered. Halorn pressed to the attack once more, a torrent of light pouring through him and down his arms. The darkness began to shrivel, though the malignant entity remained, seething and thrashing.

Then Lady Vandil joined him by the bedside, laying her hands over his. She had no authority of the Luminant Order to add. But she had belief and she had love, and both carried a potent light.

"By the Eldest," Lady Vandil gasped. "By the Sky Father, leave my husband!"

The darkness writhed. A scream of rage echoed through Halorn's mind. Then it was gone.

The archdemon had fled.

Halorn let out a deep breath, his shoulders sagging with relief. "It is enough. I can take it from here."

Lady Vandil stood back and watched as Halorn finished the task of healing. Now, with the demon gone, the blight dispersed easily everywhere his mind advanced. He pushed it out from Lord Vandil's legs, breathing strength back into the atrophied muscles. Then he cleansed the avir's head. He moved next to the chest and abdomen, cleansing and repairing each organ.

He saved the heart for last—but to his surprise, the heart did not need mending. It had stood strong against the darkness, a bastion of free will holding out when all else had succumbed. Halorn marveled, understanding now how Lord Vandil had survived so long against such a withering plague.

Once he'd finished, Halorn withdrew his hands, his awareness shrinking back to his normal senses. He stared intently at Lord Vandil's face, all too aware of the anxious stare from the noble lady beside him.

Slowly, the deathly pallor on Lord Vandil's face gave way to a healthy bronze. The avir steward took a deep, wholesome breath, and his eyes flickered open. With a cry, his wife embraced him. Tears came again to her eyes, but her face was now a bright golden hue of pure joy.

Halorn stepped back to a corner of the room as he watched the exultant reunion before him. Words tumbled from Lady Vandil's mouth as she gestured at Halorn and attempted to explain the miracle that had just occurred.

The venerable avir sat up in bed. He held out a hand and Halorn took it, dropping his eyes respectfully as the steward studied him.

"Halorn, my old servant," Lord Vandil said, his voice slightly raspy from lack of use, but still firm. "I am forever in your debt. How can I repay you?"

Halorn smiled somewhat grimly. This had been the easy part. The harder portion lay ahead. "When you are feeling fully well, go to your master," Halorn said. "Arrange for me to have an audience with him. I have words that he must hear."

"Commence fire!" the training marshal ordered.

Volthorn watched as the platoon of archers nocked arrows to strings, pulled back, sighted, and released. Each reloaded and fired at his own pace, and soon the air resounded with the hiss of arrows and the dull thuds as they impacted their targets sixty yards away.

"Cease fire!" the marshal shouted.

The archers stood at ease, waiting anxiously as an officer at the far end of the range stepped out from behind his cover and inspected the row of targets. "Fourteen hits!" he called.

"Better," the training marshal said, looking hopefully at his chief commander.

Volthorn scowled. "But still not good enough."

Normally, archery platoons needed to consistently score at least twenty hits in this exercise before they were fit to be deployed.

"We're doing the best we can," the marshal apologized. "Some of these boys never touched a bow before this year."

Boys—he was right about that. Most of the humans and avirs in the line looked to be in their late teens. The korriks, whose species reached maturity much faster, were even younger, perhaps twelve or thirteen. Towns and villages across the kingdom were scrapping the bottom of the barrel to meet their recruitment quotas.

Volthorn raised his voice to address the archers. "Keep up the hard work! We will soon face the enemy on the field of battle, but we will not face them unprepared!" He thrust his fist into the air. "Elandria!"

The archers echoed him, raising fists or bows as they joined in the war cry. But it sounded half-hearted.

Volthorn completed his review of the training grounds and headed back to his command post. As he approached the center of camp, however, he heard the dull roar of many voices. He quickened his step. Soon he could see where soldiers were massing in a field, packing together as they pressed eagerly toward something he couldn't yet see.

Then a swifter ran past him, calling out every dozen yards: "The queen! Queen Everborn is at the central parade field!"

Volthorn caught the messenger. "The queen? Why?"

"I don't know," the swifter said, tail wagging furiously. "They just told me to spread the word. She's going to give a speech!"

He darted off, leaving Volthorn standing in shocked bewilderment. "You could have given me a little warning," he muttered.

Volthorn soon found himself jostling with dozens of soldiers heading the same direction. They parted as soon as they saw the plumage of his commander's helmet, but that was usually only *after* he had managed to shove his way in front of them. Blasted stars—why hadn't he brought his horse?

Eventually he despaired of pressing through the crowd and instead skirted around the perimeter. This brought him much better results as he moved around the edge of the parade ground to a section of the camp cordoned off for him and his command staff. This was still packed with soldiers—far more than should be allowed in a restricted area—but Volthorn managed to wind his way through until he finally had a view.

Queen Adara was standing on top of a wagon at the parade field's edge, addressing the crowd of several thousand soldiers. She was dressed in an elegant floor-length dress the color of the deep blue sky, topped with a magnificent purple cloak. The jewels in her eternium crown sparkled and winked in the sunlight.

An avir's hair color was based on their general emotional state. For the past seven years, Adara's hair had always grown somber shades of blue and dark brown, a testament to her worries and her mourning over her father. But now, Volthorn noticed that the roots of her hair were growing a rich golden brown.

". . . remember the cause you fight for," Adara was saying. Her voice projected across the entire assembly, without sounding strained or harsh. "For you fight for a reason. Do you fight for me? No. I am but a single soul like any one of you, though fate and tradition have laid upon me the mantel of leadership. Do you fight for Commander Skarr? Once again, no—for he is also but a single soul, though the most brilliant strategist our kingdom has ever known."

"Thanks, Your Majesty," Volthorn muttered, not sure if he should be slighted or flattered.

"Do you fight for our kingdom? Yes, in a way—but not Elandria as some abstract concept. You fight for Elandria insofar as it represents you, me, all of us. You fight for your families! You fight for your mothers and fathers, your spouses and children, your brothers and sisters. You fight for your farms and villages, your towns and cities, your shops and marketplaces. You fight for freedom from the oppressive hand of a cruel empire. You fight for liberty to live your lives and choose your beliefs as you see fit."

Her voice seemed to amplify even more. "But that is not all. You fight for peoples and nations you will likely never see. Are we the only ones threatened by Calamar's endless ambition? No! If we fall, will Larrisa to the south be spared? Or Solapharia to the north? Or even Mitria and Marisau to the east? No! We fight for ourselves, but we fight just as much for them."

Adara made a motion with her hand, and a sergeant sprang up beside her, bearing Elandria's green banner on a long pole. She motioned to it as he held it high. "For our families! For our freedom! For Elandria!"

The soldiers took up the cry in a resounding shout. "For our families! For our freedom! For ELANDRIA!"

For over a minute the assembly cried, as the sergeant waved the banner back and forth. Then Queen Adara disappeared from Volthorn's view, climbing down a ladder attached to the wagon's side.

Volthorn pressed through the last of the crowd to reach the wagon. But it was a long time before he could talk to her. She was walking through the press of soldiers, interacting with them in small groups, giving words of encouragement, answering questions, and bestowing her royal blessing upon bowed heads or the hilts of weapons.

Volthorn watched in surprise. Was this the same young, hesitant girl he had seen crowned queen scarcely a year before? Gone was any trace of uncertainty from her face. She almost seemed to glow, her face alight with joy, her eyes fixed on each person she met.

Volthorn found Trazar standing by the wagon. "Did you know Her Majesty was coming?" he asked.

Trazar shook his head. "No idea. But wasn't that amazing?"

"Yes," Volthorn agreed. "Where did she learn to project like that?"

"I think she brought a verbomancer to project her words," Trazar said. "A great idea."

Volthorn watched Adara, nodding. He knew he should feel pleased—Adara's visit was rallying the troops at a time they desperately needed it. But instead, he felt slightly annoyed.

"You're jealous of her," Trazar whispered.

"What?" Volthorn blinked in surprise. "No, I'm not."

"You wish you could be as popular with your troops as she is," Trazar continued.

"I'm their commander, not their king," Volthorn snapped. "I can't very well have my troops swarming over me whenever I step outside my tent."

Still, he knew Trazar was partially right.

After nearly an hour, Adara dismissed the last vestiges of the crowd and turned to Volthorn and his waiting staff. "Commander Skarr," she said, her smile growing larger. "Just the korrik I wanted to see."

He bowed low. "This was quite the surprise, Your Majesty. But you really shouldn't be here, so close to enemy lines."

"I knew you would think so," Adara said. She strode past him toward his command tent, gesturing that he should follow. "Which is why I didn't tell you I was coming."

He frowned. "But the danger—"

"It's as dangerous for you as it is for me," Adara said as they entered the tent. "I can't just cower in a palace while my nation fights a war, Volthorn. Our people need to see that I'm not afraid—that I care more about them than my own security."

"Is this not your only stop?"

"It is not," Adara said. "I've been visiting cities and towns all the way up the Angerflood for the last two weeks."

Volthorn looked at her in concern. "What about your duties back at the palace?"

"Paperwork and sitting in meetings? I have delegated that to Skagar and Luviana. They're better at it than I am, anyway. For any major decisions, they are in touch via griffin courier. I need to do what only *I* can do, Volthorn, and that's to inspire my people. To give them hope again."

She gestured to a strategic map spread on his table. "And you need to do what only *you* can do: save our people on the field of battle."

Volthorn nodded briskly. "Right. Would you like an update?"

"It's one of the reasons why I came."

Volthorn planted his claws on the table's edge, taking a moment to gather his thoughts. He pointed to a cluster of green tokens on the map. "Here's our position. Eighteen thousand infantry and four thousand cavalry. I've had to withdraw down the Angerflood quite a ways since my last letter to you. We lost a small engagement last week when we attempted to defend the town of Pullan. Four days ago, Salidar almost trapped us against some marshland. I knew I couldn't engage when he had the momentum and initiative. So I pulled us back at a double march to our current position. It bought us two days of rest to regroup, resupply, and train—and hear inspiring speeches." He winked at her. Her speech, he had to admit, *had* been quite impressive.

Adara stared at the map. "And what is Salidar doing?"

"He's still two days behind us," Volthorn said. "He has to advance more slowly to give his soldiers time to claim each town they pass."

"And what are your plans?"

Volthorn folded his arms. "I have something in the works."

"And . . . that is?"

Volthorn shook his head. "I don't divulge my plans to anyone before I have to. Not even to you, Your Majesty." He kept his eyes on the map, unwilling to see the reaction on her face.

Adara responded slowly. "I understand your caution, Commander. But I feel I must know your plans." It was not a request. It was an order.

Volthorn nodded and moved to the tent door, where Trazar was waiting. "Standard procedure for strategy meetings," Volthorn said. "Keep the perimeter clear." He went back inside, working to set up a quartzite beacon and an aquamancy rune, as had become his habit. Adara watched with patient interest.

"You must promise me, Your Majesty, that you will not divulge these plans to anyone," Volthorn said.

"I promise."

Volthorn pointed to the map. "Where we are, the Angerflood makes a wide curve. Tomorrow I'm going to move the army straight north, as if I'm cutting across the loop to save time. You see this band of forest in my path? It's especially thick, dense woods—nearly impassable except by one road and a handful of obscure trails. My hope is that Salidar will follow me, trying to trap us against the wood. But I'll withdraw along this road, then make as if I'm continuing to retreat north to the next walled town."

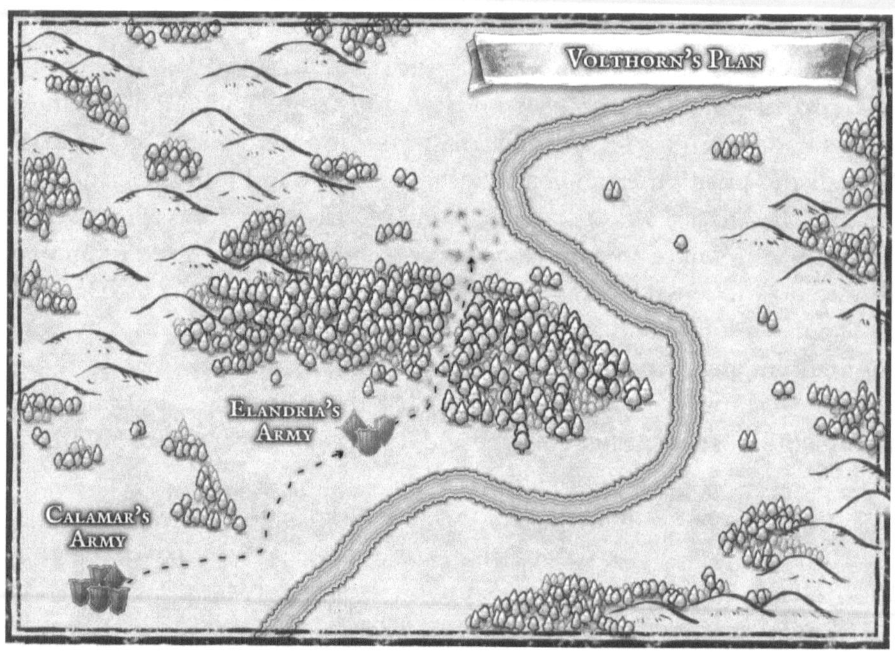

Adara nodded. "With you so far."

"But my retreat will be a feint. I'll have several battalions hidden in the woods on either side of the road's exit point. My hope is that Salidar will take the bait and march his army after me. But once half his army is through the woods—"

"You'll hit them from three sides," Adara said.

"Exactly. I could knock out half his force in one battle. Just like I did last fall."

Adara studied the map, her eyes flicking between the different points Volthorn had indicated. She shook her head. "I don't like it."

"What part?"

"All of it," Adara said. "It's too complicated. Too many things have to go right. Salidar is cunning, Volthorn. And he is a master of gathering intelligence. I worry he'll outsmart or outflank you."

"We've been through this before," Volthorn said. "War always involves risks. But I've done my best to mitigate them. I'll give the army plenty of time to withdraw through the forest before Salidar can catch up. And if Salidar discovers my trap on the other side, then the only thing he can do is sit there or march all the way around."

"I still don't like it," Adara said. "It doesn't feel right. This isn't the right place for you to make a stand."

"Then where, Your Majesty?" Volthorn said, his voice was charged with frustration. "What alternative do you suggest?"

"I don't know," Adara exclaimed, throwing up her hands. "The only thing I can think of is for you to continue to withdraw down the Angerflood, slowly retreating toward Saven, buying time without engaging in pitched battle."

"But that's what Salidar wants me to do," Volthorn said. "He would love for us to give up all our remaining territory without a fight. What did you yourself say an hour ago about fighting for our homes and families?"

"But this plan feels *wrong*," Adara said. "I can't explain it. I just feel slightly sick inside about it." She stepped away from the table. "Retreat another couple days. Then come up with something else."

Volthorn kept his head bowed to hide his scowl. "Such is your command, Your Highness."

She turned to go, but Volthorn stopped her with a question. "And what of Rendhart? Did you receive my warning?"

Adara paused for a long moment. With her back turned, it was difficult for Volthorn to read her emotions. Was she undecided about the situation? Upset at him for bringing it up?

Adara's shoulders lifted as she took a deep breath. "I did," she said, her voice tense. "And I deeply appreciate your concern. I thought long and hard about it, but elected to leave him in his post."

Never had Volthorn wanted so badly to tell her how her father had died, and who had done it. But he bit back the words. Skagar and Luviana would be furious if he told Adara without consulting with them first. "As you see fit, Your Highness," he said.

"May angels keep you," Adara said.

Volthorn watched the tent flaps close behind her, his mind whirling. Eventually his gaze returned to the map, to where a single road cut through a thick band of forest.

"So, you choose not to listen to me?" he whispered. "Then I choose not to listen to you."

CHAPTER 44

THE ELEMENT OF SURPRISE

Durrin shook his head. "No, no. Too brusque."

The young pyromancer he was training tried the move again, bringing his arm back and then stepping forward into a lunge. A small puff of fire fizzled in front of his clenched hand, then vanished.

"Still brusque," Durrin said. "Every action must be smooth and perfectly controlled. Can you feel the cords of momentum around you?"

The other pyromancer—a lad scarcely eighteen—nodded. "Yes, Master Rendhart."

"And what do they feel like?"

The lad scrunched up his nose. "Like . . . like swinging a rope."

"Think of it like a chain," said Durrin. "A chain pulling a bucket of water." He walked over to a pile of gear and grabbed exactly what he had just described. "Don't look so surprised: I prepared this metaphor in advance. Now—" Durrin spun the chain around him, leading the bucket along. "My movements must be measured and paced. If I decelerate too suddenly, the chain loses tension, and the water splashes out. And if I want to swing the bucket out farther from me, I have to swing it faster to keep the water inside." He slowed the bucket down and handed it over. "You try for a minute."

The lad went to work, swinging the bucket around him in various patterns. Durrin stepped back, watching with a critical eye, until another figure approached him.

"Captain," Durrin said, saluting the head of the training camp.

"Lieutenant Rendhart." The captain handed over a small scrap of parchment. "I've granted your request for leave. Will six days be enough?"

"I'm only going to the capital and back," said Durrin. "Six days is fine."

"We appreciate everything you've done here," the captain said. "All our best mancerers are at the front. We weren't making any headway with some of these recruits until you came along."

"Glad I could help."

"Will you be leaving soon?"

"Soon as I'm done here." He had itched to be away ever since his dream a few days before.

The captain strode away, and the pyromancer in training dropped the chain and bucket in a sigh of relief. "That's hard!"

"So's life," Durrin quipped. "Now show me the thrust again."

The youth performed the maneuver from earlier. This time, fire flickered around his wrist as he swung his arm back, and the flame released from his hand was measurably bigger. "Yes!" he yelled.

"It's all in the motion," Durrin said. "Practice with the chain and bucket, five times a day, all seven basic moves. Stay hard at it, and one day you'll be able to do *this*!"

Durrin brought his arm back before sweeping it forward. A jet of pure white flame leapt from his hand, shooting twenty feet before fizzling out inches from a nearby tent.

The lad widened his eyes. "Yes, Master Rendhart. May angels attend your journey."

"I hope they do," Durrin said. He grabbed his pack of gear and strode to where his horse waited nearby. This one, which he had bought shortly after accompanying Adara back to Saven, had cost him *ninety* shekels. Stupid inflation. But at least the stallion, whom he had named Dashing Fire, was young and decently strong. (He'd been forced to leave Raggedy Ruby in a stable in Imperium when he had left with the pirates. By now, she had probably been requisitioned and sold by the stable keeper.)

Durrin mounted Dashing Fire, turning to salute the young trainee. "Keep practicing. And remember, I'm a lieutenant, not a craft master."

"Yes, Lieutenant Master Rendhart."

Durrin tried to hide his smile with a half-serious glare. "Now you're just being precocious."

"No, Master Rendhart. Sir."

Durrin galloped away, shaking his head. Pyromancers. They were all cut from the same cloth.

The next morning, a hundred miles to the south, Volthorn sprung his trap.

Salidar had taken the bait. As Volthorn's army retreated through the forest, Salidar had followed, just a day behind. Once through the forest, Volthorn had continued to march his army north, giving the illusion that he would not contest Salidar's passage.

Then, as soon as night fell, half his army had turned and marched back, reaching the cover of the forest before dawn. These units included most of his best-trained troops, professional soldiers that had fought before in the Penandre or the Arnon Plains.

The precautions he took to ensure secrecy were herculean. Besides Adara, he hadn't shared the full details of the plan with a single soul—not even his generals or his brothers—until late afternoon the day before. Throughout the night, he deployed a thick screen of swifters to ensure no enemy scouts penetrated the forest and discovered his troops' movements. Controlling the air at night was impossible, so instead he masked the army's movements by splitting each unit up and spreading them into long lines. Officers enforced strict silence as the soldiers marched, and every lantern was cloaked to hide it from aerial eyes. Shifting cloud cover ensured sufficient darkness. By the time the morning light came, his twelve thousand flanking soldiers, split into two pincer divisions of six thousand each, were hidden under the tree canopy at the forest's edge.

A griffin flight reached him at dawn, reporting that the first battalions of Salidar's force were marching through the forest road. Volthorn ordered the remainder of his army to turn around and march to meet them.

Now came the critical juncture. If he moved too fast, he'd reach the forest before the enemy battalions had begun to emerge, and they would simply retreat the way they had come. But if he arrived too late, his pincer divisions might be discovered and attacked before he could support them.

So each hour of the morning passed like walking on hot coals. From every indication, things were going as planned. Elandrian griffins were firmly in control of the skies between Volthorn and the forest, hopefully preventing Salidar's scouts from realizing that Volthorn's army had shrunk by half during the night—or, worse, spotting where the other half had hidden itself.

Two miles out, a griffin swooped from the skies and circled around Volthorn's retinue. "Seven enemy battalions have fully deployed from the forest, Commander! They're arrayed for battle in a straight line ahead. More are issuing behind them."

"And their flanks?"

"Completely unguarded."

"Then they haven't spotted the pincer units," Volthorn said. "And now it's too late to run." He turned to two pairs of griffins walking behind his horse, giving them a nod. They flapped into the air, splitting up and winging to the right and left. Each pair would let one of the flanking divisions know it was time to deploy.

Volthorn turned to his horn blower. "Sound a light jog."

The horn blower blew three short puffs, and the army increased its pace. Soon he could see the enemy banners through a gap in the undulating hills.

"This is it," Volthorn murmured. "Our moment of triumph."

They rode over the last hill. One survey of the battlefield told Volthorn that his plan had worked to perfection. The enemy was arrayed for battle about a mile ahead. But their formation was scarcely half a mile across—already shorter than the battle line marching behind Volthorn. And to the left and right of the enemy, Volthorn's flanking battalions were emerging from the woods and forming up into ranks.

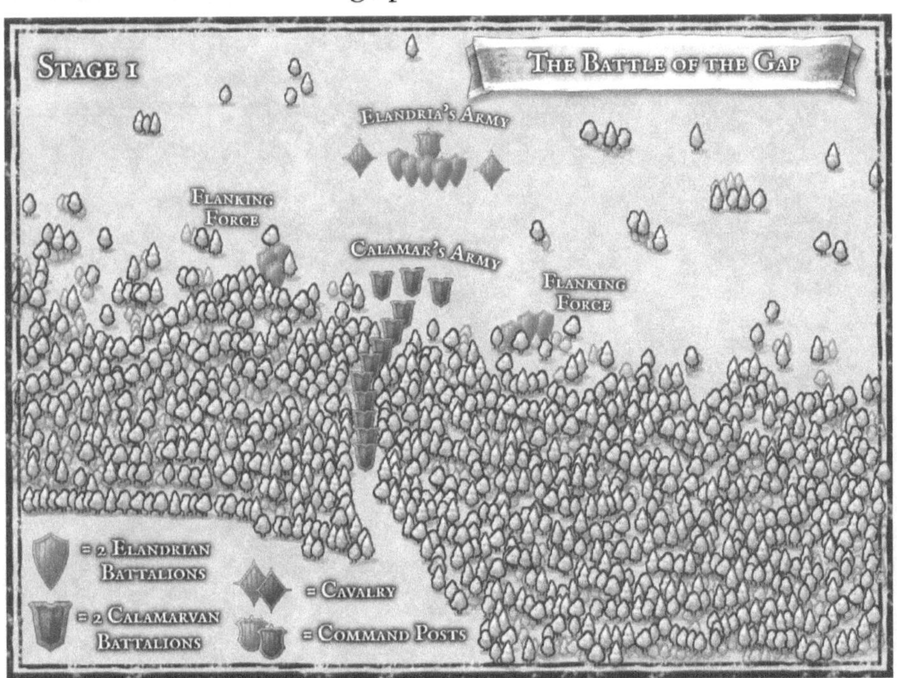

Then he paused. Something didn't feel right.

He squinted, studying the battlefield, looking for something he'd missed the first time. The ranks of the enemy looked . . . thin. There could scarcely be five thousand troops in front of them.

"Salidar's too cautious," Volthorn said, understanding dawning. "He's only sent a vanguard but kept the rest of his army back." Lord Salidar must have realized how easily he could be trapped against the forest, and so he'd sent a small portion of his army ahead to spring the trap. But if Volthorn didn't act fast enough, they could just retreat back into the forest.

Volthorn turned to his horn blower. "Sound the charge!"

A long blast sounded, then echoed down the line. The soldiers emitted a mighty roar and surged forward.

One of Volthorn's officers rode up. "Commander! We won't be able to hold our ranks for long at a full run. Not with so little training."

"We have to hit them before they can escape," Volthorn explained. Already, he could see portions of the enemy line starting to withdraw. He turned to a griffin messenger. "Tell the cavalry to deploy and hit the enemy hard!"

Volthorn and his retinue paused, letting the infantry flow around them. Then they followed at a canter behind the line. Banners, spear tips, and dust blocked Volthorn's view of the enemy. But he heard the thunder of hooves and the clash of metal as Elandria's cavalry galloped ahead of the infantry and engaged.

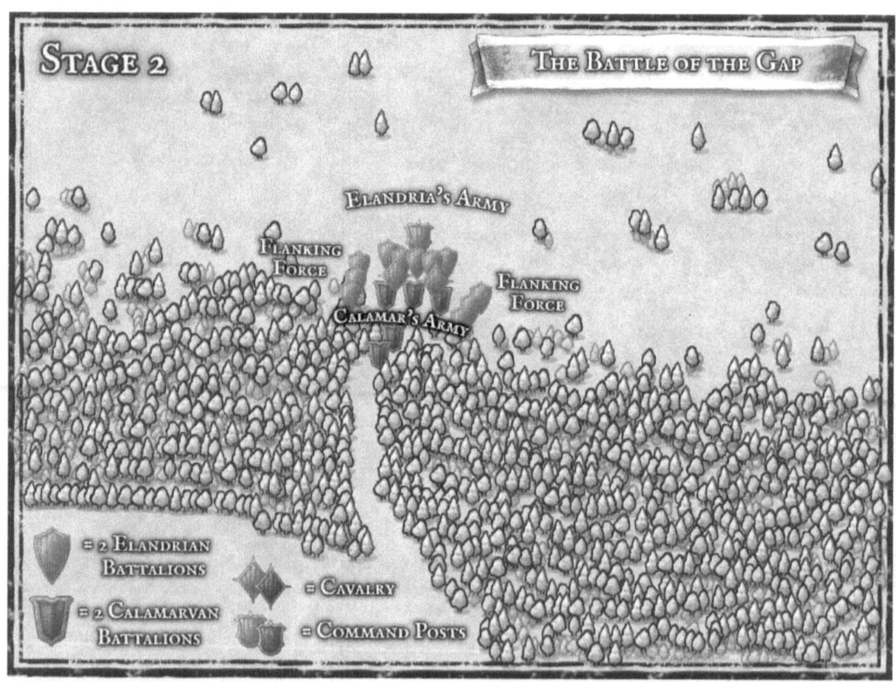

His suspicions were confirmed a few minutes later when a griffin landed next to him. "They're withdrawing back into the forest, Commander! No more battalions are on the road behind them, giving them room to retreat."

Volthorn nodded. "How many remain on the plain?"

"Perhaps four thousand."

Then Volthorn's cavalry alone nearly outnumbered the foe. This battle would be short. It wouldn't be the resounding victory that he had been hoping for, but Calamar would take significant losses all the same.

For the next fifteen minutes, he rode up and down the back of the line, trying in vain to discern what was happening at the front. The ranks of infantry finally parted to let a cavalry lieutenant through.

"Commander!" he said, raising his spear high. The tip was stained with blood. "What's left of their line has broken and scattered into the forest. We're taking hundreds of prisoners."

"What types of troops are they? Any cavalry?"

The lieutenant shook his head. "No cavalry. No heavy infantry, either. Just light infantry, barely trained at that. I've never seen such a swift and complete rout."

Volthorn furrowed his brow. He waved his two brothers over to him. "Explain something to me," he said. "If Salidar wanted to establish a foothold on this side of the forest, what troops would he send?"

"Heavy infantry, for sure," said Kelzern. "To hold out against an attack long enough to withdraw."

"And cavalry to scout the area," Trazar added.

"Then why," Volthorn said, already starting to tremble with the implications, "would he send his weakest and most poorly trained troops?"

The answer hit Trazar and Kelzern at the same time.

"As bait," Trazar whispered.

"By the stars," Kelzern cursed.

Volthorn pivoted, shouting to his aides. "Tell our infantry to disengage immediately! Get them into battle formation, facing outward to the right and left. Send word to our flanking battalions and tell them to turn their formations around!"

His command post exploded into activity as messengers accepted their assignments and scattered off. But the rank-and-file infantry were not so quickly brought up to speed. Many were in the thick of capturing prisoners. Some were already celebrating their victory. As horns began to blow and officers began shouting orders, most of the soldiers stood around in confusion, unsure where to go.

Ten torturous minutes later, a griffin dived into Volthorn's command post, nearly crashing into the ground as she pulled off a high-speed landing. "Enemy units! West of us! Closing in fast, only about two miles away!"

"How many?" Trazar asked, always the one to think about numbers.

"At least ten thousand strong."

Kelzern's eyes widened. "They must have used unmapped trailed to cross the forest during the night!"

"And Salidar has us right where he wants us," Volthorn growled. "Scattered and disorganized, with our cavalry trapped by our own infantry."

He turned back to the griffin. "Why did we just barely spot them?"

"We've been focusing on the forest road, Commander, and on keeping air superiority over the army. And just doing that has been a near thing. They've been throwing flight after flight at us all morning."

Volthorn cursed. Misdirection—the same trick he'd pulled the previous fall. Keep the enemy's perimeter focused where you want it, away from where you actually are.

"Is anyone patrolling to the east?"

The griffin didn't need to answer. Another two griffins arrived at that exact moment, nearly screaming their news. "Fifteen thousand infantry to the east, Commander! And cavalry circling around behind us!"

That was when, in the distance, horns began to blow. And blow. And blow.

They were trapped.

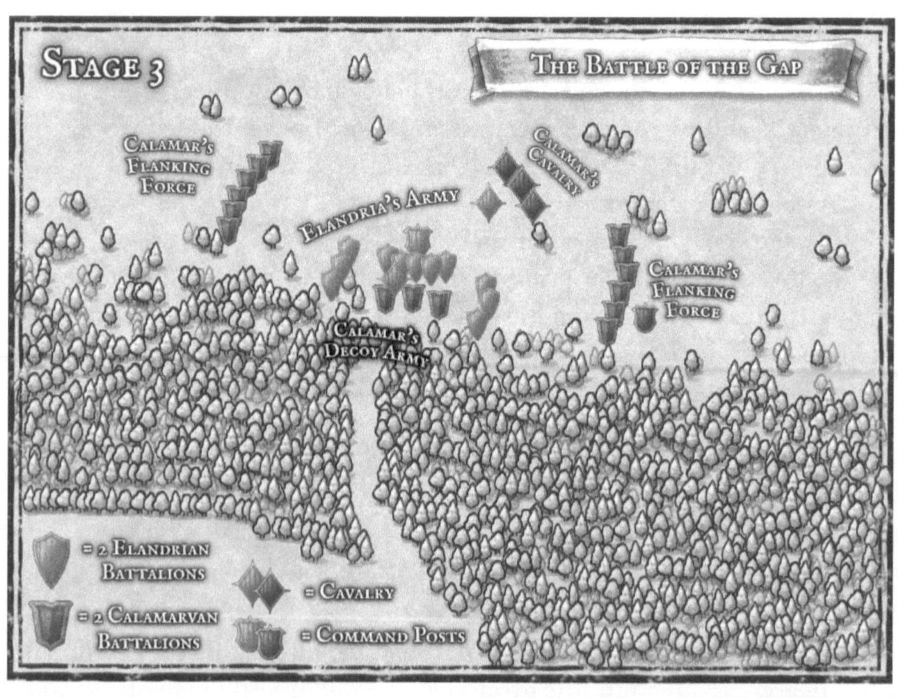

Chapter 45

Surrounded

Volthorn made a snap decision.

They were outnumbered, outmatched, and about to be surrounded on three sides, with the forest blocking their escape on the fourth. If this was the army he had commanded last summer on the Arnon Plains, he would stand and fight. But this was not that same army. His newly trained troops were already scattered and disorganized, and there was no sign that would change in the next ten minutes.

No—the day was already lost. What remained was to salvage as much of his army as he could.

He looked around. Most of his staff had already scattered, seeing to his previous orders. He turned to his brothers. "Split up and ride down the line. Tell every officer you see to get the troops in marching columns and point them north. We need to retreat as fast as possible. But *with order!*"

Kelzern and Trazar nodded, then spurred their horses away. Volthorn turned to the griffins who had just arrived with their reports.

"Go find General Drock on the west flank and General Snarltooth on the right flank." He pointed to each griffin with their respective assignments. "Tell them to deploy their most organized battalions to slow the approaching enemy. They need to buy time for the rest of the army to pull back north."

As the griffins sped away, a human lieutenant rode up to him. "Commander! I have three hundred cavalry standing by, ready to ride."

"Stars bless you!" Volthorn said. Finally, an officer doing his job well. "Enemy cavalry are closing in, circling around us to hit us in our rear. We need to head them off before they throw the entire army into disorder."

The lieutenant saluted. "I'll find and engage them at once."

"I said *we.*" Volthorn glanced over the battlefield. His brothers were already out of sight, and he could see officers starting to reform the men in ranks. He had done all he could here. Besides—he'd gotten his troops into this mess: he should help save them from it.

Volthorn spurred his horse to the north. "Follow me!"

The lieutenant waved to his horsemen, and they followed, thundering across the plain. Slowly Volthorn curved them to the northeast, aiming for a rapidly approaching column of dust.

"How many enemy cavalry?" the lieutenant asked presently.

"Probably a couple thousand," Volthorn said, matter-of-fact.

The lieutenant blinked. If he was fazed, he didn't show it. "Right."

Volthorn touched his hand to a ruby at his belt, sucking up red terracharge and pouring it into his sword. He nudged his horse closer to the lieutenant. "Let me see your spear!" he said, reaching out and pouring charge into the spear tip. He navigated his horse around the formation of horsemen, imbuing soldiers' weapons and armor with terracharge until nearly all his gems had run dry. It was the best he could do. Who knew? Maybe a few of them would even survive.

They topped a hill, and the enemy was suddenly in view: a long line of heavy cavalry, spear tips gleaming in the Sun, red banners snapping in the wind. At the sight of Volthorn's force, they bunched into a closer formation and lowered their spears.

"We'll get massacred in the first pass!" a soldier near Volthorn shouted in panic.

"Not today!" Volthorn yelled. He reached into his saddlebag and pulled out a fist-sized rock. He transferred some orange terracharge into the rock, then rode alongside the lieutenant and handed it to him. "Throw this as soon as you're in range. *Don't* drop it."

"What is it?"

"Rock-shard grenade."

Volthorn pulled another rock from his bag, priming this one as well. He eyed the distance. Arrows began to hiss around him, launched from mounted archers behind the heavy cavalry. One glanced off a soldier's helmet next to him with a flash of blue light.

Fifty yards. Close enough.

"Now!" Volthorn cocked his hand back and launched the rock into the air, deliberately aiming short to account for the enemy line's trajectory. He dropped his hand to his bag, grabbed another rock, and threw it as well.

His first rock-shard grenade impacted with a massive explosion of orange light and slivers of rock, knocking a gap in the enemy formation. The lieutenant's grenade followed a moment later farther down the line. Volthorn's second rock slammed into another point of the line. Each explosion felled a half dozen cavalry and threw the enemy formation into total disorder, as horses bucked and their riders fought to regain control.

Then they were upon the enemy, ripping into their ranks with their glowing spear tips. Volthorn pushed into the melee, thrusting with his sword and blocking with his shield, wishing he'd grabbed a spear before the assault. An enemy spear slipped past his shield, nearly knocking him from the saddle as the terracharge in his breastplate warded off the blow. Volthorn steered his horse into close quarters, lopped off the end of the spear with his glowing sword, then drove his sword through his opponent's shield and into his shoulder.

His opponent fell back, wounded, and Volthorn turned to the next foe. For several minutes he cut, hacked, blocked, and parried. Spears and shields, maces and swords, and helms and hooves flashed all around him. He was dimly aware of the lieutenant falling to his right.

Then his horse staggered from a spear wound. Sky and earth tipped as Volthorn fell from the saddle. A moment later, his vision filled with flashing hooves as another horse nearly trampled him. Its rider thrust downward with his spear, slamming the point into Volthorn's belly. His enchanted chainmail barely held, but the blow still knocked the wind out of him.

He lay for a moment, wheezing for breath.

I will not die. Not here. Not while my army still needs me.

He rose, roaring as he swung his sword. The cavalryman who had struck him glanced down in surprise, failing to react in time as Volthorn drove the tip home. He tugged his sword free and spun to face another rider, catching the soldier's mace on his shield and striking with his sword.

But the soldier was backing his horse away. Volthorn glanced about. The thick of the battle had moved away, leaving him isolated. Five mounted opponents surrounded him, weapons held at the ready.

"Look, we caught a general," one of them said, nodding toward the plume on Volthorn's helm. "So what will it be? Will you yield peacefully? Or in pieces?"

"I can take you all," Volthorn growled. He took a discrete step toward his fallen horse.

"I don't think you can," said the soldier—an officer, by the looks of him. He spun his right hand, summoning a ball of fire that he held above his head. "Drop your sword."

"All right," Volthorn capitulated, crouching to lay his sword on the ground. As he let go, he brushed a finger over an orange gem set into the hilt, drawing out some terracharge he had stored there. Then his hand shot out, reaching into the saddlebag still strapped to his mount.

"Cease!" the officer cried, throwing the fireball in his hands. Volthorn ducked, feeling the searing hit pass inches from his head. He withdrew his hand, clutching his last rock-shard grenade. He chucked it at the feet of the officer's horse, then dived for cover behind the bulk of his fallen mount.

The grenade exploded, nearly blowing Volthorn's eardrums. Even with his eyes shut, he saw the twin flashes of light: the first from the explosion, the second as errant shards impacted the wards on his armor. A piece of shrapnel nicked him in the face. Around him, screams filled the air.

He leapt up. Three of his opponents were dead; the other two clutched at wounds. He grabbed his sword and sprinted away.

He was behind the enemy line now. The ground around him was strewn with bodies of the dead and wounded, and the occasional rider galloped back or forth, but no one seemed to be paying attention to him. Once he was confident he wasn't being pursued, he removed his helmet and ran the razor-sharp edge of his blade down the base of the tall green plume, shearing it off. It would only attract attention.

He needed to get out of here, and for that he needed a new horse. He cast his eyes about. There! A riderless horse was cantering wildly across the field, obviously spooked. He dashed to it and caught its bridle, soothing it with soft words.

After a few moments, it calmed enough for him to swing up into the saddle. He almost couldn't make it—the horse was bigger than he was used to: a breed designed for humans or avirs, not korriks. He barely managed it, then prodded the horse in a course parallel to the battle line, back toward the forest.

What was the state of his troops? He rode to the top of a hill and looked about. A half-mile ahead of him, he could see infantry struggling against infantry—that would be the Calamarvans pressing on his army's left flank. To his right, he could see Calamarvan cavalry pressing the attack on his army's rear, slowly pushing back the three hundred cavalry he had led into battle. But beyond them he could see rows of green banners moving north. His heart leapt. The trap had failed to close completely. Some of his army might still escape.

He rode toward his army, desperate to get back to his men. But every route in front of him was blocked by Calamarvan infantry or cavalry. Perhaps he could wade into their ranks without anyone noticing that his armor was of Elandrian design. But what if he shoved his way to the action at the front only to get clobbered by one of his own men?

Reluctantly, he turned his horse and rode back the way he had come, to the north. He rode a quarter of an hour, keeping his distance from the back of Calamar's battle line. The farther he rode, the more sporadic the fighting looked, with pitched battles giving way to groups of horsemen riding back and forth, harassing the columns of retreating Elandrian troops. Finally, he spotted a gap and plunged his horse forward in a run.

A quartet of shapes moved to intercept him: swifters, lopping through the grass. He drew his sword and spurred his horse faster, intent to charge through before they could attack his mount.

Then he saw the green dye on their ears and tails. He pulled his horse up short. "Friend!" he cried, sheathing his sword and removing his helmet. "Friend! I'm with Elandria!"

The swifters stopped and rocked back onto their haunches, cocking their heads in surprise. "Commander Skarr?" one ventured.

"The very same," Volthorn said.

"How—"

"Long story. Find me the nearest officer!"

One of the swifters escorted him to friendly lines, then slipped back into the grass to guard the flank. Volthorn looked around. Infantry was streaming past him at a light jog. They were keeping in order—barely. To his left, a platoon of enemy cavalry thundered toward the side of the marching column. He watched with pride as his soldiers held their ranks, turning and lowering their spears to ward off the attack. The enemy didn't fully engage; they merely released a barrage of javelins before falling back.

He rode toward the rear of the marching column, shouting encouragement to the troops until he reached one of his captains. "Status!" he barked, turning his horse to ride with the flow of marching men.

"Commander Skarr!" the avir captain exclaimed, his face flashing orange in surprise. "You're alive!"

"Of course I'm alive!" Volthorn said. "What? Did you really think that leading a desperate charge against vast odds was enough to do me in?"

The captain opened his mouth, but no words came out.

Volthorn rolled his eyes. "You'll learn with time. What's the status?"

The captain recovered. "I have about a third of my battalion here," he said, gesturing to the marching men. "But more might be scattered throughout other units. Lightning Oak is behind me, and Scarlet Pine is ahead."

"Good!" Volthorn said. "Where's General Korain?"

"Dead, sir. He fell when the cavalry hit us in the rear."

"General Orrin?"

"I don't know."

Volthorn bottled up his emotions—now was not the time to grieve. "You've done well," he said. "Keep your troops moving."

He turned his horse back around and rode against the tide again. Soon he came to the end of the line. Covering the army's retreat, arrayed in a wide horseshoe formation, stood the Iron Thicket Battalion. Volthorn shook his head in wonder. This battalion had fought under him for almost the entire war, following him from campaign to campaign. Now they held their own against a withering barrage of cavalry assaults, maintaining a formidable shield wall even as they walked backward across the trampled, uneven terrain.

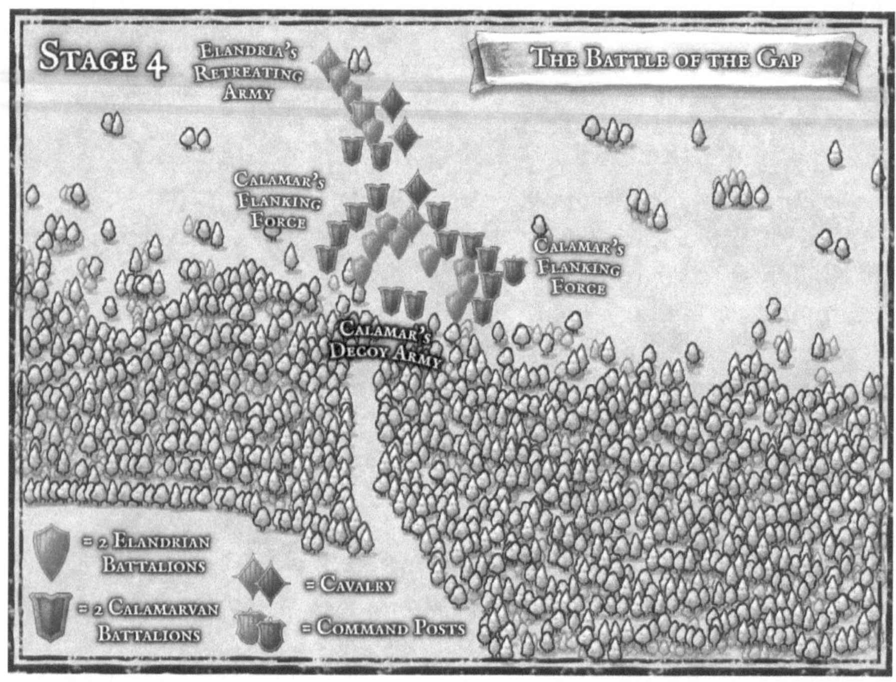

"Volthorn!"

He turned to see Kelzern running up to him. Volthorn dismounted and grabbed his brother in a massive hug.

"Thank the stars you're alive," Kelzern said. "No one has seen you since the first cavalry strike."

Volthorn broke the hug and looked around, feeling a spike of panic. "Where's Trazar?"

Kelzern frowned. "Wounded. Bad slash on the leg. He's in a wagon up ahead."

"Will he be all right?"

"I think so."

They started walking to stay ahead of the retreating rearguard. Volthorn looked around.

"What's the situation? Who's in command?"

"It's basically been me, though now it's you."

"How many troops do we still have?"

Kelzern's grimace told volumes. "We're lucky if we have seven thousand left. Both of our flanking units were cut off completely. I just heard word that General Snarltooth surrendered; I suspect General Drock did as well, assuming he's not dead. Several battalions in our own division were cut off before they could withdraw."

Volthorn stood silently for a moment, processing the loss. Two-thirds of their army, either taken prisoner or lying dead on this cursed field! He shook himself to action and handed the reins of his horse to Kelzern. "Ride up the line. Find a battalion that's in decent shape and send them back here to reprieve Iron Thicket."

"Right." Kelzern went to mount but missed the stirrup, nearly falling on his face. "Blistering beaver dams," he exclaimed. "How did you ever mount this mountain?"

"Necessity," Volthorn said as he gave his brother a leg up.

Kelzern slapped the horse's side and galloped away. In his wake, a griffin stepped forward. "Commander! Glad I found you. My flight captain assigned me to bear tidings of the battle to Saven. What I should I tell Her Majesty?"

Volthorn surveyed the mangled remains of their army as it limped away. "Describe the battle. Tell her we have six or seven thousand troops still fit to fight, possibly less. Tell her we'll be marching back toward Saven with all speed and that she should prepare the city for a siege." He hung his head, the full scale of the day's calamity finally starting to sink in.

"Tell her . . . tell her I'm sorry."

Chapter 46

Greatest of the Healing Arts

Two days later.

Durrin arrived to a capital in chaos.

Word of the army's catastrophic defeat had spread like wildfire through the city. Soldiers marched about, laying up stores of supplies and weapons. Storekeepers boarded up shop windows. Families loaded up carts with their most valuable possessions. But even as hundreds in the city prepared to flee, thousands from the surrounding farms and villages flocked to the gates, seeking refuge from the approaching hordes.

Durrin guided his horse through the turmoil, heading toward the palace. It seemed at each street corner he encountered a beggar. Of all the city's residents, the destitute were the most at risk—they had nowhere to flee to, and their meager means were stretched even thinner by skyrocketing food prices. For some reason, Durrin attracted their pleas, perhaps because he looked like the only calm one in the whole city. He gave each a coin until his purse was empty.

Confess. The word had occupied his thoughts the whole journey, growing stronger and stronger the closer he came to the capital. *Confess. Only then will you be shown how to help end this war.*

The palace was as chaotic as the city. Servants lopped down trees in the gardens. Soldiers hauled piles of rocks to the ramparts to serve as projectiles. Inside the halls, staff rushed to evacuate the more portable valuables and historical items.

Durrin strode through the corridors, following servants' directions to the royal suite. There he was ushered into Queen Adara's office, joining a queue of half a dozen people waiting to talk to her.

At the far end of the room, Queen Adara stood at a table, talking earnestly with two officers. Though still as small and delicate as ever, she had a presence to her that Durrin had not seen before. His enhanced hearing picked up their conversation despite the general hubbub in the room.

"No, no," the queen was saying. "As I said last night—turn no one away."

"But Your Majesty," the officers objected. "The overcrowding. The supply shortages."

Adara shook her head. "Supplies will not be an issue. The siege will not last for long—perhaps two months at most, maybe three. But since you're worried, we can establish this rule: villagers seeking refuge must bring at least two weeks' worth of their own victuals. Is that fair?"

The officers glanced at each other, then bowed. "Yes, Your Majesty."

"You're still worried about the siege," Adara observed.

An awkward pause. "Yes, Your Majesty. It will likely last much longer than three months."

"I will not allow that to happen," Adara said with certainty. "I have plans in the works that will lift the siege before the situation gets dire. But I appreciate your concern for the city, and for your honesty. It is much needed."

The officers stuttered their thanks, then bowed again and dismissed themselves.

Adara handled the next people in line with equal tact and confidence. Durrin paced back and forth at the end of the line, only half listening.

At last, Adara looked over at Durrin. Her eyes widened in surprise, and a wave of color flashed across her face, too fast for Durrin to discern. Red? White?

Then it was gone, and Adara smiled at him. "Durrin!"

Durrin bowed, his hands trembling. "Your Majesty. I must speak with you. In private."

Adara turned to a guard standing at attention nearby. "Clear the room, please. You can stand at the doors outside."

"Yes, Your Majesty."

As the room emptied, Durrin paced the floor. Tendrils of guilt and shame twisted around his gut. He closed his eyes, rehearsing in his mind what he was going to say. He'd practiced his confession a hundred times in the last week, but now the words felt flat and forced.

Durrin offered a silent prayer, pleading to know what to say.

The doors closed, leaving the room empty except for the two of them. Adara stood, watching him, her hand tracing the shape of her scepter lying on a table next to her. Durrin stood a few paces away from her, his head bowed, unwilling to meet her gaze.

A long moment passed in silence. He heard Adara part her lips and gather breath, but no words came out.

How would Adara react when he confessed? Would the news stun her? Would she be shocked? Overcome with anger? Half a dozen guards were in the hallway outside the door, at her beck and call. Was it even safe for him to confess?

Yes. It had to be. The angel in his dream had been emphatic. Besides— from what he had heard the last ten minutes, this wasn't the scared, fragile girl he had talked with at the Bastion. Somehow, she had changed. He hoped she had changed enough to bear the burden he had come to lay at her feet.

Adara gathered breath again. "What did you come to share?" she asked quietly.

Durrin dropped to his knees. His eyes stung, but he held the tears back.

"I have come to confess something," he whispered. "Something I should have told you a long time ago." He took a deep breath, then continued. "You should not have trusted me these last months. I am not the hero you think I am. I . . . I . . ."

He fought, and failed, to get the words past the knot constricting his throat.

"You murdered my father," Adara said quietly.

Durrin looked up, shocked. Adara's face had turned deep blue, tears streaming from her eyes.

"You knew?" Durrin whispered.

Adara slowly crossed the room, sinking down into a chair. "Not for certain. But I have suspected it for several weeks. I knew my father was killed by a pyromancer from Calamar. I knew Volthorn distrusted you. All the signs pointed to you. But I never asked my advisors about it. I . . . I wasn't ready to know for sure."

"I'm so sorry," Durrin cried, dropping his head. His tears finally broke free, streaming down his cheeks. "All the pain I have caused. To you. To your kingdom." He shook with sobs. No words could make what he'd done better. "I'm so sorry!"

Durrin shook, feeling everything again. The guilt. The shame. The regret. Tears dripped down his face until his mouth tasted of salt and the stonework underneath him glistened.

Adara did not respond. After a long moment, Durrin looked up. The queen was looking up at the ceiling, mouthing words to herself, her face twisted with pain. He bowed his head again, kneeling, waiting. In a moment, she would decide his fate. He resolved that whatever it was—imprisonment, lashings, exile, even the gallows—he would face it.

A hand touched his shoulder. He flinched, but forced himself to stay still. He could feel Adara's fingers trembling. But as she rested her hand on his shoulder, and as the seconds passed, her shaking subsided.

He looked up, blinking away the tears. Adara was staring at him, the corners of her eyes red and raw, tears still carving channels down her cheeks. But her skin nearly glowed with a deep, golden hue, and her eyes shone bright.

"I forgive you," Adara whispered.

Durrin wiped at his cheek, stunned. After everything, she'd forgiven him so easily. So quickly. "How?" he breathed.

Adara took a deep breath, turning to gaze out the window at the bright sky. "I don't know," she said. "I thought—my father—the angels . . ." she took another breath, then tried again. "I have stayed awake many nights thinking about my father's death. I have spent much time on my knees, pleading with the Sky Father for the strength to forgive and move on." She looked back at Durrin, a smile brightening her face, even as her tears continued to flow. "I guess He heard me."

Durrin felt a weight lift from his chest—a guilt that had been crushing his heart for eight years, its vice tighter even than voidstone shackles. In its place, he felt something he had missed for so many years, he had forgotten it existed.

Peace.

They passed a long moment, bonded by their mutual tears, each unwilling to break the stillness that had filled their hearts.

Then Durrin's eyes drifted to a map hanging on the wall behind Adara. His mind, now free of its suffocating guilt, grasped on a sudden idea.

He leapt to his feet. "Your Majesty! I think I have a way to end this war."

Adara's eyes widened. "How?"

Durrin strode to the map. "Earlier in my career, I spent much time among the Mitrian tribes, representing Lord Salidar's interests. I know many of their chieftains. They respect me. They will listen to me." He turned. "With your authorization, I will visit them as an official royal messenger and enlist them as allies in the war."

Adara's eyes shone. "Do you think you can persuade them to fight?"

"I will do my best. I know their ways, their motivations, and their priorities." He paused, thinking through everything he knew of the Mitrians. "There might be a way."

"Your timing could not be better." Adara leafed through the papers on her table. "We sent an ambassador to Mitria a month ago. He was met with only scorn and dismissiveness, so I wasn't going to push the matter further. But he did gain one concession. The tribes will be gathering six days from now—"

"For the annual Mitrian games," Durrin said.

"—And one chieftain promised to raise the matter in tribal assembly," Adara said. "It is only a foothold."

"But one I can use," Durrin said. "If I leave immediately, I can make it in time. I will need papers with the royal seal, pledging my status as a royal emissary."

Adara sat down, clearing a space on her table. "I'll draw that up at once."

"It may take several days for the chieftains to arrive at a decision," Durrin said, thinking out loud. "Assuming they decide to intervene, it may take another week for them to assemble a sizable force, and longer to reach here."

"You have one month," Adara said. "That's how long Saven can last under a siege—assuming Salidar doesn't launch an all-out assault before then." She dipped quill to ink, then wrote with a steady hand for several minutes. Durrin paced, anxious to be off.

"Your mission must be top secret," Adara said. She blew on the parchment to dry it. "Tell no one of your destination. Salidar has many spies, including some here in the capital and perhaps even the palace. Should he catch wind of what you are about, he will do all within his power to stop you."

Adara handed Durrin the parchment. He took it and strode to the door.

"And Durrin," Adara called.

He turned.

"May angels attend you."

Durrin nodded. Tears came once more to his eyes—this time not of regret, but of gratitude.

"I think they already do."

Adara waited until Durrin had shut the door before collapsing into a chair. It had taken all her strength to hold herself together. Now her eyes erupted with tears once more as she shook with deep sobs, letting go of all the swirling emotions from the last ten minutes. Pain. Sorrow. Loss.

Forgiveness. Joy. A moment of amazed humor even worked through her system as she watched the skin of her hands flash through a kaleidoscope of colors in a matter of minutes.

The conversation with Durrin played in her head again and again. Her suspicion had been right. Skagar's words had raised it, and Volthorn's letter a week before had all but confirmed it. Still, she hadn't wanted it to be true. She hadn't thought she was ready. Day after day, she had retreated to the shrine deep inside the palace, pleading for the strength to forgive—only to find more and more anger seething deep in her heart.

She had *wanted* to forgive Durrin. It was that desire that led her to trust him with an officer's commission, despite Volthorn's repeated objections. But the anger in her heart seemed so powerful, she had thought she would never have the strength to forgive him.

But the moment she had placed a hand on Durrin's shoulder, something had changed. A wave of love and peace had flooded her heart, sweeping the anger before it and banishing it forever.

She knew, without a shadow of a doubt, that it hadn't come from herself.

A knock at the door broke into her thoughts. She dabbed at her cheeks with a handkerchief. "Yes?"

A guard peeked his head in, concerned. "Your Majesty?"

"I'm fine," she said, conscious that the hue of her skin likely indicated otherwise. "Just processing a bit of news. Give me a few minutes."

"Chief Magistrate Cymer is here, Your Majesty. I was wondering if . . ."

She brightened. "Yes, please!"

The guard smiled. "I thought you'd say that. I'll send him in."

Adara rose and stepped to a basin of water, splashing some on her face. She dried her face with a towel, then turned to see Cymer standing in the doorway, a gentle smile on his wizened face.

"Well done, Your Majesty," he said.

She did not have to ask what he meant.

"Cymer—" she paused, reconnecting with the peace she had felt a few moments before. "Tell me the rest of Durrin's story. What happened to him after he slew my father?"

"He was captured later that day," Cymer said. "Volthorn wanted to execute him. I persuaded him not to. We invented a story and locked Durrin up in Irongate Isle for seven years. Last summer, I released him."

She stared at him in shock. "Why?"

"I had a dream," Cymer said. "A very vivid dream. I dreamed I saw Durrin clothed in light. He stood before a pair of great gates, defending them against an onslaught of evil. And I knew I must release him."

Cymer stared into a mirror, fidgeting with the end of his beard. "It was not easy, Adara. To forgive? That is one battle. But to extend trust? To trust when you have every reason not to? That is another. I knew the threat that I was unleashing upon the world. I knew all too well what Durrin was capable of, and where his allegiance lay at the time. But when I quieted my fears and asked if my course was right, I felt peace. So I trusted in that feeling."

Adara recalled many moments in the last month when she had felt something similar. "I think I understand," she said.

"Since your visit to the Bastion, you have learned how to trust. Today you learned an even more important skill—how to forgive," Cymer said. "Forgiveness is the greatest of the healing arts. To forgive is to heal the very fabric of the eternal soul."

He reached into a pocket of his robe and withdrew a small horn of oil. "Now that you have learned to heal the soul, you can be given the power to heal the body. Queen Adara Everborn, are you willing to accept the office of Healer in the Luminant Order of the Eldest?"

Adara's eyes widened in surprised. "Healer? I barely became a Light! And I still have hardly any idea what that means."

"You have done a Light's duties," Cymer said. "You have dedicated all your energy these last months to serving all and spreading light. Today, you have shown you are ready for this added mantle." Cymer's eyes clouded with worry. "And there is no time to lose. In the coming days, you will need it."

Adara nodded. "Then I accept."

She knelt and closed her eyes. A trickle of oil fell upon the crown of her head and ran down her locks of hair as Cymer spoke a series of phrases in the Numinous Tongue.

"Rise, Healer of the Eldest," he finished, reverting to Lurrian.

Adara stood, feeling somehow taller than she had a moment ago.

"In a moment, I will teach you the words of healing," Cymer said. "But first, a word of caution. It is never wrong to forgive. But trust must be merited. Be wise with when and how you extend it."

Adara furrowed her brow. "But you just said you trusted Durrin when you released him, despite every reason not to."

Cymer shook his head. "I trusted the dream and its source. I trusted that releasing Durrin was necessary. But I did not trust Durrin himself, not then. It wasn't until much later, when he had shown by his actions that he had changed, that I extended him trust. Remember what you were blessed with in your coronation." He tapped his chest. "Trust the voice in your heart."

Adara nodded, feeling a weight of sadness settle on her. Her heart was already telling her who was no longer worthy of her trust.

Later that afternoon.

Volthorn reined in his horse as he rode through the palace gates, taking in the sight of the courtyard recently cleared of trees. Good—the garrison was already enacting his orders, preparing the palace for the coming assault.

An officer spotted him and ran over to him, saluting. "Commander Volthorn! We didn't expect you until early tomorrow."

"I got an early start this morning," Volthorn said. He had hardly slept the whole night, despite how tiring the last two days had been. His disastrous defeat kept playing in his head whenever he closed his eyes.

"The queen wanted to meet with you as soon as you arrived," the officer said. "Shall I take your horse?"

"No, I'll do it," Volthorn said. He needed a few minutes to gather his wits, and stabling a horse was exactly the routine task he needed. He rode over to a row of stables lining the courtyard. Dismounting, he led his horse into the gloom, waiting for his eyes to adjust to the semidarkness.

He stiffened. In one of the stalls, brushing down a horse, stood Rendhart.

"What are you doing here?" Volthorn growled.

Rendhart looked up, feigning surprise, but Volthorn knew the pyromancer had likely felt him coming with his powers. "Commander Skarr," Rendhart said. "I thought you were at the front."

"I was," Volthorn snapped. "I thought *you* were at Nidar."

"I was," said Rendhart. "But business brought me here."

Volthorn scowled. "What business?"

Rendhart heaved a saddle onto the horse's back. "Personal matters."

"Where are you going?"

Rendhart didn't respond as he ran the saddle's straps through their buckles.

Suspicion blossomed in Volthorn's mind. "You're a sergeant in my army, aren't you? Tell me where you're going. That's an order!"

Rendhart looked up, a spark of defiance in his eyes. "I'm returning to Nidar to resume duties at my post. I came here on six days' leave with permission from my commanding officer."

"Good," Volthorn snarled, pretending he believed the obvious lie. "Then you can help them evacuate the camp. All forces are withdrawing to Saven."

Rendhart continued preparing his saddle in silence. Volthorn unsaddled his own mare and began brushing down her back. But he kept his eyes trained on Rendhart in the next stall. From the looks of his bulging saddle packs, he was planning a trip much longer than the short jaunt back to Nidar.

What was Rendhart up to? Why had he come to the palace? And where was he going now? It seemed convenient that he was embarking on a long journey right before the city would come under siege. Too convenient.

Volthorn's mind returned to his catastrophic defeat. How had Salidar prepared such a perfect trap? It was as if he had known exactly what Volthorn was planning. But that was impossible. Volthorn had told no one his plans—not even his generals—until mere hours before the battle, when Salidar's forces would already have been hacking their way through the forest.

No one—except for Queen Adara.

Would the queen have told anyone? She vowed she wouldn't. But her actions had shown that she trusted Rendhart more than she trusted Volthorn.

Of course. He scowled—why hadn't he seen it before? It was the only plausible explanation. Queen Adara must have told Rendhart his battleplans. Rendhart had then passed them on to Salidar, enabling him to perfectly outmaneuver Volthorn. But why? Was it to get back into Salidar's good graces? Or had Rendhart been a double agent the entire time?

Now Rendhart was fleeing the capital, right before a siege, with who knew how much crucial intelligence about Elandria's defenses.

Volthorn knelt by his pack, opening it and digging around among the variety of talismans inside. There—he pulled out a small, bright yellow gem. Couching it unseen in his claws, he straightened and strode to where Rendhart was leading his horse out of the stable.

"I received a report from the captain at Nidar," Volthorn said, trying to make his tone more amicable than a minute before.

"Oh?" Rendhart didn't even look at Volthorn as he doublechecked each strap on the saddle.

"As much as I begrudge it, he had only praise for your teaching methods," Volthorn said, sliding his hand up against one of Rendhart's travel packs.

"I trained under the finest," said Rendhart, still focused on the harness of the saddle.

"I know." Volthorn tucked the gem into a corner of the saddle bag. As he pulled away from the horse, he let his hand slide down the bag's side, pushing the slight lump made by the gem deeper inside, where Durrin hopefully wouldn't find it for several days.

"Well," Volthorn said, patting the horse's flank. "Take care heading back to Nidar, Durrin. The enemy is encroaching everywhere."

Rendhart mounted with one smooth movement "I hope we meet again soon," he said as he rode off.

Volthorn stared after him, narrowing his eyes. "So do I, Rendhart. So do I."

He caught the eye of the officer at the gate and waved him over. The officer hastened across the courtyard. "Everything all right, Commander?"

Volthorn kept his gaze fixed on the pyromancer riding out the gates. "Bring me a swifter you trust. One experienced with tracking."

Chapter 47

Trust

Volthorn paused at the door of the royal suite, calling his thoughts back from his encounter with Rendhart. He removed his helmet, took a deep breath, and strode inside.

Queen Adara stood at the window. She faced the setting Sun, so Volthorn could scarcely look in her direction without squinting.

Volthorn cleared his throat. "You wanted to see me, Your Majesty?"

"Commander Skarr," Queen Adara said. She slowly turned, revealing a face as blue as the darkening sky. "Why?"

His gut clenched. "Why what, Your Majesty?" he asked, feigning confusion. Though he already knew.

She strode across the room, tears lining her eyes. "Why did you violate my counsel?"

Volthorn kept his back ramrod straight, meeting her gaze. "I did my utmost to ensure the engagement would be a success," he said stiffly.

"You disobeyed me!" Adara cried. "And now our army is crippled, our country balances on the brink of ruin, and thousands of our subjects lie dead on the field of battle!"

Volthorn's blood pumped through his veins. "You were the only one I told, Your Majesty. The *only one* who knew my plans before the battle. Yet somehow Salidar predicted my every move. Explain that."

"I told no one," Adara protested. "Not a word of your plans did I utter after our meeting."

"Not to Cymer?"

"No."

"Skagar?"

"No!"

"Rendhart?" he spat out the name. "Is there anything you've told *him* that I should know?"

"Of course not!"

But there had been something—a slight hesitation in her eyes—when Volthorn had voiced the pyromancer's name. She was hiding something from him about Rendhart, something she didn't trust him about.

Volthorn broke eye contact, looking to the side. "In any case, Your Majesty, somehow Salidar knew. It is the only explanation for our defeat."

"You're dodging my question, Commander. You disobeyed me. Why?"

He bit back the response he wanted to give. *Because you're eighteen. You know nothing about military strategy. You've never seen a battle in your life.*

He spoke slowly, choosing his words as carefully as he choose his officers. "I deemed that the potential gains of the proposed engagement were greater than any other tactical situation I could contrive."

Queen Adara let out a breath and turned away. "Volthorn Skarr, if I cannot trust you to heed my instructions, I can no longer let you remain in your post. You are hereby relieved of command."

Her words cut like a knife thrust into Volthorn's gut.

"Re—relieved, Your Majesty?"

She nodded. "You have served your kingdom admirably, Volthorn. Your efforts have been herculean and your sacrifices great. But you have repeatedly shown disregard for my authority and distrust of my judgment. You ignored my premonition that my room was too exposed. You refused to inform me of the conspiracy to kidnap me. And then you engaged in a battle that I specifically told you to avoid. If I am to lead this kingdom, I need to know my officers will follow me."

The chill of shock melted into the flame of anger.

"You know my devotion, Your Majesty!" Volthorn said, squaring his jaw. "I have spent my life in service to your father and then to you. I would die, without hesitation, to defend this nation."

"I have no doubt of that, Volthorn," the queen said. "And I thank you for your passion. But my decision remains unchanged."

Volthorn's mind reeled. "But who will replace me? Who will you turn to? General Drock is dead. General Snarltooth is captured. Generals Embertail and Branoc have no experience leading infantry. I was ready to promote Captain Mern, but he was killed earlier this spring."

"I will counsel with Skagar and Luviana and decide among the available officers," Adara said.

His jaw shook with emotion. "And what will be my new command? Or will you strip me of my uniform altogether?"

"I'm putting you in charge of the prisoners of war being guarded just outside the city walls," Adara said. "I'm working to negotiate a prisoner exchange, but in the meantime, you will need to move the whole camp to the northeast, probably at least sixty or seventy miles. You'll be acting under the rank of captain."

Volthorn bowed stiffly, doing his utmost to batten down the rage, betrayal, and loss coursing through him. "I . . . accept. Your Majesty."

She gave him one last long, sorrowful look. Then she turned back to the window. "Angels attend you, Captain Volthorn."

For half a minute he stood there, trembling. He had given Elandria his all. In the last three years, he had faced death a dozen times. He had ripped victory from the jaws of defeat in battle after battle. He had clawed his way from captain all the way to chief commander, every day bending all his thoughts upon how to save his people, how to redeem himself from the failure that had scared more than his face. And today he had lost it all.

Finally, without a word, Volthorn turned and strode from the room.

The guard in the corridor saluted. "Commander, I—"

"Shut up!" Volthorn snapped, walking right past the startled guard.

He stormed through the palace, scowling at anyone who glanced at him. Adara's decision burned in his head. How could she do this? How could she strip him from command on the eve of the siege? It was organizational suicide. It was the death knoll for their military cohesion. It was—

A greeting caught his attention. "Commander! A message from your brother!"

It was a griffin, fresh from her flight. Volthorn grudgingly turned to face her. "Yes?"

She grabbed a scroll tucked into a band around her foreclaw and handed it to him. "Kelzern gives a general report of the day's movements. But he also said to tell you that Trazar's condition has worsened."

Volthorn felt like another knife had stabbed him in the gut. "Worsened?"

The griffin shifted her feet. "Kelzern didn't want to worry you too much."

Volthorn barely stopped himself from grabbing her by the neck feathers. "Trazar is my *brother*! Tell me!"

"The bleeding hasn't stopped; it's only gotten worse," the griffin said. "And he can't keep any food down."

Volthorn began to pace. "Have they given him lime water? Ragweed?"

"I know they're trying the best they can, Commander. But there's dozens, if not hundreds, of wounded to care for. Scores have died already."

Volthorn grabbed a table in his way and flipped it over, sending it clattering to the floor.

"Commander?"

"Get out!" Volthorn roared. He flipped over another table, watching from the corner of his eye as the griffin fled from the room.

He had lost everything. He had lost his command. He had lost his queen's trust. He was on the brink of losing the war—and losing his brother.

And he knew exactly who to blame.

Durrin rode for two days before he noticed the swifter tracking him.

He was camped in a meadow just outside a small village, about halfway between Saven and Elandria's eastern border. He had spent the evening practicing the fourth Kymar routine—a withering blitz of fast, jagged moves that sent fireballs in every direction. Normally, it required a large space of fireproof terrain, like stone pavers or a glacier. In the meadow, Durrin had to pause throughout his routine to extinguish errant fires. It made practicing rather tedious.

Afterwards, he stood in the middle of the glade, his feet shoulder-width apart, inhaling through his nose and out through his mouth. He pushed his consciousness outward, straining to detect every tremble of energy around him—every plodding insect, every wiggling worm, every quivering leaf. The exercise was one from Kymar's fifth scroll, to raise the awareness necessary for summoning lightning.

It was in this heightened awareness that he felt a flicker, the faintest signature of another intelligent spark several hundred yards away. But it was enough for him to recognize its owner: a particularly long-legged swifter, the same swifter who had spoken with him at the tavern he'd stayed at the night before.

Someone had put a tail on him. Who? Queen Adara? That made little sense. Perhaps a Calamarvan agent in Elandria?

He considered sneaking up on the swifter in the night. But with the combination of their keen hearing and sense of smell, swifters were almost impossible to catch unawares, especially in quiet countryside like this. And he'd never be able to chase one down, even on horseback.

Durrin decided to just settle down for the night and sleep with one eye open. He had a long journey ahead, and little time to spare. His best option was to forge ahead and try to lose his pursuer. He knew a few tricks.

⁂

"He's headed consistently southeast since leaving Saven," the griffin reported. He shook his head in admiration. "That man has covered over a hundred miles in two days."

"He must be in a hurry." Volthorn leaned over a map spread before him. The swifter tailing Durrin had gotten in touch with a local garrison, which had sent the griffin to report to Volthorn.

"Is he riding for Salidar's army?" the griffin asked. Ever since Volthorn's army had withdrawn in shambles to the capital, Salidar had advanced down the Angerflood unopposed.

Volthorn shook his head. "He's steering too far east."

"Perhaps he's trying to avoid Elandrian troops?"

"He's technically an officer in our army," Volthorn said. "And he has no reason to suppose his cover has been blown. The only thing I can think of is that he's heading toward the Mitrian Mountains."

"Then there you have it," said Kelzern, who'd been listening from the corner of the tent. "If he's not trying to meet up with Calamarvan troops, then he can't be a spy."

Volthorn eyed the map, his eyes narrowing. "Don't be too hasty, Kelzern."

"Hasty? *I'm* the one being hasty? You're tracking this man on a whim, with no evidence that he's actually a threat. It's distracting you from your duties at a critical time for our kingdom."

"My duties?" Volthorn snapped. "Move a couple hundred prisoners a couple dozen miles? Anyone in the kingdom could perform such a task."

"Then perform it," Kelzern retorted. "Perform it well and perform it honorably, and perhaps Queen Adara will promote you back to a major command. But if you insist on pursuing this rabbit chase, I will have no part in it."

"So be it." Volthorn rose to his feet. If Kelzern wasn't going to help, then he had to do this himself. "Stay here. You're in charge of the camp now."

Kelzern grabbed his arm. "And where are *you* going?"

Volthorn shook himself free, then grabbed his scabbard and buckled it around his waist. "I'm going to deal with this threat once and for all."

"How? He's over two days ahead of you."

Volthorn strode from the tent. "I have a plan for that."

He walked through the camp, toward the wooden stockades that held the prisoners of war. The anger in his veins had given way to resolve. He'd finally made his choice, and now he had only one objective.

Rendhart had to be a spy and a double agent. It was the only explanation. Perhaps he was slinking away, leaving Elandria to its fate like a rat fleeing a sinking ship. But more likely, he was headed to Mitria on Salidar's errand, to secure an alliance that would seal Elandria's fate.

It felt like every day that Rendhart walked free, a curse fell ever heavier upon Volthorn's shoulders—and upon Elandria overall. Why had their fortunes changed so drastically from the fall to the spring? Why did it seem like every decision he made this year was the wrong one? Could it be because, in defiance of justice, they had let a murderer walk free?

Well, it was time to help justice claim its own.

Volthorn reached a stockade with particularly high walls. At his direction, the guards on duty edged open the gate, looking somewhat worried but holding their tongues.

As Volthorn stomped inside, a menagerie of figures looked up, then jumped to their feet, chattering to each other in their strange tongue.

Volthorn laid a hand on the pommel of his sword, staring them down. "Who is your captain?" he barked. "The one they call 'The Barbaric'?" He glanced around. Was it the massive man lurking in the shadow of the wall, his face deformed by a scar? Was it the high-bred avir in the center of the group, wearing the strange, checkerboard skirt?

The score of warriors in front of him looked at each other blankly, then kept chattering in their tongue.

"I don't speak Hakiru, you idiots," Volthorn snapped. "I know your captain speaks Lurrian. Where is he?"

"I'm right here, you pile of half-baked shrimp kabobs," said a high-pitched voice behind him. Volthorn jumped in surprise, turning to see a snippen idling against the stockade wall, looking remarkably nonchalant despite the ball and chain attached to her ankle.

Surprise momentarily overcame his show of confidence. "You're 'The Barbaric'?" he asked flatly.

"Of course!" The snippen bowed. "Captain Twigly the Barbaric, to be precise. How may we be of service?"

Volthorn had to admire her audacity. She was a prisoner in a stockade, yet she talked as if she was haggling a deal in a tavern. Stars, she was good.

"I have a proposition," Volthorn said. "How would you like to get revenge on the pyromancer who betrayed you, regaining your cloud frigate at the same time?"

Captain Twigly took a large bite out of the apple in her hand. (Wait, where had she even *gotten* an apple? He was sure apples weren't among the prisoners' rations.) She chewed thoughtfully. "I'm listening."

CHAPTER 48

CONFRONTATION

"Pleasant weather for a one-sided fight," Twigly said from where she sat perched on the rail of the gondola. It was late in the morning, two days after Volthorn had negotiated with the pirates in the stockade.

The Hakiru hadn't batted an eye at working for their former jailers. "We stole your queen, after all," Tadgh, the crew's navigator, had said when Volthorn had asked about it. "It's hard tah be upset at you for throwing us in a stockade for that. Betteh a stockade than a gallows."

Besides their freedom and their ship, Twigly had demanded two thousand shekels of gold. After a long negotiation, Volthorn had managed to whittle it down to a thousand, but he dared go no lower. He wanted to make sure they had a reason to bring him back when the job was complete. Luckily, they hadn't asked for payment up front. His treasury access had been revoked with his demotion.

Volthorn had hoped to leave at once, but the Hakiru's ship had to be prepared first. It had floated unused for three months above a military camp, and Bjorn, the ship's carpenter, had a long and tedious list of tune-ups to perform before it was skyworthy again.

"Can't you just skip a few?" Volthorn had asked.

Bjorn had rubbed his massive chin, pretending to think about it. "Sure," he had grunted. "And next time your seamen make boat, tell them skip a few boards in hull. See how that goes."

They had finally launched early the next morning, three days after Rendhart had left Saven. The winds were favorable, but Rendhart had a long head start and was moving fast.

A message had arrived just before their departure, informing them that the swifter tailing Rendhart had lost his trail—some lame excuse about a brush fire. Now they depended solely upon the compass in Volthorn's hand.

Volthorn snatched his compass away as one of the snippens on the crew poked at it. "Watch your paws" he snapped. "You'll break it."

The snippen gibbered something in Hakiru, looking at Tadgh, the navigator. Tadgh translated. "Grimbo wants tah know how it works."

Volthorn rolled his eyes. Not this again. The whole flight, the insatiable snippen had been pestering Volthorn with questions about each of his terramantic devices. It would have been exasperating enough even without the language barrier. "I hid a gem in Rendhart's pack," he explained. "The needle's synced with it. As long as both are imbued with terracharge from the same source gem, the needle will track the gem's direction." He studied the reading. The angle had changed significantly in the last half hour. They were getting close.

Grimbo jabbered another question. "He's not sure he gehts it," Tadgh translated. "Why don't we sail directly the way the needle is pointing?"

"Because if we catch up to Rendhart, we won't know until we shoot over him and the needle suddenly spins around," Volthorn explained. "By approaching at an angle, we can sweep around him and get a fairly accurate reading of his position—hopefully without him noticing us."

From her position on the railing, Twigly fidgeted nervously. "And you're absolutely sure you want to confront him?"

"You don't want to?" Volthorn asked. "I mean, he betrayed you and stole your ship."

Twigly waved a paw. "He betrayed *Salidar*, and *you* stole our ship, if I recall. Besides, in this profession, you get used to the fact that most of your clients will betray you at some point."

Volthorn reflected on that. Durrin had switched sides on the eve of their attack. Salidar had abandoned them in the woods, at the mercy of Elandria's military. Considering that sample size of two, the snippen wasn't wrong.

"Anyway," Twigly said, "It's not too late for us to turn around. I've seen Rendhart fight. He was more than a match for four of our best warriors in a sparring bout, and you yourself saw him rip through our ranks in the snowstorm."

"Don't tell me you're *scared?*" Volthorn said, grinning at the snippen.

"Yes, I *am* scared," Twigly said matter-of-factly. "Quite scared. Terrified, actually. He can throw *balls of fire* bigger than *me!*"

"That's why your crew will attack him from a distance with arrows," Volthorn said.

"You make it sound so easy," Twigly said. "But for the record, when I said this would be a one-sided fight earlier, I didn't mean it *in our favor.*"

Volthorn rolled his eyes. "We outnumber him nineteen to one. Besides—all you need to do is keep him from escaping. I will do the hand-to-hand fighting myself."

The snippen captain didn't look convinced.

The griffin on the crew, Bladebeak, swooped into view beside the gondola, coasting on the wind. He chirped something in Hakiru, then drifted out of sight on an updraft.

"What was that about?" Volthorn asked.

Tadgh heaved on the tiller. "We've found'em."

Durrin had never been so weary.

It wasn't the exhaustion of a hard day's work, nor the breathlessness after completing a Kymar exercise. Nor was it the dull mental ache of sleep deprivation. It was the utter depletion of physical and mental reserves that came with riding fifty or sixty miles a day for four straight days, all while on constant alert for danger.

His route took him and Dashing Fire through an arid valley at the base of the Mitrian Mountains, dotted with brush and scrub oak. Now, at the end of the valley, his trail led him up a ravine cut into the side of a long line of cliffs, as if some prehistoric giant had cut a wedge out of the rock, leaving piles of boulders behind like breadcrumbs. The Sun was climbing the sky, turning the ravine into an oven.

How would he convince the Mitrians to join the war? For the hundredth time, he pondered the challenge, rehearsing the words to say, the promises to extend, the values to appeal to. This was new territory for him. He was no ambassador or negotiator. He was a pyromancer! Pyromancers preferred action over words. But he would find a way. He had to.

The Sun, the exhaustion, the preoccupation—all dulled his senses. So it wasn't until he emerged from the top of the ravine onto the windswept plateau beyond that he felt the sparks surrounding him.

He snapped upright, standing in the stirrups to extend his vision. Adrenaline pumped through his veins, pushing away the exhaustion of a moment before.

Immediately he spotted the cloud frigate. It was moored perhaps two hundred yards away, where it had been out of sight while he'd been in the ravine.

At a shrill whistle, a line of warriors emerged from behind rocks and boulders, arraigned in an arc about fifty yards ahead. He recognized them instantly: the Hakiru pirate crew. Five held bows cocked and aimed. The rest sported a hodgepodge of weapons. In the middle stood Volthorn Skarr.

Durrin glanced behind him. An additional six Hakiru had emerged from hiding at the edges of the ravine behind him, arrows nocked to bowstrings.

Durrin dismounted and slapped Dashing Fire's flank, sending the stallion trotting to the side. No sense in it getting shot by crossfire.

"It's over, Rendhart," Volthorn called, the wind trying to whip away his words. "Yield—or die."

What was going on? Why was Volthorn in league with the pirates? Durrin spread his hands in a show of peace. "What is this about, Commander?"

"Don't play dumb, Rendhart. You are a spy and a traitor. We know where you're headed, and what you're plotting."

The korrik's twisted reasoning clicked into place. Durrin vigorously shook his head. "I am on the errand of Queen Adara. She sent me to Mitria to appeal on Elandria's behalf!"

Volthorn spat into the rocky ground. "You expect me to believe that?"

"I have papers signed by her own hand."

"Forgeries," Volthorn snarled. He drew his sword. "Your lies will not work on me. Nor is Cymer here to save you this time." Volthorn took several steps forward. "Today, you pay the blood price of a king."

Durrin unclasped his cloak, letting the wind carry it away. "I do not wish to fight you, Volthorn. But for the sake of your own kingdom, I cannot let my mission fail."

"You have two options," Volthorn said. "Yield and be taken back to Elandria in chains, or fight and face a slow death by a dozen wounds."

Durrin raised an eyebrow. "I think you meant to say, 'Yield, so I can kill you without a fight.' I'll take the fight."

Volthorn gestured at the band of sky pirates. "You are hopelessly outmatched."

"I think you overestimate your chances." Durrin shifted his stance, his right hand drifting toward the sword at his waist, his left hand gathering energy.

"So be it," Volthorn said. "Fire!"

Durrin felt a recoil of energy flash through the landscape as eleven bowstrings released.

Fine.

He twisted and leapt. Eight arrows whistled past his midair form, missing him by inches. He incinerated two more with a blast from his hand. His sword leapt from its sheath, deflecting the voidstone tip of the last arrow inches before it would have buried itself in his side.

He could take them all—rip through their line with fire and sword like a whirling tornado. The archers he could take out first with well-aimed jets of fire. Then he could dance circles around the rest, eliminating them one by one, leaving Volthorn for last.

He could kill them. This wouldn't be murder; it would be self-defense. Killing them would be justified, even necessary.

No.

He would be different now. He would live a higher standard.

Somehow.

His feet hit the ground. He dropped to a crouch, spinning to gather the excess momentum from his leap and shooting his arms out toward the archers behind him. Twin jets of fire burst from his hands, not powerful enough to be lethal but definitely enough to distract them.

As he straightened, he launched into the central move of the fifth Kymar routine.

He'd practiced it only three times since his imprisonment, all in the last week and all unsuccessfully. But his battle-heightened awareness seized upon old memories, and this time, his execution was flawless.

He thrust his hands outward, then twisted them in an intricate pattern. As he did, his spark *shifted* in an intuitive way he still didn't fully understand, drawing upon a type of energy distinct from the heat and momentum he normally channeled. This energy had a crackle to it—a jumpiness that made his hair stand on end.

Azura, the pirate fastest at reloading, released another arrow. Durrin ducked, letting it whiz above his shoulder. He could feel the crackling energy building in the air around him, waiting, *wanting* to be unleashed.

He released the tension in his arms.

Rivulets of lightning arced through the air, emanating from his hands before splitting into a hundred different paths before him. The air cracked with thunder as a flash of brilliant light bathed the landscape. The Hakiru warriors staggered, tendrils of lightning leaping between the metal in their weapons and armor. For a moment, Durrin feared he had released too much power and killed them all. But when the lightning faded, the warriors still stood, fried and frazzled but still very much alive.

In front of them, Volthorn was charging straight at Durrin, completely unscathed, his armor glowing blue. Stupid terramancy.

The edge of Volthorn's sword glowed bright red—blocking it was not an option. Instead, Durrin danced away from Volthorn's attack. He counterstruck with lightning speed, slipping past Volthorn's parry and slamming a blow into the korrik's arm. But Durrin's sword merely glanced off Volthorn's mail sleeve in a flash of blue light. Durrin leapt backward, feeling Volthorn's sword slash effortlessly through his chainmail hauberk, the tip scratching the skin of his ribcage.

Movement flashed at the edge of his vision. He ducked, barely dodging a swing from Bjorn charging him from the side. Tadgh joined the fray a moment later, shouting a Dorinian war cry. Durrin swung his sword in a flurry of swings and parries, madly blocking Bjorn's and Tadgh's blows while evading Volthorn's attacks, forced to maneuver constantly to avoid getting surrounded.

His three opponents pressed to the attack, and Durrin stepped back blindly across the broken ground, leaving fire in the wake of each swing. Tadgh's longsword slammed into the chainmail on his shoulder. Volthorn's sword scored a cut on his leg. He barely blocked an overhand blow from Bjorn that would have cleaved his skull in two.

Angels help me!

An idea flashed across his brain. He flared his spark and leapt, launching himself seven feet into the air. Spinning his arms, he channeled a blast of fire downward that propelled him even higher. Then he turned the blast to the side, launching himself away from his opponents and toward a bare spot of ground. He sheathed his sword in midair.

He landed close to Azura and Krizmon. Krizmon rushed him with her spear, but Durrin caught the haft with inhuman agility. He stepped forward, grabbing the spear with his other hand and pushing it up toward the korrik's face. For a moment the spear froze in space as Krizmon threw all her strength against him. Then Durrin reversed direction and threw her off-balance. Durrin wrenched the spear from her grip and knocked her feet out from under her.

Azura pressed to the attack. He twirled the spear like a quarterstaff, shunting away her blows, then struck with a pyromancy-enhanced blow, slamming the butt of the spear into her head. She staggered, teetering on the edge of consciousness.

Durrin used a boulder to somersault over more approaching pirates. Half a dozen warriors were all around him, but he moved too quickly to be pinned down. He was a flashing, twirling, leaping melee of spear and fire, lashing out at anyone who drew near.

If this were a normal fight, he could win it handily. As skilled as the pirates were, he moved with a speed and agility far beyond them. On a dozen occasions, his spear could have inflicted a lethal wound if he let it. But he didn't. He couldn't.

Complicating the whole fight was Volthorn's terramancy. His sword glowed with so much red terracharge, Durrin feared it would slice his spear haft clean through if he blocked a stroke head-on. So he was forced to dance around the battlefield, constantly putting other warriors between him and the slower but inexorable korrik.

Durrin disabled two more warriors with well-aimed blows of his staff. The rest became wary, edging toward him cautiously in pairs, then backing off when he struck out in vigor. He thanked the stars for their overcautiousness. If they had continued to press him hard, he would have tired after another minute.

"Stand back!" he heard Volthorn call, then Twigly repeating the command in Hakiru. "Stand back! Give our archers room!"

An arrow whistled toward him. Durrin knocked it aside with his spear. The archers were drawing nearer, taking aim, as the remaining warriors bunched around them in a protective formation. He couldn't dodge that many arrows at once—not for very long. He needed a new tactic.

Durrin dropped his spear and held up his hands, wincing as the bruised muscles on his shoulder sent pain flashing through his nerves. "I yield! I yield!"

The archers kept their bows trained on Durrin, glancing at Volthorn for guidance.

Durrin shifted his spark to gather that strange, crackling energy, building it up around his raised hands.

"I have one thing to say before I die," he said, buying time as the invisible power built to a crescendo. All eyes were now turned to look at him. Good.

Only Volthorn saw it coming. "Look away!" he roared, ducking his head.

Durrin scrunched his eyes shut and released the energy. An arc of lightning ripped across the gap between his hands. Impossibly hot air surged over him as his ears nearly burst with the massive peal of thunder. Even with his eyes closed and his head bent, the flash was nearly blinding.

His opponents did not have their eyes shut.

He heard them cry out as their vision blacked out. Then he took off sprinting, running right between two of them undetected.

Only Volthorn saw where he went. "After him!" Volthorn yelled, charging in Durrin's wake.

Durrin scanned the landscape. Dashing Fire was galloping far in the distance, spooked by the blasts of lightning and fire. His horse would be no use to him. He could run back down the ravine or even leap off the cliff's edge—but that would only delay a second confrontation.

His eyes settled on the cloud frigate, moored some distance away. Perfect. Why not use Volthorn's own idea against him?

He glanced behind him. The warriors were rubbing their eyes and swinging blindly with their weapons. Only Volthorn was in pursuit, and he was quickly falling behind.

Durrin sprinted for the cloudship, pyromancy quickening his pace. He aimed a spurt of flame at one of the mooring ropes, searing through it. Then a second. Only two more remained.

Volthorn roared in fury behind him.

Something small and shiny flashed past Durrin's vision. He instinctively hurled himself to the side, twisting away from the object and tucking his head to his chest. The device exploded, filling the air with shards of rock. Several bit into his back, but his chainmail took most of the damage.

He hit the ground, rolled, and regained his footing in a split second. The cloud frigate loomed before him. He rounded the prow, slashing through the third mooring rope with a single swing of his sword. Then he severed the last rope with another plume of fire.

The ship, suddenly free, lurched into the sky. He ran forward, grabbed the wildly whipping end of the mooring rope, and swung up and around the stern of the gondola. Just as he reached the apex of his swing, he let go of the rope and latched onto one of the propeller outriggers. A swing and a leap later, he landed on the gondola's deck.

Durrin crouched for a moment, panting and gasping. He glanced over the side at the rapidly receding ground below. For the second time in nine months, the Hakiru were shaking their fists at him and yelling for all they were worth. Azura shot another arrow, but it flew low, biting through the top of the gondola's railing and sending splinters flying. Durrin ducked out of sight before they could fire more.

A sudden clatter reverberated from the prow, jerking the gondola. Durrin looked up to see Volthorn leap over the railing and land on the ship's deck, his armor glowing purple.

Volthorn straightened, drawing his sword and leveling it at Durrin.

CHAPTER 49

DUEL

Volthorn advanced.

No detail escaped his notice. Rendhart wore an outfit of chainmail and padded leather, though it was ripped and bloodied in several places. Besides his sword, he bore a long dagger strapped to his leg. His stance betrayed growing fatigue.

Volthorn pressed a hand to his armor, sucking some of the purple terracharge back into his fingers and then storing it in an amethyst on his belt. The purple energy had reversed the pull of gravity on his armor, allowing him to catch one of the gondola's loose mooring lines with a running leap and then clamber onto the deck. Leaving his armor in that state, however, would disorient him in the coming fight. He left just enough to lighten the weight. Then he touched his hand to other gems at his waist, recharging his armor and weapons: green terracharge for strength, blue for deflective energy, red to increase the sharpness of his sword.

As Volthorn reached the middle of the gondola, Rendhart swung his arm and summoned a wave of fire. It washed over Volthorn's armor and helm, its effects largely neutralized by his blue terracharge.

Eight years. It had been eight years since they had last faced each other. Rendhart had trounced him in their first encounter in the palace, but Volthorn had narrowly defeated him later that day. Volthorn had trained and drilled in the years since, while Rendhart had languished in a dungeon. Still, as the fight on the plateau had made all too clear, Rendhart was one of the most capable warriors he had ever seen. Volthorn would have to play his cards with perfect precision if he was going to win this fight.

Rendhart charged, fire rippling in his wake. Volthorn kept his feet planted, sticking to standard, proven cuts and thrusts, aiming to shear Rendhart's sword in two or slice through his armor in a lethal cut.

But none of his blows landed. Rendhart was a blur as he feinted and thrust, taking advantage of his longer blade as he danced in and out of reach, striking left and right, up and down, dodging Volthorn's thrusts or parrying at a shallow enough angle to avoid damage to his sword. Several of his blows overwhelmed Volthorn's guard but glanced uselessly off his magic wards. Volthorn felt the terracharge waning on the armor on his left side, but he managed to replenish it with his free hand before it ran out.

Volthorn advanced, trying to back Rendhart into the stern. The pyromancer circled right, summoning another wave of fire that blasted into Volthorn. Volthorn reeled back, shielding his face—the only part of him not fully shielded in armor. Rendhart followed up with a series of cuts aimed at Volthorn's head. One got through, coming within an inch of Volthorn's eye before a burst of blue light stopped its progress. Volthorn's helmet covered enough of his face that the deflective field it produced still shielded him from all but the most precise hits.

Volthorn's blade scored a hit, stabbing through Rendhart's chainmail and into his abdomen, in nearly the same place he'd been wounded the winter before.

Rendhart backed away, nearly stumbling over a crate of supplies. The gondola rocked in a gust of wind, causing them both to stumble as they fought to keep their footing.

"You cannot win," Volthorn grunted, his teeth gritted in concentration. He could not let Rendhart reach Mitria. He could not let this murderer keep harming his kingdom.

Rendhart, breathing heavily, didn't deign to reply.

They circled each other, stepping carefully over the crowded deck. Volthorn dropped his free hand to the ruby at his belt, feeling how much charge it still held. Quite a lot. He sucked power into his claws, then grabbed his sword in both hands, one claw hovering over the metal hilt.

Rendhart stepped to the attack, thrusting repeatedly toward Volthorn's face. As he parried the blows, Volthorn brought his claw against the hilt of his sword, pouring the reservoir of terracharge into the metal. The weapon's red glow intensified as the metal became oversaturated with power. On Volthorn's next parry, his sword sheared through Rendhart's blade like it was a reed.

Volthorn pressed the attack. Rendhart blocked the next blow with the stub of his sword, Volthorn's blade shaving off another couple inches. Rendhart dodged the next strike. On the next, he stepped forward, letting Volthorn's blade brush past him as he grabbed Volthorn's sword hand and clamped the blade between his chest and arm. With a twist and a blow to the wrist, Rendhart forced the blade from Volthorn's grasp.

The pyromancer twisted the blade around and took the offensive, spinning Volthorn's sword in a series of attacks. The glowing edge smashed into Volthorn's armor, each blow creating flashes of red, blue, and green light as the enchanted weapon bled its energy against Volthorn's wards.

Roaring in fury, Volthorn drew a long dagger, pouring terracharge into it. As he blocked Rendhart's next stroke, the razor-sharp blades bit deeply into each other, wedged tight. They wrestled for a moment, striving to unentangle their weapons.

Then Rendhart charged forward, slamming into Volthorn's shoulder. They both tumbled on a pile of gear, but Rendhart came out on top. He grabbed the handle of Volthorn's dagger with one hand, leaning into the sword as he drove the red-tipped blade into Volthorn's breastplate, piercing the armor's magical defenses.

Volthorn cocked a leg back and slammed his foot into Rendhart's stomach, his clawed talons nearly puncturing the chainmail. Rendhart rolled, wrenching the dagger from Volthorn's grasp. Volthorn scrambled to grab one of the weapons, but before he could, Rendhart rose to one knee and flung both the sword and the dagger out into the sky.

For a moment they both crouched, watching the still-entangled weapons spinning down toward the distant rocks below.

Then Volthorn slammed into Rendhart, grabbing him and bodily lifting him into the air. Rendhart landed a punch to Volthorn's jaw, but Volthorn powered forward through the pain, carrying Rendhart to the edge of the gondola and heaving him over the railing.

Rendhart's arms flailed as he fell, barely grabbing a rope dangling from the balloon a few feet away from the railing. He grabbed it with both hands as he slid down its length, crying out in pain as the rope burned his fingers. Only a knot at the end of the rope saved him from a fall of several hundred feet.

As Rendhart stopped with a jerk, the whole cloudship leaned to the side, off-balance. Volthorn stumbled, barely catching himself from toppling over the railing as well. He glared down at the pyromancer dandling twenty feet below him. "So close," he growled. "So close!"

Rendhart began kicking his legs, swinging back and forth on the end of the rope. Volthorn drew a second dagger. He grabbed some rigging for support and leaned over the side, dagger extended, but the rope was just out of reach of his blade.

Cursing the loss of his sword, Volthorn sheathed the dagger and loosened a pouch at his belt. He reached inside, grabbing a handful of powder. Acrid sand.

He pulled red terracharge from his belt, then poured it into the sand in his hand until it glowed red. Then he tossed it at the rope. Most of the particles missed, but some landed on the swinging rope, hissing as they made contact. The particles stuck where they landed, glowing as they began to eat into the fibers.

Volthorn grabbed another handful, but as he leaned out to throw it, a blast of fire hit him from below, scalding his face. Rendhart was still clinging to the rope with both hands—he must have summoned the fireball with his mouth.

Rendhart tucked his feet to his chest, increasing the speed of his next swing. At the apex of his arc, he launched himself free of the rope at the very moment it snapped. He yelled, issuing fire from his hands and feet. The blast of flames propelled him upward until he grabbed the railing by the stern and flipped back on board the gondola.

Volthorn grit his teeth, drawing his dagger again and charging across the deck. He touched the ruby at his belt but drew his claw away empty. The ruby had been depleted. He grabbed the last blue terracharge from his sapphire instead, using it to reinforce his breastplate.

Rendhart stumbled to his feet, his hand grasping something he'd picked up from the deck: the arrow that had nearly hit him when he first jumped onboard. Volthorn glanced at it. The tip was pure black. Voidstone.

Volthorn cursed.

Rendhart spun his free hand, summoning a blast of fire at Volthorn's face. Then he sprang forward, thrusting his arrow at a gap in Volthorn's armor. The jagged voidstone tip pierced through Volthorn's wards without resistance and left a deep gash on his thigh. Volthorn howled from the pain.

Rendhart struck again, the voidstone tip of his arrow slashing through the gauntlet of Volthorn's free hand and gouging the skin. Volthorn stabbed forward with his knife, but Rendhart shunted the thrust aside with the chainmail on his forearm, landing a kick on Volthorn's breastplate that sent him sprawling. Volthorn wheezed for breath, his vision blurry.

Stepping forward, Rendhart planted his boot on the wrist of Volthorn's dagger hand, pinning it to the deck, then pressed the knee of his other leg against Volthorn's chest. Volthorn flailed, aiming a punch with his left hand, but Rendhart caught the blow and pinned Volthorn's hand to his chest. With his right hand, Rendhart pressed the voidstone arrow tip against Volthorn's throat. The pure black stone was freezing to the touch as it pressed against Volthorn's scaly skin.

Volthorn strained to break free, but Rendhart held him fast. Their gazes locked. Rendhart's eyes were cool and hard; Volthorn stared at him, seething.

"Yield," Rendhart demanded.

Volthorn glared at him, eight years of loss and fury coursing through his veins.

"Yield!" Durrin repeated, increasing the pressure on the arrowhead.

"What are you waiting for?" Volthorn spat. "Kill me, like you killed my king."

Fire roared in Rendhart's eyes, turning them blood red. He increased the pressure on the arrow tip.

Volthorn closed his eyes, waiting for the inevitable pain. This was it. He had lost. He had given his all to defeat the murderer of his king. But today, just like eight years before, it hadn't been enough.

The pressure on the arrow tip vanished.

Volthorn cracked his eyes open. The fire had vanished from Rendhart's eyes, replaced with a wholly unexpected sight—tears.

"No," Rendhart whispered. "I am not who you think I am, Volthorn. I am not who I *was*! I already have one bloodstain on my eternal scroll. I will not add another."

He withdrew the arrowhead from Volthorn's throat. "I will not kill you, Volthorn Skarr."

Confusion swept through Volthorn's mind. What did Rendhart mean? Why hadn't he struck? Part of his mind screamed at him to rethink everything he had concluded about Rendhart for the past year.

But the fury and hatred, still coursing through his veins, saw only an opportunity.

Volthorn screamed, twisting his left hand free from Rendhart's grip. His claws flashed out, grabbing the arrow's shaft. As they wrestled for control of the arrow, Volthorn yanked his right hand out from under Durrin's boot and drove his dagger upward, the blade puncturing Rendhart's chainmail and driving deep into his side, right below his ribs.

Rendhart gasped and stumbled back. The arrow shaft finally snapped, with Volthorn coming away with the tip. He tossed it overboard, then punched Rendhart's jaw.

The pyromancer staggered back, pressing a hand to the wound in his side. Volthorn leapt to his feet, rage giving strength to his limbs. Rendhart knocked away Volthorn's next knife thrust, but Volthorn punched his ribs with his other hand. Rendhart spun his arm and summoned a wall of fire in front of him, but Volthorn simply walked through it, his wards making him impervious, and drove his fist into Rendhart's stomach.

Rendhart collapsed to his knees, gasping. He struggled to rise but failed. Volthorn raised his dagger for a killing blow, roaring in triumph.

He stopped, transfixed.

At the prow, quill and scroll in hand, with magnificent wings spread out behind her, stood an angel.

Chapter 50

True Wisdom

The dagger fell from Volthorn's trembling hand.

He collapsed to his knees, his eyes transfixed on the brilliant being before him. Her robes were of the purest white, and light radiated from her being. The quill in her hand was of pure eternium, the tip shimmering with a thousand colors.

Volthorn knew whose scroll she carried. His own.

In a flash of clarity, he saw the state of his soul reflected in the angel's eyes. He saw the anger, the suspicion, the hatred that had festered in his heart since Durrin's release. He saw how, like a blight, those emotions had blinded his judgment and twisted his reasoning. Who had caused the loss of his command, his brother, and his kingdom? Not Rendhart. No—Volthorn had done that to himself.

And he had come one dagger's stroke away from forfeiting eternity.

He fell on his face, unable to look any longer at the glorious being before him. Tears streamed down his cheeks.

"What have I done?" he whispered. "*What have I done?!*"

"Look up, Volthorn Skarr."

The angel's voice was as piercing as a chill wind. Volthorn reluctantly raised his head, squinting from the brightness radiating from the angel's robes.

"Rise, Durrin Rendhart."

Durrin stumbled to his feet, one blood-coated hand still clutching his side.

The angel stepped across the gondola's deck, her robes billowing weightlessly around her, and laid a hand on Durrin's forehead. "*Et yidivar,*" she commanded. Durrin's muscles relaxed, the pain vanishing from his face.

"Well done, Durrin," the angel said, her words smooth as flowing water.

Then she turned to Volthorn, her gaze once again reflecting the darkness that had infested his heart. He shrunk before her.

"Volthorn Skarr. Your blindness and hatred have nearly stained your eternal soul with innocent blood."

Each word cut like daggers to his heart—the pain a thousand times greater because he knew they were true.

"Leave behind your rage," the angel commanded. "Cast it out of your heart. There is still time."

Volthorn numbly nodded.

"Durrin spoke the truth: he is on the errand of your queen. And that errand cannot fail. I will steer your ship back to where the Hakiru wait. Then you must leave behind your quarrels and continue, together, to the lands of the Mitrians."

Then the angel turned to address Durrin. "You have come far, son of fire."

Durrin couldn't take his eyes off the magnificent being in front of him.

He had known power before. He had stood before chieftains and princes, kings and emperors, and the mightiest warriors and mancerers in the world.

Nothing compared to the power radiating from the angel before him.

Ever since the angel had appeared, one thought had occupied his mind. He sank to his knees.

"Tell me," he pleaded. "Do you keep my scroll?"

The angel nodded.

Despite his wounds having been healed, he trembled. "Please. Have I done enough? Have I appeased justice and expunged the stain of my sin?"

The angel looked gently at him. "You can never 'appease' justice, Durrin. Justice is an unyielding taskmaster. For an act as foul as murder, no act of recompense will ever satisfy its demands."

The words sent a chill through his heart. "Then am I doomed?" he whispered.

The angel shook her head. "The Halls of the Sun are bound not by justice, but by mercy. It is a power that flows from the Eldest, down through the ages of Time and the expanses of Forever. It heals what is broken. It strengthens what is weak. And it undoes what was done. Through its power, the scroll of your fate consists not of the sum of what you have done, but the sum of who you have *become*."

The angel stepped forward, laying a hand on Durrin's brow. "And you have become more worthy than my greatest hopes."

Durrin bowed, tears streaming down his face. The angel's touch sent rays of light shooting through every nerve of his body, replacing his despair, his regret, his pain, his loss, and his guilt with an unquenchable, unstoppable hope.

The angel stepped back. "Be on your guard," she said, her tone turning somber. "There is a balance that must be maintained, an ancient covenant that must be kept. By taking on corporal form, I have opened the door for a demon to do the same."

The words snapped Durrin back to the present. He flicked his eyes around them. "When? Where?"

"I know not the hour the demon will choose," the angel said. "Nor the place. But beware. The one I oppose possesses great power. And because I appeared to save your life, it is likely that, when he appears, it will be with the intent to destroy you."

The angel clasped her hands together. "To face him, you will need two things. In a coming day, you must gain the knowledge that you most need. You will remember where to find it. But before that, you require something you sought for a long time, only to relinquish."

The angel parted her hands. Appearing out of nothing in her grasp was a long, wooden box, decorated with swirling patterns of fire. The lid was open, revealing a scarlet scroll.

The hosts of Calamar had arrived.

From the balcony of the royal wing, Adara could see their camp three miles west of the city. Another camp lay to the south, across the Silvermoss. In total, they numbered over seventy thousand troops—nearly four times the number of troops inside the city.

Adara lowered the spyglass. "What are they waiting for?"

"More supplies," said her new commanding officer, a human named Commander Orrin. He had fought under Volthorn the previous summer, and most recently had done a capable job commanding the northern front, slowing the Calamarvan advance across the Arnon Plains. But he wasn't Volthorn. He was—well . . . dry. And unimaginative. "They're waiting to bring up their siege equipment before they surround the city and commence digging trenches."

"Siege equipment," Adara repeated. "You mean catapults?"

Commander Orrin nodded. "Those, along with battering rams, siege towers, and ballista."

"That's comforting," Adara said.

"Not really," Commander Orrin said. "It only delays the inevitable. My intelligence officers expect the enemy will commence bombardment the day after tomorrow."

Adara rolled her eyes, not bothering to point out that she had been being sarcastic. "Thank you, Commander. I'll let you see to your preparations."

"Very well, Your Majesty." He bowed stiffly and strode away.

In his wake, Skagar loped up. The swifter had been less energetic of late, and his fur had flecks of gray. The war was taking its toll on all of them.

"Your Majesty," he said. "A herald has arrived from the enemy camp and is requesting an audience."

"A herald? Did he state his purpose?"

Skagar shook his head. "Issue terms for our surrender, most likely."

"I will see him in the throne room." Adara glanced at her simple scarlet dress, debating whether it was ornate enough for a throne session. It wasn't, but she didn't care enough to change. And her advisor of fashion had fled the city the day before, so no one was around to tell her otherwise. So there.

She went straight to the throne room, talking with Skagar on the way about how to handle the inevitable call for surrender.

When the herald entered, however, he was unlike any ambassador Adara had received before. A human in perhaps his mid-thirties, he was clad not in fancy robes, nor in an officer's uniform bedecked with medals, but in simple military gear. He carried himself with assurance, but not bravado, as he stepped through the doors of the throne room and knelt before her.

The guard at the door stamped his spear. "Lieutenant Halorn Venarim," he announced. "Herald for the Imperial Seat of Calamar."

Adara and Skagar exchanged surprised glances. The Imperial Seat itself? That meant this soldier had been sent by the emperor directly.

Skagar leaned close to the throne. "He bears a low rank to be an imperial herald."

"I was just thinking that," Adara whispered back. She lifted her scepter. "Rise, Lieutenant Venarim. What message do you bear?"

The soldier stood, but kept his head respectfully lowered. "Before I speak, I must ask that my message be kept strictly confidential, heard by as few ears as possible, and that it doesn't leave this room."

Adara heard Skagar mutter in unease, but she spoke before he could. "A reasonable request, and one we are glad to grant." She dismissed most of her guards, leaving only two.

Once the guards had left, the soldier took a deep breath. "I bear a message directly from His Highest and Most Estimable Lordship, Emperor Stoneclaw the Mighty. He has traveled to the front to oversee his armies personally, reaching the war camp just this morning."

The emperor was here? Just a few miles away? Adara reeled inwardly from the unexpected news, but outwardly she kept herself calm.

"His Lordship requests an audience with Your Majesty," the soldier said. "But he requires that you go . . . alone."

"Alone?!" Skagar roared, fur bristling as he lashed his tail in outrage. "How could he demand such absurdity!"

"Hush, Chancellor," Adara said, although inwardly she, too, shrunk in disbelief. "Let him speak."

The soldier waited until they had both settled again, then continued. "The emperor has never liked this war, Your Majesty. He knew your father and mourned his loss. He would have had peace in the years since, had factions within his government not demanded otherwise."

"A powerful emperor, to let himself be swayed so easily," Skagar quipped.

"But now he has chosen to come to the front personally, Your Majesty," the soldier said, ignoring Skagar's comment. "He has seen for himself the state of the war, and it disturbs him. He does not want to see this city destroyed, nor more blood spilt on either side. In addition, he wants to avoid the additional power that his generals would gain should Elandria become a military protectorate. He wishes to talk with you of a temporary armistice, hopefully leading to long-term peace."

"Then let him send an official delegation, not a single low-ranking officer!" Skagar demanded. "Or let him come himself!"

Adara glared at him. "Chancellor! Peace!"

"You must understand," the soldier said. "For his whole reign, the emperor has had to deal with self-serving subordinates. He does not trust any of his generals to willingly pursue peace if they were sent to negotiate. But, naturally, neither is he willing to trust his own person in enemy hands."

"I understand," Adara said, cutting off her advisor before he could speak again. "His Lordship's fears are reasonable."

"He wishes to speak to you directly," the soldier said. "Yet he fears for your safety. Should his officers know of your coming, they might take matters into their own hands."

He paused, then continued in a more authentic tone. "I spoke generally just now, but we both know I speak of Lord Salidar."

"Salidar does not know about this?" Adara asked.

"Only the emperor, his chief steward, and I know," the soldier said. "No one else can be trusted, not even the emperor's closest servants. Anyone might be a spy for Lord Salidar. I took extreme measures to come here undetected." He glanced around, as if worried a spy might have followed him to the very throne room.

"The emperor asks that tomorrow morning you come alone to his camp, dressed as a simple Elandrian serving maid, one of many the army has captured and pressed into service. I shall meet you outside the gates of the city and accompany you to his tent, where he will negotiate with you personally. No other soul shall know of your coming, and he guarantees your safe return before the setting of the Sun."

Adara sank back in her throne. The soldier had laid at her feet what she had wanted since her coronation: an audience with the emperor himself, and with the emperor already sympathetic to her cause. It was a miracle!

Yet so much could go wrong. How could the emperor be trusted? Why would he call a truce with his armies outside the city? Perhaps this was a ploy for Calamar to capture her and crush her people's morale. The very presence of the emperor could be a lie, concocted by Salidar to lure her out.

But even if the emperor *had* come, and *was* sincere, and even if Salidar with his vast network of spies knew *nothing* about the soldier's errand, she would be walking straight into the enemy camp, unarmed and unguarded. So many things could go wrong.

"Who are you?" she asked.

The soldier raised his head, and his eyes caught hers for the briefest of moments. Something flashed deep in his eyes—something familiar. "I am a farmer," he said, looking down again. "I am from a village called Caradell, where my wife and four children reside."

Skagar spoke up. "And how did a simple farmer from an obscure backwater gain the confidence of the emperor?"

"In my youth, I had connections with Lord Vandil, now serving as high steward," the soldier said. "This spring, I asked him to arrange an audience with the emperor. There, I pleaded with His Lordship to take action, to investigate the war himself rather than trust Salidar's words. I brought . . . information . . . that changed the emperor's view of Salidar's intentions. The emperor listened, and he came. Since it was I who persuaded him to come, it was I whom he sent today."

Adara leaned forward, holding her breath as she listened to each word. Her heartbeat quickened. Could this possibly be true?

Skagar leaned close. "Your Majesty, a word please." He glanced at the herald. "In private."

"Leave us for a moment," Adara said. Halorn bowed and exited the chamber.

The moment the doors had shut, Skagar spoke up. "My queen, he is lying. His story makes no sense."

"He seems sincere," Adara said.

"He has to be lying!" Skagar repeated. "How could a lowly farmer ever gain audience with the emperor, much less persuade him to come to the front? And why would the emperor suddenly want to settle for peace after three years of relentless war?"

"I've already thought of all that," Adara said. She patted the fur on Skagar's shoulders, surprised at the clear resolve within her. She lacked only one detail to confirm. "I have already made my decision. It's clearly absurdly dangerous for me to accept the offer."

The corners of Skagar's mouth turned up in a smile. "*That* is the wisdom I have always seen in you, Your Majesty."

She had technically spoken the truth. It *was* absurdly dangerous. But with or without her counselor's approval, she had decided she was going to accept the offer anyway.

She ordered the soldier to be admitted back into their presence. Once again, he knelt before them, but she noticed he stole a cursory glance at Skagar. The swifter's smirk seemed to strip the man's remaining resolve. He slumped down, his head low. She imagined he thought he had failed.

"Lieutenant Halorn Venarim, herald for the Imperial Seat of Calamar." Adara rose to her feet. "We have considered the offer from your sovereign, His Highest and Most Estimable Lordship Emperor Stoneclaw, and we consider the inherent risks to our royal person too great to sanely consider."

"Well said," Skagar murmured beside her.

In front of her, the soldier didn't react. He continued kneeling, staring stoically at the floor.

"We only have a few more questions for you, before you go," Adara continued. Then she slipped into the Numinous Tongue. "Et jire aina do," she said awkwardly, struggling to remember the right words from her childhood lessons. *Look into my eyes.*

The soldier paused, confused, then obediently looked up at her. There they were—the eyes she had seen for only a moment. Within them, unmistakable, sparkled what she had thought she had seen.

"Ti ene ko Avara?" she asked. *You are for the Light?*

"To ene ko Abeam," he replied. *I am for the Eldest.*

She could hear Skagar shifting restlessly beside her. "Your Majesty?" he asked. She couldn't help but smile. Fifty years of experience, and he had never learned a sentence in the Numinous Tongue. *And he said my lessons were a waste of time.*

"Ileum, do olo ti," she said, ignoring her counselor. *Tomorrow, I will meet you.* "Kelim?" *What time?*

"Al kirum avara," the soldier said. *At first light.*

"I see," Avara said, slipping back into Lurrian. "You speak very well in the Numinous Tongue for a farmer."

"I received much schooling when I was young," Halorn said, returning his gaze to the floor. "But circumstances prevented me from studying further. As a last resort, I turned to farming."

"Interesting." Adara let just enough suspicion slide into her tone to placate the swifter beside her. "Inform His Highest and Most Estimable Lordship that we are quite anxious for peace. We would gladly end this war, and we are willing to listen to his terms. But we would find an official delegation, one that could meet within our walls, much more within our powers to accept."

"I understand, Your Majesty," Halorn said. And she knew he truly did.

"You may go," she said.

He rose and turned away, but at the door, he paused for a moment. "Di weli parab yegoro to, al Abeam," he said. *You have my word of safety, by the Eldest.*

The doors shut. Adara stepped off the dais, worried that Skagar's keen ears would otherwise hear the pounding of her heart. She could scarcely believe what she had just done. Not only had she agreed to do something so foolhardy that any one of her counselors would condemn it as madness, but in doing so, she had deliberately deceived her own chancellor!

Yet at her core, she felt perfectly at ease. Yes, the soldier had been lying about who he was. He was much more than a simple farmer—of that Adara had no doubt.

But Adara had seen something else in the young soldier. The light deep within his eyes was the same shimmer she had seen in Cymer and Sablewing. She had seen a fellow Light and Healer.

Chapter 51

Honor

"The Mitrians are a proud people," Durrin instructed his companions. "Understand that fact, and you understand nearly everything about them."

He, Volthorn, Bjorn, Line, and Twigly were working their way up a steep slope. Around them rode about a dozen Mitrian warriors: tall, broad-shouldered humans, dressed in furs, with spears in their hands and short, recurve bows tied to their saddles. Unlike most societies in Zenitha, the Mitrians were a human-only culture.

"The Mitrians are proud of their honor," Durrin continued, ticking off his fingers. "They are proud of their independence. They are proud of their heritage and their ancestors. They are proud of their cooking."

"Undeservedly," Twigly grumbled from where she rode on Bjorn's shoulder.

"I think I get the picture," Volthorn said. He dropped his voice, glancing ahead at a particularly decorated Mitrian leading their column. "Be careful with your words," he hissed. "Can't Korkor speak Lurrian?"

"Yes, he can speak Lurrian," Durrin said at a normal volume. "And I bet he's proud of it. Aren't you, Korkor?"

The human turned, showing a face split with two long scars, one on each cheek. "Aye," he grunted. "And I'm proud that I'm proud of it. Rendhart, can you tell Stubbylegs to move faster? We're going to be late to the council. And I do not like being late."

"If he didn't want to be late," Volthorn grumbled under his breath as he picked up his pace, "he should have offered us horses."

"Mitrian horses are for Mitrians only, I'm afraid," Durrin smirked. "They're too proud of their breeds to let anyone else ride them."

Volthorn closed his eyes, taking a deep breath.

Since their nearly fatal fight the day before, a tension had still simmered between Durrin and the korrik. Durrin had done his best to act amicably, but Volthorn had largely retreated within himself, spending most of the trip at the bow of the cloud frigate, staring off into the sky. Durrin guessed what must be happening under the surface. Volthorn was likely undergoing the same realignment, the questioning of his very soul, that Durrin had experienced while sailing toward Adara's kidnapping nine months before.

(Who knew Twigly's cloudship would be so conducive to life-changing introspection? Maybe she should start a business.)

By contrast, and to Durrin's surprise, the rest of the pirates had forgiven Durrin pretty much on the spot. Apparently, they weren't ones to hold a grudge. (The fact that they had stared, dumbfounded, as the angel had guided the cloud frigate back to the plateau probably didn't hurt.)

After a steep climb, the Mitrians and their guests reached the top of the ridge. On the other side stretched a massive natural bowl, carved out of the mountains on all sides. Durrin knew that normally, the bowl held only a quiet meadow. But today it teemed with life. Horsemen trotted about in small bands, weaving their way between groups of tents. Cooking fires burned. Children ran about playing games.

"There must be several thousand people here," Line exclaimed in awe.

"Twenty or thirty thousand, at least," Durrin agreed. "Every year, delegations from each Mitrian tribe gather here to compete."

As they descended into the massive bowl, a second band of riders rode up to them. Each of these wore yellow and blue ribbons fluttering from their spears or saddles. Their leader dismounted. "Durrin Rendhart," he yelled, approaching. He stopped a pace from Durrin. "So you finally decided to come and apologize," he said in Mitrian.

"Yes," Durrin replied. "I apologize for only beating you by a fox-length instead of a wyvern-length."

The warrior's hand shot out. Durrin blocked it with his arm. The warrior swung with his other arm, which Durrin blocked as well. Then he swung his leg up in a kick, which Durrin easily dodged.

The warrior broke out laughing. "It's good to have you back, Rendhart," he said, stepping forward to clasp Durrin's hand and slap him on the shoulder.

"Glad to see you're as slow as ever," Durrin said, cracking a smile.

As they continued across the meadow, Volthorn leaned close to him again. "If the Mitrians care so much about their pride, why did you block his hits? Wouldn't that embarrass him?"

"The Mitrians are proud of winning," Durrin said. "But they're also proud of keeping their cool when they lose to a superior opponent."

Volthorn scowled. "I'm confused."

"They can take some getting used to," Durrin said. He could tell that Volthorn, already tense from yesterday's events, was well out of his comfort zone here. No wonder Adara's ambassador had made little headway. "Perhaps leave most of the talking to me,"

Volthorn kicked a bush in his way. "I'd have to anyway, seeing I don't speak Mitrian."

"True."

At the center of the bowl was a large ring of colorful tents. In the middle, sitting in a circle, were about two dozen chieftains. Each sat in a finely crafted chair, with their tribe's banner—some combination of two colors—waving behind them. Most of the chieftains had one or two senior men or women from their tribe seated on the ground in front of them. In the center of the circle, one of the chieftains stood addressing the others.

"Look at that," Korkor muttered. "We're late."

As Durrin's party approached, the circle fell silent, turning to look at them.

"Will you deign to translate for my stubby friend here?" Durrin said to Korkor in Mitrian.

The man sighed. "Only because you saved my life that one time, Rendhart. But after today, you can't use that for any more favors."

Durrin smirked. This was at least the fifth time in ten years Korkor had said those exact words.

The chieftain in the middle of the circle turned toward them. "Is this the delegation from the People of the Plain?" he said, using a traditional Mitrian term for Elandria. "Whose lowly presence has the daughter of Everborn slighted us with this time?"

Durrin stepped forward, removing the cowl of his cloak. "I am Durrin Rendhart, the Fire Blade," he announced, slipping into the Mitrian tongue. He looked around the circle, making eye contact with each chieftain, noting the surprise and recognition in their eyes. "Many of you know me. The rest have doubtless heard of me. Eleven years ago, I rode with Chief Korkor and Chief Telkin in the hunt for the Tyrannosaur of Torrent Pass, joining my spear with theirs in the final charge that brought down the marauding beast. Nine years ago, I was the first and only outsider to win the Silver Axe at these games."

"But why are you representing the People of the Plain?" a chieftain called. "You hail from the People of the Sword."

"Calamar is indeed my homeland," Durrin acknowledged. "But today I come as a representative of the Daughter of Everborn." He gestured to Volthorn. "With me, I bring Volthorn Skarr, former high commander of the Armies of the Plain. He is a capable warrior and could hold his own against any one of you."

It was a risky thing to say. One of the chieftains might test Durrin's word and challenge the korrik to a duel—which, if Volthorn lost, would severely damage Elandria's credibility. Luckily, none of the chieftains spoke up. Battling a korrik was beneath them.

"Don't forget me!" a shrill voice cried in Mitrian, as Twigly stepped out of the group of pirates. She gave a low bow, flourishing her rapier.

Several of the chieftains stiffened. "You brought the Garish Ghost?" one of them cried.

"The Scoundrel of the Sky?" another said.

"The Potato Thief?"

"You can't prove that!" Twigly chirped.

Durrin gestured to the snippen. "Twigly the Barbaric and her crew brought me and Commander Skarr to these mountains."

"You mean she agreed to *work* for you?" said a chieftain on the far side of the circle. He slapped his knee. "*Now* you have my respect!"

An aging chieftain, the most decorated among them, raised his spear. "Enough drabbling!" he cried. At his word, the hubbub in the clearing died. He pointed his spear at Durrin. "We know why you have come. The daughter of Everborn has asked us to intervene in your war—to ride to your aid and break the siege of the City of the Two Rivers. Tell us why we should."

Durrin let the silence grow, making eye contact with each of the chieftains as he turned in a slow circle. Only then did he speak.

"The People of the Plain are your allies. They are your friends, your neighbors, your partners in trade. Over a decade ago, you made a pact with their king, the great Everborn. You promised to cease your raids into their borders, and you pledged your eternal friendship."

"But we did not pledge to make their war ours," a chieftain objected.

Durrin nodded. "You are correct. Which is why I come not to hold you to your duty, but to appeal to your honor. The People of the Plain need your help. One month more, and they will fall, conquered and enslaved by a cruel and unrelenting foe."

"Why is that cause to risk our lives, and the lives of our families?" another voice said.

"As I mentioned, I hail from Calamar," Durrin said. "For many years, I served their second-in-command, Lord Salidar. I know his mind. He is ruthless and greedy, always seeking to expand Calamar's borders. There are many others like him."

He turned again, slowly.

"You have seen Calamar's advance in the last three decades. First they attacked Orlan. Then Wormul. Now Elandria. Once Elandria falls, their ambitions will turn to you. You have much that they want. You control the haeber trade from Marisau. You have tin mines and silver mines. Their terramancers will covet the Leyline of Emerald Lake. Sooner or later, war will come to you."

"Let it come," a chieftain said, banging his spear into the ground. "We will show them why our enemies fear us."

"Show them now," Durrin said. "Show them now, while you have allies. Show them now, when you can take the war to them, instead of waiting until they attack your villages and children. Show them now, and drive them far away from your lands *before* they become your permanent neighbors."

Murmurings broke out across the clearing. Durrin looked at the assembled group, wondering if his words were sinking in.

One of the chieftains spoke up. "You appealed earlier to our honor," he said, his words cutting over the hubbub. "But let us talk about the honor of those who sent you. Why do the People of the Plain deserve our help? They are treaty breakers. Eight years ago, the great Everborn pledged to supply Calamar with haeber for as long as his dynasty should last. Only four years later, his daughter's regents reneged on that promise. The war is Elandria's fault. Defeat is only their just reward."

His question prompted another flurry of murmurs, but they quickly died as everyone looked to Durrin. He glanced to the side of the circle, where Korkor had just finished translating the question to Volthorn. They made eye contact.

"I have a response," Durrin said quietly, switching to Lurrian. "But it means revealing the secret you and the co-regents have hid carefully for seven years." Durrin swallowed, his body tense. "Do you trust me?"

Volthorn held his gaze, his dark eyes unsearchable.

Then he nodded.

Durrin bowed his head in return, a smile of relief and gratitude flashing across his face. Then he turned to address the chieftain that had raised the challenge. "The war is not Elandria's fault," he declared, switching back to Mitrian. "It's mine."

The chieftains stared at him with startled surprise.

Durrin took a deep breath, forcing the words out through the guilt that still lingered in his heart. "For many years, Lord Salidar plotted war against Elandria. He used every excuse, but particularly the haeber trade, to stir up animosity and conflict. But King Everborn and Emperor Stoneclaw were committed to peace, and they would not see their respective nations dragged into war. Eight years ago, at Lord Salidar's order, I assaulted the Elandrian palace and slew King Everborn with my own sword."

An audible gasp rose from some of the assembled Mitrians.

"Still, Elandria did not want war," Durrin continued. "They covered up my act, casting the king's death as an accident. For four years they delayed the inevitable, while Salidar continued to build his armies. Eventually they acknowledged that war must come, and so finally rescinded the Guarantee of Trade. But from the beginning, the architect of the war was Salidar. And I was his tool."

Durrin slowly walked around the middle of the circle, meeting each chieftain's eyes. "Only recently have I realized the extent of what I have done. Now I seek to repair it. But I cannot end this war alone. That is why I appeal to you."

His voice rose until his words thundered across the assembly. "For my sake, and for the sake of the people I have almost doomed to destruction through my crimes, come to their aid!"

Durrin fell silent.

For a long moment, the chieftains sat in stunned silence.

Finally, the aging chieftain cleared his throat. "This account certainly . . . changes the nature of the war. Do you swear that you speak the truth?"

Before Durrin could respond, Volthorn stepped into the circle. "I swear," he said, letting Korkor translate for him. "I was there the day he slew my king. This scar on my face came from his hand. All that he spoke is true."

The two exchanged glances. Volthorn's eyes were clearer than Durrin had ever seen them before. The malice and hatred from the previous months had vanished.

Durrin turned back to the chieftains, his heart swelling with gratitude for the korrik's trust. "I swear as well." Durrin drew his sword. "And if any wish to challenge my word, I will gladly prove it through trial by combat."

Trial by combat. His trump card. The ancient tradition was held in highest esteem among the Mitrians. Just to invoke it was usually enough to convince others that one was telling the truth. But perhaps today would require more than just invoking it. Durrin eyed the chieftains. Many were surely hesitant to go to war. Defeating him in combat would provide a way they could stay at home without losing their honor.

"Does anyone here challenge the word of the Fire Blade?" the aging chieftain called.

No one spoke.

Durrin turned to the chieftain who had called the Elandrians treaty breakers. He was one of the largest chieftains, a head taller than Durrin and easily twice his weight. "What about you, Chief Torgan? Do you wish to fight?"

After a moment's hesitation, the chief rose from his chair, putting a hand to his spear.

Durrin snapped his fingers, summing a flame that blossomed into the sky.

Chief Torgan paused, looking around the assembly. Several other chiefs—those who knew Durrin best—shook their heads.

Chief Torgan laughed and sat back down. "Snakes and lizards, Rendhart! We all know you can best any of us with one arm tied behind your back. I do not challenge your word."

Chief Korkor sprung to his feet. "Then I move that we ride!"

Another chief joined him. "As do I!"

"And I!"

"And I!"

The eldest chieftain raised his spear, calling the assembly to order. "Do any oppose Chief Korkor's proposition?" he asked.

Silence prevailed.

"Then we ride!"

Chapter 52

Adara Alone

Adara walked toward the enemy army, alone.

Behind her stood the mighty walls of Saven, their granite heights glimmering in the first light of dawn, their towers piercing the sky with green banners. Behind those walls she was safe, secure, and sovereign—a queen. Now she was only a lone avir maiden.

She paused at a crossroads just beyond the gates, staring to the west. Around her, a bustle of wagons and carts quickly disappeared down the northern road, another batch of citizens fleeing the city while they still could. In the other direction flowed farmers from the surrounding villages, seeking safety behind the city walls. For their sake, the city guard still opened the main gates at first light, noonday, and last light, and would until Salidar's army encircled the city completely.

Adara had slipped out with the morning crowd. Gone were her scepter, crown, and royal robes. She wore a simple dress with an apron and frock, all borrowed from the dresser of one of her handmaids. The young avir servant had approached Adara the day before, weeping tears of fear and begging permission to flee to her grandparents in a village to the east. Adara had let her go.

"You and I must look nearly identical," Adara murmured, imagining her handmaid hurrying down a path somewhere, clad in similar garb to what Adara now wore. "I don't blame you for being afraid. I might have done the same, nine or ten months ago."

How those nine months had changed her.

The massive gates slammed shut behind her, their mighty clash reverberating around the low hills. Adara looked around. Everyone else had disappeared down other roads, all steering clear of the main road leading west. She was truly alone.

Halorn, the Calamarvan messenger, was nowhere in sight.

She walked a distance from the gates, in case the guards on the walls became suspicious. Perhaps Halorn was hidden farther down the road to avoid detection. Or perhaps he was waiting over the rise with a troop of cavalry to take her by force.

"He's probably just late," Adara said, trying to reassure herself. "Calamarvan punctuality, after all," she joked. Actually, she realized, Calamarvans were quite punctual—at least the ones she had known, which were mainly ambassadors. And the pyromancer, Durrin.

The thought reminded her of her dream that morning. It had been a vivid dream—of Durrin, standing amid a circle of Mitrian chieftains. "We ride!" they had been shouting over and over. Durrin had been consulting with some of them about troop numbers, and how quickly they could reach Saven.

Was that a portent? A vision of what already was or was about to be? Or only a dream sprung from her fancy?

She cleared a small hill, and the walls of the city sank out of view. Over the next rise, the enemy camp would be visible. If there was any spot where Halorn would meet her, it had to be here.

"Hello?" she called, as loud as she dared. "Halorn? Lieutenant Venarim?" The terrain to either side was mainly flat, with wheat fields and occasional patches of trees. She saw no sign of anyone.

Uncertainty. *Release.* Clarity. *Breathe.*

Maybe Halorn was over the last rise; she wouldn't know unless she tried. She climbed the next hill, enjoying the feel of the cold morning air on her face. The daily fog from the river had disappeared, and she soaked in the Sun's rays warming her back and her hair, which now had several inches of golden growth.

She topped the rise.

The Calamarvan army lay camped before her. Tents, thousands of them, stretched row by row, section by section, two miles to either side and a mile deep. Smoke from a thousand campfires wafted into the air, casting the whole panorama in a blood-red hue. War banners snapped in the breeze. Her nose filled with the smell of roasted beef and pork, spoils of the farms unfortunate enough to lie in the army's path. Over the wind came the neigh of war stallions and the shriek of swords on whetstones.

Standing there, facing the full might of Calamar, seventy thousand battle-hardened soldiers from a far-away land, Adara wavered. For a moment, she felt like a girl again, timid and afraid.

Fear. *Release.* Faith. *Breathe.*

Every instinct urged her to turn back. Halorn had not appeared. Her mission had obviously failed. At any moment, she would be accosted by guards and dragged before some low-ranking captain to be executed or enslaved. She had no ring or token to prove her royal identity. She hadn't told a single soul where she was going. Durrin was far away. She didn't even know where Volthorn was. Should she fall into enemy hands, there'd be no rescue this time.

She glanced behind her. There was the city, two miles away, its gates beckoning safety. Behind it, the Sun climbed above the far-away slopes of Mount Terramor, as if calling her with its rays. She could still return.

"I have to go back," Adara said. "I must go back!"

Yet she could not turn back. Some force inside her held her feet in place, preventing any action except forward.

Through the cacophony of her fears came the sweet, sublime, and perfect assurance that should she continue, all would be well.

In the space between her reason and her hope, she stood balanced on the edge of choice.

She took a step forward. Then a second. Then a third.

A shrill whistle sounded somewhere. She had been spotted.

"This is it then," Adara murmured. "No going back."

She turned away from the rising Sun and walked into the sublime unknown.

After a few seconds, two horsemen galloped out of a nearby stand of trees. They carried recurve bows, but they didn't bother to load them. "Halt!" one said as they drew near.

"I already halted," Adara said, gesturing to her planted feet. "Five seconds ago."

The horsemen exchanged glances. Then the first dismounted. "What are you about?"

"Please, sir," Adara said, adopting what she hoped was a rural accent. "I was just fetchin' some firewood for the camp. Sergeant ordered me too."

She nearly winced as she said it. Why, then, would she be walking back *toward* the camp without any firewood?

"Come with us," the horseman ordered, not seeming to register the lapse in her logic. He pointed back toward the stand of trees. Adara followed, more curious than afraid.

They walked into the shadows of the trees, out of sight from the main road. Ahead, Adara saw a human silhouette, and for a moment her heart soared. But no—it was too tall to be Halorn.

"Well, well, well," came a cold voice. A familiar voice.

Her heart skipped a beat.

Lord Salidar.

"Good work, officers," Salidar said. "I can take it from here. Keep watching the road and accost anyone else approaching from the city."

"Yes, Your Excellency," the horsemen said, bowing and withdrawing.

Adara was left standing alone with her greatest enemy.

"Well," said Salidar, casually pacing before her. "What a pleasant surprise."

"Obviously not," Adara said. "Or you wouldn't be here." She marveled at the audacity in her words. Nine months ago, she had shivered at this man's feet, nearly overcome with fear. Now, there was not a trace of fear in her heart. Nor, she realized with a start, did she harbor any anger at him for ordering her father's death. Any such hatred had vanished when she had forgiven Durrin.

"I knew *somebody* was coming," Salidar said. "But I never suspected you would come yourself. You really placed that much trust in the herald who visited you?"

"How did you know?" Adara demanded.

"Please," said Salidar, waving a hand. "This is *my* army. How would I not know?"

"Where is he?"

"Ah, don't fret. He's quite secure. For now. Who knows? Maybe you'll join him before the day is up."

Adara refused to be intimidated. "You wouldn't dare arrest me, Lord Salidar. I have the emperor's personal guarantee of safety. When he finds out—"

"Ah, but he *won't* find out." Salidar smirked. "That's the beautiful thing. The emperor doesn't even know you're coming. I intercepted that meddling little farmer before he could let his master know."

The news filled her heart with dismay, but she stood her ground. "Then the emperor will suspect that something is afoot. He'll be watching you closely. And when he finds out that you've captured me, your career will be finished. Are you willing to take that risk, Salidar?"

"I see that time has not made you any wiser," Salidar sniffed. "Risk? Let's talk a moment about risk. If I let you meet with the emperor, you will try to ruin everything. Why would I *risk* you bringing down around me everything I've worked for three decades to accomplish?"

"Ruin everything?" Adara raised an eyebrow. "By bringing peace? By ending this war and saving thousands of lives, both of my people and yours? The siege will be bloody. Saven will not fall without exacting untold losses on your men."

Salidar waved a hand dismissively. "Bah! What is the blood of a few peasants, compared to the glory and expansion of Calamar? No, I cannot let you meet with the emperor. He is timid, weak, and exasperatingly sentimental. He might actually listen to you."

Adara widened her eyes. "How can you say such things of your master?!"

"I owe him no allegiance," Salidar said. "My allegiance is to Calamar. So far as the emperor lets me do what is best for my nation, so be it. But the day he does not . . ." Salidar leaned close, narrowing his eyes until they were mere slits. ". . . I will have him removed. Just as I will do with you."

He leaned back. "But I will be generous, Your Majesty. Return to your city. I would not have your blood upon me."

Adara met his gaze. "You're afraid. You're afraid that if I go missing, the emperor will suspect you. But I will not turn back."

"Afraid?" Lord Salidar's visage darkened as his voice filled with anger. "I will show you that I am not afraid! You have been warned."

A moment of silence passed.

Adara coughed politely. "Warned about what?"

Lord Salidar narrowed his eyes. "I said, *you have been warned!*" he repeated, with greater emphasis.

Adara felt her skin itching. She took a step back. "You cannot hide the truth from the emperor forever, Lord Salidar. He *will* find out that you ordered my father's death."

Lord Salidar didn't seem to hear her. He turned and peered into the woods to Adara's left. After a moment, his eyes returned to her, burning with anger. He drew a dagger from his robes. "Then I'll deal with you myself."

A cry came from the trees. "No!"

An arrow hissed through the foliage and dug into Lord Salidar's leg. He cried out in pain and crumpled, the knife dropping into the undergrowth. He grabbed his leg and rolled on the ground, hissing through clenched teeth.

Adara hesitated, unsure what to do. Every instinct told her to flee while she was still alive.

Still, she wavered. No further arrows came hissing from the shadows. Lord Salidar lay in the dirt, gasping and quivering. Ignoring her survival instincts, trusting instead in her heart, she knelt by the fallen nobleman. "I am a healer," she said, touching his shoulder. "I can take a look at that wound."

Lord Salidar snapped his teeth at her. "Go," he hissed. "If the demons have robbed me of your life this day, don't give me the pain of your pity."

Adara looked at him with sadness. "I hope we never meet again," she said softly. Then she turned in the direction of the war camp and ran.

Thirty seconds later, she broke free of the stand of trees. As she ran, she glanced back, half expecting Salidar—or soldiers under his command—to emerge from the trees in pursuit. But the woods were still.

"You, there! Girl! Halt!"

Adara ground to a stop. Two swifters had risen from the grass ahead of her, where they had been crouching almost invisible. "Identify yourself!" one barked, ears pulled back in suspicion.

Sometimes the truth was the best option. Adara pointed back the way she had come. "His Excellency, Lord Salidar!" she panted. "Injured by an assassin! He needs help!"

The two swifters glanced between her and the trees, uncertain and confused. Fortunately, at that moment Lord Salidar's pain-filled screams rose above the trees. "Help! Soldiers! Help!"

The two swifters glanced at each other, then raced toward the trees. One let out a massive howl to alert nearby patrols. Within seconds, Adara found herself alone again.

"Well, that worked out quite nicely," she said to herself, and fell back into a run.

Salidar had scarcely watched Queen Everborn slip away then he twisted to see Yorid stepping from the bushes, bow in hand.

"Traitor," Salidar snapped.

Yorid crouched next to him, eyes devoid of pity. "'What is the blood of a few peasants?'" he said, imitating Salidar's voice. Then he slapped him in the face. "Two of my brothers died for you!" he said, his face turning red. "And this is how you reward their sacrifice? Ordering me to murder a child? Threatening to kill the emperor himself?"

Salidar coughed out a tooth, then gathered air into his lungs. "Help! Soldiers! Help!"

Yorid grabbed the arrow in Salidar's leg and twisted it, causing spasms of pain to flood his leg. His cries ended in a gasp.

"Let some of your *own* blood run for this nation!" Yorid growled. "See how it feels!"

"You would kill me then?" Salidar hissed, clenching his teeth from the pain.

"And be a murderer like you?" Yorid said. "Never." He rose and disappeared into the woods.

Chapter 53

A Desperate Chance

Adara ran through the Calamarvan war camp. She knew it attracted attention, but she ran, rather than walked, for several reasons. Part of her feared that Salidar would send soldiers after her. She also needed to regain lost time. Salidar's trap had cost her a quarter of an hour. With Halorn having been intercepted, perhaps the emperor wasn't expecting her. But just in case he was, she didn't want to be late.

Finally, she ran because she could not bear to walk. Not today. Not now, when she was so close. She would either succeed or she would fail. She would either save her people or doom them. But she was tired of waiting.

Periodically, Adara stopped a camp worker—someone who didn't look too intimidating—and asked directions to the imperial headquarters. That earned her some interesting stares, but the people were always obliging and pointed farther in. Soon she spotted it: a clump of truly massive tents, surrounded by a ring of red and gold banners.

After what seemed like an eternity, she jogged up to the imposing command complex. Only then did she realize the scope of her problem. A fence of stakes had been erected around the entire complex. Gaps were frequent, but guards stood at each one. What if she tried to get into the complex and got detained long enough for Salidar to return?

Yet again, Adara considered giving up. She could wait until nightfall, slip out of the camp, then retreat to Saven.

No. She had already made her decision. It was too late to turn back.

Adara strolled forward, burying her trembling nerves under a demeanor of confidence. She decided to approach the main entrance to the complex. There, six korrik guards stood at attention, each bedecked in brilliant red uniforms and bearing heavily ornamented spears that looked both imposing but also incredibly impractical.

"Halt," one korrik said, holding up a hand as Adara approached. "State your business."

"I have an audience with His Highest and Most Estimable Lordship," Adara said. At least her tutors had taught her the correct titles to use.

Her words instantly grabbed the attention of all six guards. They looked her up and down. Adara became painfully conscious of the mud splattered all over her simple dress. She was scared to see what shape her hair must have been in. Her face started growing pink in embarrassment. No! She had to remain confident!

"I have an audience—" Adara began to repeat.

"Pass of admittance?" the first korrik barked.

"A—A what?" Adara asked, her stomach dropping to her too-flimsy slippers.

"Pass of admittance," the korrik drawled. "To get into the compound. Surly a maid with an appointment with *His Lordship* would have a little slip of paper."

Adara felt her face turning rapidly from pink to white. Halorn likely had been given such a pass. But he was nowhere to be found. She felt the paralyzing grip of panic start to close around her heart.

A single memory drove it back.

The Light is stronger than your fears.

Adara pushed the panic aside. "Who is your captain, soldier?" she asked, trying to stand tall. It helped that even though these korriks were tall for their species, she was still a head taller than them.

"A captain won't let you in either," the korrik said, "if you don't have a pass."

"I wasn't going to ask him for admittance," Adara said. "I was going to have him discipline you for blatant disrespect."

"Disrespect?" the korrik guffawed. "Toward *you?*"

"Toward His Highest and Most Estimable Lordship," Adara said. "Did I not hear you correctly, or did you a moment ago *truncate* His Highest and Most Estimable Lordship's proper title?"

The guard spluttered. "I did not—"

"You *did.* I heard it loud and clear." She turned to the other guards. "Am I not right?"

They nodded, smirking.

The first korrik looked at his companions. "That's not disrespectful, is it? I mean—it's such a *long* title! Surely His Lordship doesn't really expect us to say the whole—"

"There you go again," Adara said with a singsong tone. "Now, where is your captain?"

The korrik looked pleadingly at his companions. "You're not going to take this, are you?"

One of the others grunted. "I don't know. You about earned a flogging, I think."

"You gonna report your own brood brother, Cragaxe?"

While the korriks argued, Adara glanced around. As she had hoped, her encounter was starting to attract attention—just hopefully not the *wrong* attention. Across the compound, two humans were striding toward her, dark expressions on their faces. *Uh-oh.* Were those servants of Lord Salidar, with orders to look out for any unusual envoy?

"Soldiers, what do we have here?" a voice asked. Adara had been so intent on watching the two humans that she hadn't seen a tall avir step up. He wore ornate robes of purest silk, dyed extravagant colors: obviously a high-ranking official.

The soldiers bowed. "Your Excellency," said the one who had first addressed Adara. "This young maid claims to have an audience with His Highest and Most Estimable Lordship, but she does not even have a pass of admittance." He shot her a glance as he enunciated the full title. She smiled at him.

"Thank you for detaining her, sergeant," the avir said. He held a hand out to Adara. "I will question her further."

Adara took his hand and crossed through the gate, nodding her thanks to the avir outwardly while inwardly trying to gauge his status and disposition. He was certainly high-ranking—even Lord Salidar didn't wear clothing quite so decorated, though likely that had to do with the man's practical considerations. The avir was perhaps in his sixties. His eyes were keen, but not menacing, as he looked Adara up and down. Then he looked over at the two men, now almost upon them.

"Ah," he said. "Sir Nirvait and Master Kivald. Do you bear me any news?"

The two men stopped short, glancing at each other. "No, but—"

"Excellent. I've been gathering troop reports, but I'm still missing numbers from the Fortitude and Indomitable Battalions. Could you see about that, please? I'm afraid it's urgent."

The two men hesitated a moment, glaring at Adara like two foxes would stare at a plump chicken safe in a coop just out of reach. Then they bowed low, expressed their consent, and scurried off.

The avir watched them leave, his eyes narrowed, then strode quickly to a nearby tent. He ushered Adara inside, looked around, then followed her. "You seek an audience with His Lordship?" he asked in a low voice.

"Yes," Adara replied.

"Were you supposed to come with someone?"

This avir knew more than he was letting on. How much could she trust him? "Yes," she said slowly. "A human male, about thirty years old."

The avir nodded. "His name?"

Adara eyed him. If she said Halorn's name, would she be incriminating him? "Who are you?" she asked.

"High Lord Vandil, Chief Steward to His Lordship," the avir said.

Okay—so maybe she'd been a bit harsh on the korrik, considering here was the emperor's own steward tossing around the abbreviated form.

"And you are?" Lord Vandil continued.

Adara's mind raced. She hadn't even thought to come up with a fake name. "I . . . I'm—"

"You're Queen Adara Everborn," the steward said.

Adara nearly sprang out of her slippers. "How did you—" She bit it back. *Fool!* If the steward was just hazarding a guess, her reaction had certainly confirmed it.

"His Lordship told me to keep an eye out for a royal emissary, dressed as a common maid," Lord Vandil said. "I thought at first that you were one of the queen's servants, sent on her behalf. But only a queen would speak to me with the authority that you did."

Adara blushed. She hadn't addressed him with any title, nor had she followed the Calamarvan protocol of avoiding eye contact. Now, she realized, it was the steward who was keeping his gaze respectfully lowered. Unlike Salidar, he was honoring her status as queen and admitting his own inferiority. Well, that was a good sign, at least.

"I was supposed to rendezvous with the farmer outside the camp," Adara said. "But he never showed up."

"A man named Halorn?" the steward asked.

Adara nodded. "I believe Salidar captured him."

Lord Vandil scowled. "This whole camp is crawling with Lord Salidar's spies. Were you . . . intercepted by anyone on your way here?"

"Lord Salidar himself," Adara said. "He was about to kill me, when someone in the trees shot him in the leg and I escaped."

The steward nodded. "Yes . . . the man who claimed to have injured him got here minutes before you did. Luckily for him, your stories match. Tell me: did Salidar say anything treasonous about the emperor?"

"He said that he owed His Lordship no loyalty," Adara said, "and that his only loyalty was to Calamar. He said that as long as the emperor let him do what was best for Calamar, he was content. But the moment the emperor gets in the way, Lord Salidar will have him removed."

The steward nodded, furrowing his brow. "Then there are two witnesses against him now. If only it was possible to arrest Salidar . . . but I digress. Come. I will grant your audience with the emperor."

Half an hour later, Adara waited just a few rooms away from Emperor Stoneclaw's throne room. Well, throne *tent*, although this was by far the largest tent Adara had ever seen. It was as tall as a two-story building and at least a hundred feet long. Made from the finest materials, painted the brightest reds and golds, and bedecked with dozens of pennants and banners, it towered over the other tents around it.

Inside, the place was a maze of fabric crawling with servants and guards, all dressed in lavish uniforms sporting the imperial colors. She decided she liked the emperor's color scheme more than Lord Salidar's blue and sable.

Lord Vandil had gone ahead of her to announce her arrival to the emperor and to talk with him about Lord Salidar. In the meantime, he had given Adara access to a private room, a brush, a wash basin, and a much-needed change of clothes. Her torn and soiled maid's dress discarded, Adara now stood in a flowing green gown, tied with a silver sash. Her hair she had pulled back in a simple braid. It was a far cry from a queen's outfit, but at least she wouldn't be walking into the emperor's presence with mud all over her.

She glanced through the curtain to the antechamber of the throne room beyond. Several guards stood at attention, but Lord Vandil had not yet emerged. She had a few minutes still.

Taking a deep breath, Adara knelt on the room's rug. She touched her forehead and then her heart, as she whispered a prayer with a trembling voice.

> *"Father of Stars, hear me.*
> *Soften the emperor's heart.*
> *Give me the tongue of angels.*
> *Guide me. Lead me. Save me."*

She waited, listening to the peace that came to her heart.

Then she stood and stepped through the curtain. Lord Vandil waited in the antechamber beyond. He bowed. "His Highest and Most Estimable Lordship will see you now."

Ahh. So when guards and servants were about, he used the full title. Noted.

Adara took a deep breath and walked into the throne chamber.

The sight took her breath away. Although the room was small—perhaps twenty feet by thirty feet—it was almost as lavishly decorated as Adara's permanent throne room. Light filtered in through screens on the ceiling, illuminating tapestries depicting triumphs in Calamarvan imperial history. Gold and silver glittered everywhere. The room was heavily furnished with chairs, tables, and even couches.

And the emperor—he was magnificent. The swifter stood taller than any other swifter Adara had ever seen, with a lithe and muscled frame. His long, golden-brown fur seemed to shimmer. No . . . it really *was* shimmering. Had he dusted his fur with flecks of gold? The effect was stunning. As he paced back and forth on his raised dais, sunlight reflected off his fur, shooting beams of light through the room and turning the tapestried walls into mosaics of moving light.

A magnificent chain hung around his neck, studded with topaz and set with a massive ruby, and atop his head gleamed a matching crown. He was old—although with swifters, age was hard to gauge—but his face displayed keen intelligence, and his eyes shone with the deep well of energy common to all swifters.

This was the ruler who had let Lord Salidar wield so much control over him? Adara had expected someone . . . weaker. As much as she despised Salidar, she felt a newfound appreciation for his political acumen.

"Her Majesty, Queen Adara Everborn, Sovereign of Elandria," Lord Vandil announced, though not loud enough for anyone outside the thick, padded walls to overhear. Adara gave a deep curtsy, but when she stood, she held the emperor's gaze. This would be a negotiation among equals.

"Your Highest and Most Estimable Lordship," she said. "It is truly an honor to be granted this personal audience."

The emperor did not immediately respond. Instead, he loped off his dais and prowled around Adara, looking her up and down. She did her best to hold still, conscious of the swifter's razor-sharp claws and muscled jaw. He came so close she could feel his hot breath on her arms. If he wanted to, he could pounce on her and tear her to pieces in seconds. *And the guards insisted on searching me?* Adara thought. *What would a hidden knife do against* him?

Finally, the emperor returned to his dais. "So it *is* you," he said, his voice a magnificent purr. "I worried you would send a double. But you look and smell so much like your father."

Adara bowed her head. "Thank you, Your Highest and Most—"

"Please," the emperor said, waving a paw dismissively. "Just 'Emperor Stoneclaw.'" He looked reflective. "It's what your father knew me as."

"Thank you, Emperor Stoneclaw," Adara said. "You may call me Queen Everborn."

"Everborn," the emperor said, repeating the name slowly. "Your father was a good king. A great leader. Kind. Generous."

"He was a magnificent father," Adara said. "I try every day to follow his example."

"It was only a few weeks ago that I learned the truth about how he died," the emperor said. A growl escaped his lips. "About how deep Salidar's treachery has been all these years. It was the farmer you met yesterday who told me the news."

So that was what had convinced him to come. But how had Halorn known?

"My regents kept the secret exceedingly well," Adara said. "I myself didn't know until just a few months ago."

She waited for the emperor to respond, but he seemed lost in a memory, staring at the motes of dust floating in the dappled light of the throne room.

She took a deep breath. *It's best to get to the point*, she thought. "Emperor Stoneclaw, my purpose in coming here is to negotiate an end to the war between our two nations. Like my father before me, I seek peace."

"You are very direct," the emperor said, sounding amused. "I'm curious to hear your argument."

"You have many reasons to continue this war," Adara began. "You have won great swaths of territory, conquered mighty cities, and subjugated many of my subjects. You have won treasure and renown, and the fame and fear of Calamar have spread throughout the continent.

"To all observers, it appears that you stand at the cusp of finishing this war. Your army is numerous, well-trained, and equipped with the implements of siege. Saven is within your grasp, and once it falls, all of Elandria will be yours for the taking. You will win riches, prestige, and perhaps most importantly, full control over the haeber trade on the Silvermoss."

"When you put it that way," the emperor said, his eyes serious, "ending this conflict prematurely should be the *last* thing on my mind. Is there *any* reason I should consider peace?"

"Of course," Adara said.

"Then please, tell me what they are."

"I do not need to," Adara said. "You yourself know them. Otherwise, why agree to meet with me?"

The emperor smiled, revealing his razor-sharp teeth. He settled down onto the rich carpet of his dais, flicking his tail back and forth. "An insightful question. But I'm curious to know your thoughts. Why do *you* think I should pursue peace?"

Adara frowned. She had hoped for a more candid conversation. Maybe his trust still needed to be earned.

She took a deep breath. "First, Your Lordship, consider the unforeseen consequences of victory. Conquering Elandria, while tempting now, may be disastrous in the long run. Do you remember what happened when your father annexed the plains of Jenmar?"

The emperor looked intrigued. "They became part of Calamar. Our power and wealth spread."

"And did holding Jenmar lead to any trouble?"

"Well, yes," the emperor admitted. "My father had to deal with the Crecks, warrior tribes in the southeast."

"And what did that lead to?"

"Well, the Crecks received support from the king of Orlan, who feared our growing power."

Adara nodded. "So you invaded Orlan. And once you invaded Orlan, you had disputes with the trade guilds of Wormul over tariff rights. So you conquered Wormul. By conquering Orlan and Wormul, you then shared a border with us, and more problems ensued."

The emperor frowned. "And your point is . . ."

"My point is this: Imagine you conquer Elandria. All of it. Now Elandria's borders are Calamar's borders. What will you have? You'll find Drilandi raiders on your northern borders. They come nearly every winter. Your army will have to handle that. You'll also share a southern border with Larrissa. My father and I have maintained a good relationship with them, but that's because they don't see us as threatening. I don't think they will take kindly to Calamarvan banners at their borders. You'll also border the Mitrians to the east, a people easily offended and wrathful in war.

"So my point is this. In the last fifty years, Calamar has continually expanded in the name of protecting its interests. But the more it expands, then the more peoples and kingdoms it borders, the more enemies it makes, and the more interests it needs to protect. Does that make sense?"

The emperor eyed her shrewdly. Then he nodded. "It does."

"There are only three ways this can end. First, Calamar will grow until it controls the whole world. No offense, but I find that unlikely. Second, Calamar will overextend itself, until there's a year when it tries to fight too many wars on too many fronts, and all its hard-fought gains are lost in a few sound defeats. The third possibility—which I hope you will see the soundness of—is that Calamar surrounds itself with stable borders and firm allies. Allies like Elandria."

"And you can offer that?" the emperor said.

Adara met his gaze. "My father did."

The emperor didn't respond. For a minute, he sat crouched on his dais, mulling over Adara's words. He looked deep in thought. Adara wondered if he'd ever heard the pattern she'd described before.

Finally, he stirred. "A persuasive argument, though the future is always uncertain. Can you offer me *other* reasons I should halt this war?"

"I can," Adara said. "Continuing this war will weaken your political power." The emperor voiced no objection, so Adara continued. "We both know how powerful Lord Salidar has become. He has complete control over many of your provinces, and most of your battalions are loyal directly to him. This war has largely been fought on his terms.

"If you annex Elandria, you will find Lord Salidar's power nearly absolute. The military governors appointed over Elandria will likely come from his army and thus also be loyal directly to him. Your authority will diminish until you are little more than a figurehead, stripped of any real power."

The emperor licked his paw. "Perhaps. Perhaps not. I've reigned with Lord Salidar as vizier for nearly two decades now, and he hasn't made any attempt to seize the throne or defy me."

Adara glanced at Lord Vandil, standing in a corner of the room. The avir had turned red with anger. It was obvious he didn't like Lord Salidar. Adara glanced back at the emperor. Why couldn't swifters be as easy to read?"

"With all due respect, Emperor Stoneclaw," Adara said. "We both know the situation with Lord Salidar has grown severe. Scarcely an hour ago, I heard him threaten—no, not threaten—*state* that he would kill you at the drop of a pin should you ever oppose him. You know that I heard this, and that I was not the only witness."

Once again, the emperor didn't immediately respond. Rising to his feet, he began prowling back and forth across the dais. Finally, he turned.

"You have argued well, Queen Adara. Now it is my turn to give a reason for arranging this meeting. Perhaps I invited you as a ruse. Perhaps I wanted to make victory easier for me by eliminating Elandria's queen, sparking chaos in the capital a day before my armies strike."

Fear bubbled up in Adara. Was this it, then? Had she come all this way just to be seized and killed?

No. She pushed the fear down. She knew Halorn had been sincere. She had felt it was *right* to come here. The emperor couldn't be serious. Was he playing with her, like a cat with a mouse?

No, she realized. He was testing her spine.

"There is one more reason you should seek peace," Adara said. Her hands trembled with nerves. Did she dare say it?

"And that is?"

"Earlier this week, my emissaries finalized an alliance with the Mitrian Tribes," Adara said. "I learned of it just this morning." *Through a dream,* she thought but didn't dare voice. "Fifteen thousand Mitrian riders are already on their way here. They will arrive in five or six days. Up to ten thousand more will shortly follow. Perhaps you can survive their assault and continue your siege of the city. But you will lose tens of thousands of lives."

"You are bluffing," Emperor Stoneclaw said. But she could see the alarm in his eyes.

"Give it a day or two, and your own scouts will report their movements and numbers," Adara said. "You have never faced the Mitrians in battle. They are formidable opponents, and especially effective on the open plain, where their horses can outmaneuver any infantry."

Emperor Stoneclaw and Lord Vandil exchanged worried glances.

"Declare an armistice, and I will call off my allies," Adara said. "But attack the city, or kill me now, and they will show no mercy."

Her words hung in the air.

After a minute, the emperor bowed his head. "What I implied—about inviting you only as a ruse—"

"It was a test," Adara said. "You wanted see if I would stay calm under pressure. I knew you would not hurt me. After all, you gave me your word of protection. And emperors always keep their word."

Adara hadn't meant the words to be harsh, but they seemed to strike a chord with the swifter. The emperor's tail stopped twitching, and he looked away. "I wish I could say the same," he said softly.

"I know you knew my father well," Adara said. "I know he helped your kingdom, on more than one occasion. I know you made a pact of peace between our two nations."

"It was never officially ratified," the emperor said. He didn't meet Adara's gaze.

"You do not have to justify yourself." Adara let her tone grow soft. "I know the pressures that have been on you. The events of the past decade have not been entirely in your control. I do not blame you for breaking your promise."

She waited until he met her eyes again, then continued in a strong voice. "But I do call upon you to honor it now, when it matters most. On behalf of my dead father, I call upon you to end this war!"

For a long moment they stood, two sovereigns of warring nations, their gazes locked.

Then Emperor Stoneclaw turned away. "I wish I could," he whispered. He shook his mighty head. "I never wanted this war, Queen Everborn. I could barely stand to see your kingdom invaded. But Lord Salidar convinced me it was necessary."

"Then end it," Adara said.

"I can't."

Adara frowned. That was not the answer she'd been expecting. "What do you mean, you can't?"

"It's not in my power!" the emperor howled. His air of power had disappeared, replaced with desperation. "I'm trapped, Queen Everborn! If I order Salidar to break off the attack, I forfeit my life. Salidar's web of spies is too thick. If I move to arrest him, his soldiers will refuse to comply, and his agents among my staff will have me killed by nightfall. That's the real reason I've left him in power for so long—I've been afraid of him. And now I know for certain he's both willing and capable of killing me whenever he wishes."

He said it so bluntly. Adara wondered at the sight: the most powerful ruler in the world, so completely powerless.

"But there must be some way," Adara said.

"Actually," Lord Vandil spoke up from his corner of the room. "I think Queen Everborn can offer us the solution."

Chapter 54

Rogue

Salidar winced as the pair of snippen surgeons worked to sew up his leg. "You said this wouldn't hurt," he gasped.

"Sorry, milord," stammered the assistant surgeon. He handed Salidar an aquamancy vial. "Drink another two drops, but no more. It should numb the remaining pain."

Salidar took three drops, then leaned back, closing his eyes and waiting for the tonic to kick in as the lead surgeon finished his stitches.

He heard a rustle as the tent flap opened and a swifter stepped lightly inside. "Your Excellency," she said gingerly, in a tone that clearly harbingered bad news.

"Spit it out and get it over with," Salidar snapped. "I'm already having a bad day."

"We're close to locating Yorid," the swifter reported. "He was seen entering the emperor's compound around an hour and a half ago. We've alerted our agents to seize him at the first opportunity."

The surgeon pulled particularly hard on a stitch, and Salidar gasped in pain. "Go on," he said, waving a hand. "I know that's not all your report."

The swifter shifted from paw to paw nervously. "The emperor concluded his meeting with Queen Everborn and is now escorting her back toward Saven personally."

"Of course he is," Salidar muttered. He had been hoping the emperor would send the queen back with an imperial escort—an escort that Salidar could intercept with a faked imperial order to have her marched to Salidar's command post instead. But with the emperor himself present, that would be impossible.

"And High Lord Vandil?"

"He is with them. The steward selected their entourage very carefully, Your Excellency. We haven't a single trusted agent among them."

Alarm began to build in Salidar's chest. The situation had been slipping further and further out of his control the whole morning, and this news only made it worse. "Tell Captain Vox to ready four platoons of cavalry. And have them prepare my horse." He looked at the snippens still bustling around his leg. "Aren't you done already?"

"Almost, almost," the lead surgeon said, tying off the last stitch as his assistant wiped the area clean of blood. "Just need to wrap the wound."

Hurry, you fool, a dark voice echoed in his mind. *Make haste!*

But it took five more minutes for the surgeons to finish their work, and another five minutes for him to hobble outside, mount his horse, and wait for the platoons to form up. As he waited, he nudged his horse over to a fully enclosed wagon, unlatching and sliding open a small panel set into the side. After a few seconds, a bruised face appeared at the bars.

"Rise and shine, meddling farmer," Salidar said, hiding his scorn behind a thin veil of pleasantry. "How do you feel?"

"Like I was kicked and beaten half the night," Halorn responded dryly. He nodded at the bandage around Salidar's thigh. "Nice new fashion statement, Your Evilency."

The comment deserved a slap, but unfortunately the barred window prevented that. Instead, Salidar leaned forward. "Listen, Hal-whatever-your-name-was. You will rot in chains each day and face a beating each night until you tell me what exactly you told the emperor back in Imperium."

Salidar suspected the news had been the true nature of King Everborn's death, and who had ordered it. But how in the Void's shadow would this farmer have known?

Halorn stared back at him calmly, his face looking somehow noble. It was a bit unnerving. "I make no dealings with those in league with demons."

Salidar nearly jumped out of his robes with surprise. He wanted to grab the farmer by the throat and demand how he knew. But no. This man couldn't know. He must be using it as an expression, nothing more.

An officer rode up. "We're ready, Your Excellency."

Salidar turned back to Halorn. "Consider changing your mind," he hissed. "While you still have a mind to change."

Halorn met his gaze, a look of pure confidence in his eyes. "I promised my wife and children that I would return to them in safety," he said. "I intend to keep that promise."

Salidar reined his horse to a halt three hundred yards out from Saven's gates. He raised a hand, and the rest of the column of cavalry halted as well.

He scanned the empty road before them, then cursed. "We're too late! She's gone!"

One of his officers rode up beside him. "And the emperor? Shouldn't we have seen his retinue on the way back?"

A sinking feeling spread through Salidar's body. "He wouldn't," the vizier whispered.

"Wouldn't what?"

A horseman galloped up to them from the direction of the city. "Your Excellency!" the messenger cried. "His Lordship Emperor Stoneclaw has entered the city!"

The officers around Salidar murmured in surprise, but Salidar merely nodded at the confirmation of what he already suspected. "How long ago?"

"Five minutes. As soon as they left the camp's limits, they rode to the city at a full gallop. It's as if they were worried they'd be pursued."

Salidar turned to the officer next to him. "Lieutenant, your helmet, please."

"My helmet?"

"I need it."

The lieutenant hesitantly removed his red-plumed helm and handed it over. Salidar yanked it out of his grasp, then screamed at the top of his lungs as he slammed the helmet into the ground. Yanking a spear out of a nearby rider's hands, he shrieked again as he plunged the tip into the helmet again and again, until the spear was blunted beyond use and the helmet was covered in dents.

His officers sat in stunned silence, several of them discretely nudging their horses away from their commander.

"Thank you," Salidar said, handing the spear back to its owner and resuming his collected demeanor. "You may retrieve your helmet."

At that moment, a bell rang out from the city, its clarion ring splitting the quiet morning air. It rang a second time, then a third time. Then smaller and higher bells joined it, filling the air with their joyful din. A shout rose from the city, hundreds of voices raised in an exultant cry.

"They've killed the emperor!" an officer cried, drawing his sword.

Salidar shook his head, dread collecting in his stomach. "No. Something else is afoot." He pointed to a griffin winging toward them from the city. "See? Here come tidings."

The griffin circled above them, shouting his news. "His Highest and Most Estimable Lordship has declared an armistice! All hostilities are to cease immediately! As a token of goodwill, he and his retinue have entered the city with Queen Everborn's blessing."

Not waiting for a response, the griffin sped off for the war camp to spread the news.

In his wake, Salidar's officers erupted in outrage.

"An armistice?"

"We won't take the city?"

"But it's within our grasp!"

"The troops will never stand for this."

Salidar paid them no heed. Instead, he turned his horse and rode to the rear of the column, where a thin, sinister-looking man dressed in an immaculate uniform took up the rearguard: the overseer of Salidar's assassination team. Salidar waved him aside where they could talk in private.

"The emperor is no longer useful to me," Salidar hissed. "What are our options?"

The man shook his head. "Next to nothing. The group that accompanied the emperor was hand-picked by Lord Vandil. None of my agents were included."

"But our contacts in the imperial guard—"

"He didn't bring his imperial guard."

Salidar cursed. "Can we get someone into the city?"

"Perhaps if they loosen security. Maybe a snippen could scale the walls, or we could get a griffin in tonight. But the emperor will be suspecting it. He'll be under tight security."

Salidar bit his lip. He had a couple contacts already inside Saven, but they were trained in espionage, not assassination. And he had no quick way to reach them. "We have only a matter of hours, maybe less, before the emperor moves to arrest me," he said.

"Stage a coup," the other man said. "Seize Stoneclaw's throne and attack the city. The army will support you."

Salidar shook his head. "Not with the emperor still alive. Many of the officers would support me, but the rank-and-file soldiers would resist. Especially if he's inside the city we're supposed to attack."

"Then we're out of options."

Salidar's eyes narrowed. "Not quite," he said. "I need a moment to myself."

He rode several dozen yards away from his men, stopping in the shadows of a tree hidden behind a small hillock. He uttered a quick spell to block any sound from escaping his vicinity. Then he let out an ear-piercing scream.

"Archivous!" Salidar cried, shaking a fist. "Why? Why have you failed me? Show your demonic face and explain yourself!"

An unseen presence fell upon him, almost smothering him with its palpable evil. He doubled over in the saddle, knuckles turning white as his fingers tightened around the reins.

Imbecile! a dark voice hissed into his mind. *Spineless dog! You think this is my fault? My fault, when that royal whelp was within your power and you let her go?*

"I was shot in the leg!"

You knew Yorid was weak. You knew he would flinch at the task you set him.

Salidar struggled for breath, his ribcage feeling like it was being crushed. "No, I didn't! I swear!"

Then you are blind, as well as a coward. The pressure on his chest lessened, and Salidar gasped for breath. *But no matter. Elandria is of little concern to me. It is the Bastion that must fall.*

"I can't attack the Bastion if Elandria doesn't fall," Salidar gripped.

Can't you?

The archdemon's plan appeared in Salidar's thoughts, like a picture presented to his view. He cocked his head, considering it.

"It won't work." He shook his head. "The Mitrian tribes will get in my way."

The Mitrian tribes are assembled in one body, and are on their way here as we speak. They approach from the southeast. If you take the northern road, they will not be able to catch you in time. The archdemon laughed. *My adversary fell for my trap. By enlisting their help, she saves Elandria—but in the very act, she leaves the Bastion defenseless.*

"I'd rather conquer a kingdom than destroy a library," Salidar griped.

Destroy the Bastion, the archdemon hissed. *Then—and only then—will I give you the power you seek. Power to destroy the emperor. Power to seize his throne. Power to crush Saven and subjugate Elandria once and for all.*

"You swear it?" Salidar demanded.

A laugh cackled through his mind. *By the pits of the Void. Do you accept?*

Salidar hesitated. "What if I don't?"

Then I stand aside and let the emperor arrest and execute you. Salidar could almost see Archivous's vicious smile. *The choice is yours.*

"Then we both lose. I lose my life, and you lose your chance to destroy the Bastion."

A pause.

Do you want extra incentive? What more must I promise than Calamar's throne?

Salidar ran his tongue across his dry lips. "My soul."

The archdemon's laughter echoed through Salidar's mind. *Your soul? Your soul?!*

Salidar sat up straighter in his saddle. "Swear that if I destroy the Bastion, neither you nor any of your comrades will claim my soul if I die at night."

The laughter continued unabated. Apparently the archdemon found this idea exceptionally funny. After a few moments, the telepathic voice stuttered a response through the diabolical guffaws. *You care . . . about . . . your soul?*

"The idea of eternal agony in the Void doesn't strike me as very pleasant," Salidar muttered.

Still the demon laughed. *It's a bit . . . late . . . for caring about . . . your soul, I'm afraid.*

Salidar stiffened. "What do you mean?"

Oh, this is too funny. You don't know, because you yourself have stamped out the truth. You remember all the ancient texts of the Luminant Order, the texts your men burned? If you had read them, you would know the truth. The angels will never take you to the Halls of the Sun, Salidar. Your eternal scroll is stained with the blood of thousands, blackened with a lifetime of self-serving deeds. They will shudder just from looking at you. No, Salidar—you have been mine for quite a while now, no matter what time of day or night you breathe your last.

"I named my price!" Salidar insisted, though his mind reeled at the demon's words. "If I destroy the Bastion, you will not claim my soul!"

Very well, the demon said. *I agree. But if the Sun won't claim you and the Void won't take you, your soul will be left to wander, homeless, as a specter through the realms of mortals until the World Anchors fall and time comes to an end.*

"Better than the Void," Salidar retorted.

The demon paused. *Fair.*

A moment later, the dark presence lifted from his mind. Salidar sank in the saddle, closing his eyes and taking deep breaths, trying to organize his vortex of thoughts. After a minute, he straightened, tidied up his uniform, and rode back to his officers. They regarded him with concerned looks.

Salidar ignored them. "Head back to camp and order eight companies of cavalry to prepare to ride. Have them pack a week's worth of rations but otherwise travel light. Marshal them on the northeast side of the camp. We ride within the hour!"

Three days later.

Twigly was looking forward to a nice, long nap.

How long had it been since she'd had a day off? Not since their fateful stop at Imperium the previous summer. Since then, she'd either been stewing in a stockade, trekking through the wilderness trying to escape capture, or ferrying some great warrior or leader about somewhere to try and take out some *other* great warrior or leader. On the whole, her crew was getting quite fed up with great warriors and leaders. Good thing she was neither.

After three days of them tacking and churning to return from the Mitrian Mountains, the towers of Saven came into view, prompting a cheer from her crew. She really had to treat them once they were through with all this. Did Volthorn's pledge of a thousand shekels of gold still stand? After all, it wasn't *their* fault an angel had interceded and saved Durrin's life.

Twigly glanced at one of the frigate's compartments. Inside, she knew, rested the long box that the angel had given Durrin. The last two nights, she had seen him remove a scroll from the box and study it late into the evening. Maybe, if Volthorn failed to pay up, she could haggle for that. It seemed kind of valuable.

As they made their final approach over the capital, a griffin greeted them, directing them to dock at a plaza just shy of the palace. Twigly glanced over the side and gulped as she saw a veritable swarm of official-looking people waiting to greet them. There had better not be any bankers in that mix.

Tadgh whistled. "Dancin' dolphins! Looks like ye got quite the welcome committee." He studied the plaza more carefully. "There's a fair bit o' soldiers among that lot. We ain't in trouble, ach we?"

Durrin and Volthorn exchanged glances. "I shouldn't be," said Durrin. "And the war is over, so I don't know what else might be amiss." Word of the armistice had reached them the day before.

Volthorn didn't look as confident. "I . . . wasn't exactly authorized to leave my post. Nor requisition important state prisoners and their vessel."

Twigly's ears drooped. She hoped that didn't bode ill for the thousand shekels of gold. She had payroll coming up.

"There's the queen herself," Durrin said, pointing as they drew closer. "And Cymer."

As soon as the ship was secured, Queen Adara and her staff met Durrin and Volthorn at the base of the rope ladder. She waved for Twigly to join them.

"Captain Skarr, Master Rendhart, Captain Twigly the Barbaric," she said, bowing to each in turn.

Look at that, Twigly thought. *She used my full title. I like her already.*

"I am glad your journey was a success," Adara continued. "And I rejoice that you have returned so soon. We have urgent need of your help."

Twigly raised her paw. "By 'your help,' you mean them, right?" She pointed at the human and korrik.

Queen Adara looked down at her and gave a condoling smile. "I'm afraid you too, and your crew."

Twigly's heart sunk.

"As you should have heard already, the emperor and I have jointly declared an armistice, and are drafting a treaty to bring an end to the conflict," Adara said. "We were hoping to arrest Lord Salidar, but the day the armistice was declared, he slipped around the north side of the city and rode east with a band of his most loyal cavalry. He crossed the Silvermoss and rode east."

Volthorn cursed.

"At first, we thought he was just trying to escape arrest and flee to a foreign land," Adara continued. "But just two hours ago, a scout appraised us of their actual destination. They are heading toward the Bastion of Memory—presumably to destroy it."

Durrin sucked in a breath.

"The Whatzit of Whatnow?" Twigly asked.

"The Bastion of Memory," Adara said, turning to her. "It's, ah—"

The ancient avir beside the queen spoke up. "It's an ancient repository of knowledge and truth, whose destruction would cripple the cause of the Light and potentially tip the balance of the world toward darkness and chaos."

"It's important," Adara summarized.

"How many defenders does the Bastion have?" Volthorn asked.

"A couple dozen, maybe," the old avir said. "Normally they rely upon the Mitrians to defend them from any threat."

"But the Mitrians are on their way here, too far to the south to intercept them," said Volthorn. "Krack's crest! We walked right into this."

"How far out is Salidar?" Durrin asked.

"At the pace he's driving his troops, only about a day," the queen said. "They could commence their attack as early as noon tomorrow. We've already dispatched all the griffins we can spare, but it won't be enough."

Twigly sighed. "And I suppose that's where I come in?"

Adara nodded. "Only with your cloudship do reinforcements have a chance of reaching the Bastion in time."

Twigly shook her head. "Reach the Basta-thingy in twenty-four hours? Can't be done."

"We have two of the army's verbomancers at the ready," Adara said. "They can summon a wind."

Twigly cocked her head, calculating. "Perhaps. It'll be close."

"But the cloudship can only carry two dozen warriors at most," Volthorn objected, scowling as he looked up at the vessel above them. "What will that do against several hundred troops?"

"I will be going," the old avir said. "With Sablewing gone to the distant east, I am the closest mage in the Order and thus am responsible for the library's defense."

"You and Durrin will be going as well," Adara said to Volthorn. "And as many of our best battlefield mancerers as the frigate can fit. They're already assembled and ready, and we have supplies at hand to replenish your stores. And I will be coming too."

Her last sentence caused several heads to turn. "You're *what?*" said a graying swifter standing behind her.

"I'm coming, too," Adara said. "Our best hope is to negotiate a solution with Salidar before he attacks. As queen, I will have the most negotiating clout."

"But your safety—" said Durrin, Volthorn, and the swifter at the same time.

The queen held up her hand, cutting them off. "The Bastion is more important than my safety," she said. "But in the event of an attack, I can be whisked away in the cloud frigate. That reminds me of the other reason to send the cloud frigate: to evacuate as many priceless records as possible."

"And what if I say no?" said Twigly.

Everyone looked at her in alarm.

"My crew and I are not your subjects," Twigly huffed. "We're tired. We just flew a bajillion leagues in one week. Maybe we don't *want* to haul a bunch of crazy heroes to some distant basket-thingy of memorandum to fight a hopeless last stand."

Adara knelt at Twigly's level and clasped her hands together. "Please. I know you and your crew have sacrificed much. I know you do not owe us any friendship, nor favors. But the Bastion of Memory contains the records of hundreds of cultures over thousands of years. It is the center of an order that fights around the world to drive back the encroaching darkness of the Void. With the greatest humility and meekness, I plead for your aid."

Twigly twirled her whiskers. A queen begging for her help? She could get used to this.

Volthorn spoke up. "And we'll throw in a talent of gold, on top of the thousand shekels I already owe you."

"What?" the graying swifter behind Adara yelped.

Twigly burst out laughing. "Deal! And seriously, you thought I wouldn't help you guys?" She jerked a paw at Durrin. "Rendhart here has an *angel* on his side! A real live, bona fide angel! How am I supposed to argue with *that?*"

Chapter 55

Knowledge

The cloudship arrived at the Bastion late the next morning, after flying nonstop through the night. With several of the army's verbomancers on board summoning a stiff wind at their backs, they had made incredible speed.

Cymer offered a silent prayer of gratitude as the library came into view. It was still intact. Salidar had not yet struck.

He disembarked to find a library in chaos, as the staff scrambled to prepare the outer walls for an attack. Over a hundred griffins from Elandria had also arrived, but they could do little to assist in the preparations, nor would they do much against Salidar's battle-hardened troops. The arrival of the cloud frigate was met with many cheers and even tears.

"You came with scarcely an hour to spare," a griffin said, swooping down to meet them. "Lord Salidar's cavalry have entered the valley. They'll be here shortly."

Cymer felt the familiar—but heavy—mantle of leadership settle on his shoulders as he gave orders. "Volthorn, take charge of the defenses," he directed. "Organize the available fighters, divide them into squads, and distribute the extra weapons and gear that we brought."

He turned to Adara. "Your Majesty, you are in charge of negotiations. If you can't do anything else, buy us time. I will be in the library, overseeing the evacuation of the most precious items." Cymer turned to Durrin. "Durrin—"

"I need something from you, actually," Durrin interrupted.

"What is that?"

"An open door."

✳

A few minutes later, Durrin and Cymer stood before a pair of ornate doors at the end of the Hall of Lore. Cymer whispered a phrase too quiet for Durrin to hear, and the doors slid open.

"Are you sure about this?" Cymer asked. "We haven't much time."

"I am sure," Durrin said. He was ready.

Leaving Cymer behind, he strode swiftly into the darkness.

Up ahead, he could hear the murmur of water. His pyrosense already felt the torrent of energy that it veiled. Energy. Knowledge. Light.

Kymar's scroll had spoken of it. Energy. Knowledge. Light. Awareness. Truth. Power. Kymar had said that all these things were one. Durrin was still struggling to understood the legendary master's arcane words. Unlike all the previous scroll, the sixth scroll had held no diagrams, no new routines. Just cryptic ideas.

Energy. Light. Awareness. Truth. Kymar had said that to unlock the power of the sixth scroll, one must know the true nature of these things, and know how to combine them.

In all things, one, Kymar had written on the very last line of the scroll. *Only in unity lies true power.*

Durrin had pondered those words again and again, straining to understand how they unlocked more power than he could already wield. Last night, pondering Kymar's sayings on the cloud frigate, he had felt a flicker of something stir within him. But it had escaped him, and he had failed to repeat the phenomenon.

Sablewing had said that the Curtain would give him the knowledge that he needed most.

Well, he needed this most of all.

The chamber remained exactly as he remembered, except perhaps even more majestic. But he had no time to dwell on the beauty. Swiftly he strode down the slope to the pool, stepping through the water until he stood before the waterfall. For a moment, he paused, studying the flames beyond. Then he plunged forward.

Pain. Piercing agony like he had never felt before swept through his being. For the first time in his life, he felt the searing, scalding, blistering pain of being burned, all across his skin.

Then it was over, and all was dark. Completely dark. He tried to turn, but he didn't seem to have a body to give orders to. He was just a prick of consciousness suspended in a sea of nothingness.

Is this it? Durrin thought, panicking. *Have I been consumed? Is this what death is like?*

But the darkness around him didn't feel like death. It was just . . . nothing.

Then a speck of light appeared in front of him.

It grew brighter, flickering, pulsing, suspended in the nothingness. And in a flash, Durrin understood. He was looking at the birth of his soul. This mote of light was a shard of eternity, fashioned into the first inklings of a star.

As he stared into the depths of his spark, he found himself surrounded by memories, each one too fleeting to hold, but each impossible to ignore. He traveled back through time, steeped in memories good, bad, and mundane. For a moment he was in the snow, grabbing Volthorn by the collar. Then on the cloudship, talking to Twigly and Line. Then shivering in his cell in Irongate Isle. Then studying scrolls late at night in the Academy. Then winning a wrestling match in his youth. For an instant, he was a toddler, taking his first trembling steps.

But the memories didn't stop. He remembered falling, falling, falling through the night sky, a shooting beam of light, burning with excitement. Before that, he was a star, surrounded by thousands of other stars, each one radiant, shining, eternal. Below him, far, far below, was Zenitha. He could see the entire world in one glance: continents, rivers, mountains, oceans, all ringed by the Cosmic Mountain to the south, the Undying Flames to the west, the Endless Clouds to the north, and the Shoreless Sea to the east—except not so shoreless, not so endless, because beyond them all was the beauty of the stars, a thousand million sparks all shining. Durrin remembered eons spent solely in serene meditation.

Other memories came. As a star, Durrin had spent weeks following individual insects, zooming in on them far, far below in the untamed forests of Zenitha, watching them hatch, live, breed, and die from a thousand miles up. He had watched animals hunt and play, seasons ebb and flow, buildings come and go, kingdoms rise and fall.

He had seen other stars around him falling, falling, falling, to live a mortal life in the blink of an eye. He had watched them from their crib to their grave. So many lived only to eat and to laugh, cursing the rocks in the fields they plowed, yet not once looking up at the stars from whence they came, until their body withered into dust and they were taken by angels to the Near or Far Moons, or dragged by demons to the Void.

Other lives burned brighter. They looked up at the heavens and fueled their spark with hope or ambition. Some become kings. Some became generals. Some gained great power and riches, ruling with cruelty until their moment came, their greatness turned to dust, and they became demons, slaves of the Void, to haunt the earth and sell the misery they had bought.

Others learned to love, serve, and give. With each selfless gift, they burned brighter and brighter, until bursting from their mortal bands, they rose rejoicing to burn ever brighter in the Halls of the Sun, or to sweep the earth, spreading their light to sparks below.

Then his memory rolled back even earlier. The space beneath him was a roiling mass. Seven great stars moved to and fro. Fire, water, earth, air, life, death—each leapt into being, clashing and merging in one great harmony. But the seventh star was wrapping itself in a shroud of utter darkness . . .

One last memory swept through Durrin's mind. Before the Void. Before the creation of Zenitha. Before everything. Endless, eternal light, and in the center of that light . . .

Durrin found himself back in the chamber, standing in the pool of water, blinking in the sudden dimness. His body felt unharmed. But he knew his soul would never be the same.

He hurried out of the chamber and down the passage, hoping he was not too late.

Durrin arrived at the walls to find them lined with anxious defenders.

In the narrow valley beyond, Salidar's army waited just out of bowshot: eight hundred battle-hardened cavalry at the ready, their spears glinting in the late morning light. Durrin shielded his eyes from the Sun, studying the distant ranks. He couldn't make out Salidar, but the cluster of banners at the army's center must be where he was.

"What's the status?" Durrin asked, walking up to stand next to Volthorn, Cymer, and Adara.

"We've sent a message asking to negotiate," Adara said. "I haven't revealed yet that I am here."

Durrin pointed to a line of bonfires. "What do you suppose those are?"

"Preparation for fire arrows," Volthorn said. "It's the most logical route of attack. Pepper our courtyard and the library beyond. Keep us busy putting out flames. Then unleash a barrage of arrows and storm the walls. We've seen them building ladders."

"And a battering ram," Twigly said, sauntering up to them. "Pretty little pumpkin you've gotten yourselves in. Good thing *I* have an escape balloon."

Durrin looked down the length of the wall. The defenses were well constructed, spanning the whole length of the canyon, with crenellations, towers, and a strong gatehouse. But the defenders were few, and most were poorly trained. Salidar would probably launch an all-out assault, careless for the casualties he would incur among his own troops.

A trumpet blasted from beyond the wall.

"A herald!" Volthorn cried. "Thank the stars."

"Thank the Sky Father," Adara said.

They watched through the crenellations of the wall as a swifter, decked in the blues and whites of a herald, stopped twenty paces from the gate. Behind him, a korrik carried the standard of Calamar and a trumpet almost as long as he was tall.

"Salutations!" bellowed the swifter. "From His Excellency, Lord of the Western Provinces, Captain of the Host of Ten Thousand, Vanquisher of All Foes, and High Vizier of the Eternal Empire of Calamar, Salidar Aram."

"Former vizier," Volthorn muttered.

"To her most honored High Mage Sablewing," the herald continued, "Head Librarian of the Bastion of Memory, and to her assembled court and staff: Let all hear, so that all may bear witness, that on this day, being the thirteenth rising of the Sun in the month Anil, in the nineteenth year of the reign of His Highest and Most Estimable Lordship Stoneclaw son of Ironclaw, may he prosper under the Sun, His Excellency Lord Salidar doth invoke the ancient customs of warfare, proposing that before this field be bathed with blood, let the most honored Sablewing send forth a champion, worthy of songs, and let His Excellency Lord Salidar send forth a champion, of equal renown, and let them battle, alone and unaided. So that when one conquers by the will of the stars, and thus display the superiority of his nation in the art of war, let his opponents thus be fore-warned, so that should they opt to neither withdraw nor yield up their arms, but rather persist in their intention to fight, their spilt blood shall not stain the hems of their most worthy vanquishers."

The swifter fell silent. For a moment, the only sound that could be heard was the snapping of Calamar's banner in the wind.

Volthorn was the first to break the silence. "That rotted snail of a nobleman," he muttered. "Three weeks of ignoring my challenges on the southern front, and *now* he respects the ancient customs?"

"But why?" said Adara. "It makes no sense."

Outside the gate, the swifter called, "I will give you five minutes to respond."

Cymer, Adara, Volthorn, and Durrin exchanged glances.

"Thoughts?" Cymer said.

"Salidar doesn't know we're here," Durrin guessed. "He probably thinks the defenders are desperate and will grasp at the chance to buy time with a duel. A mancerer defending a wall is more valuable than a mancerer assaulting it, so Salidar probably wants to eliminate the library's best mancerer before his assault."

"But who is his champion?" Adara asked.

Volthorn squinted, thinking deeply. "As far as I'm aware, all of Calamar's most powerful battle mancerers stayed behind with the emperor. It's possible Salidar himself means to accept the challenge, though it strikes me as a bit overconfident, even for him."

"Maybe," said Durrin, "but a wide expanse like this is the best arena for verbomancy. Lots of room for windstorms and casting spells from a distance."

"What if he *does* know we're here?" Adara asked. "A griffin patrol could easily have spotted our cloudship."

"If so, then he must not suspect that Volthorn and I were on board," Durrin said. "He may be vain and overconfident, but not *that* overconfident."

"So who do we send?" Cymer asked.

Everyone was silent for a moment.

"I'll do it," Volthorn said.

"No," Durrin said. "You haven't replenished all the gems you depleted last week." *When you almost killed me*, he added silently, though without resentment.

Volthorn set his jaw. "So? I'm not scared of that buttoned-up ball of ice."

Durrin shook his head in frustration. *Stubborn as always.* "And when he freezes the air around you solid, and you can't breathe? What then? Don't tell me he can't—he pulled the technique on me last year. I barely managed to break free. I don't think your wards will protect you."

"I'd like to see him cast the spell while a rock-shard grenade hits him," Volthorn growled.

Durrin nearly rolled his eyes. "You're all out of rock-shard grenades."

The trumpeter beyond the walls blew a short blast on the trumpet. "I still await your response!" the swifter called.

"Impatient little kitten," Twigly muttered.

"I'll do it," Durrin said.

He waited for someone to object. No one did.

Cymer studied him for a long moment. "By rights, this duty should fall on me. But I am old, and warfare has never been my study. Durrin, do you swear to defend the cause of the Light with your very life?"

"I do."

"Then kneel."

Cymer touched three fingers to Durrin's brow, speaking in the Numinous Tongue before switching to Lurrian. "I appoint you a Knight in the Luminant Order of the Eldest. Your duty is to defend the defenseless and secure the safety of souls, even to the laying down of your life."

Durrin held his breath, waiting to feel a surge of power akin to what he felt when summoning fire. But even after Cymer lifted his fingers, he felt no different. He stood.

Adara caught his gaze. "Durrin. Will you kill him?"

She was not asking if he'd be *able* to best Salidar. They all knew he would. She was asking if he would take the man's life when he did.

Durrin pondered the question, searching his soul for the answer. After all he had done to find redemption from causing one death, could he bring himself to kill again?

Should he?

No being on Zenitha seemed so diametrically opposite to King Everborn than Lord Salidar. The man had murdered, lied, and deceived on countless occasions. For the sake of personal ambition, he had instigated a series of wars that had killed tens of thousands. Now he stood poised to destroy the greatest repository of knowledge on Zenitha.

But did Salidar deserve to die? Even if he did, did that give Durrin that right? Or would it be the greater crime to leave such a man alive?

"We shall see."

The great gates of the Bastion of Memory opened.

Adara stood in the shadows of the gatehouse and watched as Durrin stepped out of the gates. Now nothing separated him from the spears of Lord Salidar's army save a wide expanse of open ground, roughly two hundred yards long.

"May angels attend you," Adara called.

Durrin nodded, eyes fixed on his adversary.

A pair of defenders pushed the gates shut, blocking Durrin from view. Adara followed Cymer and Volthorn through a narrow door and up a series of stairs, until they came back out onto the battlements. Durrin had already walked out toward Salidar's army, standing just beyond a bowshot's length from their banners. Despite the distance, however, his clarion voice proclaimed his challenge across the field, with all the energy of the fire that Adara knew raged in his heart.

"Salidar! I accept your call to single combat! Come out! Come out and face me for the last time!"

Silence fell on the mountain and canyon. No bird sung. Only the snap of banners in the stiff wind broke the stillness. Adara shivered. She looked up to see a bank of storm clouds eclipse the Sun, sucking the land of warmth and light.

"Salidar! Come out!"

A ripple passed through the ranks of the opposing army. Banners shifted to allow a man on horseback to come to the fore. He seemed wreathed in shadows, but even from a distance, Adara could recognize the blue and sable robes.

"Durrin, my old friend," Salidar called, somehow maintaining the cool distain in his voice despite projecting across the great expanse. He was probably using a spell to magnify his voice. "I expected to see you here."

Adara's stomach twisted into a knot. Salidar had known all along they had come. Was the challenge a trap? Would they overwhelm Durrin now that they had him backed against the wall? Would they dare try?

"Let us begin," Durrin said, stripping off his cloak and casting it to the side.

Salidar's all too familiar laugh echoed across the plain. "You really thought I would fight you myself? Durrin, you flatter me. No, I have an opponent much more suitable for you."

Lord Salidar turned his horse and trotted to the side. But his shadow remained. No—that was no shadow. Something dark and sinister moved. It began to stand upright, surpassing in height the soldiers and horses behind it, until it towered over the tips of spears and even the army's banners. As it rose, it spoke with a voice dark as ice and terrible as thunder.

> *"I invoke the Ancient Covenant:*
> *Claw for Wing,*
> *Horn for Halo,*
> *Death for Life."*

Cymer drew a sharp intake of breath. "Terror from the Void!"

Adara stood riveted, a deathly fear overtaking her.

The shadow, now stretching more than twice Durrin's height, stepped forward. And in that moment, Adara's vision shifted. She saw the world for what it was on the other side of the curtain of sight.

The library behind her was a shining beacon, sending its beams of knowledge and truth into the far corners of the world. Ancient as time, it stretched its roots into the very fabric of Zenitha.

To her left, Cymer shone with a gorgeous light, radiating confidence and love. She basked in that warmth, breathing in his life-energy and letting it fill her soul.

Far above her, beyond the clouds, she sensed the faint song of angels. The Sun shone up there, and though it was obscured for now, it pulsed with life—the infinite fountain from which Cymer and the library drew.

Yet for now it was veiled. And as she looked out, she saw Durrin: a flickering lamp, faint and frail. She wondered why she should see him so weak now. He had always seemed unstoppable. Yet now he was only a spark—a candle, flickering in the wind.

And before that spark, a vortex of terrible wrath. A fiend from the depths of the darkest night. An archdemon.

CHAPTER 56

A DAY OF FIRE, BLOOD, AND TEARS

Durrin had never known true fear until that moment.

"What are you?" Durrin cried, gripping the pommel of his sword with white knuckles.

"It's good to see you again, Durrin!" rumbled the shadow, its voice grinding like chains dragged over a rack of swords. Behind it, horses and riders alike scrambled to move away, nearly trampling each other in their panic.

"Who are you?!" Durrin shouted. But he already knew that voice. He had listened to it a thousand times throughout his life.

"I am your enemy," the shadow hissed. "I am your friend. I am your archnemesis; I am your closest companion. I am the cusp of your greatest dreams and the darkest pits of your worst nightmares. And I must say, Durrin, it's nice to see you again. *Outside* your head this time."

"You are no friend of mine," Durrin said.

"Oh?" said the shadow.

Durrin drew his sword. With a flick of his wrist, fire ignited along its length. "You are a servant of the Void and an enemy to the Luminant Order! I command you to withdraw!"

For a moment, Durrin stood defiant. The shadow took a step back. Then it let out a mighty roar that shook the ground under Durrin's feet. Glowing red eyes erupted like fire from its face. Two great wings, laced with glowing red veins, unfolded from its back. It roared again, great horns slashing the air, and its scaly arm raised a spear as large as an oak tree, pulled from a rip in space itself.

"I am Archivous!" the demon roared, his voice making the very ground shake. "Archdemon of the Void! I have pulverized princedoms and toppled empires! I have vanquished foes and crushed kings! None are mightier than I!"

Durrin forced himself to swallow his fear. "Prove it."

He ducked his head. Archivous's spear clipped the tops of his hairs as it buried half its length into the ground beyond him and stuck there, quivering with the sound of a war gong.

Durrin straightened. "You missed."

The demon roared and pounded toward Durrin.

The angel had warned that the demon would take on corporal form. What did that mean? Could he be hurt by normal weapons? Killed? Durrin snapped the fingers of his left hand, summoning a plume of flame. He fed it with ever growing motions until, with a flick of the wrist, he sent it shooting across the plain. The demon raised a clawed hand, letting the blast of fire explode against the scaly hide of his arm.

"Tut, tut, Durrin, I've seen you do better than that," Archivous taunted. "Have you lost your touch without me urging you on?"

But that was only a test, to make sure the demon truly was corporal. Time for the real attack. Durrin sheathed his sword and clapped his hands together. A fireball exploded into existence in front of him. Grabbing it with his hands, he began spinning, shaping the ball of flame ever bigger, the heat warping the air around him and scorching the grass at his feet. Faster and faster he spun, until the fireball became only a blur of flame around him. He flared his spark even brighter, pouring all the energy of his soul into the blaze.

He launched the ball of fire. As it roared through the air, Durrin collapsed to the ground, but he kept his head up, eyes riveted on his attack. Never had he made a blast so large.

Archivous attempted to sidestep the blast. But he reacted too late. The raging cyclone of flame knocked the demon head over heels, his wings crumpling beneath his weight as he smashed into a boulder.

A hush fell over the battlefield.

Durrin stood upright, panting, not daring to believe it could end so easily. "Do you yield?" he called.

For a moment, the demon lay still where he lay; a heap of scaly limbs, his wings and horns pricking the air in bent disarray. Then he stirred, slowly shaking as a laugh rumbled from his throat.

"Fire?" he chuckled, lifting his head off the ground. His eyes still burned like bright embers. "*Fire?* Really, Durrin. I'm a *demon*. Fire's what I do."

The ground trembled as Archivous leapt to his feet and charged Durrin again. He extended a claw and spoke a command in a dark tongue, and his spear wrenched out of the ground and flew back into his waiting grip. "Feel the fury of the Void!"

Durrin stood his ground. So fire was ineffective? He had other tools at his disposal. He swept his hands out in front of him, then twisted them in the movements of the fifth Kymar routine, gathering that strange, crackling power to him. Twice more he repeated the series of moves, until his body felt fit to explode and arcs of light rippled between his fingertips.

Then he thrust his hands forward. A blinding bolt of lightning shot from his hands, arcing across the remaining yards and striking the demon in the wings. The valley shook with the thunderous *crack,* trapped and magnified by the canyon walls on either side. Pain coursed through Durrin's fingers as they endured the searing heat and the coursing power.

Archivous roared again—but this time, it was a scream of pain and fury. The lightning had momentarily blinded Durrin, so he could not see the extent of the damage, but he smiled grimly. The archdemon could feel pain and suffer wounds. He was not invincible.

"Watch out!" Volthorn's voice bellowed from the walls behind him.

Durrin spun to the side, feeling the archdemon's spear pass just hairs from his arm. As his vision cleared, he saw Archivous advancing on him again, one wing charred and blackened.

Durrin began to summon lightning a second time, but Archivous charged, forcing him to defend himself instead. He barely dodged a swipe of Archivous's claws as he backed away and drew his sword. Archivous swiped again and Durrin ducked, slashing his sword across the demon's arm. The demon seemed not to notice as he caught Durrin with a backhand to the shoulder.

Durrin rolled with the blow, tumbling across the grass and rolling back upright. He flicked spikes of fire at Archivous's eyes, forcing the demon to shield his face with a raised forearm. Durrin darted forward, keeping up his barrage of fiery missiles as he looked for a weak spot to stab with his sword. The wings!

Durrin ducked under a wild swing and sliced his sword deep into the bat-like membrane of Archivous's left wing. The demon roared again, sweeping his head around to try and impale Durrin on his massive horns, but Durrin slipped out of range just in time.

He had scored several hits. But the wounds he had dealt were far from lethal, and he was already beginning to tire.

Again, Archivous called his spear to his hand and stomped forward, black drops of blood dripping from his injured wing. He advanced more cautiously this time, watching Durrin for his next move. Durrin feinted left and right, but Archivous kept his spear directed at Durrin's heart no matter which way he turned.

"You cannot win," Archivous growled, malice seething in his eyes. "I will skewer you like you skewered the Everborn king. Then I will tear this library apart stone by stone, slaughtering all who oppose me."

Durrin's lungs heaved for breath, but he squared his shoulders in defiance. "Right. Like you did to Saven?"

Archivous thrust his spear forward with startling speed. Durrin's sword barely shunted it aside, even with pyromancy adding strength to his parry. Archivous thrust again and again, driving Durrin back with each exchange.

Durrin summoned a blast of fire and used it to withdraw, sprinting away across the field. Dismayed cries came from the defenders on the walls, but he was not retreating; he was only buying distance. He turned and summoned lightning again, aiming the blast at the fiend's head.

But his spark was tiring from the brutal pace of the fight. The arc of lightning was only a fraction of the power his first had been, seeming to only annoy Archivous.

And the demon kept coming.

Durrin ran to meet him, knowing that if he let the archdemon back him against the Bastion's wall, he was finished. He used a boulder to somersault over the demon's head and land behind him. His sword raked across Archivous' hide but failed to pierce it.

Archivous's tail came out of nowhere. It caught Durrin across the legs and sent him rolling across brush and rocks.

Archivous's spear came a second later. Durrin rolled, the spear's jagged edge cutting his chainmail jerkin just shy of his ribs. As the spear came down a second time, he desperately twisted to the side. Then the other side. Then he was on his feet again, hurling all the energy he could muster into his sword as he deflected impossibly powerful blow after blow.

Archivous roared, taking a mighty step forward.

Durrin ducked under a blow and ran forward inside the demon's reach, fire rippling behind him as he accelerated. He jumped into the air, caught a grip on the demon's arm, and thrust his sword into Archivous's neck, driving it with all the power of pyromancy behind the blow.

Archivous screamed, arcing his back in pain. But the sword had barely pierced the demon's hide. Durrin's arm writhed from the impact.

Then Archivous's claws caught Durrin and wrenched him away. Talons dug into his abdomen, piercing his armor and skin. Then the demon sent him spinning into the air. Earth and sky tipped and spun in Durrin's vision as he desperately swung his arms, trying to control his fall. A field of grass and rocks loomed large in his vision. He impacted the ground, rolling and bouncing before coming to rest in a patch of long grass.

Pain coursed through every receptor in Durrin's body. He lay still, his eyes clenched shut, ragged breaths escaping his lips, each inhale and exhale sending new jolts of agony through his body.

Slowly, from somewhere far away, he heard a great bellow. With sheer force of will, he opened his eyes. Through the tall grass, he saw Archivous standing some forty feet away, his back to Durrin. He held aloft something bright: Durrin's sword, a mere twig in those massive fists. With a roar of triumph, the demon snapped the sword in two.

Then the great horns began to turn. The demon was sweeping the grassy terrain around him, looking for his prey. Durrin struggled to move. His limbs screamed in pain and refused to budge. At least the grass mostly hid him for now.

The horns continued sweeping back and forth. "I know you're dying!" Archivous growled. "I can sense the agony coursing through you!"

A new wave of pain ripped through Durrin's body, causing his muscles to spasm and his spine to convulse. A stifled cry choked in his throat. He craned his head to look at his body. Rips and gashes covered his clothing and armor; blood seeped from multiple wounds on his legs and torso. One leg was twisted unnaturally, and the pain in his ribs and arms told of broken bones.

On the walls above him, he heard the shouts of dismay and panic from the defenders. Once Archivous finished him off, they would be next.

Every inch of Durrin's body trembled with pain. His vision swam red. Terror and despair closed tight around his heart.

I've failed.

I've doomed us all.

Darkness closed like a vice around his heart.

Sky Father, help me!

Chapter 57

Light

"The Sun has not set, demon. Your time has not yet come."

Archivous spun, furious, as an angel hovered a few dozen yards from him, her glittering wings shimmering.

He snarled. Not her again. "What are *you* doing here?"

"You told me once to find something less irritating to do than guard a palace. Well, here I am."

Archivous advanced on the angel, lashing the air with his horns. "Begone! You already had your appearance. You have no right to intervene now."

But the angel only inhabited the unseen plane, invisible to all but Archivous. She stood her ground, unfazed by his ranting.

"Can I not heal?" she said. "Can I not help those who invite my aid?"

"By what power do you think you can defy me?!" Archivous roared, raising his spear and hurling it at the angel. It passed right through her, of course. Stupid metaphysical constraints.

"By the power of the Eldest," the angel said.

Only then did Archivous hear the chanting on the wall above him.

The wall was in chaos. Library adherents were crying in terror or pushing for the stairs. Volthorn was bellowing orders, his voice growing more and more angry as the undisciplined defenders failed to come to order.

Adara stood transfixed, eyes riveted on the scene beyond the walls. Durrin was barely visible in the grass, his body bent and broken. Was he still alive?

Archivous hadn't noticed him yet—something seemed to be distracting the archdemon. But she knew Durrin had only a handful of seconds left.

"Rise," Adara whispered, pleading. "Get up! Keep fighting!"

In the chaos, a familiar phrase in the Numinous Tongue caught her ear. She looked over to see Lyman, the Bastion's cloudship enthusiast, a few feet farther down the wall, his head bowed, his lips moving.

Of course.

She bowed her head as well, recalling the words of healing Cymer had taught her just over a week earlier. *"Et evinal, et yidivar, et claminor, al Abeam!"*

Cymer had said that for full effect, she needed to touch the subject she was healing. That was not an option now—but her heart pleaded that the words would have power regardless. She poured her whole soul into the phrase as she chanted it again, louder, picturing its meaning. *Be whole, be healed, be clean, by the Eldest!*

Light. It cut through Durrin's pain, flashing through his mind.

Light. But it was also so much more. It was life, creation, and energy. It was healing, mercy, and strength. It was knowledge and truth. It was power.

Durrin gasped, drawing air into his desperate lungs. Pain sprouted in his ribs, but even as he breathed again, the pain receded. Power was flowing through him: a quiet, incredible power. He had felt that energy once before, pulsing in the Curtain of Knowledge. But this time it flowed through his whole body, filling his veins.

"Et yidivar!" Someone was shouting the words from the top of the wall. In response, another round of light swept through his body, pain and darkness fleeing before it.

"Et ene avara!" He recognized the voice now. It was Adara's. Other voices joined in a moment later. *"Et yidivar! Al abeam!"*

Energy flooded through him, energy like he had never felt before. Every fiber of his body revived: bones reknit; skin healed; pain fled.

He opened his eyes; the red had left his vision. For a moment, he thought he saw a glorious, winged figure hovering in the air above him. Light was flowing from the defenders on the whole, through her outstretched hand, and into his body. Then he blinked, and it was only the Sun, peeking through a gap that had opened in the glowering clouds.

An angry growl split the air. Memory swept back through him. Salidar. The Bastion. The demon!

With power coursing through his veins, he rose.

Archivous roared, glaring at the mortals on the walls above him. How dare they? How dare they intervene with their healing chants, their words of power? He drew his arm back and launched his spear at the strongest voice among them, the meddling princess who had frustrated his plans yet again. One of the defenders tackled her, knocking her out of the way a moment before Archivous's spear sheared through the stone crenelation she had been hiding behind, scattering shards of rock in all directions.

Someone chuckled to his left. "You missed."

Archivous whirled. The pyromancer stood a few dozen yards away, his body whole and unharmed. Light glowed in his eyes.

"Impossible!" Archivous roared. "Now is the day of my triumph!"

Above the human, the angel soared into the air. "You thought that Darkness would win this day," she said. "You thought to make today a fateful day. An evil day. A day of fire and blood and tears. But today is the day of the Eldest's triumph."

Only then did Archivous notice that the defenders on the wall, who had been scattering in panic just a few moments before, had regrouped.

"Attack!" Volthorn roared, dropping his sword.

Archers up and down the wall loosed their arrows. Other defenders added javelins and stones. The flurry of missiles slammed into the archdemon on the plain below, causing him to roar with pain.

The dozen mancerers that had arrived in the cloudship, some of the best mancerers in Elandria's military, followed up a moment later. Pyromancers rained fire down upon him. Terramancers tossed rock-shard grenades or launched crossbow bolts with glowing red tips. Verbomancers summoned gusts of wind that knocked rocks and tree branches into the archdemon.

Archivous howled, shielding his eyes with one clawed hand. With the other, he recalled his spear and launched it at the Bastion again. This time, it exploded in the air above the wall, raining flaming chunks of rock down on the defenders.

"Hold your ground!" Volthorn cried, as the enchantments on his armor deflected one of the pieces of brimstone. "Keep firing!"

A sound behind him made him turn. Bjorn and Tadgh had removed one of the ballistae from the cloud frigate and mounted it on the wall. Grimbo, straining to reach, touched the tip of the bolt with his paw, pouring red and purple terracharge into it until energy streamed off of it in glowing wisps. Then Azura lined it up and fired.

The glowing ballista bolt slammed deep into Archivous's leg, the first weapon to pierce his scaly hide. Archivous roared in pain. Grimbo shouted in triumph.

Growling, Archivous pulled another spear into existence in his hands. But the bolt fired by Twigly's crew had both red *and* purple terracharge.

The archdemon's body shuddered as the gravity around him suddenly increased threefold. He slammed to the ground, his furious scream muffled as the weight of his body crushed the air from his chest.

"Keep up your fire!" Volthorn roared. "We have him pinned!"

Warriors reloaded up and down the line as mancerers kept up their barrage of attacks. Archivous screamed in rage and pain, then began to crawl out of range. As the terracharge wore off, he rose back upright, shaking the earth with his pounding steps until he had escaped the reach of the Bastion's defenders.

All but one.

Durrin hurled a blast of fire, matching Archivous's pace as he pursued the retreating demon back toward Salidar's army.

"Finish what you started, servant of the Void!" Durrin called. He knew not how long Archivous was allowed to stay in the mortal realm. But he knew he could not let the archdemon escape to work more mischief.

Never had Durrin felt so alive. Light coursed through him, filling him with strength and incredibly clarity. Pyromancy came more intuitively than ever before.

Archivous whirled to face him, throwing his spear. Durrin reacted with superhuman speed, dodging it. Archivous recalled his spear and threw it again. Durrin sidestepped it easily, then spun his arms and sent a spike of flame at Archivous's leg, where the ballista bolt had left a gaping wound. Archivous howled in pain.

"Fire?!" the archdemon roared. "I'll show you FIRE!!!"

Archivous shouted a string of dark words, raising his wings and sweeping them forward. A massive column of black fire shot across the plain toward Durrin, wider than a wagon wheel, scorching the grass before it.

Durrin pinwheeled his arms, channeling the fire to either side of him. It streamed out in all directions, consuming bushes and dirt in its path, blackening the rocks with its intense heat.

Durrin took a step backward, pushed back by the unrelenting column of flames, his arms spinning desperately to direct the fire away. Sweat dripped down his face. As a pyromancer, normally he was completely fireproof. But these dark, writhing flames were no normal fire. He could feel their heat starting to scorch and burn his skin.

"*Et ene avara*," he gasped. Light flooded into him again, giving him strength and healing his burns. But it still wasn't enough. He took another step back, then another, as the wall of flames crept closer and closer to consuming him.

He couldn't do this. Even with the help of the Light, he wasn't enough. No one, not even the great heroes of old, could withstand this force alone.

Alone.

He had spent so much of his life alone. Drilling and practicing at the Academy—alone. Taking King Everborn's life—alone. Rotting in a cell at Irongate Isle—alone. Bolting through Wyvern Way—alone. He had always preferred to be alone. He had always been strong enough on his own. To rely on others was to introduce a weakness.

But memories in the year since his release flooded his mind. Hoeing wheat with Halorn. Staring up at the stars with Line. Wondering at a lamp made whole with Cymer. Rescuing Adara with Volthorn. Marshalling the Mitrians to war with Twigly and Korkor. All his greatest triumphs of the last year had come while standing, united, with others.

And he finally understood Kymar's sixth scroll.

The comprehension came to him in a flash, the pieces falling into place like tumblers of a lock. Light, power, energy, momentum—they were all the same, all different sides of the same unifying force. And that force connected everything. Everyone. It was how he could sense the energy of living things around him. It was how he could feel others' sparks, even if they were a hundred yards away. It was how he could harness the energy around him and turn it into fire.

But it was so much more.

He was not a single agent, acting alone in a world of division and competition. He was one of a hundred thousand stars, all created together, all children of the Sky Father. He recalled his visions from the Curtain of Knowledge. For eons, he had dwelt in the skies alongside his fellow stars, watching as one by one they had fallen to Zenitha to live a mortal life. Those who turned outward, who forged bonds of friendship and love with those around them, had risen with wings to join the union of angels in the Halls of the Sun. But those who had cut themselves off from the sparks around them, attempting to live out their mortal journey alone—such had fallen to the darkness.

He could not do this alone. But he didn't have to. He wasn't supposed to.

Even as he kept spinning his arms to divert Archivous's attack, Durrin closed his eyes, reaching out with his pyrosense. There. Behind him, a row of sparks marked the defenders on the wall. Adara. Cymer. Volthorn. Twigly and her crew. Lyman, Marion, and the other residents of the Bastion, plus the mancerers from Elandria. Their sparks danced with wonder and resolve as they watched him defend them, each heart willing him to stand strong. They were all united in a common cause. The cause of the Light. The cause of the Eldest. The cause of the Sky Father.

He tapped the energy from their sparks.

It shouldn't have been possible. He *knew* it wasn't possible. Pyromancers had tried for centuries to tap the energy from their opponents, concluding that it was either impossible or forbidden.

But Kymar's words held the secret: *In all things, one. Only in unity lies true power.*

Pyromancers had tried and failed—because they had tried to *take* energy. But in the bond between two intelligent sparks, energy could not be seized. It could only be given.

Power jolted through him. It felt similar to the light he had felt a few minutes before, when the faith and healing words of dozens of defenders on the wall had flowed into him, repairing his body. But this time, he could draw power—pyromantic energy—directly from the sparks in their hearts, just like how he could draw it from his own.

The power he wielded increased a hundred-fold.

With a casual wave of his arms, he scattered the column of fire in all directions, clearing the ground between him and Archivous. The demon recoiled, eyes widening in alarm.

Then Durrin held out his hand. Motes of light streamed from the chests of everyone on the wall behind him, converging on his fingers. Then a blinding ray of pure energy shot forward, colliding with the demon. Archivous howled, grasping at his chest.

Durrin took a step forward and raised his hand again, aiming for the demon's uninjured wing. Then he hit the demon's arm. Each beam of light hit its mark with arrow-like precision. Each made Archivous scream. The demon tried to throw his spear, but Durrin struck his arm every time he raised it.

Archivous stumbled backward, claws raised to shield his eyes. "Enough!" he roared. "Enough!"

"*Et ene avara!*" Durrin cried, and a brilliant light shone around him, blinding the demon further. He could barely tell the difference between the Light and the force he wielded with pyromancy. One was higher and purer, but they were two sides of the same universal power.

"Enough!" Archivous shouted one more time, then uttered something in an unknown speech. A portal of swirling shadows opened behind him, and he crouched there, flickering in and out of view, as if hanging onto the physical realm by a thread. Durrin blasted energy at him again, but this time it caused the demon little harm, as if passing mostly through him.

"Begone!" Durrin commanded. "Back to the Void from which you crawled!"

"Not quite yet," Archivous sneered. He still cowered before Durrin, but his confidence was returning. "My time is not quite up."

"Then cower until it is," Durrin said, keeping his hands raised. "I can wait."

On the far side of the field, Salidar had watched the fight from his saddle, riveted by the unprecedented displays of power. First he had shook and trembled with every strike of Archivous's claws. Now he sat in awestruck fear at the sudden and miraculous shift in the duel.

"Impossible," he murmured, almost in a trance.

Then he shook himself back to the moment and turned to his officers. "Sound the retreat. We can still ride to—"

He trailed off. His officers surrounded him, their faces tight with steely hatred. Each held his sword drawn.

"What is the meaning of this?" he demanded.

His second-in-command nudged his horse forward. The tip of his sword quivered with rage. "*Traitor!*" he cried. "You made a pact with the Void. You brought a demon into our very midst. *A demon!*"

Salidar opened his mouth. But there was nothing he could say.

"You nearly doomed us all!" another officer yelled. "If the fiend had slain their champion, what then? Would it have come for us?"

"Of course not," Salidar said. "He needed us to help him destroy the Bastion."

It was the wrong thing to say.

"This was *the demon's* idea?!" the first officer shouted. "We followed you three hundred miles, defying our own emperor, on the Void's errand?!"

"Yes!" Salidar said. "I had no other choice! But listen to me. We can still escape. The road to Marisau is open. I can lead you to—"

"To the Void?" the lead officer said. He pointed his sword at Salidar's throat. Two more officers rode up on either side, pressing the tips of their weapons against his ribs.

"It's over, Your Excellency," the officer hissed. "We're surrendering. Perhaps Queen Everborn will have mercy on us. But not on you."

The gates to the Bastion opened, and Adara rushed out, hard on the heels of Cymer, Lyman, and others as they ran to join Durrin on the field.

"Stay back!" Durrin cried, keeping his arms directed at Archivous. "He's still dangerous!"

"Not to us," said Cymer, stepping up and regarding the cowering demon. "You bested him in open battle. Rather than face eternal annihilation at your hands, he has chosen to forfeit his material form. It will be hundreds of years before he can again step fully onto the physical plane."

Durrin shook his head. "I can feel him still here. He has substance."

"A bit, yes. But he can do no more harm to members of the Order. The Ancient Covenant entitles him to a few more minutes in the physical realm. Then he must depart."

Adara pointed across the field. "Look!"

A small group of cavalry was approaching. Durrin resumed a battle stance beside her, ready to fight, but as the riders approached, their identities became clear. In the middle was Salidar, hands tied and mouth gagged. Around him rode a trio of officers, their faces grim. And last—

"Halorn!" Adara cried.

She started to run toward him, but Durrin outstripped her, bounding across the field in a few massive leaps. Halorn dismounted and embraced him, wrapping him in a massive hug. Adara stopped a few yards away, confused. These two men knew each other?

"Are you okay?" Durrin asked, holding Halorn at arm's length and glancing at his tattered clothes and bruised face.

"Yes," said Halorn, his face wet with tears as he beamed at Durrin with pride. "A million times, yes."

One of the officers shoved Salidar off his horse. The former vizier fell to the ground with a grunt, unable to catch himself with his hands tied.

"A present for Your Majesty," the officer said, addressing Adara with his gaze respectfully lowered. "We would like to discuss terms of our surrender, after . . ." his eyes flicked to the demon still glowering just a few dozen yards away. ". . . after *that* is gone."

Adara nodded. The three officers turned and galloped away as fast as their mounts could carry them.

In their wake, Cymer turned back to the demon. He raised his hands, emitting a light from his fingers.

"Archivous!" he called. "The Sun reigns in the sky. You have lost!"

Hatred gleamed in the demon's eyes. "Perhaps today," he rumbled. "But mark my vow, Child of the Sky. The day will come when the Bastion will burn. The Four Anchors of the World will be overturned. Zenitha will crack, and the Void will eclipse the Sun. And when that day comes, I will be there. I have seen it."

"What will happen will happen," Cymer said. "But you will claim no more victories today. Go back to the Void!"

Archivous crouched in the trampled grass, his eyes burning as he stared at the ring of figures surrounding him. Adara regarded them, as well: Cymer, mage of the Luminant Order, arms raised high with glowing power; Durrin, fire flickering at his fingertips; Halorn, battered and bruised but still strong; Lyman and other adherents from the Bastion, eyes firm with resolve; and Adara herself, raising her light with slender but steady hands. A ring of light extended from Cymer's hands and encircled them, shielding each of them from the demon's power.

"Go back to the Void!" Cymer repeated. The light shone brighter. "Your plot has failed. You can claim no souls today!"

Defiance flashed in Archivous's eyes. "There is still one."

Snarling in triumph, the demon spun and launched his spear at Lord Salidar.

Cymer reached out in vain, too far away to intervene.

Adara and Halorn recoiled in surprise.

Salidar stared at the demon, bracing for his imminent, unavoidable death.

Durrin stepped into the spear's path.

The bolt ripped through him, shredding the mancery he tried to summon and piercing his chest. He fell, gasping, to the dirt in front of Lord Salidar.

"No!" Adara cried, running to Durrin's side.

Behind her, Cymer aimed a beam of light at the demon. "Begone!" he commanded. Archivous gave one final growl, then twisted into nothingness.

Adara fell to her knees and stared wildly at the horrible wound. Even as she watched, the massive spear melted away into shadow, following its master back to the Void. But the gash in Durrin's chest remained. She had never seen a more horrible wound.

She pushed away the panic and pressed her hands against his heaving ribs. "*Et evinal, et yidivar, et claminor, al Abeam!*" she chanted, willing every part of her soul into the words of healing. She looked around at the shocked figures around her. "Someone help me!" she cried.

Halorn appeared at her side, light already shining around his fingers. Closing his eyes, he laid his hands on top of Adara's, letting the light flow into Durrin's body. He breathed out, brow furrowed in concentration.

After a moment, he bowed his head. "He is dying."

"No!" Adara insisted. But her healing sense had told her the same. The demon's spear had clipped Durrin's heart and punctured both his lungs. His life hung at death's door. Only their combined healing energy was holding him back, and that for only moments longer.

"Salidar," Durrin gasped. He turned his head, craning until his eyes met Salidar's gaze. The vizier stared back, eyes wide and unblinking, a look of astonished gratitude in their depths.

"My life was spared once, when I deserved to die," Durrin said. He coughed wetly. "Now I spare yours. Use it well."

As Durrin's life slipped away, he stared up beyond Adara into the glorious light of day.

"Adara," he whispered. "I see your father." Tears welled up in the corners of his eyes. "I see angels—so many angels. I see . . ."

Durrin's face gained a look of deepest wonder as his soul slipped into eternity.

SOULS AND SCROLLS

S o ended the story of Durrin Rendhart, Master of Fire, Bender of Fate.

For a long moment did Adara and Halorn kneel on that cold mountain field outside the Bastion's gates, mourning his loss.

As was the custom for pyromancers, he was cremated that evening. Halorn officiated—the only act of pyromancy he had performed since renouncing the art many years before. Thus the fire that had never burned Durrin in life consumed him in death, the flames climbing high into the sky above the walls he had died defending.

Around his pyre was perhaps the strangest gathering at such an event: Cymer, who had pardoned him. Adara, who had forgiven him. Halorn, who had believed in him. Volthorn, who had pursued him. Twigly and her crew, who had tolerated him.

And, watching silently from a distance with his limbs still bound, Salidar, who had trained, unleashed, betrayed, assaulted, and been saved by him.

They talked at length of where to entomb his ashes. His hometown? He had not been there in decades. The Pyromantic Academy at Imperium? They had denounced him. Saven? It was the scene of his greatest sin. In the end, they scattered his ashes over the field where he had given his greatest sacrifice.

Three months later.

Adara stood at the window of her royal suite, looking out over the cityscape of Saven, lit up by the fading light of a late summer afternoon.

She tapped her fingers thoughtfully, then turned to the parchment beside her and set quill to paper.

Most beloved Cymer,

With joy and gratitude, I pen you this update. I hope all is well at the Bastion. We miss you here, particularly the circuit judges, but I know you are needed more there.

She forewent the customary royal "we." Cymer was practically family.

Today was the long-awaited day, the day when Emperor Stoneclaw and I formalized and signed the treaty between our two nations. For nearly a week we sat in council together, discussing and negotiating terms—and putting up with more than one discursive sermon by Skagar. The results are far less than I would have liked, but more than I let myself hope for. Calamar will keep our provinces west of the Rugeran Mountains. They have held them for nearly three years now, and surrendering them was not something the emperor's generals were willing to do. But Meradov, the Penandre, and everything east of the Rugeran Mountains will be returned to us. What's more, we are to remain a fully sovereign kingdom, free of Calamar's control. Emperor Stoneclaw insisted on this point personally, despite demands by his generals that we become merely a client state.

The war brought much death and sowed many seeds of hate. But I am hopeful that, with time, a strong relationship of peace will develop between our two countries. The emperor's son, Crown Prince Thundertail, came to the first two days of negotiations, where he and I talked extensively. He shares his father's good heart, though he is still working on acquiring the wisdom. I am glad he is now free of Salidar's corrupting influence.

Our people are rebuilding. Just yesterday, the servants planted new saplings in the palace grounds. But this winter will be hard. Few crops were planted this spring, and even fewer were sown in haeber-rich fields. Many crops were trampled and much livestock was seized by the invading armies. The emperor has promised to send an indemnity by the fall (comprised, I am told, of a large portion of the Aram family's fortune), but gold and silver will avail little if there is no food at the market to buy with it.

Adara paused, reflecting. The haeber supply was still little more than a trickle. Almost a year had passed since High Mage Sablewing had left for distant lands in the far east to address the problem. Was she succeeding? Would she ever return? What would they do if the haeber supply stayed so low, or stopped altogether?

She had no answers. She shook her head and returned to writing.

> *Speaking of silver and gold—we finally got Twigly and her crew to leave last week! After two and a half months of eating us out of hearth and home as they, quote, 'repaired their ship,' we finally got them to take ship. We had to literally scrape the last flecks of gold from the treasury floor to make up the sixty pounds of gold Volthorn promised them. (We were a bit short, actually, but we made up the difference with potatoes.)*

> *Give my regards to Volthorn—tell him I wish him the best, as always.*

Following the attack on the Bastion, Volthorn had asked Adara for a leave of absence to stay at the library for the summer, expressing his desire to study and learn things he could learn nowhere else. While there, he was working under Cymer's guidance to strengthen the fortifications and, more importantly, to recruit and train a defensive garrison. Never again, Cymer had vowed, would the library be left defenseless to the wiles of the Void. And neither Cymer nor Adara could think of a military commander more qualified for the job. As soon as Volthorn returned, Adara planned on promoting him back to chief commander. Commander Orrin was competent . . . he just wasn't Volthorn.

> *Tell Volthorn his brother Trazar is recovering. Any danger from the infection should now be passed, though he is still very weak.*

Adara had personally visited Trazar several times. She was still getting a handle on the peculiar patterns of the Light. Sometimes she could heal someone all at once. Other times, as with Trazar, it happened little by little, bit by bit, despite all her attempts to rush it. She was learning that one didn't rush the Light.

> *I hear, in fact, that Trazar is becoming quite enamored of one of the korrik nursemaids serving in his infirmary ward. Kelzern denies it—says they're all still too young to be breaking up the broodmate band to marry and settle down. Then again, perhaps best not to mention this to Volthorn. It might make him feel old.*

Which reminds me: I overheard Skagar and Luviana talking earlier today. Skagar said that with the treaty now signed, it's time to start looking for a match for me. Something about continuing the royal line and all that important stuff. I suppose he's right. But I will desperately need your advice, Cymer, in the coming months. I am still very young and have no parents to counsel me.

Adara looked in a mirror. Her eyes had turned dark brown just with the thought of marriage. How was an avir supposed to court and find a fitting spouse when her face betrayed her every emotion?

One last bit of news. It took much urging on my part, but Emperor Stoneclaw finally agreed to add a clause to our treaty. It lifts Calamar's ban on the Luminant Order, after nearly thirty years of state-sponsored oppression. And, at his steward's request, the emperor has gifted an estate (again, formerly belonging to the Aram family) to serve as the Order's regional headquarters just outside the walls of Imperium. You and Sablewing will need to appoint a trusted and experienced member of the Order to oversee its revival in Calamar. I personally recommend Halorn.

Halorn had returned to Calamar shortly after the defense of the Bastion. The emperor had given him an armed escort to ensure he reached his family in safety.

Adara paused, looking out the window at the distant hills, where once a forest of tents had stood. Not for the first time, she thought she saw faint glimmers of light in the edges of her vision: figures in white, bearing scrolls or swords, flying through the air as they hastened back to the Sun after a long day's ministry among mortals. But as always, she blinked and they vanished from sight.

The future will bring its trials and disasters. But I trust it will also bring great joy.

Forever yours, a fellow servant in the Luminant Order of the Eldest Star,

Queen Adara Everborn

She returned the quill to its inkwell, blowing on the parchment to dry the ink before she rolled it closed.

As she sat, deep in thought, a guard rapped at the door. "Your Majesty," he called.

"Yes?" Adara replied, looking up.

"The prisoner says he's ready to meet with you. We have him here now."

"Excellent work, Lieutenant," Adara said. "Send him in."

The guard opened the door, and a tall figure entered the room. His head was bowed, and voidstone shackles clanked against his chaffed and swollen wrists. But looking into his heart, Adara could see the tender first growths of the seed of change.

"Please, Salidar," Adara said. "Have a seat. We need to talk about souls and scrolls."

Bonus Content!

Head to **jeremypmadsen.com/bonus** to download free bonus content for this story!

- Over 40 pieces of high-resolution full-color artwork, perfect for desktop backgrounds or unlock screens
- 20 musical themes, including themes for each of the main characters (Durrin, Adara, Volthorn, Salidar, Twigly, Halorn, and Archivous)
- Video commentary on the book

Follow me on social media to get news and sneak-peeks of upcoming books:

- Facebook: @jeremypmadsen
- Instagram: @jeremypmadsen
- YouTube: @jeremypmadsen

Head to **jeremypmadsen.com/game** to check out Mancery Mayhem, a card game for 2–4 players where you can play as Durrin, Salidar, Volthorn, or Talianna (from "The Aquamancer's Secret") in a magical duel for the Mayhem Cup. You can have a physical deck shipped to you, or you can buy the digital print files to print at home.

You know what would absolutely make my day? If you left an honest review on Amazon or Goodreads! Reviews are critical for helping my books reach new readers. Find quick links to leave a review at **jeremypmadsen.com/review**.

Lastly . . . I *love* to receive letters from my readers. Send me an email at **jeremy@jeremypmadsen.com**, and I promise I'll write you back!

About the Author

Jeremy P. Madsen writes clean, family-friendly fantasy stories with spiritually resonant themes.

As a child, Jeremy eagerly devoured the stacks of library books his siblings brought home. But he was too timid to check out books for himself. He had no idea which stories on the shelves were clean, and which would violate his standards.

Luckily, his siblings had excellent tastes, shaping his love of fantasy through series such as *The Chronicles of Prydain*, *Narnia*, *Redwall*, and *Fablehaven*. By 8th grade, he was writing his own stories—often acting out fight scenes with a cape and a plastic sword.

In college, Jeremy's worldbuilding was shaped by his major, ancient Near Eastern studies. As he witnessed the rise of grimdark fantasy and the publishing industry's continued decline in standards, he vowed to write stories that are uplifting, clean, and safe for all readers.

Besides his author career, Jeremy works for BK Authors, Inc. and Berrett-Koehler Publishers. He lives in Columbus, Ohio, with his wife and three children. He still wears capes.

※

Food for Thought

Twenty discussion questions for book clubs or personal enrichment.

1. Who was your favorite character?

2. What was your favorite moment of the book?

3. If you could be a master in one of the five manceries, which one would you choose and why? (Or, which of the five manceries seems the most powerful to you and why?)

4. How do the different species in Zenitha use their strengths to help their society?

5. If you could be a member of Twigly's crew, what would you love or hate about it?

6. How does the story include elements of modern technology in creative ways (such as in communication and transportation)?

7. How did Adara grow in her role as a leader? Was her country justified in putting their trust in a young, inexperienced queen?

8. In chapter 11, Cymer told Adara that she had been given the gift of wisdom, and that if she listened to that gift, she wouldn't lead her people astray. Earlier in the chapter, Adara made major decisions about the Penandre garrison and the records in the Sanctum of Kings. How did each of those decisions play out later in the story? Did Adara make the right choices? Why or why not?

9. Luviana and Skagar felt it was important to hide the truth of how King Arvanon died. What do you think? Was that a wise choice, or misguided? Even if they kept it hidden from the public, should they have told Adara sooner? Why or why not?

10. Disasters can usually be traced to multiple failures or mistakes. Think about the series of events that led to Adara being kidnapped. What mistakes did Durrin, Volthorn, and Adara each make that allowed the kidnapping to happen?

11. Adara learned how to both trust and forgive. Whom did she have trouble trusting? Whom did she need to forgive? What are the key insights that helped her change over the course of the story?

12. Volthorn had times in his career when everything seemed to be going right. At other times, everything seemed to be going wrong. What made the difference?

13. The Durrin at the beginning of the book is a different person than the Durrin at the end of the book. How did he change? What caused it?

14. Personality and character are interrelated but distinct. What aspects of Durrin's personality stayed the same, even as his character evolved?

15. Halorn and Durrin started on the same path but ended up in very different places. Why?

16. Is it wise to forgive and show mercy to someone who has hurt you and even committed crimes against you? Why or why not?

17. Salidar claims he is fighting the war to protect and advance Calamar's interests. Do you think he sincerely believes that? Or do you think that is just his cover for more selfish reasons?

18. Durrin ultimately got what he had spent much of his life seeking, even though he was no longer actively searching for it. Does life always deliver what we desire?

19. Did each of the characters deserve their ending?

20. Were you pleased with the ending, or upset? Why?

※

Continue the Adventure . . .

Ilyan the Estimable has a secret. And everyone wants to know what it is.

For 63 years, the venerable aquamancer has peddled his potions and elixirs from his little shop in Imperium. It is an established fact that his potions just work *better* than his competitors': Stronger impact. Longer-lasting results. Fewer side effects.

Rivals would pay large sums to get their hands on such a secret.

Some would be quite willing to get it for them—by force, if necessary.

If only a feisty, grammar-obsessed squirrel apprentice didn't stand in their way.

Read this novelette for free at **jeremypmadsen.com/secret**

CREDITS

Author & Publisher:	Jeremy P. Madsen
Producer & Art Director:	Kathryn Madsen
Editor:	Katrina Jackson
Music Composer:	CJ Madsen
Marketing Assistant:	Céline Taylor
Worldbuilding Consultant:	Tyler Madsen
Alpha Readers:	Audrey Jolly, CJ Madsen, Kathryn Madsen, Laura Madsen, Tyler Madsen, & Samm Madsen
Story Consultant:	Kiri Jorgensen
Side Character Contributors:	Melanie & Doug Cheney (Tadgh MacLery), David & Clayton Hansen (Grimbo), Larry & Lillian Hansen (Bjorn), Laura Madsen (Krizmon & Azura), and Tyler Madsen (Line)
Beta Readers:	Chris Burnham, Allyse Cheney, Doug Cheney, Skylie Cheney, Jacob Dayton, Joel Hansen, Larry Hansen, Talitha Hart, Matthew Jackson, Anthony Lemons, Pete Madsen, Cole McEuen, Annabel Mendoza, Thomas Ottinger, Jessica Palmer, Timothy & Mikayla Partlow, and Julia Rozier
Executive Donors:	Laura & Pete Madsen, Melanie & Doug Cheney, Larry & Lillian Hansen, Tyler Madsen, David & Wendy Hansen, Brittany Jones, and Audrey & Aaron Jolly
Cheerleaders:	The Durney Family
Personal Trainers:	Elanor, Caleb, and Bridget Madsen

Soli Deo Gloria

The Summons

In the darkest hole of the deepest cavern in the largest cave system of Zenitha, buried underneath miles of impenetrable rock, where no mortal had ever set foot and where no light had ever shone, an archdemon nursed his wounds.

Archivous hurt everywhere. His wings were torn. His arms, bloodied. His chest, scalded by that searing light. Not for thousands of years, not since the Rending, had he felt pain like this.

He had forfeited his physical form to escape total annihilation, but as a consequence, his wounds had followed him through the curtain of sight, afflicting his spiritual form. The injuries would slowly fade, but it would take months, if not years. Spiritual essence never healed as quickly as material flesh.

Buried beneath his pain, pure fury pulsed. How dare they? How dare the angels intervene, stretching the terms of their precious Covenant? How dare that meddling pyromancer defy him, defeating him in open battle! He! Archivous!

A chilling voice pierced his thoughts.

"I thought I'd find you here, cowering like the dog you are."

Archivous whirled. Even *his* eyes couldn't pierce the impenetrable darkness, but his mind could plainly sense the calculating malevolence watching him.

"Silvestra," he spat.

Silvestra slithered through the darkness. Oh, how her form disgusted him: half woman, half salamander, with four twisted dragonfly wings that she hardly ever bothered to use, instead forcing her thralls to pull her through the sky in a chariot of shadows. At the moment, she was alone—a rare event.

"Where are your minions?" Archivous sneered. "All busy running that nightmare of a logistics problem you have in the Eastern Sea?"

Silvestra drew her torso upright, the wickedly long nails on her fingers clacking the stone. "Don't forget, *Archy*, that if it weren't for my brilliant supply-chain disruption, your pet war in Elandria would never have happened." She clucked her forked tongue. "And now your little war is over. They signed a treaty last week. Did you hear the news? I imagine not, holed up here like a bat."

Archivous tried to rise, but doubled up, pain shooting down his legs. "How did you find me?" he rasped.

Silvestra laughed. "Oh, the Tyrant King knew exactly where you'd try to hide."

A spike of fear shot through Archivous's heart, displacing every other emotion. He began to tremble. "The . . . Tyrant King . . . sent you?"

Silvestra crept toward him, dragging her body over the rocks. "Oh, yes. When he heard of your disgraceful failure, he was quite . . . displeased."

Archivous began to scramble backwards, pushing himself deeper into the crevice around him, heedless of the pain lancing through his limbs. "It wasn't my fault!" he howled, shaking in terror. "The angels—that pyromancer—"

A hand clamped like a vice over his ankle, arresting any further retreat. Silvestra's eyes appeared in the darkness, glowing with a searing blue flame. When she spoke next, her voice mixed with the voice of another, vaster and infinitely more malignant.

"The Tyrant King requests your presence, Archivous."